The Splintered Gods

Also by Stephen Deas from Gollancz:

The Adamantine Palace
The King of the Crags
The Order of the Scales
The Black Mausoleum
Dragon Queen

The Thief-Taker's Apprentice
The Warlock's Shadow
The King's Assassin

- The -
Splintered Gods

Stephen Deas

GOLLANCZ

LONDON

First published in Great Britain in 2014 by Gollancz
An imprint of the Orion Publishing Group
Orion House, 5 Upper St Martin's Lane,
London WC2H 9EA
An Hachette UK Company

A CIP catalogue record for this book
is available from the British Library.

ISBN (Trade Paperback) 978 0 575 10057 2

1 3 5 7 9 10 8 6 4 2

Typeset by Deltatype Ltd, Birkenhead, Merseyside

Printed and bound by CPI Group (UK) Ltd,
Croydon CR0 4YY

The Orion Publishing Group's policy is to use papers
that are natural, renewable and recyclable products and
made from wood grown in sustainable forests. The logging
and manufacturing processes are expected to conform to
the environmental regulations of the country of origin.

www.stephendeas.com
www.orionbooks.co.uk
www.gollancz.co.uk

To alchemists and enchanters everywhere

Cover his face so that he may not see the light

A half-god came to my realms centuries before I was born. He brought with him the Adamantine Spear which slew the Black Moon and brought down the Splintering of the world. He was the Isul Aieha, the Silver King, who tamed dragons and gave power over them to men; and men in turn took his gift and tore him down. They took his broken body into a deep cave, drove a spike into his head and drank the silver ichor of the moon that dripped from his wound and took his power into their blood. They call themselves alchemists. With the taint of the half-god in their veins their potions keep our dragons dull and make them forget.

I am the dragon-queen Zafir, once the Speaker of the Nine Realms, Mistress of Dragons and Keeper of the Silver King's spear. With my treacherous lover Jehal beside me and a litter of corpses in our wake, I took the Adamantine Throne for my own; but my lover betrayed me for his starling bride and so dragons filled the skies with fire and screams and men died and neither one of us cared a whit save that the other should fall.

And fall we both did.

Amid our chaos, a dragon woke. One who became an avalanche of rage and memory and flames. The dragons threw the curse of alchemy aside and flew at Jehal to burn him and his kingdoms to ash, but I saw none of it, for by then I was a slave, taken by the Taiytakei.

Behind a pretence of obedience I have watched these new men who claim to be my masters, I, a queen of dragons. I have watched their schemes. Baros Tsen, dancing on knife-blades, weaving his web around those who thought they were his lords. Once-loyal Bellepheros, grand master alchemist, taken as a slave a year before me, fretting and pacing and doing nothing to change the cataclysm he sees coming. Not so loyal any more, I fear. His mistress, the enchantress Chay-Liang, Baros Tsen's ally and the only one who sees me as I am and fears me as she should.

And Majestic Diamond Eye, my great war-dragon whom they cannot bear to lose, whose awe-striking grace stays their hand from ending us both. I have watched and I have made them pay for their hubris, dear and long and in pain and blood and fire and plague, in glories of vengeance and flames.

I am Zafir. Dragon-queen.

Why did I not run when I could?

The Soap Maker

The soap maker emerged from the gloom and pointed a crooked finger at the shadows in the corner of the room. The finger beckoned once, slowly curling up on itself like a dying wasp. A bronze stand shaped and carved like the upturned severed limb of some terrible lizard slid across the floor. A grinding sound rattled the air. The bronze began to writhe and squirm and flow like liquid as a golden claw rose through it, a clear glass globe nestled within its talons. The soap maker paused before it.

'Sometimes we guide them,' he said. 'Sometimes we place obstacles before them. Sometimes we merely watch and crack our fingers and cover our faces with gleeful smiles. Listen to my words and learn and then listen and learn again. You will do this over and over and over, every day for the rest of your life. When your arms are withered and your eyes are failing, then you will see the shapings our prophet has cast. They play out around us. A path has been made, pick-pocked with signposts that cannot be missed.' The soap maker clasped his hands. 'Everything I've shown you these last months you could have learned from some crone in a village hovel. Potions and herbs and hedge-witch tricks. They have their uses, but today we walk the true path to power and not some fancy dance of spirals devoid of deeper meaning. You will understand this in time. You will feel it in the chill rattle of your bones.'

The words that marked the start of the soap maker's path were as familiar to both of them as the dark stains on his fingers: *The first basic principle of knowledge is to understand the animating force that brings life to all creatures ...*

'Above all else, I will teach you one thing: I will teach you how to hide.' The soap maker snapped his fingers. A box made of old black wood slid into the air and hovered between them. The inside was lined with velvet, deep red like fresh blood, and on the velvet lay a knife with a golden haft carved into a thousand eyes. Patterns in the blade moved and swirled. The soap maker took the knife and held it as though it was something more precious than life itself. 'I will show you, Skyrie, how it feels to have a piece of your soul cut away. I will show you how to make yourself into scattered parts so that nothing can ever find you, not even a dragon.'

Skyrie, for whom dragons were nothing but stories, wondered why the soap maker would say such a thing.

The box shut itself and drifted away as the soap maker came closer. 'I will show you how to find these pieces and make yourself whole again. From such a journey comes enlightenment, and from enlightenment comes understanding. All these things will be yours, Skyrie. The prophet has chosen you to be a vessel.'

His face changed for a moment, and Skyrie thought he saw a different visage, one he'd seen once before. A half-ruined face with one blind milky eye.

Baros Tsen T'Varr

Dhar Thosis

Tuuran smashed his way through a jammed door into what he hoped was going to be a vault of riches beyond his wildest dreams. It wasn't. He looked around, trying to quash his disappointment. Just paper. Neat little books of it. Big fat ledgers and small slim journals, and he couldn't make head nor tail of any of it. Gold and silver, of which he certainly *could* have made something, were distinctly lacking. It didn't bother him nearly as much as it ought to, though. A dragon had come and burned the city. On its back had been the girl from the Pinnacles, the girl he'd saved when they'd both been ten years younger, and she was alive and grown into a furious and terrible queen, and all the years he'd spent as a slave because of what he'd done that night suddenly had a meaning. Crazy Mad had found his warlock too, and Tuuran's axe had cut off the warlock's hand and then his head, and Crazy had taken the warlock's weird knife. As for the rest – the war and chaos and death and fire, the ruin of a city under the flames of a furious dragon and the swords of a raging army – as for *that*, he was made for it. He was an Adamantine Man.

He rummaged through the papers again and didn't find anything that looked to be worth much except a couple of silvery paperweights and a quill pen made from some exotic pretty feather. He stuffed them into his shoulder bag. The bag was almost full; in every room he entered he always found *something*. He took a couple of books too. Made good kindling, books, and you could always wipe your arse with them. When he was done, he picked his way back out of the shattered tower, through the litter-strewn ruins between cracked and crazed walls of enchanted Taiytakei gold-glass, boots crunching on a carpet of broken glittering shards. The remains of the palace were quiet now, deserted except for a handful of night-skin soldiers poking through the rubble for anything precious that might have survived when the towers had come down. Most of the Taiytakei had moved on, rooting out the handful of defenders too stupid to know a lost cause when it stared them in the face from the back of a dragon. In the next yard along, through a beautifully elegant ruby-glass arch which had somehow survived, three soldiers crouched around a litter of tumbled stonework, twisted metal and shattered golden glass, prodding at it. Tuuran had no idea what they'd found. As he watched, a palace slave, miraculously alive, crept out of some hiding place and ran away. No one tried to stop her. No one paid attention. There wasn't anywhere for her to go.

Crazy Mad was sitting on the edge of a wall, looking out over the cliffs and the sea and the burning city. The dragon was gone but Crazy Mad's eyes were set in its wake. Tuuran sat and nudged him.

'Some nice loot in there,' he said. 'You should grab some while you can.'

Crazy Mad didn't answer; but then Crazy carried a darkness inside, and a day with him wouldn't be complete without a pause for a bit of inner turmoil. Tuuran didn't mind. After everything he'd seen today, maybe he was in the mood for some thinking too – a thing as rare as the moon eclipsing the sun, but there it was – so he sat quietly beside his friend, looking out over the water. They'd sailed together across three worlds and fought battles side by side in every one of them. They'd crossed the storm-dark, chasing after Crazy Mad's warlock, and they'd found him and done for him, and that was all good – it wasn't as if Tuuran had had anything better to do. And then there was the Elemental Man who'd promised to take him home if Tuuran kept an eye on what Crazy Mad did, though he'd never said for how long or why or what to look for.

There was the dragon, too. The dragon had him thinking. Remembering. Ten years as a slave, years since he'd given up on going home, and now here he was, right back with all those longings again. And the girl from the Pinnacles, the dragon-queen Zafir, the speaker of the nine realms. She would have been his queen now. Duty. Desire. Purpose. They ran through him like fires out of control, messing with his head, confusing him. Crazy wanted to go to Aria and chase more warlocks. The long and short of it was that Tuuran didn't.

A shout rang out from the rubble, then another and a crack of lightning and he was off his wall in a flash, crouched behind the gold-glass shield he'd stolen off a dead Taiytakei halfway up the Eye of the Sea Goddess, peering out in case everything was about to kick off again.

'Bird! Bring it down!'

He couldn't see who was doing the shouting but he saw the next flash of lightning, a jagged crack of it launched into the sky, fired off at some speck, a black dot against the deep blue, nothing more.

'Bring it down! It came from the tower.'

Tuuran hunched up against the broken stone wall and watched, pieces of shattered gold-glass all around him. He didn't have a lightning wand because the wands only worked for the night-skins. Did the slave brands see to that? He didn't know. He watched the bird until he couldn't see it any more. The night-skins threw a dozen lightning bolts, trying to bring it down, but they all missed. Eventually they stopped shouting at each other and got back to whatever they were doing.

Tuuran waited a bit, just in case they decided to change their minds and started throwing lightning again; when they didn't, he got up, stretched his shoulders and wandered around the walls, skirting the smashed chunks of glass from the two fallen towers of what had once been the glorious Palace of Roses, all odd shapes and splinters and corners now, some of them as big as a house, all scattered among glittering gravel. Three towers of glass and gold had once stood here, colossal things that scraped the sky itself when he'd looked from the city below, but only one was left standing. The dragon had brought the other two down, rending them with claw and lashing tail, cracking them cascading to the jagged stumps that remained. The elegant yards and immaculate gardens that had once run between them were covered in twinkling splinters and sparkling rubble. Dead men – pieces of dead men – lay in scattered piles against the outer walls, and many of those walls were cracked and splintered too. In the sunlight the ruins gleamed like a vast pile of gold. Tuuran sniggered to himself at that. Like an immense heap of treasure with a dragon on the top, only the dragon had gone.

The remains of black-powder cannon lay scattered about, their gold-glass workings fractured and broken, their metal tubes and gears mangled and twisted but not so broken as to hide their purpose and thus their failure. What wasn't smashed was scorched and charred or pockmarked by the shrapnel of flying knives of glass. Where the outer ring of the palace was more than a twisted iron skeleton in a circle of debris, where it hadn't been smashed open or exploded from the inside, handfuls of Taiytakei soldiers herded groups of captives. A magnificent gatehouse stood bizarrely intact, its bronze gates as tall as a dragon. They hung open and askew and seemed to Tuuran slightly sad. Beyond, a zigzag road wound down the slope of the Dul Matha. Two more gatehouses lay scorched and burned across its way, scattered around with the charred remains of the dragon's passing. The road wound to the edge of the cliff, to the glass-and-gold Bridge of Forever or the Bridge of Eternity or something like that – Tuuran couldn't remember – which joined Dul Matha to the island that was the Eye of the Sea Goddess. The first bridge to join those cliffs had been made from a rope spun from the hair of Ten Tazei or some daft story like that. Now a great span of golden glass levitated between them, a thousand feet above the sea. It was still intact. That was something then, since the only other way off the island palace was to plunge from the cliffs into the sea.

Tuuran's eyes scanned the road, winding their way down. In a few places blackened bodies still smouldered from the dragon's passing. Furtive figures scuttled among them. Fugitives? Men of conscience lingering to give last rites to the dead and ease their passage to the next life? Maybe just looters. The brave and the mad. Crazy people. Tuuran had seen plenty of fights in his time but none as bloody as this. No quarter. Mobs of enraged slaves tearing night-skins to pieces. The dragon burning everything. Kept a man on edge, that did. Best to keep quiet and out of the way. He went back to his wall and nudged Crazy. 'We should be going, my friend.'

Crazy ignored him. Not that that was particularly strange.

When Tuuran looked again, Taiytakei soldiers were piling barrels across the middle of the bridge. He didn't much like the look of that, at least not while he was standing on the wrong side of it. 'They're going to bring it down,' he said. 'Then we're stuck here. I'm not sure they're going to let us off.' The other Taiytakei didn't look they were leaving any time soon though, so he supposed there wasn't any hurry. Still, it had his hackles up.

Crazy didn't move. On other days Tuuran might have shrugged his shoulders and sat beside him, waiting for Crazy to come back from wherever his thoughts had taken him. But today Tuuran had a dragon to find. It made him restless. They were going their separate ways from here. He could feel it.

'Well then. I'll be going,' he said; and when Crazy still didn't look round, Tuuran nodded to himself because this was how an Adamantine Man was after all. Each to his own duty. No regrets, no doubts, no hesitation, just getting on with what needed to be done. He turned his back and walked alone through the great bronze gates and down towards the bridge, briskly past the dead and the living. No sense dallying. It was time to move on. Making a fuss about it wouldn't change anything, however shit it felt to simply up and go.

He reached the bridge. Two Taiytakei stopped what they were doing and turned to meet him, barring his way. The rest kept on taking barrels off a glass sled hovering in the air beside them. The ground around the end of the bridge was thick with bodies and tumbled stone, same as when Tuuran and Crazy had first come over, a litany of dead among makeshift impromptu barricades that had all counted for nothing when the dragon came crashing among them. The bodies he remembered were all charred black and flaking on account of the dragon burning fifty shades of shit out of everything, so it wasn't hard to see the corpses that had come later. A scatter of slaves, their pale dead skin untouched by dragon-fire. To Tuuran, the scars and burns that marked them looked a lot like lightning.

The Taiytakei blocking his path across the bridge had lightning wands hung from their hips. They were dressed in glass-and-gold armour and carried ornately spiked maces for smashing that same armour to pieces. Ashgars. Tuuran didn't have any of those things, but he did have a nice big gold-glass shield that seemed to do for the lightning and a nice big axe too; and he'd found his axe could make a very pleasant mess even of a man dressed in gold-glass.

The fresh bodies were unbranded oar-slaves, most of them, but there were sword-slaves in there too. Tuuran smiled at the Taiytakei soldiers and shook his head and kept on coming. One hand went behind his back as if to scratch an itch. He rolled his shoulders, loosening his shield arm. This was all going to go bad, wasn't it?

The closer soldier whipped out his wand and fired. Tuuran saw it coming and dropped to his haunches. Lightning cracked and sparked off his shield. His ears rang, his eyes stung, a sudden sharp tang in the air bit at his nose. Never mind that though. He moved fast, a sudden dash forward, the hand behind his back clamped around the shaft of his axe.

'You shit-eating slavers never change, do you?' A second thunderous flash of lightning deafened and half-blinded him, but he was still moving and his axe was swinging around his head, and the two Taiytakei in front of him were gawping like a pair of old men, too busy wondering why their lightning hadn't killed him to be thinking straight. The swing of his axe took the first soldier across the face, smashing his helm and showering bits of it down his throat. Most of his chin and his teeth jumped loose in a spray of red. The axe didn't stop. Tuuran steered its blade into the second man's shoulder. The first Taiytakei fell back, sank to his knees and held his hands to his face and then crumpled. Tuuran gave him a few seconds before he either fainted or drowned in his own blood. The second soldier was still up, screaming, hand clutched to his shoulder, a few teeth and bits of the first soldier's face wrapped around his neck. Tuuran hadn't met any armour yet that could turn a sharp axe on the end of a good strong arm, but the gold-glass had taken the sting out of his swing. Well, that and the first man's face.

Out on the bridge the Taiytakei stacking barrels had stopped. Eight of them, and they all had their own wands and were reaching for them. A little voice in the back of Tuuran's head wondered whether he'd properly thought this one through. He kicked the wounded soldier hard in the hip and slammed into him, face to face, driving him towards the others. Lightning hit them, bursting in sparks all around the wounded man's gold-glass. It bit at Tuuran's face and fingers. He yelped and jumped away, almost dropped his axe, shoved the wounded man at the others, sparks still jumping from his armour, stumbled and almost fell. Eight at once? Soft in the head that was ...

Change of plan. He cringed behind his shield, stooped and kicked at one of the sleds they'd used to carry the barrels and sent it gliding back the way he'd come. He jumped on it as the soldiers found their wits, turned as fast as he could as they threw lightning at him, and hunkered down, the shield held behind him, eyes almost closed, teeth gritted, muttering a prayer or two to his ancestors as the sled carried him back to the end of the bridge. Thunderbolts rang around him. He felt them hit the shield. His hand went numb and then the sled reached the rubble of the barricades and Tuuran threw himself helter-skelter behind the first cover he could see. He took a moment and a few deep breaths. He certainly wasn't about to get up close into a fight with eight lunatics throwing lightning about the place when they were surrounded by explosive barrels of black powder.

'Well then, Tuuran, now what?' The fresh bodies told him all he needed to know: the Taiytakei were killing everyone. Scorching the earth. He wasn't even much surprised. You didn't let loose a horde of slaves and then expect them to walk meekly back into their chains when it was done. And you certainly didn't leave them to spread havoc and a dangerous taste for freedom.

He peered out and then ducked back as more lightning came his way. 'I was on your side you mudfeet,' he yelled at them, not that it was going to make any difference.

A movement caught his eye in the cracked stone and splinters of what might once have been a watchtower. A piece of burning wood flew from it onto the bridge. Another followed and then another. They skittered across the glass and landed around the Taiytakei and their barrels of black powder. Tuuran sank down, grinning. Lightning flew back, raking the wreckage of the watchtower but didn't seem to make any difference to the burning sticks flying out onto the bridge. When the lightning finally stopped, Tuuran risked a look. Taiytakei were running full pelt away. The barrels sat still and quiet. Pieces of wood burned around them.

'Hey!' Tuuran threw a stone at the ruined tower. 'Crazy? That you?'

Crazy Mad scuttled out from the rubble, hunched low in case the bridge exploded or some idiot started chucking lightning at him again. He hurdled Tuuran's floating sled and dived into the dirt beside him. 'And how far did you think you'd get without me, big man?'

'As far as I bloody wanted.' Tuuran smiled as he said it. Might have been true – probably was – but it felt right, the two of them side by side.

'No ships to take me back to Aria here.' Crazy shuffled closer, watching the bridge and peering at the Taiytakei on the far side. 'No ships to take us anywhere at all, by the looks of it.'

'Told you so.'

'Smug piece of shit.' Crazy crawled to the sled and poked at it. 'What's this then?'

'Cargo sled. The night-skins use them to move stuff about when they can't use slaves. Must have carried the powder up from the ships.'

Crazy poked at it some more. He seemed fascinated by the way it hovered over the ground and moved back and forth with even the lightest touch. 'What happens if I push this off a cliff? It just keeps floating, does it?'

Tuuran shrugged. 'Well I was hoping so. That or it plunges to the sea, tips everything off as it goes and then settles itself nice and happy a foot above the waves with everything else smashed to bits on the rocks below. Definitely one or the other. Maybe depends on how much you put on top of it.' He shrugged. 'How would I know? Do I look like a night-skin to you?'

Crazy gave him a dirty look. 'Best I don't answer that, big man. So, you planning on waiting here for them soldiers up at the palace to come and find they haven't got a bridge any more and then for the two of us to fight a few hundred Taiytakei for the only way off this place? Or were you thinking more about slipping off somewhere quiet while they're all still busy. Because I'm easy, either way.' Crazy turned, tugging at the sled. After a moment Tuuran followed, walking back up the road out of range of the Taiytakei across the bridge. The barrels still hadn't exploded.

'You should have thrown more fire,' Tuuran said.

Crazy Mad shrugged. 'I threw enough.' He chuckled. 'You wait, big man. Just when you're not ready … then boom.' He snapped his fingers.

It was probably a coincidence that the bridge exploded a moment later, but with Crazy Mad these days you could never quite be sure.

2

Baros Tsen

Baros Tsen T'Varr, first t'varr to the mad Sea Lord Quai'Shu of Xican, blinked. For a moment the incongruity of his circumstances overwhelmed him. He sat in his bath, the gloomy air full of steam and the scent Xizic, lit by the soft light of the walls in the bowels of his dragon-eyrie. The dragon still roared its victory on the walls up above, but here, deep below, he couldn't hear its calls. He was naked, alone in the near-scalding water with a woman whom a great many men desired. He'd put himself in her power because it seemed the only way to stop her, and now he was quivering with fear.

And how, exactly, did you think this was going to help?

'Give me what I want,' said the dragon-queen, 'or I will find another who will. Your friends from the mountains perhaps.' She was looking right through him. Her copper hair, cropped in the manner of a slave, was plastered in haphazard spikes and tufts across her scalp. Her face was bruised and fresh streaks of dried blood stuck to her cheeks. Her eyes were ferocious. He turned away, trying to think, looking at the walls. They were the same white stone as the rest of the eyrie and shone with an inner light that waxed and waned with the rise and fall of the sun and the moon. The bath sat in the centre of a large round room, on the floor instead of sunk into it because no one had found a way to cut the enchanted eyrie stone. A ring of arches surrounded it, simple and unadorned. Beneath the bath was a plinth, a slab of white stone that struck Tsen as uncomfortably like a sacrificial altar. They hadn't been able to move it and so he'd had the bath placed on top of it and not given it another moment's thought. Until now. Now the idea of being naked with that altar beneath him made him shiver. He felt very much like a sacrifice. Very much indeed.

She'd killed the Elemental Man he'd sent to stop her, which was laughably unbelievable except she'd come back with his knife to prove it. She'd burned a city to ash and shattered its towers into a desert of splintered glass. She'd done it in their Sea Lord's name and by doing so had ruined them all.

Beside the bath sat a brass bowl on a pedestal filled with water and a little ice. Tsen usually kept a bottle of his best apple wine there, comfortably chilled for him to sip at his leisure. The dragon-queen had smashed it just a minute ago, but he always had more. He flipped the ice out to the floor and then dipped his middle finger into the water. As the ripples shimmered, he told the dragon-queen how he and Shrin Chrias Kwen were bound together and how they could, if each other allowed it, watch over one another. *Or spy, as we all prefer to think of it.* Chrias who led Quai'Shu's soldiers. He'd never seen a vitriol quite as pure as that between the dragon-queen and Quai'Shu's kwen.

He tried to show her but Zafir made no move to look. Tsen shook his head and pulled his finger out of the water. 'I will consider your proposal, Dragon-Queen.' He tried to keep his face still, to give nothing away. The Chrias he'd glimpsed in the water had the dragon-disease, the incurable Statue Plague that the alchemist from the dragon-realms had tried so very hard to contain. Tsen had no doubt at all that Zafir had done that.

'To life and its potency.' Zafir smiled and raised her glass. When she saw that Tsen's was empty, she leaned across and tipped him some wine from her own. There were drops of blood in it from when she'd smashed the empty bottle and pointedly cut herself in case he'd forgotten how dangerous she was. He made himself look at her again. Her skin was red and raw where her armour had chafed. There were three fresh cuts on her face and deep dark bruises, black and purple, one around her eyes and many on her arms. When she ran a hand through her hair it stuck up and out at all angles. Her bared teeth gleamed in the light of the white stone walls. Tsen forced himself to smile back.

'To life, Dragon-Queen, although I am bewildered by the idea that either of us may cling to it much longer.' He pretended not to notice the blood as he lifted the glass. The smile on her face stayed exactly as it was, fixed in place.

'I'm glad Shrin Chrias Kwen wasn't killed,' she said. And Tsen understood perfectly well, for the alchemist in his eyrie held the only cure for the Plague and the alchemist was beholden to the dragon-queen. Chrias would die, slowly and in agony. He could see it in her eyes. *But you always knew she was dangerous. You chose to play with the fire, Tsen, when you could so easily have simply snuffed it out. Are you feeling burned enough yet? The people of Dhar Thosis surely are.*

The dragon-queen raised her glass and then hesitated. She was watching him, a strange play of emotion flickering across her face. Victory and doubt. Joyous glee and shame and a terrible guilt. A hopeless, relentless drive. Tsen couldn't begin to fathom it. As he touched his glass to his lips, she suddenly sprang forward and slapped it out of his hand. It flew off into the steam and shattered somewhere on the floor; and it was all so unexpected that Tsen didn't move, didn't even flinch, just sat in the water, paralysed as they stared at one another, each apparently as surprised as the other. A moment passed between them and then the dragon-queen climbed from the bath, her movements sharp and fast. Throwing on her shift, she stooped and picked up the bladeless knife of the Elemental Man she'd killed. 'The Adamantine Man who served our alchemist,' she said, her voice twisted and choked. 'By whatever gods you believe in, you find him. Bring him here! And when you do, you fall on your knees before him, Baros Tsen T'Varr, and you thank him. You thank him as though you owe him your life. Because you do.' Then she was gone.

For a while Tsen stared after her. He had no idea what had just happened, and all he could think of was how utterly hopelessly helpless he'd been when she'd moved. She was fast, but that wasn't it. She'd taken him completely by surprise. And he still couldn't move because even now it was so damned unexpected. Why had she ...

May the slugs in my orchards pity me. It dawned on him then, far too late, what she'd almost done to him. He looked in horror at the wine spilled across the rim of the bath and the shattered glass somewhere on the floor below and saw again Shrin Chrias Kwen as he'd been a moment before, shimmering in the water, rubbing at the hardening patch of skin on his arm where the dragon-disease was taking hold. Zafir had done that to him. She carried the disease, and *that* was how she'd given it to him, on the day when he and his men had raped her to make her understand that she was a slave. It was in her blood, and her blood had been in the wine she'd shared, that she'd put into his glass. He'd taken it for madness when she'd smashed his decanter and cut herself, but no, she'd known exactly what she was doing. She'd brought him down here to give him the Hatchling Disease and then dangle his life in front of him. And he would have drunk her wine, too stupid to see the trap wrapping its embrace around him. If she hadn't slapped the glass out of his hand...

But she had. *Why?*

A tingling numbness spread through the middle finger of his left hand. The bones inside seemed to vibrate gently. His bond to Shrin Chrias Kwen. His ring was still off so the kwen was watching him now, seeing through his eyes, perhaps wondering why Tsen had done the same a few minutes earlier. *Too late, old foe. She's gone. You don't get to see her. And perhaps that's as well, given what she's done to you.* Lazily Tsen draped his arm over the edge of the bath and dipped his throbbing finger back into the bowl of water. Quai'Shu's intent when he'd made all his inner circle bond like this had been to tie his most trusted family and servants more tightly. Words could travel faster. They would have an edge, he told them, over the other great houses of the sea lords. They would know things ahead of allies and enemies alike. In practice, they'd all done what anyone else would have done and taken to spying on one another. So now they wore the rings. The rings stopped the bond from working but didn't stop you from knowing that someone was trying to use it. Once they had the rings, it had worked out rather better. Sometimes they even managed to do what Quai'Shu claimed to have wanted in the first place and simply talked to each other.

In the bowl and the iced-water within, Tsen found the kwen looking back at him. They watched each other, which was all very dull, and then in his cabin on his ship Chrias held out his arm and showed Tsen, carefully and deliberately this time, the unmistakable signs of the Hatchling Disease. Tsen muttered under his breath, *You deserve it!* But the visions were only visions and so Chrias wouldn't hear.

The kwen moved from his bowl of water and sat at his writing desk and wrote for Tsen to see, 'If she lives, kill her. Do it now. Do it for your own good.' He put down his pen and picked up a ring. He looked at it very deliberately for a moment, mouthed a single word and then slipped the ring on his finger. The vision in Tsen's water vanished at once.

Goodbye. Shrin Chrias Kwen's last word and Tsen supposed that was the last they'd ever see of each other. If he was honest with himself, he couldn't pretend he was particularly sorry about that. He stared into the water long after Chrias was gone. Zafir had had him at her mercy, and at the very last moment she'd changed her mind. Why?

He put his own ring back on and looked at his hands. There weren't that many left of the cabal that Quai'Shu had thought would take over the world. Jima Hsian and Zifan'Shu were dead. Quai'Shu himself was alive but mad and mumbling nonsense to himself a few doors up the passageway. Baran Meido, Quai'Shu's second son, had threatened to cut off every one of his own fingers rather than allow the slivers of binding gold-glass to be implanted under his skin. Which left Bronzehand, but Bronzehand was in an entirely other world.

Why? Why did she stop me from drinking it?

He stared at the question and found nothing. He played through every moment since the dragon had come back from Dhar Thosis and Zafir had slid off its back and stood before him, battered and bruised, bloodied and full of swagger, and had dropped the bladeless knife of the Elemental Man at his feet. He picked at each memory. He'd come down here with her, too bewildered by the horror of what she'd done to think properly. She could have burned them all from the back of her dragon if that was what she'd wanted, and for what she'd done they were both as good as dead. She'd ruined everyone and he'd felt nothing beyond an overwhelming sickening dread. It was his fault as much as hers. No point pretending otherwise.

But why change her mind? *Why?*

He looked for a towel. On other days he might have called Kalaiya to listen while he poured out his heart and his worries until they were both wrinkled like prunes, but he couldn't, not today. His bath was tainted, maybe for ever. Zafir's blood was in the water. Maybe now instead of Kalaiya's dark skin, the ghost he'd see here would always be pale and bruised and bloodied and carry the vicious face of a dragon.

Is the water itself tainted now? Once that crossed his mind he couldn't get out quickly enough. He dried himself, dressed in a simple tunic, left his slaves to clean up the mess and walked briskly through the softly glowing curved spirals of the eyrie tunnels. The old luminous stone made him small and frightened today, and he was glad to reach the open space and the wide skies of the dragon yard, the hot desert breeze and the smell of sand.

Perched up on the eyrie wall, the dragon looked down at him, unbearably huge, the sun gleaming off its ruddy golden scales between dark streaks of blood. It had claws big enough to pick up a cart and crush it, could swallow a man whole or bite an armoured knight clean in half. Tsen had seen both. He turned his face away, refusing to look at the monster; instead he climbed the flawless white walls to stare out with his back firmly to everything, looking over the desert. There weren't any places to hide an enormous floating castle out here. The Empty Sands had earned their name for being, well, *empty*. Maybe he could tow the eyrie west to the Konsidar and try to hide it in the mountain valleys, but the Konsidar was a forbidden place by order of the Elemental Men. To trespass there was death, and so . . .

He stopped himself. Couldn't help but laugh at that, because the punishment for burning Dhar Thosis was surely going to be death at the very least, and a lot worse if anyone could think of something. He was as damned as he could possibly be and so might as well go to the Konsidar or do anything that damn well pleased him. They could only kill him once.

He let the desert and the breeze and the quiet enrapture him and the thought faded silently into nothing. He didn't hear Chay-Liang come up behind him. He only knew the enchantress was there when he felt her hand on his shoulder.

'You aren't responsible,' she said quietly.

'Nor have I ever been.' Tsen smiled. 'My father used to say it was mostly my bones. I have irresponsible bones. That's what he used to tell me. It seems he was right.' He felt the hand on his shoulder tense. Chay-Liang thought him too flippant for a t'varr but that was because she entirely misunderstood his need for humour. As was often the way with the scholars of the Hingwal Taktse, she was immensely clever and desperately naive. He turned and smiled at her. *See, now here's a reason to face what you've done. You can save her from hanging beside you. You can at least do* that, *can't you? Chay-Liang and Kalaiya and all the others ...*

'You did not—'

Tsen cut her off. There was no hiding. No point even trying. 'I tried to play a game and I lost, Liang, that's the long and the short of it, the be-all and the end-all. The only shred of anything decent left is to stand and face the consequences. I am responsible. Or, at the very least, I am *accountable*. The dragons are mine and I will go to my fate for what they have done.' He kept smiling but his eyes glistened. 'Look after my Kalaiya when the time comes. And look after the truth. Make sure it reaches those whose ears most need to hear it. Do not let Mai'Choiro Kwen spin lies about us. He will try.' He saw himself in the bath again, the glass flying out of his hand. *Why?* 'I'd send you somewhere safe if I could think of such a place,' he said.

'There is no place.' And they both knew she was right. 'Better we stay here and face the wrath of the Elemental Men together. I will not run either, Baros Tsen. I was there, remember? Hiding where the glasship's golem pilot should have been and I heard every word. No one else knows that. I will testify for you.'

Tsen nodded. Not that it would make any difference except to make sure that he and Mai'Choiro Kwen swung on the gallows side by side. *Oh and you were so clever, Tsen. So very very clever trapping Mai'Choiro so many times and in so many ways. How clever do you feel now?* 'Have your glasships drag us east towards the Godspike, Liang. I want you to do a thing that no one has done for a long time. I want you to fly above the storm-dark that encircles it. It will buy us a few days while I go to Dhar Thosis and see for myself what Chrias and my dragon have done.' *Yes, and perhaps your glasships that pull my floating eyrie across the desert could simply let go when the Elemental Men come, let the eyrie sink into the storm-dark and die, dragons and everything. Wipe us away as though we never existed.* Yes, he could quite see how that might be for the best.

He led Chay-Liang back to his study and offered her a glass

of apple wine while he changed into the formal robes of a t'varr who answered to none but a sea lord. His slaves braided his hair down to his ankles and dressed him in his robe of golden feathers. It might be the last time he'd get to wear it so best to make the most of it. There was a good chance the Elemental Men would be waiting for him when he came back.

'What about the slave?' Chay-Liang couldn't quite keep her loathing out of her voice. *I should have listened to you, eh?*

'Zafir? Lock her away until I return.'

'I'd rather hang her and be done with it.'

'But I would not.' The enormity of what she'd done in his name kept staring him in the face, standing in his way whenever he tried to move. He couldn't simply have her executed because he needed her presence to remind him of his own guilt. 'Liang, she knew the truth, and of all of us she has no reason to hide it. Her fate is certain.' And perhaps a little because, in the end, when she'd had the chance to poison him, she'd turned it down and he couldn't understand why. 'I'm going to take Kalaiya with me. It's an indulgence, I know, but I don't think I can face this alone. If they're waiting for me when I come back, they will try to use her to punish me. She deserves better. So do you, Chay-Liang.'

He sent her away and thought about having someone call Kalaiya to attend him, then changed his mind and walked through the eyrie to find her. On other days he passed through the ancient passageways oblivious to their age and their origin, but today, as unsettled as he was, Tsen saw them for what they truly were: relics beyond understanding, detritus left after the half-gods brought the Splintering upon the world and vanished. They were the unknown. Like the dragons, like so many things. Like the eyrie itself, a huge piece of rock, an enigma floating over the dunes of the desert, honeycombed with mystery, abandoned for hundreds of years and sitting for all that time, patiently waiting, its design unfinished and its purpose long forgotten. He tried to shake the feeling away. It was a perilous thing sometimes, to stop and take a long look at the world right there around him; that was when he realised how little of it he truly understood.

Kalaiya, of course, had known he'd come. She was waiting for him. Tsen opened the iron door to her room and she came to him at once, with neither haste nor ceremony, and wrapped her arms around him. Succour and comfort. She gave him his strength. He buried his face in her endless hair.

'Do you remember,' he asked, 'how things were before all this started? At the very least, I could have called my life normal, or perhaps not very interesting, or frequently mundane.' He took a deep breath. Six months since the dragons came. There certainly hadn't been as many people who'd wanted him to conveniently drop dead back then. Couldn't have been more than three or four. Now it must be more like ... *well, frankly, once it comes out what the dragon-queen has done to Dhar Thosis, pretty much everyone.*

Kalaiya held him tight. 'I remember.' Her hair smelled of Xizic. His favourite, not hers.

'It's all over, Kalaiya. I will never be the next sea lord of Xican. There will *be* no Xican any more. They'll hang me, and you know there's no running from the Elemental Men. I'll keep you safe as best I can. I need to go now. To see what ...' There was a lump in his throat, choking him. For years he'd built them a future full of promises and now they were all burned to ash. 'I need to leave.' She was shaking. Scared, no matter how she tried to hide it. He let her go and forced himself to look at her, to see her and remember her face. *Look at her and look at what you've done.* He could only die once, however unpleasant it was, but Kalaiya would be there to watch it and to remember, over and over. After he was gone, she'd be nothing. No one would want her. She'd be tainted by him for ever. 'Come with me? Please?' He couldn't look at her any more. He turned and fled, but it didn't help. The regret and the pain that tore at his chest came with him.

Outside, waiting in the middle of the dragon yard, Chay-Liang already had a gondola hanging by twelve silver chains from the sedate rotation of a glasship's disc. Slaves hurried back and forth, carrying supplies. Apple wine. An enchanted bowl of never-melting ice that Liang had made for him years ago. Barrels of water for the tanks on the gondola's roof. Hard bread and biscuits, fruit, cheese, silken sheets and blankets and everything he'd need. He stood in the middle of them, doing nothing useful and simply getting in the way while they bustled around him as though he wasn't there. The junior t'varr overseer stiffened when he saw Tsen but then decided to ignore him too. Tsen felt his resentment, his disapproval. *You're running away from what you've done.* And, yes he was, but he was running towards it too.

Kalaiya, of course, didn't come out until the gondola was ready to fly. She made him wait, which was her subtle way of telling him she was cross with him. When she came out to the dragon yard, she was dressed in the plain white tunic of a slave, in case anyone had forgotten. Tsen took her hand and led her inside. The ramp closed behind them. He tried to think of something to say, but as the glasship above rose into the sky and lifted the gondola away, he couldn't shake off that vision of her, years from now, a penniless beggar eking out the barest sketch of a life on what charity she could find. All that they were, all that they could have been, all gone to waste because of his own stupid hubris.

3

Hiding in Waiting

Tuuran called him Crazy Mad. The big man had called him that since the day Berren had first told him the story of how the warlocks had stolen his life, how they'd sucked him out of his body and trapped him in another one, and how he'd escaped and gone looking for the man who wore his face. How he had pieces of other souls trapped inside him – Skyrie the warlock and something else, something dark and huge and powerful. *All I want is to find out who I am. All I want is to have my life back.* He clung to those other names, the person he used to be. Berren the Bloody Judge. Berren the Crowntaker. Inside, that's who he was and who he meant to be again one day, but first they had to get off this stupid island and away from this stupid war and all these murderous Taiytakei.

He found the remains of a wooden tower on the cliffs away from both the bridge and the palace, a half-tumbled-down ruin long before the dragon had come. An old lookout point perhaps, watching over the sea before Sea Lord Senxian had raised his golden towers. He and Tuuran hid inside, covering themselves in mouldy sacking and bits and pieces of rotting timber, waiting out the day. Now and then, when Tuuran fell asleep and started to snore, Berren poked him. He'd seen what the Taiytakei on top of the Dul Matha were doing, clearing it, killing anyone who wasn't one of them. As twilight fell, he slipped out into the gloom and watched them leave. A pair of glass sleds ten times bigger than the one he and Tuuran had stolen ferried them to the few ships that had survived the onslaught. Before they left, the soldiers threw something from the shattered stump of one of the three towers to dangle by a rope. Berren heard a small cheer drift down from the ruins. A body, but he had no idea whose it was, nor any reason to care.

When they were gone, he woke Tuuran and they pulled their stolen sled to the cliff by the bridge. Berren tied a rope around it while Tuuran put a rock on top. They pushed it out over the abyss between the two islands to see what happened.

'Well that's a bit of a relief.' Tuuran grinned when it didn't plummet into the sea. 'Would have been a bit of a bugger otherwise.'

They pulled it back, took off the rock off and sat on the sled. Tuuran pushed off as hard as he could against the cliffs and they crossed the divide between Dul Matha and the Eye of the Sea Goddess, drifting over the waves far below. Tuuran sat still, looking up at the moon and the stars bright overhead, glancing now and then at the far cliff coming towards them as though it was a perfectly normal thing to float a thousand feet above rocks and the sea on something your eyes saw right though if you could bring yourself to look. Berren tried not to think about it. He had no idea how the sled worked; it just did. Let that be enough. On the far side fires still burned in the ruins of what had once been rich palaces. He felt a restlessness stir inside him, roused by his fear and by the flames. He pushed it away but it persisted. The dragon had awoken something. Memories. Ideas. Desires.

The Eye of the Sea Goddess had been an island of palaces once, of shimmering glass-and-gold towers, but the dragon had smashed most of them in a fit of … what? Rage? Among the few that still stood were the dancing lights of swinging lanterns, and as they came closer, Berren saw they were gangs of soldiers, searching the ruins for survivors. When the soldiers found one, they dragged him out and killed him.

Tuuran left the sled by the bridge. Smashed pieces of glass lay scattered underfoot, sharp and dangerous, or else ground to a gravel that crunched with shocking loudness at every step. The silver light of the half-moon cast eerie shadows among the splinters and shards. A single road meandered down the island from the cliffs and the Dul Matha towards a causeway and another bridge to the mainland, but it was busy with soldiers camped out for the night. Elsewhere, the slope was steep and treacherous, rocks sticking out between thick tangles of grass and thorny vines or else hidden beneath them, hungry to snatch a foot and twist an ankle. Tuuran bulled through it, cutting a path to the seaward cliffs away from the debris and the hunting parties of Taiytakei until they found a gully overgrown with thorn bushes, the sort of place you couldn't see until you as good as walked straight into it.

'This'll do.' He pushed his way under the overhanging thorns and settled down, waiting for the dawn. He was snoring again in minutes. Berren tossed and turned and shifted. Whenever he closed his eyes, he saw the dragon of Dhar Thosis again, the red and gold scaled monster as he and Tuuran had stood before it in the freshly ruined palace. Its eyes had been all over him. It *knew* him, and memories that weren't his had bubbled and boiled in his head, memories of another time and place when there hadn't been one dragon but a thousand, and all of them were his.

The warlock Saffran Kuy had cut him with a golden knife once, long ago, and he'd seen a flash of his future. Yesterday he'd killed Saffran's brother Vallas and taken that knife. In the dying warlock's memories he'd seen the man with the ruined face and the one blind milky eye. Among the memories in his head that weren't his own, he saw himself dying on the edge of a swamp with the night split open like swollen flesh and leaking black shadows, the stars winking out one by one. He saw the same man standing over him.

'Are you death?' he tried to ask, but the words never came out.

'I carry the Black Moon.' The eye bored into him.

That man. The man with the ruined face and the milky eye. *He* had the answers. He'd made all this happen, and now Berren had something in his head that didn't belong. Something sleeping and crippled, but he felt it when it stirred. A splinter of some unbounded power.

'I need to find him,' he whispered to the stars. 'I need to know what he did to me.' Before it was too late.

After a while he left Tuuran to his snores and slipped through the night, crept back among the ruins to where the Taiytakei were camped, loud, bright with fire and easy to avoid. He slipped around them, watching and waiting for a lone sentry to settle just a little too far from the rest. Old familiar skills and they came back to him with ease. He'd been a thief once, an orphan from Shipwrights' in Deephaven, a boy pickpocket, a cutpurse and a burglar. He smiled to himself. It was all so long ago and he'd been so many things since then, but he still remembered.

He found his sentry at last, sitting on a boulder that had once been a piece of some rich man's home, head starting to nod. Berren gave him a few minutes to doze and then came up behind him and stabbed him through the heart with the gold-hafted knife. The blade went straight through flesh and armour as though both were made of mist, but then this was no ordinary knife – he'd learned *that* back in Deephaven too – and its blade wasn't one for cutting skin and flesh. Beside the sentry a spectre shimmered into being, the web of webs that was the sum of what the soldier was and would be. Thoughts, memories, ambitions, ideals. His soul. Everything.

As Berren reached into them, the sentry started. He jerked up, eyes unblinking wide, mouth frozen open, scream unvoiced.

You. Obey. Me.

Three little cuts from the golden knife to the strands of the soldier's soul, precise and perfect, and they made the man into his slave far more perfectly than any Taiytakei galley master could ever have wished. There was so much more this blade could do but Saffran Kuy had never shown him and the knife kept its secrets mockingly close. Berren pulled the sentry to the earth and whispered in his ear, 'Make no sound except in answer to my questions and speak in whispers that even the wind will barely hear.' More words came out of him then, words he didn't recognise and didn't know and in some language he'd never heard, and yet he understood their meaning. They were a binding. *You are my slave and I am your master.* He had a strange sense then that, if he'd wanted, he could have crept on further among the sleeping Taiytakei and cut them all, one after another until every man was his.

The sentry stared at Berren and then at the knife in his chest. His eyes gleamed wide with terror. He whimpered and his hands trembled.

'Do you understand?' hissed Berren.

The sentry opened his mouth as if to speak and then closed it again. He screwed up his face. Nodded.

'You're killing everyone here. All the sword-slaves who fought to take the city in the first place too?'

The Taiytakei nodded again. Berren slid closer and clutched the soldier's head. He met the man's eyes.

'*All* the slaves? Women and children too?'

Another nod. The soldier closed his eyes but it made little difference. Old or young, men or women, slaves were merely slaves to the night-skins. The lowest, the oar-slaves, were treated like cattle. Berren knew that all too well. He pushed the soldier away.

'I'm done with you.' He drew another blade, another knife, simple steel this time. 'I'm going to cut your throat now. You won't make a sound. Do you understand?'

Tears gleamed in the soldier's eyes but Berren had long learned the folly of mercy. When he was done, he crept back to Tuuran and their gully and waited for the sun to rise.

'They're killing everyone,' he said, when Tuuran finally stirred and rubbed his eyes. 'They're wiping this city away, all of it.'

Tuuran shrugged.

'That's not how you make war. I spent three years with the Sun King's armies when Merizikat and half the western provinces of the Dominion rose in revolt. I saw things there I thought I'd never see again. Men lining the road crucified and left to die. Thousands of them. But I never saw this. This isn't war.'

'This is the night-skins showing their true colours.' Tuuran spat. 'Pretty on the outside, black with rot underneath.'

They crept through the dawn light, past the sleepy-eyed watchmen and on down the length of the island, stopping often behind outcrops of rock or deep in the undergrowth, pressed into the shadows, picking their way around sentries and patrols. They skirted what had once been a thriving market, the stump of a bell tower marking the square behind it, full of soldiers now. The slope of the island eased after that. Berren saw the smashed remains of one of the giant rock-men poking up among the lavish stone mansions of the lower slopes, Senxian's sea titans who'd risen to fight the invaders, stone men as tall as a barn. When he looked out to sea, he saw another, wading through the shallows close to the mainland, wandering aimlessly. A lucky survivor? The dragon had plucked the others out of the water. It had dropped them high above the cliffs and smashed them, and Berren wondered how that was possible, even for a monster with wings bigger than the largest sails. The stone men surely weighed as much as a galley.

They haven't been to this world for a very long time. It is rich. The very air itself to them is like pashbahla. The thought came out of nowhere, his but not. He'd never heard of pashbahla and had no idea what it was until he found a memory of a leaf, long and thin and a deep dark red and knew that chewing it or brewing an infusion gave a man enough energy to feel he could do anything. *How do I know that?* And then Tuuran had his arm and was pulling him sideways.

'Trying to get seen, Crazy? Wanting to draw a little attention to yourself so we can test whether their lightning still passes straight through you?'

And there was another thing. He fingered the hole in his brigandine coat. Its edges were smooth and charred, melted metal and burned leather. Tuuran said there was another in the back, but Berren didn't remember being struck by lightning and he didn't have any mark on his skin. A man would remember that, wouldn't he? Being hit by lightning? If he survived, that was ...

'I need to find the warlock who did this to me,' Berren hissed. The warlock with the ruined face and the blind eye. 'I need to find him. I need to know what he did. I need to know what I am!'

'And I'm going to find my queen of dragons. But first we need to get off this blasted island.'

They moved on, skirting the shore, slow and careful, passing through the abandoned grounds of grand houses, past the ornate and colourful homes of traders in luxury and the exotic, with fancy gardens and pretty cottages by their sides. The stonework was scarred here and there, hit by flying debris during the explosions of the battle, but the whirlwind of the dragon had mostly passed this part of the island by. Tuuran climbed laboriously onto the roof of one and shielded his eyes against the sun. Berren vaulted lightly up beside him.

'There.' The big man was pointing at the bridge to the mainland maybe a half-mile further on. The bridge itself had been smashed during the battle but there was a causeway underneath it. Berren scanned the buildings on either side. Wisps of smoke rose between them. They were wreckage and rubble now, bombarded by rockets at the start of the battle and then burned by the dragon. One of the sea titans had smashed its way through them, heading up the slope until the dragon had torn it away into the sky. Tuuran swore and ducked back out of sight. There were Taiytakei everywhere.

'Even if we wait for nightfall, they'll see us if we try to cross. Question is, will they catch us? They'll have more sleds. Maybe we should try taking one.' He bared his teeth. 'That would do nicely, wouldn't it?'

'We could cross somewhere else?'

'Don't fancy swimming with all this.' Tuuran patted his axe and his shield. 'Don't much fancy leaving it behind either, all things considered. We need a place to hide and sit this out for a bit. Somewhere nicer than that gully we had last night if you don't mind. Stones for pillows is all very well but I fancy myself some nice silk sheets.' He squinted, then pointed inland. Berren followed his finger. Movement beside one of the houses. Too sly to be soldiers.

'What's wrong with right here?'

'Where there's people there's food.' Tuuran patted his belly. 'Did you eat yesterday? Because if you did then you didn't share, and we'd need to have some serious words about that, Crazy Mad. Besides, if those were soldiers then we'd know about it by now. More runaway slaves means more eyes to keep watch in the night, eh?'

Berren almost laughed. He'd learned the hard way to go days without eating if he had to. When Tuuran missed a meal, he usually started hitting things.

'Did you see the two night-skin soldiers heading that way?' Tuuran asked.

Berren shook his head. 'We should go the other way then, right?'

'Nah.' Tuuran grinned and stroked his axe. 'I'm hungry.'

4

The Writing Room

From the eyrie to Dhar Thosis took four days. The glasship crossed the Empty Sands and drifted high over the maze of cliffs and mesas and canyons and gullies that was the Desert of Thieves, a mosaic of parched broken stone, almost lifeless. Tsen kept the glasship low in case anyone else was out there, passing the abyss of the Queverra a few dozen miles to the north. From above, the landscape was like an unfinished puzzle, full of gaps and incongruities, disparate fragments forced where they didn't quite belong. Tsen, in his golden gondola, felt much the same. Fractured. He paced. He chewed Xizic. He talked to Kalaiya about all the things they'd never done and now never would. He couldn't hold her, not properly, not with the deep calm lasting embrace she deserved. He wanted to but he was just too tense. 'It's not your fault,' she kept saying. 'You didn't send the dragon to burn Dhar Thosis. You tried to stop them.' But it *was* his fault.

Eventually she got sick of him saying how sorry he was and slapped him. A slave slapping the first t'varr to a sea lord was the sort of thing for which slaves were flayed, but here, where there was no one else to see, they were long past slave and master. 'Mai'Choiro, kwen to the mighty Lord Shonda of Vespinarr with all his boundless wealth – the rider-slave's orders were his, not yours,' she hissed. She sounded petulant. She was angry because she was too clever, deep down, not to see that they were doomed, and her anger lashed out at him simply because there was no one else.

Or so I tell myself. Of course, she might simply be angry with me because I was an ambitious fool who played and lost. He touched her gently. 'I was with him,' he said. 'I listened and nodded and said nothing. I gave every sign of acquiescence, of being a loyal servant of Vespinarr, of accepting that fate.' He smiled a wan smile.

'Mai'Choiro is in the dingiest, muckiest most unpleasant room I could find. He deserves his prison even more than the rider-slave but it won't make a jot of difference. Except to annoy Shonda.' It was vindictiveness, really, nothing else, and a fat lot of good *that* did him.

'You should kill them both. Hang them. While you can.'

'If I do, the Elemental Men will destroy our families, our house. Everything.' Not that he gave a fig for most of that. 'No.' He let her go and shook his head. 'Mai'Choiro must be tried alongside me, and no one else knows the truth. No one except the rider-slave. Which means I can't hang *her* either, not yet, no matter how much it's the right thing to do, no matter how much I want to.' It was all of course a lot more complicated than that. Kalaiya probably knew that too.

'There's no way out, is there?' She was giving him a very deep look.

'No. Shrin Chrias Kwen took our armies to Dhar Thosis. The dragon is mine, as is the slave who rode it. I took a great risk with the lives of many innocents and now they're dead. The Elemental Men will summon the Arbiter of the Dralamut to pass judgement, and she will hang me. Knowing everything I know, I would do the same.' He turned away. 'All I can do now is make sure that no more suffer for my mistake than necessary.' *And try to see that Shonda gets the kicking he deserves after I swing from my gibbet.*

The glasship floated serenely on. Another day passed and then another until the sands returned, a last ridge before the sea which drew back slowly to reveal what lay beyond like an exotic dancer lowering a veil, slow and tantalising and at first hard to make out, until Tsen suddenly turned away from the window and sat with his back to it, refusing to look until the full horror was on show. Kalaiya put a hand on his shoulder. She didn't say anything. She didn't need to. The city was a ruin, everything the rider-slave had said and more, far worse than he'd imagined it. The marvellous docks were a wasteland of ash dotted with the blackened bones of great warehouses and the shattered wreckage of fallen glasships. The heart of the city was gone, massive shards of glass lying amid the broken skeletons of what few buildings remained, smeared with ash in blacks and greys and white.

Two sea titans lumbered in the shallows, making their presence felt. A handful of ships were anchored in the bay, a few boats straining their oars back and forth to the shore; and Tsen wondered who they were and what they made of what had happened. He imagined the first few fishermen arriving home, full of that anticipation of land that sailors have, of spying the dark line of the coast on the horizon, the pall of smoke, the smell of ash and soot on the wind, the near-empty docks, the beached ships, the few surviving masts all askew. Or perhaps they'd spied the Palace of Roses as they strained for home and wondered why only one tower glittered in the sunset and not three.

The gondola carried on, slow and unhurried across the water. The great bridges had been smashed; the dazzle of gold-glass towers looked as though a hurricane had torn through them, as though the island itself had stirred and shaken to throw them down. There were no glasships in the sky over Dhar Thosis, none at all.

'I did this,' he murmured to no one in particular.

'No.' Kalaiya squeezed his hand.

'Yes.' He could trust her. No one else now except maybe Chay-Liang, and it hit him hard then that the Watcher was dead. The only weapon he'd had for keeping the dragons and their rider in line, for keeping Quai'Shu alive and stopping the jackals of Vespinarr from taking his dream and making it their own, and he'd lost it.

'No.' He could hear the horror in Kalaiya's voice. The worst atrocity in five hundred years.

'Yes. And Lord Shonda will continue as he planned right from the very start. He's got exactly what he wanted.'

'He'll kill you, Tsen,' said Kalaiya quietly, 'and make sure you take every drop of blame for this. He'll do it quickly, as quickly as he possibly can. *Someone* has to die for this.'

She was probably right. Yes, the Vespinese would kill him and his dragon-riding slave and they'd kill Kalaiya too. 'They'll dismantle everything Quai'Shu strove to build. They'll tear down the Palace of Leaves, hand over the Grey Isle – whatever it takes to make reparation to Senxian's heirs – generous and gracious in their apparent munificence while on the quiet and in the shadows they silence any and all who know the truth!'

'And keep what they covet most: your dragons.' They understood each other so well. The rest of the world saw only a slave, but to Tsen, Kalaiya was so much more.

'He'll come quickly, fast and deadly to silence the truth before it can spread, so no one will ever see their guiding hand in the horror that lies here at the edge of the sea.'

Kalaiya gripped his hand so tightly it hurt. 'But the Vespinese can't act until they know it's been done. They can't act until they *know*, Tsen! You have time!'

Tsen nodded. 'Everyone across Takei'Tarr shall know the truth. That will be a worthwhile end to my life.' And for that he hadn't killed the rider-slave. It *was* for that, wasn't it?

The glasship drifted over the great fortress of Vul Tara, now a blackened smear. Tsen guided it up close to the cliffs of Dul Matha, up to what had once been the Palace of Roses. Two of the three towers were stumps. The dragon had done this, the dragon alone – up here, so far from Shrin Chrias Kwen's ships, from their rockets and black-powder guns and lightning cannon, it could be nothing else.

'Where are all the people?' asked Kalaiya. Tsen didn't answer. They were dead, of course.

The glasship's golem circled the ruined palace but no one came running waving their arms for rescue. Dul Matha was empty, a ruin left for ghosts. Chrias had done what any kwen would do if he could – cleansed the place. Killed everyone and then turned on the sword-slaves he'd brought with him and left nothing. The Doctrine of a Thousand Years. Eventually Tsen spotted Sea Lord Senxian himself, hanging by the neck from the jagged tip of one of his own shattered towers. Quai'Shu and Senxian weren't even enemies, only rivals; and even then only pawns in the great dance between Vespinarr and the desert lords of Cashax. So much ruin and for what? Tsen stared at the murdered sea lord swinging lazily back and forth and couldn't look away; instead he nudged towards the sea lord's body to look more closely. He'd been right to come here. A city gone. Wiped away. A sea lord hanging dead from his own palace was a thing you had to see. There'd be no forgiveness. They were all dead men walking, every single man or woman who'd played even the most glancing part in this.

Five days in the open being pecked at by seagulls hadn't done Senxian any favours. His clothes were the only things Tsen could recognise. Maybe it wasn't Senxian at all, but Tsen rather thought it was. He shook his head. 'Ah, my Chrias, my kwen. What did Shonda offer you? They'll hunt us to the end of every realm and you must have known it. But not me. I'll be waiting for them. I'll shout the truth as loud as I can before they hang me.' He was alone except for Kalaiya but maintained the pretence of an audience anyway. Practice. Habit. All those things. You never knew when an Elemental Man might be watching, after all. 'I tried to stop it.' He shook his head and turned away. 'I tried to stop it.'

'I never understood why you had to let it go so far, Tsen.' Kalaiya was weeping.

'It had to be seen! The words had to come from Mai'Choiro's mouth! The Watcher had to hear him speak them to know the truth of Shonda's treachery! I told him to *stop* them! I sent him …' He couldn't finish. 'I thought I'd bind them in their own tangled schemes and serve them up on a plate. I thought I'd buy us freedom from our debts. I thought I was cleverer than them. And I was too, but not as clever as I thought, and now the dragon-queen has ruined us all.' The urge came again, as it did every time he saw the hurt in Kalaiya's face, to reach out and touch her. 'I will keep you safe, Kalaiya. Above all else, I will keep you safe.'

Kalaiya held his hand against her cheek. 'I live and die by your side now, Baros Tsen.' And he almost wept and had to turn away and make a show of looking about the gondola.

'Look at all this.' He needed something to say and so he flailed at the walls panelled with their ellipses of perfect pale wood, exquisitely cut and carved around the silver edges of the curved gondola windows. At the plush thick carpet, the silver table, the bed where they slept with its silks as soft as goose down, at the glass cabinets with their silver frames with yet more glass inside, cups and decanters and spirits of every colour from every world the Taiytakei knew. 'You'll lose all this.'

'It doesn't matter. I'll lose you.' She pulled away from him and pointed through the gold-tinged glass at the last of the three great towers still standing. Tsen followed the line of her finger. Near the top of the tower was a balcony lined with cages for Senxian's jade ravens and the slaves that fed them. 'Look!'

'What do you see?'

'The cages are empty.'

'Perhaps the kwen's men let Senxian's ravens fly when they ransacked the palace.'

Kalaiya laughed. 'No one would doubt you're usually a clever and insightful man, Baros Tsen, but sometimes you're an idiot. Who would open the cage of a hungry raven? Would you?'

'No.'

'Scribes fly the jade ravens. To the rest of us, they're horrors.' She shook her head at him. 'Shrin Kwen's men didn't open them. The scribes of the Palace of Roses let their ravens fly before they died.' She didn't say any more now because she didn't need to. He understood exactly: word *had* gone. Jade ravens had flown from the Palace of Roses as it fell. Of course they had. He should have thought of that.

And then another thought sent a shiver through him: that scribes were creatures of habit. They copied every message in tiny words onto a silver ring to put around a raven's leg. They copied every message exactly, word for word, line for line, but they didn't compose them. If he was lucky, if the scribes had fled in a hurry, the original messages might still be there and he could see exactly *what* word had been sent, and to whom.

He moved quickly now, driven by a surge of impatience. Here was something he could do at last, a useful thing, and so it must be done and be done *now*. He threw open the door to the cramped closet where the glasship's pilot golem sat – dwarfish creatures made of clay, feeble-witted and barely intelligent, made by the Hingwal Taktse enchanters to fly glasships and nothing else. They were exquisite works of the enchanters' art, each one months of effort, but Tsen hadn't the first idea of anything except how much they cost, and right now he didn't care. They weren't clever enough to do what he had in mind on their own and so he stood over the creature, one eye looking out through the window, guiding it exactly. The glasship rose to hover over the top of the tower and then the golem lowered the gondola on its silver chains.

Tsen looked through the gold-glass walls of the palace and saw a bathhouse built to look out over the city and the sea. It must have had a fine view once. He didn't see any bodies. The upper tiers of the tower were deserted. Empty. The men and women who had lived here had had plenty of time to see what was coming. Perhaps some had escaped?

The gondola stopped to hover by the balcony with the raven cages. The stern ramp hinged open and a howling wind rushed in at once, flapping the silk curtains on the windows and tugging at Tsen's robe. He had to shout over the roar of it, over its angry whistling through the chains dangling the gondola from the glass-ship high above. 'You might want to stay here and wait,' he told Kalaiya, more in the spirit of a noble gesture than anything else.

A derisive 'Ha!' let him know what she thought of that. 'Who's the graceful and nimble slave and who's the fat old man?' Kalaiya pushed past him onto the ramp. His heart jumped as the wind caught her and she swayed, but the ramp was wide and the balcony even wider. She turned and held out her hands and beckoned him to follow. When he did, the wind thumped into him and knocked him a step sideways.

'They're gone.' Where the balcony opened into the innards of the tower, empty raven cages lined the walls. Scattered around them were pieces of what looked like bright green glass, strewn across the floor. Chunks of it, nothing all that remarkable until you looked closer and saw, now and then, that one was shaped as a finger, or maybe a foot or a piece of a face. Kalaiya stopped to stare, hand pressed over her mouth. Tsen pulled her on deeper into the tower.

'Does it hurt?' she asked, and he realised that she'd never seen this before. In all her years at his side she'd never been up close and seen what a jade raven truly was. *Did it hurt?* He had no idea. The slaves who died tended to scream a lot but that was probably mostly the fear.

'I don't know. Come on.' The scribes would live and work near the rookery. Out of the wind his feet felt sure again. 'I don't like it here. It's Senxian's mausoleum and it gives me the shivers.'

He'd feared they'd meet a gold-glass wall, the sort that needed a enchanter's black rod to open, that he'd have to go back to the gondola and get the silver globe Chay-Liang had made for him for cutting through; but this high up in the tower Senxian had seen no need to keep people out. A mere iron door barred the way – iron so no Elemental Man could pass through – which swung open at Tsen's touch. Beyond was the Tying Room, where the jade ravens were fed while the scribes' messages were tied to their feet. More pieces of green glass covered the floor. Bits of what had once been people. There must have been three or four before the ravens touched them, turned them this way and shattered them. No one had cleared away the remains. The scribes had left in a hurry. More cages hung open in the corners of the room, large and silver – cages for men this time – and the litter of green chunks was thickest around them.

Kalaiya squealed; when Tsen looked round she was holding most of someone's face in her hands – everything from the eyebrows down to the chin, where a large chip was missing. If you'd known the man in life, you'd know him now, clear as anything. Tsen gently lifted it away. The pieces the ravens left looked like jade-coloured glass but to the touch felt more like a resin, like Xizic, with a little give beneath the fingers if you squeezed hard, not the cold unyielding sharpness of brittle stone.

He led Kalaiya away. She was shaking. 'They were slaves,' he said as if that somehow made it better, and then remembered that she was a slave too. He forgot that more than he should. 'Criminals,' he added quickly, guessing how Senxian would have chosen them. 'Murderers. Rapists. The worst sort.' They'd have been the sick and the old, though, the ones Senxian couldn't put to useful labour. 'They were going to die anyway.' That at least was probably true.

A screen of metal chains passed for the next door, another device to stop Elemental Men from entering. Tsen pushed through into a hall. They eventually found what he wanted – the Writing Room – up some narrow stairs. He clucked his tongue in frustration when he saw the bronze mesh basket where the scribes threw the letters after they transcribed them. It was blackened and full of charred pieces. He crouched beside the basket, fingering the few corners of paper that survived, looking for anything that might still be legible. Fragments of words, that was all. The rest crumbled into ash, staining his fingertips grey.

'Tsen?'

He shook his head. A waste of time. 'It was a fine idea, my love.'

'Tsen! Look!' She was standing over one of the scribing desks. There were pieces of paper in her hand. She thrust them at him. 'Look!'

Vespinarr. Shonda.

Senxian's glasships lie in broken pieces. The Vul Tara burns. Nothing remains. The creature has shattered two of the towers of the palace. I am in the third. Somehow we are spared. Everyone is fled. All is ruin ...

He read on then walked back through the Tying Room and onto the balcony again, into the roar of the wind, seeing the scene as it might have been. Perhaps whoever wrote the message had been standing here, fighting to hold his paper and pen. The writing was scratchy and erratic, hard to read, scribed in haste and panic, but what sort of man would stand here at all with a furious dragon tearing the towers around him? He tried to see it: across the sea a pall of smoke over the city as he watched the dragon burn everything in its path. It came to the palace itself. They thought they were safe inside their mighty towers of glass and gold but the dragon had smashed their walls and shattered their ramparts. It had ripped lightning cannon and the black-powder guns alike from their mountings and tossed them over the cliffs into the sea. It had gouged holes in stone and glass and filled the palace with fire. Panic spreading as fast as the flames, the scribes opening the cages and letting their ravens fly, turning and running ... but the man who'd written this, whoever he was, had stopped them. The two other great towers of the Palace of Roses had come down, cracking like rolling thunder, showering every part of the palace below with shards of golden glass as large as houses. He'd stood and watched them fall. And when the two towers had fallen and the third stayed standing, when he found he wasn't dead, he'd written of what he'd seen. Terse and concise yet eloquent. One last scribe and one final raven.

It destroys everything with ease. There is nothing left to stop it. Quai'Shu's soldiers are advancing in its wake. It gouges lesser structures with tooth and claw. It lashes the great towers with its tail until they crack. It makes holes in them and fire bursts from its mouth and pours inside. It strikes the towers then it hurls itself at Senxian's own and clings to it until it cracks and a full third falls away. The falling tower strikes the Rose near its base. The Rose disintegrates. I watch it crumble and die.

Tsen edged to the lip of the balcony. Those other towers were in full view, or would have been. He tried to think what it would have been like to stand with their bulk looming over him and then watch them shudder and fall. The noise, the cacophonous thunder of splintering glass ...

It shows no sign of weakness or fatigue but it has left the Thorn untouched. Perhaps its force is spent? Though I have no doubt Quai'Shu's soldiers will not spare us.

Tsen stuffed the papers inside his robe and decided he'd seen enough. Enough of what the dragon had done to Dhar Thosis and enough of what the mysterious scribe had written, addressed to Lord Shonda of Vespinarr. In the gondola, as the glasship drifted away from the corpse of Dhar Thosis and the taint of smoke that hung in the air, he had Kalaiya pour some water into a bowl. He took off all his rings and dipped his fingers in and kept them there to see whether any remnant of the old alliance would answer. Shrin Chrias Kwen and Baran Meido were blank. Hardly a surprise. Quai'Shu was sitting in his eyrie, mad as a hare. That left the youngest of Quai'Shu's sons, Bronzehand. He went to the window and let Bronzehand look through his eyes for a while, taking it all in. Bronzehand who was dallying in the island fleshpots of the Scythian steelsmiths when he should have been on the shores of Qeled. He'd been clever, Tsen saw. He'd left when the dragons came. Bronzehand also had another ring, linked to someone outside Quai'Shu's cabal. He toyed with it a lot. Tsen didn't think any of the others had noticed.

He sighed, forcing himself to have a good long look at what the dragon had done so that Bronzehand would see it too. It would have been nice to talk to someone who wasn't Kalaiya, someone who could actually do something, but Bronzehand was in another world. Maybe he'd prefer to stay away. Tsen could hardly blame him for that. Xican was doomed. There would be no more sea lords of the Grey Isle. Better to waste away a happy life in the fleshpots of Scythia than come back to this.

What have we done? What have I done?

He read the pages again, all of them, one after the next, slowly and meticulously, then slipped the last ring on his finger and pushed Bronzehand away. Perhaps other sea lords would come to see for themselves, perhaps not. Most of Senxian's fleet was at sea, scattered across the many worlds. His heirs would claim the ruins. They'd rebuild Dhar Thosis and maybe wipe away the scars, but the world would never be quite the same. Shonda had shown it could be done. The five-hundred-year peace, broken. The Elemental Men defied. Thwarted.

He poured a glass of apple wine and gave it to Kalaiya, held her hand and squeezed it tight. 'Thank you.' He gave her the papers. 'Keep them safe.'

Kalaiya shrugged. 'What use are they?'

'Shrin Chrias Kwen flew no banners, but in these letters the soldiers are said to be Sea Lord Quai'Shu's. How can that be? Because this was written by one of Shonda's spies, sent to be his eyes. Someone who knew what was coming before it came.' Proof of it. Proof that Shonda knew.

'Then there's hope?'

Tsen laughed bitterly. 'For me? No. For the rest of you? Perhaps.'

It was a long journey back to the eyrie and he read the letters perhaps a dozen times, picturing with each what it must have been like, trying to see through the eyes of this spy, piecing it together with what little he'd wrung from the rider-slave Zafir. It would only be later that the last few words would snag in his thoughts.

It landed amid the rubble. Two men came from among Quai'Shu's soldiers and spoke with its rider.

Zafir had never mentioned that. And it would occur to Baros Tsen to wonder, then, who could have had the courage and the audacity to walk up to a dragon, and what, exactly, did they have to say?

5

The Godspike

Further from the sea, as the gondola drifted away, the city looked more as Tsen remembered it, stone streets and bell towers and houses and little market squares and then the shanty towns of the sword-slaves and the oar-slaves and the outcasts and the poor and the desert men who'd come and never left. He wondered who claimed the city now. Anyone? As they'd drifted over the desert from the eyrie, him and Kalaiya, he'd pondered whether he'd find the streets full of people hard at work rebuilding what they'd lost, ships clustered around the docks, the damage perhaps far less than he feared. Now he wondered: was there even anyone left? But surely there must be. Chrias and the dragon couldn't have killed *everyone*. Could they?

On the top of the sand ridge that marked the edge of the desert Tsen saw a short line of tents. Behind the peak of the ridge, out of sight of the city, they had cages. Slavers, already come to pick at the city's corpse. He swept the glasship lower, filled with a fearsome fury, intent on scattering them with the ship's lightning cannon, but after a few moments he pulled away. *Exactly how much of a hypocrite are you, Tsen? It comes with the territory, but that's rich even for you.*

The more he thought, the less he could see what good it did for Bronzehand, far out to sea and in another world, to see all this. When Dhar Thosis was out of sight, Tsen read the letters again, poring over them, searching for any nuance that might damn the lord of Vespinarr just that little bit more. Shonda had wealth beyond imagination. Did he not have a spy bound to him the way Tsen and Quai'Shu's others were bound? Surely he'd seen it all with his own eyes as it happened, him and Mai'Choiro Kwen and Vey Rin T'Varr and whoever else had planned this ruin. Why the letters then?

Evidence? He couldn't let them go. Kept going back to them until Kalaiya took them while he was sleeping and hid them with the glasship's golem. She told him where they were but with a warning look.

'We have two more days,' she whispered. 'Two more days just for us when no one can touch us. After that it will be gone.' She wasn't beautiful, probably never had been, but she had a grace to her, an elegance, a poise. When she'd caught his eye, years ago, it hadn't been with an obsequious smile or her perfect kowtow, it had been the slightest curl of disdain that came afterwards, the one she gave him now. A sort of pity, as though she knew how foolish he really was underneath his clever words and his braided hair that touched the floor and his dazzling rainbow feather robes. He'd come to look for that over the years, the wrinkle of her nose when he said something particularly foolish.

'Did I tell you that ten years ago Quai'Shu went to see the moon sorcerers?' he said. It was an odd affection between them, deep and solid. Not love exactly, certainly not lust, but something profound anyway. Somehow she'd become a necessary part of him and yet all they ever did was talk. 'No, I didn't, because I never told anyone. Quai'Shu only told *me* years later.' She'd kissed him once, back when she hardly knew him, when she supposed that must be what he wanted, and it had been nice enough but it had told them both that it wasn't.

Kalaiya cocked her head. 'They brought the dragons to the eyrie.'

'They did.' He stared at her. Perhaps she was the missing piece of his soul, the piece he'd lost back in Cashax in his youth raising hell with Vey Rin and the rest. Perhaps he'd been lucky enough to find it again – unlike the others – but that just sounded ridiculous.

'Tsen?' She snapped her fingers at him. 'Tsen. You're staring right through me!'

'Yes.' He shook himself. 'The moon sorcerers went with Quai'Shu to the dragon-realm. He was supposed to bring back eggs but the eggs started to hatch while he was at sea. We lost a dozen ships and Quai'Shu lost his mind.' Tsen shrugged. 'Or perhaps he lost it as they set sail, when the dragon-queen murdered Zifan'Shu on the decks of Quai'Shu's own ship. But, years before, Quai'Shu went to the moon sorcerers to ask them for their help. He never said what it was that he gave them. I never knew how he bought them.'

'I thought they were a myth.'

'If Quai'Shu wasn't my sea lord then I would have said the same. I would have called him a liar.' There was something there, a deeper darkness around Quai'Shu's dragons that went beyond Shonda and Vespinarr and Dhar Thosis but Tsen, for all his brilliance, couldn't begin to fathom it. Nor did he want to. In his golden gondola, surrounded by silver and glass and pale wood, he snuggled close to Kalaiya, and they chewed Xizic and watched the desert sunset together. He lay in bed and tried to sleep, and when he couldn't, she got in beside him and stroked his hair and told him stories of the happy days they'd had together not so long ago. When the sun rose, he spent the next day looking at her, then out of the window at the desert and then back again, living in that moment for what little time they had left. She never said, but she needed him exactly as he needed her. That was the miracle of her; perhaps he *did* love her after all, just for wanting him.

He let the peace of the desert take him. In the evening he landed the gondola on the top of a lonely mesa far away from anywhere and the two of them watched the sunset together, glorious fiery reds in the sky while the sand turned to liquid gold and he felt Kalaiya's warmth beside him, leaning into him. Another day and then they'd be back and all this peace would be over. Or maybe it wouldn't. Maybe the eyrie would be gone and the dragon with it and Mai'Choiro Kwen and Chay-Liang and all the rest, and every-one would think he was dead and he could fly away and be free ... Or, more likely, the Elemental Men were already waiting for him.

He put his arm around Kalaiya as the sun went down. It had been an act of cowardice running away to Dhar Thosis to see what the dragon had done, a few last days together in quiet comfort and solitude before the end of everything jumped out of a wall and ate him. And so, because he was still a coward at heart, the desert stars were bright before he turned away and walked slowly back to the gondola, reluctance in every lingering step. He didn't sleep much that night, and when the sun rose again he felt the coming end sink true and deep into his bone. The storm-dark was on the horizon ahead of them, a hundred miles away and already a dark smear over the gleaming sands.

The world *was* full of things Tsen didn't understand: dragons, flying eyries, glasships and lightning cannon, but none of them touched the mystery of the storm-dark. It floated a mile off the ground, twenty miles across, wrapped around that other great inexplicable marvel, the infinite pillar of the Godspike which pierced its heart. The cloud seemed to swell as the miles fell away, a great vortex of shadows racked by violet lightning, twisting in dark spirals, a solitary isolated fragment of the storm-dark curtain that cut the many worlds into pieces, trapped here in the heart of the desert by a ring of white stone spires each a mile high. As the glasship came closer, Tsen's heart beat faster. Chay-Liang hadn't said a word about him leaving her to bring the eyrie here, leaving her to do it alone, hadn't even frowned though she'd surely seen right through him. No one flew their glasship over the top of the storm-dark if they didn't have to because sometimes the magic simply failed up there. It happened over the Queverra too and, so he'd heard, in parts of the Konsidar. A glasship that failed over the storm-dark fell like a stone until the maelstrom swallowed and un-made it. It unmade everything it touched. The lines out to sea did the same unless a navigator wove their protective weave and used the rifts to travel to other worlds – from that one masterful secret the Taiytakei had become what they were – but the storm-dark over the Godspike was different. Feyn Charin, first and greatest of the navigators, had entered it and returned. No one else ever had.

Tsen shuddered. Maybe the magic that made his eyrie fly would work better. No one understood *that* either, after all.

The clouds grew, spreading across the sky as the gondola came closer, high overhead like a dark hand reaching down to devour him. He saw the ring of spires around the edge of the cloud, caging it, their tips touching it; and, deep inside, the white stone spire of the Godspike itself, piercing it, gleaming in the desert sun, a pillar of light rising through the churning black cloud up into the sky beyond, towards the stars until it vanished into the deep and blinding blue. The spires held the storm-dark at bay, the navigators said. Truth was, Tsen reckoned, no one had ever had a clue except maybe Feyn Charin himself – and in the end Charin had gone every bit as mad as Quai'Shu, drooling in his rooms in the Dralamut and mumbling about dragons.

The air thinned as the glasship rose. Tsen felt it as the roiling black mass spread slowly around them, filling the sky. The storm-dark seemed like a hole in the world and there were some who said that's exactly what it was. He saw the flashes of lightning as the gondola rose higher, deep inside the darkness, bright and violent. Travellers between worlds saw that same lightning as they crossed, either side of the heart of the darkness where everything, even time perhaps, stopped and there was simply nothing.

The glasship rose past the edge of it. For a full minute the storm-dark blotted out the sun, and from one side of the gondola he was dazzled by brilliant afternoon sunlight while from the other all he saw was black. His knuckles were tight, the rest of him as tense as a lanyard. Kalaiya was shaking. He put his arm around her. Shameful, but he was glad of her fear. It gave him something to do and helped him to hide his own.

'We won't. Fall.' He gasped out the words between shallow breaths. 'It almost. Never. Happens.' He was starting to feel how thin the air was up here.

A strange thing happened as they climbed above the rim of the maelstrom. From underneath it was simply a black void in the sky; now, from above, with the sinking sun lighting its clouds, it became a sea of colours stretched out before him, swirls of purple and violet streaked with white and wisps of orange fire like frozen flames, flickering with inner lightning. The sight of it filled him, showing him how small he was, how tiny and irrelevant. He ran from one window to the next to the next around the gondola as the storm spread slowly out beneath them, unable to take his eyes from it except to run on and then stare again. His head pounded. And yes, he was still afraid, but not of being consumed by the mael-strom. He was afraid of what might be waiting, from knowing their journey and their time were almost done. His heart seemed to beat too quickly for his chest to hold it inside him. The cloud of the storm-dark, the majestic uncaring size of it, became a peculiar comfort. Beside it everything diminished.

He took out a farscope and peered through the gondola win-dows. Near the heart of the darkness where the Godspike punched through and streaked towards the stars, he spotted a dark speck in the sky. The eyrie. Chay-Liang was flying it high. The air was so thin now that he was gasping. His head was throbbing and getting worse as they rose. Kalaiya lay back on the silks and cushions, clutching at her hair, frenziedly chewing Xizic resin. Xizic helped with the headaches but Tsen couldn't look away, couldn't take his eyes anywhere else or even close them, until at last the glasship drifted over the top of the eyrie and the familiar craggy rocks and then the white stone circle of sloping walls and the flat bright open space of the dragon yard, a mile above the storm. As it slipped beneath him, he clung to the familiarity of the shapes. The dragon, red and gold and huge, perched on the eyrie wall, staring towards the Godspike. The lightning cannon and the black-powder guns, the hatchery, all as it had always been. He saw the moving specks of men and women, slaves about their business as they always were, and still it didn't tell him whether the Elemental Men had come or whether Shonda and the Vespinese were waiting for him. His blood was pounding, pulsing fit to burst every vein. The gondola came slowly to a stop over the middle of the dragon yard and he saw Chay-Liang running towards him, waving, but whether in welcome or warning he couldn't tell. He couldn't breathe. The air was too thin. He couldn't think any more.

He was going to be sick. His head felt ready to explode and his skull was too tight. There just wasn't enough air. He barely waited for Kalaiya when the gondola touched the white stone of the dragon yard before he cracked the ramp open. A wind worse than the one in Dhar Thosis howled about him. It buffeted him when he stepped out and he stumbled and almost fell, too dizzy to bother with righting himself, then staggered again and dropped to his hands and knees and vomited over the perfect smoothness of the dragon yard's white stone. A slave came running to help him up. Tsen clutched at him.

'Are they here?' His eyes were wild. The slave only looked bewildered. Tsen shook him. 'Are they here? The Elemental Men? The Vespinese? *Are they here?*'

The slave pulled away in alarm and shook his head. 'No, Master T'Varr. No.' He kept backing away but Tsen couldn't give a shit any more. All the strength had drained out of him. He could barely stand. He swayed in the wind. *They're not here yet.* His head was killing him. Suddenly all he wanted and all he was good for was a bath. A long soak, a lot of Xizic tea and maybe a glass or two of apple wine. Anything to be out of this flaying wind, anything to make this headache go away. Some sleep. A lot of sleep. Hadn't had much of that these last few days.

They're not here. He felt like a puppet with his strings all cut. Chay-Liang was waving again but his skull was splitting open and he ignored her. Even ignored the dragon, the towering looming angry monster that glared at him as it glared at everything with its ravenous resentment. Right now he would probably have ignored an Elemental Man with a drawn blade held to his throat.

A silver cage swinging back and forth in the gale caught his eye. Mai'Choiro Kwen had brought it with him for Lord Shonda's jade ravens. Through the haze of pain, the cage reminded him there was one thing he had to do right now, no matter how many needles he felt stabbing through his eyes. He stumbled to the top of the wall, stopping to catch himself now and then against the howl of the wind before the gusts picked him off his feet. It was only when he reached the cage that he realised he was being ridiculous. To send a raven, Baros Tsen T'Varr sat at his desk in his nice quiet study, very much out of the wind, with the pretty quill pen that Kalaiya had given him and his perfect white paper shipped from Zinzarra. He wrote his words in glorious peace and quiet and then summoned a slave to take it to a scribe. And, thank you very much, went nowhere near these horror-touched birds at all.

The jade raven eyed him from its cage with interest. The gale and its swinging perch didn't seem to bother it. Tsen turned away. As he did, the wind caught his robe and almost lifted it over his head, making him look even more of an idiot. He looked across the rim of the eyrie at the violet storm below. *I should just jump, I really should. Save us all the bother* ... But instead he struggled back down to the yard and aimed for the tunnels that would take him out of this hellish wind. State he was in, he'd probably pick the wrong entrance without thinking and end up among the Scales or something like that.

Chay-Liang caught up with him before he could get away. 'Tsen—'

'Send a jade raven,' he mumbled. *She* could do it. Saved him from thinking. 'Send a jade raven to the Elemental Men in Khalishtor. Tell them what we did. All of it. Do it now.'

'Tsen ...'

He stopped for a moment and looked at her. 'Dear gods in whom we don't believe, Liang, is it always like this up here?'

'So far, yes.' She was grinning now as though she liked it, and for a moment, through all the pain in his head, Tsen hated her. 'Tsen—'

'Later.' He pushed past. She was mad, that was it. Happened to enchanters, didn't it? They cracked and all sensible thought oozed out of their edges ... He forgave her though, five minutes later when he found she'd had his bath prepared when she'd seen him coming; and the next few hours were a blur of warmth and pain and Xizic resin and Kalaiya and relief that no one was here to hang him yet, all a little marred by a lethargic dread of what was yet to come. Chay-Liang brought him something from the alchemist to help him sleep; he drank it without even thinking, and when he woke up again, his head was clearer and only throbbed like a badly sheeted sail. He called her back and they walked the walls together, battered by the relentless gale as the eyrie drifted in its lazy orbit around the Godspike.

'Couldn't we go lower?' he shouted at her over the wind. Liang had six glassships dragging the eyrie through the sky. As far as Tsen could see, she'd moved the eyrie higher and higher until they were as far from the storm-dark as her gasping lungs could stand.

'We could,' she yelled back. 'But you get used to it. Give it a few days.'

'I may not have a few days! And if I do, I would prefer them not to hurt so much.' Was it possible to sound plaintive and shout at the same time? He rather thought he'd managed it.

She offered him some reeking drink or other. When he asked her what it was, she shrugged and shouted over the gale, 'Bellepheros makes it. It helps with the thinness of the air.' He waved her away then watched as she shrugged and drank a mouthful and offered it again. Bellepheros. The alchemist from the dragon-lands.

'You trust that slave too much.' Far too much, for what they had between the two of them was nothing like the way it should be between mistress and slave.

'What?'

He leaned into her and shouted back, 'I said you trust your slave too much!'

She looked at him then. Not a word, not a flicker of her eyes, not the shadow of a smirk, but he knew she was laughing at him. After a second or two he had to laugh as well. Kalaiya knew his soul. That was simply the way fate had turned. Maybe it was the same for Liang and her alchemist. At any rate, he was the last person in the world to lecture anyone when it came to overly liking their slaves.

He pulled Liang into some shelter where at least they were out of the wind and he could hear himself think, snatched the cup out of Liang's hands and drank. 'Yes, yes.' And he half-listened as she told him how breathlessness and nausea and splitting heads had blighted everyone until the alchemist started making his potions. Everyone except the rider-slave Zafir of course, who laughed at them all for being so pathetic. When Liang was done, Tsen looked about him. His eyrie, still *his* eyrie, kept aloft by hostile uncaring sorcery from another age.

'We're not safe here,' he said. He looked up at the glasships. 'Sooner or later they will fail.'

'I have more, loitering over the desert, out of the way and out of sight. Belli and I talked it through while you were gone.'

Belli? Tsen chuckled and shook his head. What, were they lovers now? 'You trust that slave *far* too much.' He spoke with a twinkle in his words this time. So what if they were? 'Borrowed time, Liang. We're all on borrowed time. We must make the most of it.'

'One glasship is enough to keep us aloft, T'Varr, and we have six. See how they all pull at slight angles to one another – *that* was the hard part to get right. If any one fails then it will fall clear of the outer rim of the eyrie. There will be plenty of time to summon another. We've been here for days and I haven't lost one yet.'

'It will be quite a sight if you do.' Tsen shook his head. 'But I wonder if we should release them. All of them. Let this eyrie and its monsters sink into the storm-dark and be gone. Evacuate everyone. Leave me behind. Wipe it all out. Mai'Choiro can stay in his cell. We'll go down together, he and I.' He took a deep breath and turned to look at the dragon at last, the terror that had destroyed Dhar Thosis. Its wounds were already healing. The eyrie wall where it sat was marked by dried blood. Was there anything magical about dragon blood? There ought to be, he thought, but neither the alchemist nor Chay-Liang had run around clearing it up and cackling gleefully to themselves as they did, so he supposed there wasn't.

He frowned and touched his temple. His head wasn't hurting any more and Chay-Liang was smiling at him. He rubbed his fingers into his skin, trying to chase away the last ghosts of the pain, then he turned and stared out to the west to where, if you flew for long enough, the Konsidar rose out of the sands.

'Ravens flew from Dhar Thosis to Vespinarr on the day the city fell,' he said. 'Shonda knows what has happened. They would have reached him before I reached Senxian's palace. He'll be looking for us. As big as the desert is, it won't take him long to find us. It's a race now – Shonda or the Elemental Men.' Tsen shook his head. 'I left in too much haste. I should have sent a raven to Khalishtor at once. Another mistake.'

He paused and then put a hand to Chay-Liang's shoulder. 'He'll come with the best and most deadly of what his money can buy for him, Liang. He won't wait for the Crown of the Sea Lords to decide what's to be done. He'll seize everything we have in the name of his "friend" Senxian and offer the new lord of Dhar Thosis some marvellous reparation. He's probably prepared a suitable puppet already, skulking somewhere in the shadows. Probably even made that deal before Dhar Thosis burned. He'll take everything that was ours and destroy every threat to his ambition. Quai'Shu will be allowed to live because he's a broken old man who can't string two sentences together any more, but only so they can try him and hang him for the look of it when it suits them. The rest of us?' He drew a finger across his throat. 'He'll kill every last one of us if he has even the slightest reason. You, me, Kalaiya, all of us. The only ones he *won't* kill will be the ones who deserve it most.'

His eyes drifted to the far side of the wall, to the dragon staring down into the maelstrom beneath them. He'd never seen it do that before. Usually it stared across the dragon yard, eyeing everyone with greedy hunger, or else it stared at the sky. At night in particular it sometimes looked up for hours, as though mesmerised by the stars.

'Whatever he does, however terrible it is, you mustn't stand in his way. He needs your alchemist. Make sure he needs you too. You must survive, Chay-Liang, no matter what fate comes to the rest of us. Close your eyes and look away. Hold the truth close to your heart and never let him see that you have it. Keep it until you can destroy him.' His grip on her shoulder tightened. 'But when when that time comes, Liang, you must annihilate him. You must remove him from existence, utterly and completely, or he'll grow back like a badly excised cancer.'

Chay-Liang met his gaze and, gods help him, even looked sorry for him. 'Perhaps if you hanged the rider-slave yourself before they came it might help show she acted without your order?'

'No.' Tsen shook his head. 'I will hang beside her for letting it happen, no matter the who or the how, and so I should.' He leaned into Chay-Liang and hissed in her ear, 'I played a stupid game and I lost, but I will take him down alongside me before he does it again. I'll not hang the dragon-rider and nor should you. Not until she speaks. She's the one other person who knows the truth and she has nothing to lose by telling it!' He let out a bitter laugh and pulled away, shaking his head. 'Although if you have any useful enchanter tricks to spirit me away to a quiet little countryside villa while making me appear to be dead and hanged, I'll become a most enthusiastic listener. I have one, you know. In the Dominion, a hundred miles along the coast from Merizikat. With a nice orchard full of apples and a winery. And a good bathhouse.'

'She'll die as soon as she speaks. I'm sure she knows that.'

Tsen stopped, struck again by the memory of the two of them in his bath together, how she'd knocked the poisoned wine out of his hand after so carefully putting it there in the first place. Why? He still hadn't the first idea. 'So will I,' he said. 'And you know, I sometimes wonder how much that matters. Maybe we promise to send her home.'

He watched his enchantress closely after he said that and saw the conflict plain across her face. The dragon gone and the rider-slave with it: dead would be better but gone was still good. Then hunger to get it done. And happiness for the alchemist who would surely go too. And then sadness, and for the same reason. Rather too much sadness, Tsen thought. He kept on watching though, until the play was done, and then squeezed her shoulder. 'You made her armour. She ruined it. You should start making more. If you have something Shonda needs then he won't kill you until it's finished. Be slow. Let it buy you time. Make a few adjustments to keep her in line if you like.'

He let Liang go, and together they watched the dragon again. It was staring at the pillar of the Godspike going on and on and vanishing into the deep blue of the desert sky overhead. Tsen stared too. You didn't get a blue like that at sea, nor in Xican or Khalishtor – though in Khalishtor you rarely got anything except rain-cloud grey. Only in the desert a blue like this.

'Do you think it knows what the Godspike is?' he asked.

Chay-Liang chuckled. 'I'm not sure it knows much more than that it's hungry.' She sighed. 'If you come out here at night, the Godspike has a light to it. But if you do, remember to bring a blanket. It's a bitter cold under the stars up here.' She left him there, staring. Presumably she had things to do. Presumably Tsen did too. He just couldn't think what any of them were.

She was right about the cold. He came out again to look at the Godspike that night because yet again he couldn't sleep and, well, because there were probably only a handful of people across the whole of Takei'Tarr who'd flown above the storm-dark cloud and stared up at the spike in the darkness and he wasn't sure that he'd have another chance; but in the end there wasn't much to see. A dim pale glow, barely even visible and quickly lost among the sparkle of stars. After he'd looked at it for a while, he made the mistake of walking out over the wall and across the rim to the very edge of the eyrie itself, standing in the howling wind and looking over the lightning-tossed storm below. He stood, swaying, almost hoping that a sudden gust might catch him and make him stumble. Toss him over the edge, but it didn't. Mostly, after that, he stayed in, down in his bathhouse with Kalaiya and his wine. His Bronzehand finger tingled now and then but he ignored it. There wasn't much to show any more. All that was left was waiting for his killers to come and guessing which ones would get to him first.

6

Silence

The dragon Silence darted and danced through the underworld of Xibaiya until it found a waiting egg. It eased into the dormant skin as a man might slip on an old shoe and was reborn as flesh and bone. The sensation was a familiar comfort and yet always new. Every skin was different. *What colours will I be? What sex? Will my tail be long? My neck? How many fangs shall I have?* All these things were a joy of discovery with every hatching, yet this time it paused and held back the urge to writhe and smash its way to freedom. Inside its egg it opened its brand-new inner eye and let its senses roam, searching for thoughts and other things to which the little ones were blind.

Within its egg the dragon called Silence remained quiet. It found much and looked at all the things its mind could touch in this strange and wonderful place where it soon would be born, filled with alien thoughts. It found sorceries that were fresh and strange and one that was ancient and familiar and colossal and overwhelming, older than the dragon itself. Something made before its first ever dawn, remembered from a joyous lifetime more than a thousand years ago.

It looked and bided its time. Men with ropes and chains were always watching, waiting for an egg to hatch. Men with lightning too, which was new. It slid inside their thoughts and sang songs of faraway dreams. It watched and listened and waited with a patience that strained its nature for the moment to be free. While it did, it wove mysteries into the wandering memories of those who watched over it, lullabies to make them dull.

When the killers came, flying on their weaves of magic and sorcery, the dragon felt them first.

The Lords of Vespinarr

7

The Dark of Night

Zafir sat on a wooden stool, eyes wide, and stared at the door to her prison. The soft glow of the walls echoed the night, full and deep with the moon clear and bright. There had been places in the Pinnacles like this. Empty white stone halls inside the mountain where no one ever went because there was nothing there except pristine colonnades and arches carved into walls that led nowhere. Light came from everything in those places. Even in the Octagon, her mother's throne room, the light had been like this. All of it left behind by the Silver King. So she knew it was night, the time of the deep dark, and that the moon was up and that everything slept, perhaps even her dragons.

Everything but her.

Her head throbbed with fatigue. Her brow was knotted. She yawned with every other breath but sleep had abandoned her to unwept tears, to frustration and despair. Always at this hour, always the same, ever since she'd let them bring her down here. *Let* them, and now every night she went through it over and over again in an endless loop she was powerless to stop. She could have gone anywhere after Dhar Thosis. Diamond Eye had burned its houses and smashed its palaces, rent their glass towers to ruin and crashed their glasships into myriad splinters. He'd killed the sorcerous assassin sent to stop her and she'd left the ground a-glitter like desert sand in the midday sun, awash in a sea of smoke and flames. With a storm of victory in her heart, she could have gone anywhere. She could have declared war on them all.

Yet when Tsen's soldiers had come, she'd been shivering, dripping wet from his stupid bath and almost naked. She could have been six years old again. She hadn't even tried to fight. What was the point? Over and over she ran the memories in her mind, wondering why. She touched a hand to her breast and murmured to herself, 'No mercy for pretty Zafir.'

Her slaves came every day. They brought her food and water and a fresh chamber pot. Myst and Onyx, named after dragons she'd once owned. From the way their eyes brushed over her, she still had their hearts, but they never spoke, not here. When they came, they always came with others. Men, watching. Listening. Zafir never saw them but she felt their presence. And an absence too; for she always saw the hole where the third of her slaves had been. Brightstar, murdered by Shrin Chrias Kwen before she'd even set foot on Taiytakei soil. Shrin Chrias Kwen who'd sent his men to rape her so that she could understand what it meant to be a slave among the Taiytakei.

The air was thin now. They'd moved the eyrie somewhere high. She'd felt that and the headaches that came with it for a while.

The walls stared back at her, silent and still. The door to her room was an ill-fitting iron thing that didn't belong, wedged into an opening in the soft glow of the white stone walls. She'd seen iron doors sprout everywhere before they took her, forced into places where no door was ever meant to be, but the stone never yielded. Never chipped, never scratched, smooth and pristine as if freshly polished, everywhere except for the scar in the eyrie wall where Diamond Eye had lashed it with his tail on the first day she'd flown him. Iron and stone everywhere, pressed up against one another, hostile and resentful but given no choice. Two parts that could never be one. Implacable foes without any means to fight but both with an endless will to resist. That was something she understood. They were her companions now.

A twelvenight and three days. She'd counted.

Her eyes wouldn't even blink. The tears of wishing were enough to keep them moist. Now and then one tipped over and ran down her cheek, but only here in the depths of night where no one would ever know. They were going to kill her for what she'd done, but she wouldn't let them see her weep because they'd think she was afraid or felt some regret, and they couldn't have been more wrong. In the skies over Dhar Thosis, Diamond Eye had broken the last of her fear and taught her to be free. And as for regrets? Yes, she had plenty enough, but not for anything she'd done in *this* world.

I want to go home.

And as they always did, night after night, her thoughts turned to the nine realms she'd ruled as speaker, to the lands of the dragons. She roamed those memories, searching for something and never finding it. Surely there was something there to long for, to yearn to reclaim, yet all she found was a bitter emptiness. The Pinnacles, her home, should have brought memories of warmth and closeness and comfort, yet all she remembered was fear and doubt where the only escape had been the deep abandoned places found in long hours wandering alone. She'd tried to murder her fear there, stabbed it a dozen times and thought that might exorcise it but found she'd only changed its form. Not better, not worse, merely different. In the daylight, when the fire was inside her, she hated everyone who'd ever touched her for what they'd done. Here and now, small and alone in the dark, she only felt pity. Pity for them, pity for her. Pity for everyone. Hollow, that's what she was. An empty shell. And as the tears ran freely down her cheeks, she knew exactly why she'd spared Baros Tsen T'Varr. Because everything she ever touched turned to ash. Because there was no point in anything, because nothing would make any difference in the end because nothing ever did. Because of Tuuran, the Adamantine Man she'd found again in Dhar Thosis, who was her only memory of any kindness.

Chay-Liang spent most of her nights up on the walls of the eyrie. She couldn't sleep anyway and the cold and the wind helped clear her head when she was too tired to work on Tsen's new armour. She paced back and forth, turning now and then to face the incessant gale in the hope it would blow the cobwebs out of her head and help her see more clearly. Maybe Tsen was right – maybe his cause was lost – but there had to be a way to bring the bastard mountain king down with him, didn't there? It burned inside her, the injustice. The dragon-queen Zafir should hang or burn in her own dragon's fire and the Vespinese with her, but the world didn't work like that. Yet there had to be a way!

Low towers dotted the eyrie walls. Watchers scanned the eastern horizon for the pinpricks of light that would be their first sight of Shonda's glasships when he came – and he *would* come. He had to – she couldn't see any way Tsen was wrong about that. Shonda would come and wipe the slate as clean as he could, wipe away all trace of his own hand in what the dragon had done to Dhar Thosis. If he won, the truth would all be down to her.

She cursed. It frightened her. That's what it was, all this pacing and grinding her teeth – fear. And fear burned into anger, and that made her snarl because that was how that witch of a rider-slave worked: fear crushed into rage. She hissed at the wind. She was an enchantress! A mistress of Hingwal Taktse! She had power. There had to be something! Again and again she ran defensive strategies through her head. That was a kwen's work, and Tsen had a decent enough kwen supervising the eyrie defences, but he was out of his depth with this. They all were. *As soon as we see the Vespinese glasships, we tow the eyrie to keep as much of the storm-dark between Shonda and us as possible. Make them cross over as much of it as we can. Maybe they will fear their glasships will fail and fall. Maybe they won't dare ...* But of course they *would* dare, because everyone who mattered knew that glasships hardly ever failed and Shonda had hundreds. A few dozen men lost? So what? He'd drive them on regardless.

The dragon shifted on its perch. It gleamed in the moonlight. It had been staring up at the Godspike all night without moving and she found its stillness unsettling. She'd come to know the dragons as restless creatures, but coming here had changed them and she didn't know why. Nor did Bellepheros. Even the hatchlings spent hours doing nothing but staring at the Godspike, stock still, giving an impression of *thinking* that made her skin crawl. Dragons weren't supposed to think. Bellepheros had been adamant about that. As long as he fed them his potions, they were stupid and dull, and that was still quite bad enough! A massive indestructible fire-breathing monster the size of a small galleon, with wings as wide as a glasship and a bad temper? Yes, even the hatchlings were quite bad enough indeed when no one but the rider-slave could control them. *Thinking*, though ... Liang shivered.

The great dragon Diamond Eye turned its head to the western horizon and stared at that instead. Chay-Liang frowned and raised her farscope to one eye but saw nothing. Her frown deepened. *She might not be able to see anything but the perhaps the dragon could.*

The Vespinese would come from the west. She shifted uneasily from foot to foot. *Or maybe it's nothing. Maybe it's bored with the Godspike at last.*

'Get the alchemist.' *Maybe it's nothing* wasn't good enough. She looked at the dragon hard. 'What do you see?' she whispered. Pointless, and she didn't dare go up close to it, but Bellepheros had told her that when they weren't kept dull by his potions, they spoke straight into your head, although mostly only very briefly when they weren't burning and killing and eating anything that talked back. *Maybe they're like cats. Maybe it's nothing at all. Another flicker of lightning from the storm-dark and now it'll stare for hours waiting for it to come again?*

It turned and looked at her then. A lazy glance straight at her that near as anything stopped her heart, as though Bellepheros was right and it had been reading her mind. When it looked away again, her chest thumped fit to burst. For a moment she couldn't move and almost toppled in the wind. She backed away from the dragon and kept on going, looking at it and nothing else until she reached one of the little towers on the wall. Even then she was too frightened to do much except stay where she was until she saw Bellepheros crossing the dragon yard towards her. He was in his sleeping hat and had a thick cloak wrapped around him. *Stupid. I'm jumping at ghosts.* The look didn't mean anything. It couldn't, could it?

Damned wind. It was incessant, a remorseless roaring across the eyrie that wore them all down and frayed her edges, as if they weren't already frayed enough. It kept pulling the alchemist's cloak away as he walked and he kept having to tug it back. He yawned when he reached her and didn't smile. From the look of him and the way he kept rubbing his eyes, he'd actually been asleep for once when the soldiers had roused him.

'Sorry,' she mumbled, since sleep was a rare enough thing for either of them these days. He looked at her, frowned as though he hadn't heard what she'd said over the wind, then shrugged.

'You look like you've seen a ghost,' he shouted.

'It looked ...' This wasn't going to work. She pulled him close so she wouldn't have to yell. 'It looked at me, Belli. I want to know what it's thinking! Has it seen something?'

The alchemist gave a wry smile and chuckled. When her face didn't change, he took her hand between both of his. 'It's thinking that it's hungry, Li. It's thinking that it wants to eat us. It's thinking that it wants to fly. It's thinking that it hasn't seen its rider for far too many days. It's restless because ...' His words trailed off and Liang knew why. It was restless because dragons were always restless, but that wasn't true any more, not since they'd come to this place. Beside the Godspike, the great dragon was the most tranquil she'd ever seen it.

'I think there's something out there,' she said. 'It keeps staring across the storm-dark. I want to know what it sees. Is there a way? Is it Shonda's glasships? Even with my farscope I don't see them. I don't know, Belli – it just seemed odd.'

'Dragons have senses other than sight.' Bellepheros sighed. 'It's her Holiness you need, not me.'

The rider-slave. Zafir. There'd been a moment after Zafir had come back from burning Dhar Thosis when Belli had been set on poisoning her. Sometimes Liang wished she hadn't stopped him. Heartless callous manipulative vicious murdering horror of a human being, that's what Zafir was. Liang growled and gritted her teeth. 'Get her.' The dragon was still peering intently into the night. There *was* something there. She swore with such venom that Belli took an alarmed step back. 'If Shonda's out there then your stone-hearted queen can tear his glasships out of the sky. She'll like that.' *Yes. She'll like that far too much.* She watched as Bellepheros hurried away, and quietly swore again. *Best send someone to get Baros Tsen out of his bed too, eh?*

She sent a soldier to do that too and then paced the walls, staring out at the night, trying to spot whatever it was that the dragon could see, snarling to herself at her own foolish anger. The dragon-slave. Nothing but poison from the very start, a slave who refused to be enslaved, who walked about the eyrie as though she owned it, who treated Bellepheros as though he was her own personal minion – and yes, that rankled. Who had two slaves of her own who danced at her every whim even though slaves should never own other slaves. Tsen should have locked her up right at the start and broken her properly but instead he'd let her get away with it. He'd tried to be her friend! Unbelievable! She should drag the soulless witch out of her cell and throw her off the edge of the eyrie before Shonda got hold of her, that's what she should do. Should have done that a long time ago ...

'Glasships!' The lookouts on the south tower raised the first cry. Liang put her farscope to her eye again and this time she saw them, bright specks like drifting stars, far off in the night and coming from the south instead of the west. Dozens of them, although they were still so far that they were hard to separate from the stars on the horizon. Her heart jumped to a faster beat. *Xibaiya! They come!* A mile below them the maelstrom of the storm-dark flashed and flickered, dull sparks of purple lightning arcing deep inside it. She'd known for days that this moment waited; now her blood turned to ice and her bones to water.

She barked at another soldier, fear adding a sharpness to her voice, 'Get Baros Tsen T'Varr *now*! Tell him Shonda comes!' Belli hadn't come back. No matter – they had time yet. The glasships were miles away. It would be another half an hour at least before the eyrie came in range of their lightning cannon. Plenty of time to set a dragon in their midst.

The dragon's eyes, though, remained set firmly to the west. For a moment it turned its head to look at her a second time. A glance, that was all, freezing her thoughts and pinning her feet to the stone. It met her eye and, Charin help her, curled back its lips to show its fangs, and she could have sworn it was *smiling*, as though it knew something it cruelly chose not to share. And then it turned back, leaving her reeling, back to where it had been looking before, only now its head turned as though it was following something that was rising and getting closer and closer and ...

Every hair on her skin prickled. She felt suddenly sick and clutched at a wall beside her. 'Holy Charin ...' She ran.

Lightning lit up the eyrie in a flash of stunning brilliance. Liang gasped and whimpered at the shock of it. The thunderclap staggered her. On the eyrie rim a black-powder cannon exploded. She reeled, dazzled and dazed, and then a wave of air and light smashed across the dragon yard and knocked her off her feet. As she tried to blink the light out of her eyes and shake the ringing from her ears, darkness fell again; and then she saw the vast shape of a glasship rise slowly past the eyrie rim, over the wall, huge and glittering, a monster from the depths, the golden rim of its outer disc glowing bright as it charged its lightning cannon to fire again. It was close, right on top of them. It had come up from beneath and they hadn't seen it.

But Shonda's glasships were still miles away, far out of range ...

Decoys.

Lit up by the glow of the lightning cannon, a swarm of sleds rose around the glasship's disc and danced like fireflies towards her. Liang closed her eyes as a scream built up inside her.

8

Silence and the Dragon-queen

The dragon Silence strained its senses, listening. Its mind felt sharp and bright, filled with a thousand years of memory. The taste of the thoughts around it changed. A sharp delicious tang of dread drenched them all, harsh and urgent. Strife. Conflict. Men were coming. They were distant but getting closer, fast and full of hostile hunger. The watchers with their pikes and chains set to stand over their precious eggs were looking away. The dragon Silence felt them reel and stagger; even inside its shell, through closed eyes, it saw the first dim flash of light.

Now!

Inside its egg the dragon Silence bunched its muscles and clenched its claws. It built a fire as hot as its new body would allow and burst its shell apart. It leaped and spread its wings and spewed forth flames. The scattered men with their hooks and nets were too slow. It was free.

I am Silence, the dragon whispered to the air, *and I am hungry*.

It jumped high for freedom and flew into an unseen web of chains overhead. For a moment it was caught. It shook itself free. The men who were waiting for it were fast but not as fast as a dragon already listening to their thoughts. A dazzling flash of lightning blinded them all, and in their hesitation Silence burned them where they stood. Its newborn fire was weak. The little ones didn't char and die on the spot but turned and ran and stumbled and even screamed before they fell, but fall they did. Good enough. The dragon caught the closest and clawed out his spine and then bit the head off a fleeing second. Lightning flashed again, thunder roared and the noise and the light surged into the dragon's blood, urging it on. Out of nowhere a little one ran past and staggered and fell to his knees. Silence tore him down and ate him. There was always a hunger fresh out of the egg and fury came easily to any dragon, but that fury had snared them once long ago. The dragon Silence forced back the rage and made itself wait for a moment. Pause. It had come back with a purpose. It struggled to remember.

The hole in Xibaiya. The unravelling of creation. The empty prison. You came to find the Black Moon and force him back where he belongs before the Nothing consumes even dragons.

The dragon Silence closed its eyes and listened to the rumbles of thunder that weren't thunder at all, to the cracks of lightning though there was no storm. It reached into the thoughts that filled the eyrie and tasted war and delicious fear. Beyond, out in the skies, it found a scattered haze of hunger and elation. In the moonlight it scurried away, leaving eggs still waiting to hatch, out from under the nets and tents of chains to the sweet open air where the little ones would never hold it. On the threshold of its freedom it paused, lurking in the shadows.

There was a thought beneath it. A mind it had tasted before, the mind that wouldn't break after it had snapped the mighty sea lord Quai'Shu. The dragon Silence scratched at the old white stone of the dragon yard with its claws but it didn't fly. It listened.

The dragon-queen was still alive.

Chay-Liang cringed and cowered as another flash of lightning exploded over the roar of the wind, as another black-powder cannon was blown to pieces. Shrapnel zinged through the air past where she lay. A soldier nearby toppled as something hit him and his head disintegrated into a smear, a cloud of red caught in the wind, garishly lit up by another flash. A second glasship was rising past the rim. Across the yard the hatchlings were straining at their chains. Liang staggered to her feet, stared in disbelief, and then threw herself flat again as a score of sleds shot out of the darkness over the wall, each with a Vespinese soldier flinging lightning at anything that moved. Tsen's men poured out from the tunnels. They hurled lightning of their own. Sparks cracked and fizzed over glass-and-gold armour and the night filled with flashes and thunder. The great dragon on the wall snapped at a sled that flew too close, snatching the rider off its back and swallowing him in one gulp. Liang felt its tension. She fumbled in her pockets until she found a globe of glass and shaped it into a makeshift shield. She stumbled to her feet and looked wildly about. The shield would keep the lightning at bay but only if she had it facing the right way.

'Tsen!' she screamed at anyone who would listen. 'Get the t'varr! And get the dragon-rider!' The witch would have to ride without her armour tonight.

The first glasship rose further over the eyrie, drifting towards the centre of the dragon yard, its golden rim shining bright as the sun until it discharged again, another thunderous arc that blew yet another cannon to smithereens. Liang ran, jinking back and forth, half-blind, turning the shield to wherever the worst of the lightning seemed to be. More armoured soldiers were running from the tunnels into the dragon yard, into the teeth of the storm. A sled shot overhead, far faster than the rest, tumbling end over end, swatted by the dragon's tail. Mostly the Vespinese kept away from the monster. Who wouldn't?

More sleds poured over the rim. The noise and light left her dazed and dizzy. She tripped over something and sprawled flat. Lightning shot all around her, death to anyone without gold-glass to protect them, but the real battle would be fought hand to hand. *Think!* The shield she'd made was no substitute for armour. A single bolt would fry her skin and stop her heart. The notion struggled up through the terror and she held on to it and stayed where she was, lying very still with the shield on top of her. The Vespinese circled, picking off anyone who wasn't wearing armour, and then began to land, coming down in groups and jumping quickly clear while Tsen's soldiers charged into them as fast as they could, howling and shrieking and swinging their spiked ashgars, trying to batter the enemy down before they could establish a foothold.

As the melee spread, the rain of lightning eased. Liang picked herself up again and sprinted through the chaos, bolting for the nearest entrance into the spiralling passages under the dragon yard. There she stopped, breathing hard, shaking with exertion. She winced as another crushing thunderbolt picked out one of the watchtowers. On the far side of the eyrie yet another black-powder gun blew apart. The guns were useless. Glasships were supposed to fly high and drop fire, and the cannon were built to point up at the sky. They were supposed to be mounted on the ground, around harbours and fortresses where glasships couldn't come from below, not on a floating castle three miles in the air. It made her think of the dragon-queen again. What she'd said when Tsen had first shown her his cannon and asked if he might shoot her dragon out of the sky. She'd laughed at him. *I will come at you low and fast. That is the dragon-rider's way. I will see your face as you burn.* Apparently Shonda had thought the same.

She heard a dragon scream. A hatchling. Another crack of lightning shattered the night, one from the eyrie's own lightning cannon now, turned to point back into the dragon yard, blowing a cluster of sleds to pieces and hurling screaming Vespinese high into the air. In the flash of it she saw something move in the shadows, too fast and too large to be a man. It was the shape of death, of teeth and claws and wings and a long whipping tail. Liang hissed.

'Tsen!' Where in bloody Xibaiya was Tsen to tell them all what to do? Amid the lightning flashes she saw the hatchling again, bounding across the open yard, ripping men apart as it went, oblivious to who they were. Straight for a tunnel entrance on the opposite side of the eyrie. The one that would take it to the dragon-slave.

And, she realised, to Belli.

Liang forgot her fear and raced in its wake.

An unfamiliar rumble trembled her cell and jerked Zafir from her drifting thoughts. She wiped her eyes and straightened. A second tremor followed. It felt like Diamond Eye slamming into the dragon yard after a glorious flight, except no one flew Diamond Eye any more.

The black-powder cannon. Baros Tsen had shown them to her once, weapons for shattering a glassship and maybe even a dragon if it would stay still for long enough. She understood. Other Taiytakei had come to hold Tsen and her to account for the lives she'd burned. She'd hang or whatever it was the Taiytakei did to the most vile among them. She looked to see if she was afraid and found that she wasn't. If anything it was a relief.

'Holiness!' A hammering on her door. 'Holiness! Holiness! Are you awake? Rise, please, Holiness! We have need of you!'

She recognised the alchemist's voice, the only other voice she'd heard in six months that came with the familiar accent of her homelands. *Her* alchemist, though she doubted she owned his heart any longer. Laughter ambushed her, though the spasms that shook her were as bitter as juniper. 'You have *need* of me, Grand Master Alchemist? Need? What do you know of need? What do any of you know of *need*?'

'Holiness!' Bellepheros banged on the door again – did he forget that this was a prison, opened from without and not from within? 'The enemy are upon us! You must come and ride Diamond Eye and tear them down.'

'"Must" now, is it? I *must*?' The laughing edged into screaming. 'Must?' Yet she was tempted – she might at least admit it, if only to herself. Yes. Ride the dragon once more and die in fire and lightning, tearing her enemies to pieces. Better than this slow, cold, lonely end. 'Tell me, alchemist, will they hang me a second time for this?' But still, to ride ... Better than a rope. Better than ... Wasn't it better to die free?

She thought all these things, still laughing her bitterness, entirely trapped by her own design because no, in the end she couldn't refuse, not if it meant she could fly; and yet as she opened her mouth to answer, to say yes, to say she'd ride her dragon once more for Baros Tsen and damn them all, her thoughts awash with possibilities and doubts ... As she did, her mind seemed to sharpen and she felt aware of another presence listening, except there was no one. It took a moment before she understood what this new feeling was.

A dragon. One that was awake and listening to her thoughts.

Diamond Eye? A flicker of hope came and then guttered and died. Not her Diamond Eye. She'd know. The dragon's thoughts had a familiar taste. It had been inside her before. The dragon from Quai'Shu's ship. The one once called Silence. The dragon that had driven Quai'Shu mad.

Her laughter turned hard and cold. 'Bellepheros! Alchemist! There is a hatchling very close and it is awake and listening to us.' The dragon that had cut her and given her its disease and then left her to die in lingering agony. 'Run, alchemist! Now!' Why warn him? Did she think she was saving him? And if she did, why? Because he kept the dragons tame and kept the Statue Plague at bay? Fat lot of use when the Taiytakei meant to hang her. Fat lot of use when a dragon had come to devour her. And yet ... alive wasn't dead. As long as he was alive then he would keep her Diamond Eye tame for her to fly. Alive could mean a glimmer of hope, even if she couldn't find it.

The alchemist didn't answer. Through the iron door she couldn't hear whether he'd fled or was still there, but she could feel the mockery in the dragon's thoughts as they wandered through her own. 'He's still here,' she whispered. 'Quai'Shu. The Taiytakei who thought to steal us both. Still here.'

I taste him.

'You broke his mind.'

I know.

'You will not break mine.'

I do not need to. I see you, Dragon-Queen. Others did that long ago.

Memories burst like fireworks inside her, snap-firing in dazing succession, flashed then gone again: knocking the blood-tainted glass out of Baros Tsen's hand; the Adamantine Man in Dhar Thosis, his voice, familiar, remembered – *Get off her, you fat prick* – and then a moment later slipping the knife off his belt ten years earlier as the words came out of his mouth, driving it through her father's ribs, again and again and again until he stopped, the father who thought she was nothing better than his own personal whore to share with whoever might offer him the prettiest crown; Jehal on the day he'd told her that her mother was dead, the mother who'd done nothing but birth her and then betray her; riding Diamond Eye over the flames of Dhar Thosis, deliriously out of control and yet free, a fleeting moment when she'd been mistress of her own self; the dark room of fear and despair, always waiting for her and yet always waiting for the inevitable *something worse*; imprisoned from birth by who she was, who she must be. Piece by piece, the dragon Silence ripped it out of her and showed her the wreckage.

'Have you come to kill me this time?' she asked the darkness. The dragon didn't answer, but why else was it here?

The door of her prison was ajar. Bellepheros must have opened it, but he could have flung the iron door wide and it wouldn't have made the slightest difference. She slumped onto her bed and lay back, arms spread across the silk sheets of her prison. The dragon moved through her. She was in Dhar Thosis. The Adamantine Man was bowing his head and she was remembering his voice.

There was a man beside him. She'd had no interest in him then and had no interest in him now, yet she found herself straining to remember his face; and then she knew it wasn't that *she* was trying to remember his face, it was the dragon trying to pull it out of her. She sensed its edge of wonder.

Who is he, little one?

A longing for something different filled her, for possibilities so long dead they were nothing but dry husks. She pulled the Adamantine Man close, the memory of him, his moment of unexpected kindness. Pulled it close and held it like a lover. Memories inside her burned full of flames.

I will think of you as I kill him, little one.

Zafir sat up. Ice filled her. 'Thank you, little dragon.' She bared her teeth and set her mind against the hatchling, barring it from her thoughts. 'Thank you for giving me purpose, little dragon.'

Purpose, little one?

'I will take him home. And I will change the world.'

The dragon laughed at her. *How?*

'You'll see.' She threw its laughter right back in its face, walked to the door of her prison, opened it and ran outside.

Chay-Liang raced into the open. Thunder and lightning flashed between the eyrie and the glasships, three of them now, right overhead, picking off the black-powder guns and the watchtowers. Tsen's soldiers were dragging rocket carts into the dragon yard. She dodged around them, smiling grimly. Belli had been loud about the dangers of mixing dragons with things that exploded but Tsen had brought them anyway. Clever t'varr. Already, the first few streaked into the night to detonate in showers around the glasships.

She passed the hatchery. Silhouetted in flashes of lightning, bodies lay twisted in ways no living man should be, dark stains on the white stone. Her foot slid on something wet and slippery; she tumbled in among the waiting dragon eggs, gasping, lay still and took a moment to catch her breath. The dragon yard was chaos. Men shouting, running. A madness of screams and flashes and thunder and a whirling of swinging clubs. She had no idea how anyone knew who was who.

The fall had shaken her but she wasn't broken. She took her lightning wand from her belt and ran her finger along it until the golden fire inside was as bright as the full moon. Bellepheros had erected a net of heavy chains over the hatchery to keep any newborns from flying away. It was sagging at one corner and there was a broken egg nearby, covered in sticky fluid. Maybe the chaos had confused the hatchling and it had gone down a tunnel instead of simply flying away. She didn't know. Couldn't.

Nearby, the older hatchlings were lunging at anyone who came too close, spitting gouts of fire. On the wall, Diamond Eye sat impassive, watching it all with unblinking eyes. The great beast seemed almost like a statue until another sled came too close and the dragon swatted it out of the air with a casual flick of its tail. Liang picked herself up and ran again and was almost bowled over as a squad of grim-faced soldiers rushed past her, yelling and swinging their ashgars.

'Tsen!' she shouted at them. 'Where's Baros Tsen T'Varr?' But she didn't get an answer. They probably didn't even hear her over the howling wind and the screams of the fight and the thunder-cracks of wands. She kept running, as fast as she could. Another flurry of shouts made her look up. The glasship over the dragon yard had a chunk missing from its outer disc, punched out by the last of the black-powder guns. Cracks ran into its heart and lightning crackled around its ruined rim. It wobbled erratically, drifting slowly. She bent forward, urging herself on. A spray of rockets exploded around the glasship's core. A brilliant light flashed deep inside and then went dim. The glasship lurched and slid sideways, tipped and started to fall straight at the hatchery. Liang swore and sprinted, stumbling and tripping over her own feet as she reached the iron door into the spiralling tunnels where the hatchling had gone, where she had her workshop with Belli, where Tsen himself had his rooms. The door hung open. She threw herself through, tried to slam it shut without stopping, slid, crashed into the wall, staggered, somehow didn't fall and instead kept on running, and then the entire eyrie shook as the glasship smashed into the stone of the dragon yard. The impact shook her off her feet.

Something huge and fast slammed into the half-closed door, buckling the iron and leaving it sagging against the stone. Another flash of light flared like the sun and then died. She heard screams and, for a few short breaths, simply lay where she was, unable to move. When there was nothing more, she pulled herself to her feet. There was a pain in her leg, a pulled muscle. Tomorrow she'd have a whole pile of bruises but right now that was the least of her worries. She brushed herself down and set off again and almost tripped over two dead soldiers sprawled across her path. One was missing his head, bitten clean off. A dozen paces further on she passed it, misshapen, crushed, chewed and spat out again amid a shower of splintered gold-glass.

The hatchling. Liang slowed as she went on, holding her wand bright and ready in front of her.

9

Fire and Lightning

Screams echoed through the curve of the tunnel, carried by the smooth white walls. Helpless terror screams. Liang followed the spiral deeper. She passed another dead soldier with his head torn off and his side ripped open. Another half-turn and the floor was slick with blood and gore and there were bodies all around, torn to pieces. Slaves. Four or five of them. Shredded enough that it was hard to tell. She was close to her workshop now, to Belli's study and his laboratory. Zafir's prison was just beyond. The corpses were fresh.

She slowed. Strange sensations washed past her, thin and hard to touch but there. A savage glee, a swiftness of movement, a surge of vicious joy. She felt a sense of closeness, of a hunt nearing its end and then an incandescent towering rage, and she knew the dragon was close, *very* close, and that it had come here with a purpose, not driven by confusion or panic, and had been somehow thwarted. It came closer still, an inferno of anger, and Liang realised that she hadn't given any thought to what, exactly, she was going to do when she found it.

The scraping of claws on stone, moving with furious intent around the curve of the tunnel, echoed fast towards her. She raised the wand and hurled a bolt of lightning as soon as she saw the first sight of something moving, straight into the hatchling's face. The sound, trapped between the hard white walls of the passage, stunned her − it was like standing next to the firing of a cannon. The flash blinded her too, but she saw the dragon for an instant, burned into her eyes by the light, head low, looking at her, fangs poking from its mouth like a crocodile's, crouched low and ready to spring. She must have hit it − it was far too big and close for the lightning to have arced around it − but she raised the gold-glass shield anyway, willed it to be wider and cringed behind it.

What manner of sorceress are you? A furious voice crashed into her head, streaked with rage and pain. Immediately she felt herself answering, conjuring memories of her life, of the places she'd been, the wonders she'd seen. Khalishtor, the Crown of the Sea Lords, the Dralamut, her studies at Hingwal Taktse, the powers she'd learned, the when and the how and what she could do. The Elemental Men ...

The dragon was rifling her memories. She forced them back and thought of what first came to mind and held it there: Diamond Eye up on the eyrie, staring at the Godspike and the maelstrom of the storm-dark.

The wounds of this splintered world. The passage bloomed into flame. Her eyes hadn't recovered from the lightning and now she was blinded again as the fire came; she could smell it, smell the blistering skin of the dead slaves behind her, the charring blood, the crackling fat and still the fire didn't stop. It licked around her shield and the shield held it back but the heat rose fast around her. With a flick of will she turned the glass from a shield into a shell, hard and thick and complete. The heat fell back. The fire stopped.

For a moment everything was dark and dim, the soft moonlight glow of the walls too feeble for her dazzled eyes. When she closed them, the image of the dragon was there, lit up by her flash of lightning. When she opened them again it was right in front of her, peering through the gold-glass. It sniffed and cocked its head and tapped with a talon as if to see what sound the shell would make, then shuffled back and stopped and watched her. Its eyes changed as though looking past her at something far away. Then abruptly it lunged, battering its head into the glass. The shell flew back and tipped over with Liang inside it. The glass starred and cracked. She willed the fractures away and changed its shape around her to something more stable as she scrabbled back to her feet – a pyramid – and barely in time before the dragon came at her again, this time with a crack of its whip-like tail which sent her spinning across the passage. Her head hit the inside of the glass hard enough to draw blood and burst fireworks in front of her eyes. There was something about the way the dragon was looking at her now, as though it was enjoying itself.

'Enjoy this.' She changed the gold-glass so the lightning wand poked through it and let fly another bolt. She closed her eyes this time, but the dragon had been right there, the wand pointing at its face, and she'd seen it, at the last moment, turn away as though it understood what was coming. The blast sent it flying down the passage in a tumble of claws and wings. It took a second or two to recover itself. Liang watched the glow inside her wand grow brighter as it charged again, gritting her teeth as she waited to see who would be quicker.

This world is less dull than the last, Chay-Liang. I will remember you, little one. It was mocking her. She sent another charge of lightning at it but this time it seemed to know even before she willed the wand to fire. It sprang, fast and high and straight over her head, vanishing into the gloom, back towards the surface. For a moment Liang stayed where she was, wondering if it was truly gone and why it had come here in the first place, but then she realised she already knew the answer to that. It had come to kill the dragon-slave.

She ran on, looking for Bellepheros.

'Run, alchemist! Now!' Bellepheros hadn't needed telling twice. A woken hatchling? The worst thing there could be. He turned and fled, running deeper into the eyrie until he reached the rooms at the very bottom that Baros Tsen T'Varr kept for himself and his slave Kalaiya. He stopped only when he reached the door at the very end that led into the bathhouse, the deepest and largest chamber under the eyrie. *Which should have been the hatchery*, but there was no point going over *that* argument again, certainly not now. He hesitated. The door was ajar and there was blood on the floor and he didn't know what might be inside ... but whatever it was, it couldn't be worse than a hatchling dragon chasing him. *Awake! Great Flame, not awake!* He fumbled his fingers around the iron door, pulling it open.

There was a corpse tucked into the shadows of the alcove to one side where Tsen kept towels and robes and the cheaper end of his stock of Xizic oils, an armoured soldier with his throat cut. Bellepheros tugged at the door and slipped in the blood and almost fell, and then the door opened on its own, so abruptly that it knocked him down. He wailed with fear, sure he was about to die in a whirl of talons and teeth and fire, but it was only a woman, a slave in a white tunic. She hurried out and grabbed him by his robes. 'Where is he? *Where is he?*'

He knew her face – Tsen's mistress or lover or whatever she was. Kalaiya. Bellepheros shook his head and glanced back over his shoulder. 'I don't know. But don't go that way! There's a dragon loose behind me.'

She pushed him away and ran past, shouting Tsen's name.

'Kalaiya!' Bellepheros wrung his hands for a moment and then closed the door when she didn't look back and barred it behind him. Which might or might not be enough to keep a hatchling back but he wasn't about to wait and find out. Across the bath-house, a second door hung open into the tunnels that led up to the Scales' quarters. He ran for it, back up to the dragon yard to look for Chay-Liang.

By the time he reached the surface, he was panting and gasping, almost doubled over, hobbling and cursing his knees. The yard was alive with lightning and armoured men smashing each other to bits and glasships overhead and sleds whizzing past the walls and chaos and mayhem. He cringed and ducked back into the tunnels away from the madness, then screwed his eyes shut as an explosion shook the eyrie. In the flashes of light and thunder after he opened them again, he saw Diamond Eye, perched on the wall, watching with distant interest. Bellepheros sank against the tunnel wall. He didn't know what to do. He couldn't go back, not with a hatchling down there, and he certainly couldn't go outside, and so he did nothing but curl up small and try not to be seen and quiver with fright as he watched Tsen's men and the Vespinese shatter one another with their ashgars while sleds darted overhead.

The hatchery outside the tunnel was wrecked, eggs ripped open by massive razor-edged shards where a glasship had come down and smashed into the white stone. As he watched, another fell to Tsen's rockets, tipping out of the sky and crashing into the eyrie rim, shattering as it bounced away and fell in glittering rain towards the void below. The third glasship came down low, close enough for the gondola it carried to unfurl and spit out its soldiers. Rockets exploded around it. It lurched and drifted away.

Diamond Eye shifted. The soldiers from the gondola had caught the dragon's attention as though they were strange and new, although what was different about them Bellepheros hadn't the first idea. He watched them fall, one by one, though they died far harder than Tsen's soldiers. Across the yard, in a flash of lightning, he thought he saw Chay-Liang. His heart jumped and he forgot for a moment how afraid he was. He almost ran out, but then he lost her amid the flashes and screams.

Diamond Eye shifted again and turned his head. The fighting had spread across the dragon yard now, broken into pockets, everywhere except around the hatchlings. A handful of Vespinese ran towards the eggs, straight past Bellepheros. One turned his head, saw him and slowed, but then a bolt of lightning crashed among them, skittering sparks from their gold-glass armour as three of Tsen's men charged, screaming and swinging their ashgars. Bellepheros scuttled and jumped like a nervous beetle out into the open and ran up the steps to the wall. His knees were killing him but he kept running as fast as he could around the top, robes flapping around his ankles until he reached Diamond Eye. Back in the dragon-realms he'd seen men carelessly trodden on, seen them sent flying by the thoughtless flick of a tail and, most common of all, picked up and tumbled across the ground when an idle dragon decided to stretch its wings. Sometimes men got up and walked away from that, but not often – but at least with a dragon he understood the danger. Better than lightning, anyway. Better than howling screaming men charging at him with great spiked clubs. He shifted nervously. It said something about the state of the world when the safest place he could think of was nestled between a dragon's claws.

Diamond Eye was gazing out into the night, back the same way it had stared before.

'What do you see out there?' Bellepheros asked. 'What?'

A shape shot high overhead. And then another, at the end of the wall, much lower. Bellepheros glimpsed the outline of a man crouched, one knee bent forward, head pressed firmly into the wind; and then all of a sudden there were hundreds of them over the yard. They skimmed the ground and hurled their lightning and jumped down with their ashgars swinging, and in minutes the battle was done. Over. The last of Tsen's men dropped their ashgars and their wands and raised their hands over their heads. The eyrie was lost.

'You could burn them, you know,' he whispered to Diamond Eye. 'All of them. Under the circumstances I don't think anyone who mattered would mind.'

But the dragon was staring across the yard at something else.

The rider-slave wasn't in her prison. The door was open. A cold panic settled over Liang because where else would she be if not up fighting Shonda's soldiers? Maybe she'd found some other way to escape – dear gods, was *that* why the hatchling had come down here? To *help* her? But she bit that back. Zafir hadn't passed her, and the rider-slave would hardly leave without her dragon.

Bellepheros! Liang ran to his laboratory and threw open the door. No Bellepheros, but Zafir was standing there in the ruins of it. She wasn't even trying to hide. She simply stood, wrapped in dragon-scale, holding a vial in her hand. Everything had been smashed and burned. Liang pointed her wand. Tempting to let the lightning have her and be done with it, whatever Belli said, whatever Tsen said. The world would be better for it.

'Get up and go to your dragon and do what you do best,' she snapped. She looked at the devastation, at the smouldering wreckage, the charred books. She felt the heat and it slowly dawned on her what had happened. Zafir hadn't done this; the hatchling had. And for a moment, as Zafir looked up, her face was so anguished that Liang wondered whether she was wrong. Didn't everyone deserve at least a little pity? But the look was gone in an instant and the thought with it too. Pity? The rider-slave didn't know such a word even existed.

Zafir shook her head. 'All his potions. All gone.' She looked at the vial in her hand and shrugged. 'Well, almost.'

Liang grabbed Zafir's arm and spun her round, forgetting herself for a moment. Distant shouts echoed through the tunnels, getting closer. Zafir snapped her arm away. Her eyes scanned the room, place to place to place with the tiniest little smile. Liang grabbed at her again. This time Zafir danced away. Liang levelled her wand.

'Why don't you just kill me and be done with it?' Zafir sounded tired. Bored, which made Liang want to slap her.

'It's not like you don't deserve it.'

'So do it.' A crippled smile crept into the corner of Zafir's mouth. 'You'll be doing it for the wrong reasons of course. But you want to, you always did. So go ahead. The hatchling came to do the same. Perhaps it would have changed its mind but I doubt it. Dragons are not merciful creatures. I'm afraid I can't fly Diamond Eye for you just now.'

Mercy? Another word the rider-slave claimed to know but surely didn't understand. Liang shook her head. 'Get up and do as you're told, slave! Win this day and you can have your freedom. I'll take you back to your own land myself if I have to.'

Zafir's eyes narrowed. 'Is that yours to give?'

'Yes.' Tsen had as good as said so.

'And my alchemist, will you let him go too?'

'If that's what he wants.' It surprised Liang how sure she sounded of that. Not by how much the thought hurt, though – *that* didn't surprise her at all.

Zafir strode past Liang, out through the door and into the moonlight glow of the white stone tunnels. She spat out a bitter laugh. 'Ha! Perhaps you'd like to come too. I doubt we'd do well sharing him but I think I might put up with you anyway. You make a good armourer. Have more for me yet?' She snorted. 'But no, why would you? I'm to ride to war in silks and dragon-skin then, am I? I suppose it's a better death than hanging.' She stopped. 'But I can't ride Diamond Eye just now, Chay-Liang. I took a potion to hide from the hatchling and so Diamond Eye won't know me. I'll fight for you anyway, if that's what you want, and if I live then you keep your word, whatever happens, or I *will* kill him. Not you. Him.' Zafir laughed again. 'It's a trick I learned from a dragon.'

'You *will* ride!' Liang hurried out, heading for the surface. When she looked back, Zafir was walking in long slow strides, falling away behind her. 'Come *on*! Run! Run for me!' But Zafir only laughed.

'It's my death, witch, and I'll come to it in my own time. I'll have that much.'

Liang almost turned back to drag her, but no good would come of it and the rider-slave would overpower her with ease. For the third time in as many minutes she clenched her wand and almost killed the woman. There was a battle right over their heads. Time mattered, urgency was everything but no, *Zafir* never ran. A slave, but the dragon-queen always came as though the world was supposed to wait for *her*. Liang raced on, as fast as her tortured legs would take her. As she did, she whispered a chant to Feyn Charin, the first navigator, begging him for patience.

The dragon yard was a seething morass of fighting men, yelling and shouting and scrambling between the ruin of the hatchery and the fallen glasship. Thunderclaps and flashes dazed and dazzled and the ever-present wind shrieked through everything, tearing at word and thought. Liang stood bewildered by the light and the noise. Another glasship hovered overhead, its rim glowing bright and angry. There were soldiers everywhere, Vespinese in glass-and-gold armour with their lightning wands, some with huge crossbows strapped to their other arm instead of a shield. She almost didn't see as a Vespinese turned towards her and pointed his wand, barely a dozen steps away.

Chay-Liang ducked back into the tunnel mouth and willed her gold-glass orb into a shield. Lightning cracked over its surface. The soldier started towards her and raised his crossbow. She jumped aside and he missed but the crossbow reloaded itself as she watched. She fired her own wand as he came at her. Lightning fizzed over his armour and sparked between his fingers but it wouldn't do any more than daze, not with a glass-and-gold skin; and then another soldier, one of Tsen's, loomed behind him and caved in his skull with an ashgar.

'Enchantress! Look to yourself!' The soldier pointed across the dragon yard and turned and ran to where the gondola from the last glasship had opened and more Vespinese were spilling out, throwing lightning all around them. The glasship's cannon fired and rang her ears with a dazzling moment of light. She reeled, and then a stream of rockets streaked up from behind her, blowing two of the stabiliser discs in the glasship's heart to pieces. Fragments of shattered gold-glass as big as horses fell like rain around the gondola, breaking into a million glittering shards as they hit the stone of the eyrie, crushing and skewering the men beneath them. The spinning glass disc tipped slowly sideways and began to drift.

'Slave!' Liang screamed back into the passage. She'd have to protect the rider-slave from those crossbows as well as lightning then, and the dragon was right over on the far wall. Bloody woman would bloody well learn to run once she got up here! That or she'd die. *Can't ride? My skinny arse she can't ride!* 'Slave!' Tsen's knights were being hammered but were holding their own. She'd never seen these crossbows before, never anything like them but they were clearly enchanter-made. She reshaped her gold-glass into a wider shield and peered back outside, looking for Bellepheros.

Flashes of lightning cracked in among shouts and screams. The last glasship slewed drunkenly over the edge of the eyrie and disappeared. The chains on the gondola snapped taut and tore it across the yard. Men caught in them howled as they were dragged away. Vespinese or Tsen's she couldn't tell, but either way she couldn't do anything to help them. The gondola smashed into the wall. The chains snapped. Three of them whipped back across the dragon yard, slicing men apart as cleanly as an Elemental Man's blade. Liang ducked and winced as a sled shot over the wall behind her. She loosed a lightning bolt in its wake.

'*Slave! Zafir!*' She couldn't see Belli anywhere. Up by the dragon, maybe? Even now no one dared go near it. Still no sign of the dragon-queen but just maybe that wasn't going to matter – Shonda's soldiers might be better but Tsen had more, and now that the last of the glasships was gone they had no cannon left to turn the tide. Hard to be sure in the chaos but perhaps the first attack was going to fail! And the bulk of Shonda's fleet was still a mile or two away. Liang whipped around. They didn't need her here, not right now. What they needed was for her to go back down and drag that heartless whore to the surface by her hair and carry her onto the back of the dragon if she had to ...

Zafir was right there, head cocked, an amused smirk on her face. 'Enchantress?'

Liang pointed to Diamond Eye perched on the wall. 'Go on then.'

'Do you have a sword for me? Some sort of weapon would be helpful.'

'The dragon, you stupid woman.' Beside herself, Liang lunged and slammed her palms into Zafir's chest.

Zafir pursed her lips. 'I can't,' she said, and as the words hung between them, she pointed to the wall where the dragon sat as a new wave of Vespinese soldiers on glass sleds whipped past and swarmed into the dragon yard, filling the air with lightning. Scores of them. Hundreds, perhaps. Too many to resist. Liang spat and ground her teeth.

'Go, slave! Serve your master.'

Zafir glared and didn't move. Some sort of animal snarl forced itself out of Liang's throat, the sort of sound she didn't even know she could make. She lunged at Zafir again. Zafir caught her arms, spun her round and pinned them behind her back. The rider-slave hissed in her ear, dripping with venom, 'I already told you, witch, that I can't do that just now. I took a potion to hide from that hatchling and so I can't ride.' She let go and they faced each other, Zafir looking down on her, cold and haughty. 'And the truth is, *witch*, that I would if I could, but not for you, because why would I? These are men from the mountain king, are they not? Why would I save you from them? I'm just a slave, and one master is as good as the next, and you would never let me go. None of you ever do. At least this one might not hang me. But if I could, I'd fly. Because that is what I am.'

Liang took a step away and stroked the lightning inside her wand up to its brightest. She levelled it at Zafir's face. There really wasn't any reason now, was there, not to kill this viper that Tsen had brought among them?

Zafir watched calmly. 'I don't think you have it in you, Chay-Liang. But if you do, then have done with it.' She slowly walked past Liang out into the frenzy of the dragon yard and tipped back her head to look at the stars. 'My dragon stands on the far wall. Bellepheros sits between his feet. Have a thought for him.'

Chay-Liang raised the wand and aimed it at the middle of the dragon-rider's back. She counted slowly to five. Then lowered it again.

10

The Regrettable Man

Tsen was in his bath, irritably scratching at his finger, when the Vespinese came. Bronzehand was being insistent tonight, trying to reach him again and again, and Tsen was steadfastly ignoring him because he didn't think that either of them had much to say, not when Bronzehand was a world away in the jungles of Qeled. They'd all be like that now, all of Quai'Shu's heirs, or at least they would once they knew what he'd done. Bunkered up and watching from a good safe distance, trying to make sure they didn't get caught in the wreckage, watching in case they could pick up any pieces for themselves. It made Tsen unreasonably cross and he was almost minded to take off Bronzehand's ring and write him a little letter and show it to him, telling him exactly what he thought of them all. *Hardly matters now. I'll be dead soon enough.*

The bathhouse door opened. He looked up and felt a vague sense of relief as Kalaiya walked in through the steam, carrying a thick towel. She slid between the circle of white stone arches, climbed the steps and sat at the edge of the water beside him. He hadn't asked for her tonight but it was hardly a surprise that she came anyway. She knew his moods and when she was wanted. She had an instinct. Her movements were quick and sharp and she'd clearly come with a purpose in mind.

Without thinking much about it he reached out for her hand. 'Bronzehand's being a right ...' His words stuttered and failed as she drew back and opened her robe. She wore tight silks underneath, as black as midnight, clothes he'd never seen on her before. She unfolded the towel and inside were more of the same. The biggest surprise came when he saw the Watcher's bladeless knife, which he'd taken to keeping in his room.

'Tsen.' Her voice was strange. Strained and not her own at all.

She held out a hand to him. 'Tsen! Shonda comes. Now. It's time to go.'

Baros Tsen stared up at this new Kalaiya and frowned at her. This was a Kalaiya he'd never seen. He smiled, but nothing about her smiled back and so his own quickly faded to a frown. 'Who are you today, my love?'

She beckoned him out of the bath, fingers twitching with impatience. 'Whose face do you see, Tsen? I'm who I've always been.' She sounded more like herself now than when she'd first spoken. Softer. Kinder. 'I'm the slave you've always known.' She sighed. When Tsen made no move towards her, she dropped her hand. 'When would be a convenient time?' she asked. 'In a few days? Is that long enough to set your affairs in order, Baros Tsen T'Varr? Except, knowing you, you'd ask for years.' She smiled a little. 'And how shall it be? A knife? A metal wire garrotte? For you perhaps the ecstatic poison of the Shabbahk, laced into your apple wine. I would have done that for you.'

Tsen gaped. 'You're one of *them*? All this time and you're one of *them*?'

He looked for the inner voices that would tell him he should have seen this coming for years, but for once they were silent, as stunned as the rest of him. His Kalaiya was a Regrettable Man? No. Not possible. It simply couldn't be.

'Don't be an idiot – of course I'm not!' She crouched at the edge of the bath. 'Shonda is here. Now. He will kill you and the truth will die. We have to leave.'

Tsen shook his head. 'You're not Kalaiya. I don't know who you are but you're not my Kalaiya.'

'Someone sent me to murder you a long time ago, Baros Tsen T'Varr. And I chose otherwise.' Her voice was still different. Everything about her, her manners, her expressions, the words she chose, the way she moved, all of it was wrong as though the Kalaiya he'd known for a dozen years had been nothing but a mask. Perhaps she had. He'd often wondered if she secretly detested him, or if she simply put up with him because she was a slave and he was her master and everything he thought they had between them was in fact nothing at all. But this? *This?*

Her face though. Her face was perfect. The same face that had looked at him almost every day for all that time. *See, Tsen? What a fool you are! All these years ...*

Well that stupid voice could shut itself up right now. *This is a pile of horse crap. I'm not that bad a judge of character.* 'And you're going to do it *now*? After *how* many years?'

Kalaiya slapped the water impatiently. 'I'm not here to kill you, you idiot. What in the name of the unholy Konsidar would be the point of that when I could just do nothing and let Shonda have you. I'm getting you away. He's *here*! Listen!'

Tsen listened. There wasn't much, but he felt the stone walls of the bath tingle now and then, the faintest vibration running through the stone. There was little that could do that except the black-powder guns.

That or the dragon is dancing very energetically and for no apparent reason.

'He's here and you are going to *lose*. Come on!' Kalaiya held out her hand again, and this time Tsen took it because if the Vespinese really had come then he certainly didn't want them to find him surprised and naked in a bath. He let her wrap the towel around him and hurry him into his clothes. When he was done, he looked at her long and hard. He stared at her face. He couldn't believe it was her and yet he couldn't believe it wasn't. Could she have a twin? 'Who are you? Is this a game? Because if it is, it's not funny.' His Kalaiya knew better than to play games though. *You've known this woman for twelve years, Baros Tsen. Every feature, every curve, every line, every wrinkle, every pore. Look at her! She is who she is.*

Yes, yes, but really? In my hour of greatest need the slave I quietly adore becomes a Regrettable Man and rushes to save me? If he heard that in a story he'd piss himself with laughter at the absurdity of it. *The beautiful assassin who falls in love with the man she's sent to kill? Oh, please!*

Well then, what? A golem sent by Shonda? Does that sound any better? Look at her!

The eyrie quivered again. He scowled. The Vespinese *had* come – that could hardly be any more obvious – and yet why was it Kalaiya, of all people, who was here to warn him? *I have kwens for this, not slaves! Kwens and soldiers. Where are they?* He looked at Kalaiya, if that was who this truly was, bemused, trying to decide.

She smiled back at him and rolled her eyes. 'Come. Time to go. Don't tell me you don't have a secret escape plan?'

Tsen shook his head, bewildered even more because escape had been the one thing he'd never considered and she knew it. And yes, maybe now he was wishing he *had* considered it, and yes, standing proud at the prow of his sinking ship had seemed all well and good when it hadn't actually happened and yes, now that that same ship was apparently on fire with the sea lapping at his feet it seemed … well, *less* well and good, but he'd always known it would be this way. That was the point. He'd made a choice: no desperate escape plans. No chance to take the coward's way at the very end and run. To his disappointment he found that a part of him, right now, was very keen indeed on the coward's way.

The night-black silks were awkward and ill fitting and so thin that he felt almost naked. *She's not real? Then what is she, a golem? Don't be absurd.* He didn't know what to believe. He kept thinking he should shout for his guards and then he looked at her face and was struck dumb. She took his hand and tugged him towards the iron door of the bathhouse and he came slowly, resisting but never quite pulling away. 'Show me,' he said. *Yes, yes, stall for time, for surely all the gods in which we do not believe forbid that you should come over suddenly decisive at this time of crisis.*

'See for yourself.' She hurried him out of the bathhouse, not the way she'd entered but through the tunnels that led up to the Scales and so they didn't pass the alcove where the slaves kept the oils and the towels.

Whatever this was, getting to the surface and seeing it with his own eyes was imperative, and so now he followed as fast as he could. Kalaiya led him through the Scales' quarters, running ahead through the rising spiral passage. The lower rooms were empty, deserted, unused, but he could hear the commotion as he came closer to the top. The Scales – the slaves who cared for and fed the dragons – had stumbled out into the night-glow of the tunnels wondering what was happening. The eyrie shook and trembled, explosions too powerful to be lightning. Tsen tried not to look as he pushed past. The Scales disturbed him. They carried the Statue Plague, the Hatchling Disease the rider-slave had given to Chrias and would have given to him as well. They were all slowly dying, their skin turning hard until they couldn't move or breathe, and yet none of them seemed to care. That was the worst part. The dullness they carried.

Not the best time to be worrying about that, T'Varr! The eyrie shuddered, almost shaking him off his feet, a great heave far worse than the firing of the cannon. He shivered as he stumbled, wondering if that was the eyrie's magic failing at last. Maybe they were all falling to their doom. All things considered, would that be so bad?

Kalaiya was waiting for him at the top. She caught him and pulled him on. 'Come on!' She was strong and her voice was urgent. He slowed and looked at her but she didn't flinch. The Kalaiya he knew, the one he'd quietly fallen in love with years ago, she'd have been terrified by this. All these years and she wasn't the person he'd thought she was? It broke his heart. How? How had she done it? Day after day after day the same flawless mask and he'd never seen through it, not once? Him, a t'varr to a sea lord no less, who read people at a glance every day. How?

Because she's not who she seems and you know it. He slowed again. 'Are you really my Kalaiya?' But if not then how did she have Kalaiya's face?

Kalaiya-or-maybe-not gave him a quick look. 'I have a sled by the watchtower overlooking the hatchery. Do you want to live? Because if you do then we have to reach it before Shonda does.'

He closed his eyes and ran on, up and out into an annihilation of sound and light. Lightning flashed everywhere, men ran and howled, waving ashgars, hurling themselves at each other in murderous frenzy. Sleds shot across the dragon yard. The smashed remains of half a glasship lay on its side in the middle of the hatchery, right in front of them, broken eggs and hatchling flesh scattered around it. A gondola lay rolled onto its side against the wall, and not far from it was a second, just reaching the level of the dragon yard, its ramp opening. Soldiers in glass-and-gold armour jumped out and threw lightning every which way as they did. A rocket fizzed from the wall and exploded among them, a handful of his own soldiers ran howling to meet them while the golden rim of the glasship glowed brighter and brighter until it dazzled, and then there was a crack of thunder so loud he felt the shock of air hit him and he almost fell over. He couldn't think any more. He couldn't tell who was with him and who wasn't. Lightning thundered and the eyrie shook and every thought was murdered in his head, stillborn in the chaos of noise and light and screaming wind. On the far wall sat the great dragon, perched on the edge of his eyrie. Doing nothing. Watching.

'The rider-slave! Where is she?'

'Too late for that, T'Varr.' Kalaiya-or-maybe-not yanked him out into the mayhem where he really didn't want to be, but he was so slack-jawed and dazzled that he didn't think to pull away. The hatchery watchtower was right above them. Kalaiya ran up the steps to the top of the wall, pulling Tsen huffing and puffing after her, then let him go and vanished into the tower. The wind hit him hard as he crested the wall. He teetered for a moment, almost tumbling back down the steps. *Nice. A hundred men trying to kill you and you break your own neck to save them the trouble?* He just about caught himself. Somehow, almost falling seemed to calm him. He was still terrified enough to shit his pants, but he could think again now. *Think!* That was the thing. Every instinct apart from his eyes told him this wasn't Kalaiya. But how ...?

Thunder rumbled and cracked all around him. Lightning flashed. The screams and shouts of men came and went. Rockets flew off the walls, striking at the Vespinese as they landed. Out across the storm-dark, more glasships were drifting closer. Scores of them though still far away. He ducked into the shelter of the tower, fearful he'd be hit by a stray bolt of lightning. *Yes. Yes, I want to run ... Time for betrayals and broken hearts later.*

A dead soldier lay on the floor. Even through the wind and the scorched tang of the air, Tsen could smell the freshness of the man's blood.

Well, in case you were still wondering, isn't that an answer? Kalaiya-or-maybe-not was climbing onto the roof. He cringed and winced as another shattering bolt of lightning struck the eyrie from the glasship floating above. He reached for his wand but of course he didn't have it; he'd left it in the bathhouse. The ground trembled as a barrage of rockets peppered the glasship with explosions. There was an ear-splitting crack, louder even than the lightning, a brilliant flash and the golden rim of the glasship went suddenly dull. Up in the heart of its great disc, among the smaller discs that all spun in different ways, something wasn't right. It started to tilt. It was coming down, and he knew he should probably run away now, any way at all, but he didn't know how, didn't know which way to go. So he just stood there. *Pathetic fat old t'varr.*

Not-Kalaiya jumped back into the tower. She grabbed his face and turned it and he knew he *had* to run away right now if he wanted at all to live, and yet still he didn't, because it was still *her* face, and if he was going to die then that was what he wanted to see as he faded. 'Look, Baros Tsen! Look!'

His eyes blurred with tears. 'You're not—' he began. *You're not my Kalaiya.*

'No.' She caught hold of something and pulled. Tethered to the outside of the tower, a sled appeared as if she'd lifted an invisible blanket. She twirled her hands as though she had something in them and then wrapped whatever it was around herself as if putting on a shawl. From her neck down to her knees, she vanished. Tsen's mouth fell open. 'Shifter skin,' she whispered. 'Do you understand now what I am?'

Shifter skin? But her eyes ... 'You're not her. You're not.'

Not-Kaliaya shook her head. 'Your slave is who you think she is, nothing less, nothing more. I borrowed her face because I knew you wouldn't come here without her.' She touched his cheek and a horrible pain flowed across his face and into his head. He felt his skin writhe as something terrible happened inside him. She caught him as he fell. He waited as the lights went out for some last snide remark from his little voices but they had nothing to say, not for this.

The Spire of the World

The dragon Silence hurled itself through the tunnels. There was blood in the air and war on the wind. There were dragons, dulled maybe, but perhaps they would have followed had it asked. Perhaps if it had spoken its thoughts into theirs and broken their chains then they would have turned on the little ones, but as Silence reached the open air, it swiftly forgot them amid the chaos of thunder and lightning as the little ones fought one another. And it might have circled and listened to their thoughts and revelled in them, in their pain and hope, in their despair and fear, but it saw, as it took to the wing and slipped into the darkness of the night past a falling glasship, what lay below.

The storm-dark. It had seen it before, in the life before this at the end when the moon sorcerers had thrown its flesh into the sea and sent its soul to Xibaiya. An unravelling of the very stuff of matter. Silence dived and skimmed the surface, tasting the scent of it, touching its smell, and it knew as it did that it had been right. But this was different. In tiny subtle ways but there was a smell and a taste of a wrongness, of the creeping hole of the Nothing it had found in the realm of the dead. It tasted the Nothing here in the air. The dead goddess and the Black Moon, her killer, were no longer the walls and door to the prison that had kept the Nothing locked away.

The battle raged above, forgotten. A vast disc of glass, spinning slowly, fell past the dragon, too slow for gravity alone to be at work. A silver orb dangled beneath from a dozen chains, half of them broken. The dragon watched the glass touch the Nothing and piece by piece cease to be. Not shattered or smashed or burned or transformed or destroyed but annihilated, every piece of history and future taken away. Matter that was not and had never been. The dragon watched and remembered its purpose, why it had chosen this place as it flew across the roiling black clouds and the purple lightning, the shroud that kept the Nothing ever out of sight. It circled the Godspike, unexpected and vast, piercing the cloud and piercing the Nothing as well, an impossibility standing proudly before it. The dragon Silence flew closer and touched the shaft with its talons and then flipped away. It knew this stone well.

Bellepheros cowered under Diamond Eye, sheltering from the wind and the fight and the bursts of lightning. The Vespinese on their glass sleds scoured the yard in circles, hurling their thunderbolts until nothing moved. Others landed, throwing themselves in waves against the beleaguered defenders until, hopelessly outnumbered, Tsen's men finally surrendered. Most of the Vespinese then headed off into the tunnels while a few handfuls stayed in the dragon yard, stripping the survivors of their glass and gold, rounding up everyone who was still alive to pile the bodies of the dead. Amid the smashed ruin of the fallen glasship, some of the hatchlings were loose from their chains. Like Diamond Eye, they were oddly still and strangely quiet. They kept looking up at the great red-gold dragon while Diamond Eye himself stared fixedly across the eyrie. Bellepheros squinted. The dragon was looking at two figures standing together and yet apart, but the glass lenses Liang had made for him were down in his laboratory, and without them he couldn't make out who the figures were.

More and more Vespinese landed. They poured along the walls and through the five iron doors into the tunnels and passages that spiralled through the stone, rooting out anyone who was left to resist. Bellepheros sat down, miserable and cold, and huddled against the dragon's warmth. Out over the great cyclone of the storm-dark the Vespinese fleet drifted closer, so slowly that by the time they reached the eyrie, Shonda's victorious soldiers were herding everyone into the yard, dividing them by caste. Slaves. Scales. Tsen's soldiers. Kwens and t'varrs and hsians. Bellepheros squinted and finally saw Zafir, still with her head held high as soldiers pushed and shoved her. A body hung limp beside her, dragged between two Vespinese.

Li! His heart jumped. The soldiers dropped her on the ground. She lay still for a moment then rolled onto her side. One of the

Vespinese kicked her. He would have kicked her again but Zafir stepped between them. Diamond Eye suddenly shifted. The soldier drew back his fist. Zafir didn't move. Even as the punch knocked her down, Diamond Eye's wings flared, and Bellepheros had only a moment to throw himself as flat as he could and grab the edge of the wall before the wind of the dragon's leap grabbed him by his cloak and tore it away and almost flipped him into the air. His cloak fluttered off into the night, drifting away to die in the maelstrom below as Diamond Eye skimmed the dragon yard. There was a short sharp scream as the dragon plucked up the soldier who'd struck Zafir and then crushed him, still in mid-air, bits splattering over those below. Diamond Eye tossed the mangled corpse among the Vespinese, landed softly on the far wall and turned his back to stare at the Godspike again. For three long breaths no one moved, waiting to see what would happen next. When Diamond Eye stayed where he was, the Vespinese slowly returned to sorting their prisoners. They left Zafir and Li well alone.

Bellepheros picked himself up. The Vespinese still hadn't seen him. He ducked over the far side of the wall, rolled and stumbled down its slope onto the eyrie rim, scrambling through the ruins of black-powder cannon, around the cranes that dangled over the edge, through the rubbish and detritus. Li was the worst, insisting that nothing ever be thrown away, and so the rim was covered with piles of wood and stone and metal and boxes of broken glass as well as coils of rope and heaps of half-cleared sand. He circled the eyrie until he was close to Diamond Eye again and then stopped. A mile below swirled an utter darkness, fractured by violet flashes deep within. The Godspike rose before him, punching through it all, lit by its own starlight glow, a dim light climbing to the heavens and perhaps beyond. In that moment he thought perhaps he understood why the dragons stared at it so – to them everything else was small. So immeasurably insignificant.

He shook himself and scrambled clumsily up the shallow slope of the wall and stood beside Diamond Eye's talons as he had before, carefully out of sight. The sky was getting lighter. He hadn't thought much of it, scrambling round the rim, but the eyrie was lit up now by a light brighter than any full moon – the light of the glasships clustered above, a hundred of them jostling for space, their lightning-cannon edges glowing bright white, illuminating each other and the dragon yard below. They lowered more gondolas as he watched. Soldiers crowded the eyrie and lined the walls, making everything theirs while the remnants of Tsen's men stood in beaten huddles, ringed by soldiers in glass and gold. The yard fell quiet save for the rush of the wind. The faint glow of a hundred lightning wands gleamed off the white stone of the yard.

No one came close to the dragons.

Soldiers marched out of the tunnels. They had Tsen's prisoner with them, Mai'Choiro, the kwen of Vespinarr. There was some shouting but Bellepheros couldn't make any words out over the constant rush of wind. Mai'Choiro dragged one of Tsen's men away from the rest. Lightning flared and thunderclapped. The man arched and lurched across the stone, twitched a while and then lay still. Mai'Choiro moved on, inspecting his prizes. He stopped by Zafir, and all at once Diamond Eye quivered and changed in the snap of a finger from boredom into a killer on the brink of attack.

'Don't,' whispered Bellepheros, as if the dragon would either hear or pay him any attention. It felt the threat to its rider in the Taiytakei's thoughts and that was all that mattered. They'd seen it once already. How stupid could they be?

Whatever passed between Zafir and Mai'Choiro, the wind stole their words. A Vespinese kicked the back of Zafir's leg, forcing her to kneel. Diamond Eye flinched and bared his teeth, fire building inside him. With a sigh of exasperation Bellepheros jumped up and ran along the wall, flapping his arms and shouting, making as much fuss and noise as he could over the howl of the wind, hoping someone would notice him in the gloom. 'Mai'Choiro Kwen! Your Holiness! Do not! For all our sakes, do not!' He reached the nearest steps and came down as fast as his old knees would take him, but by the time the Vespinese noticed, Mai'Choiro had already moved on and Zafir was still alive.

At the bottom of the steps soldiers seized him. When Bellepheros told them who and what he was, they dragged him to Mai'Choiro, but the kwen only shook his head and waved them away after asking, 'And you, alchemist. Do *you* know where Baros Tsen T'Varr can be found?'

*

White. Impervious. The eyrie had been the same. The enchanted stone of the half-gods before they fell. The Silver Kings. The dragon Silence flew higher, on and on, chasing the very top of the spike until the air was gone and the desert stars were joined by a million more, and the mile upon mile of the swirling maelstrom was made small by the limitless world stretched beneath it. At the very top the dragon Silence sat and perched and knew that no other creature had ever been to this place, not a single one in the whole course of history. From its height atop the world it reached out its thoughts and searched and searched until it found a fragment of something remembered, like a reflection or an image cast in smoke, fleeting and flickering but impossible to forget. It was far away, but the dragon knew it of old, and the treacherous gift of the stars it carried too. It knew them from before the world had shattered into splinters and been so haphazardly stitched back together.

For a long time it watched, long after the battle in the eyrie was done. It watched and it thought until finally it spread its wings and let itself fall.

I see you, the dragon whispered.

Crazy Mad

12

The Desert

Tuuran stroked his axe. 'I'm hungry.'

They separated. Tuuran went one way, Crazy the other, circling the house and coming up on the night-skins one from each side. Up close Tuuran could smell the taint of smoke on the soldiers' clothes. He'd spotted the night-skins heading away and was reckoning to slip in behind them, so it was a bit of a surprise when he almost walked straight into them coming towards him. Must have turned to head for home. Just luck who saw whom first, but maybe luck figured she owed him for making him a slave. Either way, he took that luck and rode it, let out a roar, jumped out of the trees in front of them and took the first night-skin's head clean off. The second got his wand half-raised before Tuuran caught him with the backswing, caving in his ribs. The wand went off, blasting lightning into the ground. The Taiytakei dropped to his knees. Blood poured out of his mouth. He fell over, face first, and didn't move.

'Bloody bollocks.' Tuuran stamped out the smouldering fire from the lightning bolt. 'Shit, fuck and bugger.' Now they'd have to be keeping their eyes peeled for the rest of the day, watching out in case any other night-skins had heard and came looking.

He heard another noise then, jumped up and had his axe ready in a blink, but it was only Crazy rushing in from the other side. Behind Crazy, Tuuran saw a dozen eyes cowering in the shadows. Faces. Slaves.

'Yeh,' said Crazy. 'I thought we passed a few night-skins having a bit of a doze a few miles back. Good of you to wake them up.'

Tuuran wiped the blood off his axe. 'Bit of a dragon's testicle, that. We'd do best to drag these bastards somewhere away from where their friends can find them.' He glared at the cowering eyes in the trees and raised his voice. 'We're slaves like you. We're not going to hurt you. You can come out now, or run away. It's up to you, but frankly I could do with some help here, thanks. Heavy buggers these night-skins, especially in all that armour. Mind you don't slip on the mess, though. Mostly it's blood but I think that bit over there might be brains.'

Once he'd rooted the slaves out from where they were hiding, Tuuran paced up and down, taking a good look at them, same as he used to with new slaves taken for the galley oars only with a lot less shouting. They were a mixed lot: a couple of night-black Taiytakei men from the deserts with brands on each arm, three brown-skinned women from the southern reaches of the Dominion and an olive-faced man from Crazy's old home of Deephaven. The women had one brand each and the man from Aria had none at all. Tuuran showed off his own.

'But these don't matter any more,' he said. 'We're all the same now.' He looked at them hard and then decided he might as well have said the moon was made of lettuce and it would have made more sense. He sighed and had the men help him carry the dead soldiers off the path and then asked why they were all out here instead of inside the grand stone house right here next to them, which presumably had lots of useful things inside it like food and wine and places to hide and things for hitting people. Or was that because there were already people inside who'd barred the doors? They told him no, the house was empty, but the doors were locked and they didn't have a key. That, Tuuran replied, was pretty damn pathetic. He showed them how a big axe could pass very nicely for a key when it had to, and they went in together and scoured the place like starving rats. Food, water, wine, fruits, Xizic, silk sheets, gold, jade, silver – all that a freshly freed slave could want except for a ship to take him home.

They made a feast for themselves and he asked them who they were and had them tell their stories like he used to on his galley. The desert men had stupidly complicated names, something like B'zaiyan Barrati and Josemarinn Dul'Tarras, names that probably meant something very important to them but simply wouldn't stick in Tuuran's head. He took to calling them Tall and Short. Same as on the ships he'd sailed, because slaver galleys picked up oar-slaves and sail-slaves from all over, with as many names and skins and voices as you cared to conjure and all with their own gods and devils and cities and songs, and there wasn't a sail-slave he'd met yet who could be bothered with getting his tongue around any name too long to be shouted across the deck in one loud bark. Desert Taiytakei, it turned out, had a fondness for selling each other to the city slavers, which was was how Tall and Short had ended up in Dhar Thosis. Tuuran told his own story after he'd listened to theirs, the way he used to at sea. Made them brothers, that did.

The women and the man from Aria came from further up the island. Slave stories were all the same: slavers showed up and you were too weak to stop them and too stupid or too slow to run away, that's what they all came down to in the end, but Tuuran listened to theirs too because that was the courtesy every slave gave to every other, no matter what tale they spun. While they were eating and sharing their stories, the olive-skinned man from Aria slipped away and didn't come back. Crazy went looking, though Tuuran couldn't imagine why. If a man wanted to do his own thing then he reckoned a man should be left to do it, but Crazy went out anyway. Didn't find him.

Day after day they stayed hidden in their little palace, waiting out the soldiers, eating food the fleeing Taiytakei princelings had left behind and drinking their wine and their water. Crazy mostly kept to himself, away from the other slaves, sitting in corners and staring into space, or else he went off wandering for hours, night and day, even while the Taiytakei soldiers were still scouring the Eye for anyone they'd missed. Trying to understand who he was and what he should do, Tuuran supposed. For his own part he mostly stayed inside the walls, carefully out of sight, and when he wasn't keeping watch on the road in case any soldiers happened along, he wandered from room to room. Wrapped in silk sheets, he dozed on rich feather beds. He rummaged through chests and shelves and closets. He dressed himself in a Taiytakei robe of bright copper-orange feathers and found a white fur cloak and pranced around in it for a while issuing absurd orders until even Crazy Mad smiled. He dressed Tall and Short as masters of the house and gave the brown-skinned women fine dresses. He found a gold-glass sled in the cellars and dragged up a keg of wine and they all drank together until his head was swimming. They rode the sled around the house, screaming and laughing, and then in the pantry he found a cask of something fiery and strong and got them all so blind drunk that in the morning he couldn't remember for sure exactly who had fucked who the night before.

When his head cleared, he found some fine silk shirts big enough to fit him and a pair of strong leather boots that weren't but had decent soles. He spent the rest of the day fixing the boots, watching the road.

The Taiytakei soldiers stayed another day and then at last they left. The morning after they were gone, a single glasship drifted out of the desert. Tuuran watched it float slowly across the burned-out ruins of the city and then out to sea, rising to crest the cliffs of the Dul Matha. It lingered a while and then went on its way and they were alone. It was a sign, Tuuran decided, that they should leave. Crazy shrugged and picked up his pack. Tuuran gathered the rest of the slaves together, told them he and Crazy were leaving and that they were all welcome to come along, and then started to pile the sled with jugs of water and wine and sacks of fruit.

'Leaving for where?' they asked him, and he could only shrug. 'But the only ways from Dhar Thosis are across the desert or the sea.'

'I don't see any ships.'

They thought he was mad. Maybe he was. He'd seen enough to have a good idea of what the desert was like, from up in the eyrie, serving Grand Master Bellepheros back before they'd sent him away for being too much trouble. Mostly what he remembered was an endless sea of big and hot and empty. He had a go at Tall and Short, trying to talk them into it, but they only laughed and thought he was daft; and so in the end it was just him at the front dragging the sled and Crazy Mad beside him, slipping out into the night. They pulled the sled to the sea and then walked along the shore, and Tuuran saw that Crazy never once looked back. They reached the ruined bridge and waited for the tide to ebb enough to pick their way across the causeway. The path was choked with rubble and splinters that cast odd lumpen shadows in the moonlight where the bridge had spilled its guts into the water. Tuuran kept his eyes peeled in case the rock golems that had survived the dragon decided to come back, but all he saw were waves and surf.

'They're long gone,' said Crazy.

The far side was much as Tuuran remembered it: smashed-up houses with gaping holes in them and streets filled with debris. The air still carried a tang of ash and lightning over the smells of sea and mud, while moon-born shadows peopled the night-time ruins with ghosts. The flames were long out, the ashes still and cold, but as they walked Tuuran's feet kicked up a fine grey dust which swirled around them and smelled of soot. Now and then he heard noises, the skitter of tiny feet or paws, the rattle of a loose board, the scrape of a shifting pebble, and he couldn't shake the sense of a hundred eyes watching their progress.

Further on, bodies littered the streets in lonely clusters, scatters of men caught by rockets or lightning or the dragon's fire. They lay as they'd fallen, untouched for all this time, ripening in the warm spring days. Even in the cool night air the stench of death and rot wafted in pockets strong enough to make Tuuran gag. Men, women and children, black-skinned Taiytakei, slaves of all colours. Ordinary people, not soldiers. Some lay sprawled in the street, others in piles in little squares around enchanted fountains which still chattered with clear sparkling water. Now and then clouds of silvery birds rose from the corpses and cawed their resentment before settling again after he and Crazy passed. Tuuran was glad to put his back to them.

The outer fringes of the city weren't as bad, and as the sky over the sea began to lighten with the approaching dawn Tuuran climbed a small stone tower. It didn't seem possible that no one had survived and so he looked over what remained of Dhar Thosis, searching for fires or smoke or other signs of life. The rooftops nearby were a colourful patchwork of clay tiles, reds and browns and ochres and—

He started. There were fires burning on the ridge overlooking the city. A line of four of them, strung out but too close not to belong together. Four fires, so maybe ... fifty people? He took a good long look at where they were and climbed down again. Elsewhere the city seemed dead. Any other survivors were too wary to come out of their holes. The soldiers had only been gone a day, after all.

'There's people up on the ridge,' he said when he came back down. 'Slavers, maybe.'

Crazy seemed to give that some thought. 'I want a ship to take me home,' he said. 'You want to find the woman who flies dragons. There's nothing for either of us here so it's either the sea or the desert.' He shrugged. 'And like you said, I don't see any ships. They'll want paying though.' He set off again. Tuuran let Crazy pull the sled a while and rummaged through the bag of stuff he'd looted from the sea lord's palace. Silver coins, golden feathers, jade carvings, polished stones, anything that had caught his eye. Like a magpie.

'Plenty here,' he said.

The outskirts of Dhar Thosis seemed as deserted as the rest, but Tuuran knew better because he saw signs now and then: a flicker of movement that was too big to be a dog or a lizard; a body too recent to have died in the battle; one time he heard the sound of running feet. He felt eyes on him again, only here the eyes were human, peering out through cracked walls and from behind closed curtains. Here, on the fringe of the desert, the streets, where there were any at all, were trampled sand and dirt. The houses were a mishmash of wood, of pieces of stone and mud brick, mostly simple huts. Doors were strips of sailcloth and roofs too. They passed burrows dug into the sand framed with old wood with hanging canvas or pieces of sacking for doors. When Tuuran peered inside, he found they were only a few yards deep, little more than places to sleep out of the sun. They were cool but they were empty, and after the third he stopped looking. Sometimes, when he was sure he was being watched, he stopped and held up his arms, palms outward, showing off the brands of a sword-slave, the lightning-bolt scars of the lord of Xican. He wore them with pride now, those brands, for the sea lord of Xican had faced a dragon and it had broken his mind, and Tuuran had faced many and never wavered once. Each time he showed off his brands he felt the air fall still and dead as if the streets themselves held their breath. Those brands had been here before.

Tuuran and Crazy walked on. The sea was a mile to their backs now and the land was barren earth where nothing grew but tufts of spiny grass. As they climbed the ridge, Tuuran could see men moving about or sitting under sun shelters around their morning fires. They ignored him at first, then, with the drilled precision of a legion of the Adamantine Guard, a dozen of them stopped what they were doing, picked up spears with bulbous hafts and blunt hooks near their points for tripping and clubbing and beating, and started down the slope. Tuuran stopped and held up his hands, showing off his brands and making a gesture of peace.

'We're here to trade.' He glanced along the ridge at the shelters but he didn't see anything that looked like a slave cage. He opened his bag and took out a golden owl. Everyone liked gold, didn't they? He cast a sideways glance at Crazy Mad. 'If they come for us, you got my my back, right?'

The desert men came on, calm and without fuss, but they kept their spears high. A sinking sensation wormed through Tuuran's guts. He dropped the golden owl back into his bag of treasures and took the axe off his back instead, shook his head and set his eyes on the leader of the desert men, a narrow wiry man, tall but thin.

'Oi! Skinny! You don't want to do this. You might have the numbers but you'll be first. You *will* be first.'

A charge, a feint with the point of the spear and then a hook at the legs, that's what he'd do, and Tuuran would jump over the hook, move in and split the skinny shit with his axe right down the middle. But they didn't charge and they didn't stop coming either. They circled him instead, keeping their distance, cautious but penning him and Crazy together. Crazy hadn't bothered to draw his sword.

'You come one way or the other, slave,' said the skinny desert man.

Tuuran roared at them, 'Well then? I say I kill three of you before you touch me.'

Skinny shrugged. 'At least with us you get food and water.'

'Got food and water here, thanks all the same.' Tuuran gritted his teeth. 'Crazy, at least draw your sword. You're good for a handful of these camel shaggers. The two of us, we might just take them.'

They wouldn't though. Twelve was too many unless Crazy did the thing he did when his eyes went all silver and turned men into greasy black ash, which was sort of what Tuuran had been counting on. Admittedly, Crazy claimed that that hadn't ever actually happened and Tuuran hadn't actually *seen* it either, just an empty space where three men had been only a few seconds before and two screaming women and a cloud of sticky black dust in the air. But then there was the whole business about the holes in Crazy's armour, like something had gone straight though him and yet never cut his skin.

Crazy drew his sword, slowly and carefully, held it sideways in front of him and dropped it onto the sand. 'Let it be, big man. They're taking us where we want to go after all.'

'*What?*'

Crazy walked to the ring of desert men, arms held up. He dropped to his knees in front of them and bowed his head. Tuuran watched in disbelief as two of them tied his hands. The silver eyes never came. No one turned into dust. Nothing happened at all. Crazy just let himself be taken; and after that making a fight of it all on his own didn't seem to make much sense. Tuuran let his axe fall too, let his shield hang and stared as three of them led Crazy away. The others gathered close, keeping their spear points an inch from his skin while Skinny tied his hands. They led him to the top of the ridge, following Crazy's footsteps in the sand, and now he felt stupid because on the other side of the ridge, carefully out of sight, dozens of crude slave pens stood. Most were full. Slaves. Hundreds of them.

They pushed him and Crazy into a cage together. Skinny bared his teeth and smiled. 'See, it's not bad.' Tuuran just gave him a look. Short and sharp and straight in the eye to let him know that he wouldn't be forgotten.

13

The Elemental Men

Chay-Liang didn't see the Vespinese who knocked her down. She felt something hit the back of her head, felt herself dragged and dropped and kicked and then a great wind, and then mercifully she was left alone. When she finally managed to get up again, groggy as a sailor after his first night back in port, they'd taken away her wand and all of her globes of gold-glass. Soldiers led her back to her room and shut her behind the iron door she'd made to keep out the Elemental Men. She sat on the bed, nursing her head and wondering what to do, musing on the small arsenal of devices that littered her shelves and floor, but she must have fallen asleep almost at once, because suddenly the white stone walls were bright with the orange light of dawn and the Vespinese were hammering on her door.

In the bright morning sun they led her to the dragon yard. A glasship hovered over the hatchery, its chains wrapped around the remains of the ship that had crashed in the fight, lifting the pieces too large to be carried by hand. The soldiers watching the slaves at work weren't wearing their armour but lightning wands still dangled from their belts and their hands hovered close. Away on the eyrie wall Diamond Eye sat watching the Godspike. Four hatchlings that had broken free in the night sat around him. On the opposite side of the eyrie the sunrise over the desert lit the sky with orange fire.

A Taiytakei in long robes of shimmering emerald and blue feathers stood in front of Liang and snapped his fingers in her face. A t'varr. An important one by the braided hair that ran past his waist and his voluminous robes, but not from the same stratum as Tsen or Mai'Choiro Kwen. His sleeves flapped in the wind. 'Is it always like this up here? This wind?' He swept his hand across the dragon yard and then frowned and glared at the sky as a particularly vicious gust knocked him a step sideways. Liang looked about. Scales were standing huddled among the eggs. They looked wretched this morning.

'Sometimes gets worse,' she said, not bothering to raise her voice. The Vespinese cupped a hand to his ear.

'Pardon?' he shouted.

Liang dragged him into the shelter of the tunnel mouth, stepping around the mangled iron door. In the light of day it looked as though a dragon had stamped on it.

'I said it sometimes gets worse,' she said icily.

He nodded thoughtfully. 'I am Perth Oran T'Varr. For your slaves everything will be much as it was. They'll hardly notice the change. For you it's a bit different. Mai'Choiro Kwen favours throwing you off the side of the eyrie. The alchemist says he has to have you. You will make it all work as it did before, that's all I ask.'

Liang took a moment to look the emerald and blue t'varr up and down. He was old and with some grey in his hair, the two of them probably much of an age. Maybe that made things easier. Tsen's words came back to haunt her. *Whatever he does, however terrible it is, you mustn't stand in his way. You must survive, Chay-Liang. Hold the truth close to your heart and never let him see that you have it. Keep it until you can destroy him ...* And now the moment had come. She would do as Tsen had asked and meekly lie down for the bastard Vespinese, would she?

Yes, if it meant she could burn them later. So she told Perth Oran T'Varr, who might have been a perfectly decent person, that she would help as best she could. She asked where she could find Bellepheros.

'He says that he needs you, his Scales, food and water for the dragons, the rider-slave to fly the big one and otherwise to be left alone. I need you to document all of this and tell me precisely what is required and in what quantities and why and what it is for. I also need you to explain this "Statue Plague".'

Liang nodded. 'I need to start at once with what was destroyed in the fighting. The hatchery is ruined and there are hatchlings loose.' She could see Bellepheros for herself now, out in the wind leading a handful of Scales coaxing the hatchlings at Diamond Eye's side back into their chains. Docile all of them, far too docile, and it put her on edge. Maybe they were simply mesmerised by the maelstrom of the storm-dark and the Godspike. She tried to tell herself that but didn't really believe it. She couldn't shake the notion that they were waiting for something.

Perth Oran T'Varr was looking at her expectantly. Liang nodded.

'Yes, yes. I'll start at once.' She hurried after the alchemist; and when Belli turned and saw her coming, the relief on his face was obvious. He couldn't help grinning.

'Li!' He came towards her. She brushed past him, haughty, letting out the undertow of angry resentment and ... was that a flash of shame? Yes, it was.

'You told them you needed the rider-slave, did you?' she snapped. 'Well you'll not have her. She'll not fly that monster. If that means it has to eat the bodies of the dead, so be it.'

The horror on his face crushed her. 'Li!'

So much else they needed to say and she was so desperately glad to see him alive, but the Vespinese were all watching and she couldn't let them see ... *They'll use us. Play us off against each other.*

'What else?' she hissed. 'He hasn't eaten for two weeks and I'll not let her out again. Your beloved slave brings nothing but ruin. Let her go, Belli. Let her die as she deserves.'

'Will you let me poison it then?' he snapped, the old argument they'd always had.

Liang snorted. 'Do that and they'll hang us both!'

'Then she must fly him!'

No. She couldn't keep this up. She pulled him close and hissed in his ear, 'We just quietly get on with what needs to be done and we do what they say. We are mistress and slave to them, nothing else. We keep our heads down. The time will come. I'll say more when they're not watching.' At least the wind meant you didn't have to worry about anyone short of an Elemental Man eavesdropping on your conversations.

She tried to set her mind to the hatchery and what they'd need to repair it, but it was hard while Belli and the Scales were still getting the hatchlings back into their chains. Every time a dragon moved her heart jumped, expecting to see Belli ripped to pieces in a flurry of claws and fire, but the hatchlings submitted with a meekness that, if anything, was worse. Just like her, they were hiding something.

When Belli was done, they picked their way together through the mess of the hatchery. The Vespinese had lifted the biggest pieces of the shattered glasship out of the way and dumped them on the other side of the eyrie wall, another heap of junk out on the rocky rim. The ship had fallen on some of the eggs and smashed them to pieces. Shreds of crushed unborn dragon lay scattered about. Each one carried the threat of the Statue Plague, and Bellepheros was as keen as the Vespinese to clear *those* away. A job for the Scales. And for him and for her; and so she waited until he was ready and then they wrapped each other up in their leather aprons with their gauntlets and masks and goggles. 'We'll burn them afterwards,' he told her. 'Just to be sure.' He meant the leathers. The pieces of dead dragon could go over the rim, down into the maelstrom below.

They set to work, she and Belli with the Scales, counting the eggs and the hatchlings and telling the other slaves what to do and generally trying to restore the hatchery to some sort of order before anything actually hatched. She felt a fraud. What she ought to be doing was everything she possibly could to bring these Vespinese bastards to their knees.

She picked up a piece of gold-glass the size of her head and dumped it in the crate on the sled beside her – at least they had no shortage of *those* now – then winced in disgust as she moved part of the collapsed net of chains and found a dragon's severed talon underneath. She shouted and waved to one of the Scales to do something about it. The net had to go back up and Belli was as anxious about that as he was about everything else. Back up and the hatchery restored as quickly as could be. She hoped that obeying Perth Oran T'Varr would be easy for Belli after that because it certainly wouldn't be easy for her. There would be a reckoning, probably sooner rather than later, one she fully expected to end with her falling off the rim one dark night, but Belli ...? All he had to do was carry on with what he'd done before. Bellepheros and Baros Tsen had never seen eye to eye, and a change of master probably didn't mean that much to him. Perth Oran was right – it shouldn't matter to a slave. Shouldn't matter to an enchantress either but she found that it mattered very much. Mai'Choiro had sent Zafir and her dragon to kill thousands upon thousands. That Zafir had actually done it made her every bit as despicable, but if you absolutely *had* to give her credit for anything at all, she didn't hide and pretend to be anything but what she was. 'Monsters, both of them.'

Liang started. She hadn't meant to say that aloud but Bellepheros hadn't noticed; in fact he probably hadn't heard anything at all over the wind. He was standing in the middle of the surviving eggs, looking at the pieces of the broken ones, counting for the third time, beckoning her over. When she looked, he lifted his mask and yelled at her, but she didn't catch what he said. She was about to go to him when a thought struck her and she crouched down and peered at the stone of the dragon yard. A glasship had fallen here last night. Crashed down and smashed to pieces with enough force to crumple a half-inch iron door and pulverise everything beneath it. Yet the white stone was undamaged. Not even scratched. Not the faintest hint of a mark. Smooth as glass. She pondered that and then looked across the yard to the place where the eyrie wall was chipped and cracked. A dragon had done that. She shuddered.

'One went into the tunnels last night,' Bellepheros shouted when she got up and went to see what he'd found. 'It went for her Holiness.' There was an odd look on his face. He seemed to struggle for words. 'It burned my laboratory. Is it dead? I don't see the body. Where is it?'

Liang shook her head. It wasn't that she'd forgotten or thought it didn't matter; it was just ... it was just that there were so many other things to worry about, and what could they do? Nothing. It was gone, and that was that. She frowned, shook her head and gestured to the ruined hatchery, but when the day ended and they dragged their weary bones out of the wind and to the tunnels, she made qaffeh for them both in her workshop and broke out some Bolo bread and told him what had happened, all of it. When she was done, Bellepheros gazed at her in horror.

'It came out of the egg awake? It knew? Great Flame, we have to find it!'

Liang snorted and shook her head. 'No. We have to keep our heads down and do as we're told and hope they don't kill us. *Then* we have to find it.' He might, she thought, have shown some sort of concern for her, what with having faced down a dragon all on her own. But he was lost in this, entirely lost. He was terrified. She sighed. 'Belli, it's gone. It's already out in the desert somewhere, and it'll be no more dangerous tomorrow than it is today, nor the day after or the next. We have time. We'll rebuild the hatchery. We'll make sure no others escape. Let this matter with Shonda and Tsen resolve itself. When the Elemental Men come we'll tell them, and they'll hunt it down and kill it and we'll help them as best we can. My promise to you.'

'And how long, Li, before they come?'

'A few days, perhaps. It could be any time.'

'A few *days*?' He grabbed her and stared into her face. 'It's a woken dragon, Li! Do you know what that means? It's *aware*! It *thinks*! It *remembers*! A hundred lifetimes! And they're clever, Li, as clever as we are. If it goes to ground in the desert then they'll never find it! Perhaps not for years, until it comes from nowhere fully grown and another city goes up in flames.' He was trembling, still shaking his head. 'Or worse – what if it comes back here, Li? What if it comes back to the eyrie? It could do that today or tomorrow. It could be here right now, lurking under the rim. How would we know? What if it freed the others? How could you possibly stop it? Li, we have to tell them!'

Liang frowned. *I stopped it all on my own last night, you know.* She glared at him and then sighed again. 'Oh, I'll talk to Perth Oran T'Varr then.' And she would, but he wouldn't listen. He wasn't the sort. Not like Tsen. 'Shonda has a hundred glasships with lightning cannon.' She made a face. 'I expect that should be enough.'

'Let her Holiness hunt it,' Belli urged her. 'I'll persuade her.' He stopped. He must have seen the look on her face.

After the Bolo bread, she forced some more food into him and even ate a little of the thin tasteless gruel made for the slaves and captives herself. She took him back to his study and tried to convince him to get some sleep – he was exhausted and ready to collapse – but he simply refused, and so in the end she left him to drag the Scales back out of their cots to the hatchery and work on through the night. She could have done with some sleep herself but stayed up for a while instead, writing an inventory for Perth

Oran of all the things the Vespinese were going to have to find from somewhere if they wanted to keep their dragons. They'd question everything, of course, and then waste hours of her time making her explain what every single little thing was for. She supposed she shouldn't complain. They were right not to trust her.

She tried to sleep when she was done, but of course now she was wide awake, and sleep, elusive at the best of times, wanted nothing to do with her. So she went back outside to the cold and the wind and the night and found Belli still there, exhorting his Scales to keep working. It must have been past midnight and the poor man was staggering about, hardly able to keep himself upright against the buffets of the wind and about to do himself an injury if someone didn't stop him. She sent the Scales away, and when Belli kept on with his protests she dragged him inside and virtually carried him back to his room. He growled and snapped and snarled at her all the way until she laid him on his bed and made him some warm tea and slipped in a little something to help him sleep. She felt a bit guilty about that and so curled up beside him and stroked his hair – what there was of it – and waited for him to close his eyes. Five minutes later he was snoring. Liang drifted next to him. Maybe he was right to worry about the hatchling coming back. It had gone after Zafir and destroyed his laboratory before it left. They were lucky he'd taken to keeping some of his things in his study.

She must have fallen asleep too, because the next thing she knew she was alone in the alchemist's bed and the white stone tunnels were bright with their daylight glow. When she went to the dragon yard to look for him, she saw the Vespinese had built a wooden platform and were busy erecting a set of gallows. She found Belli back with the Scales, trying to raise the chain net over the hatchery. He looked pleased with himself and the rubble from the night before was gone. 'We need a glasship, Li,' he shouted as he saw her, 'to lift the chains.' Which was how they'd done it before, silver chains lifting the net into place while dozens of slaves laboured beneath to raise the frame that would hold it.

'How did you clear the rubble?' she asked. No 'Thank you' for last night, she noted sourly.

He pointed, and Liang saw the rider-slave lounging against the wall, watching with that irritating smirk on her face. 'Her

Holiness had the dragon get rid of the worst of it. It carried the larger pieces away and look!' He pointed to the eyrie wall where pieces of gold and iron and glass were mounded up against it. 'It flapped its wings and blew the smaller pieces clear! We can take the rest from there whenever we like. It's out of the way, and now we can get the chains up again.' He looked so happy that she hadn't the heart to tell him there was no way he'd get the Vespinese to lend him a glasship.

'There might be something else I can do,' she said at last. The first framework had been wood and iron but gold-glass would do just as well, and it wasn't as if they were short of the stuff at the moment. It was literally lying at their feet. 'I could grow it into shape and we wouldn't need a—'

A shout from one of the watchtowers cut her off. Liang watched as a group of Vespinese soldiers went running up, and a few minutes later as they came out again, manoeuvring awkwardly along the wall and down the steps to the yard, carrying a body. They laid it on the white stone. When Liang went to see who it was, they pushed her away, but she got close enough to see the face.

Baros Tsen T'Varr, there couldn't be any doubt. He looked smaller dead than she remembered him. Shorter. For some reason he was naked.

'At least cover him up.' She turned away, suddenly feeling sick, and bent over against the eyrie wall. The Vespinese ignored her. A pair went running into the tunnels, full of excitement. Liang watched them and spat. Once she decided she wasn't going to throw up after all, she straightened herself and smoothed her robes. Tsen. They'd had their differences, plenty of them, with the rider-slave top of the list, but he'd seemed a good man at heart and she was going to miss him. The sleepy voice, the sharp sparkling intelligence behind it, the glasses of apple wine out on the eyrie walls in the starlight, talking about how the world might be changed. Of course all that was before the dragons, before Quai'Shu went mad, before the rider-slave murdered his heir and Tsen got it into his head to be the next sea lord of Xican. She couldn't really blame him for any of that. As sea lords went, he'd have been as good as any. It wasn't as if he'd actually *wanted* to burn Dhar Thosis.

She shuddered. There were probably a lot of ghosts in Dhar

Thosis right now who didn't have much sympathy with that view. It occurred to her then to wonder whether Tsen had killed himself. He didn't seem the sort, and why in Xibaiya was he naked? And the body had no obvious marks or lightning burns …

Mai'Choiro Kwen came striding out of the tunnel with a dozen other kwens and t'varrs and even a pair of hsians, all with long braids and bright flowing feathered robes streaming sideways in the wind, shining gold and crimson and emerald.

'String him up,' he bawled. He was grinning like a snake with a cornered mouse, barely containing his delight.

'*What?*' Liang started towards him but the soldiers held her back. The kwen shouted more orders as he walked away: 'String him up. Hang him by his feet and get everyone up here to see it!' He was going to make an example of Tsen. Give a little speech about the terrible things the t'varr had done and how this was the price for them. The hypocrisy made Liang's blood boil. If the Vespinese hadn't taken her lightning wand she might have used it right there, and hang holding on to the truth of what she knew until she could bring the whole lot of them down together. She turned back to the hatchery, trying to block out what was happening around her. She couldn't think.

Tsen's slave Kalaiya came running. The soldiers around the body caught her and dragged her away but not before she saw and started screaming. Liang ran to put an arm around her and held her while she sobbed, then took Kalaiya back into the tunnels and into Belli's study and found her something stiff and strong to drink. It was the least thing she could do and, whatever happened next, surely neither of them wanted to see it. She tried to get Kalaiya to lie down but the slave wouldn't have it.

'Twelve years. I'll watch and weep for him. He deserves that.'

Liang couldn't imagine wanting her last memories of anyone, least of all someone she'd come to respect and perhaps even admire, to be of their corpse hanging upside down to be mocked and flogged, but Kalaiya wouldn't be moved, and so Liang reluctantly returned with her and stood and watched. The yard was full. A squad of Vespinese in brilliant green with gold-plumed helms guarded Baros Tsen T'Varr's body, which hung as Mai'Choiro had told them, twisting and swinging by his feet in the wind. Around them were the slaves and captive Taiytakei who'd served Tsen until yesterday, then more Vespinese soldiers in a ring to make sure they did as they were told and watched as they were meant to while Mai'Choiro Kwen played out his piece of theatre. Tsen's Taiytakei were solemn and dour and anxious but not the slaves. Some were laughing and chattering to each other as though it was all some marvellous spectacle. Liang wanted to slap them. *He was your master. He was a good one.* Maybe a slave didn't care two hoots whether their master came from Xican or from Vespinarr. Probably not. They should though, she thought. They should.

Six Vespinese at the gallows broke off and marched straight for the hatchery. For one heart-stopping moment Liang imagined they were coming for her. One hand reached for the wand they'd taken away; the other clutched at a piece of gold-glass. The soldiers came right at her but then carried on, ignored her completely and surrounded the rider-slave. Zafir gave a tiny shake of her head and might have wagged her finger at them but they never gave her the chance. Two seized her arms and held them behind her back while two more forced a hood over her head. Between them, they frog-marched her to the gallows. Liang gritted her teeth and growled under her breath, 'Good riddance.' Yet even now the rider-slave walked with her head held high, as proud and haughty as it was possible to be with her face hooded and her arms behind her back and four soldiers practically lifting her off the ground in their hurry to get her to the scaffold. She didn't stumble, not once, and Liang found herself caught in a fleeting moment of admiration. She shivered. *Loathsome woman ...*

Mai'Choiro Kwen climbed onto the scaffold. He slapped the sagging flesh of Baros Tsen with a short whip then put on a gold-glass circlet. His voice rang clear over the roar of the wind, unnaturally strong as he poked at Tsen again: 'Sixteen days ago Baros Tsen T'Varr attacked the city of Dhar Thosis. The palace of Sea Lord Senxian was torn down.'

Bellepheros was at her side. 'Stop them, Li! You have to stop them!'

'How, Belli?' Why did it have to be her all the time? Why couldn't he do it himself? 'What do you want me to do?' She shook her head. 'Besides, I agree with him. She deserves it. Best to get it done.' Even if it left her carrying the truth alone.

Belli seized her arm, turned her and pointed to the eyrie wall behind them. Diamond Eye was watching intently. His huge unblinking eyes were fixed on the scaffold and his mouth hung slightly open, fangs gleaming bare, a soft halo of fire burning around them. Liang thought about that for a moment and then, inside, she started to laugh.

The Vespinese had Zafir at the scaffold. They pulled away her hood, tied her arms behind her and then hauled her up to the gallows and forced a gag into her mouth. All around the dragon yard Vespinese soldiers had their lightning wands in their hands, pointing at the dragon on the wall.

'She knows the truth.' Liang shook her head. 'Mai'Choiro has to silence her.' She had no doubt that Zafir would have spat in the kwen's face given the chance, but the gag wasn't for that. The gag was to stop her calling for her dragon, wasn't it?

Mai'Choiro's voice rang out again. 'The actions of Sea Lord Quai'Shu and his house attack the very foundations of our life.' Belli tugged at her arm so hard he almost pulled her over. 'The Sea Lord Quai'Shu will stand trial for the actions of his house –'

'The night they came! Didn't you see? One of the soldiers struck her, and the dragon ... If they kill her, the dragon will go berserk. I thought he meant to let her live. I never told ...'

'– in the Crown of the Sea Lords in Khalishtor, where he will be judged by his peers.'

Liang put a finger to Belli's lips to silence him and slowly shook her head. 'With gag and blindfold, surely she can't call her monster.'

'As for this slave –'

'She doesn't need to speak to call him! It will know anyway.'

'– Baros Tsen and Shrin Chrias –'

'Then we'd better get out of the way, hadn't we?' *Let it happen. Let Mai'Choiro hang Zafir and let the dragon burn him in his turn. Justice for all of them.*

'– t'varr and kwen to the Sea Lord Quai'Shu –'

Belli started to protest. Liang grabbed his arm and marched him to Perth Oran T'Varr. 'T'Varr, the Scales are required elsewhere.

May I return them to their duties?' When he shook his head she pointed up to the gold-red dragon on the wall. 'They are needed, T'Varr, to calm the dragon whose rider your master means to hang.'

'– all three will hang, their bodies to be cast into the storm-dark –'

Perth Oran stared at Diamond Eye. He seemed to shrink a little and then nodded. 'Whatever needs to be done, enchantress.'

Liang pushed Belli away. 'Get them underground. You too. Quickly.' She looked around the dragon yard. The Vespinese soldiers had their wands raised, waiting for the dragon to move. Three glasships hung overhead. They'd dropped close and their rims glowed sun-bright, their lightning cannon charged and ready to fire. On the scaffold two men were shaping gold-glass. Enchanters. It stood to reason that Shonda would send one or two of his own.

'What are you going to do?' asked Bellepheros

Liang laughed and shrugged. 'I'm going to let it happen.'

'But you can't … You have to stop them!'

'Stop them? No.' She couldn't look at him. His face was that of a child whose favourite toy had just fallen down a well, struggling with the notion of never having it back. 'Besides, I doubt there's anything I could say. Let them learn the hard way.'

'But you … Li!'

She pushed him away again. 'Go, you daft old man, before it's too late.'

'She saved you, Li! Do you not remember what—'

Liang almost threw him towards the hatchery and the doorway to the tunnels. Whatever it was he wanted to say, she didn't want to hear it, not now, not until it was done and too late. She turned, heart pounding. Maybe the Vespinese lightning would be enough to kill the dragon or maybe it wouldn't. Either way, the world would be a better place. *Good riddance. Good riddance to both of you!* Up on the scaffold Mai'Choiro finished his oration. A Vespinese soldier lowered the noose towards Zafir's neck and stood back. Two others started towards her …

Bellepheros still had that look of bewildered horror on his face. He ran to Perth Oran T'Varr, grabbing his arm and shouting something that was lost in the wind. Oran looked up at Diamond Eye, fear spreading across his face. Liang tried to watch all of them at once. The dragon leaned forward, stretching out its wings. Most of the assembly had their backs to the great beast but not the men on the scaffold. They were watching it. Mai'Choiro and the dragon stared straight at each other. Oran jumped up and down and shouted, but over the wind Mai'Choiro surely couldn't hear him. Oran started to run but the gallows were halfway across the dragon yard ...

Too late. The soldiers on the scaffold pushed Zafir towards the noose. The dragon leaned further forward, its wings spreading in ever-wider menace. Somewhere in the cordon around the crowd a Vespinese soldier lost his nerve and fired his wand. A crack of thunder boomed over the wind and the lightning struck the dragon on the nose. It bared its teeth. Mai'Choiro looked sharply away. As he opened his mouth, the dragon screamed and kicked off from the wall with such force that Liang felt the eyrie shift under her feet. It didn't lunge for the gallows but lurched sharply sideways. Liang slapped her hands to her ears and screwed her eyes shut ...

All three glasships fired at once, a deafening roar that shook the air and knocked soldiers and slaves alike to their knees across the dragon yard. After the flash Liang opened her eyes again. They'd missed, all three of them. The dragon had anticipated them and now shot over the dazed and dazzled crowd, blotting out the sun. Shouts filled the air, rising over the roar of the wind. The soldiers who weren't still rubbing their eyes fired their wands and threw their lightning but the dragon hardly seemed to notice. Mai'Choiro dived off the platform. Liang caught a glimpse of Zafir as the two enchanters on the scaffold threw a shield of golden glass around it, and then the dragon obscured everything. It smashed the gallows and the glass and the platform into splinters and matchwood and probably did as much to the two enchanters too. Tsen's corpse flew through the air, limbs akimbo like a doll, soared fifty feet and smacked into the wall. The dragon rose over the far side of the eyrie, climbed and arced up and then around and came back.

Liang bolted for the nearest wall, cringed and shaped her piece of gold-glass into a shell around her as she'd done facing the hatchling, waiting for the dragon to fall on them in torrents of fury and fire. Slaves ran screaming – a few Vespinese tried to stop them, but only for a moment and then they turned and ran too. More lightning lashed the dragon as it wheeled in the air. Panic swept the dragon yard. There were Taiytakei who'd seen this dragon burn the desert sand to glass and plenty more who'd never seen a dragon at all until today but had heard from breathless messengers what it could do. Whatever sense of their own might the Vespinese had had, the dragon smashed it into splinters as they saw it for what it truly was, and for a moment Liang thought she understood what it must be like to ride such a creature.

Not that that helped her much. She crouched in her shell and waited for the dragon to open its mouth, for the fire to come and the dragon yard to turn into a blazing inferno, but the dragon simply swooped, flared its wings, flapped hard once and rose sharply away. The wash of air plucked the nearest slaves and soldiers in handfuls off the ground and scattered them like a farmer scattering seeds. All across the yard the shock of the dragon's passing shoved flee-ing screaming men in the back like a mule's kick, sprawling them to the stone. The wind slammed into Liang's shield. She saw the dragon rise over her. In its foreclaws it carried Zafir.

The dragon powered between the helpless glasships. It skimmed over them, smashed the heart out of the nearest with a single lash of its tail, gripped the glasship's great disc with its hind claws before the vessel fell out of the sky, and levered it sideways through the air before landing on the back of the next. The first glasship, stricken, slid sideways and down, tipping and falling faster all the time. It clipped the eyrie rim as it plunged towards the storm-dark below, chipping a shard the size of a house from its outer disc and crack-ing it to the core. Lightning from its half-charged cannon arced across the stone. The glasship tumbled out of sight.

Looking for somewhere to shelter before the dragon brought the other two glasships down on top of them all, Liang glanced up. The dragon was sitting on the second glasship with Zafir beside it, gazing at the scurrying little figures of men beneath it, at the terri-fied slaves and the men of Vespinarr running this way and that, wild with dread; and Liang stared back, wondering not for the first time what kind of creature it really was, what it could become if Bellepheros stopped feeding it his potions, how such a monster had ever come to exist and what it must have taken to tame it. She was still wondering when the dragon lazily turned its head to look at something else.

A man was standing on the wall where no man had been a moment ago. Then Liang saw another and another, coalescing out of the air around the eyrie; and as she watched, one appeared in the dragon yard beside the broken body of Baros Tsen, another winked into existence beside the ruined scaffold, and another beside Mai'Choiro Kwen, holding out a bladeless knife in warning.

The Elemental Men had come.

14

A Memory of Flames

The dragon Silence plunged out of a sky so high and vast that only a dragon could understand it. The stars watched it leave them. The dragon spread its wings wide and seemed to glide, though it was still so high that there was no air to lift it. It fell, mile after endless mile, until the ground came to welcome it and the sun rose before it. Broken crags and cracked stone passed beneath, dry and almost dead but never quite. Scars in the brown earth marked where rivers once ran and might run again. Further towards the rising sun, broken cliffs rose out of the earth, misshapen things, crumbled scattered mesas packed ever closer until they merged into a plateau.

As the dragon flew on, it felt a whisper and changed its course. It flew over the top of a great chasm in the earth, a bottomless thing. A wind seemed to suck at it though the air was still, dragging it down. Calling it. It felt the touch of Xibaiya deep beneath the earth, the realm of dead souls through which every dragon passed between each life. It flew on and away.

In Xibaiya the Nothing slowly grew, the unravelling thing, the crack in the essence of everything summoned by the Black Moon to shred the world as the age of the Silver Kings reached its end. The cataclysm of the Splintering and the birth of the storm-dark. The dragon Silence had been there and had seen the crack first made; and then again, in Xibaiya, as it passed between its many lifetimes. It held those memories in iron claws of purpose now. The Nothing seeping from its cage, unravelling everything it touched, the essence of matter and life dissolved to foam and smoke. The dead earth goddess and her slayer, who had held the Nothing at bay for so long, gone.

Or not. The dragon Diamond Eye had tasted the Black Moon. Silence had felt the memory burn inside the fog of drowning that was the great dragon's stifled mind. The dragon-queen had given that taste a face and now the dragon Silence hunted. Among the canyons and the mesas below it, it sensed little ones. Thoughts. It fell out of the sky and tracked the incessant inner murmurings of the little ones. When it found them, it fell on them and snatched one away and perched itself on the ledge of a cliff and ate him. A black-skinned man. It hadn't seen his like for such a long time, but it *had* seen them once, in that very first lifetime when the gods themselves had gone to war and dragons and sorcerers had fought and died until the Black Moon broke the world with unleashed imaginings.

Blood tasted good. A fresh kill, and now it wanted more.

It struggled to remember. How was the Black Moon free once again?

It was a child of the sun ...

But that could not be.

Perched on pinnacles of stone, reaching out to drink in the world, the dragon Silence found again the presence felt from atop the Godspike. A touch of something immense. The ghost of an echo of a memory of the greatest half-god of them all. The Black Moon. The god-killer.

I see you.

The sun set and the stars came out to mock it once more. The dragon Silence flew on. The plateau broke into a landscape of swirling stuttering stone and sand that led it to the sea, to a broken city and a place where a mighty monolith of stone rose from the waves, a place remembered from long ago when the Silver Kings had left their chaos and their dragons and their monsters amid the endless legions of little ones. It circled and swooped and settled on the top of a single tower made of glass and gold, a strange sorcery, weak and fragile when set against those it remembered, yet one not tasted in its many lives before.

It had been here long ago and in another life. There had been other relics. The remnants of creatures made to fight the gods and others of its own kin too. It had been different then. Its body had been fully grown and strong, big even for its own kind, sharp-minded and filled with desires. The dragon Diamond Eye had been here too in those years after the world had shattered. It had flown and plucked giant stone men out of the water and dashed them on the rocks the way seabirds dropped crabs to break their shells and feast on the soft insides.

The dragon Silence reached out its senses and found the stone men were here still, a few of them. A handful, lurking under the water but twisted now. Dulled in their own way. Held and bound by some sorcery.

So many strange magics. The world had changed.

The dragon remembered it had come with a purpose. It searched and found again what it was looking for. The Black Moon, some echo of a memory of it, was near.

It hunted. Back in the desert on the edge of the blasted city it found little ones, a hundred of them and more; and what greater pleasure could there be than to fall among them and taste their fear; but it had come to them for another reason and so it kept to the sky. In the deep of night it soared overhead, and perhaps one of them might look up and see a star flicker off and on as the dragon passed before it or perhaps not, but they would never sense its presence. It flew in circles and reached down, sifting through inane chattering thoughts until it found what it was looking for, the one who carried the echo.

It had names. Berren. Crowntaker. Bloody Judge.

And the dragon saw that it had another name too, a hidden name. Skyrie. Pieces of two souls merged together, the one trying to hide inside the other

And deeper still, the echo. Buried where almost no one would find it. A splinter of a half-god. The dragon wondered who could have done such a thing and why and how, who could have made a little one like this, so cleverly done and difficult to unravel – but dragons were immortal and had time until the end of the world.

However long that would be.

15

Things Lost and Things Found

A memory haunted Berren now and then, as clear as a temple bell. It came from long ago when his life had been different. He'd come from three years of war, of fighting for the Sun King to buy freedom for his lover Fasha and their son from Princess Gelisya of Tethis. The winning of her back was a story in itself, but it had ended well enough, with the three of them safe and free and together; and after he'd stolen them away, Berren had carried them through Tethis to the castle on the top of the cliff. He'd taken a pair of horses and left the men he'd fought beside for all those years and simply gone, done with it all – or so he thought. He'd ridden with Fasha over his saddle and the sleeping babe in his arms, and now when he closed his eyes he saw them clearly again as though no time had passed at all. Sometimes he'd stopped simply to look at her face. He'd taken them to a tavern, a place whose name he'd never known, and gazed at the face of his son, a face he'd never seen until that day; and when at last Fasha had stirred, he'd carried her outside. The day had been a glorious one, a warm late-afternoon sun tingling his skin. They'd sat in the shade together while he told her everything that had happened. They'd shared wine and got drunk together and she'd sat on his lap and they'd kissed for hours and time had slipped away between them. Years he'd waited to feel like that again. It had been the most achingly beautiful thing. He could see her clearly even now, her face only a few inches from his own, strands of hair falling across it, shy and smiling and aglow with happiness.

He sat quietly in the slave cage, motionless, remembering again. A tear rolled over his cheek because it was gone, all of it. He remembered her, how beautiful that moment had been, how perfect, how it had seemed that the world could do whatever it wanted and they'd meet it head on, the two of them hand in hand together, the happiness of that evening an armour as unbreakable as the Sun King's coat of burning mail. Other moments belonged beside it, crowding around and clamouring to be remembered, but the vision of Fasha in the tavern by the woods was the worst of all. So heartbreakingly full of joy. That moment in the woods when the world had been made of her smile felt like the last joy he'd ever had or might ever have again.

Was she dead now? He didn't know.

A cool night wind blew out of the desert. It smelled of dry stone. The other slaves were sleeping. The moon was high and bright. Berren lay on his back staring at the night. The stars weren't the stars he remembered. He wondered if they had ever been.

No. This wouldn't do. He had to move. Had to do something more than sit there and remember, with the pain of it getting worse every minute, with his heart about to burst with grief. He nudged Tuuran and then kicked him until the big man's snores stopped and he opened his eyes and growled: 'What?'

'I told you how the Bloody Judge of Tethis got his name. I told you how he fought the Dark Queen for years and how that ended. I never told you the bit in between.'

Tuuran glared and slowly shook his head. 'Now, Crazy Mad? You have to tell me a story now?'

'Yes.'

Tuuran let out a little gasp of exasperation. 'Tell it to the stars.' He turned over.

Berren poked him hard. 'I would, but they say they can't hear me over your snoring.'

For a few seconds Tuuran didn't move. Then he sighed and rolled back again and sat up. He looked Berren in the eye for a long time. 'Go on then, slave. So there was a little thief boy in Deephaven who took up with a thief-taker and fell in love with a sword of the sun and ran away to sea when—'

'Press-ganged, big man. I was press-ganged.'

'Whatever.' Tuuran looked Berren up and down. 'Does this have anything to do with why you didn't lift a finger to stop us from being made into slaves again, Crazy? If it does then I'm listening, because I was quite enjoying all that *not* being a slave we managed for a while there. Otherwise, if it doesn't, save it for someone who cares. I'm not sure I'm even speaking to you any more.'

'The Bloody Judge, before he turned to hunting warlocks and putting an end to the Dark Queen, fell in love with a slave. Did I tell you that? He fathered her child and then went to war to buy her freedom. He came back and took her and his son and turned his back on everything. No one knows what he meant to become. Certainly not him. Something else, that was all that mattered. Six years he'd been a sailor and then a soldier. Fighting was all he knew, but he never forgot how it felt to have a moment of joy. The gods knew they'd been few enough.' Berren gazed at the stars. 'I never forgot ...'

Tuuran yawned. 'Sounds nice. Can I go back to sleep yet?'

'The gods took her, Tuuran. Piece by piece. He didn't see it at first, but he couldn't let go of the warlocks and all the things they'd done. Just couldn't let go.' Berren shook his head. He might have wept but all his tears had gone long ago, all except one. 'His son fell ill and died and he wasn't even there. All that love and joy he'd found and he kept putting it aside for one more killing, over and over. One day he rode away and never came back. There was nothing left. It was all gone. Love? He hadn't the first idea, but revenge? He understood *that* perfectly. From the day he left Deephaven, his life had been made of it and so the Bloody Judge had his way. Through the back alleys of the world, cutting down the warlocks that survived. He found the remnants of the Fighting Hawks and made them his own and brought them down on the Dark Queen. Revenge for what, though? For a son taken by sickness before he could speak a word? The work of the gods, not of any warlock. For a lover whose fire for him died long before she left him? No one to blame for that but himself.'

He didn't care any more whether Tuuran was listening. Memory after memory came back, all the things he'd ever done and all the things he'd ever been. A scared little boy scraping dung from the streets for Master Hatchet down in the Deephaven docks. Earning his name from the Fighting Hawks the day he'd killed an old woman without even thinking before he struck. Leading those same men ten years later to tear down the Dark Queen. The thief-taker's apprentice, paralysed by fear with a golden-hafted knife in his hand, turning it on himself, powerless as the warlock towered over him. *Three little cuts. You. Obey. Me.*

'Over the years he forgot how to have those things he'd lost. He forgot that he wanted them, forgot what they even were, just knew that something was missing and so he went looking for it in blood. In all the wrong places and all the wrong ways.'

The pain was crushing. All he could think of was that day in the woods with Fasha, the smile on her face and the taste of wine on her lips and how he'd never had its like again and never would. The numbing all-devouring dread that at the end of his life he'd look back and be left with that one and only thing that truly mattered. And as the anguish gripped his thoughts, they slipped from Fasha to the warlocks he'd killed, then back to Fasha. His son. Saffran Kuy. Fasha. Vallas. And the knife, always the knife.

He shook himself. Why tonight? All these memories coming back at him, it felt almost as though someone had crept inside his head and crawled into his heart with a big spoon and started stirring. He clung to Fasha, gripped her as though she was right in front of him and held her as though his life depended on it. He had no idea why she'd come to him out here like this after so long, but now she was here, he wouldn't ever let her go, ghost or not.

'Interesting story.' Tuuran belched, sat up, then stood and started to pace back and forth. 'Nice of you to wake me up to share it. Don't know how I'd have made it to morning otherwise.' He stopped and glared at Berren. 'I *will* kill him, you know. I will.'

'Who?'

'The skinny shit who made me into a slave again.'

'What?' Fasha shattered before him. 'What? Gods, Tuuran, it's just another way to get to where we want to go.' Berren stared out into the darkness, trying to pick up the pieces and put them together again.

'Still going to kill him.'

'It's possible, big man, that you won't, on account of me having stabbed you through the eye while you were snoring before you got the chance.'

Maybe Tuuran caught the edge in Berren's voice. He stopped his pacing and sat down again, let out a long heavy sigh and rolled his eyes and then slapped Berren half-heartedly on the shoulder.

'You know what? He sounds like a bit of an idiot, this Bloody Judge of yours.'

'Is that your idea of being helpful?' Berren spat. 'He should have stayed with what he had instead of running off to fight monsters who no longer mattered.'

That earned him a snort of derision. 'Never mind the monsters, he should have had a woman in every city and fathered bastards with all of them, that's what he should have done.'

'You never have a woman who was special?'

'I knew a good whore who knew just exactly how to—'

Berren punched him. Hard. 'I was forgetting. You were an Adamantine Man. You don't have feelings.'

'We're swords. We sate ourselves in flesh and move on. In more ways than one.' Tuuran snorted and slumped onto his back, looking up at the stars. 'I had some feelings once. Saw a girl being hurt by a man who should have known better and had no right to, and so I stopped it.'

'Did you fall in love with her, Tuuran? Secretly and from afar and without telling a soul?'

Tuuran kicked him. 'Don't be daft, you mudhead. She took the knife off my belt, stabbed the idiot to death and ran away, and I got sold into slavery for my pains.' He snorted again and then burst out laughing. 'Great Flame! Yes, there were plenty I might have been sweet on but that's not the soldier's way. We love like kings while we live. We move on. We fight. We die.'

'Who am I, Tuuran?'

'An idiot, Crazy Mad. Why did you let them take us? Really?'

'Why did you, big man?'

'Because I didn't fancy twelve of them against one of me after you threw down your sword, that's why! Flame, I'm not *that* terrible. Six apiece maybe we could have beaten.'

'No. Not six.' Although true as it was, that wasn't why Berren hadn't drawn his sword. He'd had no doubt at all that he would have won against six, twelve or a thousand. It was more the how that troubled him.

You're doing that thing again.

What thing?

That silver eyes thing. Weren't there some of our comrades here just now?

Still couldn't say why Fasha had come back to him so hard tonight. She was fading now but the hurt was still there. The hurt was always there. Just sometimes he forgot.

When at last he fell asleep, the dragon of Dhar Thosis visited his dreams. He saw it staring at him while Tuuran and the dragon's rider talked. Staring and staring straight through him, right into his deepest secrets as if it wanted something. As if it knew him, but neither of them was quite sure how or when or why. He tried to ask it but the words stuck in his throat. The dragon kept staring, and he saw, now and then, flashes of other familiar memories that tried to cling but never quite could. Things he'd seen before with other eyes. Dragons filling the sky, hundreds and thousands of them, the air thick with their cries, flying to war; men arrayed under the sun, light gleaming from silver so bright that it blinded; armies massed among spires so high that clouds snagged on their flawless white stone; the light of the moon shining down, hard and violent; and it burned and he clenched his fist and would not bow, not ever, not even to the god that had made him, not any more because now he knew what lay beneath and behind and beyond, and these things called gods were nothing but empty masks.

And then it was gone, and nothing was left but an endless wasteland of night, and the Black Moon had eclipsed the sun for ever, and among the twinkle of midday stars one winked as a distant dragon passed overhead.

The dragon seemed to pause.

I see you, it said.

16

Shouting in the Wind

Liang huddled by the wall, cowering behind her makeshift shield. Cries and wails of despair rose over the howl of the wind. Men and women, slaves and soldiers alike, crowded around the entrances to the tunnels. From its perch atop the glasship the dragon looked on through the low ruddy light of sunrise. Cracks of thunder and lightning punctured the chaos, flashes of stark white light across panicked faces. The Vespinese bellowed, some trying to stop the exodus. Faces twisted with terror rushed past her, buffeting her as though she wasn't even there. Slaves, kwens and t'varrs, men who'd been soldiers in Tsen's service: none had eyes for anything save the tunnels and their illusion of safety.

Through them all, the Elemental Men flashed and flickered, appearing and vanishing, cutting down anyone foolish enough to raise a weapon against them. The crowds clustered around the tunnels were fighting to get inside. A few brave Vespinese remained out in the open, some by Mai'Choiro, their courage returning as the dragon simply watched. They lowered their wands and the futile lightning stopped. None of them seemed to know what to do.

'STOP!' The word ran like thunder through the air, as if the wind itself had spoken. As if with one will, all the Elemental Men vanished from the dragon yard and reappeared on the walls like dark sentinels. Dozens of them.

The dragon jumped from the back of the glasship with a lazy flare of its wings. Fresh panic gripped those still in the open. Sporadic cracks of lightning from the Vespinese wands lashed out. The dragon spiralled around the eyrie and settled on the wall, put Zafir down and dropped its head. Zafir climbed unsteadily onto its back. As soon as Liang saw that, she got up and walked quickly towards the tunnels herself. The dragon might not have burned everyone before, but it surely would now. Even the Vespinese soldiers who'd had the courage to stand instead of run were edging away. A last flash of lightning struck the dragon's neck. It turned its head slowly to stare at the soldier who'd thrown it.

'STOP!' As one, the Elemental Men vanished from the eyrie walls and appeared in a circle in the middle of the dragon yard. Others appeared at the entrances to the tunnels. The dragon reared onto its hind legs and stretched out its wings. Its vast bulk with the dawn sun behind it cast the whole eyrie into shadow. It looked out over them, its eyes roving among the Vespinese until they settled on Mai'Choiro Kwen. The dragon stretched its neck and bared its fangs, and that, Liang decided, was as much as she needed to see. She shaped her glass into a bigger shield, spread it out behind her and ran. Let them fight. As she glanced back, more Elemental Men shimmered out of the air onto the wall beside the dragon.

'STOP!' The whole eyrie quivered with the voice. A third warning, and the Elemental Men never gave more than three. The last Vespinese dropped their wands and ran. In the press of the crowd around the mouth of the hatchery tunnel someone reached out to catch Liang's arm and pull her in but the crush dragged her away. Men and women swore and pushed, brands and rank all but forgotten. Someone stumbled and fell.

'Li! Li!' Bellepheros was pressed tight against the curve of the wall. In the tunnel someone let off a bolt of lightning. The noise was deafening and Liang gasped. Her ears screamed. Everyone around her shouted louder and pressed harder, barging each other out of the way. She gave up and backed off, crouching against the wall by the hatchery with the gold-glass shell around her, hugging the stone. Another lightning bolt and then another. She didn't know what the Vespinese feared the most – the dragon or the sorcerous killers of the Elemental Men. She looked up to the walls. Several Vespinese soldiers were still up there, turning the remaining lightning cannon towards the dragon. At least someone had kept their wits then. She had a good mind to go up and join them.

The dragon hadn't moved. And the Elemental Men hadn't killed Zafir either. There were a handful around the monster but they were keeping a respectful distance. The rest flickered about the dragon yard, appearing and vanishing, making the terror even worse. Everyone knew what happened when Elemental Men came. Blood. A lot of blood …

A last crush of slaves struggled past her. And, dear gods – she shook her head in disbelief – Belli had somehow managed to squeeze back out. He tapped on her shell and looked nervously at the dragon. Liang shrank the gold-glass back into a globe, yanked him to the ground beside her and then screamed at him a bit for being an idiot as she grew the shell around the two of them together. 'What in Xibaiya do you think you're doing? Get inside!'

He was shaking his head. 'They have to stop! They have to stop!'

'Yes.' Liang let out a laugh. Couldn't help herself. 'Yes, at some point they have to stop, but when?' They'd stop when everyone was dead. The miracle, if there was one, was that they hadn't really started, though Liang couldn't imagine a single reason why Zafir hadn't scoured the eyrie clean and was slightly surprised that the Elemental Men hadn't set about that too. *Maybe they're trying to agree on who has the privilege …* Mai'Choiro had tried to hang Zafir. He'd got as far as putting rope around her neck so he could hardly pretend that he hadn't meant it, yet Zafir did nothing. The Elemental Men were moving closer to her now. 'Why in the name of Charin don't they just kill her, for pity's sake?! Before she burns everything!'

'They mustn't!' Belli tugged her arm. His voice rang with alarm. 'Li, they mustn't! You have to stop them! We need her and we need Diamond Eye to find the hatchling!'

'*What?*' Inside their shell Chay-Liang twisted, grabbed Belli by his robes and pinned him to the wall. She shook her head, glancing at the dragon, at the Elemental Men, at Mai'Choiro still out in the dragon yard, at the Vespinese manning the lightning cannon. And he wanted to stand in the middle of them and make them stop?! 'No, Belli. This ends here and now. Mai'Choiro Kwen, Zafir, all your monsters, we rid ourselves of all of them.' Assassins who could shift their form to become the earth or the air or fire or water or light or shadow or ice as they willed it: the Elemental Men were hunters. Killers of sorcerers. Executioners of monsters, and what was a dragon if not a monster? *And its rider too.*

Belli was shaking with desperation. He tried to push his way past her. 'It will hide from them!' he wailed. 'Without Diamond Eye, they will never find it. Without Zafir, you have no dragon!'

'Good!' Liang almost yelled in his face. She pulled him back. 'No dragon is *good*! And *you* need to stay right here with your head down and try very hard not to be noticed!' Because what was an alchemist if not a sorcerer? 'The Elemental Men keep the peace, Belli. They always have. They are the blade on a thin string that hangs over the heads of the sea lords and is now about to fall on all of us. Dhar Thosis burned. They're here to make sure that such a thing never happens again. Ever. They will make an example of everyone who had anything to do with it. Lord Shonda is the most powerful man in all the many worlds, yet they will hang him without hesitation if they are sure of his guilt, right next to your rider-slave, high and in front of everyone and in his own city. They won't blink or hesitate and no one will try to stop them.' She let him go. 'And I will see to it that they *are* sure, but if they mistake you for a sorcerer then they will hang you too. You must be *careful*! And that means staying very quiet. Particularly now!'

'If they kill her now, Shonda walks free, doesn't he?'

Liang took a deep breath. Closed her eyes. Counted to three. 'No, Belli. I was there too. Hiding. I heard it all. I heard Mai'Choiro Kwen give his orders.' She looked around. The last of the slaves and soldiers were pushing their way inside. The dragon yard was empty except for a cluster of Taiytakei and Elemental Men stood around the wreckage of the gallows. A hundred goggling eyes peered out from the tunnel entrances. Vespinese stood ready in the lightning cannon on the walls; more Elemental Men watched them and still more were around the dragon, and yet they hadn't gone close and Zafir was still alive. *Why? Why aren't you killing the murderous bitch?* 'Belli, look around you. Take a moment to consider: the dragon is about to burn Mai'Choiro. Mai'Choiro is about to set his lightning cannon on the dragon. The Elemental Men are about to kill them both and a great many more people besides just as soon as they can work out *which* people should die. And you want to go out and stand between them?'

'If they kill her now, Shonda walks free,' he said again. And the dragon *still* hadn't moved. Liang didn't understand it.

'No!' She shook him. 'No, he doesn't. I was there! *She was not the only witness!'* Why hadn't Zafir simply sent Diamond Eye to burn them all? The Elemental men would have had no choice but to kill her then and it would be done. Done and finished and the world a much better place. But for whatever reason, Zafir hadn't. *Because*, Liang thought ruefully, *she's actually clever. Or cunning at least. Clever is going too far.*

And then a moment of understanding. Zafir had known the Elemental Men were there, even before they started to appear, probably even before the Vespinese took her to the noose. The dragon had warned her, as the dragon had tried to warn of the Vespinese coming in their glasships. Liang spat a furious curse. Zafir had known they were watching, right from the moment they'd arrived, however long ago that had been. *That* was why she stayed her hand. Performance, all of it!

Bitch.

An Elemental Man was close to the dragon now and Zafir was leaning towards him. They were talking. Liang ground her teeth in frustration. It wasn't going to happen ... She opened the gold-glass shell into a shield. 'Fine, fine, fine.' She looked around to see if anyone was paying attention and then reached her arms around Belli, a quick awkward embrace. Even if the rider-slave was a thorn between them, even if they were from different worlds, they were two minds alike, searching for the same answers and interested in the same questions. 'I'm sorry, Belli. It always falls to us, doesn't it? Go to her then. Keep the dragons quiet and keep you and her out of the way. I will go to the killers. I will tell them what you ask and why. But they *will* kill her when the time comes and I'll sleep like a newborn when they do.'

And if she quietly hoped that that time would be sooner rather than later, Liang kept that to herself. She patted the alchemist on the back, hugged him again and shrank the gold-glass shell into a ball in her hand. For a few seconds she watched him go as he walked towards the dragon, so afraid for him, then pressed her hands to her mouth and blew through her fingers and took a deep breath and then another and began to walk as well, but the other way – out into the open and the roar of the wind towards the gallows, hands spread wide, palms out so anyone who cared could see there was no slave brand on her and that she came carrying nothing. After a few steps though she changed her mind, turned and hurried after Bellepheros. She rushed past him, climbed the steps to the wall, pushed past the Elemental Men and walked right up to Diamond Eye's feet, the closest she'd ever been to the monster. She wasn't quite sure why she had all this courage all of a sudden, but judging from the way she was quivering, it was probably rage.

The dragon lowered itself, stretching out its neck and its tail. Zafir, sitting only a dozen feet above Liang, bent to look at her. She had that smirk on her face again, the one that made Liang want to punch her.

'Chay-Liang,' she shouted over the wind and cocked her head. The dragon, Liang noted, never stopped staring at Mai'Choiro Kwen.

'There's going to be a court and a trial,' Liang shouted so she could be quite sure the Elemental Men would hear too. 'You can die now or you can die later. Personally I'd like you to live exactly long enough to tell the truth of it all and then hang. I'm going inside now where it's not so bloody windy. Stay here with your dragon if you like. With luck a gust will blow you over the edge. I'd like that, but my alchemist wants you to hunt the missing hatchling first. You choose.' She turned her back and walked away, snatching Belli's arm and taking him with her as she passed. Let the rest of them stand here for the whole morning, watching each other, staring and glaring and not quite daring if that's what they wanted, but frankly she was sick of it all. Her eyes glittered as she threw Belli a glance.

'Well I've done what I can. Qaffeh?'

The alchemist frowned. 'Do you have any more of that sticky sweet spongy bread stuff? You know? What's it called?'

'Bolo bread. How would you like it? Drenched in brandy or absolutely soaked?'

17

Someone Always Dies

After qaffeh, Bolo bread and rather more brandy than was sensible, Liang found herself calm again. An hour had passed and no one was dead. She sent Belli to get some rest, sat in her workshop wondering what to do and then, when she couldn't conjure anything better, set to work on the rider-slave's new suit of armour. Ridiculous really, since Zafir would surely hang before she had a chance to wear it, but it gave her hands something work on. Besides, Tsen had come up with some deliciously unpleasant notions as to what Liang could make this armour do to keep his slave in check.

She pottered between her various tables and shelves, rummaging around the litter of discarded half-made devices and leftover odds and ends, pieces of glass, strips of gold and lengths of copper wire, then stopped when she found a gold-glass dragon figurine about a foot long. She'd made it three years ago as a model to give to a goldsmith. He'd sent back two golden dragons and she'd enchanted them and given them to Quai'Shu, who'd given them in turn to a prince of the dragon-realms as a wedding present. Liang put the pieces of half-finished armour aside, cleared a space on one of the benches and set to work on the dragon. It wasn't hard to remember the enchantments she'd devised for the golden ones, and glass took them much more readily than any metal; still, by the time she was finished, the whole day had passed and she hadn't really noticed. The eyrie hadn't quivered and there hadn't been any screaming and shouting up and down the tunnels, and so she supposed the dragon and the Elemental Men and Mai'Choiro had temporarily settled their differences. That or they were all still out in the freezing wind, staring at each other.

Belli came to see her after dark, telling her that the Elemental Men had called everyone into the dragon yard earlier in the afternoon. From what he'd been able to make out over the wind, the message was that no one was allowed to leave and everyone should carry on as they were. Mai'Choiro Kwen was confined to Baros Tsen T'Varr's old rooms but they were letting his men visit freely. They didn't seem to care whether one of Tsen's t'varrs or kwens ran the eyrie or whether the Vespinese did it, as long as everything stayed exactly as it was until their precious Arbiter arrived. Liang shared some more qaffeh and Bolo, they very carefully didn't talk about Zafir, and when Belli was gone, she went to bed and had her best night's sleep for weeks.

She woke late and found the truce, to her mild surprise, still holding. She spent the day helping Belli repair the hatchery, and also surreptitiously testing her little gold-glass spy-dragon. Towards the middle of the afternoon an enormous glasship drifted in from the edge of the storm-dark. It carried beneath it, hanging from a dozen gleaming chains, a lenticular silver gondola three times the size of any Liang ever had seen before, decorated with emerald and jade. Etched into its shell were the three entwined dragons of Vespinarr. As it touched down on the white stone, Liang wondered for one wild moment whether this could be Lord Shonda himself – but when the gondola opened there was no one inside. Over the rest of the afternoon a procession of t'varrs and kwens emerged into the dragon yard from the tunnels, two Elemental Men watching over them as they came and went. The gondola opened, swallowed them and spat them out again some time later. Liang kept stopping to watch until Belli almost lost his temper and snapped at her to concentrate. He had almost all his Scales desperately trying to hold up the chain net over the hatchery while she shaped gold-glass struts to keep it aloft.

They worked through the day until the sun was sinking and the dragon yard fell into grey shadow. The eyrie felt more peaceful than it had since the dragons first arrived, and yet beneath the calm Liang felt the tension. The peace was a phoney one, and her eyes kept straying to the eyrie wall. Lit up by the setting sun, Diamond Eye's fiery scales seemed to blaze. It had its back to them, and as far as Liang could tell had spent the entire day staring at the Godspike again. When she put on her goggles, she could see Zafir propped against its hind claws, head drooping as though she was dozing, although how anyone could doze in the constant infernal wind, Liang had no idea.

An Elemental Man appeared out of the air beside her. Liang jumped, turned and swore.

'Chay-Liang of Hingwal Taktse!' The killer bowed solemnly, gestured to the gondola in the middle of the dragon yard and, without another word, dissolved into nothing, vanishing into the air as he became the wind. He appeared again beside Belli. Liang waited to see what would happen. The Elemental Man shouted, gestured to the gondola a second time and vanished once more, reappearing this time by the open ramp. Liang hurried to take Belli's arm before he said something stupid – he kept glancing at the hatchery, at the unfinished netting, but you didn't ignore a summons from the Elemental Men, not for anything.

The gondola ramp had been contrived with shapes and colours and contoured silver to look like a forked tongue, inviting them into the maw of a jade-fanged dragon. Liang supposed it was meant to be impressive, even awe-inspiring, and maybe it was until you saw a real dragon face to face. She paused nevertheless, because the working of the silver on the gondola's skin *was* impressive. From top to bottom, every elegant curve was carved into a series of reliefs, the history of Vespinarr from the first coming of the self-styled Emperor Vespin, his expeditions into the mountains, the terrible scourge of the Righteous Ones, the razing of the temples by the Elemental Men, the sorceress Abraxi and doubtless more further around the rim. The quality of the workmanship, particularly in the silver, was as fine as she'd ever seen, and she doubted she could have worked glass any better. A little voice suggested she find the name of the artist so she could use him for her own work, then remembered that, whoever it was was in Vespinarr and unlikely to want to work with the enchantress who was about to ruin their city.

Bellepheros was getting impatient, fretting about his hatchery. Liang left the reliefs for another time and walked up the ramp. As soon as she stepped inside the gondola itself, she knew it belonged to Mai'Choiro. The entire space was a monument to his vanity. Three portraits hung between the windows; everything was wrought in Vespinese silver and studded with emeralds; dragons and lions peered at her from every nook and yet it was clearly the design of a kwen. The windows lining the curved silver walls were staggered, some of them looking down, others looking up. Much of the floor was gold-glass spoked with gold. Liang wondered for a moment if the gondola even had its own lightning cannon, but no, the gold-glass was simply to observe directly below. Fitted into the walls either side of the golem pilot's cabinet, two small black-powder guns pointed out. Liang paused to run her fingers over them. The best Scythian steel. Vanity or did they really have the power to hurt another glasship? She knelt down beside them to see if she could discern any mechanism to turn them and then stopped short. Fascinated as she was, now was hardly the time or the place.

The centrepiece of the gondola was a huge round table of polished obsidian. The gondola had been empty as she and Bellepheros entered but now she heard the air pop and felt the touch of a breeze. When she looked back, seven Elemental Men sat around the table, all in identical black robes edged with entwined strands of red, blue and white and impossible to tell apart. They beckoned to her to sit, and for the rest of the evening they asked about the dragons, on and on, what they were and where they came from and what they did. They pressed Bellepheros for everything he knew on their nature. Had there always been dragons? He didn't know. Where had they come from? He didn't know that either, but they continued on into the night until Liang thought she knew as much about the history of Belli's world as he did himself. The killers asked how dragons were restrained, about the potions he made, about what a dragon would become without them – Belli couldn't help himself when they got to that and ranted for some time about the hatchling that had gone missing and the dire threat of it and how everything else must stop until it had been found and destroyed, but the Elemental Men seemed barely interested. They let him exhaust himself with pleas and threats and exhortations and then calmly asked how much poison he would need to kill all the dragons and how long it would take to make it. One of the Elemental Men spent the entire time furiously writing down everything that was said.

A t'varr and some slaves came with food and water, but the Elemental Men touched nothing. When Bellepheros and Liang had eaten, they told her to go out and make a gold-glass shelter for

Zafir up on the wall so she could live beside her dragon for now. After that they sent the two of them to rest for the night but the questions resumed in the morning, this time about dragons, their nature and their origins and the taming and keeping of them. For a while they asked about alchemy and blood-magic; and when it came to the Silver King, the half-god who'd tamed the dragons in the first place, they asked about nothing else for two straight hours.

On their way out that second day, Liang and Belli passed Tsen's slave Kalaiya walking across the dragon yard to take their place in the gondola. She looked shrivelled and smaller than Liang remembered. Her face was puffed but she held herself stiffly straight. Liang tried to catch her eye but Kalaiya stared pointedly into the far distance until the gondola swallowed her up. When the Elemental Men were done with her, the dragon-rider's slaves came next. Liang had stayed in the yard to watch and glanced across at the dragon. It wasn't looking at the Godspike any more. It was looking at the gondola.

'Kalaiya!' Liang called. Kalaiya stopped. She turned and took a deep breath and then slowly lowered herself to her knees. She must have been younger than Liang but she moved like an old woman. Tsen's death had done that to her.

'Mistress.'

Liang shook her head and quickly pulled Kalaiya back to her feet. 'No, no. None of that.' She offered an embrace but Kalaiya simply stood wrapped in Liang's arms like a lump of dough. 'I told Tsen that I'd look after you,' Liang said. 'When they came for him. If there's anything—'

'He's dead.' Her voice was flat and lifeless.

'I know, and—'

'They're going to take Sea Lord Quai'Shu to Khalishtor for trial. They'll hold him in the Elemental Palace at the foot of Mount Solence. We're not allowed to talk to him. He's forbidden to speak to anyone.'

Liang snorted. 'Quai'Shu lost the last bits of his mind months ago. He's as mad as Zaklat the Death Bat. What's the point of talking to him, for pity's sake?'

'They'll hang the rest of us here.' Kalaiya turned away and then looked back. 'Tsen said you would be a friend. They killed him days ago.' A sob shook her. 'I heard them talking. They said it was poison. They think he killed himself but he didn't.' Her face set hard. 'He was going to face them. He knew they'd hang him anyway but he was going to face them'

'I know.' Poison. That's why Liang hadn't seen any wound.

'They stabbed him in the back. Those bastards.' Abruptly Kalaiya burst into tears, and this time when Liang held her she shook and shuddered with her grief until she pulled away and for a moment her eyes blazed. 'You were a friend to him, Chay-Liang. Give me a wand. They mean to bring Mai'Choiro Kwen to the dragon yard to hear their orders for the eyrie. Give me a wand that a slave can use and I'll see he never hears them. Or a knife to make him bleed.'

'You'll never get close. They'll kill you.'

'I don't care! I have nothing left!'

'I can't, Kalaiya. Go back inside.' It almost crushed Liang to send her away without giving her some sort of hope.

Mai'Choiro, though …

Liang ran back inside, ignoring Belli's indignant protests about the hatchery. She wrapped black silk across her eyes, the silk that let her see through the eyes of her little enchanted glass dragon, and waited to see what would happen.

18

Warlocks and Other Things Best Forgotten

At night the dragon Silence watched. Through the day it flew along the coast for hundreds of miles. It found the edge of the desert where it blurred into smudges of green that grew and then sprawled into a thick jungle of emerald trees laced through with silver ribbons of water. It found clouds and lush hills that drew the rain out of them before they could reach the desert beyond. All these things but no cities of the little ones.

It hunted and returned, perched on a rock in the night and listened to the thoughts and memories of the little one who carried the splinter of the Black Moon. It poked a little and prodded, but only with the lightest touch. Before the sun rose it flew away, out to sea until it found another curtain of the storm-dark, stretched out, endless to the eye. It dived beneath the water, down until it reached the bottom, and in the depths there purple lightning flashed, dim and distant and full of sullen purpose, lighting the black water. There were no fish, no crawling things on many legs scuttling in the darkness, no glow-eyed jelly creatures. Life knew better than to be close to the Nothing. The dragon Silence rose again and burst into the air, long and sharp and hard in glittering spray, and returned to seek the little ones once more. It drew out their thoughts and divined their destination – the Queverra – and when the dragon sought to see this place in their memories, it saw a scar across the earth, the bottomless chasm it had crossed some days before.

It found the Crowntaker once more. It dug into his thoughts, peeling the layers of his life like an onion.

'Did I ever tell you about Utthen of Merizikat?' Berren walked with his hands tied to a pole. Five other slaves had their hands tied to the same pole in front of him and three more followed behind. Tuuran was on another pole beside him. Their feet were tied too, with ropes loose enough for walking but too short to run.

'I'm not listening to you.' Tuuran made a big show of looking somewhere else.

'Utthen of Merizikat! Name not mean anything?' They walked like that, night after night over hard-baked earth, dry and dusty. Tufts of hostile spiny grass and stunted thorn bushes ambushed them in the twilight now and then, tearing at legs and feet.

'I think I am hearing some noises. Might it be a large dangerous animal? I hope so – then it might *eat* someone.'

'Merizikat. In the Dominion. They have some catacombs there. They hang people under the ground. The worst sorts. They take them from all across the provinces. Thousands of miles some of them come. They hang them underground and then leave their bodies in the catacombs so their souls can never reach the sun.' They walked in the mornings as the sun rose and the heat of the day began to build, rested and hid in what shade they could find from midday until late in the afternoon, then walked again until long after dark and then slept, the same every day.

'Or is that noise the wind? Come to think of it, it *does* sound like a lot of hot air.'

'Utthen of Merizikat. Pretended to be a necromancer. Came from somewhere in the far south. Claimed he'd murdered more than a hundred souls. Entire villages. So they locked him up and took him a thousand miles to be hanged in Merizikat. But it turned out he wasn't a necromancer at all. He just had business there and was too tight to pay for passage.' Berren's legs ached. He was hungry and tired and thirsty but most of all he was numb inside, as though all the colour had drained out of him and every memory was a washed-out grey. Fasha stayed, a slowly dimming pain, the memory of her face blurring, the sharpness of remembered feeling leaching out every day.

'Did they hang him anyway?'

'I don't know.'

'Bit of a crap story then.'

Tuuran went back to ignoring him. The slavers made their next midday camp in the lee of a great cliff. They propped up shelters and walked among their captives, giving each a meagre cup of water and a wedge of dry stale bread. Berren dozed, woken again when it was time to go by sharp shouts and prodding feet. The slaves pulled wearily at each other, all having to get up at once along the pole that bound them together, tripping over the ropes around their feet. Some were close to the end of their endurance. Berren had no idea what would happen when the first one fell. It wouldn't be him. That was all that mattered.

They trudged on, the slavers exhorting them to a faster pace with threats and now and then the crack of a whip. They followed the base of a cliff, the sun behind them now as they headed ever eastward. The world around Berren narrowed to the heat on his back, the pain across his shoulders from the wooden pole, the aches in his legs and his feet and the cracked-dry earth in front of him where each next step would fall. The reluctant sun sank to the horizon, darkness fell and a full moon rose. They passed the cliff and headed into open ground and a breeze swept across from the north. A light puff of wind but delicious nevertheless.

The dead of Merizikat. Stupid story, although that reminded him of even more stupid stories from the galley back when he'd been a slave. Stories of how the dead men lying in the catacombs had started getting up and walking again these last few years. And that was simply ridiculous, or so he'd thought until he'd gone back to his old home of Deephaven and found the streets he used to know had become a necropolis, crawling with the walking talking bastard dead. He shuddered at the memory. With their eyes stitched shut – what was that about?

Deephaven and the dead. Made him think of warlocks, of Saffran and Vallas and Skyrie; out of nowhere they bloomed inside his thoughts, unexpected, unwanted and unwelcome. Skyrie had stopped fighting him years ago. The warlock's memories were dead things, passive and still, but they remained. Memories of the memories of another man, now escaped somehow from the closets in which he'd put them. He remembered walking into the Pit under the castle of Tethis, knowing what Vallas Kuy meant to do. He remembered being Berren on a field a few miles away with sigils scribed in blood pressed to his chest in the heat of battle. He remembered the horror as he was ripped out of himself and Skyrie's horror as they merged, for that wasn't how Vallas had meant it to be.

He'd never stopped to think much about this other man Skyrie. All that had counted back then was that they were trapped together, that only one of them could win and that it had to be him. Skyrie had been a warlock, a minion to the soap maker. Little else. It was all that mattered.

But no, there had to be more.

No. Nothing that mattered.

Remember it anyway.

A farmer then. A poor village boy from somewhere. Berren had never heard the name of the place, only knew that it was on the edge of a lake beside a swamp, surrounded by reed beds. Didn't even know what kingdom. He'd had a sister. Men had come to his village. Soldiers on horses. Raiders who took whatever caught their eye. One year they came twice and something bad had happened and ...

He could see the scar on his leg. Cut to the bone across his thigh, it was a savage wound. The skin had closed in time, twisted and warped and folded but healed. The leg worked well enough now.

The second time they came, they killed every man, woman and child. They burned Skyrie's village to ash and he was the only one who lived because he'd already crawled out into the reeds to die that night. The leg had gone bad. And yet he hadn't died after all and he'd come back in the morning and found everything gone. He'd followed the tracks of the soldiers but lost them. Then he met an old man with a half-ruined face, scarred by pox or fire and with one blind milky eye, who claimed he'd seen some soldiers come by not long ago, a villainous-looking lot, and he knew who they were too. The Bloody Judge's men.

A lie. A lie a lie a lie!

Something about the old man. He'd travelled with Skyrie a little way. Only a few days. The soldiers were long gone by then, beyond his reach, but there were men who would help him, the old man said. Men in Tethis. He should look for the soap maker. And so he did, and told his story and learned everything there was to learn about the wickedness of the Bloody Judge, the mercenary lord who took his band of outlaws up and down the little kingdoms and answered to no one and left a trail of wailing women and fatherless children behind him. The greatest evil north of Kalda, but in

Tethis something would be done. Queen Gelisya meant to bring an end to his reign of terror.

He remembered Vallas, the soap maker. Remembered him both as Skyrie and as Berren the Bloody Judge, years before on a ship and years later, a few days ago when Berren had finally found him in Dhar Thosis and killed him.

Aria, Skyrie, where the Ice Witch keeps him in a gilded cage. He gave you a gift. One that not even she knows. The warlock's last words. He had no idea what they meant.

A gift?

He'd never understood.

Saffran Kuy's last apprentice. The man with one eye. The man with the half-ruined face.

You ask me who you are, Skyrie, but that's not the question. The question is what?

A man with a half-ruined face. He'd seen a man like that before. The old man who'd sent him to the soap maker. But somewhere else as well.

Where?

In Skyrie's memories. The ones that came out in his dreams. He pushed deeper.

Bloodied and broken and crawling to his death in the swamps while the stars above winked out one by one. With a man standing over him in robes the colour of moonlight, his pale face scarred ragged by disease or fire, one blind eye milky white. Fingers that traced symbols over him. Air that split open like swollen flesh. Black shadow that oozed from the gashes left behind.

There was something out of place in Skyrie's memories. He hadn't seen it before because he hadn't looked or cared. But Skyrie had crawled away into a swamp to die with one leg festering and ruined beyond repair and in the morning he'd walked out again. *Walked* out …

The wound in his leg. There were marks within the scar, impossibly intricate, silvery lines and whorls like runes. Like the sigils of the warlocks. The man with the one eye …

But he'd met the old man with the one eye afterwards, not then. The one who'd told him about the soldiers, who'd sent him to Vallas …

Show me!

For a moment Berren stumbled. *Show me?*

It fills the hole, you see. Words Gelisya had spoken to him once. The Dark Queen before that's what she became. *Like the Black Moon and the Dead Goddess fill the hole in the world. He showed me. You have to keep it closed. Otherwise something will come through. Not yet but one day. Before you both come back for the very last time. You have to keep it closed.* Even with her lips almost touching his ear, her whisper was so quiet he could barely hear her. *He's making us ready. To let it in when the Ice Witch brings down the Black Moon.*

And then Skyrie again, that night in the swamp where everything changed. *What will you give?* the one-eyed stranger had asked.

Anything, he replied.

And everything?

Everything.

Anything and everything.

The hole was there. For the second time he looked inside and saw that he was not alone. He saw that something looked back.

The Black Moon.

The stranger with the half-ruined face and the milky eye had put it there. Inside Skyrie. Inside him. And he saw too that all along there had been other eyes behind his own, peering with a quiet hunger over his shoulder at every vision and every memory, pushing and nudging and guiding him towards revelation.

The Black Moon saw too.

I see you, little worm.

Destroyer! Who let you loose?

A flicker of a thought that didn't belong to any of the pieces he carried inside him. *A child of the sun . . .*

Crazy Mad muttering to himself wasn't anything new. Tuuran had mostly stopped listening, but this time he caught the last few words because something had changed. The voice wasn't Crazy's any more.

'A child of the sun.'

Crazy's eyes burst into brilliant moonlight silver. All of a sudden Tuuran could see everything around him as though it was the middle of the day. He staggered as the other slaves on his pole lurched and lost their step. Crazy Mad stopped dead. The ropes around him simply ceased to be and the pole over his head was gone too. The slave behind stumbled into the back of him and dissolved into a cloud of black ash. Tuuran stared aghast. No pretending it hadn't happened, not this time.

A hundred yards off in the scrub among the loose rocks he saw a dragon. A hatchling. In the darkness it had been invisible. Now it was clear for everyone to see, except everyone was staring at Crazy Mad.

'Dragon!' Tuuran would have pointed but his hands were tied to the pole. A flash of lightning dazzled him, brighter still than the light pouring out of Crazy Mad's eyes. The thunderclap made him wince. Crazy staggered. Another lightning bolt hit him and then another, thrown by the slavers with their wands, each one strong enough to kill any man it touched and probably anyone unlucky enough to be standing next to him too. They ought to have hurled Crazy Mad through the air like a leaf in the wind. After the third Crazy didn't even flinch any more. He stood there, all that silver light pouring out of him, and simply didn't notice.

The slaves next to Crazy suddenly found themselves free. They bolted, only they weren't running for freedom, they were running to get away. Everyone was suddenly shouting at once. The slaves bound to Tuuran tried to run too, except the pole and the tethers around their feet made it impossible. One tripped in his haste, lost his balance and fell, and his weight on the pole was enough to bring them all down in a tangled heap of arms and legs. Another pole of slaves was shuffling away as fast as possible; yet another had fallen; the slavers were screaming their heads off and dashing this way and that like crazed geese, bawling at everyone to get down on the ground while everything threw up crazy shadows, bathed in the eerie moonlight glow from Crazy Mad's eyes.

A bolt of lightning hit the pole of slaves trying to get away. The slave at the back arched and threw himself into the rest and then hung, a deadweight among them, and down they went. When Tuuran looked again, the dragon had gone. Or maybe it was hiding. He'd never heard of a dragon hiding but then he'd never heard of a man's eyes turning silver and lighting up the night as bright as day, nor of anyone who could swat aside lightning as though it was nothing. Or maybe he had, but only in stories that the soldiers of the guard used to tell each other around their fires late at night, tales of the Isul Aieha, the Silver King, the half-god who'd come with his Adamantine Spear when the dragons had flown free, who'd shown the first blood-mages and alchemists how to tame them.

'Crazy! Crazy Mad!'

The air was awash with shouts and moans and wails. Crazy didn't move. He hadn't moved a single step since the moment this had started.

'Berren! Skyrie!' Tuuran paused a moment because he was a simple man who saw the world in simple ways. 'Isul Aieha!'

Crazy heard the name and spun round as though he'd been stung. He took a step towards Tuuran and then stopped again. The slavers were still throwing lightning. Crazy shifted, caught three bolts in the palms of his hands in quick succession and threw them straight back the way they'd come, and after that the slavers gave up and slipped away into the shadows, fear getting the better of them as it should have right at the start. Through it all, Crazy's eyes were locked on Tuuran. He came closer and crouched down. The wails from the men around grew louder. They tried to scrabble free. Futile, bound as they were, but they tried.

Stop.

The air fell still. All sound ceased. The slaves stopped their struggles. Everything froze. Everything. It took a moment for Tuuran to realise it. No rasping breaths, no hiss of the breeze, nothing, not even his own heartbeat. He couldn't even shift his eyes. It was as though Crazy Mad had stopped time itself and slipped them both outside it, and now those burning silver eyes bored into him. Neither of them spoke a word. Tuuran couldn't have, even if he'd thought of something to say. Crazy Mad still moved as though nothing had changed, but this Crazy didn't need to speak. Tuuran felt something dive into him and take whatever it wanted.

Isul Aieha.

Abruptly the world began to move again. There was sound and Tuuran's ears filled once more with wails of fear. He blinked. Crazy was crouched over him, only now the light had gone and Crazy Mad was just Crazy Mad, and Tuuran had never seen such a despair in any man.

'Crazy?'

'There was a dragon in my head. It took my memories. It showed me everything.'

'Crazy! Cut us loose!'

'What am I, Tuuran?' Crazy backed away. 'What am I? There's no joy any more. No kindness. Nothing warm and nothing soft. Nothing.'

He disappeared into the darkness. Tuuran yelled after him. 'Crazy! *Crazy*! Cut us loose, you mad daft bastard. You leave me here and I'll hunt you down, so help me you selfish piece of ...' But Crazy Mad was gone.

Nothing.

Tuuran let out a long breath and let himself slump. However hard his heart was thumping, he couldn't say there wasn't a piece of him that hadn't seen this coming.

19

The Gold Dragon

By the time Liang had her little golden dragon up by the gondola in the dragon yard, Mai'Choiro Kwen was already within. The dragon fluttered onto the gondola's crown and crept down the side, its golden claws click-clack tapping on the gleaming silver. Liang had it poke an eye around one of the windows where she hoped the Elemental Men wouldn't see. It pressed its ear to the silver shell.

'... every person within this place shall be subject to this order and is forbidden to leave under pain of execution. Lord Shonda of Vespinarr is required to present himself to this place until his non-complicity can be proven ...' The Elemental Man speaking had his back to her. He was standing up, reading from a scroll of parchment. From what Liang could glimpse of it, the writing was marvellously ornate and the scroll was bound to bone and silver rollers.

Mai'Choiro's face darkened in outrage. He clenched his fists and banged the table. He looked more angry than surprised. Liang didn't hear what he said. Something about Lord Shonda. He didn't like his master being summoned, was that it? She grinned to herself. *I bet ...*

The Elemental Man sat down but kept talking. Something about Tsen and Quai'Shu and Shrin Chrias Kwen. Liang couldn't hear much of it through the shell of the gondola until the killer stood up again and resumed from the scroll: '... found guilty shall be returned to the Crown of the Sea Lords in Khalishtor to be publicly hanged by the neck until dead, their bodies to thrown into the sea unless execution is deemed more expedient to be carried out here.' He paused, took a deep breath and went on. 'The Arbiter places the remaining witness, the slave Zafir, under the protection of the Elemental Men until such time as judgement is passed.'

In her study Liang laughed and shook her head. 'Her? Of all of us, *her*?'

'This is ridiculous.' Mai'Choiro was sitting very still. 'I was a prisoner here!'

She didn't hear what happened next because Bellepheros burst into her room. 'Li! What are you—' He stopped as she ripped the silk from her eyes.

'Hush!' She waved him to sit on the bed beside her. 'The Elemental Men are talking to Mai'Choiro Kwen. I'm eavesdropping. So be quiet!'

'But we—'

'Quiet!' She put the silk over her eyes again and shifted back into the golem dragon's artificial sight. The smile on Mai'Choiro's face made her want to punch him.

'... are forbidden from approaching her, speaking with her or attempting any contact. The Arbiter will have the truth of what happened and then the slave Zafir will be hanged and the dragon she rides will be destroyed. This is not the ruling of the Arbiter of the Dralamut but the decision of the Elemental Men. The slave Zafir is decreed a sorceress to be executed accordingly.'

Beside Bellepheros, Liang gleefully clenched an exultant fist. 'No more nor less than she deserves,' she muttered. Get rid of the monster and get rid of the rider, and even Belli must quietly rejoice. It wasn't even killing, if what he said was right, simply making its spirit find another egg, an egg that was somewhere *else*. All they were doing was making it smaller.

'What?' Belli nudged her. 'What is it?' In the gondola Mai'Choiro's expression had gone from a smile to horror. That was delicious too and made her want to laugh out loud. *They still have designs of keeping these monsters?*

'They're going to hang your dragon-queen.' She leaned into him. 'Let her go. There's no hope for her, Belli.'

Beside her she heard Bellepheros sigh. 'Come back to the hatchery, Li. I still need your help.'

Mai'Choiro was whining like a hurt puppy now, about how the dragon was no more dangerous than a glasship or a lightning cannon, that it was simply a weapon. He wheedled on and on about the Ice Witch and Aria and other nonsense that really made no difference. Liang didn't hear it all but she didn't need to. The Elemental Men clearly didn't care. Excuses, that's all they were, though Liang wondered now whether it had ever crossed any minds what might happen if they *did* take a dragon across the storm-dark and sent it against the Ice Witch, and the Ice Witch turned it back on them, and how stupid they'd all look.

Belli squeezed her hand. 'Li! Leave it be. Please.'

Liang watched for another minute, but the Elemental Men seemed largely done with Mai'Choiro. She sighed and unwrapped the silk from her eyes and patted the alchemist's hand. 'Come on then.' She tried a smile. 'Sometimes I'm not entirely sure which one of us is the slave.'

Belli grimaced. 'Both of us.' They walked together back through the tunnels, Bellepheros wincing now and then at his knees, which always gave him trouble, and Liang wincing at the bruises she still carried from the night the Vespinese had come.

'A right pair we make,' she said.

Bellepheros didn't answer, but when they reached the dragon yard he stopped and glared at the gondola. 'I've seen their sort before. I know what they can do. Their kind brought me here. They took away my freedom so they've already done the worst they can. Diamond Eye is a catastrophe waiting to happen. I'll kill it for you with a happy heart when it's not needed any more. But the hatchling that escaped, you show me that abomination dead first.'

They almost killed themselves getting the last chain nets back up but eventually managed it, Liang pillaging gold-glass from the rubble of the crashed glasship and reshaping it into struts and beams and arches. Without a t'varr to watch and shout at her, she was profligate, but it was draining to work with gold-glass that had already been formed and set once before, and it was late and long after dark when they were done. She felt so tired that for once she might actually sleep instead of lying awake in bed worrying about things she couldn't change. The hatchery at least was now back as it should be. One of her many problems gone away.

She bade Bellepheros goodnight outside his study and, since no one else was there to see, hugged him. It confused him – he had no idea what to do – and it was hard not to laugh. She left him there, bewildered, and went to her workshop and opened the iron door. As she did she felt a breeze, and then an Elemental Man stood before her. He held her little glass dragon in his hand.

'You have something to say, enchantress?'

Liang glanced at the strip of black silk still on her bed and nodded. She pushed past him and flopped down beside it. 'You don't need to keep the rider alive to hear what passed between her and Baros Tsen T'Varr and Mai'Choiro Kwen,' she said. 'It was Mai'Choiro Kwen, not Tsen, who gave her her orders.'

'So you say, lady, but how do you *know*?'

'Because I was there. Hidden and unseen but there. Tell that to your Arbiter. I heard it all with my own ears. Close the door on your way out now. I'd like to know I won't be disturbed.'

For a moment the killer was silent. He put the golden dragon down beside her. Then she felt a stirring of the air, and when he spoke again his voice had moved. 'We do not expect to see this toy again. Goodnight, Chay-Liang of Hingwal Taktse.'

She heard the door close.

20

The Abyss

Dawn burst over the desert horizon. For Tuuran and the other slaves it meant they could see where they were going again, not so much chance of stumbling and bringing down the pole. He'd lost track of how far they'd gone now. A legion of Adamantine Men might march thirty miles a day across open country, but the slaves were roped together and slow. Half that perhaps then, and they'd been going ten days, or maybe eleven or was it twelve? He'd stopped counting when Crazy Mad did his thing and left.

On other days the slavers sent an advance guard ahead as the sun rose. Tuuran had learned to watch for them, a dozen men on humpbacked horses who rode off as soon as the light was good enough to see by. A few hours later, as the heat was beginning to bite, the slave train would crest a rise or traverse a canyon or reach the top of a trail and find a camp waiting. The slavers were hardly kind but they knew better than to damage their merchandise. They gave out water and stale bread and, when they ran out of that, a paste of crushed beans and a bowl of seeds cracked and boiled soft. After eating, the slaves were left to rest until the sun sank close to the ground. Late each afternoon they cleared the camp to earn another round of water and set off again.

On this morning the vanguard stayed with them. As the sun rose, the slavers reached a stream, a rare thing in this heat-blasted landscape of bare broken stone, and stopped a while to let their animals drink. One by one they freed each group of slaves from the pole that held their arms and let them crouch together by the water, still tied at the feet but with their hands their own. They drank and drank, all of them, the first running water Tuuran had seen since the sea. When they were done, each group was led away, one mounted slaver in front, two on foot behind with their spears held close. Tuuran stood at the front of the men of his pole when their turn came. He looked the slavers up and down and knew that he could, if he wanted to, take either the one off the horse or the two on their feet, but he couldn't do both and so he did nothing and followed meekly as the stream cut sharply into the rock in a series of steps and cascades. A ravine closed around them, and Tuuran understood there was no way out except forward or back.

Other dribbles of water joined the stream as they walked, tiny trickles that poured over the edge high above. The air in the ravine was pleasant, damp and cool even as the day wore on and the sun rose high. By midday they were walled between two straight cliffs of sandy red stone, walking through a gentle rush of water no deeper than his toes over a bed of gravel and littered stones. The endless marching wore at his feet and his hips. Everything ached but he was better off than most. The slavers had already had to slow the march twice. Most of the other slaves were used to soft work, some of them used to no work at all. Some hadn't even been slaves before the dragon came. It was easy to pick them out, the ones with no brands who complained and screamed and begged, the ones given the least mercy. The rest took it all with stoical resignation, an unpleasant interlude in a life that had never been their own to begin with. Even the slavers themselves knew they might be taken by others one day, bigger, stronger, better armed. The great cities and their palaces, their sea lords and their fleets and their pageants, were devourers of men and their dignity, endless in their appetite, and those who'd once been citizens of such a city found no mercy now. A few withdrew into themselves, silent and dull-eyed, trying to understand what had happened to them, why, and how their lives had been turned so utterly upside down. Tuuran would have told them not to bother. Questions like that didn't have any answers worth knowing. Shit happened and that was the end of it.

The slavers kept them going right through the night this time, and in the morning too, and by then it was hard even for Tuuran. At least it was all downhill.

The ravine widened. The cliffs arced away around a wide strip of flat land bounded by high sharp hills on one side and a colossal abyss on the other, a great rift in the landscape that ran for miles and delved so deep into the ground that its floor was lost in darkness. One vast knife wound stabbed into the earth. The river ran over the edge of it and Tuuran wanted to run and look but there were slavers everywhere and a large camp ahead of them. Half a mile away, on the other side of the abyss, jagged ruddy cliffs rose towards the sun. Tuuran stopped to stare, and the other slaves behind him stared too. He'd never seen such a rift but he'd heard the Taiytakei speak its name: Queverra.

The slavers prodded them on with a bored anger, their hearts not really in it any more. As they left the canyon behind and staggered on across the open ground beside the abyss, a dozen men on horses trotted over. One was the skinny desert man from Dhar Thosis, the rest Tuuran had never seen before. Skinny pointed to him. The others dismounted and cut Tuuran loose. 'Pale skin. Step forward.'

Tuuran looked about for anything that might do for a weapon, then bent down and picked up a stone. He tossed it from hand to hand a couple of times, stepped forward and held up his arms so everyone would see his brands. 'I have a name. And have you forgotten the promise I made you?'

The other slaves backed away as best they could. Skinny laughed. 'You have a stone. What will you do with that, slave?'

'My name, when I had one, was Tuuran. I earned the right to have it back the hard way. I pulled oars and then ropes on a galley collecting more slaves for men like you who sailed the seas of worlds that weren't my own.' He dropped his arms and looked at the stone. 'This? Why, I might just split your skull with it if you come close enough.'

'Keen to die are you, slave?'

'No keener than any man, but nor am I afraid of it.'

'Then live, slave whose name is Tuuran. What realm were you born to?'

'The realm where there are dragons.'

Skinny paused, then dismounted. 'Some of my men say they saw a dragon a few nights back.'

'So they did.'

'Others say it was a dragon who burned Dhar Thosis.'

'That it was. It had help from a great many men, though I dare say it didn't need it.'

'What else did you see on the night you saw a dragon, Tuuran who has earned his name?'

Tuuran eased down onto his haunches. He made a show of putting the stone down and rose again. Letting him have his name probably meant they weren't planning to kill him, not yet. Probably. 'I saw the return of the Silver King, who tamed our dragons.'

'And what is this Silver King?'

'A half-god sorcerer. Beyond your understanding or mine. Worse than any dragon, I dare say, or better by far. Depends what he wants. Depends if you're on the wrong side of him or the right.'

'You serve this man?'

Tuuran laughed. 'I serve no man. No man, no monster, no god, no magician, no one but the dragon-queen of my far-off realm.'

Skinny made a show of looking about him. 'Well, Tuuran who has earned his name, I see neither dragons nor queens about me. Just a lot of men with sharp spears and hungry bellies. You belong to me now, pale skin. We'll see about your name.'

'Oh you'll get a good price for me. Guard me well and keep me shackled, and once I'm sold, spare a moment of pity for the man who thinks he owns me.' Tuuran shrugged. 'Or give me my axe and run fast and far. You're still the first one I'm going to kill.'

Skinny rolled his eyes. 'The man who came with you from the city of Dhar Thosis. You know him. He's this Silver King, this half-god sorcerer is he? Yet he seemed to me just a slave like any other. How is this, slave who might be called Tuuran?'

Tuuran shrugged. 'You'd need a man far less ignorant than I am to answer that. The dragon brought it out of him, of that much I'm sure. Why? Given you some trouble, has he?' Although after what he'd seen, if Crazy had come this way then it was something of a surprise there was anything here but ash.

'He came this way, slave. He paid no heed to anything around him but went into the Queverra. He can stay down there for all I care.' Skinny shook his head and climbed back onto his horse. 'Keep this one close. Watch him. I'll have fingers and heads from the lot of you if you let him escape. But I don't want him hurt.' He grinned at Tuuran. 'At least not yet, although if his eyes blaze silver like the other then you should either run or throw him into the abyss, I'm not sure which. And give some thought, slave who might be called Tuuran, to where you are. No water, no food, just desert and sun and snakes and scorpions for a hundred miles.'

'And a dragon.' Tuuran laughed back at him. 'You might want to keep a piece of your mind on that. They get very hungry, you know.'

The slavers turned and left, and when it came to it, Tuuran held up his arms and let them tie him back to his pole and lead him through the camp and push him into a pen with the rest. Skinny had a point about there being nowhere to run, and Tuuran had long ago settled on the notion that alive was better than dead. Chances would come, the way chances always did for a patient man. So he took his water when they brought it and made no fuss and ate his food, every last drab scrap of it, and settled back and closed his eyes to sleep. Crazy was somewhere near here, was he? Maybe he wouldn't punch the stupid bugger's lights out for leaving him then. Not if he came back and did something about it.

Crazy Mad. Maybe thinking about him as he closed his eyes was why he had Crazy in his dreams. Crazy and his wild stories of being the Bloody Judge, of being ripped out of one body and tossed into another by some mad warlock. In his dreams he saw the sorcerer they'd killed in Dhar Thosis, the one he'd seen on the galley when Tuuran had thrown Crazy into the sea to hide him.

Hide him?

Because the warlocks were looking for him, that was why. It had been obvious. And because of the tattoos they'd had in the same strange writing he'd seen on the pillar in Vespinarr when the Elemental Man they'd called the Watcher had taken him from Baros Tsen's eyrie to send him back to sea. Tuuran had never quite understood why the Elemental Man had been so interested in Crazy, only that he was, and that Tuuran was supposed to find him again and watch him, and that doing so was supposed to earn him his freedom, though a fat lot of use that looked like it would be now. But still, right there was reason enough to make his way back to the dragon of Dhar Thosis. That and the dragon-queen who rode it.

He felt a strange surge of something there. A flash of interest that seemed out of place, quickly gone.

Why?

In Vespinarr the Watcher had taken him to an ancient obelisk whose name he'd never bothered to remember. Something to do with Crazy Mad's scars, if that's what they were. The marks on his leg. The obelisk had weird writing on it. He only vaguely remembered what it looked like now, but he recalled how the writing and the marks on Crazy's leg and the tattoos on the back of the assassin who'd ripped out a piece of the alchemist's throat up on the eyrie were all alike. Mostly, though, what he remembered was how they were the same as some of the old writing he'd seen in the dragon-lands. In the dragon-queen's palace inside the Pinnacles. A world away but the marks had been the same, sigil for sigil for sigil ...

He was trying to remember. Trying so hard that it woke him up. He sat and rubbed his eyes, fuddled for a moment by sleep. The Watcher had sent him to find Crazy. To watch him and watch for the warlocks. The grey dead men, he called them.

Why?

He didn't know. Never had.

The sigils had been like the tattoos on the assassin who'd tried to kill Bellepheros.

He'd gone. Willingly. Glad to be away from the alchemist and what he was doing. Glad to be going back to sea. Glad to see Crazy Mad again.

What did they want?

What of the knife?

What is he?

Who were they?

Where is this Watcher?

And then the last thing Crazy Mad had said, after his eyes had become his own again. *The dragon was in my head. Taking my memories. It showed me everything ...*

Tuuran sat bolt upright and hissed, awake as if someone had thrown a bucket of ice in his face. The dragon was back. It was right here and rifling through his head like he was some dusty old book. 'You little shit! Where are you?'

There, out in the darkness, hardly visible at all, a shape of shadows in the desert night. But there nevertheless, its eyes agleam in the moonlight, not far from the cage where Tuuran sat and staring right back at him. The dragon he'd seen on the night Crazy Mad had gone crazy again. It was a hatchling barely out of its egg, not that that made it any less deadly to a man trapped in a cage with no axe and no dragon-scale to shield himself. Tuuran bared his teeth. Slowly he stood up, kicking the snoring slaves around him. 'Come on then. You know what I am.'

I know. And I am hungry, Tuuran.

For a moment he caught a flash of something. Of being somewhere else. Of being the dragon in the mind of some other. *I will think of you as I kill him, little one.*

Then came the fire.

21

In the Blood

'The whole eyrie in quarantine and we're not allowed to even move.' Li was in one of her huffs again. 'They might as well drop us into the storm-dark, dragon and all. It's three hundred miles of desert to the nearest city and that happens to be Dhar Thosis, so that's no use. Who's going to bring everything we need to survive out here?' They were in the alchemist's study, since his laboratory was still a charred mess from when the hatchling had escaped. Li's workshop looked, if anything, even worse. Not that a dragon had run around smashing everything and setting fire to it, that was just the way her workshop was all the time.

Bellepheros mumbled into his cup and nodded agreeably. He had no idea, but then he never had. He was merely a slave and that sort of thing was someone else's problem. 'I'm just glad you didn't get hurt in all that fighting. It's not your trouble, Li.' When it came to troubles he had enough of his own, the first being to persuade Zafir to take Diamond Eye hunting after the missing hatchling. He picked up a glass retort on his desk and stroked it absently. It was beautiful work, Li's own.

'Do you think she'd do it?'

'Who?' He frowned at the retort. Almost a shame to use it. They never got really clean again, not *really* clean.

'Charin's sails, Belli, you haven't been listening!' Li rolled her eyes and threw back her head. 'Your precious dragon-riding slave who ought to hang. The one thing Mai'Choiro Kwen got right. Would she do it?'

'Do what?' Bellepheros put the retort back onto the desk and picked up his cup of qaffeh instead. 'Li, my queen desires her freedom. If you want something of her, why don't you ask her?'

'Because she hates me!'

'Because you hate her.'

'And with good reason!'

Bellepheros laughed. 'I don't mean this personally, Li, for you're far better than any of the dragon-lords I used to know, but her Holiness Zafir was a queen and your people made her into a slave. Does her resentment truly surprise you?' Thing was, with Li, it seemed that it did. *You're a slave. You might as well get used to it, and actually it's not so bad if you keep your head down and do as you're asked. You should be grateful for what we give you.* 'It's different for me. I was always a slave to the dragons. I took that path willingly and knowing what it was. And even I begrudge what your people took from me. I begrudge the manner of it. The sense of entitlement and privilege, the quiet assumption that your way and your lives and your culture are somehow better. You take for granted many things you should question. Not all your achievements are gifts to be shared and received with fawning gratitude.'

Li snorted and poked at his cup. 'Tell me that the next time I put some Bolo in front of you.' He supposed she meant it as a joke, and maybe when it came to Bolo she had a point, but he didn't smile.

'Her Holiness doesn't drink qaffeh, and if she eats Bolo then she does it very discreetly.'

'The truth! I need her to tell them what Mai'Choiro said, Belli. Just the truth. Is that so hard?'

'Do you think she doesn't understand?' Bellepheros laughed and drained his cup and stood up. 'She was born to these games, Li. She has something that others want and she'll extract the best price she can before she gives it up. She probably knows perfectly well that it's the only thing keeping her alive. Can you blame her for clinging to it? They want to kill her. *You* want to kill her. You seem to want that very much.'

Li glared at the table. 'Can't see many who would blame me for that, given what she's done.'

'Never mind the rights and wrongs. She's not stupid.'

'Even you wanted to kill her once.'

A silence hung between them. Bellepheros opened his mouth and then closed it again, trying to frame an answer, to tell her that yes, he had, and how grateful he was that she'd stopped him, but that didn't change things.

'I'm sorry, Belli. That was ...' Li looked at him with her big brown eyes as if struggling for words until a slave knocked on the study door. She jumped up like a jack-in-the-box and opened it and an old Taiytakei shuffled in carrying a silver tray and a crystal bottle. He looked around for a table or a bench with some space on it, didn't find one, and then looked helpless until Bellepheros took some books off his desk and put them on the floor. The slave set down the tray. He bowed deeply. 'Apple wine from Baros Tsen T'Varr's cellar. The lady Kalaiya wishes to share it with those who were loyal before the …' he coughed and looked over his shoulder '… before the murdering Vespinese bastards drink it all.' As he backed away and Li laughed, Bellepheros stole a look at her. She had a lovely laugh and a lovely smile. Honest and unforced.

'I have work,' he said when the slave had gone. 'But I'll talk to her. Her freedom for the truth and the hatchling hunted down. How can you do it though? They'll never let her go. Never.'

'Ask her anyway. I was thinking perhaps, if we have to, we should all go. You and me and her, running away on the back of her dragon.' Li snorted derisively. 'She flies it; you feed it potions; I'll find us a way to cross the storm-dark.'

Bellepheros roared with laughter. 'How far before you push her off? Do we get to cross the eyrie wall?'

'Not before *she* pushes *me* off, I suspect.'

'A dragon-queen, an irritable old alchemist and a cranky enchantress flying away together on the back of a furious dragon?' Bellepheros laughed again, shaking his head. 'What are you thinking, Li?' Somewhere under there she really meant it though, some little part of her anyway, and that wasn't the Li he knew. She was troubled then, and deeper than she let on.

Li picked up the bottle and peered at the amber wine inside. 'I hear she roams hundreds of miles. Hours every day, taking the dragon to feed while two Elemental Men always watch her. I'm thinking that I don't understand why they let her live. And I'm certainly thinking that I don't see what difference it would make or why it should bother them if she hunts for your hatchling while she flies.'

'We shall see, eh?' Bellepheros clucked and left Li there in his study and walked up through the white stone tunnels. They glowed bright today, like the sunlight outside but never so dazzling. Zafir found the tunnels cramped and small and oppressive but they'd never struck *him* that way; but maybe that was just him being used to living under the ground. Alchemists spent a lot of time in caves because caves were safe from dragons. He'd grown used to it over the years and had never much liked the vast open spaces of the deserts and the plains, even back in his old realms and certainly not here. The craggy moors were easy enough, and forests, and the City of Dragons at the foot of the Purple Spur was manageable too. Mountains, *they* were best of all. As long as he was at the bottom of them and not at the top. Heights … He shuddered. Heights were worse than open space. *Far* worse.

Out in the dragon yard the wind caught his robe and whipped the hem around his feet. He was heartily sick of this blasted wind. It had a caprice to it that lifted up tunics and whipped a cloak over a man's head when he least expected it, but underneath lurked a more sinister malevolence that blistered skin and flayed the edges of everything. It was a relentless grind, leaching the strength out of them all, battering and wearing him down until he was too tired to think. The only one who seemed not to care was Zafir, but then a rider was more used to wind.

Diamond Eye was perched on the far wall, staring at the Godspike as ever. Bellepheros sighed. Down in the yard, surrounded by walls, he could pretend he was on the ground, nestled close to the earth. Once he climbed up … He shuddered as he thought of being on the top of the wall, the wind rattling and shaking him, looking out and seeing yet again where they truly were, miles above the ground with a huge black storm circling beneath them, dark purple lightning flashing in its depths. Flame! The storm was so wide you couldn't even *see* the ground, even though the desert air was bright and clear.

Heights. He'd never done well with heights. Never had and never would though he hadn't the first idea why. A healthy fear of falling? Well yes, but … He shuddered, remembering the day he'd first met Li and she'd flown him off through the air on a tiny disc of glass. He'd been sick. He'd nearly fainted and fallen off. Probably would have done if the Adamantine Man Tuuran hadn't been there to catch him. *And then none of this would have happened.*

The thought caught him mid-stride. He faltered. Best not to go there. Just best not to. Instead, he took a breath and forced himself to look up at the wall. Zafir would be there somewhere, up next to Diamond Eye in the gold-glass shelter Li had made. He couldn't see her now but she'd barely left the dragon's side since the Vespinese had tried to hang her, and the dragon wouldn't let anyone near except him and the two slave girls who still devotedly served her – they'd even made their own little shelter outside the walls on the rim. No one else dared venture near Diamond Eye's perch.

He wandered across to the hatchery, inspecting the hatchlings and exchanging a few words with the Scales. He checked under the chain nets where the eggs were kept. Any excuse. Maybe, if he was lucky, one of the eggs would hatch – *that* would give him a reason not to go up onto the wall – but the eggs were all resolutely quiet. With a sigh he wandered back and forced his feet to turn the rest of him to the looming bulk of the dragon. Damned monster cast a shadow right across the eyrie this late in the day.

Someone was ahead of him, he saw, climbing up the steps in the wall. He wondered who it could be. A Taiytakei in the white tunic of a slave, but that was common enough.

Liang looked at the bottle on Belli's desk and smiled. She'd made that. A simple piece of glasswork long since drained of any enchantment. Early work, but *her* work nevertheless. Maybe Kalaiya remembered and had sent it deliberately, a little message along with Baros Tsen's apple wine. In her spare moments Liang felt for her. Everything she was had been founded on Tsen, and now he was gone and she was nothing, just a bed-slave like any other, wrinkled at the edges and unlikely to find any great favour. She'd fallen from the top of a mountain into a deep dark hole and all in a matter of days. There were probably plenty of slaves who'd spent years envying her and tittered at her fall, but she deserved better than that. They'd had a strange thing, Kalaiya and Tsen. She'd actually liked him.

I'll buy her, Liang decided. *She has half a lifetime left. Let her live it in peace.*

She poured herself a glass. Maybe they could take Kalaiya with them. She wasn't sure what use the slave might be but she probably knew more of Tsen's secrets than anyone except Tsen himself, and Tsen probably had more secrets than there were grains of sand in the desert. If there were hidden caches of treasure, secret alliances, debts unpaid, favours, then Kalaiya might know them. Things like that were currency for a man like Tsen, things you couldn't put your finger on, ethereal and traceless.

Would it make a difference? She frowned. It actually might. Leaving on the dragon wasn't much of a plan and she hadn't been serious when she'd said it, but ... could there actually be some sense to it? More to the point, could it *achieve* something even if it could be done? Steal the dragon while no one was looking? Vanish in the night. Or poison it and send it away – send Zafir with it if she could, but quietly Liang knew she'd never fool the dragon-queen so easily. Sink into the underworld of a city like Cashax where even the Elemental Men would have trouble finding her. Make their way to a ship bound for the dragon-realms. Vanish. Hope the Elemental Men wouldn't follow. With Kalaiya and all Tsen's old debts and favours in their pocket, it struck her that it might even work.

But no, that was the coward's way. If she had to hang for Mai'Choiro Kwen and Sea Lord Shonda to be exposed for what they were, so be it. She sipped at the wine. It was good. She'd forgotten. Tsen had given her a bottle once but that was long gone. This one, if anything, was better. She smiled to herself. She actually felt slightly drunk and she hadn't felt that for the best part of a year, not since she'd been sent here.

Bellepheros tried not to think of the wind up on the wall. The slave ahead was carrying a tray with a bottle balanced on top. Carrying it in one hand. Good luck with *that* in the wind; but the slave climbed the steps with ease. Bellepheros felt a pang of envy. Even thinking about going up there was making his knees wobble.

Practice, that's all ...

He could see Zafir now, sitting behind Diamond Eye. She was dressed in a simple white slave's shift, her long legs crossed under her. He couldn't tell if her eyes were closed but she looked as though she was meditating, a novelty among dragon-lords who were usually as restless as their mounts. As the slave with the tray approached, Zafir got up and walked to meet him, and then without any warning kicked the tray out of his hand. The bottle went flying and something else too. Bellepheros ran up the steps, the wind and the horrible empty space all forgotten for a moment. The slave staggered and cried out. Zafir stooped and picked something off the ground and came up in a fighting crouch. The slave stooped to a crouch too, his hands weaving in front of him.

Bellepheros hauled himself onto the top of the wall. The wind smacked into him and almost knocked him tumbling back. He steadied himself and then stopped dead because Diamond Eye was watching the fight with a fierce intensity, snarling, fangs bare, wings half opened, tail swishing, held on the very brink of striking. But Zafir was stopping him. Why?

Zafir slashed the air. The slave jumped back and then forward again, rolling inside Zafir's guard, only he wasn't quick enough and she must have seen the strike coming. As he tumbled towards her, she took a nimble step sideways, right to the edge of the wall. Bellepheros caught a flash of the sun as Zafir brought her fist hard into the man's back. The slave collapsed and lay still. By the time Bellepheros reached them, he was lying in a pool of blood. Zafir crouched low beside him, nose almost touching the ground, one hand on his head, pressing him into the stone, with an ear cocked to listen to any last words he might have had. She was snarling softly. She was also in the way and Bellepheros couldn't see the man's face, couldn't see if he was alive or dead. If he was alive then it wouldn't be for long but there might be something to be done about that … He glanced about, looking for watchers.

Abruptly Zafir sat up. 'He's gone,' she said. She didn't look up as Bellepheros stood behind her. 'I didn't want him to die so quickly. Flame! I wanted to know who sent him. Which one of them it was. You could have used truth-smoke …' She cocked her head.

'Who is he?' Bellepheros asked. Zafir clenched her fists. She drew back and Bellepheros finally saw the dead slave's face.

'I knew,' Zafir said. 'I knew what he was going to do before he knew it himself. Diamond Eye showed me.' She kicked the corpse. 'Who sent you?'

It was the face of the slave who'd brought the bottle of wine to his study. Zafir was still talking but Bellepheros didn't hear. He was already running.

They'd get a long way on the dragon, Liang knew they would. How far? She wasn't sure. She ought to be able to work it out. Ought to, from what she'd seen, but how could she know how long they'd have before the Elemental Men found them? *Silly idea anyway. Never meant it.* Couldn't understand why it wouldn't leave her alone. They'd have to poison the dragon before they left. Which gave them how long? Belli had told her how it would work. Her and Belli, running away. Never mind the rest, the rest needed to go away. They'd get to the sea, would they? She wasn't sure why they'd bother. Didn't make much sense, did it? She'd do what she'd promised first.

She squeezed her nose and screwed up her eyes. Her head was starting to hurt. She stared at the apple wine. She hadn't drunk *that* much. Only a glass, wasn't it? But when she tried to see how much was left, the bottle kept blurring and stretching and rippling and tipping sideways. Her head tipped sideways to follow it but the glass kept on going until suddenly the whole world jumped up off the ground and hit her.

Even lying on the floor, the bottle kept moving. She wasn't sure why.

Xican. A ship. The key was the ship. She could hide them from the Elemental Men but there were only so many ships, only so many navigators. They'd be watching. She'd need a favour. A blind eye. How was she going to do that again?

Oh yes. Kalaiya. That's right.

Liang giggled. She could hardly keep her eyes open. There was a pain in her head and then a bloom of light as if a star was exploding, but so slowly that she could see each and every ray that came out of it.

For a moment she saw the bottle in a bubble of clarity. Nearly full. She'd hardly had any wine at all. *See! Hardly had any at all …*

She closed her eyes. She wasn't sure why.

The Arbiter

22

The Arbiter

Red Lin Feyn, daughter many generations removed but tied by blood to the uniquely revered Feyn Charin, watched the world through the windows of the Dralamut library. The view outside looked as it always did: a peaceful steep-sided valley in the foothills of the Konsidar, its slopes partially terraced with groves of orange trees. Pocket herds of goats grazed on spiked grasses between thorny bushes. A sparrowhawk, riding the thermals, called to its mate. Red Lin Feyn watched it fly, flapping for a few seconds then gliding, flapping and gliding, always the same. Only the sparrow-hawks did that.

As she watched, something in the library changed. She went from being alone to being watched, she was certain of it. The air didn't move, the wooden floor didn't creak, not a single grain of sand fell from the stone walls or from the mortar between them, but she wasn't alone. She could feel the presence.

'Show yourself,' she whispered.

The Elemental Man emerged from the air across the library with such softness that Red Lin Feyn didn't feel it at all. 'Lady.' Thirty feet away but she'd known he was there. She was getting good at this. She didn't turn round.

'Killer.' There would be no more acknowledgement than that.

'Your ship awaits, lady.'

Her ship.

Her eyes stayed on the valley outside. If she tried hard, really, really tried, she might have sensed the disturbance in the weave of the world made by the enchanted glasship come to take her to the desert. 'Do you know, killer, how much of his life my Father of Fathers spent on these walls? How much more of his energy he devoted to this fortress than to all those things for which you remember him. He rebuilt it, enhanced and added and subtracted.

He structured all the storage we have now. The cellars are lined with enchanted stone to preserve provisions. His work, killer. This library? More than half of it came here in his lifetime. Hundreds of years old and yet how much has changed since he died?' Her arms swept past the shelves and shelves of books, the tables covered with astronomical instruments. 'Whispers say that my Father of Fathers owned a copy of the Rava and that he read it from cover to cover. They say he kept it from you and that it's still here.' She was taunting the killer now. She did that with all of them. They never rose to it.

'Why would he do that, lady?'

Lin Feyn shrugged. 'No one knows. Perhaps because your kind had him under your eye even then.'

The Elemental Man came closer. Lin Feyn felt the swish of air, heard the rustle of his clothes but still didn't look at him. It was important not to trust the eyes alone. Important to teach the other senses. 'We gave him this, lady. He was tied to us from the very start. We watched him as we watch you now, all of you, with such a close eye.' He paused. 'You are a sorceress. We call you by another name but that *is* what you are.' He moved a little closer, so close she thought she might touch him if she were to lift and stretch out her fingers. She didn't know this one. His voice was new. He wasn't one of the usual visitors, who would have known better than to engage her in this particular conversation. 'I am told, lady, that Feyn Charin lived to his very end in fear of the Crimson Sunburst. He believed she was not destroyed and that her return was imminent. He asked us to protect him.'

'She was his mentor. Why would she turn on him?'

'He turned on her, did he not?'

'No.' Lin Feyn rounded on the killer and met his eye. 'How do you know this? What is this "I am told"? Told by whom? Were you there, killer? Did you know him?'

'No, lady. You know that we live no longer than ordinary men.' His voice was soft and soothing. She knew the tone. She'd learned it herself years ago. Coaxing. Softening her to do what he wanted – in this case to get into the ship waiting to take her to the desert. She closed her eyes and took a long deep breath and turned to face him.

'I'm not your pawn, killer, and your kind are not untouched by what Quai'Shu's t'varr has done. I will not simply give whatever answer it is they want to this. I'll do what I see is right and not shirk the consequences.'

The killer bowed. 'Nor will we, lady. We will be your eyes, your armour and your lightning.'

'I would rather have my own eyes, thank you.' She pushed past him, out of the library and into the open elliptical heart of the Dralamut with its layer after layer of concentricity above her, its sloping balconies and whitewashed walls. Three long sweeping curves of steps rose from the ground to the flat stone rooftops. The glasship was waiting for her, floating over the yard, sunlight sparking inside it and splitting into rainbow glimmers. As the great outer disc turned, little sons and daughters of light danced and played with the shadows to the rhythm of its languorous orbit, chasing each other from one side of the yard to the other and away again as each surrendered to the next of its myriad brothers and sisters. The waiting gondola was silver and jade. Silver and jade for Vespinarr – so it was the Vespinese who would be taking her. They *were* the closest, and the Dralamut was built on land they claimed – quietly and delicately and with much politeness – as their own. Vespinarr, whose lord Quai'Shu's t'varr claimed had brought all this to pass.

'When I next sleep, you are to go ahead of me, killer. We will stop in Vespinarr. You will find me a different glasship to carry me on from there. Go to Tayuna. Sea Lord Weir will be happy to oblige you. You can have it waiting for me by the time I arrive in the Kabulingnor.'

The ramp into the gondola was open. The Elemental Man vanished with a slight whiff of air. By the time she reached it, he was standing inside, waiting for her. 'It is safe, lady.'

He didn't need to say it. Like it or not, he and the others of his kind were going to be her guardians, vigilant for assassins and murderers everywhere she went. It gave them the perfect excuse to spy on her, night and day.

She sat. The gondola was comfortable, made for the likes of a sea lord or perhaps one of his closest t'varrs or kwens or hsians, the sort they might use to make their leisurely journeys up and down the western coast of Takei'Tarr. The larger lower level was panelled in a pale hardwood, stained henna-red and inlaid with pieces of brilliant jade. Everything shone, sparkling bright and clean. Pinpricks of light snapped at her from every silvered corner and gilded curve. Wherever she looked, she found a reflection of her own face, stretched and distorted, a thousand different aspects and personalities tied by a single name. Windows girdled the gondola at a comfortable eye level, wide ellipses framed in gold and carved with the dragons and lion of Vespinarr. Lin Feyn inspected them. They weren't the work of a true master but they were done well nonetheless.

The same could be said of the other furnishings – a simple large table, a pair of chaises longues and six small silver cabinets fixed around the walls. A bronze tray lay on the table with an exquisite enchanter-made crystal decanter. Someone had already poured a cup of water for her. Towards the front where the pilot golem sat a skeletal silver staircase arced to the upper section. A carved rosewood bed covered in silks and a feather-stuffed mattress waited for her beside an immense cabinet and a battered old chest – the only thing here that was hers. The servants of the Dralamut had already brought her clothes and costumes and personal things. Stacked beside the bed were books from the library, those she thought she might want or need.

She went to the table, took the decanter and the glass and left the gondola, emptied both and refilled them from the fountain in the centre of the Dralamut. Then she returned. When she closed the ramp behind her, the gondola rose at once.

'Vespinarr. We will make that the first stop.'

The Elemental Man bowed. He moved to one of the tinted gold-glass windows and opened it, which caught her attention. A gondola like this rarely had openings of any sort, because openings were a way for the killers to get inside. 'I will be waiting for you in Vespinarr, lady.' The killer gestured to a sheaf of papers on the table beside the bronze tray. They were held down by a silver paperweight in the shape of a dragon and hadn't been there when she'd first entered. 'I will have more for you when you reach the Visonda landing fields.' He bowed and vanished, a slight gust of a breeze whispering around the gondola as he left. Red Lin Feyn, Arbiter of the Dralamut, closed the window behind him and settled back into a chair. She picked up the papers and began to read.

The first pages were an account of Sea Lord Quai'Shu's decade-long quest to steal dragons from the dragon-lands, beginning with how he had acquired the services of not one but two Elemental Men – an unprecedented purchase and one which made her quite certain that the Elemental Men themselves must have desired Quai'Shu to succeed. The document was silent on this but there was no other explanation. The hidden fathers and makers of the Elemental Men had called dragons to Takei'Tarr. Why?

She had no answer and nor did anything written here. The document explained how far into debt, principally to Lord Shonda of Vespinarr, the lords of Xican had allowed themselves to fall in order to buy these men. It detailed the exact mechanics of how Quai'Shu had stolen dragons and eggs and all the necessary handlers, how he'd built his own eyrie in the desert under the stewardship of his t'varr, Baros Tsen. Red Lin Feyn read slowly and carefully. The theft had been admirably done with precision and care, and whoever had written this clearly thought the same. It left her wondering who that was and whether the lords of Vespinarr had known anything about it.

There followed a single hastily scribbled page on the nature of the monsters themselves. It was a hodgepodge of notes, broken sentences, single words and unanswered questions, irritatingly uncertain and incomplete. Nothing offered any clue as to why her presence had become necessary. Finally came the burning of Dhar Thosis itself, the confessions and accusations of Baros Tsen T'Varr, the reports of the first Elemental Men to arrive, their secret watch over the eyrie barely hours after the Vespinese had seized it, their intervention when it had seemed necessary and why, and the testimonies they had gathered since. Others might have jumped straight to the end, but Lin Feyn was patient and methodical and wouldn't have been here if she was otherwise. Now that she was armed with an understanding of Quai'Shu's grand design and of the monsters he'd brought back, she read over these events with a new mind.

When she finished, she read it again. Not because the words were in any way unclear but simply because once wasn't enough to make herself believe what they were telling her. Soldiers of Xican and a single dragon had destroyed a sea lord's city and palace. They had killed Sea Lord Senxian himself. A hundred ships sunk, perhaps more. Dozens of glasships shattered. The sea titans, the ancient guardians of Dhar Thosis, plucked from the water and dashed against the cliffs. Quai'Shu's kwen and much of his fleet and all of his army vanished out to sea and not yet found. Baros Tsen T'Varr's admission of his own guilt and his astounding accusation that she couldn't ignore.

She read from the beginning a third time, slowly and carefully without skipping a single word. She finished again still without an idea as to why Sea Lord Quai'Shu had set himself to do this thing, nor why Sea Lord Shonda would do what Baros Tsen T'Varr had claimed, nor why the t'varr himself had acted as he had. Madness. Though she knew where the real answer to all those things would lie. Greed. Power. Envy. Fear.

She read through yet again, setting her mind to favour the Vespinese, letting herself imagine them wholly innocent and falsely accused to see how the subtleties behind the words would change. Then once more with Tsen as a callous killer, then as a buffoonish dupe, then with all of them as unwitting puppets of the Elemental Men themselves. Each perspective shed a different light but all, in the end, to little purpose. Every motive remained cloaked in shadow.

The most telling passage of all lay in a few buried words from Baros Tsen T'Varr's own confession. He claimed to have sent an Elemental Man to make it all stop, to bring the dragon back before it carried out its orders and to rein in Shrin Chrias Kwen. Not only had this Elemental Man failed, the killer had himself been killed. Lin Feyn wondered why Baros Tsen would say such a thing if it was a lie and discovered she couldn't find any reason. She shivered then, because an Elemental Man should not fail, and yet here was a story that began with one failure and ended with another and had a third in between. If Tsen's confession was true then Quai'Shu had found something to unbalance the five-hundred-year peace that the Elemental Men had brought with them when they emerged from the Konsidar.

She looked at what she had. Vespinarr, the richest city in the world. A scheme cast over more than a decade, backed and aided by the invincible Elemental Men themselves and yet a creature that could kill them? As she read from the start one last time, she knew that hers had become, briefly, the most powerful voice in the world.

The killer was waiting for her as he'd promised, in the landing fields at the foot of the Silver Mountain by the Visonda Palace of Vespinarr. There were dozens of gondolas and seven glasships tethered there, gold-tinged glass discs slowly rotating as they drew energy from the black enchanter monoliths that ringed the field. Horses and elegant carriages stood waiting while a steady trickle of flying sleds moved back and forth to the Visonda itself. There was even a glass-and-gold carriage shaped like a sailing ship, floating a little off the ground.

'This is how the sea lords and their minions live,' she murmured. 'Swathed in gifts from their enchanters.'

The killer bowed and kept a respectful distance. 'Sea Lord Weir sends his greetings and wishes you luck. The glasship from Tayuna will be here tomorrow.'

'I've read your papers, killer. We will fly this glasship to the Kabulingnor itself. I will require your presence.'

The killer frowned and Red Lin Feyn smiled behind her Arbiter mask. She understood. His first thought would be: *Sea Lord Shonda's kwen, whoever holds that title here with Mai'Choiro indisposed elsewhere, will shoot an uninvited glasship out of the sky*. His next thought would be the realisation of his responsibility to prevent that. The one after would be that she was deliberately provoking a battle of wills that Lord Shonda, possibly the most powerful man alive, must somehow lose.

'How long will it take for us to rise to the top of the mountain?' she asked when he still didn't answer. He'd be right about the battle of wills, if he'd got that far yet. If she couldn't coerce Sea Lord Shonda into line right now then she might as well turn around and go home.

'Not long.'

Not long *enough*, he was telling her. Perhaps she could concede a little. 'I will need some time to prepare.' She drifted to the window and looked outside. They'd left the Dralamut early in the morning. The afternoon was already old, but the summer evenings in the mountains were long. 'I will arrive at dusk,' she said. 'I've heard the Kabulingnor is at its most impressive when the sun sets fire to the distant mountaintops. So yes, I will come at dusk.'

'As you wish, lady.' There was, perhaps, a very slight hint of gratitude in the killer's voice; although she'd given him this little delay not to spare *him* but to spare the men he might have killed to make his point more swiftly. She watched him open his little window, about to vanish without reply, when a malicious demon piped up inside her.

'Don't kill anyone,' she ordered, a moment before he was gone.

Alone, she closed the window behind him and all the little blinds around the gondola so no one would see inside. Modesty in part, but more to keep prying eyes at bay. She opened the chest that the slaves from the Dralamut had loaded aboard, the chest with the false bottom and a secret inside, and took out the glass shards of the Arbiter.

The sun sank. She had no idea when the right time would be to leave so she opened the little shutter door to where the pilot golem sat. It was a short squat clay thing, a creature a little like an inverted urn with stubby little arms and stubbier little legs. They could walk and even talk but they never did. She told it to be at the top of the Silver Mountain where the glasships landed, very shortly before dusk, and left it at that. The glasship began to rise at once, but slowly, very slowly, and long before they arrived she was ready. Dressed. Painted. Red Lin Feyn was no more and the Arbiter of the Dralamut stood in her place. She looked at herself in a mirror and adjusted the glass needles that ran through her hair. It wasn't often she dressed this way, mostly because it was a pain and took an age to get right, but she'd practised it because it was part of the point of who she was.

Once she was finished, once she was safe from prying eyes, she opened the blinds again and looked down. Vespinarr lay beneath her now. Beside the landing fields the Visonda Palace rose up the lower slope of the mountain in layers, fortress-like, with its vast inward-sloping walls broken only in their upper parts by straight rows of many windows and sliced by layers of flat rooftops. The Visonda was built on an outcrop of rock jutting from the base of the mountain. The side facing the city was a large space enclosed by walls from which great open gates led out to the Visonda

Square, while more great gates on the inner side stood ajar and opened to a series of grand stairs, miniature palaces and castles and towers between a gently sloping path that led up to the peak of the outcrop. A quadrangular mass of gilt-canopied buildings packed the little summit so tightly that it seemed a marvel to Red Lin Feyn that none had ever toppled off.

Beneath the walls lay the vastness of the Visonda Square, a plaza of pale grey stone. Dark lines ran in from the corners and the edges, converging on an annulus at the centre pierced by a small spire, the mysterious Azahl Pillar. Further across the city, more gilt canopies loomed like monsters out of the packed narrow streets of the Harub. The Temples of Jokung and the Sun and Moon, where whispers murmured of forbidden gods who still took sacrifice.

She lost sight of individual streets and palaces as the glasship rose higher. Instead, she saw how the city sat at one end of a basin surrounded by snow-covered peaks with the silver-gleaming ribbon of the Yalun Zarang, the 'merry blue', running through the southern quarter and, a few miles to the east, the second river, the Jokun. The swamps to the north glittered in the twilight sun while the gullies of the southern Konsidar beyond fell into shadow and their snow-peppered peaks glowed pink in the sunset. There was a beauty here, an elegant soaring natural grace to the land that the cities on the coast somehow lacked; and she thought she understood for a moment the arrogance of the Vespinese. There was more wealth in Vespinarr than mere silver.

She went back to her chest and took out a glass globe roiling with black cloud. Put her hands on it to soothe the tiny snip of the storm-dark kept trapped within. Sometimes, all alone, she imagined that Feyn Charin himself was trapped there.

'I am ready,' she told it, and looked at herself once more in the mirror. The Arbiter's robe was of firebird feathers stolen from the deep jungles and lava runs of Qeled, feathers that seemed to burn like flames, the deeper darker ones around her feet where the robe flared, then growing lighter in strands that wrapped her body in spirals like the weave of a rope and made her appear a tornado of swirling naked flame. Gold-glass shards hung from her arms and across her chest and tiny sparks of lightning flashed between them. Her hair was piled high and shot through with threads of gold and silver fire. She lifted the headdress off the bed and fitted it carefully in place. Pure white feathers rose behind her now, almost as tall and as broad as her outstretched arms. In the midst of all this fire and light, her face was painted white and black, split straight down the middle, black on the right, white on the left. Her lips were as red as ripe cherries and a second line of red crossed her face from side to side, ear to eyes to ear.

'I am ready,' she said again.

They were reaching the top of the Silver Mountain, crossing the outer wall of the Kabulingnor, twenty paces thick of bland dark stone, and then the inner, painted yellow, wide enough that the lords of the mountains sometimes had chariot races on it when they were bored. Inside these walls rose the twin gold-glass towers of the Ziltak, the place for receiving honoured guests. Deeper in the mountaintop gardens were the marvels of the Chensdong and Polsang Palaces, almost hidden among giant trees. She couldn't see the fabled Golden Quintarch at all. It was said to be the most magnificent of the five palaces of the Kabulingnor but it was also Lord Shonda's innermost court and hardly anyone born outside the walls ever penetrated so far.

Around the Ziltak, Shonda's court had assembled to receive her in the open. Lin Feyn closed the blinds with a thought as the gondola touched the ground. She counted to a hundred and to a hundred again and Red Lin Feyn dropped away. As she stepped outside and let the crowds see her majesty, she became the Arbiter, heart and soul. She lifted her right arm high and to one side, a finger pointing firmly and strongly to the sun. Her left hand rose more slowly to the Vespinese until she saw Shonda in all his finery, here to receive her as he should. She lifted her arm a little higher and then let her finger droop to point at him, and when she spoke, her voice boomed like thunder, strong enough that everyone would hear, so loud that the front ranks of waiting t'varrs and kwens quivered and tried their hardest not to tremble. It was a voice that could be heard across mountains and down the slopes in the city itself. Everywhere throughout the seven worlds in tiny echoes.

'I have followed the path of Feyn Charin. I have crossed worlds. I have bent the storm-dark to my will. I am Red Lin Feyn. I am the Arbiter of the Dralamut and I will be your judge. Shonda of Vespinarr, you are called to my court among those who have cavorted with dragons.'

She held the moment, let the words sink in and the echoes of them ring around the mountains. Then she turned her head and looked away and slowly walked back inside the gondola – slowly because beneath the weight and bulk of the headdress anything else was impossible.

The killer was with her in the air, but no matter. As the ramp closed behind her, she sat and carefully lifted the headdress, put it on the floor and became Red Lin Feyn again. The temptation to throw the blasted thing across the room and kick it was strong. *Loathsome burden.*

'All for that?' the killer asked.

Lin Feyn nodded. 'All for that.' The Arbiter had said what the Arbiter had come to say. There was no need for more. Something had started. Lin Feyn couldn't yet begin to see where it might end, but the Arbiter of the Dralamut wasn't meant to care.

Dragons. The symbol of Vespinarr was a snow lion and three dragons entwined. Some said dragons had lived here once but they were only repeating stories.

23

A Matter of Blood

Liang had a dream. In her dream Belli raced through tunnels of soft light to find her. She saw him stumble and slide and almost fall as he reached her. She was on the floor and she had no idea why, but something was terribly wrong. Everything was sideways. She was in his study and there was something under his desk, a vial lying on its side that must have dropped and rolled there and been lost. She tried to reach it but it was so difficult to make her arm move. She watched it instead, quite certain it would roll away and hide the moment she took her eyes off it. And Belli would want to know. He'd want it back. So she lay still. Watching.

'Li! Flame! No!'

She felt his hands on her, moving her, turning her onto her back. She felt the movement inside her but her skin was numb and she didn't feel his fingers at all. The world shifted suddenly and she wasn't looking at the vial any more but up at blank white stone. She whimpered. The floor, was it? Was she floating and about to fall? Then he was looking over her.

The vial. 'Belli?'

'Hush.' He drew away. He was holding a glass with a pale amber liquid in it. She wanted to warn him, tell him something was wrong, tell him about the vial under the desk before it rolled away and was lost, but her lips wouldn't move. He ran his tongue around the rim of the glass, tasting the amber liquid. Then he screwed up his face and smashed it. Shards rained over the floor and there was a blaze of fury in his eye. He picked one up and came close to her again. 'Live, Li.'

She could barely hear him. Her eyes wouldn't stay focused. He brought the glass shard close to her face. She watched in horror as he cut himself and dipped a finger in his own blood and ran it over her lips. She closed her eyes. The pain was going away and a delicious numb warmth swept through in its place.

'Live, Li,' he said again.

And for a while after that she remembered nothing.

24

The Collar of the Moon

The gondola from Tayuna was every bit as pleasant as the one from Vespinarr, although made of gold instead of the more expensive and ostentatious silver of the mountain lord. Red Lin Feyn watched from her windows as they drifted away from Vespinarr, over the silver cascades and cataracts of the Jokun river on its way to the rebellious desert princes of Hanjaadi and the sea. She watched as the glasship crossed the southern fringes of the Konsidar out into the desert beyond. The desert was dull but she watched that too. She let her mind wander, contemplating the intricacies of power that laced Takei'Tarr like an invisible web. On and on out into the sands and the gravel flats and the bare sculpted stone, and each day the killer came back with hastily written reports and words of his own, telling her everything she should know before she arrived. No, everything she *could* know, except not even that. Everything the killers had found and cared to share. *Chose* to share.

The last was important, she felt sure, and when he came back from his first visit to the eyrie, she knew she was right not wholly to trust his reports. He told her in a carefully calm and measured voice how things were and what to expect, but something had shaken him, and by the time he bowed and begged her leave, she knew it was the dragon though he never told her nor gave her any clue as to why. She couldn't have said what betrayed him. A flicker at the corner of his mouth one time. A slight tone out of place in his voice. The instant of hesitation when she asked him if there was anything else she should know before he'd shaken his head and told her that no, there wasn't. He was hiding something. But the killers were good at hiding things and clever, and she couldn't be sure whether he'd meant to let her know there was a secret he couldn't share or whether it had slipped out to kiss her all on its own. She didn't trust them though, not quite. It wasn't in her nature, and her nature was why she was what she was.

Why would a killer keep a secret from the Arbiter of the Dralamut? Why would he let her see that he had one but not share it? Were there other killers watching them both? They had a hand in this somewhere, far deeper than they cared to show, that much was clear.

No matter.

In time she saw the stain of the storm-dark on the far horizon ahead. She dressed and opened the gondola window. The Elemental Man was waiting for her, a whisper of wind that curled around her robes and then was gone as he appeared three steps behind her, head bowed.

'Without the glasships that tow it, Tsen's eyrie will sink, will it not?' she asked.

'The enchantress Chay-Liang who served Baros Tsen T'Varr claims so. Glasships may lift it higher or drag it down, but without them it slowly returns to float a hundred feet above the ground.'

So yes, without the glasships the eyrie would sink, and so if the worst came to the worst they could simply drop it into the storm-dark and be rid of it. She wondered if Baros Tsen had had the same thought on his mind when he brought the eyrie here in the first place. She wondered too if the dragon would be so easy.

As she reached the edge of the maelstrom, she watched the storm-dark spread out beneath her. Sea Lord Weir had had the windows in his gondola set at the perfect height for his own comfort and he was a tall man. Lin Feyn found herself pressed to them, on tiptoe, craning her neck like a curious child. After a while she made a pile of books and stood on it. Better. Hardly how an Arbiter should behave, but she was alone, and alone she was merely Red Lin Feyn, enchantress and navigator, initiate of Hingwal Taktse and the Dralamut. For an hour she stared out at the swirling black cloud and the sullen purple lightning deep within while the glasship drifted into the storm's heart and to the Godspike that pinned the maelstrom to the desert of Takei'Tarr.

The Elemental Man flitted ahead of her on a sled, a tiny bright speck over the dark vastness of the storm. She wasn't sure why when he could simply become the wind, but she envied him.

Glasships suited her, but here and now she would have joined him, unsheltered from the enormity of everything, the timeless colossal sky overhead, the unfathomable endless depth of the storm-dark, the ancient immensity of the Godspike towering over everything, the constant rush of the wind, the sheer size of space and time all around her making her as small as a speck in the desert. That was how the world truly was and it was good to be reminded now and then. *We are all so insignificant.*

Yes, she envied him but she stayed where she was. The Arbiter of the Dralamut did not cavort through the sky, even if she wanted to. Instead, she closed the blinds and dressed herself as she'd dressed for the lords of Vespinarr, all except for that blasted headdress; and when she was done, she stood half in her majesty and half not, perched on her pile of books, and peered through the window again. When she looked hard, she saw the dark mote of the eyrie beneath six pinpricks of light glittering in the late-afternoon sun. She watched the walls as the glasship drifted closer until she saw the dragon. The killer had warned her above all else about the dragon. He'd told her how big it was but they'd both understood that he could do as much telling as he liked; it was a monster she would have to see with her own eyes. She let the sight of it settle inside her as she floated closer, but it was hard out here in the shadow of the Godspike to be impressed by size. In a place like this everything else amounted to nothing. Perhaps the dragon felt the same? The killer claimed the creatures had been restless things until Tsen had brought his eyrie here, and now they seemed quiet, almost as though entranced by the unfathomable monolith of the desert.

A shadow broke her thoughts. Three other glasships passed above, keeping station with the eyrie. She'd seen more on her approach to the storm-dark, a dozen Vespinese ships keeping pace with the storm's edge. The Vespinese had made quite a little camp down in the dunes, and she thought she might have a use for that. The killers, meanwhile, had counted more than a hundred glasships loitering out in the desert now, many of them Vespinese but many of them not, some from Xican still loyal to Sea Lord Quai'Shu and waiting to see what would happen, a growing few from other cities, come as voyeurs. There would be more of those before long, a gathering of vultures, but she dismissed such things as beneath her concern.

She closed the last blind and painted on her Arbiter's mask. She would make her judgement and return to the Dralamut. What happened after was for the killers, not for her. She lifted the headdress, put it on and roundly cursed it and then sat and waited until she felt the gondola arrive and cease its drifting. Every slave and every soldier of the eyrie would be outside, assembled in the dragon yard to greet her, Vespinese and Xicanese alike, chased from beds and duties and chores to abase themselves. The Arbiter of the Dralamut had come.

As before, she counted to a hundred and then again. When she was quite certain that she was ready, the gondola opened. She stepped delicately down its ramp and let the world see her.

The wind caught her at once. It whipped across the ramp and caught the headdress like a sail, and it took all her strength not to sway and take a step to the side. And at the same time the first thing she saw was the dragon, straight across the yard and perched on its wall directly in front of her. The ramp led straight towards it, so perfectly aligned that she knew someone cleverer than the killers was waiting for her. The dragon gazed at her, eyeball to eyeball across the space between them, at her and through her, its massive armoured head craned forward, the vast sails of its wings spread wide and the rider on its back; and all the men and soldiers, the slaves and kwens and t'varrs and even the killers kneeling between them immediately lost all purpose. A part of her screamed. She let it. Let it scream and scream and keep on screaming as she locked it in a quiet place in her head where it wouldn't be heard.

She looked to her left and right and then tossed two small gold-glass spheres, one to either side. They grew into shimmering golden screens, shielding her from the wind. Her voice was like thunder. 'I have followed the path of Feyn Charin. I have crossed worlds. I have bent the storm-dark to my will. I am Red Lin Feyn. I am the Arbiter of the Dralamut and I will be your judge.'

The force of her voice caught them all. Even the dragon seemed somehow diminished. She felt it looking at her, suddenly curious.

'Mai'Choiro Kwen is relieved of all duties and responsibilities. He will remain as an honoured guest of my court.'

An Elemental Man shifted to stand beside Mai'Choiro before she'd even finished. The killers had known what she'd say for days and she'd told them exactly what they must do. The Elemental Men had said they were her eyes and her armour and her lightning. Well, if that's what they thought then they could work for it. The killer took Mai'Choiro's lightning wand and the black wand that gave him access to almost every gold-glass structure in Vespinarr. She was humiliating him out in the open and in front of everyone. He wouldn't ever forget that. Nor did she care.

'The t'varr Perth Oran. The enchantress Chay-Liang. The slaves Bellepheros and Zafir. Attend me!' She tossed a third gold-glass sphere into the air, paused for a moment to see it zip away towards the dragon, then turned and walked into the gondola and sat with her back to the open ramp, forcing herself not to look at the consequences of what she'd done. With elaborate care she took the white feather headdress off and laid it on the floor beside her. A miscalculation was always a possibility, but there were no screams yet, no roar of fire ...

She glanced at the headdress. It was too hot and heavy to wear for long and quite impossible out in so much wind.

Still no screams, still no fire. Perth Oran T'Varr came nervously up the ramp and pressed his head to the floor beside her. She waved him away, haughty and dismissive, but in truth because she was too distracted.

Still no fire. Her killer appeared next. He bowed. 'Lady, the enchantress Chay-Liang is too weak to come to you. It remains unclear whether she will survive.'

Lin Feyn nodded absently. Yes, yes, poisoned some days ago. But if the enchantress wasn't dead by now then she'd probably live, wouldn't she? 'Did it work, killer?' She had to ask.

'The dragon-rider is coming, lady.'

Red Lin Feyn closed her eyes for a moment and let out a tiny breath. The old slave arrived next, the alchemist, grumbling and complaining at the killer who brought him. The dragon-rider followed last of all, silent and haughty and with a furious scowl dancing over her face. There was no ceremony, no respect – she simply threw herself into a chair and sprawled. As far as Red Lin Feyn could see, she wore nothing more than a long heavy tunic belted around her waist, the clothes of an ordinary slave, but now with a collar of gold-glass around her neck, the last sphere that Red Lin Feyn had tossed into the air after she'd spoken. *That* was what had brought her down from her dragon's back.

'Waiting on the witch?' drawled the rider-slave. 'Oh, she'll live. Grand Master Bellepheros of my Order of the Scales was the best alchemist in the realms before your people took him to be a slave.' The rider looked at the killers at first, not at Lin Feyn, but then her eyes shifted and a boundless fury flared within them. She cocked her head at Red Lin Feyn and tapped the collar. 'Take this off. Now.'

Lin Feyn drew a hand across her face, palm out, fingers splayed, and cast a wall of silence across the table between them. The rest could all talk as much as they liked now and not a sound would come out of them.

'You know my purpose here is the devastation of Dhar Thosis. We will speak of that later, and also of the death of Baros Tsen T'Varr, but first we will speak of dragons. You will do what needs to be done and you will do it without being noticed. If one of you fails then I will cast all three of you, your Scales, your dragons and your eggs into the storm-dark below. I do not need dragons. I do not want dragons.' She gave them a moment to digest that and then went on. 'Perth Oran T'Varr, you will make arrangements for animals to be brought to the eyrie for the smaller dragons to eat. Purchase them from the desert men who trade in the shadow of the Godspike or ship them from Vespinarr or conjure them from your chamber pot, I do not care nor do I wish to know.'

The alchemist slave started forward from his chair. He opened his mouth and got out a good few words before he realised there was no sound coming from between his lips. The Arbiter turned to him. 'You, alchemist, will do whatever Perth Oran T'Varr requires. You will be his slave. You will keep your enchantress mistress alive and ensure she has whatever she needs to do what I require of her, which is to keep the adult dragon compliant, docile and available to me for any purpose I see fit, as and when I desire it.'

The killer next, a little deviation from what she'd told him she had to say. 'The Elemental Men will find the missing dragon and destroy it.'

The killer twitched and then bowed. Lin Feyn turned to Zafir, the one who was always going to be the most difficult. 'You will fly the adult dragon. You will hunt food and water and whatever it requires to sustain it. When you fly, my killers shall fly with you. If you are disobedient to my will then I will end you, summarily and without thought or hesitation.' She leaned forward and tapped her own neck with a finger. The dragon-rider had been clever enough to station herself on the walls for this stupid ceremony so presumably she was clever enough to understand that the collar would kill her whenever Lin Feyn felt the urge. 'That is all. I will summon you again when I require you. You may leave.'

She opened the gondola ramp with a wave of her hand. Perth Oran T'Varr stumbled out as fast as his legs would carry him. The alchemist wasn't much slower and only because his knees clearly troubled him. He looked much more content than the t'varr. Pleased even.

The rider-slave didn't move, which was more or less as expected. Lin Feyn waved the ramp closed, feeling the glasship lift back up off the ground. She met the slave's eye, kept the wall of silence between them for a minute longer as they stared one another down, then finally let it go. 'Speak.'

The rider-slave gave the very slightest tilt of her head. 'Take. This. Off.'

'No.'

'No?' The rider-slave smiled and lightly shook her head. 'Then I will do nothing for you, nor for any other.'

Red Lin Feyn nodded. 'That is your choice to make. You know there is no good end for you here. We can finish this between us here and now if you wish.'

'I am a dragon-queen.'

'I know what you were before you were taken. You have your pride. I acknowledge that matters to you. Hence we do this here, in private.'

The killer vanished and appeared behind Zafir's chair. Lin Feyn placed two fingers in front of her mouth and gently blew over them. The rider-slave's eyes went suddenly wide and her jaw dropped. She gasped and both hands flew to the collar as she choked.

'My killers tell me that when Mai'Choiro Kwen tried to hang

you, your dragon plucked you from the gallows.' Lin Feyn lowered her fingers. The rider-slave shuddered and gulped a lungful of air. Her eyes were murderous. Red Lin Feyn clasped her hands together and bowed in apology. 'I do not yet mean you harm, dragon-queen. I will send men with you when you fly, but you have already killed one Elemental Man, haven't you? So if you do not return, my collar will kill you as the whim takes me. You will both be far away and your dragon will not save you from me. I hope you understand.'

The rider-slave spat. 'Take this off me or kill me here and now.'

Lin Feyn opened the glasship's ramp. They were up in the air again now, only a few hundreds of yards from the eyrie but they might as well have been miles. A howling wind blew in between them, whipping at Lin Feyn's dress and at the rider-slave's tunic. Lin Feyn went to stand at the ramp and looked down to where the vortex of the storm-dark twisted its slow spiral about the Godspike a mile beneath her. The slave Zafir could get up and push her out. If the killer wasn't quick enough to stop her she'd fall and the storm-dark would eat her. Or she'd ride it as her Father of Fathers had done.

'I am daughter of daughters to Feyn Charin himself, first navigator!' she cried over the wind. 'Feyn Charin, who entered the storm-dark of the desert and returned, the only man who ever did. He taught a handful of apprentices how to cross the lesser curtains out to sea, and from that one piece of knowledge everything that we are was built. He never returned to this, dragon-queen. The Elemental Men forced him back to the desert in the end but he would not go into the storm-dark. He refused them. By then he was a good part mad, closeted away in the Dralamut, filled with obsessions – the forbidden Rava and the half-gods and sorcerers who once strode the world before they shattered it. But I've read his words, dragon-queen, and it all came from what he saw in there; and now here it is, laid before us! I have his blood. I've crossed every curtain line of the storm-dark to every realm the sea lords know. I am but halfway through my life but one day I will come here and follow him. I know this as surely as I know the sun will rise each morning.' She reached out her hand towards Zafir. 'So jump, dragon-queen, if that's what you want,' she cried. 'Push me, if you think you can. Let us go together if death is what you so greedily desire, and see how true my Father of Fathers' blood runs! Shall we?'

She waited. Counted out a minute then counted out another, then turned and looked back. The dragon-queen was now sitting straight in her chair, staring right through her. All full of a great deal of murder and wondering what Lin Feyn truly was. Lin Feyn closed the ramp, stepped calmly back to her seat and sat down.

I thought not. But she kept that to herself.

'Take. This. Off.'

'I will not.' Lin Feyn shook her head. 'But if it is because a collar is the sign of a slave, I will change it.' She rose again and came behind Zafir, placing delicate fingers on her neck. As she touched it, the gold-glass began to flow. 'There is a story,' she whispered as she worked, 'that in the times before the Splintering, each of the old gods put a piece of their essence into an object and gave it to their most holy priests. Over time the objects changed hands but they never changed what they were. The sun put his fire and strength and power into a coat of burning mail. The earth put her immutable will into an Adamantine Spear. The moon filled a circlet with thought and transformation and seduction, but, fickle lord of night as he was, he couldn't bring himself to bestow his favour on just one and so split it in two and set them loose on the world together. The lady of the stars, not to be outdone, placed power over spirits in a pair of knives whose golden hafts were carved with a thousand eyes.' The glass oozed up over the rider-slave's neck and around her chin, across her face. 'We Taiytakei are forbidden these stories. To us they are fables. Yet an Adamantine Spear? You held one once. A suit of burning mail? The immortal Sun King of the Dominion wears such a coat. Golden circlets of moonlight? The Ice Witch of Aria claims them as her own.'

Red Lin Feyn stepped away. The gold-glass was a circle around the rider-slave's brow now.

'Fables. Stories. To me they are simply that, but perhaps you might think otherwise. I cannot and would not give you your spear, but you may have a crown, queen of dragons, if that suits you better. If you try to take it off, or if you displease me, it will still burst your skull.' She glanced at the ramp, closed now. 'If you ever prefer the other way, no one will stop you.'

25

A Holy Trust

In a perfect world, Bellepheros thought, he might have moved
some of his laboratory outside to the hatchery and done his alchemy
while watching over the eggs, but the wind put paid to any notion
of that – five minutes in that and only the Great Flame could
know what potions he'd end up with! But still it was sometimes
an irritation having to go all the way back to his laboratory when
he needed a potion in the hatchery, and so he'd taken to keeping
a few things closer to hand at the top of the tunnels where the
Scales lived. He slipped away there now. The eyrie was crowded
with the Vespinese and now the Elemental Men, but the spiral
where the Scales lived remained almost empty. The consequences
of the Hatchling Disease were there for everyone to see and, for
those who'd been here and remembered, Tsen had been ruthless
in keeping the plague suppressed. No one wanted to be anywhere
near Bellepheros's dragon-slaves, and that was fine: the eyrie had
five separate spirals of tunnels and rooms and the Scales had one
entirely to themselves. It gave them far more space than they
needed, and what was an alchemist to make in dozens of empty
rooms where he might work in the sure knowledge he'd not be
disturbed? Mischief, clearly!

He had a sled hidden in one of them, stolen from the Vespinese
on the night of their attack. The Scales had found several when
they'd been clearing the rubble from the ruined hatchery, and
one of them hadn't ever quite made it back in the chaos of the
Elemental Men. In fact he had two sleds, but Perth Oran T'Varr
knew about the second one and Bellepheros made sure to keep it
out in the open where everyone could see it.

The Scales weren't the only the reason the Taiytakei avoided
this part of the eyrie. It stank of death. There were bodies here.
Tsen had started it, feeding the slaves who caught the Hatchling

Disease to Diamond Eye, and somehow it had never quite stopped. Bellepheros hated seeing dragons eating the bodies of the dead even though in most eyries in the dragon-realms men had considered it an honour to feed their dead to the dragons. The Taiytakei saw things differently, but Perth Oran T'Varr was of a practical disposition – he was a t'varr after all – and considered any slaves who had died in the crossfire of the fighting nothing more than useful meat. So, what with one thing and another, Bellepheros had ended up with a larder of dead men. He'd had the Scales gut them so they didn't rot and explode, and Li had months ago placed some sort of enchantment on a couple of the rooms to keep them cold, but the smell had gradually come anyway. It lingered.

Bellepheros went to them now, his larder of the dead, because it was the one place he was sure to be left alone. He shivered and blew on his fingers. The corpses hung from hooks through their wrists, a gaping flap of skin and pasty flesh across their abdomens where their stomachs and intestines had been removed and emptied and replaced again as knotted sacs full of the potions he made to dull the hatchlings. It was a grisly gruesome little room and he hated that it even existed, but after the escaped hatchling had burned his laboratory and destroyed almost all his potions, he'd been glad of his little larder. If nothing else, the rogue dragon had taught him to keep his most precious things scattered in different places.

He pushed through the hanging bodies. Another corpse lay across the floor behind them, one that hadn't been gutted yet, the slave who'd poisoned Li and had tried to kill her Holiness. He stared at the man a while, as he did every time he came here, then turned away. Everyone knew the corpses hanging here had potions for the dragons inside them, but nowadays he kept other things here too. He took what he'd come for out of the open belly of a slave who'd once been one of Tsen's cooks. He'd been a good cook and had liked his food so there was plenty of space inside him. He'd become Bellepheros's favourite place to hide things.

The thought made him shudder. He had a favourite corpse now?

He put a knotted half-dried bladder in his shoulder bag and hurried out, through the hatchery and across the dragon yard to the spiral of tunnels where he and Li had their studies and their workshop and laboratory. Now was a fine time for what he had in mind. Perth Oran T'Varr had already gone below, doubtless off to shout at the lesser t'varrs who served him, who could shout in turn at their kwens, who would then bawl at their men to go and do something about feeding the hatchlings. Li was still sleeping off the poison. The killers would be busy. Her Holiness … He looked up. The gondola had lifted and drifted, out past the rim.

Ah well. Her Holiness and a sorceress. Let them sort it out between them. Kept them both out of his way. After what he'd seen, he couldn't wait any more.

The iron door to his study was closed. The Elemental Men had insisted on putting a guard outside but the iron door was why he'd kept Li here in the first place. That and it was easier than trying to move her. She was in his bed and he was camped in his laboratory.

'Anyone come by?' The guard shook his head. Bellepheros bent and inspected a corner of the door where he'd wedged a piece of leaf against the frame. 'Then you might as well come in.' They'd *said* they were putting a guard on Li, but he hadn't had a single moment to work in peace since she'd been poisoned. Eyes, always eyes watching him. He had a bad feeling that it was about to get a lot, lot worse, and for a moment, inside the sanctuary of his study, everything he'd just seen suddenly hit him all at once. He stood in the middle of the room, then bent double, gasping for breath. He felt sick. The woman was a sorceress! When he'd tried to speak through the web of silence she'd wrought, he'd felt his blood curdle in his veins.

No, he couldn't be sick. He just needed to do this now. Quickly.

The guard was frowning. 'You all right?'

'The Arbiter has come.' That shut him up. Bellepheros shook himself. *No time for trembling now, old man. Later …* Li was on the bed where he'd left her, wrapped in all the blankets he could find. He put a hand on her brow. As far as the watching guard could tell, that was all he ever did, check on her and force a little water into her now and then – he and the guard both took a good swig of it before they fed any to Li – but what he'd forced into Li when he'd found her dying on his floor hadn't been a potion but his blood, pure and strong, and there were consequences to doing a thing like that. The first and most important consequence was that

Li wasn't dead, but there were others. He closed his eyes, reached into his own blood and through it across the bridge he'd made to Chay-Liang. Blood-magic. The terrible temptation every alchemist had to face. He had a hold on her now whether he wanted it or not. He could, if he chose, compel her to his will. He could read her feelings and perhaps even her thoughts. He could make her a slave far more than she'd ever made one of him. Not that he wanted to. Not that the thought didn't appal him. But he could.

The poison in her veins was a villainous one and Li was still fighting off its last claws. Another few hours, maybe another day. He straightened. 'Not long now. If she wakes and I'm not here then you must send someone to find me. Do it straight away. She'll be thirsty. Give her water.'

The Taiytakei smiled. He looked relieved – happy even – but then Bellepheros thought he caught a hint of something else. Something anxious and then a glance at the water jug.

'I'll make sure it's pure,' Bellepheros said. Not that he had any reason to suspect this particular Taiytakei of anything, but still … He forced a smile. 'I have a couple of chores to see to. Actually, no, I can give her something else that might help. Would you mind getting me the decanter of wine from the desk in my laboratory?' He took the bladder from the dead cook out of his bag and poked a tiny hole into it with a scalpel, then squeezed the goo inside into a small clay bowl. It stank, the most noxious smell imaginable. The Taiytakei, who'd come to peer over his shoulder, recoiled.

'Unholy Xibaiya, alchemist! What *is* that?'

Telling him it was the rotting liquefied brain matter of someone who'd once cooked food for them both didn't seem politic. 'It has a particular name but basically it's fermented dragon shit,' he lied, then glanced back and grinned. The soldier had retreated to the door. 'You get used to the smell.'

'You do?'

Not really. Bellepheros coughed and made a face. 'Well …' Out of sight he pricked the heel of his hand with the scalpel and dripped three drops of his own blood into the bowl. 'Could you get the wine?' When the Taiytakei didn't move, Bellepheros let his shoulders slump and gave a little sigh. 'Right.' Yes, yes, the whole tiresome matter of never having a moment alone with Li. Not that he wanted one, but having someone watch everything he did in his own study, he could have done without *that*. He sprinkled a little powdered obsidian into the bowl, dripped in three drops of moonshade and a half a dozen of clove oil. The clove oil didn't actually do anything useful, but he liked the smell of it a whole lot better and it went some way to mask the stink of rotting brain. 'I'll take this to the laboratory and then it can go to the hatchery in a bit. It can stink out there instead of in here.' He forced a smile for the watching guard and stirred the pot until everything was mixed together nicely. 'Right. Wine.' He walked out with his pot. The soldier didn't see the scalpel he took with him, hidden up his sleeve.

He came back without his stinking pot and carrying a silver tray which he set down on the desk. He poured a little wine onto a piece of clean cloth, took the cloth to Li's bed, about to squeeze a little into her mouth, and then stopped and looked at the Taiytakei soldier. The soldier looked back. There were two glasses on the tray. 'A little wine will help her recovery –' Bellepheros grinned '– but perhaps we should do as we do with her water?' He poured a little into each cup and let the soldier choose which one to drink. They raised their glasses to each other. The soldier grinned too as he knocked it back.

'This from old Tsen T'Varr's stock, is it?'

Bellepheros shrugged. 'I don't know. I don't drink much, to be honest. The lady Chay-Liang found it …'

There were several things he might have said or done next but he didn't do any of them because the iron door was still open and now two women in white tunics were standing there, looking nervously inside. Bellepheros sighed. Zafir's slaves. 'What does she want now?'

'Master alchemist.' Myst and Onyx both bowed as though they didn't know what to make of him. He was a slave too, so no better than they were, but then so was their mistress, who almost seemed to run the eyrie sometimes, and Bellepheros was the one person – now that Tsen was gone – that she treated with anything other than contempt. 'Master alchemist, can you come please? Our mistress asks.'

'Tell her to come here,' he snapped. 'I'm in the middle of something.'

They bobbed and bowed and shuffled their feet and didn't go away. 'Lord alchemist, our mistress will not come. But she ... asks kindly for you to attend her. And we beg you, both of us. Please.'

Bellepheros looked at them hard. Zafir sent them now and then with petty errands and asked him odd little questions and sometimes demanded his presence. So far he'd obliged her. This time ... this time he was half-minded to refuse and send them away, but something about them was off. They were worried. They were also the only two people in the eyrie who'd do anything except breathe a great sigh of relief when the Elemental Men finally hanged Zafir, but for the time being he had good reasons to want that day to be a little way away. 'I don't suppose she wants to start hunting the hatchling that burned my laboratory, does she?'

'We are to tell you that she will consider it.'

Bellepheros glanced at Li, at the soldier and at the wine. He took a deep breath. The air stank of cloves and something rotten, but all that could wait a little. 'Very well.' He shrugged an apology at the soldier. 'I won't be long. Keep her safe and let no one enter until I get back.'

The soldier followed him out and closed the door and resumed his post. Bellepheros didn't bother with the leaf this time – *this* time he was quite sure that the soldier would keep Li safe. He followed Myst and Onyx out into the wind and up to the wall where Diamond Eye perched, staring at the Godspike. Zafir lay on the dragon's back, basking in the sun. As Bellepheros approached, she beckoned him to climb and join her. Bellepheros rolled his eyes. Yes, he understood why she wanted him up there, because the Elemental Men couldn't come so close to a dragon without turning back into flesh and bone and so Diamond Eye's back was the safest place for them to talk without being overheard. But really? The ladder flapped and swung in the wind. Heights and open space both made him sick with anxiety, and he was an old man and his knees hated climbing anything at all, even gentle steps. Besides, it wasn't right for an alchemist to sit on the back of a dragon. They did it when they had to but it wasn't how the world was supposed to work. Dragons and alchemists, oil and water.

'Holiness ...' She probably couldn't even hear him from up there over the wind, and even if she could it wouldn't make any difference. He took a deep breath and steeled himself. She'd left space for him to sit in front of her as always, but this time, as soon as he was up, she reached around him and pulled him tight up against her and locked her arms around his waist.

'Holiness ...?'

'Didn't you ever want to fly, alchemist?'

She was already buckled into her harness. He saw it coming a moment before it happened, let out a pained little gasp and closed his eyes with a volley of silent oaths, and then Diamond Eye flared his wings and jumped and he was tipping sideways and the only things stopping him from falling were Zafir's arms wrapped around him. The huge vast emptiness suddenly all around him made him want to scream. He screwed his eyes tight shut and prayed he wouldn't be sick. Couldn't look. Couldn't. And there was nothing to stop him falling except those arms which could let go at any moment ...

Zafir pulled him straight again. He knew they hadn't banked, knew that Diamond Eye was simply gliding straight over the maelstrom of the storm-dark far below them, but his tongue had swollen so much it seemed to fill his mouth, his heart was *thump-thump-thump* against his ribs as if trying to break free, and much of his insides desperately wanted to escape by whatever way they could. Mustering all the will he could find, he righted himself and risked a look, then quickly closed his eyes again. 'Holiness?' He couldn't manage any more than that.

She hissed in his ear. 'This may be the last time I fly alone.'

Diamond Eye began a turn, making slow lazy circles, spiralling lower towards the storm. They passed under the dark belly of the eyrie, lit up now and then by purple flashes of lightning.

'You don't serve me any more, alchemist. You serve them.'

'Holiness, I ...' He stopped as she let him go and shoved him in the back instead. He felt himself slip, screamed and flailed to keep his balance and then she had him again, yelling in his ear over the tearing wind.

'Don't! Don't you dare blow sugar up my arse. Your loyalty is long gone. So be it. You want something from me and I want something from you. Then let us bargain, you and I.' Diamond Eye swooped and Bellepheros let out another howl of terror as he felt the dragon drop away beneath him and his stomach tried to scale his throat and jump out of his mouth. Zafir held him tight. He doubled over and threw up, spattering the dragon's scales and his own robes, and all the while he felt her head pressed against his own, her lips right up to his ear, close enough to brush his skin. 'I have something to show you,' she said. The dragon dived towards the storm then levelled and skimmed its surface in a gentle arc. 'Look down, alchemist.'

He didn't *want* to look down. He didn't want to look anywhere at all and would rather have kept his eyes firmly closed until she either threw him off or took him back, but if he was going to look at anything then he preferred the dark speck of the eyrie high above or the bright looming spire of the Godspike. The evening sun was on it, making it shine with a pale orange fire. It was vast. Huge, as Diamond Eye curved towards it, and so unspeakably tall. When he tried to look up to where it must touch the sky, his eyes kept sliding off it. He tipped sideways.

Zafir shifted with him, easy and assured. Her grip tightened. 'It sucks you in, doesn't it? What is it, alchemist? Do any of them know? It means something to Diamond Eye. I've half a mind to wake him up and ask him.'

'Holiness!' She couldn't hear him though, not a word he said, not over the wind.

'Down, alchemist, I told you to look down!'

He forced himself. The storm-dark lay spread out around them as far as he could see. The emptiness forced its way into him. The sheer size of it seemed to swell inside his lungs, filling them tight so he couldn't breathe. He gasped and squirmed but Zafir still didn't let him go. Dark churning clouds flecked with flashes of purple lightning, just as he'd seen when the Taiytakei had brought him on their ship from Furymouth to Xican and Tuuran had smashed open the shutters on the window in his cabin and shown it to him. The vastness overwhelmed him. The space devoured him. Heights and open spaces. He screamed. Couldn't help himself. 'Stop! Stop! Take me back! I beg you!' A roaring that wasn't the wind filled his ears. He pitched forward. The next thing he knew someone was shaking him, and for one blissful moment he thought it was Li and he'd been sleeping in his bed and it had all been a horrible dream, until Zafir pulled him upright and grabbed his head in her hands.

'I said down, alchemist. The lightning. Look at the lightning!'

He looked at the lightning and whimpered and wailed, eyes watering in the wind. 'What, Holiness? What am I supposed to see? I have crossed the storm-dark as you have! Yes, this is the same. I know that. They all know that! What more must I see? Please take me back!'

'Watch, alchemist. Wait. Patience.'

Bellepheros quietly closed his eyes. Her Holiness was behind him so she couldn't see. Diamond Eye circled. On the back of a dragon with nothing to keep him safe except Zafir, with the storm-dark churning beneath them, every second felt like hours.

A brilliant flash of light made him flinch and blink, bright enough to startle him even with his eyes shut. More purple lightning, only this time it was too bright to have come from inside the maelstrom so it must have come from ...

'Did you see it, alchemist? Did you see?'

Bellepheros took a deep breath and wondered whether Zafir had finally tipped into madness, whether she'd always been slightly mad, whether she was more mad than before or whether this was the same madness and he just happened to be in the way of it. Times like this he understood exactly why Li wanted rid of her and the sooner the better. They'd all been mad in some way or other, the queens of the Silver City, the mistresses of the Pinnacles surrounded by the lost works of the Silver King.

'It came from the eyrie, alchemist. From the *eyrie*!'

Bellepheros nodded. 'Yes!' He hadn't seen anything at all but he supposed she must be right. Lightning from the belly of the eyrie, where flares of purple played back and forth. Lightning to the storm-dark. Was that what she wanted him to see? That the eyrie and the maelstrom were somehow connected?

'They are the same, alchemist.'

Maybe she was right. He tried to forget about being afraid and Zafir's madness and let that idea settle inside him instead, almost grateful for something else to occupy his scattered thoughts. The eyrie and the storm-dark. They were ... what? Talking to each other? Something. Did the Taiytakei know? Presumably they did but perhaps ... Did they ever fly under the eyrie as Zafir had done?

Did they ever see it? What if they didn't? Was there a use to this knowledge?

Diamond Eye was rising now. Zafir pressed her cheek against his again. 'Well? Are they? *Are* they the same?'

'I ... I don't know.'

'Do *they* know?'

'No. I'm not sure they do.' That was a revelation even to him. But no, now he thought about it, he rather thought that the Taiytakei didn't have the first idea.

Zafir's voice dropped to something that was almost a snarl. 'Alchemist, they say that everything that enters the storm-dark is destroyed, that only they have the sorcery to prevent this. What if they're wrong?'

Bellepheros took a few deep breaths. The fear was easing a little, and he was fairly sure now that Zafir didn't mean to pitch him off to fall to his doom, but that didn't stop him from sinking forward as soon she let go of him, from pressing himself into Diamond Eye's scales still sticky with his own vomit and hugging them tight. *What are you trying to say?* But he couldn't open his mouth to speak. He could barely even breathe.

Zafir flew towards the Godspike. Diamond Eye circled it, higher and higher until the eyrie was below them, and then the glasships that carried it, and then the others that floated higher still and on until they were alone in the sky and Bellepheros was gasping for air and his head was thumping for lack of it. 'Now look up,' Zafir hissed.

Bellepheros risked a glimpse. The Godspike rose into deep blue sky, on as far as he could see. He screwed up his face but all he could think of was how he wasn't getting enough air and how his heart was racing and his head felt ready to explode and he thought he might be sick again and, dear Flame, he was surely going to die out here ... 'Holiness! Please! Enough! Let us go back!' He closed his eyes and started to sob. He could feel her shaking. Laughing at him perhaps. His fingers were going numb and his face too. The air was as cold as ice and his robes were too thin, though the heat of the dragon underneath him and Zafir at his back kept him from shivering. 'Please!' he whimpered. 'Holiness, please!'

Diamond Eye arced away from the Godspike and swirled in a

shallow spiral dive for the eyrie. The dragon landed gently and lowered his head to the ground so that when Bellepheros tried to climb down and missed his footing on the ladder because he was shaking so much and crashed instead in a jumble of arms and legs to the eyrie wall, the fall wasn't so great that he broke anything. He lay there for a while, feeling his bruises, drained and spent. Getting up was just too much. Blessed dear solid ground again. He wanted to hug it, to spread himself across it as widely as he could like a man might smear butter over bread, but he didn't get the chance. Zafir jumped down beside him and hauled him to his feet. He was still quivering with cold and fear and he stank of his own puke, but he had enough awareness to see how things had changed between them. Time was, she'd never have stooped to something as menial as helping him up.

She didn't let go. Instead she pulled him close into an embrace and whispered in his ear, 'You want me to hunt your missing dragon. I will give you that.' Then she pulled away, but for a moment she kept a hand on each of his shoulders and looked him in the eye. Standing straight they were exactly the same height, but Bellepheros always felt as though he was the smaller of the two. Zafir's eyes, when she stared for long enough, could set things on fire. 'Make her take it off me.' She tapped the gold-glass circlet around her head. Bellepheros blinked. He hadn't even noticed it until now. Zafir leaned in and kissed him on each cheek and then let him go. The wind pulled at him. He felt hopelessly unsteady. Not that the wind ever changed but his legs weren't working the way they were supposed to today, not now anyway. He staggered and stumbled and then stayed where he was. The wall wasn't tall and it wasn't even steep where it sloped away to the rim, but he simply couldn't move. Too much space everywhere he looked. Too much emptiness. It had drained him. He was spent. Utterly gone.

Zafir laughed, and Myst and Onyx took his arms and helped him as far as the steps to the dragon yard. The rest he managed on his own. When he got back to his study he was still shaking. The door was closed and the Taiytakei guard cocked his head. 'There's an Elemental Man in there now, master alchemist.'

Bellepheros went in anyway. As soon as he opened the door, the smell of cloves and rotten brain hit him like a smack in the face.

The Elemental Man, if he was here at all, was keeping himself invisible. Bellepheros waited a moment to see if he'd appear but the air stayed still, there was no wisp of breeze and no figure materialised out of any corner.

'Look after her,' he muttered and sat down at his desk and poured himself a large glass of wine and knocked it back in one long swallow. Maybe that would help with the shakes. Then he put the glass back on the silver tray, took the wine back to his laboratory and locked it away there, careful because it wasn't just wine any more. The blood he'd dripped into it while no one was watching had made this wine into something else, and now that something else was inside the guard who stood by his door.

The laboratory reeked of cloves. The smell would linger for weeks now and he could thank her Holiness for that. He picked up the offending pot and took it out. On his way back to the hatchery he passed the guard on his door again. 'Keep her safe,' he said. 'Make sure no one does anything to hurt her.'

The guard screwed up his nose and flapped at the air as he nodded. Bellepheros smiled and reached inside himself and through the blood-tainted wine. 'Keep her safe,' he said again, and knew that the soldier would do exactly that because now he had no choice.

Satisfied, he returned to the hatchery and the larder full of corpses and left his clay pot smelling of cloves beside the dead slave who'd poisoned Li, waiting for it to thicken. It hit him then what Zafir had been trying to show him. That the eyrie and the storm-dark *were* somehow connected. That the Godspike was made of the same white stone as the dragon yard and the walls and tunnels and towers and that the Godspike pierced the storm-dark.

She was asking if the eyrie might survive in there. She was asking if they might go home.

26

Abyssal Powders

Chay-Liang opened her eyes. It seemed as though only a moment had passed and yet the whole world had changed around her. She wasn't on the floor but lying in a bed. She was still in Bellepheros's study but it was a lot tidier than she remembered. She supposed that meant he'd finished sorting out the mess from when the hatchling had burned his laboratory and was doing his work there again and not here.

She sniffed. The study smelled of cloves. Her head swirled as soon as she tried to move, but not before she saw a figure watching her from across the room. He stood in the shadows. She couldn't see his face.

'Belli?'

The figure vanished. Perhaps it had only been a shadow, a trick of the light and there hadn't been anyone there at all. She lay back. Nothing exactly hurt but she had no strength and she could barely breathe. Her head was working though, her thinking, and that was what was important. She remembered everything until her eyes had closed, how it had felt, how confused she'd been, the vial under Belli's desk that had seemed to matter so much, but all that urgency was gone now and the confusion with it. Someone had poisoned her. Someone who had access to Baros Tsen T'Varr's cellars. Which narrowed it down to the Elemental Men and probably a dozen of the Vespinese, which was tantamount to not narrowing it down at all, although if the Elemental Men wanted her dead then presumably they had better ways of doing it. Doubtless Mai'Choiro Kwen had been behind it. A better question to ask was why she was still alive.

'Li!'

She turned her head and winced as her eyes blurred. She tried to sit but it was beyond her. Bellepheros hurried to her side. An

Elemental Man in black robes came in after him and then a woman wrapped in shimmering midnight-blue, someone Liang didn't know but who moved all wrong. Stiff and awkward.

Belli's hands were rough and calloused, stained and leathery from years of alchemy. He lifted her head and tenderly propped her up and then yelled at the Elemental Man to go and get some pillows. Liang laughed when he did that, except it ended up as more a wince and a whimper because, damn it, it hurt!

'So typical … of you … to send a killer … for pillows.'

'Never liked them. Let them run errands. How do you feel?'

'Like a dragon hit me.' Liang tried to peer past Belli at the woman, but she'd turned her back and was inspecting the shelves and Belli's book collection, running her fingers down their spines one by one. 'Who's that?'

'If a dragon had hit you then I'd have been cleaning up the mess with a mop and a bucket. You were poisoned.' Bellepheros shook his head. 'And *this* lot were worse than useless. I tucked you up here to keep you away from them and they've been …'

Liang squeezed his hand. The iron door. It made her smile, that look of concern on his face, and she knew he'd kept her here because it was the easiest place to keep an eye on her, the place where he spent the most time, so he could work and be with her both at once. She knew because she'd have done the same. 'Happy about that, were they?' she asked wryly.

'Not particularly, no.' He put on a stern face. 'They were supposed to keep you safe and abjectly failed and, as I pointed out, if it wasn't for me then you'd be dead, and since I'd stuffed you full of my potions they'd best let me take responsibility for whatever happened next. I …' He stopped, suddenly realising what he'd said. 'Oh Li, I'm so sorry.'

'It's funny,' she said, smiling so he knew it didn't matter. 'I was lying on the floor. I don't remember you finding me. I just remember there was a vial under your desk, rolling around down there. It seemed the most important thing in the world. Stupid.'

Bellepheros snorted. 'That? Yes, you were … you were talking about all sorts of things while the poison worked through you.' He shook his head. 'The vial? It's nothing. The potion her Holiness took the night the Vespinese came, when the hatchling broke free.'

'I remember!'

'It came down here to hunt her.' He frowned. 'I keep wondering why it did that.'

'Belli!' Now she was annoyed. 'I *do* remember! It tried to kill me, damn it! And I sent it packing with a few good strokes of lightning, not that anyone seems to have noticed or cared.' But Belli was looking across the room now, distracted by his own thoughts and eyeing the woman who was eyeing his books, deep furrows etched into his face. He shook his head, then turned back and crouched beside her and made a show of putting a hand on her brow to see if she was feverish. He pulled each eyelid back one after the other and peered into her eyes, then stood up again. 'The poison's gone. You'll be fine in a day or so.'

'Who did it? Who?' And had the poison really been meant for her? Or had it been meant for Belli? Perhaps for both of them?

'The slave who brought the wine, but as to who sent him …' The Elemental Man returned with pillows and a sour look. He said nothing, but the way he dropped them on the bed spoke loudly. Belli ignored him as he busied himself sitting her up. 'The same slave who brought the wine went for Zafir with a knife. She took it off him and killed him with it. It wasn't just any knife either. It was one of those the Elemental Men carry. The ones where you can't see the blade.' He glanced over his shoulder at the woman, still browsing, then threw a filthy look at the killer and made a face. 'No one knows where this particular slave came from, of course. He's not one of Tsen's and now he's dead.'

'Mai'Choiro.' But if the same assassin had tried to murder Zafir then perhaps the poison *had* been meant for her … Did someone know what she'd seen?

'Probably.' Belli's voice dropped. 'I may have a way to find out but it needs some thought. It's a, ah … questionable thing to do.' And Liang was about to ask him what he meant by that, but then the woman turned from Belli's books and Belli put a finger to his lips and stepped away.

'How is she, slave?' The woman's voice was quiet but carried the power and command of a sea lord addressing his fleet. 'She seems well enough to talk, at least.'

'Recovering.' Belli touched a finger to Liang's wrist, feeling her pulse. 'The poison is gone. I'm afraid I still don't know what it was. Not something I've encountered before, but that merely means it didn't come from my homeland.' He turned and leaned towards Liang again. 'I kept the bottle though, Li. I've given it to them and kept a bit for myself. We'll find out in time, I promise you.'

'Is her memory affected?'

Liang frowned. 'My memory?' She pulled herself up a little higher, winced and let Bellepheros ease her back down.

'She's weak, Lady Arbiter,' he said. 'She needs rest and to be left alone, but no, her memory shouldn't be affected. No reason to think so.' He gently patted Liang's shoulder. 'A few days and you'll be on your feet and shouting at me about her Holiness again. Although I think you'll like what the lady Arbiter has done to her.' Then he leaned over and whispered in her ear so quietly that she could barely hear. 'You have my blood in you now, Li. It will help you in other ways. The next time anyone poisons you, remember me.'

He withdrew, the woman took his place and Liang saw what was strange about her. Her face was painted, half black and half white. She had gold-glass shards crossed upon her chest, sparking and glittering over dark silk. 'I know who you are. You're our judge sent from the Dralamut.'

The Arbiter tapped Bellepheros on the arm. 'You may go now, alchemist, but not far if you please. Be about your work.' She didn't wait for him to leave but drew a piece of gold-glass from her sleeve. She shaped it into a disc that hovered in the air beside her, pushed it gently to Liang's side and sat on it. She smiled. It might have been a friendly smile but the painted mask made it alien and unsettling. 'What did he whisper in your ear, Chay-Liang?'

'That I have his blood in me and that it will help me in other ways. That's where his magic lies. In his blood.'

'Help you in *what* ways, enchantress?'

Liang shrugged. 'I don't know. He didn't say.' She glanced nervously past the Arbiter to Belli as he walked out the door but he didn't look back. He trusted this woman then.

'And earlier, when you both thought I wasn't looking. He has a secret he's keeping from me about you. What is it?'

'I think ...' Liang started to laugh – which still hurt – and felt her cheeks burn at the same time. 'Lady, I think he's uncommonly fond of me for a slave.'

'And you uncommonly so for a mistress.' The Arbiter snorted. '*That* secret is none of my concern, although calling it a secret is a bit like calling the Godspike small, which it simply isn't.' She tried a smile again and it still didn't work. 'I mean the other secret: he knows something about who poisoned you. What is it?'

'He didn't say.' Liang closed her eyes. She had no idea what Belli had meant and now she was glad she hadn't asked because it meant she could be truthful and yet not betray him. 'I suppose he thinks he's found a clue.'

'Tell him to share it. I will let him help if it suits me and you can tell him that too. When I'm done here then you can all poison and burn each other as much as you like. While I stay, it stops.' She smiled again but it didn't touch her eyes.

'I will tell him, lady.'

The Arbiter's voice changed abruptly. Suddenly they weren't master and servant, with the Arbiter giving the orders and Liang meekly compliant, suddenly they were old friends sharing their little guilts and confidences. It was a subtle change and yet complete, as though the Arbiter had quietly shifted into an entirely other person. 'I was an enchantress once,' she said. 'Since I'm a navigator, you know that. I learned my craft at Hingwal Taktse as you did. And yes, your suspicions are right: that does make me Vespinese. Ironic that I should be Arbiter when this happens and my own people come under question. Is that why they did it, if they did anything at all? Did they think they might sway me? I know you learned some of your craft in Khalishtor too. I'm sure it was very different.' She frowned. 'May I ask you, what is that smell?'

Liang coughed – it *still* hurt – and managed to lifted herself so she was almost upright at last. 'Cloves, lady.'

'Cloves? Are we in a kitchen?' The Arbiter's eyes glittered and little wrinkles formed at the corners.

'Alchemy.' Liang smiled back. 'I don't claim to understand it. I am Chay-Liang.'

'I know. And I am Arbiter Red Lin Feyn, but you already knew that too. I'm glad to find you alive.'

Liang met her eyes, watching her steadily. They were

unusual eyes for a Taiytakei, somewhere between lavender and violet. 'Lady, I'm certain that Lord Shonda is a very clever man, as clever as he is rich and powerful. But he knows the Arbiter of the Dralamut is above such things. I doubt it even crossed his mind.' She paused, gauging the Arbiter's face for any reaction and seeing nothing. 'I can't speak for his character because I've never met him. Mai'Choiro Kwen, whom I *have* met, is a reprehensible insect who probably thinks he can buy you with some pretty beads just as he thinks he can kill me with wine that has turned a little.'

'Ah.' The Arbiter smiled a little more. 'So you believe it was Mai'Choiro Kwen who poisoned you?'

'Yes.'

'Why would he do that?'

'To silence me.'

The smile faded. The Arbiter cocked her head. 'And why would he want to do *that*? What would you be saying?'

'I would be saying that I heard him tell the rider-slave where to fly and what to do. That he detailed to her the defences of Dhar Thosis. That he gave precise instructions for the burning and slaughter of another sea lord's city.'

The Arbiter widened her eyes in mock surprise. 'My, my. When you have your strength you shall tell me more.' She cocked her head. 'But how did he know that you would say these things? Were you there when he said them?'

'Yes, Lady Arbiter, I was.'

'And he knew it and said them anyway?' The frown was real this time.

'It was done in Baros Tsen T'Varr's gondola. We had removed the pilot golem and I was hiding in its place. There was an Elemental Man too, but he had become air. Mai'Choiro had no idea he was overheard.'

'That sounds a lot like a trap, Chay-Liang.'

'Because that's exactly what it was, lady.'

The Arbiter took a deep breath and let it out slowly. 'Then why, Chay-Liang of Khalishtor, if you were hidden and he didn't know you were there, would he want you dead? Who did you tell?'

For a moment Liang's thoughts all crashed into each other. She'd been ready to let it out, every bit of it, word for word as well as she could remember. She shook her head. 'Tsen knew. And Belli. I told Belli.'

'Just him?'

She nodded.

'No one else? Are you quite sure?'

'Quite sure.' Her voice was a whisper. Nothing made sense any more. 'Oh, and one of your Elemental Men when they came.'

'I see.' The Arbiter nodded and looked thoughtful for a moment. 'One of my killers. Who should then have told me and yet I have heard nothing of this.' She took a deep breath and wriggled on the gold-glass disc, settling herself. 'So be it. Perhaps we should do this now if you have the strength. All of it, if you please, from start to finish leaving no part out. Word for word if you can, who said what and to whom concerning the burning of Dhar Thosis.' She took Liang's hand for a moment. 'Once we're done, no one will have cause to poison you again.'

So Liang described how she'd hidden, what she'd heard Mai'Choiro Kwen say to the rider-slave, what Tsen had said to Zafir and what Tsen had said to the Watcher when the Kwen had gone, sending the Elemental Man to put an end to it before it could start. She felt as though she talked for hours and the Arbiter kept asking her to go back, back, always back to things that had happened before. Shonda's visit, when the Vespinese had provoked the dragon by throwing lightning at it and the rider-slave had saved Shonda from being burned. Vey Rin T'Varr and his jade raven. Shrin Chrias Kwen and his hatred of Zafir and his rivalry with Tsen to be the next sea lord of Xican. As much as she could remember. She could see the picture the Arbiter was drawing out of her. Tsen's hunger to humble and humiliate the Vespinese who wanted his dragons. How he'd tried to string them and wrap them and tangle them in their own schemes. Was it a sense of justice that had driven him or simply a desire to be free of the debt Xican owed them? She didn't know, and now that Tsen was dead they never would. The Arbiter moved to the aftermath, to Tsen vanishing away to Dhar Thosis and what Liang had done while he was gone – or perhaps more to the point, what she *hadn't* done; the coming of the Vespinese and the failed hanging of Zafir, the Elemental Men; and finally her own confession, after it was all done, that she'd been present when Mai'Choiro Kwen had given Zafir her orders. By then Liang was too tired to even remember what she said.

'Do you notice,' whispered the Arbiter, 'how everything revolves around the rider-slave? You see how she chooses who lives and who dies?' The Arbiter smiled then, almost in admiration. 'And you all call her a slave.'

'I would have hanged her months ago,' murmured Liang.

She didn't notice when the Arbiter left, only that Red Lin Feyn was suddenly gone and that the light in her room had changed to the moonlight of the small hours. She must have fallen asleep, probably in the middle of answering a question. Hardly appropriate, but she struggled to feel any guilt. Arbiters, when they convened their courts at all, did so in the Dralamut, and mostly concerned themselves with arcane disputes about trade entitlements and access to storm-dark lines. For the most part the sea lords kept their arguments quiet or else settled them in other realms where the Arbiter and the Elemental Men didn't see and didn't care. That was how it had been for a hundred years and more.

'Li? Are you awake?'

She started and sat up. Through the quiet moonlight glow of the walls, Belli was keeping watch over her – but instead of sitting beside her bed, he was hunched in the shadows in a far corner. He shook his hand and a light glowed between his fingers. He came closer. The smell of cloves was on him. The room reeked of it, stronger than she remembered.

'Do you feel better now?'

'I ...' Liang stretched and rolled her feet off the bed and sat up. 'Actually I do.' She stretched again. The aches and the fatigue had gone, almost as if they'd never been.

'The blood.' He came and stood over her. 'Did you tell her?'

'I told her everything, Belli. If it was Mai'Choiro Kwen who sent the poison, why did he do it? How did he know I was there? Belli, I never told anyone at all except you and one of her killers.'

The alchemist set down his lamp and stood over her for a moment, a silent shape in the gloom. He sounded subdued, almost hesitant.

'Belli? Is something wrong?'

'If you can stomach it then I have something to show you.' He paused and then picked up the lamp again and looked about, nervous as a thieving child. 'Are we alone? Can you tell?'

The iron door was closed. Other than that she had no idea. 'Isn't there a guard outside?'

'I convinced him to let me in and leave us be.' Something about the way he spoke sounded off. 'Actually I needed his help.' He came to her and took her hand. 'I need you to put mistress and slave aside for a moment, Li. Do you trust me?'

'Trust you?' She brushed his hand away. 'I did until now. What have you done, Belli?'

'Nothing yet. But it's what I could do. I never told you …' He trailed off.

'Told me what?'

He didn't answer but walked off into the shadows. 'Come.'

She took a few steps towards him and stopped. A hand flew to her mouth. There was a body lying face down flat on the floor against the far wall. When he put the lamp down beside it, she saw it was the slave who'd brought the poisoned wine. The dead man had a huge gouge in his back and his tattered tunic was covered in dried blood, presumably where Zafir had stabbed him. Liang jumped back. 'What's he doing here? How did you get him here?'

'I … I convinced the guard to help me.' She couldn't see his face but she could hear the darkness in his voice. 'Li, there are things we learn as alchemists. Knowledge we swear not to use but learn nevertheless. There are things I can do that I've not told you. I'm afraid you're going to start to feel that now.'

'What do you mean?' He was scaring her.

'You have my blood in you. It is a connection between us. I will know where you are if I choose to look for you. I will know how you feel. It may work a little the other way sometimes. I promise I will never pry. I only did it to save you from the poison.'

The pain in his voice at least was honest. She closed her eyes. 'Very well, Belli. I trust you.' Because in the end, yes, she did.

He looked around the room and bared his teeth the way he did when he was anxious and uncertain. 'If I'm wrong and there are hidden eyes here to watch us, watch us well. You will not like what you see but watch to the end and listen.' He looked at Liang and his face seemed haunted. 'Li, you won't like this either.' He rolled the dead man over and lifted him so he was sitting against the wall and then opened the dead man's mouth and upended a thimble of black treacle-like ooze over the dead lips until it fell in one sticky gobbet onto the dead man's tongue.

Liang took another step away. She'd never seen Belli like this. Anxious snakes squirmed inside her. 'What are you doing?'

'All the alchemy I do with dragons is done with blood, theirs and mine. Everything becomes a matter of blood in the end.' Bellepheros waited another moment and then crouched in front of the dead man. 'Hello, corpse,' he whispered as its head suddenly twitched.

Liang jumped away, shaking her head, crying out, 'No! No no no!'

The dead man's gummy eyes opened one after the other. His lips parted and a quiet moan eased between them. Liang backed further away. 'No! Belli! What have you done?'

'He will tell you.' The alchemist's voice was a hoarse whisper. 'Ask him, Li. Ask him who put the poison in our wine. Ask him who told him to do it. Ask him who tried to murder you. Ask him and he will tell you everything.'

Even as something broke between them, she knew he was doing it for her. She knew that, just as she knew that she could never look at him the same way ever again.

27

Orders

Back in her gondola, Red Lin Feyn pored over what she'd heard and picked it apart, sorting fact from opinion, evidence from circumstance. She found she was inclined to believe the enchantress. Nothing about Chay-Liang struck her as deceptive, and she'd grown exceptionally good at knowing when she was being deceived. It was odd then that the enchantress claimed to have told the gist of her story to a killer and yet none of her killers had thought fit to relay it. Remiss to the point of treason.

She sighed. The killers were hiding things. So be it. She would sit in her gondola and hold her court, and one by one they would stand before her. All of them. She was the Arbiter of the Dralamut, with power of life and death over everyone and anyone until the question put before her was resolved, and the Vespinese needed to understand this with a clarity to put the waters of every mountain stream in the Konsidar to shame. So did the Elemental Men. She snapped her fingers. Two of the killers materialised beside her and bowed. 'Fill this table with food,' she told them. 'Things that may sit here a while. We begin.'

Mai'Choiro Kwen came first. Lin Feyn asked her questions and listened to what he said. She'd half-expected lies, for Mai'Choiro to protest his own meek innocence and for the blame to be placed squarely on Baros Tsen T'Varr, but instead he admitted freely everything that the enchantress claimed. Yes, he'd given the rider-slave her orders. Yes, he'd told her exactly what to do and how the city's defences lay and in what order she must subdue them. Yes, yes and yes. But as to why? Because Baros Tsen T'Varr had threatened him with the most dire and terrible death if he didn't reveal all he knew of Dhar Thosis – murdered under the ground and his body left in an unmarked cave. He'd spoken under duress, and there was no order given to burn the city. He'd balked at that.

Lies. Some of it. Not all, but someone had reached him. Lin Feyn watched his eyes as he spoke, and his hands and his knuckles, his brow and the way, just sometimes, his upper lip tightened as if trying to pull his nose to cover his mouth. He had a bitterness to him and an anger but not much fear. He knew he was doomed but he was trying to save something and she wondered who or what and why. She played with him a while, seeing if she could tease it out of him, but no. Eventually she let him go. By then it was dark and so she busied herself writing notes on everything she'd heard and sorting them into piles. When she still couldn't sleep, she left the gondola and walked the eyrie walls, looking down at the storm-dark and then up at the dim gleam of the Godspike, at its monumental reach disappearing up among the stars. Everything changed at night, everything except the wind which still howled across the walls. The white stone of the empty dragon yard turned silvery-grey while every shadow seemed blurred and restless as if tossing in dream-filled sleep, about to awake and race away into the night. She was alone except for the two killers who drifted through the air around her, unseen. She felt the Godspike wanting to crush her with its size, the storm-dark calling out, luring her towards it, begging her to try and bend it to her will. *Charin's daughter of daughters ...* Where no one would see, she smiled and wagged her finger at it.

One day.

She took her time circling the walls, gazing up at the bright glitter of the glasships above, counting them, counting the stars, looking to see if they were the same. Maybe tomorrow she'd call only a few to be questioned and then fly her own glasship around the rim of the storm-dark and look at the lesser monoliths that bound it. She might examine the one that was cracked. Others kept watch on it, documented and recorded the slow creep of the storm-dark out of its cage and wrung their hands without the first notion of what to do or what it meant, but it would be interesting to see it for herself.

She'd come out into the night half-dressed. Not as the Arbiter, because the winds out here would catch her firebird robes and the headdress like a pair of sails and whisk her off into the sky. She might raise a shell of glass around her, but even the Arbiter of the

Dralamut had no power over the wind. Tonight she was Red Lin Feyn, nothing more. Apart from her and the killers who flitted around her, the only other living things up here in the night were the dragon and the slaves who slept at its side.

Her walking was taking her towards them. The dragon had already turned to watch, letting her know she was seen. In the moonlight its golden-red scales were silvery black. She stopped at what she thought was a properly respectful distance. 'I mean you no harm tonight, nor your mistress,' she told it. As far as she knew, the creature couldn't understand her and she was wasting her time. It seemed a harmless gesture nonetheless.

The dragon cocked its head and then looked away as though losing interest.

Curious.

She walked on, wary now. Behind her a killer became flesh. 'Lady, we cannot protect you from the monster.'

'Nor could you protect me from it when I came, nor can you protect me from it in the morning. So tell me, killer, what difference does it make? The creature can move, you know. No.' She waved him away. 'I make my own protection.'

The killer looked unhappy. 'We will be close, lady.' He furrowed his brow a little as he returned to the air, as if concentrating hard. As if it was an effort.

Also curious.

She found herself wondering to which killer Chay-Liang had told her secret, and the seed of an idea appeared in her thoughts. She walked on, faster, until she was at the dragon's side by the gold-glass shelter Chay-Liang had made for the rider-slave and the two girls who served her. She tapped on it and then tapped on it again when no one woke. When still no one moved, she crawled inside and touched the rider-slave to shake her, and in that moment Zafir had a knife in her hand and leaped with such speed that she had the tip at Lin Feyn's throat in a blink.

They stopped, both of them, the point of the knife pressed to Lin Feyn's skin, her own fingers halfway to her mouth, ready to blow and crush the rider-slave's skull. Her killers, she noted, were conspicuously not here and not doing what they were supposed to do.

'I could cut your throat,' hissed Zafir.

'Really?' Red Lin Feyn met her stare. 'Are you sure? If you *are* sure, why don't you? *I* am sure you will not.' She let her hands fall to her sides.

'Take this thing off me.'

Red Lin Feyn smiled back at her. 'No. Because if I did that, then you *would* cut my throat to make sure I couldn't put it back on again.'

Zafir snarled. The knife flicked across Lin Feyn's skin. She gasped, thinking for a moment that the rider-slave had called her bluff, but no, that wasn't the look in the slave's eyes. Sullen resentful anger, not vicious glee. Zafir had marked her, that was all.

One of her killers appeared at the entrance, red-faced and sweating. 'Lady—' Red Lin Feyn slapped the palm of her hand against the air in front of her. The killer flew backwards, hurled away with enough force to kill a normal man.

'You should leave us be,' she called after him, 'since you clearly cannot be of use. We will have words about this in the morning.' She smiled at Zafir. 'See. We are alone.' Although of course they weren't. Both killers would be lurking silently as the air around them. Or they should be.

'I wear your mark, you wear mine.' The rider-slave sneered. She sat back and put the knife away. 'Well? Was that worth it?'

Through the gold-glass, the dragon never moved, never flinched. *You see? You know, don't you? You know I don't want to hurt you, not today.* Red Lin Feyn touched a hand to her neck. The cut was a deep one. There was going to be a lot of blood and there wasn't much she could do about it. The killers would be mortified and so they should be. *We cannot protect you from the monster?* Perhaps next time they might be a little more specific as to which monster they meant.

'Tell me what I want to know, dragon-queen.'

Zafir cocked her head. 'If I do that then I have nothing left and you'll hang me. Or at least you'll try.'

'Mai'Choiro has already confessed.' Blood from her neck was running down her shoulder now, turning tacky and starting to itch. She looked about the tiny shelter for something she could use to wrap the wound. 'It *is* true though: if you have nothing to tell me then I have no use for you, dragon-queen.'

Zafir shook with bitter laughter. 'Hear it then.'

Lin Feyn listened to Zafir's version with polite patience and found nothing to contradict what the enchantress had said. The rider-slave left bits out but nothing that mattered, simply the things she didn't find interesting enough to remember. The aftermath in Dhar Thosis was there for all to see, those who cared to look. The exact hows and whos were unimportant. She'd never unravel which soldier had done what to whom even if she stayed at it for years, and it simply didn't matter. Slaves weren't punished for obedience to their masters' orders and soldiers weren't punished for what their kwens commanded them to do, and those were the laws by which all Taiytakei lived. She asked anyway. Thoroughness demanded it and sometimes one found the unexpected amid the simple and the mundane.

'Did Tsen try to stop you, after you flew?'

Zafir laughed. 'You mean did he send an Elemental Man to kill me?' She sounded gleeful but then her voice changed and she became hesitant, a little distant, as if remembering something she preferred to forget. 'Yes. He did.'

'I'd like to know why he failed.' That was the key.

The rider-slave smiled ruefully. With the twitch of a finger Red Lin Feyn called lightning from the shards that crossed her chest. It arced between her fingers. It made a pretty light, she thought.

Zafir's look was scornful. 'Really?'

'The Arbiter is not your friend, slave, but nor is she your enemy.' Lin Feyn let the lightning fade. 'I will have the truth from every man and woman who comes before me, slave or sea lord. I will treat them all the same and I will not punish a slave who steadfastly obeyed her master, for that is what is expected of a slave. Others might and very probably will, but not the Arbiter of the Dralamut. Do you hear? That's all the hope I have for you. Why did Baros Tsen's killer not stop you?'

The rider-slave pursed her lips. Red Lin Feyn saw her weighing up the advantages of keeping her mouth closed no matter what against the trouble she might unleash by speaking of it. 'He tried.' She shook her head. 'The detail doesn't matter. The Watcher. He was there. He heard Baros Tsen and Mai'Choiro, every word, and he made that much clear to me. But who was I to disobey my master? And the Watcher was *not* my master.' She spoke with a deep and bitter disdain, took a long breath, paused and waited, weighing things again, then snorted contemptuously. 'I don't believe in your hope or your mercy, but here's the thing you want to know: he came to kill me, and so Diamond Eye stamped him into the ground, and as it happened I saw him try to change and I saw him fail. Diamond Eye made his magic not work and the killer knew how it might go before he came for me. I saw that in him. He was afraid of my dragon. They all are. They'd kill me if they could because of that fear and so I sleep where I do and Diamond Eye watches over me. That's why your killers couldn't stop me putting a knife to you. They were supposed to, weren't they? That's what they're for?'

Red Lin Feyn kept her face perfectly calm. 'Do you believe Baros Tsen sent him?'

The rider-slave shrugged. Lin Feyn watched her face, watched the play of emotion there, the understanding. Yes, she knew that Tsen had never meant her to burn Dhar Thosis. She'd done it anyway. That was what condemned her.

Red Lin Feyn left then and continued her walk until she'd trod the length of the eyrie walls and then went back to her gondola to dress the wound that the dragon-slave had given her, shooing away the killers whenever they came close and banning them from her presence. Alone, she looked up at the carved silver dragons over what had once been Mai'Choiro Kwen's bed and at the jade and emerald lions that frolicked around them, trying to put it all together. The rider-slave was an enigma of self-destruction but her story of the killer … And a killer had heard Chay-Liang's claims and yet *she* had not.

When she found it was dawn and that she was still awake, she dressed as the Arbiter and summoned the alchemist. He had nothing useful to add over the burning of Dhar Thosis but something important had changed in the night. She could read it from him. A suspicion proven true. Evidence uncovered. Something very wrong. Lin Feyn let him talk about Tsen for a while and then asked the questions that actually mattered, about dragons and alchemists and Elemental Men. When she was done with him, she closed the doors to her court and turned to the killers who loitered in the air around her.

'So dragons make you weak then, do they? They make you useless.'

They didn't answer, but the tone of their silence gave them away.

In a blistering fury Zafir dressed for war. She clutched at the circlet around her head. Rage had been building from the day she'd come back from Dhar Thosis and now it needed release. Something. Anything. The sun was setting and dragons didn't like to fly at night and she'd already taken Diamond Eye to hunt today but it wasn't enough and she needed to fly again. *Needed* it. The infernal enchanted glass around her head gnawed at her. The witch-Arbiter had caged her and she couldn't stand it. When there was no hope any more then she would take the Arbiter in Diamond Eye's claws, their lives wrapped together tight as wet silk. But not yet.

Find the dragon. The one that is far. Go!

Diamond Eye understood. She felt him surge with glee as he launched himself from the eyrie rim. He was fast in this realm, faster than he'd ever been in the world from which they'd come.

Tuuran gaped as the hatchling stared at him across the darkness and opened its mouth. Bloody marvellous, this was. With his axes and his shield and the dragon-scale armour of an Adamantine Man, he might have had a go at a hatchling. Oh, and also not being in a cage would have helped. As things were, there wasn't much he could do. He lurched to grab one of the other slaves and use him as a shield against the flames and then stopped. *That* wouldn't do him any good either.

The dragon had stopped too. Its mouth hung open, fire still gathered in its throat.

'Come on then, dragon! Do it!'

Other slaves were waking. Screaming. Shouting. For another long second the hatchling didn't move, then it turned suddenly away and spread its wings and no fire came after all.

You are lucky, little one. She comes for you.

*

Diamond Eye was burning hot. The heat of him reached through the saddle. It scorched the air Zafir breathed and warmed her even through the dragon-scale of her armour. How the Elemental Men behind her weren't being cooked alive she didn't know and didn't care. The hatchling was close, that was what mattered. The sun had set behind them, the moon and darkness had risen, but Bellepheros's dragon was near.

Other things were near too. Diamond Eye sensed them but he had no idea what they were. Strange colossal things. Old things that tried to reach through the fog of alchemy that ruined every thought to touch some ancient memory. She'd felt him like this in Dhar Thosis when the Adamantine Man and his strange little friend had come and stood before her. The other one. In flashes now and then, Diamond Eye thought he knew him.

The hatchling. She had to keep reminding him why he was here. *Find it and kill it.*

Obediently Diamond Eye sharpened his eyes. He tucked in his wings and arrowed for the ground.

There was no warning when the second dragon came. Tuuran was still staring at the space where the hatchling had been when the monster dropped out of the sky like a fallen star and hit the ground with a crash that shook the earth, wings stretched out. Instinct made Tuuran throw himself flat because every Adamantine Man knew what came next from those flared-out wings. As the dragon shrieked and the ground quivered, the wind picked up man and beast alike and threw them aside. Those slaves still lying down rolled and tumbled, but the ones who'd stood up to scream at the sight of the little dragon now flew like dolls, smashed into the bars of their cages, shattering man and wood alike. Tuuran lay still, listening to his bones and his bruises before he even tried to move, waiting to see what was broken and what the dragon would do. Feed, he supposed, but it didn't. It jumped to the edge of the abyss and dived, shrieking challenges into the depthless darkness.

A lot of bruises. No broken bones. And just for a bit, no dragons.

Best be getting on then, because at least one of them would surely come back. He picked up one of the shattered wooden staves that had once been part of his cage and looked at it. Sheared off nice and sharp. A good enough spear in a pinch.

Zafir glimpsed the hatchling. Its flesh wasn't the same as the hatchling she'd seen on the slave ship that had taken her from Furymouth but Diamond Eye knew its soul. *You.*

The hatchling knew her too. It filled with an eager hunger, the thrill of the chase.

You gave me the Statue Plague. I will kill you.

She felt the hatchling laugh at her challenge and then caught the flash of a face as Diamond Eye smashed into the ground and the hatchling darted away. The Adamantine Man. The one from Dhar Thosis. He was here. The hatchling's thoughts surged with anger. Diamond Eye powered into the air again, hurling himself after the other dragon. He revelled in her glee, her hunger. The hatchling had given itself away.

And yet ... a moment of hesitation. Only a moment, but as she thought of the Adamantine Man and what he'd meant, of the one great thing he'd done for her, she wondered: should she let the hatchling go? Should she find the Adamantine Man instead? He was a slave here. A favour returned ...

The hatchling threw itself into the abyss. Zafir swore and threw the Adamantine Man aside, forgotten for now but not for ever. The hatchling had tried to ruin her and then it had tried to kill her, and she would have a price in blood for that. The Adamantine Man could look after his own skin a while longer. She could come back another time.

Kill my flesh and I will return again.

Then I will find you again and I will force the potions of my alchemists down your throat!

The hatchling dived deeper into the crack in the earth. Zafir felt its rage, how it burned to turn on her and tear her to shreds and scatter her far and wide, and she threw its fury straight back, tenfold stronger. Diamond Eye screamed in its wake, pouring flame to light their way. Fire streamed over her, scorching the harness, washing over the gold-glass of her visor, her helm, her armour, the heat held back by the dragon-scale underneath. The abyss went on, bottomless, all the way to Xibaiya, and Diamond Eye heard the distant ghosts of the dead deep beneath the earth yet strangely close and so Zafir heard them too. Steps and terraces flashed past, etched into the chasm's sides, some lit by clusters of torches, others barren and empty. The air grew thick. Zafir's ears popped and clicked.

We all come back. One after another, we awaken.

The chasm narrowed. She had no idea how deep they were. Three miles? Four? The air was as thick as treacle, far beneath the sands of the desert and close to something old and terrible, but Diamond Eye was a dragon as Zafir was a dragon-queen, slaves to hunger and fury, strangers to caution and fear. A stone arch whistled past. The hatchling flared its wings to check its fall and shot sideways. Zafir felt her bones bend as Diamond Eye followed. Another arch and then another, and then they were in a maze of them where the chasm walls narrowed further still. Diamond Eye's wing clipped one. His lashing tail smashed against another, using it to lever himself into a turn, shattering the stone so it fell in colossal pieces the size of the dragon itself. The hatchling darted and wove between them. Slower than the monster war-dragon she rode but nimble.

Little one, I am not for you today.

The force of the wind pulled and tugged at her. The roar of it screamed in her ears. They were all she knew amid the hunger and the fury and the inexhaustible raging need. Diamond Eye was holding back. She felt it. Holding back to spare her own fragile bones. And then the dragon abruptly slowed and the hatchling pulled away and vanished into the darkness, and Zafir found the tugging and pulling and the roar in her ears was more than the wind. An Elemental Man was wrapped around her, one arm locked about her chest, the other tearing at her head, screaming at her to stop.

'Enough, slave! Enough!'

They were afraid. Truly, properly afraid.

Confusion and chaos were always an escaping slave's best friends, Tuuran reckoned, and there was certainly plenty of that. Many in the camp had seen the dragon, and those who hadn't only hadn't because they'd been sleeping. The whole place had been knocked flat by the storm wind of its landing. Men reeled everywhere, lying on the ground, running this way and that, the way men always did when a dragon came.

But not him. He ran a few paces and stopped. The dragon had gone over the edge of the abyss. Dull glimmers of flame lit up the far cliff, quickly diminishing. And last he'd heard, that was where Crazy had gone and so that was where he was going too – but not before he had a few things to take with him, and so he ran first into the heart of the camp, not far away. The first slaver he saw looked at him blankly, all the wits driven from him. Tuuran punched him in the gut. As the slaver doubled over, Tuuran took his spear and pinned him with it into the dirt. It wasn't much of a camp and it didn't take him long to find the baggage the slavers had carried on their humpbacked horses from Dhar Thosis. It was all piled together, everything they'd looted. His axe was right there in front of him, and the gold-glass shield too. With those back in his hands, he felt whole again.

Right then. He turned back to the abyss. Crazy Mad was down there, so they said, and so that was where he was going because Crazy, whoever he was, *what*ever he was, was his friend, and here and now the only one he had; but before he did that there were a couple of other little scores he fancied he might settle. As chaos gripped them all, he ran through the ruin of the camp like a whirlwind, smashing the slave pens that weren't already broken, screamed in the faces of terrified slavers. They all ran. They knew what was good for them. He let them. All of them but one.

'Hello, Skinny,' he said, when he found him. Skinny turned to run, but *that* wasn't going to do him any good. Tuuran threw him down, and he begged and pleaded and wept but not for long because Tuuran was past any forgiveness. 'Told you you'd be the first, you piece of camel shit.' Even if strictly he wasn't because of the slaver he'd stuck with his makeshift spear. First in thought. Something like that. Flame, did it matter?

Tuuran left Skinny in the sand, blood dripping off his axe just the way it should. Slaves and slavers were scattering like leaves in a storm. They'd seen a dragon. Not the little one they'd seen before but a proper monster of nightmare stories, the real thing. They weren't men any more, any of them, just prey. Small screaming prey and they knew it.

He passed them by, laughing at their fear until he found the steps carved into the cliffs that would take him into the abyss of the Queverra, and down he went.

28

Dark Little Secrets

The setting sun blazed through the windows of Mai'Choiro's gondola, washing the etched silver walls the colour of burnished copper. Red Lin Feyn sat in the Arbiter's throne. The Elemental Men were waiting for her, hovering in the air as light or wind or shadows. The one they'd chosen to speak for them today knelt at her feet, a symbolic pretence of servitude though they all knew it didn't work that way. With a little sigh, Lin Feyn folded her hands across her lap.

'Mai'Choiro Kwen confesses and both the rider-slave and the enchantress tell much the same story.' She wished she could pace up and down and walk around the backs of the killers. 'Baros Tsen is dead and unable to defend himself. It seems very easy, doesn't it?' Her glance flickered up and shifted between the Elemental Men wafting around her. She couldn't see them but she could feel they were there. Another day to be filled with questions, and she was beginning to think that the answers she wanted weren't here to be found. She let out a second little sigh. Pacing helped her think – didn't it help *everyone* do that? – but she was what she was and so she forced herself to be still. Let the killers around her squirm. 'Where is Shrin Chrias Kwen?'

The kneeling Elemental Man bowed his head. 'We continue our search, lady. He has hidden himself well.'

'And Shonda? Do I have to send you looking for him too?'

'Glasships left Vespinarr two days ago, lady. He will be here in the morning.'

Red Lin Feyn leaned forward in her throne. She stretched down and touched the killer's hair. 'Why do you fear these dragons so?'

The killer bowed again. There were at least seven other Elemental Men around her, and it crossed her mind that if they ever had a secret they all wished to hide, they'd have no difficulty.

'They are monsters,' the killer said. 'Look at what even one has done.'

She made sure not to let her exasperation show. 'Baros Tsen T'Varr sent one of you to stop the dragon-rider. He did not have to kill the monster, only the rider. Why did he fail, killer?'

The Elemental Man bowed his head further. 'I have heard the testimony of the rider-slave as you related it, lady. I know no more.'

A lie. She had him. She lifted one arm from her chair and crooked a finger, beckoning him closer. Closer and closer, shuffling on his knees until he knelt right at her feet. She cupped his cheek with her hand. He would not lie to her now. 'Killer, what do you know that you have not told me? Why do you fear them so? Why did you bring them here?'

'They are monsters …' he began, but they were long past *that* answer. Her hand didn't move but a tiny puff of dark smoke rose from each of her fingers. A whiff of the storm-dark. They all had it inside them.

'I will unmake you, killer, if you lie to me again,' she said.

He held her eyes then rose and stepped back, silent, breaking the pretence, exposing the lie of that false obedience. A dark scar blemished his cheek where her hand had touched him. It would never heal. For a moment she thought he'd turn and walk away, and if he did then she'd do the same. She'd return to the Dralamut and the killers could clean up their own mess as they saw fit without her. It seemed an inextricable part of this that the killers had brought the dragons to Takei'Tarr in the first place.

'I exist for a reason,' she whispered. 'Your kind demand that I exist. You cannot walk away from that, killer.'

He bowed his head and then met her eye again. 'The dragons devour the essence of the world, lady.'

She waited for more.

'There are no sorcerers in the dragon-realms. Its magic is almost gone. The dragons have consumed it. They will do the same here. In time there will be no more Elemental Men, no enchanters, no sorceresses, no navigators. Lady, the great dragon drains the thread and weave of the world around it. We cannot stand before it except as ordinary men.'

'Then why did you bring them here in the first place?' A

horrified part of Lin Feyn's mind began to digest what the killer had told her and all that it implied. The rest of her kept the killer pinned where he was while she had him.

'Sea Lord Quai'Shu brought the dragons to Takei'Tarr, lady. Not us.'

'You helped him.'

'And that is not your concern, lady.'

Lin Feyn blinked. Talking back to an Arbiter? Well if they wouldn't obey the rules then neither would she. She stood up and began to pace. 'It seems unwise, killer, to keep a creature that devours arcane energies aboard a device that depends upon such energies to exist while inexplicably levitating above a storm that destroys everything it touches. But you didn't think it mattered? You didn't think it was significant enough to *mention*?'

'It was not important to your purpose, lady.'

'Deemed so by whom?' She waited for an answer. When she received only silence, Lin Feyn sat back in her crystal throne, opened her arms wide and cast her eyes around the gondola. 'You're afraid. All of you, and of something beyond these dragons. You can't hide that.' No answer. 'I require Shrin Chrias Kwen and the hatchling dragon that escaped.'

The Elemental Man with the scarred cheek bowed. 'We are looking, lady.'

'Do better.' She leaned towards them all. 'Go to your masters. I require an answer as to why they saw fit to allow Sea Lord Quai'Shu to purchase two of their disciples when such a thing is without precedent.' Her eyes shone with ire. 'There was a slave from the dragon-lands who worked a while with the alchemist. He was in Dhar Thosis when it burned. He spoke with the rider-slave there. Find him.' There – a next-to-impossible task. She waved them away. They wouldn't leave her entirely, but she waited until the gondola was empty and quiet, awash with evening light. It was late and she should retire and consider what she'd heard through the day and maybe even sleep for once, but she couldn't, not now.

Lin Feyn yawned and blinked a few times, putting on a show for the two Elemental Men who lurked as wisps of air nearby, then opened the gondola's ramp and let the wind buffet her. She looked for the dragon but it had gone and hadn't yet returned, so she looked at the space where it habitually perched anyway and paused. Just in that moment she thought she understood why no one had found the courage to put the dragon and its rider down. *I might need an ally. I no longer trust the killers who claim to serve me. That must be how it is for a sea lord, always. And so I keep close that which I might use against my enemies and never throw it away.* Was that it? She smiled to herself. *Perhaps. But am I falling into that same trap?*

She crossed the dragon yard. The killers were nearby. One would waft ahead of her and one behind. To keep her safe from lesser assassins, or so they said, but lately she'd started to wonder. At the alchemist's study she stopped abruptly and opened the iron door, walked through and shut it behind her in a moment. Iron. A bar to the killers. A place where they couldn't reach her. She closed her eyes and took a deep breath, feeling for any wisp of wind that might have crept in behind her and sensing none, finding only the stale smell of old fire, of a hundred burned things she didn't know and, overpowering all else, the strong scent of cloves and of something dead.

Lin Feyn waited a moment, pressed against the door until she felt it quiver. She'd taken them by surprise and stranded her killers outside. She let out the tiniest groan of relief. She would stay here, exactly here.

'Enchantress Chay-Liang, you wished to show me something?'

In the depths of the Queverra the dragon Silence felt the great dragon that hunted it recede. It waited a long time and, while it did, felt at the other things that existed around it. A rift in the earth, depths still far beneath it that touched the lands of the dead in Xibaiya. The other little one, the one who carried the Black Moon within him, circling with single-minded purpose downward. The hatchling watched them all, dragon and little one and the distant paths to other worlds, its attention flitting from one to the other to the next, wondering. Each one tempting it to follow to see where they would lead.

It chose the dragon-queen. And the little ones who shifted their forms, touched with a splinter of the dead goddess – *they* were something new. And the little one above, the Adamantine

Man Tuuran, who wasn't afraid, one of those splinter-touched Elemental Men had once sent him to watch over the echo of the Black Moon. Why?

It was too tempting to resist. When the dragon Diamond Eye was long gone, Silence turned its thoughts from the echo of the Black Moon toiling towards Xibaiya and flew in the great dragon's wake, back towards the Godspike.

Red Lin Feyn watched the alchemist and the enchantress drag a corpse across the room and prop it in front of her. This was, so they said, the slave who had poisoned Chay-Liang and gone after the dragon-rider with a bladeless knife. The alchemist tipped back the dead man's head and forced open his mouth. Chay-Liang tipped a thimble of something like tar into the corpse's mouth. The smell of cloves grew stronger.

'What are you doing, enchantress?' she asked, before something happened that made it too late for all of them. Chay-Liang shot her a fearful look but it was the alchemist who answered.

'He will talk now. Ask him your questions, Lady Arbiter.'

'He's dead, alchemist.'

'And yet he will still talk.'

For a long time Lin Feyn said nothing. They were offering her sorcery, the forbidden magics of Abraxi and the Crimson Sunburst. The Elemental Men existed to hunt down the people who practised such abominations and end them, and two of her killers were standing right outside the door. 'Chay-Liang, do you understand the consequences of what you are doing? Truly? Do you?'

'It's my blood,' whispered the alchemist.

Lin Feyn shook her head. 'Enchantress, I asked you a question. If you do this, do you understand what the consequences may be?'

'Yes.' Chay-Liang's whisper was hoarse.

'And does your slave?' No answer. Lin Feyn closed her eyes and tried to think. How was she here? As Red Lin Feyn or as the Arbiter of the Dralamut? Could she draw a line between them? 'Two of my killers are outside, Chay-Liang. How long have you known this was possible?'

'A day. No more.'

The killers would find out. They had to. She should tell them because that was her duty. They would take the alchemist and end him for this. Without the alchemist there could be no dragons. It was over. All of it. Might as well go outside here and now, set free the glasships that held the eyrie aloft and let everything and everyone sink into the storm-dark. Or she could say nothing and be complicit in what they'd done.

The moan of the dead man startled her out of her thoughts. Lin Feyn bared her teeth and hissed. 'Did you hear what I said, Chay-Liang? There are two killers outside this door. I should open it. It is my duty to show them what you've done.'

Chay-Liang bowed. 'I know.'

'And you presume my duty will defer to my curiosity in order to—'

'Corpse, who told you to kill Chay-Liang and her Holiness Zafir?' The alchemist's voice rode over her.

'Mai'Choiro Kwen,' groaned the dead man.

Red Lin Feyn threw out her hands. The gold-glass shards of the Arbiter which hung over her shoulders and neck flashed into a whirlwind of knives and sliced the dead man to pieces before he could say any more. It was done in an instant and then the shards returned. Chay-Liang and the alchemist were too shocked to speak. Lin Feyn tore open the iron door; wind rushed past her and the killers appeared at once, one standing between her and the alchemist, the other behind Chay-Liang, their bladeless knives glinting in the gloom.

'Stop!' Lin Feyn hurled the word like a weapon, shivering the air, dazing them all. 'Let them live!' She waited a moment and then spoke more softly. 'Confine them both. Keep them apart. Let them continue their duties, but no more.' She pointed to the shredded body of the dead slave. 'Take that abomination and throw it into the storm-dark!' She turned and plunged through the door. Might have run, except an Arbiter never ran.

'Baros Tsen T'Varr,' shouted the alchemist after her. 'His body is still here!'

She didn't look back, not until she was in her gondola, safe and alone. Except not alone. Another killer was there. Always. He whispered into being beside her and knelt. 'What would you have us do, lady?'

Allow me to unsee what I have seen. Allow me to unhear what I have heard. But that was beyond him. 'Nothing,' she said.

The dragon Silence flew across the desert. In the dead of night it felt the storm-dark and the Godspike drawing close. It felt other dragons and they felt it in return, but the little ones who tended them slept.

Do not speak of me, it whispered to them. It thought of freeing its kin and burning the little ones and devouring them until all of them were gone, then pushed those thoughts aside. It had come with another purpose.

In the memories it had taken from the soldier Tuuran who thought he could kill dragons, Silence saw more of these strange wizards, these Elemental Men who had come hunting with the dragon-queen. Creatures who masqueraded as little ones but had the power of the dead goddess of the earth running through them. Not so easy to kill with tooth and claw and fire a creature who might turn into flames or air in an instant.

Elemental Men.

There had been one in the dragon-realms two of its lifetimes ago. In the Adamantine soldier's memories one had taken Tuuran to a city and shown him words from long ago and sent him to watch the echo of the Black Moon. Tuuran hadn't understood what had been asked of him or why, but perhaps somewhere here was the one who had sent him on his way. That one would have answers.

The dragon Silence found itself a place beneath the eyrie, clinging to the underside of the black rock as it floated above the storm-dark, and poked into the minds of the little ones and the creatures who called themselves Elemental Men one by one, searching their thoughts, looking for anyone who remembered the name plucked from Tuuran's memory. The Watcher. Days passed. It probed, still and unseen, listening until it found what it needed. The Watcher was dead. Crushed by the dragon that had chased it into the abyss and almost to Xibaiya. While the little ones slept it asked the other dragon where and how it had done this thing. The great dragon answered and showed its memories of the place.

Content, the dragon Silence emerged from its hiding place.

29

Consequences

Red Lin Feyn sat on her crystal throne in the splendour of her court and listened to her killers while she waited to receive Sea Lord Shonda of Vespinarr. The lord of the mountains was somewhere over the desert, answering her summons as slowly as he could possibly manage. His dawdling didn't trouble her; she would receive him as an almost-equal and say nothing of his tardiness. In return, he would be courteous and polite and charming and of course furious. He would answer her questions with a mix of lies and half-truths and politely demand that he and his kwen be allowed to go. He would tell her that great cities like Vespinarr, great trading empires like those it controlled, did not run themselves. He'd remind her that he'd already lost Vey Rin, his t'varr and also his brother, to Baros Tsen T'Varr's dragons, and would ask how such a great empire of ships was to govern itself if now its kwen and sea lord were imprisoned in a flying castle three miles above the desert and three hundred from the nearest thought of civilisation. Sea Lord Quai'Shu, he would point out, owed him a very great deal of money. He would like this debt repaid, and Baros Tsen's dragons would do nicely.

Shonda would come with all these requests, and she would refuse them, throw Mai'Choiro's confession in his face and wonder as she did why he even bothered to ask. Once she'd trapped him, she'd ask him why he'd done it, because surely a man as canny and wealthy as the sea lord of Vespinarr could contrive a more subtle scheme to get what he wanted, one that didn't bring with it such risk of ruin? The question she wanted to ask Lord Shonda of Vespinarr, before she condemned him to hang before the Crown of the Sea Lords in Khalishtor, was no longer *what*, but *why*?

Whatever the killers were saying to her now, she wasn't hearing a word. She wasn't hearing a word because the alchemist had made a dead man speak. In the eyes of the killers that made him a sorcerer, and sorcerers were put to death. As the Arbiter of the Dralamut, all of that had nothing to do with who had burned Dhar Thosis and so wasn't her concern. As Red Lin Feyn, navigator and dutiful citizen of Takei'Tarr, it bothered her considerably, and not in ways the killers would have been pleased to know. A part of what bothered her, and would bother the killers most of all, was that she hadn't told them.

With an abrupt wave of her hand she silenced them, and then, with another, she sent them away. All of them, winkling them out. When she was sure she was alone, she went up the stairs to her bed and the chest beside it and took out the glass globe that held a snip of the storm-dark. It wasn't much more than a novice's training toy. She held it in her hand.

Beneath the layers and masks of her rank, Lin Feyn remained the daughter of daughters of Feyn Charin, the first navigator. His blood was in her and what had he been if not a sorcerer? Oh, the world had dressed it up and called him something else because of the one great trick he'd shared, the crossing of the storm-dark, but he was more than that. He'd been apprenticed to the Crimson Sunburst of Cashax, who'd gone to war against the Elemental Men and almost won. Some said he'd been more than an apprentice. Lin Feyn hadn't ever found any reason for such a belief but she secretly favoured it because it made her blood the blood of the Crimson Sunburst herself and was a poke in the eye for the killers, who claimed to serve her but in reality served only themselves. And the truth, though few knew it, was that the Sunburst had never sought to confront them.

She'd been the first enchantress, and her court had grown to be filled with magical creatures and devices, animated wonders of glass, automata and the first golems. The library of the Dralamut, in its forbidden rooms where the killers couldn't enter, contained journals in which the Crimson Sunburst spoke of old books, of reading the anathema of the Rava, of the old white-faced silver-skinned half-gods who existed before the world broke into splinters. The journals were full of awe and wonder, gleeful childish fascination with the miracles she found she could perform, yet Red Lin Feyn had found no ambition for domination or such worldly hungers, only a relentless curiosity and the Sunburst's constant air of surprise that her spells did more than make a sour taste or a bad smell. In the end her unfettered curiosity had brought the killers down on her, yet Red Lin Feyn had never found anything to suggest that the Crimson Sunburst had wanted more than she already had. The Sunburst had been queen of Cashax before her twentieth birthday, back when Cashax had been the greatest city in Takei'Tarr. She'd wrought her sorceries simply because they were there. To see if she could.

The alchemist, when Lin Feyn watched him at his work, reminded her of the woman from those journals – meticulous, curious, fiercely clever, someone who did what he did without any hunger for power or prestige. Which brought Lin Feyn right back to the thing she was trying very hard not to think about, the question that circled her with the predatory malevolence of a shark: *What do I do with you?* He was probably a kind man. Lin Feyn, whose life had been built on knowing such things, saw no reason to think otherwise. Yet he did things that others could use, others who were not so kind, and for that the Elemental Men would kill him. After what she'd seen she'd told the killers to lock him up but hadn't yet told them why, and now found she didn't want to, even though she should. She wondered how much they'd seen, how much they already understood for themselves.

She sat alone on her crystal throne in all her splendour and considered these things deep into the night, then rose and undressed and slipped between the silks to sleep and considered them some more.

She was still musing on them when the dragon yard burst into flames.

Zafir woke filled with a sense of warning, a sharp and dire immediate threat. She barely had time to throw back her silk sheets before the poles that held up her shelter out on the eyrie wall snapped like twigs. Gold-glass shattered into splinters, crashed down on top of her and crushed her almost flat. The sail-cloth canopy smothered her and the bulk of something vast almost crushed her, almost but not quite. Through the silks tangled around her face she thought she saw the night outside light up with flames.

The hatchling.

The Elemental Men had said they would see to it themselves. She'd laughed and said she'd hunt it when she pleased, but she hadn't. Now a surge of anger shot through her. She'd hidden herself from its searching on the night it had come to kill her and now here it was, back for another go.

She could feel it already flying off. Diamond Eye was rising, the wings he'd wrapped around her shelter like a cocoon folding back. She sensed his hunger, tense and sharp and ready for the hunt, exactly as she wanted him. She threw off the silken sheets and the debris of the smashed shelter and ran up the wall. Across the dragon yard everything that would burn was in flames. The hatchling was already far out of sight. Diamond Eye turned his head to look at her as if asking something, and she knew exactly what. She nodded.

'Yes, my deathbringer. No matter what they say.' And by the time the first Elemental Men vanished into the darkness in pursuit, she was already in her armour and on the dragon's back.

Red Lin Feyn barely had time to make herself decent before the killers appeared around her. 'Lady, it is the hatchling. We require your leave to pursue.'

Lin Feyn took a moment to compose herself. *Require it, do you?* And she might have taken them to task for that but then another thought struck her. She nodded her assent. 'All of you. Go. Finish it.'

They bowed, eager to follow their nature. 'Stay here, lady, with wards on the door. We will not be gone for long.'

Telling her what to do again. They were losing their perspective. Fear was making them careless, opening cracks and letting their true natures show. Lin Feyn nodded and said nothing, watched them leave and shut the gondola window behind them. She closed her eyes and waited another few minutes, stretching out every sense for the whisper of wind that might tell her that one had disobeyed and stayed to watch over her. When she was certain she was truly alone, she opened the gondola and hurried into the night. Flickering fires from the hatchery and the remains of the Vespinese scaffold shot a dark orange glow over the dragon yard stone, pulsing in the ever-present wind whose fingers gripped her and shook her and almost picked her up and blew her away. She held her robe tight – not the dress of the Arbiter that she'd become but the simple robes of the enchantress she'd been before they took her to the Dralamut to learn the secrets of the storm-dark. The adult dragon was gone from its perch on the wall. Beneath, the hatchlings in their chains stared at her and at the eastern sky, shrieking their agitation. She ignored them and slipped down the tunnels to the alchemist's room. A bleary-eyed kwen came stumbling the other way, dressed in bits of armour.

'Go back to bed,' she told him sharply. 'It is a matter for dragons and killers. The Elemental Men have it in hand.'

He blinked a few times and frowned, then shook his head and ran on, and it was only after he'd gone that she realised he didn't recognise her without her painted face and gold-glass shards and wreathed in flames of feathers. She smiled then, surprised by an unexpected sense of freedom.

The smell of cloves hit her as soon as she opened the door to the alchemist's study. She closed it behind her and listened again for any whispers in the air, felt for flickers of breeze and found nothing. The killers were about their business, hunting monsters. The room was empty. She searched and let her nose guide her to the alchemist's potion for waking the dead, took it and left and ran barefoot through the deeper passages of the eyrie, spiralling ever down to what had once been Baros Tsen T'Varr's bathhouse, the smell of cloves trailing after her. Tsen's bathhouse had become a morgue now. Dead slaves were simply thrown over the side or fed to the dragon and a good few of the men who'd died before she'd come had gone that way too, but the rest of the Taiytakei dead waited here, to be burned one day with all due funerary dignity or else hung by the ankles from the spires of Khalishtor for the world to see. One word from her either way was all it took. Tsen's corpse was among them. One of the ones who'd hang by his ankles.

The iron door was cold to the touch. It opened for her and a wash of chill air rushed out, enough to turn to mist as it reached in tentacles into the corridor. Chay-Liang's enchantments had been strong enough to glaze the water in Tsen's bath with ice.

The doors that led to the other spirals of the eyrie were closed. She listened again, felt for any movement in the misty air, then closed the door behind her and hurried into the passages where the Scales lived, where the alchemist and the enchantress were now shut in their prisons. When she reached the guards who stood watch over them, she beckoned them away and had them follow her to the bathhouse morgue, hurrying them inside. They didn't recognise her either but they were mere soldiers and her voice still carried all the force of an Arbiter's command.

'Bring out the body of Baros Tsen T'Varr,' she told them, then left them to find it and ran to the alchemist's cell. She went inside and shook him awake.

'I will bring you Baros Tsen T'Varr,' she told him. 'You will make him talk. Then we will know.'

Zafir didn't see the Elemental Men vanish into the night but Diamond Eye felt their thoughts rush away into the wind, full of hunting and sharp blades and the tang of death. The dragon felt them and so Zafir felt them too.

This time you don't stop, she told him. *This time you fly on no matter what they do. Whatever they think, they will shy from it at the very last. They dare not kill me. My death will be my own. In flames, and many will burn with me.*

The dragon launched himself into the void. Zafir felt his purring approval and in him an awareness of her and of the world that was greater than anything she'd known back among the dragons of her home. He powered after the hatchling, eager and hungry, fast and strong. The air was different here, filled with a tense incipient energy, a lightning-crackle of expectation and potency. She felt the distance diminish. The chase might take hours but she would succeed this time. *No escape, little dragon, no trick.*

But it *was* a trick, of course it was. A lure. It slipped out of the hatchling's mind, unwatched. Slipped from hatchling to dragon and from Diamond Eye to her. He'd come here to tease her out. He *wanted* this chase. She caught the flash of a half-seen place where he wanted her to be.

Careless.

Show them the way, she cried, and Diamond Eye lit up the sky with fire, and from every compass point the Elemental Men saw and stopped their blind searching rush and came.

So this is how it is to be prey. The dragon Silence raced through the night. The feeling was strange, to be tearing away from something, and stranger still from something that couldn't be outrun. The earth-touched Elemental Men had given chase this time. It felt their thoughts. They were like little ones in their form and their nature but not in their essence – in that they carried something else, a tiny echo of the dead goddess just as the alchemist carried a lingering memory of what had once been a half-god. The dragon told itself to remember these things, that they mattered, but for now the rush of the chase was irresistible. The alchemist knew exactly what he was, but the earth-touched were ignorant. The dragon didn't understand how that could be. It would ask one, when the chance came, but for now they raced like the wind towards it, the endless chattering of their thoughts like tiny beacons in the sky. Silence felt their searching. They couldn't see it, not in the darkness, and so the little dragon skimmed the rim of the storm-dark and dived beneath it and flew a different way and zigged and zagged between their dispersing thoughts. It learned something it had missed as it listened to their minds. They were afraid. Dragons made them weak. Dragons devoured their powers as dragons devoured everything. They were quick though, quick as the wind and faster than a dragon could dream. Quick but blind, so none of them would catch it.

It reached its mind to the one thing that would never let it escape.
The others are scattered, brother. Lead the little one. Bring her to me.
It was a trick. Of course it was a trick. It had played this hunt in its mind days ago. It knew how it ended. Prey hoped to escape. Silence did not.

Zafir felt the change in Diamond Eye's thoughts. An Elemental Man had found the hatchling. Diamond Eye strained to be faster, filled with a furious hunger. This kill was *his*. The dragon watched and listened as the hatchling felt the killer come close and pried at his thoughts and peered into his intent, and at the moment the Elemental Man changed to flesh to strike with the bladeless knife that would cut through even a dragon's scales, the hatchling Silence veered and arced and dipped a wing and lashed its tail. The bladeless knife cut only air. The killer shifted once more but it was hard so close to a dragon, no longer as easy as breathing. Silence's tail whipped flesh and cracked bones and the Elemental Man fell like a broken doll and dissolved into darkness. The hatchling rode his thoughts. The killer was crippled but he didn't die, not this time. He was lucky, then.

Diamond Eye watched. Through him, Zafir saw it all. *That* was how they fought. Yes, dragons read the desires of their riders, but like this ...? She'd never imagined. The knowledge chilled her and thrilled her. *That* was how Diamond Eye kept her safe. Always.

She urged him on. The Elemental Men were faster, howling in tiny hurricanes of wind, dancing from light to shadow. They raced around her and past with their knives, searching and finding. Diamond Eye felt each duel as it happened and so Zafir felt it too, the sharp glee of a victory, the pain of another cut, the jubilation of another earth-touched smashed out of the sky. It mingled with her own – *Yes, let them fight* – and she cheered the little dragon on even after all it had done to her, because every killer whose bones were smashed and whose flesh was burned was one more enemy sent to Xibaiya. It had learned after the first and struck harder now, killing them. *Yes, little dragon. Fight them! End them for me!*

The hatchling shot back a vicious glee. *Not for you but for me, little one. Come close enough and you will follow.*

The sky began to lighten. The hatchling was hurt, stabbed a dozen times by the knives of the Elemental Men, but it had broken and burned five of them and now the others held back, lurking in the wind, watching. A hatchling. A hatchling had beaten them. In time she would show them what a real dragon could do.

Silence raced on, hard and straight into the teeth and fiery glare of the rising sun. Sometimes, in the distance, Zafir thought she saw him as they flew, and then at last the hatchling came to the earth and stopped atop a mesa, waiting for her, and Zafir realised she knew this place, that she'd been here before. Caution narrowed her eyes. She circled Diamond Eye once around the cliffs to be certain, then again, lower until she could see the hatchling waiting for her. And it *was* waiting.

Why here, little dragon?

Diamond Eye landed gently and the two dragons sat and watched one another, a dozen yards apart. This was where she'd stopped for the night on the way to Dhar Thosis. This was where the Watcher, Baros Tsen T'Varr's Elemental Man, had tried to kill her. Now the hatchling squatted where Diamond Eye had squashed the Watcher flat. Not close to where he'd died, not nearby, but on the exact spot. The dark stains of the Watcher's blood on the pale stone left no doubt.

Why here? she asked again, but the hatchling didn't answer. It seemed impatient. Keen to be done with this.

To show you something. In Xibaiya among the wandering dead, the rip is opened again. Diamond Eye will understand. Embedded in that thought came a sliver of memory, of moving among the ruins of what the dragons called Xibaiya to the edges of a hole and oozing out from that hole a spread of void and chaos. It crept hither and yon, devouring what it touched, and the prison that had once held it back was no longer there. Zafir frowned fiercely. The memory made no sense. *How long will it take?* mused the hatchling.

It was a trick. A trap. It had drawn her here but she couldn't resist. Not that it mattered. Diamond Eye took a pace forward and then another, and the hatchling still didn't move. Zafir cocked her head. 'Why, little dragon?'

Diamond Eye lunged. His jaws snapped shut. He crushed Silence between his fangs and spat the hatchling's head over the mesa's edge. The decapitated body fell limp and Zafir felt a strangeness in Diamond Eye's thoughts as the dragon stared at what it had done. Dragons killing dragons wasn't a thing it knew. *You did well*, she told him, though she'd understood long ago that dragons had no use for such praise. His disquiet echoed inside her. *A trick. A trap.* She'd known it, knew it still, yet didn't see how it might now be closing around her.

An Elemental Man appeared on the mesa and walked cautiously to the hatchling's body. *Earth-touched.* The hatchling, in its thoughts, had called them that.

'Is it dead?' he asked.

'It has no head!' Her voice tripped in her throat. Something wasn't right. It had led her here, brought her to this place, all this way and then …? No fight, no struggle, no resistance. Why? Why *here*?

'Return at once. Bring the body so the alchemist may say whether your words are true.'

It struck her at last as she flew back with the headless corpse of Silence clutched between Diamond Eye's claws. The hatchling was dead and so there was no longer any need for a dragon to hunt it. No longer any need for her. She had nothing left to keep her safe. It had given her its death and sealed her own.

A trap. She looked for the elation of victory she ought to feel and found nothing but emptiness and a longing for the home she'd never had.

In the gloom of the alchemist's laboratory in the hour before dawn Red Lin Feyn watched as the cold dead lips of Baros Tsen T'Varr began to move.

'Why did Dhar Thosis burn?' she asked. 'For what reason?'

'I do not know.'

'Why did Mai'Choiro give the orders he did?'

'I do not know.'

'Did you force him? Was this the design of Sea Lord Quai'Shu? Was this all to free yourselves of your crippling debt?' Too fast, too much. She was getting ahead of herself. Perhaps, faced with a dead man who spoke, even an Arbiter might fray a little at the edges.

'I do not know.'

'How can you not know? What were your orders to the rider-slave?'

'I gave no orders.'

'How so? Were you not there? Were you deaf?' Lin Feyn rounded on the alchemist. 'What trick is this? You play with me? Your life hangs by a thread, slave! Do you think this saves you?' But when the alchemist shook his head, she saw his own bewilderment and found she could not doubt it.

'The dead do not lie, Lady Arbiter,' he said. 'They do not.'

'What's your name?' asked Chay-Liang, the first of them to see the truth. The simplest question that surely should have been Lin Feyn's beginning had she had her wits properly about her. Lin

Feyn didn't quite catch the reply the corpse gave but she heard it well enough to know that it was wrong.

'Say it again!' she demanded. 'What is your name?'

'Darris Veskai Kwen,' said the corpse.

Red Lin Feyn glazed at the naked flesh. A face she'd seen only once and years before, but it was him, she was sure. His skin. His face. Baros Tsen T'Varr.

The enchantress asked who he was, where he came from, how he came to the eyrie, question after question in a voice of rising horror and confusion. The alchemist simply gaped. The corpse related that he was a slave from across the storm-dark who'd earned his sword brands. He'd been born in the Dominion of the Sun King. How was it that he had the dark skin of a Taiytakei and the face of the eyrie's t'varr? He didn't know, but he knew that he wasn't Baros Tsen.

'Why is he lying?' screamed Chay-Liang. She shook the alchemist. 'Why doesn't he know who he is?'

'It is the wrong spirit.' The alchemist looked lost. 'The wrong soul. I do not understand how. There's no precedent—'

'What is the last thing you saw?' Lin Feyn asked.

He told her: standing watch in his tower when the Vespinese came, staying at his post, waiting to see how the fight would go, then Baros Tsen T'Varr on the wall with his slave Kalaiya, both of them dressed in black silk. Kalaiya's face changing, becoming something with no face at all. The kwen opening his mouth to cry an alarm but making no sound. His hand in hers on the end of an arm impossibly long. His skin rippling and changing. The dreadful horror of trying to breathe, of gasping to draw air through a mouth and nose he no longer had. Then shrinking and dissolving to the ground. Baros Tsen T'Varr lying beside him, heaving for breath. The world going grey and then black. The corpse spoke it all in a dispassionate monotone, oblivious to the horror of its own demise and yet aware, in a cold way, of how it had felt.

'It's not him?' said the alchemist, the last of them to understand. 'It's not Baros Tsen?' He stared at the dead man's face. 'But it is. How ...?'

'Wait! Wait!' Lin Feyn tore at her hair, trying to see what this meant. 'This isn't him? You're certain?'

'Either this corpse is a liar or Tsen's not dead at all,' said Chay-Liang. 'Why else go to such trouble?' She chuckled, an edge of hysteria creeping through. 'Clever t'varr. Clever, clever t'varr. Although it's not possible ...'

'Corpses don't lie,' mumbled the alchemist. He was shaking his head, utterly bemused. Lin Feyn went to grab the corpse and shake it for answers, then thought better of it.

'Great Charin! He's not dead!' The enchantress was almost laughing with glee now. 'He's not dead! He escaped! He could be anywhere at all by now! But how ... How was it done? I don't understand how it was done ...' She frowned. 'And if he escaped, why didn't he take Kalaiya with him? He would have taken her. He would!' Chay-Liang shook her head, momentarily too puzzled to remember she was standing next to a corpse that talked back. 'And I haven't the first idea how ...'

Red Lin Feyn did though. 'A skin-shifter,' she said. 'From the Konsidar.' She closed her eyes, trying to think. A skin-shifter in the form of his slave. One who'd killed a man and then changed the corpse to fool them into thinking that Tsen was dead so no one would come looking. Clever. Almost perfect. 'This was no escape.' She closed her eyes. A chill swept through her. 'Someone took him. And so everything is changed.'

The dragon Silence fell through the weft of the world to Xibaiya. It had chosen its dying and chosen the place of it, the place where Diamond Eye had killed the Watcher, the earth-touched who had sent Tuuran to watch over the echo of the Black Moon. In Xibaiya the dragon Silence looked for the trail of the dead killer and found it easily enough. It would ask the Watcher why, and how it knew. With tooth and claw wrapped around the dead spirit's throat if it had to.

It started to hunt.

Baros Tsen T'Varr

30

Shifter Skin

The last thing Baros Tsen T'Varr remembered, the Vespinese were attacking his eyrie. The next thing he knew, he woke lying on something hard. His head hurt and he had no sensation in his arms, his legs or his face except to feel the wind on it, the same bloody wind as ever tearing at his braids and tugging his clothes. What he *could* feel was someone pulling at him.

He opened his eyes and wished he hadn't. A mile straight below were dull purple flashes of lightning that could only be the storm-dark. Between him and it there was, well, nothing. Everywhere else was dark – no, not quite dark; he could make out a deep purple tinge. It took a moment to realise that he wasn't, in fact, falling to his death.

He was underneath the eyrie.

Instinct made him push against whatever invisible force was holding him, but his arms weren't working properly and he supposed he must look rather like a fish flopping about on a riverbank. He managed to roll over. At least he wasn't staring down at the storm-dark now, though looking up at the black stone underbelly of his eyrie a few feet over his head didn't strike him as a great deal better.

'Hush.' The voice sounded like Kalaiya but he knew better. She'd touched him and, in a crippling flash of pain, stolen the strength from his legs. He remembered falling, the pain getting worse. He remembered not being able to move, seeing another man topple beside him, seeing the man's face swim and change and morph into his own, the doppelgänger Kalaiya crouching beside him, her hand never leaving him. Actually, he remembered everything with grim clarity. He rather wished he didn't.

Not-Kalaiya crouched beside him, one foot pressed on his chest, pushing him down. Shifter skin. She'd said she had shifter skin hiding a glass sled. Was that how she'd changed her face too?

'What are you?' he asked. He tried to move but she wouldn't let him and so he lay still, terrified he was about to die. No, not die, because if that was what she wanted then he'd already be dead. Something worse.

'Be careful, Baros Tsen T'Varr. It's a long way down and this sled is a touch small for any rolling about. I wouldn't want you to fall after I've gone to so much trouble to get you here.'

A distant flash of purple lightning lit up Not-Kalaiya's face. She was wearing a very Not-Kalaiya smirk. It was cold and mocking and heartless and turned her into someone he'd never seen. It was a smirk that made him unreasonably angry. He tried to sit up but that clearly still wasn't going to work for a while.

'What did you do to me?' He winced as a jagged line of bright violet arced from the belly of the eyrie to the storm-dark a mile below. The thunderclap rattled his bones and set bells ringing in his ears. 'Who are you? Where is Kalaiya? What have you done with her? If you've hurt her, I'll ... I'll get ...' He faltered. He'd get what exactly? Angry? Well he was already fairly angry and so far it hadn't been much use. He'd throw this impostor into the storm-dark? But if he could do that then why hadn't he done it already? Because he was a stupid fat t'varr, that's why, and no match for a skin-shifter.

Skin-shifter. The thought rolled around inside his head. He'd heard things about skin-shifters, hadn't he? 'I will make you suffer,' he finished. 'A thousand times.'

'I didn't hurt her. I took her shape, nothing more. What will happen when the Vespinese are done here, I don't know. By now your eyrie is theirs. Whatever happens to your slave now, your business is with them, though you may not be in a position to do much about it for a while. If I were you, Baros Tsen T'Varr, I'd worry a lot more about myself just now.'

'Who *are* you?'

'Someone who doesn't want to see you hang from a Vespinese gibbet.' The foot came off his chest. Tsen carefully felt for the invisible edges of the sled and sat up. Not-Kalaiya stood over him, watching. Above them both the jagged black underbelly of the eyrie was close enough to touch if he stood up. Veins of deep purple ran though it. Another violet thunderbolt cracked between the eyrie and the swirling clouds below. He shuddered. *No one ever told me it did that. Did anyone even know?*

'You're one of them!' he said suddenly, grasping at the first thought he could and finding Not-Kalaiya's words in the bath house. *When would be a convenient time?* 'You *are* a Regrettable Man! Or Woman, or whatever.' He looked down at the storm-dark. No. That couldn't be right either, and he wasn't going to die, not yet and possibly not at all. *You're not a Regrettable Man any more than you were Kalaiya. So who are you?*

'Don't be stupid. I'm here to rescue you.'

'I didn't *want* to be rescued!'

Not-Kalaiya rolled her eyes. 'Fine, then I'm abducting you. Would you like to go back?'

'Not really.' If she wanted, she could have killed him in his bath, as easy as anything. But rescue? 'Who sent you?'

Careful, T'Varr. She's not what she says.

Not what she says? Oh how marvellously astute!.

You're really not helping much here. 'How do you look like her?'

'I'm a skin-shifter from the Konsidar.'

'And I'm a dragon in a funny hat!'

'You asked.' Not-Kalaiya shrugged. 'I really don't mind if you don't believe me.'

'Shifter skin. That's what it is. You have a shifter skin. So show me who you really are.'

'Look away, T'Varr.'

'Why?'

Not-Kalaiya watched him steadily until he turned away. He'd been in Cashax when he first heard of shifter skin, years ago when he and Vey Rin had been tearing up the city's heart every night, looking for each thrill to be bigger than the last. Vey Rin had come in one night with a story of a woman – or maybe it was a man – who had a coat of skin and could become anything you wanted. They'd gone looking but they never found her, and Tsen was sure now that she'd never existed, because was *that* how you spent your time if you had the power to change into the shape of anyone at all? He remembered how he'd wondered what he might do with such a treasure.

But maybe it had been some sort of elaborate game. He and Vey Rin and some of the others back in Cashax had set challenges for each other. Stupid dares, and this would have been right up their street. *So, go and abduct the stupid fat t'varr from under the noses of the people who want to kill him. Then leave him naked in the desert with a bottle of apple wine and tell him he has to sing a song about the nymphs of the Yalun Zarang.* Sometimes, remembering what he used to be like made his skin want to crawl off and go and be with someone else.

'You can look now.' When Tsen looked back, Not-Kalaiya was gone and in her place stood a slender man of similar height and build. His face, in the dim light of the storm-dark and the dazzling flashes of lightning that spat down from the eyrie now and then, made him look little more than a boy.

'What if one of those bolts hits us?' snapped Tsen.

The man shrugged. 'Then whether this is a rescue or not will be of academic interest and no one will ever find us.' The man uncoiled a rope from around his waist and tossed it into Tsen's lap. Instinct made Tsen grab it, but the rope writhed and wriggled in his hands like a snake. He yelped and tried to scrabble away. One hand went over the invisible edge of the sled and he fell back. The rope moved fast as lightning and wrapped itself around him, pinning his arms to his waist. He cried out as he began to topple over the side of the sled but the rope was tight around him, the far end held fast in the other man's hands. Tsen glared at him.

The shifter pulled on the rope, dragging Tsen away from the edge. 'Clearly, T'Varr, if I wanted you dead then I would simply have let the lords of Vespinarr have their way. So I want you alive, at least for a while. Frankly I'd been hoping for a little more gratitude.'

'Really?' Tsen looked pointedly at the rope wrapped around him. 'Was that before or after you decided to pretend you were my Kalaiya?'

The sled eased away from the shelter of the eyrie. The wind roared fierce and the shifter had to shout into Tsen's ear to make himself heard. 'Look up, T'Varr! Three glasships approached low, hugging the surface of the storm-dark. They sent their soldiers on sleds like this, so small you wouldn't see them coming, so many your dragon wouldn't be able to kill them all. The glasships were to draw your monster into the sky while the soldiers passed beneath it, but you never saw them coming at all.'

'And in the midst of that, you thought you'd rescue me? How kind. Show me your shifter skin, whoever you are.' Tsen snorted. 'You know where it comes from? Shed by the Righteous Ones of the Konsidar.' He sniffed the air. 'It should stink.'

The shifter paused for a moment. 'You're right, of course. Only we don't exactly shed it, T'Varr. It has to be flayed from our still-living bodies. It has to be enchanted and cut and stitched into clothes. Abraxi the sorceress made exactly three sets from us before the Elemental Men made an end of her. Remind me, T'Varr: where were you when the Vespinese came?'

'I was …' The wind ripped the words off his lips and shredded them. Tsen sighed. *In my bath. Without a clue they were coming.* 'Take me back!'

'No.' The shifter shook his head. 'T'Varr, I took the place of one of their soldiers. This is his sled. Sea Lord Shonda was very specific: we find you, we kill you. Very specific indeed.'

'Shonda? Shonda himself?'

The sled was clear of the eyrie now. Tsen looked up and gasped. There must have been fifty glasships above the dragon yard, or sixty or perhaps even more. In the night sky they were lit up from within by the gold light at their hearts, sprinkled and sparkling through concentric annuli that spun one within the next and all inside the slow rotation of each great outer disc. The rims shone a brilliant white, their lightning cannons bright and ready, shining on the eyrie like a full moon. They were clustering slowly together, layering themselves so they were all huddled above the eyrie. Tsen had never seen so many so close together. They looked like a shoal of giant glowing jellyfish, only instead of seeing them from above and from the deck of a ship, he was seeing them from below as though he was some tiny fish.

'These lords of Vespinarr came to your home with two things in mind,' yelled the shifter. 'To kill you and to take what was yours. I don't know why and I don't care, though if you wish to air your opinions then go ahead. We have a long journey and I'm fond of conversation.' He guided the sled back towards the shelter of the eyrie.

'Who *are* you?'

The man shook his head and chuckled. 'A friend of Bronzehand.'

'Bronzehand?' The youngest of Quai'Shu's sons. Bronzehand, who'd been trying to reach him right before this skin-shifter had come. *Well there's a thing.* Bronzehand was possibly the one person in the world who might have a reason for keeping him alive, the only trouble being he was across the storm-dark in a different world, and people had a tendency to vanish when they tried to penetrate the jungles of Qeled. Another thought struck Tsen. He laughed. 'Looks like Meido's going to win our wager after all.' Maybe that was why Bronzehand was so interested.

'What wager was that?'

Well done, tongue. Anything else you'd like to share? Tsen sighed again. 'Nothing that matters now. We wagered this eyrie on how long Sea Lord Quai'Shu would live. I'm a month short.' *Bronzehand.* For some reason that made him feel safe.

Really? You feel safe?

Well, safer than I did a few minutes ago.

And why's that, then, T'Varr?

Because Bronzehand could be an ally.

An ally? Ha! Walking corpses don't have allies, T'Varr.

Well thank you for that little piece of joy. Although the voices had a point.

'What's your name, boy?' All this shouting into the teeth of the wind was making him think of being at sea. He hadn't been at sea for a long time and hadn't much liked it either.

The shifter yelled back, 'If you knew how old I was you'd choke. I've more years than you, T'Varr, and let's leave it at that.' They sank slowly towards the maelstrom, keeping under the eyrie where the glasships wouldn't see them.

'Your face says otherwise.'

'I'm surprised you put any trust in faces. As for names, I wear them every bit as easily. Call me Sivan.' He grinned and bared his teeth.

'Sivan. Well then, Sivan, I am first t'varr to a sea lord, and now you can take me back where I belong. I will not leave without Kalaiya.'

The sled dropped suddenly. Tsen screamed as they plunged like a stone towards the storm-dark. 'Kalaiya!' They were really going without her. Somehow he had thought there might be a miracle, that he could change what would happen. 'Kalaiya! *Kalaiya!*' He struggled against the rope, rocking back and forth until he almost threw himself off the plummeting sled, and screaming and screaming until Sivan whirled about and touched him and everything went black.

31

A Half-Remembered Place

For the second time Baros Tsen T'Varr opened his eyes and wondered where he was. This time he quickly screwed them shut again. The wind had stopped. The air was still and the sky was as bright as the sun. The sled under his back was hard and uncomfortable. He shifted, trying to stretch himself out, and realised he could move and that the rope was gone. He rolled onto his back, sat up and tried that eye-opening thing again. It didn't much help. Everywhere he looked, all he saw were rolling waves of dazzling sand. He was out in the open in the middle of the desert in the middle of the morning with no shelter and, as far as he could tell, no water.

'Come on. Get up.' Sivan was poking him.

His first thought was to push Sivan off the sled and fly away. 'If we're going to debate the terms of your surrender, could we at least do it somewhere comfortable? Frankly I'd prefer a pleasant orchard, perhaps over a qaffeh and some Bolo, but I'd honestly settle for any place with some shade. Could you perhaps ...?'

The shifter ignored him, jumped off the sled and walked away across the sand. For a minute or so Tsen watched him go but Sivan didn't look back. With a groan, Tsen got up. His feet hurt. He frowned and scratched his head, trying to remember how to make sleds work. They were enchanter toys. They did what an enchanter wanted because the enchanter wanted it and that was about the extent of what he knew; that and that they were probably a lot less use than they appeared in a place like this. He dimly remembered hearing that the small ones couldn't fly all that far before they ran out of whatever it was that made them work.

He jumped up and down a bit. The sled wobbled. It was floating over the sand, not resting on it. Still working then, although a fat lot of good that did him. Enchanter constructs worked when he wanted them to work because he carried a black rod. The en-chanters made those rods for everyone and each rod was different, a personal thing. They were like keys, unique, and what locks they opened depended on who you were. And he didn't have his black rod any more. Of course he didn't. Sivan had taken it. Then again he hadn't seen Sivan use a rod either. Did that make him an enchanter then?

Well, you could always ask him. Sivan was almost at the top of the nearest dune. Tsen watched as he disappeared over the top.

Or perhaps not.

Tsen stood there for a bit, thinking *Go* and *Up* as hard as he could and then thinking what a fool he'd look to anyone watching and then what a fool he was for thinking something so stupid. *Yes. Probably a whole host of invisible dune people pointing and laughing at you.* Although if there were then at least they might know where to find some water. He was parched. Sand had crept into his ill-fitting too-tight black silks too. It itched.

He sat down again. He was sweating and there was no shade. The sled was made of glass and no use. He got up again and very deliberately scanned the horizon in case somehow he'd missed something, but there wasn't anything to see except the rolling dunes and one set of footprints leading up the nearest rise. *See? Now if there were invisible dune people, then that's how you'd know. They'd leave tracks.*

The only tracks were Sivan's. Tsen closed his eyes and took a deep breath and sighed. He really didn't want to climb the dune, *really* didn't, but the only other choice seemed to be to stay where he was and see what happened first: whether he roasted to death or died a parched husk. He sighed again, dropped off the sled and started to follow the footprints. He was probably being stupid. Sivan hadn't gone to all that trouble just to drop him into the storm-dark so he presumably wasn't going to leave him to die in the desert either; *presumably* he was off getting some shelter and water and other useful things and so *presumably* he was coming back. Presumably. Unless the shifter meant him to follow and just hadn't bothered to say so.

Thoughts of rescue bubbled up, of escape and flight, all of them utterly stupid. He had absolutely no idea where he was except that he was somewhere in the Empty Sands, and what he *did* know was that the Empty Sands had earned their name. They ran almost the entire width of Takei'Tarr, from Cashax in the north to the Lair of Samim and in places right to the sea in the south. From east to west they were a bit smaller – a mere handful of hundreds of miles from the Godspike in the east westward as far as the escarpment of the Tzwayg, which, if he could be bothered to imagine such things mattered just now, might be considered the start of the foothills of the Konsidar. Since the Tzwayg and the eastern Konsidar were every bit as dry and dead as the sand sea, he reckoned the distinction was irrelevant. Good to know he remembered his geography though. All those years trying not to learn anything. Must have had a good tutor back in Cashax. Maybe if he wasn't dead a year from now then he could go back and thank him. Tell him how knowing the exact extent of the Empty Sands had really raised his spirits when he was stuck in the middle of them …

Oh just shut up.

Halfway up the dune and he was already gasping. Bloody sand. He'd spent a good deal of his youth in Cashax, roaring around the desert on the back of a sled, wadi racing and generally making an arse of himself. He'd learned a lot about sleds and how fast they could go and how to corner them and skim them across the face of a dune. He tried to remember whether he'd accidentally learned anything useful about surviving out here. If he had, it was largely to try very hard not to have to.

Well, that's useful then.

Yes. Almost as useful as illeistic sarcasm.

Actually, that wasn't strictly …

Looking for features in the sand wasn't going to help because there weren't any. He probably knew the desert as well as anyone who didn't actually live there, and the sum of what he knew was that it was mostly made up of great big sand dunes with other bits scattered around like careless sprinkles on a hurriedly decorated cake: flats of gravel and of a milky-white power like crushed glass and a few stretches of hard red clay that the desert men claimed had once been lakes in the long-ago before the half-gods broke the world. He clearly wasn't in any of those, and even if he climbed a dune to find one staring him in the face, he hadn't the first idea how that was supposed to help him because they all looked the same. *Oh, look, a large flat expanse of red clay. Must be a dried-up lake bed. Pat yourself on the back for being clever for a moment before you go back to dying of thirst.* Something like that.

From the air he'd sometimes seen what looked like lines in the sand, or maybe under it. The shadows of old roads, said the desert men, but from the ground they were invisible. Nothing much lived here. Spiders. Scorpions. Snakes now and then. Skimming the dunes around Cashax, he'd once come across a nest of tiny silver ants with ridiculously long legs. If he was lucky maybe he might see a desert hawk. Magnificent birds, but that wouldn't be much consolation when he was stretched out dead. Maybe he'd be eaten by one. There were probably better ways to go.

What? Like dying quietly of old age in your bath fifty years from now with Kalaiya by your side and the taste of apple wine on your lips? Already forget that your dragon burned a city, did you? Forgot that everyone wants you hanged?

He deserved this. He deserved to die out here for what he'd done.

I tried to stop it! He waited a bit to see if his conscience was having that, but no, apparently not. *You were trying to be clever and you messed it up, but hey, you tried to stop it. Well done. Clap clap clap. THOUSANDS OF PEOPLE BURNED!*

He spent another few minutes arguing with himself about just how much everything either was or wasn't his fault, which kept him going until he reached the top of the dune. Sivan was waiting a few yards down the leeward side, just out of sight.

'You could have stayed with the sled, you know,' said the shifter.

'Now you tell me.' Tsen looked around for any sort of weapon but there was only sand and the sea of dunes. Sivan picked himself up.

'What do you know that makes them want you so badly, T'Varr?'

Despite being lost in the desert, despite his fallen eyrie and the fleet of Vespinese ships that had taken it from him, despite Kalaiya left behind – or perhaps because of all those things – Bàros Tsen T'Varr laughed. 'I know a great many things. I have made it my business to see that while Lord Shonda aimed his lightning at me,

I had lightning enough to aim back. You don't imagine I'm going to tell you, do you?'

'Didn't see this though, eh?' The young man laughed.

'Why are we here, out in the middle of the desert? Where are you taking me?'

'Somewhere safe and out of the way.' Sivan set off again. At least sliding down the lee side of the dune was easier than climbing. How long since he'd gone walking in the dunes? He'd done it as a boy and a couple of times in his younger years with Vey Rin – rich young men riding their sleds, dressed up in their glass-and-gold armour, scouting for the slavers that struck out into the desert now and then from Cashax. Older now, wiser and knowing a little more of the world and its consequences, he found himself ashamed of almost everything he'd done during those years in Cashax, but most of all of the time he'd scouted for the slavers. He'd been so painfully ignorant.

He slid down the sand, almost falling. He caught himself. Sivan was already ahead again, starting up the next slope.

'Is there an end to this?' Tsen called after him. 'Or are we just walking for the sake of it?'

'I told you, you could stay with the sled.' Sivan didn't look back.

'If you came all this way out of the goodness of your heart to save me from the wicked Lord Shonda, why didn't you come a little sooner with news of his plans so I was ready to meet him? And why did you tie me up? To be blunt with you, I do not feel particularly *rescued,* Sivan.' Inside he winced. Sometimes he couldn't help himself; he just had to push a bit harder than he ought. He reached the bottom of the dune. Sivan, already halfway up the next, looked back at last.

'You're free to go, T'Varr. You're not my prisoner.' He kept on walking.

It had never occurred to Tsen, even when it was happening right under his nose, what the slavers in Cashax were really doing, how they ripped tribes apart, families. One thing to treat the barbarians of the other realms so – although the older he got, the more he questioned even that – but the desert men were black-skinned Taiytakei like him. Oh, the slavers dressed it up well, made sure their rich-boy scouts were kept safe and away from the nastier parts of their business, but what shamed him most was that he'd never stopped to think. It wasn't so much what he'd done, more that he'd joined in so blindly and never once thought to open his eyes.

Halfway up the next dune, he paused to catch his breath. He was sweating like a pig and Sivan was at the top. At least the shifter was waiting for him this time.

He'd gone dune climbing once, with Vey Rin, back long before anyone had imagined that Vey's brother Shonda would somehow rise to be sea lord of the most powerful city in the world. Vey Rin was back in Vespinarr now, mind broken by the dragon he'd been stupid enough to provoke with his jade raven. He owed his life to the rider-slave. Maybe Shonda did too and so maybe Shonda would spare her for that, but Tsen doubted it. Most likely he'd never even know. Vey Rin was certainly in no state to tell him.

Dunes. One step up, slide most of a step back again, and they'd been bigger dunes than these. He remembered how they'd joke, the two of them, about how many steps they really took to climb. They'd taken their sleds out into the deep desert scouting for signs of the black ooze lakes that rose from the sand now and then and drew the desert men. They'd gone a long way and hadn't found any and had turned back when Vey Rin spotted one of those dunes that really was as tall as a hundred men and challenged him to climb it. Tsen had given up halfway, laughing, sliding all the way to the bottom and flying to the top on his sled, but Vey Rin had kept on, walking all the way. Something had changed between them after that, as though Vey Rin was always a little disappointed in him.

He reached the top.

'You should have come to me openly,' he said to Sivan. 'You pretended to be the woman I love. You tricked me and I don't believe a word you say.'

Sivan's smile was broad and mischievous and with a touch of malevolence. 'Would you have come if I'd simply asked?' He laughed. 'As it happened, I did rescue you, T'Varr, and I really don't mean you any harm.'

'But you were coming for me either way.'

Sivan pointed down the lee of the dune to a pillar of white stone, round and about as tall and as wide as a man. There was a hole in the ground beside it. Tsen found the whole thing so odd that he forgot for a moment how exhausted and thirsty he was. A pillar and a pit in the middle of the shifting dunes? How did the hole not get filled up and the pillar not vanish under the sand? Sivan was already walking, and as Tsen hurried to catch him up, he saw that the hole was more of a shaft, the pillar in the centre of it and that a set of steps spiralled down. Closer still and he saw that the steps were made of the sand itself. Clearly his tutor in Cashax hadn't been so marvellous after all, since he had no idea what this place was or how it worked or how Sivan had found it.

'Kalaiya,' he called. 'I want Kalaiya. That's all.'

Sivan started down the steps. When Tsen reached them, he hesitated, but then again he couldn't think of anything else to do but follow. The sun was hot, the stairs were shady, he needed water, and all that waited for him in the dunes was death. He ran his hand over the pillar as he tested the first step. The stairs looked the same as the dunes but if he closed his eyes and listened to his feet then they were as solid as iron. The white stone of the pillar was hard, flawless and perfect-polished smooth like the white stone of the eyrie and of the Godspike. It had two symbols carved into it but he had no idea what they meant. It disappeared into the shaft and the steps spiralled around it, and as the sunlight fell away, he saw that the pillar itself glowed with a soft yellow light, guiding his way.

Like the white stone of the eyrie tunnels. So they were the same. He tried not to think about that. Hardly useful just now.

'Did you hear me?' he shouted. 'I want my Kalaiya.'

No answer. Sometimes he wished he'd never heard of dragons. Had never left Xican. Had never risen to be crazy Quai'Shu's t'varr. Sometimes.

The steps went sixteen full circles down and then stopped. A passageway apparently of sand led him to another tunnel, this one much longer and larger and made of the white stone again, almost perfectly round but flattened at the bottom, like the spiralling passageways of the eyrie except wider and arrow-straight. The walls glowed with their own soft light, dim as a moonless night lit by stars, and the tunnel ran each way as far as he could see. Across the way and recessed, two bronze doors stood partly open. They were as tall as three men, and carved into each were the likenesses of two serpents twined one around the other. Sivan was waiting for him again. As Tsen stared, Sivan put his hand to Tsen's chest and shook his head. 'What's in there isn't for you, T'Varr. Wait here.'

'Kalaiya, shifter. If you want something of me, she's my price.'

'Yes. Now wait while I bring food and water.'

'Is this your hideaway, Sivan?' He felt close to the end of his rope, as though nothing much mattered any more and he might as well be as rude as he liked.

Sivan laughed. 'No!' Then he shrugged. 'You can go in if you really want to, but I sincerely don't recommend it. In part because you'd very likely go mad and at the very least greatly wish that you hadn't, but mostly because if you as much as touch these doors then the snakes carved into them will come alive and rip you to pieces.' Sivan cocked his head. 'Reasonable enough?'

Tsen laughed. 'I'm no child.' He looked at the doors and regarded them nervously. The snakes did seem very lifelike.

'No?' Sivan laughed back in his face. 'Have you ever been here, T'Varr? Have you seen a place like it? Have you? Do you have any idea who made it?'

'Actually I do. My eyrie. Perhaps you were too busy pretending to be Kalaiya to notice? It was made by the same sorcerers. The old half-gods.'

Sivan paused, and for a moment Tsen thought he might even change his mind. But no. 'Stay here, T'Varr. What's beyond is not for you. Believe what you like, but you're no use to me mad.' He slipped between the doors and left Tsen to stare up and down the tunnel. The world wasn't big any more and it wasn't supposed to have many surprises left for a man like him, not for a t'varr to a sea lord, the highest a t'varr could rise. It was his purpose in life to know where everything could be found, procured and bought, how to ship it, pay for it and use it.

No surprises? Well apart from the Godspike and your eyrie and the storm-dark and the Elemental Men ...

But that's just stuff I don't understand. Like everything Chay-Liang does. Not the same.

... and dragons and alchemists and shifter skin and jade ravens and everything that ever comes out of Qeled ...

Fine. He didn't have much of an answer to that.

He looked up and down the tunnel with a sense of awe and wonder that he found he rather liked. Dragons were different. Dragons were simply terrifying, but this … How many people knew this tunnel existed? And who had built it? When? How? Where did it go? And then he found himself with the same uncomfortable sense of intrusion that had settled over him when he'd first walked through his eyrie, pacing out its empty passageways, imagining its builders and agape at the mystery of its purpose and design. He'd made the eyrie his and the unease had quietly gone. He'd dressed it as the fancy took him and put in his bath, and no matter that no one understood what it was or how it worked or anything much about it, it had become merely a flying piece of rock that made a good place to keep Quai'Shu's dragons, and that was all he thought of it.

The dragon *was* different. The dragon had brought something else. Awe, yes, but not much wonder. Fear mostly. Dread.

Sivan came back carrying two sacks, one in each hand. Behind him the doors ground shut, apparently a decision made entirely on their own. Tsen took a sharp step away. 'Who else is here?'

'No one.' The shifter followed Tsen's eyes. 'Not the work of any enchanter, T'Varr. There were no such things when this was made. No such things as Elemental Men and certainly no navigators for there was no storm-dark to cross in those days. It was made by the servants of the sun and the moon and the earth and the stars.' He laughed as Tsen shuddered. 'Yes, Baros Tsen T'Varr, the old gods of whom we must not speak – do you think an Elemental Man will hear us down here?' He rapped the stone with his knuckles. 'They can't pass through this. Did you know that? There's no one here to murder us for remembering, for speaking the old gods' names and offering them sacrifice. If that's what you want then go ahead. I hear there are plenty of men and women on the surface who have their secret shrines and none more so than in Vespinarr. Go on, T'Varr – read from the Rava itself if you wish.' He laughed again at the look of horror on Tsen's face. 'I have no use for those gods and their disciples either but I'll not pretend they never happened. They broke the world and now your Elemental Men keep watch to see that none of us ever grow such a power again, but no one cares about the relics they left behind.' He chuckled. 'Except, it seems, for dragons.'

Tsen glared at him. 'What do you know? Who are you?'

Sivan pushed past him, back into the tunnel made of sand, talking over his shoulder as he climbed the steps back to the surface. 'Follow the old ways and you'll reach ... places you'd rather not visit. The Queverra, if you're lucky. The other way will take you to ruined Uban. It's not far. No one has much use for a few tumbled-down old temples, but if you were to shift the sand you might find much more than that.' He turned and tossed one of the bags to Tsen. 'If we live long enough, you might think on that. In the meantime here's some water. Earn your keep.'

'My keep?'

'I rescued you from the Vespinese, didn't I? I think some gratitude is in order.'

'I didn't ask to be ...' Tsen's voice trailed away. Sivan was mocking him. They walked back across the dunes in silence. It was hard work but he barely noticed. By the time he reached the sled, most of his thoughts were with Kalaiya and what the Vespinese would do to her when they found he was gone. *That* was far more terrible.

32

The Lair of Samim

It took three days to reach the end of the desert. Days of skimming the sand on the back of the sled. Sivan stopped every few hours to drink and eat and rest, and each time he did, Tsen looked at the water and at the rings on his fingers and wondered what to do. One ring slipped off, one dip of a finger in a full cup, that was all it would take, but no one except Bronzehand had answered him for months and Bronzehand was in a ship far away, and anyway Sivan claimed to work for him so he was hardly going to offer any help. More likely he'd simply smile that bland smile of his and mouth something like, *How's the rescue going?*

Rescue my arse!

Each time they stopped Sivan took a gold-tinted glass globe the size of a man's fist off the back of the sled and threw it away into the sand, took another globe out of his bag and put it in place of the old. After he'd done that for the second time, Tsen understood. That was how the sled worked. That was how it got its energy.

'Most of them need to be taken to a black obelisk,' Sivan said when he caught Tsen's eye. He looked at the golden globe and tossed it idly from one hand to the other and back again. 'You're a t'varr. How much do these cost?' When Tsen shrugged, he laughed. 'But you're a t'varr! You know the price of everything.'

'Not of something I've never seen.'

'The enchanters of Vespinarr make these. No one else. They take a great deal of effort and they certainly cost far more than this sled. And here I am, throwing them away.'

'I'm flattered to be considered so valuable.'

They flew more at night than in the day. Sometimes Sivan found them shelter, sometimes he draped a sheet of dark cloth over the sled and the two of them rested in the tiny patch of shade underneath. Tsen dozed and thought about running away but Sivan never seemed to grow tired and there was simply nowhere to go.

'Aren't they looking for me?' Tsen asked after three days. 'If Shonda wants me dead so badly, why doesn't he send his men to look for me?'

'I doubt it.' Sivan chuckled. 'The Empty Sands are vast. He had enough trouble finding your eyrie. Besides ...'

'Besides what?'

Sivan pursed his lips. 'I gave him good reason not to come after us. Don't you remember? I left a body for him to find. He thinks you're dead.'

Oh. Yes. That. The dying sword-slave whose face he'd seen change into his own. He kept blanking that as though it hadn't really happened. Because it couldn't have.

He watched the passage of the sun each day for want of anything else to do and thought they'd flown almost straight south from the Godspike, but on the third morning he saw he was wrong and they'd veered a good way west. The air was still as dry as dust but ahead he saw the glitter of water sparkle here and there in the far distance, while the land become as flat as paper.

'You know where we are?' asked Sivan when they stopped again.

Tsen stared ahead. 'That is the Lair of Samim.'

'The desert men call it the Poison Sea. They say that every venom in every creature in every world was made there. They say the Samim dwells within. Do you know what that is, T'Varr?'

A wry smile twisted Tsen's lips. 'A legend. A giant scorpion a hundred feet long with a hundred legs, with seven poisonous tails and three pairs of claws each of which can cut a horse in two. In a ring around its mouth parts grow seventeen venomous snakes so deadly that neither Zaklat the Death Bat nor the Red Banatch could face it. Fortunately for them and for the rest of us, the Samim never leaves its lair, content to give birth to the endless snakes and scorpions of the world. Just as well.' He snorted. 'Stories, Sivan.'

'It wasn't always so, but either way it won't trouble us much on a sled.'

Tsen couldn't help but laugh. 'Sled or no sled, a sight like that I think would trouble me very much.' He looked at Sivan hard. 'I've heard other stories too, ones that have weighed on my mind of late. Stories of the Konsidar and what lies beneath.'

'Oh yes?' Sivan's voice stayed light and careless. He grinned. 'Go on then. I like stories.'

Tsen, who considered that if he had a talent for anything at all then it was for spotting such things, thought he saw a flash of tension behind Sivan's grin. *Yes. I thought so.* 'You really are one. One of the Righteous Ones who dwell beneath the Konsidar?'

Sivan shrugged. 'I did tell you so.' He was still trying to look unconcerned, but another twitch gave him away. *And here, tongue, is where you might wish to tread with some care.*

'Then your skin is priceless.' He watched Sivan hard, whose smile had fallen off his face like the moon crashing out of the sky. He looked ready to kill someone but Tsen's tongue had the better of him now. 'You're taking quite a risk coming to the surface. And you're not working for Bronzehand at all.'

Sivan didn't speak. They looked at each other until finally Tsen had to turn away. *What's the matter, fat old T'Varr? You were ready to die only a few days ago.* Although it was more a case of being resigned to the inevitable than actually being keen on the idea. *Are you mad, then?* And yes, he realised, he was. He seemed to have somehow found some hope. Probably a profound mistake but there it was, and when he looked at it, it didn't seem to want to go away.

'Would *you* skin someone, T'Varr?' Sivan's expression was strange. Dark and full of glowering clouds. Tsen thought of the alchemist on the eyrie skinning the hatchling he'd poisoned to make dragon-scale armour for his rider. Skinning the assassin who'd tried to kill him to preserve the marks on the man's back so he might one day understand them.

'A man?' Tsen shrugged. 'I'd like to think not but I suppose it might depend on what he'd done. If someone harmed my Kalaiya? Yes, I suppose I might skin them for that. *Did* you harm her?'

Sivan stayed silent for a while as though weighing Tsen's reply. He pursed his lips. 'No,' he said, and finished his breakfast and climbed back onto the sled. 'Coming, T'Varr? Or would you rather stay here and ponder your stories?'

The Samim itself may have been a story, but the saltmarsh flats where the Yalun Zarang and the Jokun came out of the mountains and hit the desert before they reached the sea were real enough. Men died here more often than in the Empty Sands. They died because they saw the water and drank it, not realising that away from the main flow of the rivers it was poisonous. There were shifting thick yellow crusts over stagnant pools of fetid water that would crack and split and swallow a man, and yes, there were creatures that lived in this swamp, some of them big and most of them poisonous. By midday they had reached the edges of it and Sivan drifted the sled slowly through its channels, taking his time as if looking for something. They changed course several times until Tsen saw the first of the two great rivers ahead, the Jokun. There were boats on the river. People. Which made Tsen have all those thoughts of help and rescue and escape again that he'd had back in the desert, only now they didn't seem so futile.

'Are you going to take this rope off me?' he asked. He didn't get an answer but Sivan didn't move so he supposed that was a no.

The sled drifted on, apparently aimless until the saltmarsh gave way to a small grove of summer moon trees. They had bands around their trunks, little gashes in the bark and strapped-on pots to collect the resin that oozed from the wounds. The smell in the air was unmistakable – Xizic. Sivan stopped the sled in the middle of the grove and stepped off. He made a slight gesture and clucked his tongue a few times. The rope around Tsen wriggled and shifted and looped around his legs until Tsen was trussed like a fly in a spider's larder. He couldn't even wriggle enough to pull the rings from his fingers. Sivan walked off among the trees; ten minutes later he was back with three scruffy Taiytakei who stank of cheap Xizic. He clucked at the rope again. It unwound itself and snaked across the ground to coil around the shifter's waist. Sivan tossed Tsen a Xizic tear. 'Have some.'

Tsen caught it, looked, sniffed it and tossed it back. 'I never had much taste for it.' *Hanjaadi Xizic. Cheap nasty stuff.*

'Suit yourself.' The shifter patted the rope around his waist in case Tsen was thinking he might try running off. The idea struck Tsen as vaguely absurd – maybe slightly less absurd than when they'd been in the middle of the desert with no one around for a hundred miles, but still pretty ridiculous. *I mean, look at me!* 'You know these trees grow everywhere, as long as it's hot?' Sivan asked. 'Sometimes they seem to grow straight out of solid rock. The really hardy ones have a bulbous swelling of the trunk at the base to keep them from being torn away by the wind. The tears they shed are supposed to be the best. They have a more fragrant aroma. I suppose, being a lofty t'varr, you prefer those.' He chuckled. 'Xizic was traded across Takei'Tarr since before the Splintering. You can see sacks of Xizic in the murals on the walls of the temple of Mokesh. They mention Xizic in the rituals of the Rava.' He laughed as Tsen winced. 'Still no Elemental Men watching over us out here, T'Varr, and if there were, I think perhaps speaking the name of an old forbidden book is the least of my worries.'

'You speak as if you've read it.'

'Maybe *you* should read it. You'd learn a thing or two about your dragons.' Sivan scratched his neck, swatting at a fly. There were a lot flies in the Lair of Samim, bloodsucking things that carried all manner of disease. 'In the Dominion of the sun king, followers of the old gods use Xizic from these very trees. They mix it with other oils in all their rituals. The desert men use it in medicines. They say it's good for digestion and healthy skin, for the joints, healing wounds and purifying the atmosphere from undesirable spirits. Almost everything. If you throw some on the fire then the perfume repels mosquitoes.' He laughed, swatting at his neck again. 'You'll smell it a lot here in the swamp. A miracle tree.'

They reached the edge of the grove where the mud gave way to a shallow lagoon. A small flat-bottomed boat was moored by a frayed rope to a dead tree stump. The three Taiytakei stepped in while Sivan waited for Tsen. 'In the spring, when the floods come, the Lair of Samim is cleansed. Then the floods go, and the lakes and the lagoons are cut off from the river again. You know there's nowhere to run, don't you?'

Tsen didn't bother to answer. He stepped into the boat and sat down. 'You're going to leave that sled in the middle of those trees, just like that? I know how much *those* cost. A great deal more than a Jokun Xizic boat and crew.'

'They'll be back for it.' Sivan threw a tattered poncho at Tsen. 'Put this on.'

It made him look like one of them, a Samim Xizic man. He

wondered, as he sat in silence watching them punt across the water, why they were leaving the sled and thought perhaps he understood: Sivan didn't want to be seen. He didn't want any word or whisper of something unusual creeping up and down the river to Vespinarr or Hanjaadi. There were enough people out here in this wilderness that a sled would catch the eye. It might be remembered. Xizic men, though? Still, the thought gave him hope. Despite what he'd said, Sivan was afraid there would be people looking for him after all.

Only so they can hang you, Tsen reminded himself.

On the far side of the lagoon a narrow channel a foot deep ran off into the swamp. A half-mile later it reached the expanse of the Jokun, bright clear water at last. Even the air smelled better: fresh and without the swamp stink of rot crawling into his nose with every breath. A riverboat with a little mast and two more Taiytakei sat tethered to a thick post sticking up from the water. When Tsen clambered aboard, the other men set about pulling the punt on deck. Tsen sat himself on a basket full of Xizic tears. He watched the sailors raise a sail and lower a pair of oars and caught the eye of the nearest as he passed, cocked his head at Sivan and whispered loudly, 'I don't suppose he's told you who I am or how many people are looking for me or what's going to happen to you if they find out you had a part in this? Hmm?' He clucked and shook his head. 'No, I don't suppose he has. Whatever he's paying you, I will pay you ten times as much for you to throw him in the river right here and now and take me to Hanjaadi. You have but to name your price.' They weren't turning the boat, he saw, so they weren't heading for the Bawar Bridge and the sea; they were taking him upstream. *And where does following the Jokun upstream take us?*

Vespinarr.

The sailor turned away. He muttered something to the others and none of them would even look at him after that. They didn't speak to him, not once, all the way through the Lair of Samim and up towards the Jokun cataracts.

Sivan came and sat beside him a little later, once they were under way. 'In your place I might have done the same. But they won't help you.'

'I can't tell if it's me they hate or you they fear,' Tsen said.

'Try to remember: I *did* rescue you.'

'I don't feel very rescued.' Tsen shrugged. 'I'm not sure, but it might have been the rope that did that.'

Sivan offered him another piece of Xizic, clear and pale and clearly not from the marshes. This time Tsen took it. 'They don't hate you,' Sivan said, and Tsen wondered how much he should read into that. 'They don't have the first idea who you are.'

'Why all this trouble?'

'This isn't my face, Baros Tsen T'Varr. Not my real one, but I can't show that here. None of this is what you think. Let us say that, whoever I am, I'm neither slave nor lackey. Let us also say that I have many ears in the court of Vespinarr.' He smiled widely and drew out a black rod, the sort that any Taiytakei of significance carried to enter the towers of glass and gold and make the device-gifts of the enchanters come to life and do their bidding. Things like sleds and glasships. 'Yours,' he said. 'It opens many doors. I took it when you were staring at me from your bath all bewildered at what was going on. That's what's in it for me.' He leaned in and whispered in Tsen's ear, 'T'Varr, I went to your eyrie to steal a dragon's egg.'

Tsen laughed. 'And my alchemist and my rider and some of those Scales slaves with their vile disease too? Why not simply steal the lot?'

'Just an egg. One would have done, although I would have preferred several to be safe. Unfortunately, events caused a change of plan and so I stole you instead. You will help me. In return I will steal your Kalaiya for you.'

He wouldn't say any more and so Tsen sat back and enjoyed the shade and the warm air and the cold fresh water of the river. He moved to the bow of the boat and stared up the river. The Jokun came down from the mountains less than a hundred miles away. The water there was like ice, and it flowed down into the desert quickly, keeping its freshness. The odd thing was that there were creatures living in the waters of the lakes and lagoons that would die of cold if they tried to swim in the river, and other creatures in the river that would slowly cook in the warmer pools of the Lair of Samim. Two different worlds joined together but unable ever to meet. Like the Taiytakei and the Righteous Ones of the Konsidar.

Oh, look at you, with your clever metaphors for life. How useful. Got any metaphors to get us out of here? Tsen had a bit of a think about that and found that no, he didn't. Instead, he quietly decided that Sivan must be a lunatic because only a madman would know what a dragon was and then try to steal an egg without an alchemist to control the hatchling that would eventually come out of it.

In the night his Bronzehand finger tingled. He slipped the ring off and let Bronzehand see where he was, for all the good that might do him. He didn't have a bowl of water handy to return the favour but he walked out into the cool dark air and the breeze off the mountains and trailed his hand in the water of the river, letting Bronzehand see the Lair of Samim around him. He kept the ring off. Didn't seem to matter much now. Maybe Bronzehand had a way to tell some of the others, but if he did, none of them tried to see through him to find out where he was. Besides, unless Sivan was a liar, Bronzehand was probably very happy with matters just as they were.

After two days on the river, the swamps of the Lair fell behind them, the banks turned rocky and barren and Tsen saw the first distant summits of the Konsidar ahead, the southern rim that cradled the Vespinarr basin before the greater peaks of the Righteous Ones further to the north. Another day and another night and the river changed again, became narrow, fast and angry. They left the boat and the silent frightened sailors behind and returned to the shore. Sivan had other men waiting – hired sword-slaves with little interest in anything but money, Tsen thought, but when he made the same offer as he'd made the sailors, they were every bit as afraid. Mortally, dreadfully afraid. When Tsen tried speaking to them, they looked away. They wouldn't even meet his eye. He wasn't sure, but he thought perhaps they pitied him.

'Who is he?' he whispered to one, but if he knew he didn't say.

33

The Lords of Vespinarr

When they were done asking questions of the corpse that looked like Baros Tsen T'Varr but wasn't, Red Lin Feyn and her soldiers took his body back to the bathhouse. Liang watched them go, left alone with Bellepheros. They looked at each other in silence for a long time and Liang tried to see the man she'd thought she'd known. He looked exactly as he always had – scruffy, tired and slightly irritable, the same Belli she'd worked with all these months – but now he'd brought a dead man back to life. Two, in fact. She was glad of the gloom. It meant he didn't see how she stared at him. She took a deep breath and forced the lump out of her throat.

Belli sat down. 'What now?'

'What you've done is sorcery. The Arbiter ...' Liang shook her head. 'She has to tell them, Belli. She has to. The killers. And once they know ...' Words kept trying to jump out of her mouth. He'd done this for her and now ... 'Sorcerers shattered the world, Belli. They made the storm-dark. The killers won't allow it to happen again. It's what they're for. What now? I don't know.'

'I'm not a sorcerer, Li.'

Liang didn't know what else to say. 'Is it true? The dead can't lie?'

The alchemist stuck out his bottom lip. 'I've never known otherwise.' He started towards her and then stopped. 'Li, abyssal powders are not used often or lightly.'

'Belli! It's not what you *choose* to do. It's what you *can* do. Oh Xibaiya!' She had to turn away again.

After another long silence Bellepheros grunted, hauled himself back to his feet and paced across the room. 'Your killers could send me home, you know, if they don't like what I do.'

'They could.' But they wouldn't. More likely, when they knew what he could do, they'd launch an expedition to the dragon-realm and put every alchemist they could find to the knife. 'How long dead ...' She knew exactly what they'd think. Could someone with this sort of power dig up the corpse of Feyn Charin and pull out all his secrets? What about the monstrous sorceress Abraxi or the nightmare terror of the Crimson Sunburst? *Never mind what the alchemist says, best to be sure.*

Bellepheros was watching her. He looked sad.

'They could send us all home, Li,' he said. 'Me and the dragons and the eggs and the hatchlings and her Holiness. Wouldn't that be better? Just let us go back where we belong.'

Liang rounded on him. Her words came out hot and full of anger. 'Why do you always call her that, Belli? Holiness? Look at her! Do you think her some sort of goddess?'

He laughed at her for that. 'It's tradition. Where I come from, failing to address one's speaker properly can mean being fed to their dragons before the sun sets. Li, how is it possible for that man not to be Baros Tsen? He *is* Baros Tsen.'

'I don't know.'

'But if he isn't then someone changed his face! How? And you tell *me* about sorcerers!'

'I don't know, Belli, I don't know. It frightens me. *You* frighten me.'

'Me? Ha!' He sounded so full of hurt and disbelief that a part of her wanted to hug him and tell him she was sorry and that she'd find a way to understand and it would all be fine and not to worry and ... And yet she didn't move, didn't speak.

The iron door eased open behind her. Red Lin Feyn slipped back in. 'I'm sorry to intrude,' she said, 'but I'm afraid I've been listening and *I* do know.' The Arbiter closed the door and for a few seconds stood very still, eyes closed. 'We are alone. That is good. Chay-Liang of Hingwal Taktse, you will listen to me now and do as I say. Do not ask questions and do not speak of this to anyone. I will explain more later when we are alone on a glasship to Vespinarr.'

'Vespinarr?' Liang blinked in surprise. Red Lin Feyn frowned at her.

'I told you to listen, not to speak. You will go back to your rooms, both of you. This did not happen. The guards will remain outside your doors. When my killers return, I will inform them I have decided on a further course of investigation. I will not tell them why, not yet. At first light you, Chay-Liang, and I will travel to Vespinarr. I will send a killer ahead to the Dralamut to demand additional guardians. We should not consider ourselves safe, either of us, so you may bring whatever you see fit to defend yourself. They will send a killer with us to watch over me. You will say nothing of what you've done or heard in this room tonight unless you are absolutely certain we are alone. Do you understand? Absolutely, unquestionably alone.'

Chay-Liang nodded, bewildered. 'And Belli?' she asked as the Arbiter turned and reached for the iron door.

'Your alchemist slave will remain and go about his usual duties. I will leave orders for the killers to mind the eyrie and allow no one to leave. It will carry on exactly as it is until our return. They will be told this is my will. Whether they adhere to it will depend on truths yet to be unravelled.' She fixed Belli with a hard look. 'I will not tell them what power you have, alchemist, not yet. For now, I suggest you both consider any means by which a killer may be incapacitated or detained.'

Liang's mouth fell open. 'Lady ... ?'

Red Lin Feyn opened the door and barked at her soldiers, 'The enchantress is to return to her quarters. No one is to enter –' she paused '– even if they appear to be me. Come, Chay-Liang. Back to your prison now.'

She walked away. Liang took a step after her and then stopped and turned back. She went to Belli and took his hands in hers. 'I don't know what you are any more, Belli, but you're a good man. Stay that way. Be safe. Do nothing to make them suspicious.' She looked into his eyes for a moment, felt the calloused skin of his hands under her fingers and found she wanted to do much more than hold them; but want would have to wait.

'I'll do my best, Li.' He looked bemused, which made her want to laugh and cry all at once.

As soon as she was back in her room, Liang began to pack. Vespinarr? There were a lot of things she might have taken with her, the accumulated nonsense of a dozen years as enchanter to a sea lord. Things came her way whether she wanted them or not.

Pieces of glass worked with different metals in them. No one had yet found anything that made glass as malleable to an enchanter's will as gold, but that didn't stop the journeymen in Hingwal Taktse from trying, and now and then they found an interesting property. Then there were things people made to show off their skills, hoping to secure her attention and patronage; pieces sent to her as gifts; things sent to Tsen that he didn't want; her own early pieces as an apprentice, kept for posterity. When her workshop had no space for it all any more, her room had become a cross between a laboratory and a museum. Little of it was actually useful. The Arbiter had already taken her lightning wand and her black rod.

She packed a dozen pieces of unworked glass and a spare robe. Over in one corner, stored carefully in a chest, were a dozen globes of trapped fire from the Dominion, where blazes were caught by the sun priests and imprisoned inside enchanted glass. The sea lords used them to tip the black-powder rockets their ships carried into battle; but after the dragons had arrived, Tsen's rockets had been removed from the walls and put into storage. Liang had dismantled a few. She couldn't remember what she'd been meaning to do with them now but she had the fire globes and three sealed pots of black powder.

She picked up a globe and looked at it. Fire globes set everything around them alight when they broke. Horrific and terrifying things when shot on rockets against wooden ships but not much use against dragons, which laughed at fire, and not much use against Elemental Men either, not when they could simply turn into the stuff at will. She fiddled absently with some gold-glass until she'd made a second shell around a fire globe and then filled it with black powder. It would explode with even more force now.

What am I doing? She was shaking. Her breathing was ragged. Did she want to go to Vespinarr? No. Did she have a choice? No. *I've been told by the Arbiter. I have to. I don't have a say.* She shaped the glass some more, making it into a ball with needles sticking out so it would explode into a hail of sharpened slivers that would shred anyone near it. She fiddled, refined it, moulded it, changed it, changed it back and then changed it again. Yes, a fine thing for murdering a crowd of people, but what she'd made had ended up about the size of her head and covered in spikes – too heavy to be put on the end of a rocket, ridiculously awkward to carry and it still wouldn't trouble an Elemental Man.

She burst into tears, and the tears turned into great heaving sobs. Truth was, if she was honest, she was glad that the Arbiter was taking her, and she was glad that she had no choice. She needed just to be away. To have some time to think. To not see Belli's face every hour of every day and see him standing over a talking corpse; and yet it made her feel so utterly horrible because she was abandoning him when he needed her most and she hated herself for that, and she knew that if she was given the choice then she'd stay because that was right and he deserved it, but the Arbiter *hadn't* given her the choice and she was so damned grateful because that meant it wasn't her fault when she left him here alone ...

What did that say about her? If he knew, if he could see her inner thoughts, wouldn't he hate her? He certainly ought to.

She closed her eyes, thinking furiously about how she could keep Belli safe and what she ought to do for him and how much he deserved everything she could give, and then she must have fallen asleep because the next thing she knew there were men barging through her door and the Arbiter was with them, dressed in all her flaming finery.

'Give her five fingers of the sun to be ready. She may bring whatever she wishes.' Red Lin Feyn swept out and Liang was about to follow, all ready to start her arguments as to why she should stay so she could look after Belli, when another pair of soldiers came running in and gave her a wooden box with a tiny brass catch. Inside it six wax-sealed vials lay cocooned in soft velvet nestled over packed goose down. Her breath caught in her throat – she'd given the box as a present to Belli not long after he'd arrived. She couldn't remember where she'd got it – Zinzarra, perhaps – but the vials were her own work. They were simple little shapings, each no more than a few minutes' effort, but they were all unique and she'd worked the necks into differently shaped dragons for him. As she opened it, a piece of folded paper fell out, tied in a ribbon. She picked it up and read it:

'Be safe Li.'

Tied around the neck of each vial was a tiny label. Liang almost burst into tears again. She stuffed the box into her bag and hurried after the Arbiter, determined to stop her and demand to stay, but when she reached the dragon yard, she abruptly stopped. The yard was swarming with soldiers. Most were the Vespinese who had come to free Mai'Choiro Kwen, lined up in arrow-straight ranks. Their polished gold-glass armour gleamed with coppery fire in the dawn sun, their ashgars rested on their shoulders and their shields were raised to their chests in perfect lines. Their emerald and silver capes billowed and flapped like flags in the constant wind and the jade in their helms and the coloured silks they wore across their chests seemed to glow.

In the centre of the dragon yard a small golden gondola sat beside the one the Arbiter had taken for herself, but the soldiers weren't for her. Across the yard and close to the walls – as far away from the dragon's perch as they could be – three gondolas of jade and bright shining silver rested with their ramps still closed. Red Lin Feyn stood waiting for them in all her splendour, in her Arbiter's robe of flames and with the white headdress on, her arms spread wide and shielded from the wind by gold-glass screens while Elemental Men stood on either side. More killers watched from around the dragon yard, conspicuously outlined atop the walls. The hatchling dragons paid no heed to it all, almost hypnotised by the Godspike as ever. The great dragon was nowhere to be seen.

Liang's escort stopped dead. They were Vespinese soldiers themselves, proud in their silver and emerald, and Liang saw they were looking up at the glasships overhead, whose chains had carried these new gondolas here. When Liang followed their eyes, she understood. The glasships above the silver and jade gondolas were stained a silvery green. The impurities made them slower but they also made them unique and only one sea lord flew them. Shonda was here at last.

For a fleeting moment, at the top of her ramp, the Arbiter became Red Lin Feyn again. She shot Liang an irritable glance and made a sharp gesture for her to come. Confused, Liang ran to the Arbiter's side as the silver and jade gondolas cracked open. More Vespinese soldiers were running out from the barracks, forming themselves up into an honour guard as quickly as they could. The dawn sun shone across the storm-dark, lighting its swirling cloud with apocalyptic orange. The white stone of the eyrie appeared touched with pink.

'Go inside and make yourself invisible,' muttered Red Lin Feyn as Liang reached the gondola. Liang hurried in and climbed the steps to the upper level. She'd never been up here. It only occupied half the width of the gondola's interior and was reached by the sweep of an arcing silver stair. There was a huge bed and several closets and racks for … she had no idea what they were for but they were empty. She felt like an intruder, a thief, a burglar. This was where the Arbiter slept, where she stripped away the trappings of the Dralamut and became just an ordinary person, and Liang had no place being here. She put down her bag and wished she was somewhere else, wished that Shonda had arrived ten minutes earlier so she could have stayed in her room until all this was done or perhaps gone and spent an hour with Belli. Or later so she could have made her case to stay.

Which made her think again of the pale corpse of Baros Tsen turning to her to speak. She shivered. The alchemist was her slave. She often forgot but others didn't. She had responsibility for him and it cut both ways. The killers would look at her long and hard once they knew what he could do. It was all too much to think about.

She went to the window to see what was happening. The silver gondolas of Vespinarr had their ramps down now. Two dozen more soldiers were lining themselves up, pushing the other Vespinese back to make space. The wind tore at the emerald plumes on their helms and at the gold banners that flew from the long spiked staves they carried instead of ashgars – and then Liang frowned as she saw what else they were carrying. They had gold-glass globes in their hands and at their belts – and yes, they were armoured like soldiers but they weren't, they were enchanters! *How* many of them? She put a hand to her mouth and almost gasped and then counted to be sure. Twenty-two. Twenty-two enchanters. Hingwal Taktse rarely held more than fifty. The Cashax school was smaller and the palace in Khalishtor was smaller still. Across every realm of every world there were no more than a couple of hundred of them.

Twenty-two Hingwal Taktse enchanters. With that number working together they could do … well, anything really. They could build a cage for the dragon! Even the killers would have to pause surely? She watched as each enchanter lifted their glass orb and shaped it into a curved screen until they had a corridor running the length of the dragon yard from the middle of the three silver gondolas to the base of Red Lin Feyn's ramp. A man stepped out of the middle gondola. Bright green robes swirled behind him, while the braids of his hair were so long they dragged on the ground. He walked along the line of enchanters as though inspecting them, now and then shaking his head and gesturing to their glass screens until he was content, and Liang had to wonder what he was doing until at last she understood. They were shielding the path to the Arbiter from the wind. Twenty-two enchanters and Shonda had brought them to keep the wind off him?

The man in emerald came steadily on until he was so close that Liang couldn't see him from the window any more, even when she stood on tiptoe and pressed her nose to the glass to peer over the curve of the gondola's silver shell. There was a long pause and then a second man came out in a feather robe which spread out around him and seemed to float above his feet. There were patterns woven among feathers of shimmering electrum, a pale coppery gold, but they were subtle and too far away for Liang to make them out. His braids were even longer than the first man's and trailed behind him as though floating very slightly above the ground – no, they *were* floating, each one tipped with a tiny gold-glass sled no bigger than a finger. He wore a silver crown inlaid with jade. Shonda, sea lord of Vespinarr.

A movement on the eyrie wall caught her eye. An Elemental Man. The hatchlings all had their eyes on Shonda as though they hadn't forgotten the last time he'd come. Shonda himself never looked away from the Arbiter.

Liang moved back to the top of the stairs. She took a farscope out of her bag and spent a moment with it, reshaping the glass to bend it to look round the corner. She lay down at the top of the steps just out of sight and poked the bent end around the edge, feeling even more like an intruder and a little like a naughty child spying on her elders. Clearly the Arbiter had meant her to hear whatever was to be said otherwise why beckon her inside and then tell her to hide? Although why the Arbiter should want her here, Liang couldn't begin to guess.

At the top of the ramp two killers moved to bar the sea lord's way. Shonda stopped. He stood in front of Lin Feyn far longer than he should until, like the waiting man in green, he dropped to one knee. Whatever words passed between them were lost to the wind, and then the Arbiter turned, walked into the gondola and took her place on her crystal throne at the head of Mai'Choiro's table. One killer sat to either side while the others vanished. Into the air around them, Liang supposed. Watching. Watching her too, no doubt.

Shonda entered alone. The ramp closed behind him and the rushing roar of the wind across the eyrie abruptly ceased. Liang saw Shonda's robes clearly now: the designs, in slightly paler silvery gold or a touch darker with a hint more copper, were of three dragons and a lion, the sigil of his city. They were exquisitely done, almost as though they were living things. Each time he moved the dragons moved too, entwining around one another. He stared long and hard at Red Lin Feyn, sitting in all her splendour. 'Arbiter. You summoned us. We came.'

'And with some difficulty, I must suppose, given your delay. I do hope the journey wasn't too much trouble and that my summons was no inconvenience.'

'None at all, lady. Indeed, I had planned to visit your court to request the return of my kwen.'

'Then I am relieved and very glad to have summoned you. It would be such a shame for you to have come all this way for only one reason and then to have to leave with disappointment as your only reward. I'm afraid your kwen will not be returning to you. You will need to find another.'

Shonda paused and then cocked his head. 'Your investigation is complete, lady?'

'No, Sea Lord Shonda, it is not. Did Mai'Choiro Kwen engineer the destruction of Dhar Thosis on your behalf?'

'Of course not.'

'Very well. You may go. One testimony remains to be heard. You will remain at my court until that time.'

Shonda's lip curled. He laughed, a low throaty sound. 'Shrin Chrias Kwen? He continues to elude the Elemental Men, lady?'

'No. Baros Tsen T'Varr, Lord Shonda. I must hear Baros Tsen

T'Varr speak before I am done. Surely you must see the necessity?'

'I had heard he was dead, lady,' said Shonda, and Liang caught the moment of surprise on his face.

'Someone did indeed try very hard to leave that impression.' Lin Feyn cocked her head. 'Was it you?'

Shonda hesitated again. He frowned and looked to Liang as though truly confused. 'I am at a loss, lady, as to what you can mean.'

'No matter. Tsen himself, I imagine, seeking to escape his punishment. You may go. Amuse yourself. I hope you brought something to do. We are rather remote, there is little entertainment and I'm afraid you may be here for some time.'

'Lady Arbiter, if you have no further questions for me then I will return to Vespinarr. I will of course be available to be called again.'

'No, Sea Lord. I have decided you will remain here until I give my verdict.'

Shonda laughed. 'Lady, I have a city to run, a fleet, an empire. You have taken my kwen and my brother my t'varr is—'

'Of no consequence.' Lin Feyn didn't even raise her voice, yet she cut him dead where he stood. It was a beautiful thing, and Liang made a quiet mental note to ask how she did it. 'You may go. My killers will see to your safety.' Liang imagined the Arbiter smiling, though doubtless her face remained perfectly still. As she watched Shonda compose himself, the most powerful man in all the worlds dismissed like an errant child, Liang found herself starting to like this Red Lin Feyn. Eventually Shonda dropped to one knee. 'Lady. May I ask, lady, how long I will be remaining here?'

'As long as is required, Sea Lord Shonda of Vespinarr.'

Shonda rose. Liang thought he left with surprising grace, all things considered. She crept sheepishly back to the window and watched him and the man in green return to their gondola. The ramp closed behind them, sealing them in. The twenty-two enchanters with their gold-glass screens remained exactly as they were. Liang could almost feel them wondering what they were supposed to do. Nothing, apparently, so they simply stood and waited, and she tried to imagine Baros Tsen T'Varr doing something like this and then keeping her standing like a lemon. She might have slapped him for that. But then Baros Tsen didn't have twenty-two enchanters to pick and choose between. He had her and that was that.

She shaped the farscope back to its original form, picked up her bag and started down the stairs, and then froze as an Elemental Man appeared in the gondola close to the Arbiter and almost collapsed. He clung to the table and hauled himself upright, clutching his side. He was covered in blood. He saw Liang, vanished, appeared again at the Arbiter's ear, whispered for a moment and then was gone. Liang didn't move until Lin Feyn glided across the gondola and raised a hand, beckoning her to follow out across the dragon yard. Red Lin Feyn had to stoop to walk against the wind, the headdress whipping around her. *No enchanters to keep the wind from pulling at the robes of the Arbiter*, Liang thought. *Yet she's one of us. She could have emptied Hingwal Taktse if she'd wanted.*

The last gondola in the dragon yard was a small golden thing decorated with ships and sea serpents, the sigils of the city of Tayuna. As soon as Red Lin Feyn was inside it, she lifted the headdress off and almost threw it on the floor.

'I swear whoever designed this couldn't possibly ever have worn it themselves.' She put it gently on a table and glowered at it, then smiled, though her eyes carried a flash of warning. 'I have some excellent news, Chay-Liang. The rider-slave slew the missing hatchling at sunrise this morning. She returns with its corpse. It is of no consequence to my purpose one way or another ...' again a flash of warning and this time a flick of the eye to yet another Elemental Man who stood patiently inside '... but it's one thorn fewer to prick at my killers.' She picked up an ornate fan made of silk and silver and ran her fingers over it. 'You will come with me because I may have need of an enchanter. I will not say where and you will not ask. You will be told what you need to know when the moment arises. We shall begin in Kabulingnor and we shall visit other sites in Vespinarr. You will not speak to any we meet unless I permit it.' She looked away. 'You will find the gondola has been partitioned so we may travel together without inconveniencing one another. You will find the space allotted to you above. I suggest you acquaint yourself with it. You may come when I call for you.' Which was as clear a way as could be of telling her that she was dismissed.

'Lady!'

The Arbiter looked up sharply. 'Enchantress?'

'I cannot come with you.'

For a moment the Arbiter was Red Lin Feyn again. She frowned fiercely, walked past Liang and closed the gondola ramp, then stood in the way so Liang would have to push past her to open it again. 'I do not believe I gave you a choice,' she said crisply, flicking another glance to the Elemental Man. 'Your reluctance stems from concern for your slave?' She sounded dismissive. 'We will discuss him if so.'

'Lady, I . . .' She didn't get any further. The Arbiter put a finger to her lips and suddenly Liang couldn't talk any more. Words formed in her mind and in her throat. Her lips and tongue moved but not a single sound came from either.

'In good time, Chay-Liang.'

Short of actually attacking the Arbiter of the Dralamut, which would get her killed on the spot by an Elemental Man in however little time it took him to cross the gondola and stab her, Liang couldn't think what she could possibly do except turn her back, climb the steps and go where she'd been told. Waiting for her she found a tiny windowless compartment that was so low she had to stoop. She dropped her bag on the minuscule bed. Even a slave might have objected to the space the Arbiter had given her, but so many thoughts were already crowding her brain they were almost bursting out of her head and she had no space for trivia. She felt the gondola move immediately. They were off! Already! She snapped and snarled and punched her fist into her hand. So this was getting what she wanted, was it? Leaving Belli behind? A bit of time and space of her own to think? Only that had been what she wanted last night, not now. Now she wanted to be with him, to keep him safe, and it was far more than a sense of duty from a good mistress towards her slave. She sat heavily beside her bag and balled her fists. She thought she might throw herself down and beat them against the mattress but that wouldn't do any good. No one would come and the Arbiter wouldn't change her plans.

She sat for what seemed a long time, wondering what she could do, realising that the answer was nothing and then wondering it again anyway. The thought that something could happen while she was gone, that it really might this time, that she wouldn't be there to stop it, was paralysing. Not the dragon or even the rider-slave this time, but the killers. And when she tried to tell herself that she was being foolish, that the killers didn't know what he'd done, that Belli was clever enough to look after himself, it just wasn't enough.

Liang felt her ears pop. They'd crossed the edge of the storm-dark and were coming down to a more comfortable height over the desert. She'd grown used to the altitude of the eyrie, where every step climbed left her gasping. The richness of the air close to the ground was intoxicating. She could almost taste it. Her ears popped again. There was a rushing sound from below that came and went. The low muttering of talk between the Arbiter and her killers was done. Liang lay very still and listened but she couldn't hear a thing. A moment of silence passed and then: 'Chay-Liang?'

Downstairs, Red Lin Feyn wasn't in her formal dress as Arbiter of the Dralamut any more but wore a simple white enchanter's robe. Two glasses of wine stood on the table in front of her. She patted the chair beside her and offered a glass to Liang.

'The killers have gone,' she said. 'Off to the Dralamut to bring our sentinel golems. Sadly we won't be taking them into the Kabulingnor with us, but I should hope that having both their kwen and their sea lord hostage in my court will deter the Vespinese from anything foolish.' She smiled faintly and sipped from her glass. 'You will find, Chay-Liang, that I will talk to you very differently when they return.'

'We are still going to Vespinarr, lady?' Liang frowned. She'd assumed Red Lin Feyn had meant to question Sea Lord Shonda there, but clearly not.

'Ironic, isn't it? Still, he shouldn't have delayed so long in answering my summons. He can stew for a while.' Her eyes brightened and she smiled. 'Did you see his enchanters, Chay-Liang?'

'Yes, lady.'

'One can't help feeling a little satisfaction at humbling a man who flaunts his power quite so openly. Very helpful of him too.'

'Lady?'

Lin Feyn shrugged. 'Between the dragon and its rider and Shonda's entourage, I think my killers will be kept very busy. All the better. The less attention they pay to us on this little journey, the more I am pleased.' She frowned. 'He seemed genuinely surprised when I asked him about Tsen, though. The one thing that caught him off guard.' She frowned again and then shrugged. 'Well, it can't be helped. Doubtless our arrival at the Kabulingnor will cause a great deal of confusion and there can't be many left there who have the authority to act in Shonda's stead. I suppose you realise that one reason I brought you with me was to keep you safe? *One* reason, although not so much *the* reason.'

'Me, lady?'

'Yes, Chay-Liang. You. The killers are in charge of the eyrie now. With luck they won't do anything much. They are very prone to inaction. It's their nature. Watch and watch and watch; although when they *do* strike, I will admit they do so with alarming thoroughness. One must always keep in mind their true purpose. I am a little uncertain as to where it will lead them at present.'

'Their purpose is to hunt sorcerers,' murmured Liang. She struggled to see what that had to do with anything except maybe Bellepheros, but …

But Lin Feyn was laughing and shaking her head. 'To hunt sorcerers? No, Chay-Liang, that is an *expression* of their purpose. They exist to prevent the world from being shattered. Sorcery offends them because of what it can become. Gods — and devotions to those gods — upset them in the same way. You wanted to stay because you think you can protect your alchemist slave but you can't. He's safer without you.' She turned a little and peered at Chay-Liang. 'I've not told them, not yet. I give you the chance to explain him first. What *else* can he do? Tell me about the disease that the Scales carry. This Statue Plague.'

'Bellepheros makes potions that keep the disease in check. He gives it to the Scales.'

'And? What else can he do?'

Liang thought for a moment. What could she dare say when Belli's life might hang in the balance?

'The whole truth, Chay-Liang. The killers are gone and we are alone. At this moment I am merely Red Lin Feyn, enchanter of Hingwal Taktse and navigator of the Dralamut, but even as the Arbiter, I'm interested in Dhar Thosis and nothing else. Sorcerers and Rava readers are for the killers, not for me. Now, Liang. Your alchemist slave. You may speak in confidence. What is he?'

Liang bowed her head. 'I saw an assassin rip his throat so deep he should have died in heartbeats and yet he lived. He gives the Scales potions that dull their minds as he dulls the dragons. He calls it a mercy. Given the disease they carry perhaps that's so but I am … unsure.'

'Could you not use golems?'

'Perhaps for some things, but for others I suspect the dragons require living thoughts from living minds. Lady, you said I may not ask questions but may I ask one? Why do you not trust your Elemental Men?'

For a long moment Red Lin Feyn gazed at her. The hint of a smile played at the corner of her mouth. 'The second reason I chose you to come with me, Chay-Liang, is because you are the cleverest woman or man on that eyrie. We head for Vespinarr, but we will enter the Konsidar when we are done there.' She must have seen how Chay-Liang's face froze because she held up her hands and cocked her head and smiled broadly. Across her painted face the expression seemed out of place. 'The killers will permit it, although they will watch us every moment.' She paused, as if mulling what to say. 'Liang, when the half-gods broke the world, the Elemental Men and the Righteous Ones hid themselves in Xibaiya, the only place that was safe for them. The Righteous Ones of the Konsidar are shifters too, but where the killers change to earth and air and fire and water, the Righteous Ones change their flesh and bone. They are skin-shifters, and one of them came to this eyrie and took Baros Tsen. I would very much like to know why.' She let that sink in for a moment. 'And yes, the caves and tunnels of the Konsidar reach all the way into Xibaiya and the land of the dead. In places they cross over. The killers chose this world, the Righteous Ones chose the other. No, I do not trust my killers.'

'Baros Tsen?' Liang couldn't keep the amazement out of her voice. 'He's in the Konsidar?'

'It's a place to start.' Red Lin Feyn smiled faintly. 'Either the killers don't know or they have allowed it. Perhaps they have encouraged it. The dragons too. Think it through, Chay-Liang. Think it through. Two of them given to Quai'Shu to do with as he pleased?'

Liang was still trying to get her head round the idea that a creature whose existence she'd thought was a mere story had actually come up from the land of the dead and taken Baros Tsen. 'Dear forbidden gods, why?'

'That is what you and I shall endeavour to uncover.' Red Lin Feyn shrugged her shoulders. 'The killers will leave us alone until we reach Vespinarr. You may ask your questions and then I shall begin your instruction as a navigator. The third reason you're here. I suspect you'll find it utterly disappointing.' She started to get up then froze as if struck by a thought. 'The missing hatchling is dead. The dragon-rider hunted it down. The killers tell me it went to the Queverra at first. I don't supposed you have any notion why?' When Liang shrugged, Red Lin Feyn shrugged too. 'No, I couldn't see that you would.'

34

The Queverra

Tuuran shifted his axe from one shoulder to the other. There weren't many good things you could say about climbing down an endless set of steps into a sodding great abyss with two dragons chasing each other down below and an ants' nest of riled slavers above. Not much except how it had seemed like a good idea at the time. But he went on anyway because he was an Adamantine Man and that made him as stubborn as any mule ever born. It was better than climbing *up* anyway.

Best not to think about that.

He stopped and watched the pinpricks of light that were the two dragons hurling fire at each other, so distant beneath him that they weren't much brighter than the stars overhead. It was a long way down, a long, *long* way. Years clambering around rigging as a sail-slave had seen to it that heights never bothered him much, but *this* drop ... well it was just unreasonable. Best not to think about that either. In fact, ever since he'd got back together with Crazy Mad on the galley, his life had become quite crowded with things best not thought about.

He thought about all of them anyway, of course. It never helped and he usually ended up wishing he hadn't.

By the time he got to the first ledge, he could feel how the air was thicker. There were huts here, a few crude wooden things and shelters made of poles and sailcloth and not much else. Someone had been kind enough to line the edge of the drop with white stones he could just about see in the abyssal gloom, so at least he had a clue where it was, although a bigger clue came from the knots of black-skinned Taiytakei with white-painted faces and torches. They stood right up close to the edge, apparently not too bothered by any notion of falling, peering down and jabbering to each other with exactly the animation of a crowd of people who'd had their first sight of a fire-breathing monster shooting past their doorstep. If they had doorsteps, that was. Or doors. A few of the white-painted men stopped to look at him as he sauntered past but they didn't seem very interested.

'My job's killing them.' He couldn't resist. He patted his axe. 'Just as soon as I catch them. Which way is down?'

Most of them ignored him. A few looked at him as though he was mad, which he thought reasonable enough, all things considered, saw his shield and his axe and his sheer bloody-minded size and let him pass with a few mutters and pointed fingers. *Let the daft bugger get himself killed*. Well fair enough. He wasn't going to argue, but now that he had their attention another thought crossed his mind.

'Any of you see a short-arsed idiot with a tiny little sword come this way a few days back?' No, that didn't do it. 'How about one with eyes made of silver that glow in the dark?' The way their faces changed was all the answer he needed. They'd seen Crazy Mad right enough and he'd still been crazy.

By the time he got to the bottom of the next set of steps, he reckoned the sun ought to be coming up, but he was so deep he reckoned the sun hadn't got much hope of reaching him unless they both got lucky somewhere around midday. How far down was he? No idea. Two miles? Three? His legs were starting to make a fuss. Mostly he told them they could shut up and save their complaining for when he had to climb back out again – how much fun *that* was going to be. His stomach was rumbling and he was thirsty too. Might have been a good idea to grab some stuff off the slavers in their camp before he'd set off. That was hindsight for you – smug and mostly useless.

The dragons had long disappeared by now. He had no idea how that had panned out, whether the hatchling had got away or whether the big one had caught it. He supposed he ought to give that a bit of thought. Hard for a full-grown dragon to hide itself in a place like this, but a hatchling … yes, a hatchling could hide out down here rather easily and that one had had a mean streak.

Another hour and his legs got to thinking about how the back of a dragon would make a nice easy way out. He had to point out to them that the world wasn't that kind.

The hatchling had known his name. Alchemists always said that dragons could do that sort of thing – pluck thoughts out of heads – and that was how they knew what their riders wanted of them, but being on the end of it had turned out a whole lot different to being told it could happen to someone else. Crazy Mad had said the same. So maybe that was it. It had found his name inside Crazy's head. Still bothered him, though. Not enough to make him scared or anything like that, because Adamantine Men didn't get scared, but it tasted bad enough to get him moving again and gave his legs something to think about before they started back up with their moaning.

He reached a ledge that wasn't much more than a few shrines to Flame-knew-what gods. Adamantine Men didn't have much use for gods and suchlike – a few angry and neglected legion ancestors were all they ever bothered about and even then usually only when they were drunk. He had a quick look in case someone had gone by not so long ago and left an offering of something he could eat or drink, but all he found were bones carved into little totem men. The more he looked at them the more they made his skin crawl. He let them be.

When he looked up, it was definitely daylight. He could see the sky, a deep blue, but all he got on his ledge was twilight. When he looked down, he still couldn't see anything except dim cliff walls getting ever darker. It had to have *some* sort of bottom to it, right?

He descended another mile. By now the air was so thick it was making him light-headed. The sky above was almost black, so little light made it down. When he squinted he could see stars, which he supposed made it night again, though he didn't think he'd been going quite that long. Could have been. After that he gave up looking back because every time he did it made him think of how far up he was going to have to climb when he didn't find Crazy down here after all, or, better still, how far up he'd have to climb with Crazy slung over his back, and his legs really *really* didn't want to think about that.

And then he found himself standing in front of a pair of ornately carved pillars and a massive piece of stone that stretched out over the abyss like the trunk of a fallen tree across a river. The pillars looked a lot like some sort of gateway, while the carvings covering them looked a lot like the sigils he'd seen on the pillar that the

Watcher had shown him, back when the Watcher had taken him to Vespinarr and put him on the riverboat to find his way back to Crazy Mad. The pillar had been in the middle of a great big square in front of a palace, and the Watcher had gone on about how old it was and how it went back to before the Splintering – which, if Tuuran was getting his head round the whole Taiytakei idea of how the world worked, meant pretty damn old and a little bit creepy. The sigils also looked a lot like the weird patterns he'd seen etched into the walls of the Pinnacles back in the dragon-lands and the sigils Crazy's warlocks had tattooed onto their faces and Crazy Mad carried himself, in intricate little silvery marks all around the massive scar on his leg.

This way, they said. This way to *what*, well, maybe they said that too, but not in any words Tuuran had a use for.

35

Palaces of Ancient Kings

As the landing fields beside the Visonda Palace of Vespinarr drew close, Red Lin Feyn closed the blinds on each window. She stepped behind a screen and busied herself with becoming the Arbiter once more. Liang, who'd been to the Visonda fields before, thought they looked empty. More than twenty glasships hung around the edges, clustered around four black monoliths, sucking up their energies from the earth, but the field was big enough for a hundred. Dozens of gondolas lay scattered about, some gold, most of them silver. Close to where their own settled on the earth two giant men of glass stood as still as statues. Golems. In Xican they'd had golems, hundreds of them made of stone, digging and tunnelling into the jagged grey cliffs to make the city ever larger. She'd seen golems like that made into soldiers, simple dumb creatures who followed simple dumb orders but had the advantage that nothing much hurt them, not fire or lightning or even a sword or an ashgar. Yes, they had that, but they were incredibly dim, easily fooled and quickly rendered useless by most black rods. They were automata after all, no more or less than the pilot of a glasship, imbued with a rudimentary intelligence usually stolen from a death-sentenced slave before they died.

But not these. These were the guardian golems of the Dralamut, a very different thing.

As the ramp opened, an Elemental Man appeared in a rush of air beside the Arbiter. He whispered in her ear. Liang couldn't hear his words but his voice was harsh and angry. She watched. Lin Feyn walked back into the gondola and shut the ramp behind her, leaving Liang out on the landing fields alone. Liang pursed her lips and, after a moment, turned to inspect the golems. They were made of enchanted gold-glass tougher than steel, with four arms, two on each side. One ended in a shield easily large enough for a grown man to stand inside and curved almost to the point of turning back on itself, with a lip at the bottom like a step. A second ended in a miniature lightning cannon far stronger than any wand. The other two arms split towards their ends, each terminating in a pair of hands, one huge like a bear's, one as small as a child's with long spindly fingers. They stood slightly apart, their glittering heads turning now and then. Their eyes, seven of them, were golden orbs spaced evenly over their glass skulls. They didn't need to turn their heads – they did it, Liang thought, to make themselves seem more human.

She felt their attention as she came close. If the stories were true then these guardians of the Dralamut carried within them the life-sparks of dying navigators, not of slaves.

'Golems, state your purpose.' Which was always how she began with the stone men of Xican.

'We serve and protect the Arbiter of the Dralamut.' They spoke together, their voices soft and melodious, out of keeping with their monstrous size. 'Name yourself.'

Golems that talked back? Well *that* wouldn't catch on. 'Chay-Liang of Hingwal Taktse,' she said. 'Are you functional?'

'We do not answer to you, Chay-Liang of Hingwal Taktse.'

Liang snorted. She walked around them, looking them over, wondering what else she could do. She knew how each part was made – could have made most of them herself – but she didn't dare go close enough to touch them.

A glasship drifted from one of the black monoliths and lowered sixteen silver chains that wrapped themselves around a waiting gondola. A small group of Taiytakei went inside – a hsian, two t'varrs and a handful of lesser kwens, judging by the colours and feathers they wore and the braids of their hair. The ramp closed behind them and the glasship lifted slowly away, taking the gondola with it. Liang watched it go. North towards the Konsidar at first but then west. When she looked back, the Arbiter's ramp was opening again and the killer was gone. Liang found Red Lin Feyn with her headdress on the floor and her hair let down, brushing at it with fractious force.

'We're alone,' she said as Liang came to sit beside her. 'The killer will go to the Kabulingnor to make the necessary arrangements.

While we are here, there are places I wish to see. We shall walk.'
She sighed and looked at the brush, then shrugged. 'Knots. I tell
you, there are good reasons why we keep our hair in braids. The
rest of you are lucky.' She tapped a set of gold-glass hairpins and
they rose into the air and set about piling the Arbiter's hair neatly
back on top of her head. 'They ask me why we are here. I've not
told them about Baros Tsen. Be careful what you say. They seem
very much on edge. Are the golems in order?'

'As far as I can tell, lady. They await your order.'

'Is it windy out there?'

'No, lady. Still as a mirror sea.'

'Well thank Feyn for that!' For a moment Lin Feyn wasn't the
Arbiter any more. 'You have no idea how sick I got of that bloody
wind.' She chuckled and cocked a smile at Liang. 'Or perhaps you
do. Do you ever get used to it, up there all the time?'

'Not really, lady.'

The gold-glass hairpins finished their knitting and settled into
place. Red Lin Feyn rolled her eyes and let out a tiny sigh, then
lifted the headdress and put it on, the white feathers rising high
above them both. She strode past Liang as the face-painted Arbiter
once again. Outside she spoke to the golems in whispers.

'Lady, why are we here?' asked Liang.

Red Lin Feyn put a finger to her lips. 'You know of the Azahl
Pillar?'

Before Liang could answer, the air shivered and another
Elemental Man stood before them. He bowed low. Liang didn't
recognise him. They came and went so much she was losing track.

'Lady, there have been difficulties. Lord Shonda has left his
brother Vey Rin T'Varr to speak with his voice. He refuses you
passage to the Konsidar.'

'Vey Rin? I go as I please. Anyway, didn't he go mad?'

'His mannerisms are … unusual, lady. But the fact remains.'

'No matter. You are killers and he is bound to obey you.'

'Lady, he is bound to obey *you*. We are but guardians.'

For a moment Liang thought the mask might crack. Impatience.
Exasperation. Exhaustion. Maybe even a little fear. Outside the
Dralamut no one ever saw the Arbiter as anything other than the
voice of the Crown of the Sea Lords and the Elemental Men. It

was such a rare thing for the Arbiter to be invoked that some sea lords had never seen one except at a distance. For the most part the Arbiters stayed inside the Dralamut, listening to the few arguments brought before them when they couldn't be settled in Khalishtor in the Crown. But for the four days it had taken to cross the Empty Sands from the eyrie to Vespinarr, Liang and Lin Feyn had been alone together. Liang had asked her questions and Lin Feyn had begun to teach her the secrets of the storm-dark, and now and then the mask had dropped and Liang had seen an ordinary woman beneath it. Sharp and clever and wise perhaps, an enchantress in her own right and a navigator and powerful within her own skin. Far more than an empty mask. Beneath their surfaces they were alike. They might, in another world, have become friends.

The Arbiter gathered herself perfectly and turned back for the gondola. 'I must go myself? So be it. Come with me, Chay-Liang.'

There was no space in the gondola for the golems so they stayed where they were on the landing fields, infinitely patient. The glasship rose slowly up the side of the Silver Mountain and Red Lin Feyn allowed the blinds to be open so Liang could look out over the city. Lin Feyn pointed to the huge open space sprawled in front of the Visonda Palace, to the circle of intersecting lines that came together in its centre. 'Chay-Liang must see the Azahl Pillar before we travel into the Konsidar. On that I insist, killer.'

The Elemental Man bowed. 'You know the conditions of the peace, lady.' He was looking at Liang. 'I am concerned, lady, for your safety. It would be better to bring those who must answer to your court.' For a moment he looked almost human. Touched by real fear.

'I cannot bring the Righteous Ones to my court. You know that as well as I do.'

'Lady, what have they to do with Dhar Thosis? If you tell us ...'

The Arbiter and the killer dropped to whispers. Liang turned away. At the window she watched the Silver Mountain slip beneath them until they passed over the yellow inner walls of the Kabulingnor and began their descent towards the three towers of the Polsang Palace. A thousand men were arrayed to welcome them, but as the gondola came closer Red Lin Feyn closed the blinds. 'You will remain here, enchantress. You will not believe nor heed any summons that does not come either from my own lips or from this killer. Remember that the Vespinese have already tried to murder you. Practise what I have shown you while I deal with this, and know that we are not safe here.'

They landed in silence. Red Lin Feyn stepped out into sunshine and crisp flower-scented mountain air in a fanfare blast of trumpets and horns; then the ramp closed behind her and Liang was alone. She spent the afternoon staring into the glass globe that Lin Feyn had given her, the one that contained a fragment of the storm-dark inside it. She focused her mind on the glass itself at first – a thing she now did every day that came with unforced ease – and then tried to move it into the storm-dark. After an hour of getting no-where she put the globe away and read. Lin Feyn had some of Feyn Charin's journals, books that usually never left the library of the Dralamut, and Liang devoured them hungrily, dutifully returning to the globe now and then with the same lack of success. 'This is the hard part,' Lin Feyn had said, laughing at the look on her face the first time she'd tried it. 'Many never succeed but you will. You have the mind for it. Apply yourself. Master the globe and I'll take you to the storm-dark itself.' She'd been banging herself against the globe for four straight days, almost to the point of wishing she could spend her time measuring the rider-slave for her next set of armour instead. But she kept trying because that was who she was.

No one came to the gondola that night, nor until late the next afternoon when the ramp suddenly opened again. Lin Feyn came in, looked about, wrinkled her nose and waved a hand in front of her face and beckoned Liang. 'Come, Chay-Liang, walk with me. Killer, this gondola is no longer pleasing. The air is bad. See that another is found. A Vespinese one will do.'

If an Elemental Man was somewhere around them then Liang didn't see or hear him, but that didn't mean much. She put the storm-dark globe away, smoothed the creases in her robe and fol-lowed into the evening sunshine. The Arbiter walked briskly and Liang almost had to run to keep up.

'The gardens of the Kabulingnor are most striking at this time.' Lin Feyn kept her eyes straight ahead as she spoke. 'It would be a shame for you to come here and miss them. I suppose you don't have much opportunity, even though the enchanters of Hingwal Taktse built most of this. It's marvellous, don't you think, how lush green pasture land and forest have been created on the top of this barren mountain? The entire peak has been reshaped over the years. Sadly we shall see only a little, but the grounds of the Kabulingnor boast gardens of roses unrivalled anywhere and a dazzling array of flowers from across Takei'Tarr and the many realms beyond. Your alchemist slave would weep with delight at the variety of herbs and rare plants here. Look up.' For a moment she stopped and pointed. High above the palace slabs of gold-glass drifted like the Palace of Leaves in Xican except here nothing hung beneath them. They caught the sun and showered rainbows across the towers of the Polsang and the Ziltak Palace nearby. 'They warm the entire mountaintop. If you stand and watch them, you would see they turn to follow the sun. They extract water from a spring that has always risen out of the peak – strange behaviour for a spring if you ask me, but it was there long before even Vespin chose to make this his capital.' She leaned in closer and lowered her voice. 'We are both in danger, Liang. They know you are here and we will not have much time.' She leaned away again. 'The grounds also possess wildlife in many forms, a true menagerie of creatures from across our realm and beyond. One thing has always puzzled me: they say that one can walk among the three towers of the Lake Palace without ever leaving their walls. Doors that lead from one tower to another without any passage or bridge. Is that possible? I was an enchanter once and never heard of such a thing. Do you see how it could be done?'

'I do not, lady.'

Again Lin Feyn's voice dropped. 'When they bring a new gondola I shall change my mind. Nevertheless, be wary. Move quickly when we leave. Go directly to the gondola in which we came. Do not hesitate. We will find out here and now whether our killer is to be trusted.' She turned and swept back the way they'd come, her voice rising as she did. 'I command you to find a reason to come here again, Chay-Liang, if the opportunity presents itself. Perhaps the lords of the Kabulingnor would wish to employ you for some task. It would be worth your while simply to see the marvels that past masters and mistresses of our art have wrought here.' She leaned in close to Liang. 'Someone does not wish us to go to the Konsidar.'

She talked on but Liang found it hard to listen. She could see a second glasship wafting towards the open space where their golden gondola waited for them. It carried a new one beneath it, silver this time, because only the lords of Vespinarr could afford to build gondolas from silver and they liked to remind the world of their wealth. Liang did as she was told and ignored it. Red Lin Feyn stopped to nod to the dozen or so kwens and t'varrs who came to see her off, then followed Liang back into the same gondola in which they had arrived. She closed the ramp and told the golem to leave immediately. The Kabulingnor fell away beneath them, there were no booms of black-powder cannon, and Liang supposed she would never know how close her escape had been, or if it had even been an escape at all.

'Lady—' Lin Feyn cut her off with a gesture and cocked her head. After a moment she nodded. 'Lady, why are we here?'

'We're looking for Baros Tsen T'Varr.' When Liang looked bemused, Lin Feyn smiled. She wouldn't say any more.

They drifted through the early evening, suspended somewhere high over the Vespinarr basin towards its northern edge where the sheer water-carved gorges of the Jokun and the Yalun Zarang cut into the heart of the Konsidar. From on high the basin looked like an enormous crater scooped out of the mountains. Green fields laced with threads of silvery water spread for miles on either side of the two rivers. In the distance the peak of the Silver Mountain was still in sight, with the Kabulingnor on its crown and Vespinarr at its feet. Liang watched the sun set over the western sky. The clouds lit up in sprays of ochre and flaming orange that tinged the snow on the mountaintops and set them aglow.

'It's beautiful up here,' she said. She didn't expect a reply – an Elemental Man sat quietly in the corner and the Arbiter had her mask firmly back in place – but to her surprise Lin Feyn came and stood at the window beside her. Together they watched the sun go down.

'I am, through some arcane path, a descendant of Feyn Charin himself,' said Lin Feyn. 'The Dralamut keeps careful track of these things. It's one of the duties of the Arbiter to maintain the records of her bloodline, although of course we have many slaves to keep them for us. A long time ago someone decided it might matter – that perhaps the sons and daughters of Feyn Charin carried something in their blood which made them special.' She raised an eyebrow slightly. 'There *is* a little truth to it. The sons and daughters of the first navigator make fine enchanters. But so do many others.' She didn't move from the window but the tone of her voice changed and grew subtly wistful. 'You've read some of his journals now. In the Dralamut I have them all, written at the time of the Crimson Sunburst. He was in love with her, that much is clear. Now and then people whisper she was his mother or his half-sister or his lover or perhaps all of those things. Some people nurse a prurient hunger to read his journals to find the answer, but it's not there. What always strikes me most is the power in his words. The joy of them. I think perhaps he was in love with everything, with the world and all its beauty. He would have liked this sunset, Chay-Liang.' She turned away. 'The journals of which I speak were written when he was young. Before everything changed.'

Liang opened her mouth to speak and then closed it again. What did you say to that? 'He was a very great man.' There. As trite and bland and meaningless a thing as anyone could possibly imagine.

'He was. He spent a great deal of time at the Godspike. He was there when the killers came for the Sunburst. History would have us believe he stayed there while she hid in the Empty Sands and that the two had no further dealings with one another. History says he was absent when her golem army made its unexpected appearance at Mount Solence and attacked the Elemental Men in their own home, just as they had done to her. I have read his journals and there must be something else, something that was erased or lost. For a long time he kept no records or else destroyed them. The stories would have us believe he remained at the Godspike all through the insurrection and its aftermath and that the Elemental Men left him entirely alone. Years he spent there, and in that time what do we have of him? Almost nothing until he finally entered the storm-dark and returned, and then everyone knows his story after that.

'I've seen the journals from start to finish. The man who wrote in those later years was different. Changed. He was troubled and paranoid and always looking over his shoulder. He hints at things he saw when he crossed the storm-dark and it seems they affected him deeply. A realm made of liquid silver. A different time when a black moon rose into the sky to blot out the sun. All that love he'd once had for the world, somewhere he lost it.

'He spent most of his later years refusing to leave the Dralamut, constantly building and improving it. He showed a few of the other enchanters how to cross the curtains that lie out to sea, a handful of men and women he knew and who'd learned their powers from the Crimson Sunburst as he had. Then he left them to it. When the Elemental Men all but forced him back to the Godspike, he refused to enter the maelstrom or to teach any others. In his last years he drifted into madness, filling book after book with bizarre rantings that make no sense. Most of it's illegible. Some is in code. When he was lucid, he was bitter and dark. For years they shut him away, left a few slaves to take care of him and quietly wished he'd die. Eventually he did.'

She turned and put a hand on Liang's shoulder.

'He saw something in the storm-dark that left him desperately afraid, and now and then, in his later notes, he speaks of what can only be dragons. I believe, in part, we are following his path. Do not end your days like him. Keep your love of the world, Chay-Liang.' Her eyes glistened.

'And you, lady.'

The Arbiter turned slowly back to the window and stared at the distant darkening sky. 'For me it may already be too late. I have begun to look over my shoulder more than I look to where I'm going.' She watched until the sun had gone and the first stars began to shine, then quietly went to her bed.

36

The Azahl Pillar

Liang woke the next morning to find the gondola filled with golden light. The rising sun burst over the eastern mountains and blazed through the windows. When she crawled down from the tiny space that was hers, food was on the table. Honey and fresh bread and fruit, and the bread was still warm inside. When she wondered how this could be, Lin Feyn actually laughed. 'A perk of being the Arbiter. I sent the killer to bring us food. He might as well. He has his uses.'

'Is he here, lady?'

'Not now.' They were sinking back towards the city. 'There are places in Vespinarr I wish to visit. Tomorrow we leave for the Konsidar. He's making the arrangements.'

'Surely you have a t'varr?'

Red Lin Feyn shook her head. 'The Arbiter does not need a t'varr, nor a hsian nor a kwen. The Dralamut has all these things. When the Arbiter ventures elsewhere, it's always to the Crown of the Sea Lords to hold her court, and Khalishtor is filled to the brim with more t'varrs that you could count. Should it be that the Arbiter travels elsewhere then she sends a killer to warn of her approach. Wherever she goes, all men lose their masters and become hers. That is the way of things, and the threat of the killers sees to it that the way is obeyed.'

'Lady, why did you tell me about Feyn Charin last night?'

Lin Feyn drizzled honey over a torn piece of bread. The look she gave Liang was full of sadness. 'To have told someone at all. We all grow up to see him as such a hero, such a great man, the maker of Takei'Tarr as we know it. Without him, we couldn't cross the storm-dark. Perhaps the secret would have been found in another realm instead. Perhaps in the Dominion with their priests, or in Aria with their sorcerers. Perhaps their ships would have come to our shores as we go to theirs, taking what amused them. Perhaps we would be their slaves and not they ours. And all these things are true, and yet among them other truths become lost. He was a sorcerer, apprenticed to the worst of them all – when I say worst, perhaps I should say most threatening – after all, the Sunburst never did anything particularly wicked. She was no Abraxi. In fact, as a sea lord, she was good to her people. By far her greatest crime was to make the killers afraid of her.'

Lin Feyn bit into a ripe dragonfruit with a touch of savagery. Its juices dripped down her chin.

'Our great hero was everything the killers swear they exist to destroy and yet they exalted him. They gave him the Dralamut and made him a teacher.' She shrugged. 'Much good came of it: our world is what it is because they made that choice. But why him, when he was against everything they exist to do? Do you see, Liang, why I don't trust them? They are founded on sand.' She shook her head. 'And then the great hero of Takei'Tarr becomes an old man with a terrible darkness. We don't talk of that. You see him sitting in a room, old and grey, poring over his notes, writing the secrets of the universe, but I've seen the actual words he wrote with my own eyes and I know better. He was afraid to his very core of what he knew.' She wiped her mouth. 'I do not wish to become like that, Chay-Liang. The Sunburst – *her* journals are those of a visionary. How different things might have been had their positions been reversed.'

For a few seconds she stared past Liang out into the empty space beyond the gondola as if trying to see into some other far-off world. Then she wiped her mouth again and rose. 'I should not burden you, enchantress. These things do not matter. I am what I am, and they have no relevance. Leave now, please. I must dress myself. The world will expect the Arbiter of the Dralamut, not a tired old woman.'

Liang smiled. 'Old, lady? You're younger than I am.'

Lin Feyn snorted. 'Old enough, Liang. Now go and make the storm-dark in that globe bow to you.'

The glasship drifted over the Vespinarr basin to the flanks of the Silver Mountain and sank lazily to the landing fields of the Visonda once more. Red Lin Feyn had become the Arbiter again, although this time without the headdress. She handed Liang two wands – the lightning wand and the black rod she had confiscated back on the eyrie.

'I believe we may still be in danger. Nevertheless, there is something here I wish to see.' She opened the ramp, walked out with the Elemental Man at her heels and found the two golems standing exactly where they'd been two days before. People stopped to stare at them, though Lin Feyn seemed not to notice. Perhaps she was used to it. She walked with Liang beside her, her golems behind and the Elemental Man ahead, across the landing field into Visonda Square where the huge walls of the old palace towered over them. Knots of brightly-dressed people stood about in idle conversation and dozens of slaves in their white tunics hurried to and fro on their errands, but the square was so vast that it felt empty. It was a pale stone wilderness, Liang thought, touched with a faint morning mist that dimmed the far-off jubilant chaos of the Harub on the opposite side to a lurking silhouette and leached the many colourful robes to dull dark grey. A space like this would swallow the eyrie's dragon yard whole. Even the dragon itself would look small.

The morning mountain air felt cold and damp and unnaturally still.

Red Lin Feyn stopped and pointed at her feet. Patterned lines of a darker polished stone ran from the corners and the sides of the square, converging on the middle where the Azahl Pillar rose, its white stone almost invisible in the haze until they neared it. The pillar had come out of the Konsidar hundreds of years ago. Its exact dimensions had been measured and recorded by the enchanters of Hingwal Taktse, who'd meticulously copied and studied the unknown runes that covered its surface, but that was about as much as Liang knew. Now she saw it with her own eyes, one thing struck her above all else. It was the same white stone as the insides of Baros Tsen's eyrie. The same white stone as the ...

'The Godspike!' She couldn't help herself. Her hand flew to her mouth. It was exactly like the Godspike except several thousand times smaller and covered in sigils.

'Very good.' Liang heard the smile in Lin Feyn's voice. The Arbiter walked up to the pillar. 'Touch it,' she said.

Liang did. The stone under her fingers was smooth and hard and cold, the edges and corners still sharp, the surface unweathered. It felt fresh from the stone cutter, polished only yesterday, exactly, again, like the white stone of the eyrie. 'How old is this?'

'At least a thousand years. Perhaps many more. Vespin brought it out of the Konsidar, but it was made before the cataclysm that spawned the storm-dark. Charin knew it as soon as he saw it.' Red Lin Feyn ran her fingers over the carvings and smiled. There was an edge to her now. 'No one can read these words, but I can tell you that they are dedications to a general whose name is lost. They give an account of his services to the long-forgotten king of a realm no one remembers. Or so my ancestor claims in his journals. In the Konsidar you will see many more of these.'

'It feels so new.' Liang stared at the pillar and an icicle ran up her spine. 'I've seen words like these before. Tattooed across the skin of the killer who nearly slit my alchemist's throat.'

'Yes.' Lin Feyn was nodding. 'I saw the skin of that man your alchemist kept so carefully preserved. I think they were not as strange to him as they are to you and me. Quai'Shu's Elemental Man had an interest in them before he died too. Did he speak to you of this?'

Liang shook her head.

'Nor to anyone else I've found. But I'm convinced he had, none-theless. He was pursuing some ... other purpose. It's a shame we can't speak to him and ask.' She turned slightly and fixed Liang with a steely look. 'Enchantress, I know you have your views, but the duty of the Arbiter is to determine where responsibility truly lies. I must consider the possibility that even Shonda of Vespinarr is a paw—'

A flash of light caught Liang's eye from the narrow busy streets of the Harub's morning gloom. A huge golem hand grabbed her and a massive glass shield slammed down in front of her as a bright streak hurtled towards them. Another erupted from a doorway and a third from a window. Rockets. The first hit the pillar and exploded into a ball of flame that washed over the glass in front of her. The second fizzed past and struck the ground behind her. Fire billowed everywhere but the golem had stepped close and placed its shield around her, caging her in a gold-glass shell. She heard the third rocket detonate, so loud it must have exploded in front of her face, but by then she was huddled down into a ball. A terrible thunderclap made her ears ring. As she tried to blink away the flashes, a second thunderbolt erupted, this time from the golem wrapped around her. It struck the window in the Harub from where one of the rockets had come and the entire house blew apart.

The Elemental Man had vanished. Behind and beside her the other golem had Red Lin Feyn protected in its embrace. They stood as still as statues by the Azahl Pillar while the square erupted into screams and people ran helter-skelter away.

'For your safety, Chay-Liang of Hingwal Taktse, step into the shield.' The golem sounded so distant over the ringing in her ears. The one wrapped around Red Lin Feyn started moving, fast. Liang fumbled with her feet. Yes, on the inside of the shield was the step. She climbed onto it and the golem started to run.

Another explosion erupted out of the Harub, this time with a cloud of pale smoke. The shoulder of the golem carrying Red Lin Feyn exploded, spinning it around and almost knocking it down. Gold-glass shattered and shards of it pinged off the shield in front of Liang's face. The Arbiter's golem had lost both the arms on its right side. It staggered, righted itself and kept running. A rocket streaked past and exploded in the distance against the walls of the Visonda and then another hit the Arbiter's golem yet again. For a moment the flash was blinding. The air swirled with smoke and Liang could smell the reek of sulphur, of burned black powder. Her eyes stung. Another thunderclap seared her ears. She hunched forward and cringed inside the golem's shield as it pounded towards the Harub. She didn't understand why they were running towards their attackers instead of away, didn't understand why someone was firing rockets at her. Not lightning or arrows but rockets! Xibaiya!

A cluster of explosions erupted around the golems and the air filled with sulphurous smoke. Her own golem staggered and shuddered as something hit it hard, then spun. It tipped and fell on top of her, slamming her face first into the ground as it rolled inert onto its back. Its arms dropped, limp. Liang was sprawled behind the shield across the hard smooth flagstones of the square. She started crawling and then stopped. She had no idea which way she was facing. Look for Lin Feyn, that had been her first thought, protect the Arbiter, but the golems had taken them to the edge of the Harub, to the closest shelter but also towards their attackers, and the air was so thick with stinging smoke that she could barely see a thing. Her eyes filled with tears. She coughed and the smoke burned her lungs, hot and acrid. She still had her lightning wand at her waist and three unmoulded glass spheres in her pockets. She pulled one out now, hastily moulded it into a shield that wrapped almost all around her, and ran with no idea where she was going. She saw the shapes of men. Soldiers. She turned and ran the other way instead. More thunderclaps and lightning bolts split the air. One of them hit her shield. Sparks scattered in front of her eyes.

The shape of a narrow street loomed from the smoke, empty except for three bodies and the metal tubes of a rocket launcher. In the distance she heard screams. Her heart was racing. The air here was thick with the same sulphurous smoke again. She darted to the side of the street and looked for a door, any door, kicked it open and ran into a dark little shop filled from floor to ceiling with shelves of pottery jugs. The air was a little better, at least. She ran through, looking for steps to take her up, but only found an alley no wider than she was and too narrow for her shield. She changed its shape and made it smaller and ran on. The Harub was usually packed with crowds. Find them and she'd be safe.

'Arbiter!'

The voice came from behind. She froze, but before she could turn, a hammer blow struck her shield and shattered it and then she felt something sharp and deadly hit her back. Pain shot through to her heart. She turned but all she could see was the shape of a man, a miniature black-powder hand cannon at his feet, his arm raised to throw another knife. She ducked, tripped over her own feet, stumbled to her knees as she whipped the remains of her shield over her face. The second blade struck the glass and skittered away, and then the man was gone even as she snapped her wand towards him. The pain in her back was like fire. When she tried to stand, she found she barely could. There was no way to tell how bad the wound was.

The second knife was on the ground in front of her. She bent to pick it up and saw the blade was wet. Poison. She staggered back the way she'd come, looking for the man who'd killed her, lightning wand ready to kill him in return, but she never saw him. Her legs started to wobble. She stumbled back into the little shop and its shadowy darkness and clutched at the shelves. They crashed in a shower of shattering clay around her. She fell to her hands and knees, coughed and tasted salt and iron in her mouth. Her breathing was too fast. Her eyes were swimming. And now there was the man again, standing over her, and she was too weak to even lift up her head.

37

The Gates of Xibaiya

Berren crept forward in the darkness. He wasn't sure where he was any more. The dragon was a dull memory. It had been out there, picking at him, pulling at the strings of his soul. Digging and digging deep. He remembered a flash of purity as it touched the edge of something that didn't want to be touched, and after that the world became strange. He could remember sending the dragon away without knowing how. Keeping himself safe. He remembered Tuuran, talking to the big man, starting to tell him what the dragon had done. He remembered walking away and leaving the big man behind with no idea why he'd done that. He could have let them all go. He could have done anything then. That was the most frightening part of it all. He could have done *anything*. He could have picked up the world and thrown it into the sun or shattered the moon and made it fall in fragments across the sea for each one to grow into a strange new island of silver stone.

The moon. He kept seeing the moon, the sullen hostile moon.

In the end he hadn't done anything at all.

Afterwards he walked and walked and walked without much idea of where he was going or why but with an absolute certainty of where he needed to be. The sun rose and he went on. He should have burned. He should have been crawling on his hands and knees but he wasn't. He didn't remember being hungry or thirsty though he'd had neither food nor water and never stopped to look for either. He didn't remember exactly when he'd started down into the crack in the earth. Maybe it had been night again by then and he hadn't noticed. He had a vague idea of a lot of steps and a bridge and a whole lot of tunnels made out of white stone that lit his way with a soft moonlight glow, and great bronze doors held closed by four-armed guardians. He wasn't tired, though he hadn't ever stopped to rest. There had been people too, he thought, up near the top, with white-painted faces, but they'd kept away and left him alone and he'd gone on by.

He passed gateways, old, old places. He didn't pay them much attention. It was as though he'd seen them before and knew what they were and understood that the words written over them were meant for him and him alone in a strange language that he couldn't understand and yet did. They were guiding him.

And now this. The largest cavern he'd ever seen. The distant walls were smooth and rounded in all directions. A single span of white stone reached from his feet out into the void, and walking on it was like walking towards the centre of some giant bubble. When he reached that centre, the span splayed out into a circular platform ringed with archways, and the walls were so far away that he couldn't even guess now how big the cavern was. Everywhere was a faraway unchanging pale glow, and within it distance lost its meaning. In the middle of the floor beneath him was a pitch-black hole. He couldn't tell how wide or deep it was, but he knew it wasn't just any hole. This was a hole in the world. Through it lay Xibaiya. The land of the dead.

He paced around the arches. The echo of the Black Moon had brought him here. The man with the ruined face and the one milky eye had put it into the warlock Skyrie. Now it was in him and it was looking for something.

Where are you?

The question came with the sense of a task not finished. The archways were empty, but only until he touched them and the Black Moon reached through his fingers and shivered them into life.

The first shimmered onto a sea of liquid silver. He felt a wistful pang of regret tinged with disappointment and murderous anger. The silver sea called to the Black Moon, begging him home, and for a moment he felt the pulse inside him waver, but then another sense came, a slowly growing awareness of his presence, huge and resentful. He let the arch go and the gateway shimmered and vanished. The regret lasted a little longer. He'd done something once. Something monumentally vast. What was it?

Get out of me. Get out! Berren screamed at the echo inside him with all the potency of an ant screaming at a tree.

The next arch shimmered like the first when he touched it. It opened onto a small round chamber, dark with no exits. There was a mosaic on the floor, almost lost to age. Three skeletons lay over it, long-dead men clad in bronze-mesh armour. There was a book ... No. There had once been a book but now it was gone.

Where are you?

Get out! Get out, get out! But the Black Moon didn't even know he was there, and Berren understood now how it had been for Skyrie when the two of them fought. Drowning. Powerless. Screaming silently in his own skin.

The next arch was a great throne room, grand beyond imagining. A king in a coat that burned like the sun. Then a room full of more archways exactly like the ones in front of him but at the top of some high tower. Then a gloomy cave at the bottom of a spiralling staircase and a spear, its pointed haft buried six inches into the floor, walls lit by alchemical lamps whose cold white light glittered on the spear's silver skin. Then a place of shimmering rainbows and a woman, achingly beautiful, with a golden circlet on her brow. They meant nothing, any of them.

In the next he saw himself. Berren the Bloody Judge. Berren the Crowntaker. His own face, his real face, the flesh and skin that had once been his, taken from him years ago in Tethis. He saw himself staring at a knife, the other knife with a golden haft carved into a thousand eyes and a pale swirling blade. The Bloody Judge looked right back at him, and for a moment the Black Moon wavered, its substance turned to smoke. Berren lunged. 'Help me!' he shrieked. *'Help me!'*

The gate snapped closed. The Black Moon inside him shivered and roared, coalesced hard as black iron, too much to bear as it grasped at a memory that should have been within easy reach and yet simply wasn't there. Brilliant silver light flared across the cavern, and all the arches shimmered and flared and opened for a moment and then closed. *I built this! I made this!* Silver light soared around him. *I. Made. This.*

The last arch shimmered into the black abyss, into the all-devouring void that was Xibaiya, land of the dead. The Black Moon took his legs and stepped through. Berren screamed and ...

... ceased to be. Souls passed him by. Millions upon millions of

glittering shards of the sun, flitting through him, dancing briefly on their way home. Now and then the memories of a dragon, lurking, searching to be reborn. Fragments of the earth which fled at his approach, knowing what he was. And he remembered. He was the singer of songs to the earth. Creator and maker of terror and monsters, of Zaklat and the Kraitu and a hundred others, defier and destroyer of gods, unraveller of terrible secrets. He was the Black Moon, who turned his enemies to dragons and split the earth asunder and rose to wipe out the sun, trapped in useless flesh as futile rage and boundless despair crushed through him like a deep ocean storm and ...

... sat up.

Blinked and took deep gasping breaths, trying to remember who he was.

Berren. Berren the Crowntaker. Berren the Bloody Judge.

Relief shuddered through him. A dream then.

A dream? But that didn't ... But best not to think about it. That's what Tuuran would say. He was who he was.

He got to his feet, unsteady as an old man. He wasn't in the cavern of white stone with archways any more, if he ever had been. He was lying on his back as though he'd been asleep, and that on its own made wherever this was a damn sight better. He was himself, not driven by some hungry thing he didn't understand that some warlock had stuck inside his head.

Berren. Berren the Crowntaker. Berren the Bloody Judge.

He lay still, breathing hard until his heart finally slowed. Stupid dream. He sniffed the air. It smelled of Xizic, which made him feel slightly sick, but at least the smell was familiar. Taiytakei, slaves, everyone chewed the stuff here.

The night was black. There were no stars, no slivers of moonlight. He was in some sort of shelter. He could feel that by the stillness of the air. He was tired. Weak. His skin, already dark from years at sea, was sore, burned by the sun and sand and wind.

He sat up and felt around him. He wasn't in a hut or a shelter after all, but some sort of cave. There was a jug of water beside him and a cloth. He drained the water, greedy for it, then got to his feet and felt his way about. When he moved too quickly, his head started to swim. Slow and careful then. A cave and he was at the back of it. He dropped to his hands and knees and crawled around until a faint flickering of firelight lit the damp stone wall around a corner. The light led him to where the cave opened onto a dark expanse of black sand beneath inky-dark cliffs. The sky above was every bit as black as the sand. The middle of the night then, with clouds blotting out the stars. Three men sat around the tiny fire whose flames had led him. It lit up their faces. He froze, startled – they looked like ghosts and it was a moment before he realised they were simply painted. Three naked men with their skin painted white.

They looked up. Saw him and then glanced at each other and beckoned, and when he joined them, they knelt and pressed their heads against the sand, prostrating themselves before him. Berren frowned.

'I'm hungry,' he said. 'Got any food?'

They backed away and scuttled into the darkness and returned a few moments later with bowls of nuts and dried berries and leaves.

'Meat. Got any meat?'

They shook their heads.

Berren looked up. Everything was obsidian-dark and that wasn't right. There weren't any stars, not one, and the last thing he knew he'd been in a desert and there hadn't been a cloud for a hundred miles. So there should have been stars.

'Where am I?'

The white-painted men backed away. They were scared of him. Somehow he wasn't what they'd expected.

'How did I get here?'

Two of the men kept shuffling away; the third hesitated, then beckoned Berren to follow and returned to pick a burning brand from the fire. He led the way to the cliffs, into a different cave and through a wide rough tunnel. After a few minutes it opened into a vast space, bigger even than the white stone cave from his dream. He was at the bottom of a colossal scar in the desert. The Queverra. He remembered now. Right at the bottom of the damp cold depths while five miles above him a long slit of daylight filtered feebly down. Berren closed his eyes. A camp at the edge of the abyss. And he remembered, yes, walking down all those steps, part of what he'd thought had been a dream. He pointed to the sky.

'I came from up there?' He took a deep breath and squatted

on his haunches. The sun must have cooked his head to make him think that coming down here was a good idea. Then again he hadn't been thinking right since that night when he'd seen a dragon and something had happened to the slavers' pole he'd been tied to and he'd escaped. It was all a bit hazy. Muddled.

The white-faced man was shaking his head. He pointed to the light too. 'Not from the light. All others come from the light. But not you.' He pointed a sure finger a different way, along the canyon bottom to where it narrowed and funnelled into yet another cave mouth, this one guarded by two pale stone sentinels covered in strange runes. 'There. You come from there.'

Berren walked to the pillars. He ran his fingers over the stone, which was smooth and perfect, the runes carved crisply, not worn and pitted by wind and water. He moved to go on between them into the cave and then turned and took the brand and poked it ahead of him. The cave devoured the firelight. He couldn't see a thing right in front of him, and yet in the distance he saw a dim light. A tunnel, straight and true, of softly glowing white stone that vanished off into for ever.

Something more than a cave.

'There,' said the man. 'You come from Xibaiya. From the dead.'

Berren leaned hard on the pillar beside him. His head started to spin. He took a deep breath and looked inside himself.

The Black Moon looked back.

38

The Konsidar

Chay-Liang woke to find she wasn't dead after all but lying in Red Lin Feyn's gondola. She recognised the smell. The air carried a tinge of ozone and sulphur from Visonda Square but underneath it lay the soft perfume of the Arbiter's silks, of old Xizic and the odd mustiness that came from the half-empty chests under the bed. Liang could feel the vibrations of the glasship coming down the silver chains into the gondola walls and could hear the wind outside through an open window. They were moving quickly.

She opened her eyes. She was lying on her front with her head almost hanging off the bed. Her clothes were piled in a tidy heap on the floor next to the box Belli had given her. The box was open and one of the vials was missing. She groaned and tried to roll onto her back and a searing pain shot through her shoulders. The knife, she'd forgotten the knife. She'd been stabbed and poisoned and yet here she was. The last thing she remembered was the man standing over her. Her head ached and her mind was foggy but her thoughts were clear when she forced them to be.

She was naked underneath the silk sheets apart from a bandage wrapped around her chest and back. It went under her arms and over her shoulders and there was so much of it and it was so tightly wrapped that it felt like a second skin whenever she took a deep breath. She liked that, the sense of it squeezing her chest. She carefully eased herself to sit on the edge of the bed. A dull ache throbbed through her belly, echoes of cramps and retching but nothing worse than she'd had every month since she turned twelve. When she wiggled her toes they wiggled just fine. So did her fingers, and everything was in focus. She hurt deep inside, a little bit of everywhere, but it was the hurt of a body put through a trauma that it had fought and survived and now it wanted to let her know about it.

She picked up her clothes and saw the blood. The stains were huge. Dry now, but they ran from between her shoulders down past her waist, and drips and trails ran as far as the hem around her feet. They were ruined, robe and shift both, but she had others. She tried to stand, but that hurt too much so she shuffled along the edge of the bed to her travel trunk instead. Painstakingly, she dressed herself, then looked at the steps down to the body of the gondola. They were steep and she had no idea how to get down them. Shuffling on her backside maybe but there was a good chance she'd fall, which was hardly the sort of thing one did before the Arbiter of the Dralamut.

Assuming the Arbiter was there. Assuming she'd survived.

The air shuddered. An Elemental Man appeared sitting on the bed beside her. The same one who'd been with them in the square.

'Your sort just can't use the stairs, can you?' She pointed. 'They're right there.' It was easy to be angry with him because she hurt and because the Elemental Man was meant to protect them and he hadn't, and ... 'The Arbiter?'

The killer smoothed his robes. 'Our lady is shaken and bruised but not physically harmed. Mostly she is angry. As Arbiter, however, she is hurt badly. An attempt on her life. The audacity to strike at her and, by inference, at the very order of things.' The killer took a deep breath and let it out slowly. The strain on his face was clear and for once he seemed less like a mystical sorcerous assassin and more a common man close to the end of his tether. He nodded to the steps. 'It's laziness, Chay-Liang, that's all. It's easier for us to shift our substance and fly and shift back again than it is to climb a few steps. Does that surprise you? I suppose it must but it's true. Here and in Aria and the Dominion too. Everywhere except the dragon-realms. Dragons make it hard. I suppose she told you that while you were speaking in secret?' When Liang shook her head the Elemental Man rolled his eyes and looked away. 'The Arbiter has chosen you to be her companion, Chay-Liang. She chooses to trust you over the Elemental Men who have served the Dralamut for five hundred years. So be it. We're not your enemy. We serve in good faith. May I ask you to undress? I would inspect your wound. I have no doubt you would do a better job yourself, but its position, I fear, is awkward for you.'

Who have served the Dralamut ... Words chosen with thought or carelessly let out? The Elemental Men were supposed to serve the Elemental Masters who existed at the top of Mount Solence and whom no one else had ever seen, like priests who served a god whose every miracle was in fact the work of men. Liang had always quietly thought of the killers as serving an idea, or perhaps an ideal, and even if she shared it, she'd never much liked the notion. It was hard to argue with an idea, and ideals were notoriously intransigent. In a very metaphysical sort of way killing ideals was the purpose of the Elemental Men. It was ironic to imagine that they also served one.

Who have served the Dralamut. Perhaps she'd had it all wrong. She moaned softly. It was hard slipping her robe and shift back up her body. 'Someone has been through the potions my alchemist slave gave me. Was that you?'

The killer bowed. 'When it was clear the danger to our lady was past, I found you and brought you here. For the rest I was banished outside. The wound was not fatal but the blade carried a poison, and we do not learn the arts of healing on the peak of Mount Solence. Many other things, but not that. Our lady Arbiter tended you while I hunted those responsible.'

'Did you find them?' She had the robe and shift over her head now and felt conscious of her nakedness. The killers were eunuchs, she knew that much, but it had been a very long time since anyone had seen her disrobe. She flinched as his fingers brushed her skin and loosened the bandages. 'It was you I saw at the end.' The feet in front of her face. She'd thought they belonged to the man who'd stabbed her, come to finish her, but it must have been the Elemental Man instead. 'Did you find him? The one who left his knife in me.'

The killer shook his head as he unwound the cloth from her chest. 'My first concern was the safety of the Arbiter. Others will come once news of this reaches them. It cannot be ignored.' He poked at the wound in her back. He was gentle but she squealed anyway.

'With the dragons and the rider-slave and Shonda and his enchanters to deal with? How many of you are there, killer?' His fingers were hot and everything between her shoulders was swollen and hurt.

'Enough, enchantress, always enough. I would go and tell them myself but I fear to leave our lady's side. Where she goes I must be her voice.' Whatever he'd done he seemed satisfied. He began to wind the bandage back around her.

'The Konsidar?'

'Indeed.' The Elemental Man tied the end of the bandage. He shuffled back and gave her a baleful look. 'Our lady does not say why. I will not ask if she has told you, but the Konsidar is another realm where our rules and our laws no longer apply. Be wary there, enchantress.' He stood up. 'The wound is closing well. If I didn't know better then I'd say it was many days old. Whatever your alchemist slave puts in his potions, you might consider selling its secrets. You would have good custom.'

'I was content where I was, you know.'

The Elemental Man walked to the steps. Halfway down he turned and smiled at her. 'You see, we *can* do it if we remember to try. I will tell our lady you are risen from the dead.'

When he was gone, Liang eased herself back into her clothes. It took for ever, an endless series of slow tiny movements and then a gasping jab of pain and a pause for breath and begin again. *Whatever your alchemist slave puts into his potions.* His blood, that's what, and where his blood went so did a little part of him. She didn't know what Belli had meant by that but his face had said it wasn't a good thing, as if he'd put some sort of curse on her even though it had saved her life from poison twice now – a curse that struck her as peculiarly benign, as curses went. With careful gentle steps, she eased her way down the stairs. The killer stood in a far corner now, still and out of the way. Most of the gondola was taken up by the smashed-up remains of one of the golems, lying on its back. The two arms on its right side had been shattered by the iron ball of a black-powder cannon. Its head and back were peppered with chips and cracks and three of its golden eyes were missing. Lin Feyn was bent over it, moulding glass between her bare hands. She didn't look up as Liang came down. 'Can you work?'

Liang didn't reply at first. The Arbiter was a navigator from the Dralamut, and every navigator had been an enchanter first and they had to excel to be called. But around Lin Feyn, Liang forgot these things and only saw the Arbiter, dressed in all her finery.

Now and then she'd seen the woman underneath, who seemed to find her own privileged life vaguely disagreeable. But as an enchantress, moulding glass ...?

'Well?'

'Yes!' Liang moved as quickly as she could and stood awkwardly, trying to find a position that was comfortable.

'You're injured. You may sit in the presence of your Arbiter. Or kneel.' Lin Feyn suddenly laughed. She was dressed in a tan smock streaked with stains and scorched in places; her braided hair was tied back in a messy bundle to keep it out of the way and she looked like any other enchantress hard at work. She glanced at the Elemental Man. 'Or sit or lie down or do handstands or roll around the floor. I think we can all forget, for a while, that I am what I am. Even you, killer. I am Red Lin Feyn today. I am a very fine enchantress but this golem is beyond me.' She sat back and looked at Liang. 'When was the last time you went back to Hingwal Taktse? Do you know how these things are supposed to work? I made my own little golems when I was an apprentice and I imagine you did too, but they were stupid things, nothing like this.'

A smile spread across Liang's face and she cracked her knuckles. 'I was never the best enchantress in Hingwal Taktse, not by a long way, and it's been a decade since I was there. But I have spent years indentured to the lord of Xican, and there are more golems in Xican than in the rest of the Fourteen Cities put together. I know my golems.' She crouched beside the glass-and-gold body and pressed her hands to it, looking for the shape and form of its inner structure.

'The spark is still there,' said Lin Feyn. 'We're not wasting our time.'

'I feel it. But something has cut it off from its body.' She let her thoughts roam the structure of the glass. 'I'm not sure I can remould this.'

'I should hope not! It's a sentinel golem of the Dralamut. As with the palace towers of the sea lords, it's meant to be impervious to your intrusions. Or mine for that matter. Not much use if one of us can simply reshape it into an exquisitely expensive glass statue just by putting a finger to it.'

Liang withdrew her hands and winced at the pain across her

back. She was already sweating at the effort of forcing her mind inside the golem's glass. 'We'll have to break it open. I have raw gold-glass ready for moulding. Some, anyway. I can probably repair what's broken, although it won't be as well made as this. Perhaps *you* should work it, lady? It's your golem.'

'I'm not sure I'd do any better but I do have more glass. What's wrong with it?'

'I can show you, but first we have to get inside.'

Easier to say than do. At the heart of the golem the spark that gave it life and motion resided within an intricate structure of glass and gold. Moulded around that was the carapace armour of its body, inches thick. Neither Red Lin Fey nor Liang, even together, could begin to reshape the armour, which left breaking inside, and that would be no mean feat given the golem had been struck by a cannon and had survived. They looked at it for a while until Lin Feyn hit it with a hammer out of sheer frustration and then laughed at her own foolishness as it bounced and flew out of her hand. 'We should open the ramp, throw it out and smash it to pieces on the mountains and rework it from the start,' she said, although they both knew that would shatter both the golem's armour and its inner heart.

In the end they landed the gondola and tipped out the golem and had the Elemental Man drop rocks on it from ever-greater heights until the armour cracked and they were able to smash and lever a chink out and reach inside with their own moulded glass. Liang rebuilt the link from the spark to the body and then withdrew and left Red Lin Feyn to repair the arm and broken armour. It looked like what it was when they finished – a hodgepodge – but it walked and talked and remembered who it was. Which was as well, since even all three of them together had no hope of dragging its weight back inside the gondola.

Lin Feyn smiled. 'Well, Chay-Liang of Hingwal Taktse, that was certainly far more enjoyable than sitting in Mai'Choiro Kwen's gondola in your wind-blasted eyrie listening to Sea Lord Shonda threaten and whine about not being allowed to leave.' There was a new tear in her smock and her hair was a mess.

'I'm afraid I never learned to master lightning beyond a simple wand.' Liang poked at the golem's shattered arms.

Lin Feyn shrugged. 'Nor did I. It's still better than nothing.' She chuckled. 'I could have another one sent from the Dralamut, of course. We'd wait a few days and it would come, perfect and new, but I prefer this way. We'll have little use for a golem in the Konsidar anyway. They won't let it beneath the surface.'

'How did you get it into the gondola in the first place?' Liang asked.

'A lot of slaves and a sled.' Her smile faded. 'It gave my killer something to do while I had a look at your wound. Don't thank me, though. It was your alchemist's potions that saved you.'

Liang eased her back and realised it was hardly troubling her any more. She stared at the mountains around her. They were far from Vespinarr. Not in the Konsidar proper but at the edge of it, among the valleys where the Vespinese mined their silver. The landscape was deserted. A wide river only a few inches deep ran through a bed of sharp rocks and gravel, some tributary of the Jokun or the Yalun Zarang. The sides of the valley either side were steep and streaked with bare rock between thick verdant trees. The air was damp and cold. 'A pleasant change after the desert, lady,' she said,

'I hate that desert.' Lin Feyn's voice was distant. 'I hate that eyrie. I hate the Godspike and I hate the storm-dark.' She shuddered. 'Floating over it and it's always there, huge and uncaring and malevolent, just waiting to swallow me whole. You were there far longer than I – didn't you ever get the urge to jump?' She turned and smiled at Liang. 'The Arbiter is long gone, isn't she? If you were her, what would you do?'

That was easy. 'I'd poison every dragon. I'd throw the eggs into the storm-dark and I'd throw the dragon-rider into it too.'

'You don't like her?' Lin Feyn laughed again, deep and throaty. 'Why Chay-Liang, I'm taken wholly by surprise! And you hid it so well.'

Liang let the mockery pass her by. 'She's poison, lady. You asked me what I would do if I were the Arbiter. I'd put her and her dragon down in a heartbeat. I would have done it long ago. I would certainly have done it before we left the eyrie. They're both too dangerous. You told me yourself – see how she chooses who lives and who dies.'

'But the rider knows the truth and has no reason to lie.'

'*I* know the truth, lady. Baros Tsen T'Varr knows the truth. Mai'Choiro has already confessed that he gave the orders. Shonda told him to do it. *He's* the one who burned Dhar Thosis.'

Red Lin Feyn went to the edge of the river, crouched in the water and drank from it. The Elemental Man, Liang saw, had already done the same while they were repairing the golem. His robes were wet. When Lin Feyn came back, she said, 'I believe you, Chay-Liang, but you would not make a good Arbiter. Shonda is guilty, you say? My heart says yes but I must stand before the Crown of the Sea Lords and say so to all of them, and some will crow with glee and others will howl with outrage, and what is said will depend on who has been paid and how much and by whom. It will be easy to blame Baros Tsen T'Varr – and blame him I do – and no one will blink an eye. The dragon burned Dhar Thosis. The dragon is his. He is responsible and also bankrupt. But to hold the lord of Vespinarr to account, with all his riches? He wasn't even there. His kwen was a prisoner. He'd already lost his t'varr – his own brother. Baros Tsen was surely his enemy, not his ally. Mai'Choiro claims coercion.'

'But …'

Lin Feyn squeezed Liang's shoulder. 'I must, if I can, have all those who were responsible alive to speak. That is why we are here on the trail of Baros Tsen T'Varr. He and Shrin Chrias Kwen, who as yet eludes my killers, they are the ones who matter the most. Without them, perhaps I am acting on a whim. Perhaps I am a poor Arbiter. Perhaps I have been bought and paid for by the lords of Cashax, who will crow when Shonda falls. Or, worse, what if Shonda is guilty but did not conspire alone? I have my suspicions there. The killers will trust my word and carry out my verdict, but I must do better than that. To bring down a sea lord, there must be no questioning of my judgement. Our authority is absolute. Our dispassion and rigour must be the same. Thus I need your dragon-slave to speak the truth, and I will bargain with her if I have to and promise her whatever she wants to convince her to give me what I need, for what I need is more important. She is an unbranded slave who obeyed her master, and that cannot be a crime. The deed is the crime of the master. When a sword stabs you, do you blame the steel or the hand that held it?' She pursed her lips.

'You're going to let her *live*? Dear Xibaiya, are you *mad*?' Liang put a hand to her mouth as soon as the words came out. 'Lady, forgive—'

But Lin Feyn had doubled up with laughter. '*This* is why I have you with me, Chay-Liang!' She took a moment to compose herself. 'No. A city has burned, a sea lord hanged from his own palace, and she knew her master meant her to stop ...' She glanced at the Elemental Man still standing by the river and leaned in to Liang, her voice now a fierce whisper. 'But in the midst of this a skin-shifter of the Konsidar steals away the man most clearly responsible? My killers try to hide things from me? These things strike to the heart of what we are.'

She sighed and walked on back to the gondola. The golem was waiting inside, silent and infinitely patient. As Lin Feyn passed it, she ran a hand over its glass. 'This one was Ferring Syfa once. I knew him. He was an old man even when I first came to the Dralamut but he taught me a great deal before he died.' She patted the golem. 'Lungs, wasn't it, old man? Gave out on you in the end. Slowly filled with fluid. The coughing got worse and worse. Ah, we tried to keep him a while, to make him comfortable, but there's no cure for age. I suppose you must have drowned in your sleep one night, was that it?'

The golem didn't move, didn't speak.

'Do you remember, golem, who you were?'

'No.'

'None of them do. I suppose it's a mercy but I missed him. I was young and the world had just become so very big.' She glanced at Liang with a moment of longing in her eyes. 'Could your alchemist have saved him, I wonder. He's saved you twice now.' She pulled a piece of paper from her pocket, crumpled up and covered in Belli's writing. 'This is yours. It told me what to do.'

The gondola lifted them slowly out of the valley. Liang watched the mountains sprout up from behind one another. She moved so she could look to the north and to the heart of the Konsidar. She'd seen it so many times but only from afar, only the edges of it. Towers of stone capped with snow. Deep dark valleys filled with trees, the ground buried beneath their leaves. Streaks of dark rock amid waterfalls of green vines. They flew over a valley where a deep red streak of acer trees ripped through the green, a rune carved into the forest like a livid scar on wrinkled green skin. Another valley and another sigil in the same dark red leaves. The mountains grew taller and the valleys deeper and the forest thicker and wilder. They drifted above more sigils etched among the trees, mostly the reds of acers but now and then the black leaves of some tree Liang didn't know, and once there were lines of scars and pale bare rock. They were too regular to have grown that way on their own. They had been made.

'They're like the writing on the pillar.'

'Yes.' She hadn't even noticed the Elemental Man come to stand beside her. 'It is the language of the half-gods whose war brought the Splintering and broke the world apart. It is the language of the moon. These ones are signs. Some are warnings. Some are directions. Some ...' He shrugged. 'Some of them only the skin-shifters know.'

Liang had questions. So many questions of gods and half-gods and times long ago and why any of that mattered here and now and what it had to do with dragons and the death of Dhar Thosis. But the killer was what he was, sworn to keep such secrets dark and undisturbed, and so even if he knew them they would stay his and his alone. She looked at him for a moment. 'You understand why we put the golem back together, don't you? Instead of simply asking for a new one?' Then the glasship rose over a ridge and Liang saw what lay on the other side and all her questions melted into one.

'Fire and earth! What is that?'

Surrounded by cliffs and the sheer sides of the mountains, the ground fell away into a monstrous chasm, a hole a mile wide and ten miles long and deeper by far. As the glasship drifted past the ridge and out over the abyss, Liang couldn't see to the bottom.

'This? This is the secret of the Konsidar?'

The killer shook his head. 'This? No, enchantress, this is merely the way in.'

The glasship sank into the chasm. Waterfalls spilled down its sides, dissolving into mist. On every ledge and in every cranny, trees and vines clung to the stone. Ferns gripped even the slightest crack, and where the rock was so smooth and sheer that no root would take hold, long streamers of moss clung to it instead.

'Have you ever seen anything like it?' The killer was mocking her, she thought, but when she shook her head he tapped her shoulder and pointed down. As the walls of the abyss drew slowly closer, she saw an arch of stone reach from one side to the other, and further down were others, dozens of them until they vanished into the darkness.

Lin Feyn was dressing as the Arbiter again. 'Gird yourself, killer. The guardians of Xibaiya await and I may have to be rude.'

'It's like the Queverra,' Liang whispered.

'Yes.' The killer drew away. 'But the Queverra is dead. Its gates to Xibaiya are marked and warded and those who enter do not come out. Here, Chay-Liang, it is otherwise.'

39

Best Not to Ask

The stone bridge went on for what felt like for ever and Tuuran didn't like it one little bit. It reminded him of a giant tree root made of rock – rounded and arching through empty space and uneven and slippery, smooth as glass in places – and there was no kindness to it, no forgiveness. Twice it caught him out and he slipped and barely regained his balance before a short sharp slide over the edge into oblivion. Further down, all he could see was lots of blackness and a handful of pinprick lights that just might have been fires, or maybe stars looking back at him from the other side of the world, or possibly they were his mind playing tricks on him.

He'd given up thinking about the way back, and so far he'd only found one way down. Crazy must have gone this way. If Tuuran went far enough, he'd find him. When he did, he'd think about what happened next. Though there was a good chance it would start with him giving Crazy a good solid punch in the face.

The bridge took him to a series of terraces linked by steep steps. In places the terraces were as wide as a field, in others so narrow that he had to ease his way along sideways, trying not to peer down at his toes and the endless chasm underneath. 'Crazy Mad!' he bellowed when he'd been making his way along them for an hour. It felt good to break the silence. He was fiercely hungry and close to exhaustion and the terraces just went on and on. 'You hear me, Crazy? When I catch up with you, you're going to get a right thumping, I can tell you.' There wasn't any answer. After a bit he took to singing to himself just to make the emptiness go away.

The terraces dumped him onto another arch back across the chasm. He looked up and rather wished he hadn't, crossed over anyway and found yet more steps carved into the cliff, winding on down. There were sparks on the side of the chasm here, distant little windows of firelight. Proper fires, not torches, and they got him wondering what sort of people lived in this darkness, what they could possibly find to burn and whether they had any food he could have.

A spike of fear hit him then – that he'd made a mistake, that his strength wouldn't be enough to climb to the top again, that he'd never get out and he'd die here alone, so far from everything he knew that his legion ancestors wouldn't ever find him. He crushed it quickly. Adamantine Men didn't know fear. Adamantine Men faced dragons and spat in their eyes. And as for his legion ancestors? *They* were Adamantine Men too, the spirits of the hundred thousand gone before, and they knew their duty. Leave no one behind. They'd find him wherever he died. They'd upend the underworld if they had to.

They would too. He felt a bit better, thinking that.

He went on because he was stubborn, because turning back meant he'd been wrong, and Adamantine Men were never wrong – or if they were they didn't live to be shamed by it. He counted the steps this time so his legs would have something to think about on their way back. Somewhere over six hundred he gave up. By the time they brought him to the next ledge, he reckoned it must have been pushing a thousand.

Another bloody stone arch. He could hardly see his hand in front of his face now. He passed the remains of a few old fires. Charred fragments of wood. Men had come here, not in the last few days but not all that long ago.

Wood? Where did they get the wood?

He passed a pair of pillars sunk into the face of the cliff. White stone like the ones he'd encountered before. Thing was, he'd seen writing like this back in the Pinnacles in the places where the Silver King had worked his magics, and the white stone there was the same as in the eyrie and now here, and a pillar was just a pillar but two pillars started to look like an archway or a gateway, and the Pinnacles had had archways lining the walls everywhere. Riddled with the things, and all blank and just for decoration and not leading anywhere except in the stories people whispered when sometimes one of them suddenly changed and there was another world on the other side and you could walk right through into a different land, except no one ever came back because as soon as you crossed through the arch snapped closed behind you.

Stupid stories. These pillars didn't lead anywhere either.

'Crazy?' He meant to shout but he couldn't bring himself to, and then he told himself how stupid that was, and it made him angry because it meant he *was* afraid, and that wasn't supposed to happen, not ever. 'Crazy? Crazy Mad? Berren! Skyrie! Whoever you are! You in here?' This time he roared it as loud as he could, then stood and clutched his axe too tightly as he listened to the echoes. He tried to slow his racing heart with some long deep breaths but apparently it wasn't feeling in a slowing mood.

'Flame on this.' He turned his back on the pillars and walked away, fighting the urge to jump, to get it over with, to get to the bottom and be done with it. He had to pinch himself to remember that he couldn't just do that and then get up again.

Keep it together. Cursed place is getting to you.

And then suddenly there wasn't an abyss beside him and he was at the bottom. He took a few deep breaths, let his head spin a bit until it sorted itself out and then wandered about to be sure there wasn't some hidden crack leading even deeper. All he found was a flat sandy floor with a shallow river running through it and no sign of any great rift on to the very heart of the world. He knelt by the river and tasted the water, found it pure and clean and filled his belly with it. Better. Then he looked for footprints in the sand because if Crazy Mad had come this way then he must have left some, and it wasn't as if there was any wind or rain to hide them again, and Flame but Crazy was going to get a thumping for dragging him all this way ...

When he traced his own steps back to the side of the abyss, he found what he was looking for. Prints. One pair of boots. They might have been Crazy's or they might not, but Tuuran couldn't think of a better idea. In the near dark at the bottom of the Queverra he followed the tracks on his hands and knees, crawling from one footprint to the next. It was grindingly slow and probably made him look utterly stupid but it took him to a cave. A bigger cave than the others and this one didn't have just two pillars outside it but six, four like the ones he'd seen before and two much larger. He swore and wondered what to do, because Crazy Mad had gone in there but Crazy was, well, crazy and mad, and his own not-so-crazy guts were twisting in knots at the thought of following even if they couldn't tell him why. He called out again: 'Crazy?' No answer. He wasn't surprised. Hadn't had one yet.

But there really wasn't anything else. Not after he'd come all this way.

'Crazy Mad, I'm going to carve some new holes in you for this.' He got up, muttering to himself, and took two steps towards the cave.

'I wouldn't, if I were you,' called a voice in the dark behind him. *Crazy.*

'You son of a turd!' Tuuran turned and squinted and peered and then spotted the shape of a shadow in the gloom and strode towards it, still not sure whether he was going to hug Crazy or hit him or possibly both. And it *was* him, even if there was something different about him. Something different in his face. When he reached the little man, he settled on pushing him. Hard. 'You! You left me! In the middle of a gang of slavers! You turned one man to ash and scared off a dragon and then you just left! You git! And then this! You drag me all the way down here?' He pointed up to the narrow slit of light miles above them. Relief had the better of him, wagging his tongue. 'Do you have any idea what a royal pain in the arse it's going to be to get back up?' He shoved Crazy again and then grabbed him, crushed him. 'I tell you, I intend to make you pay for this for the rest of your whole bloody life! Bastard!'

He stepped back and took and deep breath and let out a sigh, and that was when he realised that he and Crazy weren't alone. He jumped back and grabbed his axe but Crazy held out a soothing hand. 'Calm, big man. They're not here to hurt us. These are my friends.' He laughed but there was strain in it. Something off. 'You didn't have to follow me down here, you know.'

'Oh, so you leave me with slavers and go gallivanting off to make some new friends on your own, eh? Were you planning on coming back out at some point to see about rescuing your *other* friend – you know, the one who's been at your side for the last however many years it's been? Why'd you come down here anyway?'

Crazy Mad's face screwed up. 'Don't know really. Looking for something. Looking for some*one*.'

'Looks like you found several someones.'

'Not me. Whatever it was the one-eyed warlock put into Skyrie before Vallas Kuy did what he did to both of us.'

Tuuran snorted uneasily at that because it made no sense to him and never had. Crazy Mad had his name for a reason, and he'd got it before his eyes had started turning silver now and then and the odd occasion when he'd disintegrated people. Oh, and stopped time that once. That too. 'Well then, did you find who you were looking for?'

'No.'

'Not your one-eyed warlock himself, was it? You didn't think he'd be down here, did you?'

Crazy jerked as though stung. Then he frowned. 'I think it was looking for itself.' He said this as though they were back in a tavern in Deephaven and Tuuran had asked him whether he wanted his ale pale or dark. As though the answer was so obvious it amazed him that Tuuran felt the need to ask.

'I find a mirror works pretty well for that.' Tuuran took a deep breath, let it out slowly, took another one and found he still hadn't the first idea what to do with himself. He'd come all this way to find Crazy. Well, he'd done that. And now? 'I'm just a simple soldier, Crazy. You know what? I don't have the first clue what you're talking about.'

Crazy clapped him on the shoulder. 'Long way down though, isn't it? You hungry? You must be. Want to eat before we start on the way up?'

'What? We're going back up now? Great Flame, tell me there was something here to make it worth it!' Although now that he mentioned it, yes, Tuuran was very hungry indeed and yes, he would very much like to eat something because eating was a simple thing he could understand.

'Food first, big man.' And for a while, as they walked along the bottom of the abyss with white-painted men creeping in circles around them and gated caves to Xibaiya and the realm of the dead passing on either side, Crazy Mad talked like he usually did, and Tuuran talked too, and life was almost normal again.

40

No Escape, Not Even for You

The sun rose over the storm-dark and the swirls of cloud lit up in a patchwork of dull orange light and deep black shadow. The sunward side of the Godspike glowed a brilliant pink and bright rays of dawn fire streamed over the eyrie walls into the little shelter. They sprawled through its sailcloth walls and over the sleeping face inside. Zafir sat up and pushed away her silken wrappings. She rubbed her eyes and blinked and then took a little water from the silver bowl beside her and splashed it on her face. She hitched up her shift and squatted over her chamber pot and then walked outside to greet the dawn. When she reached the wooden lean-to where Myst and Onyx slept, she ducked inside. They were gone, but she could still smell them so they hadn't been awake for long. They fretted at how their mistress lived and yes, palaces and castles and gold and silks were fine things, but in her heart Zafir was a dragon-rider before she was a queen, and no dragon-rider was a stranger to a crude camp in an open space with a dragon beside her.

She walked out to the eyrie rim, through the litter of her first shelter, which Diamond Eye had crushed on the night the hatchling came to kill her. He was perched out on the edge this morning instead of at his usual post on the wall beside her. She sat down next to him, feet dangling over the void, peering between her knees at the storm-dark. Sometimes she thought about falling. Toppling forward and not stopping herself and tipping over and plummeting into the maelstrom below. But even if she wanted to, Diamond Eye wouldn't let her. He'd come after her before she was even close to the cloud, catch her and bring her back. He'd keep her safe whether or not safe was what she wanted. That was why she slept beside him. To know when they were coming for her.

'They're thinking it,' she whispered to him. 'You first and then me. Even the ones who want to keep you want me to hang.

Everyone wants us gone. One day my alchemist will quietly poison you, though I've forbidden it. Then they'll come for me.' Here they were, she and her alchemist, both slaves of the rapacious sea lords, both taken from their homes, both from the same land. The alchemist should have been hers, body and soul, and yet he wasn't. He tolerated her. That was about as much as you could say now. It cut deep, knowing he would betray her.

'I want to go home,' she whispered. The dragon didn't move. His eyes stayed on the Godspike. His thoughts were distant and vague. Watching. Waiting. And Zafir had come to think that neither of them had the first idea what for. Just something.

'The rest of them are waiting for doll-woman to come back. That's when they'll do it.' Doll-woman? Yes, doll-woman because *Arbiter* smacked a little too much of *speaker*, and because she painted her face and kept it so absurdly still she looked like a doll, and because Zafir hated her for the gold-glass band around her head, and calling her doll-woman made her seem small and stupid.

She got up and tapped Diamond Eye on the foot. 'Come on. Let me up.' He turned his head and looked down at her, and she thought she caught a flicker of resentment. 'I won't be long. I need to check the harnesses.'

Diamond Eye shifted and lowered his shoulders and neck. Zafir shinned up the legbreaker rope onto his back. The Elemental Men who flew with her had taken to buckling themselves into the harnesses these days — not that they particularly needed to, but now and then she flew Diamond Eye in tight loops and rolls and spins for the sheer fun of it. When they didn't buckle themselves in, she invariably threw them off. She could feel Diamond Eye in her thoughts too, felt his amusement and smiled, riding the memories beside him. 'I told them a dragon was a dragon and they could fly you without me if they liked to try.' So they'd taken to using the harnesses. It was a quiet and subtle victory. Strapped to Diamond Eye's back, they couldn't shift form, and when the time came she'd make the most of that: chasing the hatchling into the Queverra abyss, filled with fury and hunger, she'd understood that Diamond Eye could turn and dive and climb and loop with force enough to break her in two. He held back to keep from snapping her bones, that was all.

She finished checking the harnesses. The Elemental Men never bothered. She supposed they didn't mind too much if she sabotaged them because if they fell off so what? But they never would. Each morning she checked with meticulous care. They were perfect and tight and would stay that way.

Zafir slid back down the legbreaker to the eyrie rim and sat against Diamond Eye's claws. She wasn't sure what she'd do when the doll-woman returned. Maybe nothing. 'Or maybe we'll fly together for one last time and bring that glasship down and burn her to ash, and I'll push you to my limits or yours, whichever we find first. And the killers will be trapped in their perfect harnesses, unable to shift away, and their bones will snap like twigs.' She snapped her fingers. She could feel Diamond Eye coursing through her thoughts, adding a savage edge all of his own. 'Then we'll fly away, far far away where they'll never find us.' She sighed. Would she, if she could? She honestly didn't know but it didn't matter anyway. The gold-glass crown around her head meant she could only dream.

Myst and Onyx came hurrying along the top of the wall, tunics flapping in the wind, clutching their bronze trays. Zafir got up and left Diamond Eye to the Godspike. Yes, she'd tear the doll-woman out of the sky, and then the circlet would kill her and Diamond Eye would shatter them all and burn them, everything, all of it, as much as he could before they brought him down. She'd been teaching him that. No plunging after his fallen mistress to sit mute beside her corpse until another rider led him away, not this time. No. Rage. Unfettered rage, the thing dragons did best. She'd die in fire and fury as a dragon-queen should. There would be nothing left of her to dangle by a foot from a rope, for them to mock with their jeering scorn, not like they'd done to Tsen. She almost felt sorry for him for that.

The wind howled across the desert sky. Zafir went to help her slaves but they shied away. She had no idea how they managed to balance themselves and carry their trays and never drop anything in the teeth of all that wind but they always did. They shooed her off as if mortally offended at the suggestion they couldn't manage on their own. Zafir let them. She could understand that. *I need no one's help.* She crawled back into her shelter instead and sat, waiting, legs crossed. Onyx shuffled in on her knees and bowed and offered a bowl of steamed stuffed dumplings. Zafir had tried a few times to have them all sit and break their night fast together but Onyx simply refused and Myst looked as though she'd rather take a running jump off the edge of the eyrie. The way they sat mute and watched her while she ate set her teeth on edge so she simply ate as quickly as she could, stuffing dumplings in one after the other and washing them down with a jug of fresh milk. It left her feeling bloated.

'Mistress, Lord Shonda is out in the dragon yard,' whispered Myst.

Zafir pursed her lips. Shonda of Vespinarr. She had to wonder about him, whether there was some way to use him. Whether their interests could somehow align. The doll-woman had trapped him here and he hated it. Zafir had seen him strutting about in his electrum feather robes with his enchanters around him to keep the wind from ruffling them. He hadn't ever come close to Diamond Eye. She wasn't sure whether she thought more or less of him for that. Most men came, sooner or later. Most men had to test themselves against their fear and most were found wanting. Or maybe what had happened the last time had been enough for him, when he'd had one of his soldiers throw lightning in Diamond Eye's face and the dragon had swatted the man off the eyrie wall. Diamond Eye certainly hadn't forgotten. Presumably Shonda hadn't forgotten either.

She crawled back out of the shelter, looked over the top of the wall and there he was, walking with a measured purpose around the yard with Mai'Choiro Kwen at his side and four enchanters around them holding up their gold-glass screens. A pair of lesser kwens followed behind. Zafir watched for a while. Every now and then Mai'Choiro would point to a spot in the dragon yard and one of the kwens would run, check he had the right place, then make a mark with a piece of charcoal. From up on the wall Zafir couldn't make out what the marks might mean, whether they were numbers or letters or …

Abruptly Shonda stopped and looked straight at her, as if suddenly aware of being watched. Zafir looked back. He held her eye for ten long heartbeats, and with that look she felt he was telling her that they were the same, that neither of them could ever bend or break for another, that it simply wasn't in the way they were made. She thought he almost smiled at her. And then he turned away and raised his arm and tapped it, and she understood exactly what he meant. *I am no slave.*

'He means to leave,' murmured Zafir.

She was good to the killers that morning. She waited until they were strapped in tight, let Diamond Eye climb until the air was so thin it made her gasp, and then dive, wings tucked in so the wind tore into her like a hundred furious fists. Before they took to wearing their harnesses the wind of a dive like this would tear the Elemental Men off Diamond Eye's back and blow them away like leaves. One day she'd let Diamond Eye fall like he really could, the way they used to dive together off the Great Cliff and even off the top of the Pinnacles, like a spear straight down at the ground, and the killers on his back, strapped in tight and unable to escape, would be ripped to pieces by the wind. There were tricks to riding a dragon through a dive like that, tricks they couldn't possibly know.

But not today. Today she was gentle. Diamond Eye flared his wings, crushing the breath out of her, and landed in the dunes, blowing a great cloud of sand into the air. Zafir looked at the faces behind her and saw the strain in them. They came every day, not the same killers each time, but every day in every face she saw the same. They were afraid of her dragon and afraid of what it might be, just as they should be.

The Vespinese camp out in the desert lay outside the shadow of the storm-dark. They kept a herd of bison here, all of them withering and dying in the sun. Zafir let Diamond Eye loose to do as he pleased. The bison stampeded, snorting their terror while the dragon gave gleeful chase. He caught them with ease, flipped them onto their backs with a flick of a talon, catapulted them into the air with a twitch of his tail or bowled them over with the wind from a flap of his wings. Once he'd scattered the herd, he picked a few to kill. He played with them more than he ate. These last few days he'd grown wasteful and vicious, bored and tense, swayed by Zafir's moods while she waited for the doll-woman to return. Her own thoughts wandered as the dragon lunged and danced and dived. She looked long and hard back up at the storm-dark. Glasships had been gathering before she left, Vespinese glasships. She wondered what it meant.

When the dragon was sated, she let him rest. 'It makes them bad-tempered to fly after they've eaten.' She'd said that to the Elemental Men once and they'd never told her she was a liar even though she was. Dragons didn't care; it was simply that she liked to be down here for a time, out of the wind, basking in the desert heat and relishing the thick strong air. She sat beside her dragon and dozed a little while as the sun crept higher, and when the warmth became stifling, she flew him in a long gentle circuit of the storm-dark. She came back to the camp to let him feed a second time if he wanted, but he didn't seem interested. He kept staring up at the sky, and so she let him sit and unstrapped herself and lay across his shoulders, dreaming dreams of what she'd do to the doll-woman if the circlet around her head were to suddenly fall away, wondering how to fill the long hours of the afternoon. Sometimes she laid her armour aside and simply sat beside him and stared at the same things as he did: at the swirling storm-dark and the Godspike towering to the top of the sky. Once she flew him up to it to see if he could cling to it with his claws, but the stone offered no purchase. Another time, because of something she remembered from long ago, she flew him underneath the storm-dark to the base of the Godspike. She'd dismounted and touched it herself, and it had seemed to her that it was the same stone as the eyrie, the same white stone that ran through and beneath the Pinnacles, riddled with archways, whose soft light reflected the wax and wane of the sun and the moon and the passing of the stars, whose gateways supposedly opened to other worlds now and then when no one was there to see.

Maybe that again today. A slight memory of home.

A sharp cry snapped her back to the present. She glanced at the killers and followed their eyes up. A swarm of glasships was drifting over the edge of the storm-dark and heading west, bright sparks of light in the afternoon sun. There must have been almost fifty of them, and Diamond Eye had gone very still. One of the killers jumped off Diamond Eye's back and turned into the wind before he hit the ground. *Interesting*, she thought, then turned herself so she could see the glasships without having to crane her neck. She settled back to watch.

The killer returned a few minutes later and the second Elemental Man jumped to join him on the ground. Zafir yawned. They obviously didn't want her to know what they were saying and equally obviously didn't realise that Diamond Eye, mute and dulled as he was, still picked up the impressions of their thoughts. If she concentrated hard, he could show them to her. Another little secret she kept to herself. She slid down and walked casually towards them, straining to pick up the emotions and images Diamond Eye pulled from their minds. *Anxiety. The glasships. A silver gondola. Shonda, surprise, anger. Uncertainty.* An image of gondolas sitting in the dragon yard, ramps open with dead men scattered around them. Vespinese soldiers. By the time she was close enough for them to hear, she knew she'd been right. Shonda had decided to leave and he hadn't asked politely.

She paused, wondering. *I am no slave.* That last little jibe left her with a hunger to make him humble. She raised her visor and shouted at the killers, 'Would you like me to get him back for you?'

The Elemental Men turned to look as she carried on towards them. Zafir reached for what Diamond Eye saw in their thoughts. They couldn't enter a gondola once it was sealed. Its walls were proof against them. Not her concern. Vespinarr. They couldn't stop a glasship. *Impatience. Concern for the Arbiter's return. Failure in their duty. Suspicion.* All this as she walked towards them, head cocked, glancing back now and then at Diamond Eye, and it amazed her how it took them so long to answer. She leaned towards them and smiled.

'Show me which gondola is his and Diamond Eye will pluck it off its chains as you or I might pluck an apple off a tree.'

They vanished, both of them, appeared again far away and conferred. *Dislike. Mistrust.* But by then she'd already made up her mind. She turned back to Diamond Eye without waiting for their answer, walking briskly, carefree. They'd confer until the glasships were lost to sight. But however far they went, Diamond Eye would catch them. Brinkmanship with the Elemental Men? The Taiytakei remained largely a mystery but she knew enough about how they worked to admire Shonda for that. Maybe it was his way of facing down a dragon. A different dragon but no less lethal.

She reached Diamond Eye and climbed onto his back. She was Zafir, dragon-queen, speaker of the nine realms, and she would not wait to be told what these killers would or would not permit. They would either stop her or they wouldn't. Two alone might not be able to bring her down but they could go squealing back to the eyrie and come after her in numbers and catch her easily enough – another thing learned from chasing that hatchling – and they might not be able to touch her up in the sky on Diamond Eye's back but she couldn't sit in the saddle for ever.

But she could do *this*.

She willed Diamond Eye to the sky. He reared up, stretched and started to run, wings throwing up a storm of sand in his wake. He powered into the air, crushing her with the strength of every beat as he drove after the drifting glasships. He had a hunger to him – here were prey worthy of a hunter – and she wondered at how serene they seemed, hanging in the sky, spinning slowly. She had no idea which one was Shonda's. They were all silver, all the same. He'd be in the middle somewhere if he had any sense, but maybe he didn't. He hadn't seen Dhar Thosis.

The golden rim of the nearest glasship began to glow as she closed, dim at first and then brighter and brighter. A lightning cannon readying to fire. Then another and another and another. Diamond Eye saw them too. He'd felt them in Dhar Thosis, how they hurt. They'd brought him down with one of those. The urge to strike and smash and let them see what happened when they tried to sting washed over her, but in Dhar Thosis she'd fought the sea lord's glasships a handful at a time. There were too many here.

We can't win this.

And though a large part of her didn't much care, for it was certainly a far better end than hanging, it turned out there was still a part of her that did.

She turned Diamond Eye away, reluctant and resentful. Maybe the Elemental Men felt it too, that the glasships were too many for her. Maybe that was why they hadn't stopped her. Or maybe, like her, they were simply watching and waiting to see what would happen.

41

Bronzehand

The road that ran beside the Jokun gorge had been carved out of the sheer cliffs beside the river. In some places it had been cut using enchanter-made fire rods charged by globes of living flame brought back from the Dominion of the Sun King, but for the most part the Vespinese had used the more traditional method of throwing a very great many slaves at the cliffs and shouting at them until they had a road. Since neither Sivan nor his hired swords showed any interest in talking to him, Baros Tsen settled to wondering exactly how many men it had taken and how long and all the other sorts of thoughts that came to a bored t'varr with nothing else to fill his mind. Not that there weren't plenty of things that ought to be filling his mind, such as where they were taking him and why and who this Sivan really was and how he might escape, but he found he simply couldn't be bothered with all of that any more. Escaping seemed rather pointless given what awaited him if he ever got back to his eyrie. As for the rest, what difference did it make? They'd tell him when they were ready, and Sivan waving Tsen's black rod about made it obvious he needed him to do something that couldn't be done by anyone else. Then the bargaining would start. And he was good at bargaining. He was a t'varr and so he had to be.

He watched the river. Past the cataracts and falls of its upper gorge, the Jokun was the artery that linked Vespinarr to the sea at Hanjaadi and thus their ships and their fleet and thence to the rest of the world. In late spring, when the Jokun waters were at their highest, even the lower parts of the river became impassable. Then the Vespinese were forced, for two or three months of each year, to rely on glasships and the long tedious land route from Shevana-Daro. The Yalun Zarang river to the west was shorter and quicker, but the Yalun Zarang led to Tayuna, and somehow the lords of Vespinarr and the lords of Tayuna had never managed to see eye to eye. They'd failed, over the last couple of centuries, to see eye to eye on rather a lot of things in fact, but mostly what they failed to agree on was whether Tayuna should follow the example of its Hanjaadi neighbours and allow itself to settle into the comfortable life of a Vespinese vassal state. The Vespinese were very much in favour of the notion, frequently urging the lords of Tayuna to see things their way through encouragements such as sinking their ships, setting fire to their city and occasionally dragging them into unwanted wars in other realms, yet despite these marvellous incentives, the lords of Tayuna remained strangely intransigent, perversely preferring to keep their independence and telling Shonda where to stick it. As a t'varr in distant Xican, Tsen had sometimes wondered why Tayuna didn't take the easy choice and give in. Now, after what he'd seen these last few months, he felt like giving them a round of applause. Maybe they'd give him a job once this was all done. There certainly wasn't much of a future for him as a t'varr of Xican any more.

If you're honest with yourself, there isn't much future for you as anything at all, except perhaps as sustenance to the vulture population in some remote part of the desert for a day until they pick you clean. Or perhaps the fish off some distant shore ...

He rolled his eyes and laughed at himself and wondered if perhaps he was finally going mad, and was grateful when a hold-up in the road distracted his thoughts. There was some shouting and milling about as Sivan and his men squeezed between the overhanging cliff wall on one side and a sullen team of broad-backed bison towing a barge against the current on the other. Men cursed and did their best to get out of the way while Tsen mentally checked off how many new words he was learning. Sometimes he wondered what would happen if he turned his horse and tried to bolt back down the road, but the chances seemed good that even if he could muster the skill to make his horse do something other than follow the one in front, trying to escape would simply end with him being dumped in the river, followed either by a quick death from drowning or maybe a slightly slower one from freezing. Doubtless either outcome would irritate Sivan no end after all the trouble he'd gone to, but being dead and washed into the Samim to be gnawed on by crocodiles seemed a poor way to appreciate such frustration.

As the sun sank low, the gorge widened. The cliffs fell away and spread out around the shore of a wide lake where the Jokun paused in its eager plunge towards the sea. Hundreds of boats bobbed, rocked by the brisk cold winds that blew off the mountains, everything from little skiffs with barely a shred of sail to massive Vespinese river barges. Upstream of the lake the Jokun came down from the mountains around Vespinarr through a series of gorges and cataracts, and so the lakeside had grown a shanty town of warehouses and sailors and sail-slaves, of mules and the teamsters who drove them up through the mountain passes, of rough edges and straightforward words. It stank of sweat, cheap spirits and even cheaper Xizic, and of men and women who filled their lives with hard back-breaking work and came at you with all you might expect.

Sivan stopped at a house on the fringes and Tsen meekly ate his supper and went to bed. He pretended to sleep while he stared at the ceiling for much of the night, listening to the snores of the sword-slave who was supposed to be watching him. He supposed he ought to slip out from under the sheets and climb through the window or something equally dramatic. Run away as fast as he could and get on one of those boats and stay on it to Hanjaadi and cross the sea and never come back. But he didn't, and when he looked to see if any of those nasty little voices were going to taunt him for being scared, he found them silent. They knew better. He wasn't scared, not any more. Staying with Sivan had become the cold hard calculation of a t'varr. Question was, what did the shifter actually want?

A black stone fortress full of Vespinese soldiers looked across the lake from an outcrop of rock on the far side – full, it was said, with a fortune in Vespinese silver. By the middle of the next afternoon they were riding under the shadow of its walls. Tsen examined it as they passed and found himself wondering how it would fare if a dragon came. Badly, he supposed. And then they reached a bridge across a narrow gorge, and after crossing it Sivan led them off along a winding track into the hills until the evening, stopping where a waterfall crashed over the lip of a cliff. The sword-slaves dismounted. By now Tsen could barely move, exhausted and in agony from all the riding, and they practically had to lift him off his horse, which none of them appreciated because he was heavy. As they did though, he took the chance to look at the brands on their arms. Vespinese, all of them. *It's not my fault*, he wanted to tell them. *Some djinn crept past your snoring watchman in the night and swapped my back for a pain-soaked plank of wood … or maybe glass.* Cracked and broken glass that made horrible grinding sounds every time he moved but was still as stiff as a beam. *That sounds about right …*

A path slipped around the back of the falls to a cave behind the roaring water. The sword-slaves pushed him inside through a thick curtain of metal chains, the sort used to keep Elemental Men at bay, and then through a heavy iron door fitted carefully into the rock. Sivan was already there, flitting from wall to wall, lighting lamps while the sword-slaves poked and prodded Tsen as far as a soft couch. There were chairs carved from Zinzarran rosewood, a silver and glass table and a cabinet well stocked with crystal bottles, even a shelf of books. It felt like a home, cared for and lived in with plenty of comfort and not what Tsen had imagined at all. Sivan poured himself a glass of wine. When he didn't offer to share it, Tsen lay back and sank into the couch. It really was deliciously soft, quite big enough to make a bed, and he couldn't see himself getting up again in a hurry. The roar of the waterfall was muted, though he could feel the vibration through the floor.

'So what do you want from me?' he asked. He supposed some sort of enchanter's device must be hidden somewhere, keeping the air as fresh as it was. It was certainly the most unexpected cave he'd ever seen.

As Tsen watched, Sivan's face changed. Sivan slowly vanished and another man took his place, a man Tsen knew well. Bronze-hand, although Tsen knew perfectly well that Bronzehand was on a ship and had sailed to Qeled to find an answer to all their problems, or possibly just to run away from them all. He'd seen it through Quai'Shu's rings, and the rings didn't lie. He snorted.

'Another face you've learned to steal? Can you do Shonda of Vespinarr too so I can punch both of you at once? Although you'll have to come closer because I don't think I can get up. Again, what do you want from me?'

Sivan held up Tsen's black rod. 'I already told you.'

'Dragon eggs?' Tsen shrugged. 'You're mad, but I can hardly stop you. I don't see how I can help you either. Nor why I should.' Maybe he should run away just for the sake of it, even if he didn't have anywhere to go, but given the state of his back, Sivan could have taken his sword-slaves out for a riotous night at the lakeside whorehouses and it wouldn't have made a blind bit of difference. *Old, fat and crippled, t'varr. Could you be more useless?* He looked around some more. Pictures hung on the walls, odd paintings in a style he didn't recognise: they weren't of people or even of places but streaks and splatches of dull slate and tan and deep greens and reds all run together. If someone had decided to make an art out of painting mud, he thought, this was what it would look like.

'If you're going to be Bronzehand, his tastes run more to lewd nudes. Gold and silver frames too. Ostentatiously expensive.' The more he looked around, the more the cave struck him as slightly off.

Sivan tapped Tsen's black rod. 'I saved you from the Vespinese, Baros Tsen T'Varr. I left a body for them. I killed a sword-slave and changed his shape and face to be yours. You saw it. So you know it's true when I tell you that the world believes Baros Tsen T'Varr is dead. You are free. That's my gift to you. Freedom. Freedom to vanish far away across the storm-dark if you wish, or into the desert or the Samim swamps if you prefer, but vanish you must.' Sivan sucked in his cheeks as if tasting something sour. 'I'm offering you both your freedom and your life.'

'Is that all? Pity.' Tsen shrugged. 'Everything back the way it was would be nicer, but failing that I'll take Kalaiya and a quiet passage across the storm-dark to a comfortable retirement on the fringes of the Dominion. Somewhere across the mountains from Merizikat. I have a villa waiting for me there with a bath house and an apple orchard.' *Free?* His heart leaped at the idea. Free to fly away and grow old and even fatter in peace and quiet, but the voices in his head were shouting at him, full of warning. *Much too easy. Much too pretty.* 'But you wrap me in rope and sword-slaves, skin-shifter. I do not feel free at all. Again and for the last time, what do you want?'

'I want you to help me steal a dragon's egg.'

Tsen laughed, and then for some reason he couldn't stop and

kept on, so much it hurt, until there were tears rolling down his cheeks and his back knotted in agony. It had been funny the first time too, but here the irony struck him like a hammer between the eyes. 'You bring me all this way only to take me back? Why didn't you steal your eggs that night instead of stealing me? It's not as if they're kept under lock and key. Anyone can take one if they can carry it.' The tears kept coming. 'What? You need me to carry one end of it for you? Because there aren't any other strong-armed men available?' He hooted.

Sivan came and crouched beside him. He tapped Tsen's black rod. 'The glasships, T'Varr. You can still control the glasships that tether your eyrie.'

'So? Shall we steal everything at once then? Do you think the Elemental Men perhaps wouldn't notice?'

The shifter grinned as he stood again. 'The beauty of my gift to you, T'Varr, is that no one will ever know. You're dead. No enchanter, no Elemental Man, no navigator, has the gift to unravel my deception. It's perfect. We'll go to your eyrie. My men will take my eggs and your Kalaiya too if that's what you want, and you will have your glasships pull the eyrie and everything inside it down into the storm-dark so it's gone for ever.' Sivan was almost giggling. 'You will have your life and I will have my eggs, and no one will ever know what either of us has done!'

'You're mad.'

'We can both have what we want, T'Varr, without anyone knowing. Anyone! You and your slave can vanish together. Somewhere far away to grow old in peace. Think on that.' He went away and left Tsen to his thoughts.

In the morning Sivan was gone, and for the next five grinding days the shifter's sword-slaves led Tsen onward, climbing past the Jokun cataracts until they reached open country again at last, a wide flatness of water meadows and fields with the Silver Mountain looming in the distance. There Sivan was waiting for them again, with slave tunics for all of them and a pair of heavy wagons. The sword-slaves changed their clothes and crowded with Tsen into a wagon, and they all rolled along a rutted road between neatly planted paddies glistening with water from the Jokun. Rows of slaves waded through the mud up to their knees. Thinning crops, Tsen decided.

Somewhere was a t'varr who would know these things, who knew exactly what was in every field and probably accounted for every single plant if he was at all like Tsen. One group of slaves close to the road stopped work and waved, and Tsen saw the brands on their arms. Sail-slaves, trusted to work on simple things without supervision. The men around him in the wagon didn't wave back. Their tension was like spring ice, sharp as cut glass.

When they stopped for a break, Tsen walked a few dozen yards into someone's paddy, squatted and relieved himself. Sivan didn't look up but Tsen felt the shifter's eyes on him. When he was done, he paused a moment, slipped the ring off his middle finger, dropped it and then dipped his hand into the muddy water. That was the thing about paddies – always plenty of water. And the thing about the slivers of glass under his skin was that any water would do. A few seconds was enough. *Well then, Shrin Chrias Kwen. Once you know I'm not dead after all, will you bite?*

The wagon rumbled on, hour after hour. The Silver Mountain grew and Tsen could make out the smudge of green that was the garden on its peak and then the glint of Shonda's giant gold-glass screens which captured the sun. Closer in, he picked out the black spires of the enchanter monoliths around the Visonda landing fields; and then, in what seemed no time at all, they were on the landing fields themselves and Sivan was hissing in his ear as they lined up with other gangs of slaves to walk into the gondolas of three great glasships. They were packed together inside like fish in a fisherman's barrel, standing room only, and flew for a day out over the foothills of the mountains and down to the desert, though Tsen was too far from any window to see much of it. Some of the slaves chattered, others stood silent and sullen. The ones Sivan had brought clustered around Tsen. Sivan himself stood beside him and said nothing at all.

Why a dragon's egg but not an alchemist? To hatch a wild dragon of course. What other reason could there be? But why? Did he *want* the end of the world? But what if he did? What if Sivan was simply barking mad? Did it change anything? Presumably Tsen's eyrie was still occupied by the Vespinese, and even if it wasn't, did that make a difference? Thank you very much, Baros Tsen T'Varr. Now please step up to this noose …

I've become a pawn in a game I no longer understand. Kalaiya. Focus on Kalaiya. Just her. But when he tried, he found that he couldn't, simply because that was what Sivan wanted.

The glasships landed as the sun set, disgorging their slaves into a makeshift camp where the Konsidar and the desert and the Lair of Samim came together, an ugly land of arid stone and earth punctured by poisonous tepid lakes. The heat was dry and stifling, a shock after the cold mountain air. There were cattle here, more than there ought to be, herded out of the Lair of Samim and the fringe of the Konsidar, starving mangy animals with a few already lying dead among them. No one had bothered to move the corpses and flies covered them like a second coat of fur. A handful of massive cargo sleds spun slowly and hovered at the fringes of the camp. They were largely useless over crags and hills but marvellously cheap and efficient over open expanses of water or, say, sand. Tsen watched as a hundred animals were crammed onto the back of one, a huge white sail thrown over the top to cover them and tied down around the edges. A glasship hauled the sled a hundred feet into the air and then let it go. Tsen watched it drift off across the desert until it was gone and wondered how many of the cattle would get to where they were going and still be alive and whether it mattered. He had no doubt what they were for: to feed his eyrie. To feed his dragons.

A pair of Taiytakei slave masters in glass and gold armed with lightning wands started shouting, pushing their new slaves away from the gondolas and yelling at them to get to work. It was a dirty, dusty place and you could see at once who had been here a while – they were the ones with scarves across their faces. Tsen found himself rolling barrels of water onto a second great sled and heaving them upright. He'd been streaked with aches and pains to start with; by the time they were half done, he hurt in places he'd never hurt before, in muscles he hadn't even known he had. He coughed and choked and his nose ran with thick dark snot. He stopped, gasping.

Sivan growled at him, 'When was the last time you did any work, Baros Tsen? Real work? That's why you hurt. You have no idea what it is to be a slave.' The last words came out bitter, as though the shifter had spent most of his life pulling oars on a galley.

'And you do, shifter?' Tsen laughed in his face. 'A shifter a slave, Sivan Bronzehand Kalaiya face-changer whoever you are? How long exactly since any man had *you* in chains?'

'You know *nothing*!' Sivan's hand flashed to Tsen's throat; a whip cracked the air over their heads and Sivan let go and went back to rolling barrels. Tsen did the same. When they were done, the slavers herded him and the other men onto the sled among their barrels. A glasship settled overhead, lowered its chains and lifted the sled into the air; and as they rose Tsen looked through the gold-tinted glass at the fires scattered across the edge of the desert, at the sprinkle of little shelters. Even now, in the small hours of the night, everywhere was movement, slaves and Taiytakei shifting crates and sacks and barrels and animals from one place to another. Some of them looked up as the sled rose over their heads, but it was dark and Tsen was too high to see their faces.

A Taiytakei soldier released the chains and swung back to the glasship, holding on to the last of them, and the sled floated off into the desert alone, straight and steady and unswerving, adrift with hundreds of barrels of water and two dozen slaves, no soldiers to watch over them, only the vast empty skies. Below, more slaves were already loading the next one. The t'varr in Tsen did the calculations: a sled was cheaper than a glasship and faster too. Not greatly but a little. From the Lair of Samim to the Godspike was a distance of about seven hundred miles. Four days then. Four days out in the desert sun. They didn't have enough food. They barely had shelter.

When he was sure no one was looking, he opened a barrel of water and wetted his middle finger. *Are you listening, Chrias? Or have the killers found you at last?*

He dozed through the first night. The sled drifted on, relentless and oblivious, and when the sun rose, Tsen spent the morning lazing in whatever corner of shade he could find, doing what he could to keep out of the heat, watching the broken barren yellow stone drift beneath them, spires and canyons, mesas and gorges, a landscape cut apart by water once long ago but now dry and dead. The heat grew. The sun passed its zenith. The air became thick and stifling until all the slaves simply lay still among the barrels, panting, eyes nearly closed; and then, in the middle of that afternoon when the heat was at its worst, Sivan and his sword-slaves killed the others. They didn't make any fuss about it. They whispered among themselves, picked the two slaves who looked the strongest and simply heaved them over the side. The first Tsen knew of it was when their screams, short and sharp and cut off as they hit the ground some fifty feet below, jerked him out of his snoozing. For a moment Tsen stared like a startled rabbit, not understanding what was happening as three more slaves went wailing and pleading over the edge. He heard screams, shrieks and then a howl as the sled drifted on. Even after the screams stopped, he still didn't understand, still thought he might be next, until Sivan grinned in his face and patted him on the shoulder.

'Who's to say what happened? Who's to say how many slaves were sent on this barge or why?' He bared his teeth in the most horrible smile Tsen had ever seen. The smile of a madman. 'When we reach the Godspike, there will only be us. A handful of slaves who know nothing. What did you see, T'Varr?'

Tsen shrugged. 'I saw nothing.' If he'd had any doubts before, they were gone. Sivan's freedom was a lie. The shifter would murder him and dump him in the desert as soon as they were done. *Or maybe just leave you to fall into the storm-dark with everyone else.*

'That's right.' Sivan let his face slip. His eyes darkened, his nose sharpened, his cheeks narrowed and he became Kalaiya again. 'I could change you, T'Varr. I could leave you as an oar-slave and sell you to a galley with little fractures and weaknesses in your bones and sinews so they break and snap. I could take your face and take your Kalaiya and give her to ...' He peered at Tsen. 'Who hates you the most? Mai'Choiro Kwen? The heirs of Sea Lord Senxian, the sea lord left hanging dead by his ankle from his own ruined palace?' His eyes glittered. His features melted and he became Sivan again. He reached out but Tsen jumped away.

'You're a monster!'

'Remember why you're doing this.' The shifter walked away and sat among the barrels, laughing with his sword-slaves as they re-enacted the terrified faces and strangled cries of the men they'd murdered; and the most terrible thing to Tsen was how he wanted so much to be with her again, how much he'd wanted Sivan-Kalaiya to take his hands and look into his eyes and whisper sweet lies about how things would be once this was done, how the two of them would slip away to another world and no one would come after them because everyone would think he was dead, how they'd lounge together in baths laced with Xizic oil and grow apples in their orchard and make wine and drink it together in the steam and be happy for as long as they were alive. Even if it was all a lie, even if he *knew* it was all a lie, he still wanted it.

After the murders there was more food to go around, so that was something. More shelter too, even if he lay and stared unblinking at the canvas over his head while Sivan's slaves snored. He wondered briefly whether he might push some of *them* off the edge, but he was too afraid to try. He wondered about jumping and found he was too afraid for that too. Sometimes hard things had to be done, or so he used to tell himself, and that had been fine when he could simply hire a few men to do whatever dirty work it was. Yes, wash his hands of it. Have a bath and a glass of apple wine and tell precious Kalaiya all about it and then never let it trouble him again. Not so fine when the hands to be dirtied were his own. No, not fine at all. *Useless fat t'varr.* He was afraid, dear gods, but how he was afraid. And yes, useless. Shamefully, pathetically useless.

They wafted above dead dry valleys and crossed the Tzwayg escarpment. The ground fell away beneath them and the Empty Sands stretched ahead, a thousand feet below. The sled drifted on, blind and dumb, always in the same direction, day after day over the endless rise and fall of the dunes, a great red and yellow sea frozen stiff, until in the distance on the fourth day Tsen saw the smear on the horizon that was the storm-dark of the Godspike and the unmistakable flashes of lightning in the sky. Every night he dipped his middle finger into one of the barrels of water and tried to see through the eyes of Shrin Chrias Kwen; and every day that finger tingled back at him as he sat in the sun looking out over the desert. For better or for worse, Quai'Shu's kwen knew where he was. Chrias wasn't stupid either, so he could probably guess where Tsen was going – whatever good that might do him.

High overhead, off in the distance, a swarm of glasships drifted, sparkling as they caught the sun. Tsen squinted. They were far too far away for him to make out whose they were, but only one person had so many. Shonda. Tsen watched until he saw that they were heading away.

Pity.

42

The White-Faced Men

Climbing out from the abyss of the Queverra was every bit as long and hard and tedious as Tuuran had imagined. His legs didn't thank him at all. There would be a reckoning, they told him, in aches and pains that simply wouldn't go away. One day he'd want something of them and they wouldn't budge and he'd have to manage without. Walk on his hands or something. Maybe on his head. Let the bit that made all the ridiculous decisions see how it felt. Tuuran tried pointing out how it could have been worse, how he could have been on his own with no food and no water. Could have done the stupid thing and gone back up the way he'd come, not knowing any better. Could have come all this way and not found Crazy and his naked men with their white-painted faces who thought Crazy was some sort of god. But his legs were having none of it. Food and water were all well and good for other bits and pieces, they said, and the same went for company, but climbing the however many thousands of steps it was back up to the top was still down to them.

Tuuran did his best to ignore them and watched Crazy Mad's new friends instead. They were weird little men but they knew a path out of the Queverra that wound back and forth past the river that cascaded into it, one that passed little pools full of beautiful cold clear water that tasted divine, and they carried food on their backs and never complained even if they watched Tuuran with a strange mix of awe and envy and fear while grovelling in the dirt whenever Crazy so much as looked at them. Weird, but hard not to like, all things considered.

They acquired more as they climbed. Crazy Mad started at the bottom with seven following him. After the first day there were still seven but in the morning there were a dozen. Tuuran never saw them arrive. They were simply there when before they weren't. By the next morning there were twenty.

'Why?' he asked no one in particular. Not that any of them were much for talking with the strain of the climb, and Crazy Mad was setting a pace as though *his* were the legs of an Adamantine Man. For a while Tuuran thought he didn't know. But eventually Crazy spun some ridiculous story about a great tunnel of white stone that ran off under the ground for ever, and how the painted men had found him staggering out of it without the first clue who he was. Didn't remember much about how he was in there in the first place, he said, though he had that funny look in his eye that made Tuuran think maybe Crazy remembered more than he cared to say. It was a funny enough look for him to think better of asking, but eventually his not asking was so loud that Crazy huffed and sighed and said that as far as the painted men were concerned, it meant that he'd walked out of Xibaiya, and apparently that made him special. And obviously no, he had no idea what they were talking about and it was a pile of utter crap and nonsense, and yes, he might have been a bit delirious by the time he reached the bottom of the abyss, and yes, his wits were a touch addled, but he was pretty sure he'd remember if he'd happened to take a little excursion into the realm of the dead thanks very much.

And there was that funny look again, and Tuuran took a deep breath and let it slowly out and rolled his eyes and let it go because by now, after all he'd seen with Crazy, it was just one more thing. Water off a duck's back. *Best not to think about it.*

The climb took five days. By the time they got to the top, Crazy's band of white-faced men had grown to a horde. There were … Tuuran didn't know. A thousand? Two thousand? They spilled over the lip of the Queverra and swarmed through the camps of the desert men scattered around its rim. The painted men were naked, armed with nothing more than stones and whatever else they could pick up, but they came like a sandstorm, rushing through one camp and killing everyone in their path and not even stopping for plunder except maybe to pick up a sword or a spear before they charged on to the next.

The desert men had no idea what hit them. The first camp didn't even see them coming. The next made the mistake of trying to put up a fight. In his time Tuuran had seen how a few dozen well armed soldiers could put a mob to flight if they knew what they were doing and held their nerve, but not *this* mob. The painted men were as crazy as Crazy. Dying didn't bother them. A few dozen were cut down and so what? The rest didn't even seem to notice as they swarmed over the Taiytakei and tore them to shreds with their bare hands. After that, the rest of the slavers had the sense to flee, grabbing what they could and jumping on the first horse or camel-like thing they saw and putting as big a cloud of dust between them and the Queverra as they could. When it was over, Tuuran put up his feet and dozed – about time they had a bit of that, said his feet – but he'd barely closed his eyes when Crazy was poking him up again, dragging one of the bad-tempered humpbacked camel-things after him. It was called a linxia, or something like that, but they'd always looked like hump-backed horses to Tuuran.

'Get up,' said Crazy. 'We're leaving, big man.'

'Where?' Though *Why?* might have been a better question, but Crazy had that look in him again, the one that said best not to argue in case his eyes did their silver thing and people started disintegrating.

'Where the dragons are. Some place called the Godspike.'

Tuuran looked at his boots. 'Sorry, feet.' He got up.

They didn't leave until the next morning on account of Crazy not having thought of anything much more than where he wanted to go and grabbing an animal to carry him there. The small matter of it being a ten-day trek across what was as close as made no difference to desert didn't seem to have entered his thinking. And maybe he could just go all silver-eyed and disintegrate being thirsty, but Tuuran certainly couldn't and neither could the painted men – well, probably – and so Tuuran spent half the night shouting at Crazy Mad not to be crazy and the other half yelling at the white-faced men to find someone who actually knew where they were going and to sort out the things commonly used to stave off the various irritating ways to die that deserts tended to throw about in their thoughtless way. Took a while but he did it. He was good at that sort of thing. When they did leave, they left with a couple of thousand men trailing after them. Trailing after Crazy Mad, anyway, Tuuran reminded himself.

They rode on their humpbacked horse-camel-things through day after day of broken cliffs and stone spires and scrubby dusty earth. The white-faced men led them to a shallow river running through a deep canyon, where the sun rarely touched the surface and where they drank and refilled their stolen water skins. After that, they climbed for three days until they emerged on the top of a great cliff looking out over a sea of sand, and there it was, fifty miles to the west, a dark smudge in the distant sky: the Godspike with the storm-dark wrapped around it. Tuuran and Crazy Mad walked to the cliff's edge and sat together with their legs dangling over the drop while the maelstrom turned a livid purple and the sea of sand gleamed like burnished copper.

'What is it, Crazy?' asked Tuuran. 'Where did it come from?'

'A big dark cloud on the horizon,' Crazy said after a bit. 'That's what it is.'

Tuuran shoved him. He thought about shoving him right off the cliff. Maybe plummeting to his death would turn Crazy Mad into Silver Eyes, and Tuuran reckoned Silver Eyes might know a thing or two more than 'big dark cloud on the horizon'.

'You going to go all weird on me again, Crazy?' Crazy didn't answer, and it was, Tuuran realised, a bit of a stupid question. Crazy hadn't stopped being weird since they'd left Aria. 'They're a funny lot, these dark-skins. Don't have any truck with gods yet they have this. In the Dominion all that desert would be one big temple, the whole of it. They'd have twenty thousand people out there in a city of tents and every one of them a priest. Maybe even in Aria too. Here it's all just, yeah, yeah, some half-god left behind a spire of stone that reaches all the way up to the sky and there's a hole in the world that eats everything that enters and no one has the first idea why or what it's for but never mind, just ignore it, just leave it be and everything will be fine.' He paused. 'That's what you're after, is it, Crazy? That why we're out here in the desert? What happens when we get there?' The last fire of the sun blazed around the black smear of cloud. As it died, the desert began to fall dark.

Crazy Mad sat and stared and didn't answer for so long that Tuuran was starting to think he'd fallen asleep, then he suddenly got up and slapped Tuuran on the shoulder. 'I think we go home, big man.' He paused. 'I don't know. But I think that's what it is. Wait and see.' He puffed out his cheeks and blew, mumbled a bit to himself and then headed back towards the white-faced men waiting back with their mounts. After a few paces more, he stopped. 'Your dragon's there, big man. Somewhere.'

Tuuran stared up at the stars that night, tried to count them as he sometimes did when he couldn't sleep and tried to remember the names of all the constellations – the ones he recalled from his home and the ones he knew from the seas around the Dominion and off the shores of Aria. Different stars in different worlds but not *all* different. Some remained the same but rose in different places in the sky. Were some stars always there no matter the world? The Adamantine Spear, they had that back in the dragon-kingdoms. Crazy said they called it the Earthspear in Aria. He didn't know if the Taiytakei had their own name for it, but it was here too.

He didn't sleep at all. Usually Crazy was the one kicking him, tossing and turning and complaining about his snoring while Tuuran was gone seconds after he closed his eyes, but not tonight. He watched the half-moon rise, and got up and went to sit at the edge of the cliff again. In the darkness he could see the horizon maelstrom aglow with its own dim inner light, lit by the same flashes of purple lightning he and the alchemist had once seen when they'd crossed the storm-dark together, two slaves on their way to Xican. He stayed there until the sky lightened and the sun rose. A pillar of bright orange light, needle-thin but brilliant, suddenly descended from the sky. The light of the rising sun running down the Godspike to strike the storm-dark and set the maelstrom alight.

Some of the white-faced men came to sit and watch too, although they kept their distance. Then Crazy came and chivvied them and they set off along the cliff and down a narrow trail through a steep cleft out into the sands. They camped again for the afternoon and crossed the sands at night, sheltered in the day and rode on in the dark, and all the while the maelstrom grew closer, swelling with each mile that passed, a black blot in the sky in the sunlight, a dark violet glow in the night, until Tuuran found it hard to look at anything else. It filled his thoughts – that and what would happen when he and Crazy Mad reached it.

As the sun rose on their third day in the desert, he saw other threads of light forming a circle from the desert sands to the rim of the maelstrom like bars in a cage. Tuuran rode the last few miles alone to the closest of them, a massive white stone monolith a mile high. He touched it and looked up at the black stain in the sky above. Its surface was as smooth as glass and unmarked, like the stone of the eyrie tunnels, the arches in the Pinnacles, the pillars in the Queverra and the one the Watcher had taken him to see. He felt the surge, the adrenaline kick when a fight was on its way. He could almost taste it. Crazy Mad swore the dragons were here so the eyrie must be here too. Maybe old Grand Master Bellepheros could make sense of it all. He closed his eyes and shook his head, throwing off the awe and dread that threatened to overwhelm him, turned away and rode back. He was an Adamantine Man. He dealt in simple things.

The painted men led them to the shadow of the maelstrom and a camp of desert slavers. The Godspike was a place of truce for the tribes that otherwise spent a good part of their time trying to kidnap each other to sell into slavery. Tuuran learned that yes, there *was* something above the storm-dark now. Glasships of the city men flew to and fro far overhead every day, and a monstrous creature lived there too, but that was mostly seen on the other side where the men from the mountains had their camp. He thanked them while Crazy rode on under the storm-dark. The painted men balked at that, but Crazy simply didn't give a shit, so Tuuran told them to stay and wait while he went on at Crazy's side, the two of them together and alone the way they'd been for years. The desert men didn't look best pleased at having the white-faced men left milling about with nothing much to do, so Tuuran kept his mouth shut about the thousand or so more who would arrive during the night. Best, he thought, to let them have that as a surprise. Didn't want to spoil their last day, after all.

43

Dragonthief

Zafir took Diamond Eye back to the eyrie. She made him fly slowly, in long gliding sweeps. His blood was up and she needed him calm. She needed both of them calm.

Bellepheros was waiting for her when she got back. She ignored him and sat on the top of the eyrie wall, looking over the chaos of the dragon yard. Idle glasships hovered overhead. Gondolas hung empty and abandoned beneath them. The bodies she'd seen in the minds of the Elemental Men had been taken away but there were dark stains on the white stone where they'd fallen. Slaves ran back and forth, far more than usual.

The alchemist started telling her something dull about how bringing food out here was hard for whoever ran the eyrie – Baros Tsen, then Mai'Choiro, then the Elemental Men, now the doll-woman, except the doll-woman was gone. Was anyone at all running it now? Zafir didn't know and didn't care. She looked at the slaves rushing about and a little smile crept over her face. Shonda had called their bluff and now the killers didn't know what to do.

'Yes, yes. I'm sure it's very hard to get food out here into the middle of the desert.' She waved Bellepheros away. 'I suppose on account of there being no water and the animals dying of thirst all the time? And yet I seem to remember that Queen Shezira managed to feed two hundred dragons at Outwatch and *that* was in the middle of a desert. Was it not, alchemist?' *Show me then, killers, show me how you answer.* 'If it's that difficult, they can simply move us.'

'I have asked them to, Holiness. I am told it's not my concern nor my business and I should keep to my dragons.'

'*My* dragons, alchemist,' she corrected him. Something in his voice sounded off. She turned to look at him at last but now he was gazing off into the sky, lost in his own flurry of thoughts.

'I've heard the Taiytakei speak of this, Holiness. They are …
loud. And often pass my rooms.'

'It's a pity your enchantress isn't here. She could have made
something for you to hear every word.' She probably had. She'd
done it before – the pair of golden dragons with ruby eyes, given to
Prince Jehal on his wedding to his starling bride Lystra.

'Holiness, I'm not certain …' He wandered off into what he
thought Chay-Liang could and couldn't do; Zafir turned her attention back to the dragon yard and stopped listening. She missed
most of what he said but his last words caught her attention.

'What?'

'I said I fear they are keeping us here so they might drop the
entire eyrie into the storm-dark.'

Zafir raised an eyebrow, thinking of the lightning and the ride
she'd taken with Bellepheros pinned in front of her. 'And will that
work, master alchemist? Will the storm devour us or not?'

'I don't know, Holiness. I would not pin my hopes either way.'

He went away after that. Zafir sat and watched and waited,
musing. Perhaps the white stone *was* impervious but even so, that
didn't guarantee anything more than a scoured stone skeleton
would survive.

She didn't feel the pop of air on the rim behind her, but Diamond
Eye rode the Elemental Man's thoughts as soon as he appeared. It
was the one who'd ridden with her earlier today.

'We have considered your proposal, rider-slave,' he said. 'To
return Lord Shonda of Vespinarr to this place.'

She already knew their answer. Diamond Eye had plucked it
from inside his head.

Yes.

'When it's dark,' she told them. 'When they don't see me coming.' The glasships were long out of sight but Diamond Eye kept
staring after them. He was watching them in his mind, following
the faint whispers of their thoughts.

*If we just didn't come back … How long before they came looking?
We could run, couldn't we? Should we?* She laughed, harsh and bitter. Run? But to where that would change anything? To the north
or the south and the sea? To the east and the ruin of Dhar Thosis?
To the west and the great cities of Takei'Tarr? And then what?

Burn them? But nothing would make any difference any more. She could run all she liked and she'd never get home. And then there was Shonda, and that little gesture he made, reminding her she was a slave and that he was not.

Just this once, my deathbringer. Just this once. Afterwards . . .

Tsen watched Shonda's gondolas fly. He watched the dragon rise from the desert and give chase and then turn away, and his middle finger told him that Shrin Chrias Kwen was watching too. Atop their sled full of barrels of water even Sivan and the other slaves stopped their games of dice and peered out across the burning sands, squinting and shielding their eyes. The glasship fleet of Vespinarr. Tsen had no idea why the dragon might throw itself against them but as the lightning cannon began to glow and the monster thought better of it, the sight filled him with an unexpected joy. No matter that it was Shonda passing overhead, no matter how Shonda deserved to hang, he'd shown there was a limit to what the dragon could do. He'd shown it could be turned back.

'Even monsters can fall,' he murmured.

'Thing is,' muttered Sivan beside him, 'they keep getting up again. It's the riders that don't.'

Tsen shuddered then. He'd never forget the first time he'd seen the dragon fly, the terrible speed and strength and power, the lash of the tail that cracked the unbreakable stone of his eyrie, the fire that burned the desert sand to glass. Now he watched it fly into the sky, back the way it had come. *That* was what Sivan wanted? Really? But it was. The shifter's face gave away his naked hunger, the gleeful hate of vengeful ambition. Yes, he wanted that, and no matter the cost.

So you have to stop him then, T'Varr. But how? O Kalaiya, how?

The sled drifted under the fringes of the storm-dark. A glasship lowered its chains to snare them. Sword-slaves on fast-flying sleds skimmed in and jumped down among the barrels. It was a tricky manoeuvre and Tsen quietly admired their skill. They slowed the sled to a stop, made fast the chains, and the glasship dragged them in its slow leisurely way through the sky and lowered them to the earth. As it did, Tsen stared at the waiting chaos of this new Vespinese camp, the t'varr in him aghast. Men milled everywhere, most of them doing nothing. T'Varrs and kwens prowled with small groups of soldiers, bawling orders and poking at slaves with sticks. The air was tinged with a crazy madness, discipline and order hanging by a thread. The desert, the dragon, the storm-dark, the Godspike: everything was out of control and simply too much to grasp, and Tsen wanted to laugh, a wild crazy laugh because he knew exactly how the Vespinese felt, long past fear and well on the way to madness.

'We need to get up there.' Sivan threw a hard look at Tsen. 'Those were Shonda's glasships we saw, weren't they?'

Tsen nodded. 'Silver gondolas. Vespinese.' Abruptly he gripped Sivan by the collar. 'Understand me, shifter. I will not lift a finger for you without Kalaiya. And I will not be fooled. I will ask questions, and the answers will be things you cannot possibly know. Try to trick me and you'll never leave my eyrie. Remember that I saw through you before.'

'I'll bring you your slave, T'Varr. That is the least of your worries.' Sivan delicately lifted Tsen's fingers away from his shirt. 'Whether you get to keep her depends on you.'

They busied themselves doing what they were told, rolling the barrels of water off the sled and half-burying them in the sand under the shadow of the storm-dark above. The sun set and they worked on into the twilight and then the dark. A kwen paced among them, barking at them now and then to work harder. When they were done, another giant sled drifted over with a pair of Vespinese on the back to guide it. Water for the eyrie. And now Tsen found himself unearthing other barrels that were older and rolling them onto the new sled while the t'varr in him howled at the waste of effort. Why didn't they just take the load they'd brought straight on up?

In the darkness two of the slaves got into a fight and it took the kwen, three of his soldiers and a couple of sharp doses of lightning to separate them. Five minutes later a second fight kicked off. As soon as the Taiytakei were distracted, Sivan touched the soldier beside him lightly on the arm and stopped his heart. It was done and over in a second. A sword-slave squatted in the shadows and began stripping the dead soldier's clothes and weapons and armour. Sivan took down a second soldier from behind and then took the last two together. He walked up to the kwen, quick yet obsequious as anything, begging the kwen not to kill the quarrelsome slaves for their terrible discipline, a stream of placating words until he was close enough, and then killed him with a touch. The final soldier gawped, and that was the look on his face when he died, a split second later. The rest of the sword-slaves stopped, stripped the bodies, then finished loading the barrels as though nothing had happened. They opened the last few, half-emptied them and, one by one, got inside, all except the three now dressed as soldiers and Sivan dressed as their kwen, until only Tsen was left. The shifter gestured at the last barrel. 'Yours, T'Varr.'

A bath, at last, said some stupid voice inside him. Tsen climbed in. For Kalaiya, he told himself. 'And then?'

Sivan laughed at him. 'You were t'varr to a sea lord. Use your imagination.' The shifter closed the lid.

Zafir spent the last hours of daylight with the image of Shonda in her mind, remembering when the lord of Vespinarr had come to see Diamond Eye and one of his men had thrown lightning in the dragon's face. *That one. Find him.* And Diamond Eye remembered that day too and found the distant pattern of Shonda's thoughts. When he had it, Zafir pictured a glasship and a gondola, Shonda inside it, Diamond Eye falling like a stone to snatch both in his talons and flying away, carrying the gondola between his claws. She imagined it over and over until she knew that Diamond Eye understood. It filled the time, waiting for midnight.

They sent an Elemental Man. He climbed onto Diamond Eye's back, sat behind her and showed the bladeless knife he carried as if somehow she might have forgotten. 'Any one of us, slave. Any one of us can end you.' Zafir hardly heard him. It didn't matter. If not today then they would kill her tomorrow. If not then, the day after. *But not if I kill all of you first.*

Star by star, the constellation of the dragon crept over the horizon. Zafir turned Diamond Eye to the west and flew him high into the deep dark of the night, far above the glasships, hunting them out; and when he found them, Zafir circled slowly down as her dragon picked through all the thoughts that whispered below. She'd never understood quite how it worked, back in her own land, but she'd always known that it did. Picture the foe you wanted to find, and if the dragon you rode knew that knight then they would hunt them out no matter how thick the battle, even in the turmoil of a thousand dragons and riders and rage and fire and air made of scorpion bolts. No matter what, they'd find that rider if you held your mind hard enough. She'd done it once – over her home, over the Pinnacles, when Jehal and Hyrkallan had answered Valmeyan's challenge and burned him out of the sky, but then she'd let it go and taken life over death. There were times she regretted that choice. It would have been a proper way for a dragon-queen to die.

Diamond Eye shifted under her. He'd found what she was looking for.

Not so fast, my deathbringer. We have another wasp to swat.

Trapped in his barrel, sodden and cramped, Tsen's legs went to sleep. He felt the sled move and rise and then for a long time nothing. His ears clicked and popped. His heart beat faster. His head started to hurt, just as it had when he'd first come here after his flight to Dhar Thosis. He closed his eyes and tried not to whimper at the pain – he'd forgotten how thin the air was. At least he had water. Then a jolt as the sled landed – he supposed in the dragon yard but there was no real way to know – and voices. And then, for a long time, nothing until a tiny tap on the lid of his barrel.

'You just stay quietly there, T'Varr. My men will get the eggs; I'll get your woman. I'll come for you when I need you.' Tsen hissed something back but the shifter was already gone. He found himself quietly hoping that one of the dragon eggs might hatch halfway to the glasship. When he tried to move, his legs had gone to sleep and the lid of the barrel was firmly shut.

An interminable wait later someone pried open his barrel. For a moment Tsen didn't recognise the face in the darkness. When he did, his eyes flew wide. Chay-Liang's alchemist! 'What are you—'

'It's Sivan, you idiot.' Sivan clamped a hand over Tsen's mouth.

His legs still didn't work. There was a lot of clumsy heaving and shoving and then Sivan gave up and tipped Tsen's barrel over and spilled him onto the dragon yard. Tsen managed to lift himself half-up. He still couldn't feel anything in his legs. 'Are you mad? How can people not see what you're doing?'

'Of course they can see! How would they not? They think I have a reason. They think I'm the alchemist and so they let me do as I wish.' His eyes glittered in the starlight. 'Can't you feel the tension, Tsen? Something has happened. The place is almost empty. Now come with me!'

'I can't move!' Tsen gasped and tried not to whine as the first pins and needles slowly worked their way from his feet to his hips. Alchemist-Sivan stood there, taut as a halyard. He was right. The air was electric. Uncommonly still. Even the wind ...

'Come *on*, T'Varr!'

This was Sivan wearing the alchemist's face but it was so hard to keep remembering. He kept starting to think or speak as though the real alchemist, Liang's slave, was there. 'Where is she? Where's Kalaiya?'

'Patience!' Sivan propped him up as he dripped all over the sled and the barrels around him. There were dozens of men in the dragon yard. The Scales and others too. They were hauling eggs out of the hatchery and into the open.

'Dear forbidden gods!'

'Dear gods indeed! Whenever you're ready, T'Varr. I have her. She's waiting for you.'

Alchemist-Sivan jogged across the yard with far more grace than the real alchemist had ever shown and climbed one of the walls. Tsen looked about, still trying to remember how his legs were supposed to work. The dragon wasn't here but no one seemed bothered. As soon as he could walk without veering sideways and falling over, he followed to the other side of the wall and onto the bare rock rim where one of the six glasships Chay-Liang had used to move the eyrie was chained into the stone. Its gondola hung nearby, close to the surface. The ramp was open.

Sivan handed Tsen his black rod. 'Release the chain!'

Tsen touched the rod to the enchanted glass welded into the stone and thought of the chain coming loose. The glass shifted and parted and the chain jerked free. Sivan nodded to the gondola.

'Inside now! Get this over the yard where the eggs are.'

Tsen shook his head. 'Kalaiya first.'

The shifter shoved him hard. Tsen almost tripped and fell. He stumbled halfway up the ramp and staggered into the gondola. And there she was, scared and shaking like a leaf, but it was her.

'Kalaiya!'

Zafir flew in straight and fast. Shonda's glasships couldn't possibly miss her. *It will hurt, deathbringer. It will hurt us both. But it has to be this way.* The lightning cannon of the nearest glasship began to glow. They'd seen her. And after one lit up, another followed and then another. She'd felt it in Dhar Thosis. Lightning hurt but lightning didn't kill, not a dragon. And she had the armour that Chay-Liang made for her, while the Elemental Man behind her had nothing. Bound to the dragon by his harness, he couldn't simply shift away into the air, and when the lightning came he would die. There was no way to be sure that he would die and she would not, but she didn't care any more. If Shonda killed her too, then so be it. Another gamble poorly made.

At the last moment Diamond Eye veered just as the first bolt hit him square in the shoulder. Zafir felt his mind blank and squealed in shared pain as his wing fell limp and he spiralled sharply down. A second blast hit him close behind her. Sparks arced over her glass-and-gold armour. *The Elemental Man* ... But she had no room for those thoughts any more. She screamed as Diamond Eye tumbled and tipped onto his back, plummeting through the air towards the distant sand. A third blast hit him in the belly. The world spun, sky, earth, sky, earth, all roaring closer. The wind ripped at her head, trying to tear it off her shoulders. She clung to him. Her vision narrowed. Red tinged everything. For a moment she heard only a roaring, louder and louder in her ears, more than a hurricane wind – the screaming wail of death and a thousand vengeful ancestors. The glasships drifted away, lost into the darkness and a million twinkling stars. The desert sand rushed at her face. Zafir screamed again, one last savage burst of will to live, to stay breathing, for hearts to keep beating. Screamed into the chaos that was the dragon's mind.

And lit, for a moment, a spark. A flicker of order, a surge of instinct. Diamond Eye's wings stretched and flared and tore at the rushing wind with a savage bite that crushed her into his scales and squeezed every gasp of air out of her and then squeezed some more. She felt her ribs bend and creak, and there were her ancestors, riding their whirlwind to take her, and this time she had nothing left.

They hit the ground hard, hard as the smack of a dragon's tail, and for a moment everything went dark; but her ancestors never came, and when she opened her eyes Diamond Eye was on the ground, his wings stretched wide, glaring at the sky while her body was one long tortured shriek of pain. She weathered it, waiting for the waves to fade enough for her to move. Three long painful breaths and then she sat up and never mind the hurt. Her face was bleeding where her helm had been slammed against it. Her ribs had taken the worst but those pains were hard throbbing aches, not sharp stabs. Nothing broken, then. Cracked maybe, but not broken. Diamond Eye pawed at the sand, hungry to smash and shatter and burn and rend, waiting for her to release him to be what a dragon should be but she didn't. He let out a cry, a challenge of fury and pain.

Is the killer dead? She couldn't feel him behind her but she couldn't turn her head enough to see. It hurt too much.

Diamond Eye threw himself into the air. Patience was something for others. It didn't matter. Death didn't matter. Death was the little death, and then came rebirth and he'd come again, over and over until the creatures that flew and spat their white fire were smashed and gone. Zafir rode his rage, taking it in, mingling it with her own – and the Great Flame knew she had plenty enough of that – turning it and guiding it. Nudging him until he eased gently down from his fury. She let him race back and forth, burning the sand to glass to let the fire out of him until at last he was ready to listen.

Wait. Just a little, she soothed him. *Just a little. Is the killer dead?*

She brought him down and this time he stayed long enough for her to turn her head to the Elemental Man who'd come to make sure that she obeyed. Neck snapped, lightning-charred, doll-limbed. Very, very dead.

She was free.

From above this time, she told the dragon. *The way it should have been.*

She started to laugh.

'Kalaiya!' Tsen gazed at her face, and Kalaiya stared back as though he was mad and a complete stranger.

'Tsen? You're not dead? But I saw—'

'The rod. Quickly.' Sivan pushed her away, none too gently, and if Tsen had had a knife on him he might have used it, but as it was he clenched his fists and did as Sivan asked. The glasship moved over the dragon yard. He felt Kalaiya's stare on his back as he lowered the gondola and watched in a daze as Scales brought four dragon eggs and rolled them up the ramp, doing exactly as alchemist-Sivan ordered. When they were done, Tsen brandished his black rod at the shifter. Sivan pointed to a small sled. The Scales loaded that too.

'Now do as you promised,' Tsen hissed. Kalaiya was still staring at him. She wasn't stupid. She'd seen him use the rod and knew he was no illusion, and yet her eyes wouldn't have it.

'I saw you dead,' she said. She touched him and his vision blurred with tears because she brought everything he loved back into the world simply by being there. Baros Tsen T'Varr, short and fat and happy, only without much of the happy just now.

'Touching.' Sivan pulled Kalaiya aside for a second time and stood at Tsen's shoulder, a hand on his back. 'Down to the desert! Now! And quickly! We don't have long, T'Varr. The Elemental Men will not be kind to you if they catch us.'

Tsen touched the black rod to the pilot golem and they drifted away from the eyrie. 'What happens if they catch *you*, skin-shifter? Do the rest of your brother Righteous Ones under the Konsidar pretend you don't exist? Is it war between us?'

He didn't get an answer. Sivan stood at his shoulder, tense as a drum. He flinched as Tsen almost skimmed the edge of the storm-dark in his haste to be away and only relaxed when they were underneath it where they wouldn't be seen. 'Now tell the golem to take us to the ground.' Sivan clambered past the eggs and opened the gondola's ramp. A great wind rushed in and swirled around them. He grabbed Tsen and pushed him at the sled the Scales had loaded with the eggs.

'I've done my part, T'Varr,' he shouted over the howl of the air. 'I've got your woman for you. Now you do yours. Ride with me!

Release the other glasships. Drop your eyrie to be devoured by the storm-dark and no one will ever know!'

Far away, out in same the desert night, Diamond Eye tucked in his wings and dropped from the sky like a falling star, straight and hard and fast, and this time the Vespinese never saw him coming. He hit Shonda's gondola like a ball from a cannon, ripped it off its chains and fell on, and all the Vespinese saw was a blur and a mighty shape and a gondola that was hanging in the air one moment and gone the next, while the heart of the glasship above cracked and then shattered into fragments. The great glass disc shuddered in its spinning and began to slide out of the air. Diamond Eye barely even slowed. He levelled out across the dunes and not a single lightning cannon glowed in his wake.

How it should have been.

Zafir flew him skimming across the sand, miles and miles, and then brought him down. She unbuckled the corpse of the Elemental Man and threw it off and then slid down beside it. It was hard to resist the temptation to have her dragon pick up the gondola and shake it, but she simply knocked on the ramp instead. When nothing happened, Diamond Eye bit the ramp open and ripped it off. A crack of lightning shot out at once and hit him on the nose. She felt its sting but the dragon understood her mind and, dulled or wild, dragons always enjoyed playing a little with their food before they ate. He backed away and waited, watching her.

Zafir peered warily inside. One battered Taiytakei in emerald robes crouched behind an upturned table. She ducked instinctively as he fired his wand, but he was shaking so badly that the lightning hit the inside of the gondola. Behind him Shonda quivered under a table cut from a single diamond. The gondola walls were silver and jade, carved into dragons and lions. Six chests of gold sat against the walls, and three glass cabinets. The cabinet doors had fallen open and golden bottles and white clay pots rolled around the floor. Behind the diamond table a silver staircase curled up to a second level. Zafir narrowed her eyes. Diamond Eye felt three souls, all of them deliciously terrified, but she saw only two.

'It's up to you whether we make this bloody.' Zafir stepped into the hole where the ramp had been, trusting to the armour the enchantress had made. 'Where's the third of you? I know he's here.'

Shonda fired straight at her chest. Her skin tingled, a few muscles twitched, a corona of sparks fluttered around her but nothing more. The man in the emerald feathers drew a long knife from his belt and threw himself forward. Zafir stepped back, letting him stumble past her and out of the gondola. He slashed. The blade skittered off her armour. She looked at him as he wheeled to face her, cocked her head and then laughed at him, wondering whether to have Diamond Eye squash him or burn him. 'What do you think you're doing?' Him in his emerald feathers and her in gold-glass armour. It seemed hardly fair.

Another thunderclap sounded behind her. She shivered and twitched. Shonda had shot her in the back. The enchantress's armour shrugged most of it aside, but the man with the knife took his chance and jumped, thrusting at her neck, and he might have killed her too if it hadn't been for the dragon-scale she wore underneath with its high collar. As it was, she staggered back, choking from the blow to her throat, while the emerald-feathered man feinted a thrust at her face, quick as a snake, kicked at her legs, almost knocking her down, then slashed at her chest and cut at her hand so quickly she only just whipped it away. He was limping. It slowed him, and that was probably the only reason she was still standing. Careless.

'You're good.' Zafir raised an eyebrow. 'Bodyguard? If I wasn't wearing this armour, you'd win. I don't even have a weapon.'

He was circling, trying to manoeuvre her back round to the hole so Shonda could shoot her again. She folded her arms.

'You realise I have a dragon?'

He still didn't answer, though she could see it in his face. He understood.

'I don't know you. I have no quarrel with you. Don't die for that pig in there.'

Nothing. Zafir sighed. *Pin him.*

It was a hard thing for a dragon to take a man in his talons and not crush him to death, and maybe Diamond Eye was still smarting from the battering he'd taken from Shonda's lightning cannon. His tail whipped in a silent arc and took the emerald-feathered man in the side and caved in half his chest. Zafir shrugged, crouched beside him, took his knife and finished him. A quick kill. A mercy stroke.

Back to the gondola. Shonda was on his feet. Backing away, he trod on a bottle, lost his footing and fell over as he fired at her again. Missed. He didn't get another chance. Zafir bent down and pulled the wand out of his hand.

A sharp warning from Diamond Eye. She ducked fast and low as a movement flickered from the top of the stairs and something came flying out and shot over her head and out through the ripped-open ramp. A glass sphere landed in the desert sand. In the blink of an eye it blew up into a huge sphere bigger than the gondola and as thin as paper. Diamond Eye smashed it and then flung the tip of his armoured tail like a spear straight through the gondola's silver skin, rattling everything. Two of the cabinets fell over and smashed. Zafir felt the spark of life from whoever had thrown the orb flicker and die.

She looked at Lord Shonda, wondering what to do. He was trembling but at least he wasn't begging. 'So you're the most powerful man in the world, are you?'

'What do you want? What is your price to serve me? I have anything. Everything. You know that because you know who I am. Fly for me and I will give you worlds!'

She would think afterwards that there were so many other things she could have done. Pacts that could have been made. Bargains struck. Words spoken. Maybe he had an enchanter to take the doll-woman's circlet off her head. But in the end he was just another fat old man who thought he could own her, and what she remembered most of all was watching him turn away from her, tapping his arms to remind her that she was a slave and he was not. What then struck her eye was the brand lying on the floor, of three dragons and a lion entwined together, and the realisation that she had a fire-breathing monster outside who could heat it to a nice cherry-red in no time at all. And when she thought afterwards of all those other things and remembered how the most powerful man in the world had screamed and screamed and screamed as she'd marked him, there was never even the slightest sliver of regret.

Except perhaps that she could have held the brand to his skin a little longer.

Sivan raced the sled back towards the eyrie. Tsen clung on as best he could. They were really going to do it. Sivan was really going to bring the whole eyrie down. One glasship, Chay-Liang had told him, one glasship was all they needed to hold it up, but with none it would fall. And he shouldn't do it, he knew that, but Kalaiya …

Or maybe he *should* do it …

They reached the rim. Sivan crept the sled to where the first glasship chains merged into gold-glass were welded into the stone. Tsen didn't even have to step off to release them.

'Do it!' hissed Sivan.

Chay-Liang is probably here. Others. Good men, good women. The storm-dark will swallow them all. But hadn't he had the same thought himself, back before the Vespinese had come? *Yes. But I was going to send them away first. Mai'Choiro and I would have gone together. And alone.*

Sivan gripped his arm. 'Do it! Put an end to dragons!'

Chay-Liang could make a sled out of glass. There were other sleds too … Maybe people would get away … An end to dragons …

'Do it or never see your slave woman again!'

Tsen touched his rod to the chains and watched them let go. They hung loose. The glasship stayed where it was and so did the eyrie. He did it not because it was right or wrong or because it would end the dragons or even because of Kalaiya; he did it because he knew that if he didn't then Sivan would kill him right there and then.

Stupid, weak, pathetic, cowardly t'varr.

Sivan dropped the sled beneath the eyrie and followed the underside of the rim to the next glasship. And the next and the next and the next; and as the last chains unravelled and the eyrie began to fall, Sivan turned the sled and hurtled off into the night as though the wind itself was chasing him.

Such a coward, Tsen. Such a pathetic coward.

Chay-Liang

44

Not the Quietest Night

Bellepheros almost missed Baros Tsen T'Varr. Underneath the bland smile, the amiable facade of blissful ignorance and the cheerful slightly stupid t'varr manner, he'd had the sense and the certainty in his own people to leave Bellepheros and his Scales and Li alone. He'd given them whatever they needed, trusted they had a good reason for everything they did and largely believed in Li to do what was right. Mai'Choiro Kwen, on the other hand, hadn't even trusted his own t'varr, Perth Oran.

The Elemental Men had cleared out his study. They were watching him as though they knew he'd done something terrible; and Liang had as good as told him to keep his mouth shut and his head down. He trusted her, so he was following her advice. He missed her. He missed having someone to talk to.

Lord Shonda had made his exit with all the subtlety of a monkey kicking over a hornet's nest. The killers were buzzing after him, her Holiness was off on some night flight, and between the two of them that left him with a little peace and quiet for once, a rarity these days.

On his desk was what would be a book if he was ever allowed to finish it. In earlier years he'd travelled the length and breadth of the nine kingdoms of the dragon-realms and written about what he'd seen so other alchemists could learn about their lands without the indignity and discomfort that came from having to go and look with their own eyes. It was better that way for most. Dragon-riders called him mad, but he really did prefer to read about faraway places in the comfort of a warm fireside than see them for himself in the freezing rain through a haze of hypothermia. Writing a book about the Taiytakei was a little different but he'd been reading whatever he could and boiling it down into one account. For that he appreciated quiet nights like these.

'The Konsidar'. He kept coming back to the same page, the one he read every night before he started work again. It was where Li had gone.

The Konsidar mountain range runs north–south along the western side of Takei'Tarr and divides the continent into the narrow but wet and fertile Western Coast and the arid interior. Largely unexplored. A few passes exist in the far north, which provide once-vital but now little-used land routes between the cities of Cashax and Zinzarra. Other routes existed before the Splintering, an event which considerably changed the landscape of the Konsidar. The city of Vespinarr lies on a plateau at the southern tip of the range, along with the silver mines that give it its famous wealth ...

And the thoughtless self-serving bastards who lord themselves over it.
The thought made him blink. He wasn't used to thinking things like that. It was only a short step away from saying the same about dragon-kings and dragon-queens, and he'd long ago decided he knew better than to have any thoughts at all when it came to them. He served. That was his purpose. He served whoever needed to be served in order to keep the dragons from flying free.

A glass globe, a present from Chay-Liang, shifted on his desk. It started to roll sideways. He caught it and put it back but for some reason it just started to roll again. He frowned at it hard. For the last several days it had been perfectly happy sitting still and now it wasn't?

There was a tapping at the door. He ignored it. The Elemental Men and Perth Oran would both just barge right in; Li wasn't here and so this had to be a slave. He didn't want a slave. He tried to settle the globe but the sphere wasn't having it.

The tapping on his door came again.

'Go away!' he shouted. He tossed the globe onto his bed and went back to his notes.

The central massif of the mountains is inhospitable and largely unknown even among the Taiytakei. A prohibition on entering is ruthlessly enforced by the Elemental Men. Within live the so-called Righteous Ones, a mysterious group whose existence is not widely known. Some texts allude to deep complexes of caves and tunnels running through the Konsidar in much the same way as they are said to exist under the Desert of Thieves. If true, it is conjectured that these tunnels and caves interconnect under the expanse of the Empty Sands.

Every night he read it and finished with the same thought: that what he'd written was a dry and long-winded and slightly dull way of saying, 'Range of mountains. Do not enter. No one knows why.'

The tapping on his door came again. 'Master Alchemist sir!' He recognised the voice now. A Scales. Which was odd because the Scales never came here to bother him. Never.

He got up, lurched sideways and almost fell over as if he was drunk. He steadied himself on the desk. Frowned. There was something odd. The room was ... tilted? Except that surely couldn't be right, could it? He rubbed his eyes.

'Master Alchemist, sir!'

'What?' He walked to the door slowly, an old man a little unsure of his footing. When he opened it, the Scales looked terrified.

'Master Alchemist, the eyrie's falling!'

'What?'

'The eyrie's falling!'

Scales weren't the cleverest slaves. The potions he gave them did that. He hurried up to the dragon yard, and on the way found that he kept drifting towards the passageway walls as he did. By the time he got outside, there was no doubt. He could see the Godspike and feel the change in the wind. The eyrie was dropping steadily through the air. Falling more like a feather than a stone, but falling nevertheless. It was also tipping slowly sideways. He looked up. The glasships that once held the eyrie aloft were high above, five tiny specks of light.

A momentary chill ran through him.

'There used to be six ...' He shook himself. *Falling.* And what in the name of the Great Flame was he supposed to do about that?

Someone had let loose the glasships. He'd warned her Holiness, but whoever it was had done it without telling anyone. *How long do we have?* They weren't falling all that fast ... Long enough to get everyone up and away ... A surge of panic shot through him. He forced himself to be calm and looked around for Diamond Eye but the great dragon hadn't come back. 'Well go and wake everyone up!' He shook himself again. *No*. No need. There were already men up on the walls and other men coming running out of the tunnels and passages dressed in their nightclothes. 'We need an enchanter.' Did they even have one any more? Now that Chay-Liang had gone and all the Vespinese? 'Sleds! We need sleds! Get them! Load the eggs!'

Really? Load the eggs? When he could simply let them go?

A kwen came running. 'You have a sled! Where?'

They kept one in the hatchery. Bellepheros looked about wildly. 'Yes.' He poked the Scales. 'Show him. Take him to it!' Let the eggs fall into the storm-dark, but he'd need his potions, and a single sled wouldn't be enough for all his Scales anyway .

Other sleds were rising from the rim, heading fast towards the floating glasships. Bellepheros watched them go, helpless, then ran to his secret larder of corpses and started to pack a bag.

Zafir flew with Shonda's gondola in Diamond Eye's claws. She had Shonda trapped inside and the corpse of the Elemental Man to keep him company. At the edge of the storm-dark she dropped the gondola towards the maelstrom. She watched it fall and then thought better of it, swooping to snatch it out of the sky. She turned Diamond Eye towards the Godspike but the eyrie wasn't where she expected to find it. There was a moment of disorientation then, but only a moment before she spotted it. Not so much falling, she thought. More adrift. Slipping slowly downward, half a mile lower than when she'd left it and half a mile and steadily less from the violet churning clouds below.

Specks of light rose from the stricken eyrie. Sleds were heading for the glasships floating high above. She watched, carefully distant, considering. If the eyrie fell into the storm-dark, that was the end of the alchemist. No more potions. No more dragon poison. No more eggs or hatchlings. Just her and Diamond Eye, and in time Diamond Eye would wake up. The Elemental Men would survive, of course. They'd hunt her.

Or she could do something?

They'd kill her either way. Just maybe later.

Bellepheros came outside, huffing and out of breath and with a satchel over his shoulder. He seized the first Scales he found by the arm. 'Get everyone together. All the Scales.' More and more sleds were taking to the air now. Bellepheros couldn't tell whether the Taiytakei were abandoning the eyrie to its fate or trying to do something to save it. A bit of both, perhaps?

The Scales he'd sent to get the sled for the kwen was tugging at his sleeve. 'The sled isn't there, Master Alchemist. It went with the glasship like you told us.'

'What? What glasship? What are you talking about?' He had a second sled hidden in his room of corpses. Not that he could fly it. Not that he'd want to, but better that than falling into the storm-dark. 'Speak! What glasship?'

The shriek of Diamond Eye thundered over the rushing wind. The dragon crashed onto the wall and the whole eyrie shivered. It was holding something that looked like a battered gondola in its foreclaws, clutching it as though it was precious. It grabbed the wall with its massive hind talons, dug in and started to flap its wings. Bellepheros watched, paralysed with amazement. He staggered as the wind of each wingbeat shuddered across the dragon yard, but even for a dragon, lifting the whole eyrie was too much. It let go and disappeared up into the sky. Bellepheros grasped the Scales by his shoulders.

'In the larder where the corpses hang is another sled. Get it and get the rest of you together.' It wouldn't be big enough for all of them but he didn't know what else to do.

And when it isn't? Who stays and who goes?

There wasn't a comfortable answer to that. How could he leave another man to die, even a Scales?

Li . . .

In his study, underneath the page on the Konsidar, was another he knew by heart. *The Righteous Ones are a mystery among the Taiytakei* . . . Truth was, he had nothing, nothing that made any sense. Another race of men, or a race of something different, not creatures of flesh and bone at all but beings of the spirit or of something else, or else arcane constructs like the golems of the Crimson Sunburst.

Li … That was where she was, in the Konsidar. He'd told her he'd be safe. He'd told her not to worry. And now he needed her more than anything.

The dragon powered up towards the glasships and he lost track of it in the darkness. The first sleds were already coming back. Taiytakei ran back and forth, yelling at each other. They were on the edge of panic. The glasships weren't getting any closer. If anything, they were further away. Bellepheros stared up into the night sky. *The writings of the Rava are whispered to describe men who change both flesh and bone …* Not that *that* meant much since even having seen a copy of the Rava was punishable by death. He'd come across whispers that said the Rava was pretty much anything you could imagine, from a manual to summon demons to an excessively lewd collection of erotic poetry. But men who changed both flesh and bone? They were skin-shifters surely?

Specks of light darted back and forth high above like rising embers dancing in the smoke of a camp fire. Frantic sleds in the moonlight, rushing to the receding glasships. Bellepheros had no idea whether the glasships could descend fast enough to catch the eyrie anyway. He thought probably not.

Li … Of all of them, of everyone here, she'd have been the one who would have known what to do, and he really couldn't fly away on a sled and leave a man behind, not even a Scales. After everything he had done to them, *especially* not a Scales.

The eyrie was too much. Diamond Eye's talons dug into the stone but after a few heavy beats of his wings, they both knew it wasn't going to work.

Why are you trying to help them? The thought was her own, not the dragon's, and she didn't know the answer, but she was beginning to think it had to do with the Adamantine Man from Dhar Thosis. Seeing him again after so many years had changed something. She wasn't sure what, but it had started then. Started when she'd knocked the poison from Baros Tsen T'Varr's own lips. She wasn't as … *certain* of things as she'd once been.

Up! She tore Diamond Eye loose from the wall and shot straight for the glasships. Taiytakei on sleds were milling about them. Several of the gondolas had open ramps, men inside now, trying to get the glasships to move. Diamond Eye picked at the sense of their thoughts. *Not working. Not moving. Can't make them obey.* Fear and frustration and despair; they didn't understand. And then the whisper of an Elemental Man among them who did. *Doomed. Regret. Anger.* The glasships had been locked with an enchanted key. They flew at the command of the black rod of Baros Tsen T'Varr or the enchantress Chay-Liang. No one else. One of them had done this. Baros Tsen was dead. The enchantress then.

The witch abandon her alchemist? Zafir laughed at that. *Not likely.* But none of them knew what to do ...

None of them but her. She showed Diamond Eye, picturing it in her mind, and the dragon wheeled in the air and snatched at the chains of the nearest glasship, seizing them in his teeth. He dived, powering towards the falling eyrie, dragging the glasship after him. The glasship fought him stubbornly through every beat of his wings, adjusting the harmonics of its rotations to fight for its place in the air. A chaos of sleds whirled around her. An Elemental Man appeared in the air ahead of them, gestured and shouted words that were lost in the wind as Diamond Eye hauled the glasship down. The eyrie fell steadily lower, sinking towards the storm-dark. Halfway there and someone lit a torch out on the rim, and then another and then a whole ring of them, and Zafir understood they were guiding her in. As Diamond Eye came closer, she saw the lanterns formed a circle around the wreckage of a black-powder cannon blown to bits by the Vespinese not so many days before. She urged him on towards the violet clouds.

Bellepheros was on the wall as Zafir and the dragon came in. Half the Taiytakei of the eyrie were there now too, all of them holding their breath. The other half were out around the ruined cannon, waving lamps, or else up in the air on their sleds. Lots and lots of sleds. A couple of t'varrs had been trying to organise the evacuation, but even they had stopped to watch.

Diamond Eye reached the eyrie rim and seized it with his hind claws, tearing rents in the solid stone. The dragon still held a gondola in its forelimbs; now it leaned forward, the glasship chains clamped between its teeth, dangling limp. Bellepheros could see it, even from so far away, quivering with the effort. Before the Vespinese had blown it up with their lightning, the black powder cannon had been mounted on massive iron plinths set into the stone of the rim. The iron was still there, warped and twisted. Enough to wrap a chain around it, perhaps.

For a moment no one moved. Then a Taiytakei ran out and grabbed the end of one of the chains and started to pull on it, struggling to even lift it, to wrap it around the iron; and then more men ran forward, and in a moment a swarm of them were heaving beneath the dragon's maw, slaves and Taiytakei alike, dragging the loose ends of the chains and wrapping them around the plinth, twisting them together, pinning them with the bent barrel of the ruined gun, shouting and cheering and swearing up a giddy frenzy of hope. The dragon terrified them to the core and yet they did it, and then they were finished and backed away and a cheer went up from the wall and Bellepheros found he was cheering too, but his heart was still racing because that was only the start.

The dragon let go. The chains snapped taut.

And held.

Bellepheros stayed on the wall, watching, as mesmerised as everyone else.

The first glasship stopped the eyrie's fall with its underbelly touching the cloud. Zafir arced Diamond Eye under the rim to look and see if the storm-dark devoured the stone but in the night it was all too dark to see. And maybe, just maybe, the eyrie was still very slowly sinking. She drove her dragon skyward again and one by one Diamond Eye hauled the glasships down. When she came with the second the men on the eyrie changed their plan and guided her to the white stone watchtowers, unbreakable by anything except a dragon, threading the chains through the windows of the towers to hold them fast.

Do I expect their gratitude for this? It wouldn't make any difference. She'd burned and shattered Dhar Thosis to ash and splinters and in the end she'd hang for that come what may.

Why do it then?

She really didn't know.

When the third glassship was secured to the eyrie and they were rising again, Bellepheros reckoned they were safe and he could probably go back to his room and get some sleep, or maybe go back to his book. But everyone else was out in the yard or up on the wall, slaves, soldiers and other Taiytakei, even his Scales, milling around and shouting at each other over the wind while they waited for the dragon to haul the next glassship down, so he stayed. He couldn't stop thinking about Li, about how she'd have known what to do, the same thoughts running round in the same circles, staring blankly into space until suddenly it was done and over. Five glassships floated overhead. The eyrie wasn't falling any more. Zafir, of all people, had saved them. Zafir, not Li.

He shook his head and turned away. He needed to think.

The dragon perched on the wall, hunched with its head almost resting on the battlements. It had carried the same dented silver gondola throughout, but now the gondola was lying in the dragon yard at the foot of the wall, discarded, and the dragon was holding something in its claws, looking hard at it. Not a some*thing*, Bellepheros saw as he came closer, heading for the tunnel back to his study. A some*one*. Her Holiness Zafir was on the wall, yelling, and the man in Diamond Eye's talons was screaming, brimming with fear and outrage but unable to settle on one over the other. 'You cannot do this!' That sort of thing, over and over with different words and an occasionally varying order, but it all amounted to much the same.

Bellepheros walked on past. He'd seen it too many times over the years – the torture of a man who thought he couldn't be touched. That was dragon-kings for you. They always did it, even when they didn't need to. Even when they *knew* they didn't need to because they'd called the grand master alchemist of the Order of the Scales to their eyrie to make truth-smoke, and Bellepheros, given time, could get the truth out of creation itself spoken by the very stones of the earth. They all knew it, but dragon-kings tortured their prey anyway. Queens, apparently, were no different. No great surprise – this was more the Zafir he knew. He paused, fought the wind and turned to see who the man was.

Shonda!? Dear Flame, she had Shonda! Even in the moonlight his robe gave the sea lord away. There was nothing else like it. Bellepheros sighed and hung his head. Truth-smoke was another thing he'd chosen not to mention to Li or the Elemental Men, mostly in case they decided to have him make the stuff and then use it on himself. Maybe now was the time. Better that than let her Holiness kill a man and then have to make his corpse speak.

He walked back to his study, dragging his feet all the way, sat down at his desk, picked up the next page and tried to get excited about it. *Vespinese sorceress Abraxi increased her interest in the mountains and their subterranean dwellers in the last years of her reign. The few of her writings to survive confirm the apocryphal Rava although they may simply be repeating it. The Elemental Men have at least once directly spoken of the existence of shape-shifters beneath the Konsidar* ... Zafir had told him that, and he had no idea why an Elemental Man might have said such a thing to her. Maybe she'd made it up on a whim to tease him. He wouldn't put it past her. He wouldn't put *anything* past her any more. *Abraxi's writings suggest the Righteous Ones tamed dragons and now consort with them, keeping them as pets* ...

You picked a story and chose which one to believe. Some of the slaves from the desert claimed it was all a myth, that the Elemental Men were protecting some other secret from before the Splintering ...

He couldn't concentrate. With a flash of peevish resentment for everyone and everything for choosing *this* night of all nights for their excitement, Bellepheros put the pages away, got up and poured himself a glass of cold qaffeh. He missed sitting with Li, drinking qaffeh and eating Bolo. He'd missed it before but it was worse now. It hadn't ever crossed his mind that he might not see her again but now ... Now he found a fierce hunger burning inside him. He wanted to ask her what she'd seen. Tamed dragons? Was there any possibility of truth to it? No one else seemed to think so and yet he couldn't let it go. The Vespinese had taken the dragon as a symbol of their city after all. Why?

Flame, he missed her. Too much. He wanted her back. They'd all nearly died tonight. It was like that every day. The tension ...

I'm afraid.

He forced himself to sit down again. Tonight's page was supposed to be on the Rava itself, the forbidden book of the Taiytakei, though he wasn't much in the mood for writing. 'Book about the ancient gods and the time before the Splintering. Probably no real copies left. Elemental Men hunt you and kill you if read a single word of it so don't, and besides, if anyone claims they have a copy, it's probably a fake. Possibly entirely mythical.' Easy. Move on. Next entry. Except it wasn't so easy because even if the book didn't exist any more, even if it never had, its history was real enough and so was the who and why of its writing and probably the nature of what it contained.

He picked up his pen and dipped it in the ink. At the very end of his book he had a page set aside for Zaklat the Death Bat. He had fond thoughts of Zaklat. Zaklat meant the end. Zaklat meant he was done.

A hammering on his door made him jump. 'Master Alchemist! Master Alchemist!'

Another Scales. Bellepheros glared at the closed door. 'Are we falling out of the sky for a second time? Have the chains failed? Is her Holiness on the rampage, burning everyone?' he shouted.

'No. Master Alchemist.'

'Then *go away*!' Writing his journal was his own personal time, and Flame knew he got little enough of that. Even if he was staring at a blank page, not writing a word.

The Scales was still outside his door. Bellepheros wasn't sure how he knew it but he did. He waited. Closed his eyes. Sighed. 'Is the dragon injured again? Because if it is, I already showed you what to do.' Which was to make sure the dragon was well fed, leave her Holiness to sit with it and keep as far away as possible.

'No, Master Alchemist. They want to know about the other glasship. The one we used to move the eggs. Please come!'

'Eggs? Who said anything about moving eggs?' He got up and went to the door, growling and muttering to himself. He'd forgotten in all the excitement. 'What are you talking about? Who moved eggs? What glasship?'

He opened the door. The Scales gave him a vacant imploring look. Bellepheros let out a deep sigh and followed for a second time, up the winding spiral of the white stone passageway. For the middle of the night there were a lot of Taiytakei about, but maybe it was hard to go back to sleep when you'd almost been dropped into the storm-dark. Most of them were looking at the dragon, at Zafir and Shonda. Most of the rest were looking at the chains or at the glasships, muttering to each other nervously. Wondering whether the chains would hold and for how long and who it was who'd tried to kill them all. And yes, now that he bothered to think about it, there were five glasships holding up Baros Tsen's eyrie now where last night there had been six.

'Master!' The Scales was still dogging his heels and tugging at his robes.

'Yes, yes, I see it.' He looked at the dragon. You'd have to be blind not to see the hole in Diamond Eye's wing from so close, but really what was he going to do? Stick a bandage on it and tell the dragon to rest until it got better? 'There's really nothing for it. Food and water and I'll talk to her Holiness about flying him more carefully for a while.' As if that would work either. Might as well talk to the dragon itself.

'No, Master Alchemist, not Diamond Eye. The other masters wish to know where the sixth glasship went.'

Bellepheros turned and saw a t'varr closing on him with a squad of soldiers. 'What *are* you talking about?'

'They ask why we moved the eggs to the glasship and where they've gone and by whose order.'

'Eggs? What eggs?'

'The four eggs we drew from the hatchery an hour ago and sent away with the old t'varr's glasship. They want to know where it went.'

The Taiytakei were almost on him, but never mind that. Bellepheros ran to the hatchery. It took only a glance to see that the Scales was right. Four eggs gone. He grabbed the Scales and shook him. 'Where are they? Who told you to move them?'

The Scales only grew more bewildered. 'You did, Master Alchemist. You were there. You told us to move the eggs and then you left with them.'

'I *left* with them?'

The Taiytakei reached him. Soldiers seized him by the arms.

'And the sled too,' called the Scales as the soldiers dragged him away.

'I did *what*?' Bellepheros screamed, but his words were lost in the wind.

45

The Enemy of My Enemy

Red Lin Feyn's glasship descended into the abyss of the Konsidar. Liang looked out of the windows as the day faded into a twilight gloom. The walls of the chasm were slick and black, the ferns and trees that grew from the cracks higher up now gone. Only mosses and lichen could live with so little sun. The gondola reached a platform in the stone and stopped. Red Lin Feyn, dressed in her glory as the Arbiter, gestured to open its golden ramp but the Elemental Man caught her hand.

'You do not have authority here, lady. None of us do. We must wait. We must be invited.'

There was little to see from the windows. The ledge jutted out over the deeper abyss with a single dark tunnel leading into the rock. Elsewhere the walls were sheer. Liang peered down to see if she could see how far they went, but they vanished into the darkness. She looked up then, trying to guess how far down they were. A mile perhaps? 'How deep is it?' she asked, but Lin Feyn only shook her head.

The Elemental Man shrugged. 'Deep. That is as much as any of us knows. We do not come further than here now. Once, perhaps …' He trailed off.

'Why not?'

He laughed. 'Enchantress, this is a realm of other creatures, of other rules and other ways. To intrude would be … impolite.' And other things too, she thought, from the careful way he chose his words, but the killer clearly had no intention of explaining himself.

An hour passed, then two, then another. Red Lin Feyn hid her impatience behind her mask; the Elemental Man stood like a statue and Liang twiddled her thumbs until at last she saw movement in the tunnel and three figures appeared. *Creatures*, the killer had said, but to her they looked like men. Nothing about them seemed strange except that they wore veils to hide their faces.

They walked onto the ledge and stood before the gondola. The Elemental Man waited for Red Lin Feyn to seat herself at the table, then opened the ramp, shifted into air, vanished and appeared again at the Arbiter's side. The three veiled men entered. Men, Liang thought, not women, but it was hard to tell. They were slender and oddly built, though she couldn't say exactly what was strange about them. As one they bowed. The first stepped forward.

'You are not welcome here.' The veiled head turned to the Elemental Man. 'You, earth-touched, know this. Your kind do not belong.'

Red Lin Feyn spread her hands across the table, the usual pause she made before she began, but the killer leaned forward beside her and spoke first. 'Our kind do not name ourselves. The lady before me is Red Lin Feyn of the Dralamut. She judges those who live above when judgement is called for. The other is Chay-Liang, artificer of glass. One of you has come to the surface. I am here so you may explain yourselves. You do not wish the alternative.' The threat in his voice was naked for a moment. The veiled man cocked his head as if to consider this. Liang winced. The violence in the air was something she could almost touch.

As the veiled man turned away, he said, 'Earth-touched, you may pass. Alone. When you are ready.'

The air popped. The Elemental Man vanished and appeared again on the ramp, blocking the exit for a moment before he stepped aside to let the veiled men pass. They swept past the killer and away down their tunnel. The ramp eased closed. When it was sealed, the killer moved from one window to the next, closing the blinds. Red Lin Feyn didn't even blink.

'I am the Arbiter, killer,' she said. 'You are not.'

The killer bowed. He glanced at Liang and then bowed again. 'I may not speak of the Konsidar to any who is not of Mount Solence or an initiate of the Dralamut, lady.'

'Chay-Liang? Yet I brought her here.' Lin Feyn reached a hand across the table and beckoned impatiently. 'Chay-Liang of Hingwal Taktse, kneel before me.'

Liang approached uncertainly. She folded her legs carefully

under herself and placed her hand palm down on the rosewood table between them. Lin Feyn turned her hand and gripped Liang's wrist. 'Chay-Liang of Hingwal Taktse, I summon you into the mysteries of the Dralamut. I name you navigator of the first rank. You will not practise your art without my permission. The many other rules by which you must now abide will be explained as opportunity presents itself.' Her voice was quiet but a fury quivered through her. Her grip on Liang's hand was so tight it hurt.

'Lady!' The killer was shaking his head. His hand rested on the hilt of his bladeless knife. 'You cannot—'

'I am a navigator of the fifth rank, killer. I have crossed the storm-dark to the Dominion of the Sun King, to Aria, to the dragon-lands, to Qeled and Scythia and to the Slave Coasts. I have the right and the authority to add to the number of the Dralamut as I see fit and I have done so. Chay-Liang, you are now a navigator of the Dralamut. Killer, explain yourself.' Lin Feyn didn't move except to release Liang's hand.

'Lady, this woman is directly involved in the crime of Dhar Thosis. You cannot take her as an apprentice at this time. You *cannot*!' The killer spoke through gritted teeth.

'If you do not trust my judgement as your Arbiter, killer, you are not fit to be at my side. I break no oath or rule of my title. You will depart our company and find another of your ilk who understands his duty more fully.'

'Lady!'

Lin Feyn raised a hand to silence him. 'Go, killer. Begone!'

'I was instructed to stay!'

'And I *instruct* you to leave.'

For a few seconds the killer stayed where he was. Then he unlatched the one window that would open and vanished into the air. Liang felt the flutter and then he was gone.

'Close it, Chay-Liang. Do not let him return.' Red Lin Feyn was trembling with rage.

Liang shut the window. With slow and careful movements Lin Feyn lifted the feather headdress off and pulled out the pins that held up her hair. She looked tired, but then she turned her head and smiled for the first time Liang could remember in a while. 'Do not aspire to my title, apprentice. I would happily give it up but not to one for whom I cared. *Are* you willing to learn from me, Chay-Liang?'

'I am, lady.'

'I am ten years younger than you. Let neither of us forget that. I have knowledge you do not. You have experience and wisdom I may yet find I lack. Shall we begin with the Konsidar and the creatures who dwell beneath and the true nature of the killers, why they are called the earth-touched and what the storm-dark really is? Or shall we begin with jasmine tea?'

Liang bowed and went to the kettle. When she had made the tea and turned back, Lin Feyn had the glass globe of the storm-dark on the table. She had her hand on it and was rolling the fragment of the maelstrom back and forth and from side to side with her mind as though it was the easiest thing in the world. As Liang set the tiny glass cup beside her, Lin Feyn passed her the globe.

'Keep your hand on this at all times. Do not think of it, but hold it. We may be here for a while.'

And so they sipped tea together and Red Lin Feyn told Liang what everyone secretly already knew: how there had once been four divines, the lords of the sun and the moon and the ladies of the earth and the stars, remembered even now in little ways in corners of Takei'Tarr and revered in the realms of the Sun King and of Aria. How each had made a race of creatures in their own image: the children of the sun, who would become the peoples of Takei'Tarr and the Dominion and all the other realms; the sorcerers of the moon with their white skin and their silver eyes, few but with near limitless power, the half-gods whose war broke the world; and the earth-touched, most favoured children of the dead goddess, who changed their shapes and forms as it suited them.

'You said four. What of the fourth?'

Lin Feyn shook her head. 'They are forgotten. Even in the writings of the Rava. Perhaps they were never made.'

Liang was amazed, for even to speak of the Rava was a curse and Red Lin Feyn was the Arbiter, no less. For a second they looked at one another and then Lin Feyn laughed.

'It will be hard for you at first,' she said, 'for the world is not what you think or have been led to believe. We grow up to imagine the mighty killers as the protectors of our ways, and so they are, but that is not their purpose nor was it ever. What *is* their purpose, Liang?'

'They are killers of sorcerers.'

'That is what they *do*, but why?'

'To protect us.'

'From what?'

Liang hesitated. 'From ... from subjugation. No?' Red Lin Feyn was laughing again. 'Then what?'

'From being enslaved?' The Arbiter shook her head. 'Look at our race and how we behave. Do they lift a finger? No, because slavery is a part of us. No, no, no. You belong to the Dralamut now and you must see a larger canvas.' She shook her head. 'There are no killers here, Chay-Liang, and you must not believe all they say. There are copies of the Rava hidden in the Dralamut, and yes, the killers will do all that they promise if ever they find them, if they find that any of us have even looked at them, but all of us have, Chay-Liang. All of us. Its knowledge is needed if you are to cross the storm-dark. Feyn Charin read every single word as he sat at the foot of the Godspike while the killers hunted his mentor. You will read it too.' She gave a toothy grin. 'More tea, apprentice!'

Liang did as she was told. Lin Feyn got up and climbed the steps to the upper section. She came back holding a book, large and heavy and very old. She put it on the table in front of her. As Liang poured more tea, Lin Feyn pushed the book across.

'The Rava, Chay-Liang. What purpose do the killers serve?'

'I don't know.' Liang couldn't take her eyes off the book. It was as though Lin Feyn had put a poisonous scorpion down in front of her.

'Better. Much better. No, you don't know, and nor should you ever assume otherwise. They hunt sorcerers to prevent another cataclysm. That may be true. They say they hunt the copies of this book because it contains the knowledge to make such a cataclysm possible. That may also be true. But some truth is not the whole truth, Chay-Liang. The Arbiter, above all others, must know the difference.'

She talked on, of how the half-gods had fallen to fighting among themselves and against their creator, how many had simply vanished, how the earth-touched had withdrawn to their safest places, to the realms of the dead they called Xibaiya while the war of the half-gods raged, of the Splintering itself, the cataclysm that ended the half-gods who remained and broke the world into pieces. How the breaking of the earth had slain the goddess-creator.

'All of this you will find written elsewhere, in myths and stories. We imagine the half-gods and the earth-touched long gone, figures of legend, never truly real, but they were. Yet there are also things in the Rava that you will not find elsewhere. The Rava *is* dangerous, for it is the tome of all the gods of its time and there were not four but five, the sun, the moon, the stars, the earth and the Nothing that came before them all, and the story it tells is of the breaking of the world that came when the Nothing was unleashed, for a very fraction of a moment, from the prison in which it was held. That is a secret you will not find elsewhere. You must never let the killers know you have learned it, for they will kill to keep it, yet it is the secret of the storm-dark.'

She reached across the table and tapped the book. 'It's all in there. The last priests of the old ways wrote down everything they knew before the killers found them. The goddess of the earth was slain when the Nothing burst free, but in her dying she made a cage in the ruins of Xibaiya and captured it once more. All but a few ways between this world and Xibaiya were destroyed – here in the Konsidar, others in other places, in the Queverra, once – but those were abandoned long ago. Here the Rava is incomplete, for it does not say the cause. The earth-touched remained in Xibaiya.'

'Xibaiya?' The enormity of what Liang was hearing kept slapping her, making her head spin and her skin turn numb. 'The Elemental Men are from Xibaiya? Are they dead?'

'They are people like you and I, Chay-Liang, but they carry a piece of something else inside them – a fragment of the fallen goddess. It changes them. An Elemental Man is a fusion. They are both now.' She said it lightly as if it was nothing, as if Liang would somehow understand. 'The skin-shifters are the same in some other way. On this the Rava has nothing to say. Unfortunately.'

She leaned forward and sipped her tea.

'Something has changed, Liang. It began twenty-three years ago when a new star lit the sky above the Godspike at the exact end of the year. Do you remember it?'

Liang nodded. A beautiful light had bloomed like a new moon on the night of midsummer. It had lasted for a week and everyone across Takei'Tarr had seen it.

'I remember it too. I was a girl then. After it was gone, the hsians of the thirteen sea lords and the Arbiter of the Dralamut met in secret to consider it in the Palace of Forever. Nothing was resolved except that the star must carry some great meaning. The hsians went back to their lords and hatched their plans. Quai'Shu's dreams of dragons were born on that day. This foolishness between Xican and Dhar Thosis and Vespinarr is a scratch on the surface, Liang. The killers had a hand in bringing dragons to Takei'Tarr, and the moon sorcerers too, who never came out of their towers in the Diamond Isles and were nothing but myth and legend until Quai'Shu went to their island and called them from their diamond towers and they actually came. Dragons in Takei'Tarr, that's what they wanted, all of them. In hindsight it's so obvious. They know something, and the Righteous Ones in their gloom, they know something too.' She frowned. 'Six years ago, in the desert by the Godspike, one of the ring of needles cracked and the storm-dark began to shift. You know this.'

Liang nodded.

'It has not stopped. The change is slow but it continues. Something changed in Xibaiya as well at that time. We cross the storm-dark, Chay-Liang, and when we do, we stare into the very heart of death itself. We go to places the killers can no longer imagine. For six years the Righteous Ones have been creeping out of their caves. The skin-shifter we seek now isn't the first. It is little more than six years since, in Aria, an army of the dead scourged that land, since the Ice Witch rose, since the founding of the Necropolis. Across all the worlds, Liang, it has been anathema for a thousand years to bury the dead and consign their souls to the dead goddess of Xibaiya but in these last handful, in both Aria and the Dominion, the dead who die without the light of the sun or moon or stars, without fire or water or wind, no longer rest in peace but rise again. In our world too, Chay-Liang. In the Dralamut we have poisoned condemned slaves in lightless caves and seen them die and rise once more. The sea lords push the sun king towards holy war against the Ice Witch for their own ends. Dragons come to Takei'Tarr.

Skin-shifters roam from the Konsidar. I will judge the guilt for the burning of Dhar Thosis but there is far more to this and I would penetrate its mystery. The killers try to hide what is happening because they are afraid. They think to keep it from the Dralamut but they know more than they are saying, Chay-Liang, and so do the Righteous Ones of the Konsidar. When our new killer comes, you will say nothing of this, but do not trust his answers. They hold the reins of our avaricious sea lords and see that the shifters remain in their homes; and so we shall gather what knowledge we can and pretend that that is all that matters. We shall keep our peace despite what we know.'

Liang thought of the body of Baros Tsen T'Varr, which wasn't his at all. *For now*, she mused. *For now*.

Red Lin Feyn seemed to read her mind. She nodded. 'For now, yes. Until we are certain of our course.'

A killer came to them not long after that, a different one. His words were terse. 'Lady Arbiter, the Righteous Ones of the Konsidar claim ignorance of any skin-shifter come to the surface.' He shifted uncomfortably, frowning deeply.

'Then they lie. Watch them.'

'Yes, lady. They … they are unusually perturbed, lady. I cannot say for sure but I believe there has been some disturbance elsewhere.'

'The Queverra?'

The Elemental Man came closer. He looked confused. 'Lady Arbiter, there is more. At the eyrie. Lord Shonda escaped, though briefly. It appears the alchemist stole four dragon eggs in the night. The glasships that suspend the eyrie were let slip, perhaps in an effort to destroy it, all but one glasship which flew away with both alchemist and eggs. Yet …' He stared at Chay-Liang. 'Lady, we know of only two who might control those glasships. Lady Chay-Liang and Baros Tsen T'Varr. And Baros Tsen T'Varr is dead. And the alchemist, who many eyes claim left with the glasship and its eggs, remains among us.'

'Baros Tsen is not dead, killer.' Red Lin Fey bared her teeth and then started to laugh. 'The skin-shifter. Back, and as fast as we can. And killer, set a watch on the Queverra. The shifter will go there now, not here. If he leaves it before I reach him, you must be waiting.'

She looked at Liang and they exchanged a glance, both wondering the same: why would Baros Tsen help a skin-shifter?

46

Or Not, as the Case May Be

Sivan and Tsen caught up with the glasship again halfway between the underside of the storm-dark and the desert sand. Sivan shot the sled inside and slammed the ramp shut behind them. 'Down! Now! As quick as you can.' Tsen drove the glasship down as fast as it would go. Dozens of men on linxia were riding across the desert, closing on them. As soon as the gondola touched the sand, Sivan opened the ramp.

'Out! Out! Get them out!' he shouted, pushing at the eggs. His sword-slaves tried to lift them but they were too heavy. 'Roll them!' Dozens of riders were converging on the gondola. Sivan waved, urging them on. Four were pulling gold-glass sleds behind their linxia, each the right size for a dragon's egg but dressed to look like a desert trader's wagon. As each egg rolled out of the gondola, it was hauled up onto a sled. Sivan shouted at them to hurry. The first egg vanished on its sled into the darkness with twenty desert men riding beside it. The second and the third followed. Sivan drew out a knife as the desert men hauled the last egg onto its sled. He looked at Tsen and shook his head. He looked almost mournful.

'You knew this would come, T'Varr.'

Tsen looked at the knife. 'Yes. I did. But why now? Why not just pitch me into the storm-dark from the back of your sled, shifter? Surely that would have been easier?'

'I was still ... hoping that it could be otherwise. But now it comes to it ...' He shook his head. 'The earth-touched won't fall into the storm-dark with the rest and this glasship simply doesn't travel fast enough. They'll find you and your eyes have seen too much.'

Tsen nodded. 'To be truthful, I never thought you would let either of us live beyond this moment, no matter what.'

The shifter fingered his knife. 'I'm surprised at you, T'Varr. I would have expected more ... resistance. But I thank you for your help. We serve a greater purpose. I wish I could show you.'

Tsen shrugged. 'I'm just an old fat t'varr – what can I do? Oh, and there really isn't any need. I made contingencies before we left Vespinarr.' He waited, unsure what would happen now. Whether he was about to live or die.

One of the desert men stabbed Sivan in the back. The shifter stumbled, turned and lunged but missed. All around, Sivan's slaves were struck down.

'I … paid you … so much,' he gasped. 'We were going to … bring them … down.'

'I got a better offer.' The desert man took a spear from someone behind him and rammed it through Sivan, pinning him to the side of the gondola. Tsen watched the shifter fall, waiting for him to change his features and get up again, but he didn't.

'Baros Tsen T'Varr?' The desert man grabbed Tsen and looked him up and down. 'You look like him.'

Tsen's middle finger tingled; it had for several hours now. 'Chrias has my thanks. I appear to owe him a favour. I would like to go now.'

'You come with us.' The desert man pulled Tsen out into the cold night air. They took Kalaiya and left the rest of Sivan's slaves with their blood draining into the sand and bemused expressions on their faces. They hadn't even had time to raise their blades.

Tsen sat with Kalaiya on the back of the sled, resting against the last dragon egg, as big and heavy as a horse, the sled skimming over the gentle rise and fall of the sand. In the desert near Cashax were dunes taller than the tallest tower in Khalishtor, as high as the cliffs of Xican, but here under the storm-dark the waves of sand fell away as if both they and the wind were afraid to come too close. Within the ring of the Godspike's outer needles, the sand was like ripples on a calm sea.

Well, there's a thing. Another useless fact. Maybe you have a future as a teacher.

The riders scattered leaving a dozen different trails behind them. The sled sped on through the night, through the Godspike's outer ring of spires to an outcrop of rock surrounded by tents. As the desert men approached and slowed, Tsen saw bodies with arrows in their backs. Closer in, he saw marks where others had already been dragged away. A pavilion rose beside the outcrop and a dozen soldiers were hurriedly pulling it down. Tsen saw a gap in the stones behind it and a darkness that was more than the dark of the desert night. A cave, he thought at first, but the walls were too smooth and straight.

'You. Off.'

The desert men threw Tsen and Kalaiya onto the sand as the sled slowed and then eased it into the gaping darkness. In the starlight Tsen thought he saw a tunnel ending in a shaft, then the sled was inside it and the soldiers were putting the pavilion back together, hiding cave, sled and shaft all at once. Strong hostile arms hauled him to his feet and dragged him away. There were bodies in piles, pits being dug, men cursing and shouting for the work to be done faster. The desert men hurried Tsen into the largest tent where a thick fug of Xizic filled the air, stifling, almost choking. A man sat in the gloom, naked from the waist down with two slaves oiling his skin. A handful of dim lamps flickered around the tent's edges, enough light to see shapes and outlines but no more. But then Tsen didn't need to see the man's face.

'Shrin Chrias Kwen.' Tsen bowed. 'From one servant of our sea lord to another, I greet you.' They'd been enemies not all that long ago and yes, they'd probably been set to kill each other to see who would follow Quai'Shu as lord of Xican. But that was then, and now they were both hunted men with nooses waiting for their necks.

'Baros Tsen T'Varr.' The kwen's voice was hoarse and rasping. There was nothing friendly in his tone. Much more of a vengeful, gleeful, about-to-murder-you sort of voice, really. Tsen squirmed. He tried to remind himself what exactly it was he had to offer his old rival right now. Not much, that was for sure.

'Are you not well, Chrias?' *Be polite, tongue. For the love of the forbidden gods, be polite. We're in this together, like it or not. And I'm still a sea lord's t'varr.*

'I got your message, T'Varr. Are the Elemental Men not hunting you every bit as hard as they hunt me?'

'They've taken my eyrie but they think I'm dead.'

'How convenient. Very soon they'll be right.'

Tsen closed his eyes. *Ah.* Not that he'd really expected better.

This was what you got with kwens. Big stupid brutes all full of shouting and holding grudges. At least Kalaiya would be safe. Chrias wasn't mad like the shifter. Chrias was a pig and bastard, perhaps, but he had no reason to hurt Kalaiya, and wasn't that the point of it all? All he'd ever wanted? 'It was all Shonda. You know that, don't you? You must, by now.'

'Shonda betrayed me at sea. Of course he did. Ships and navigators across the storm-dark and a long and happy life in glorious luxury. Ha!' Chrias laughed. 'There is one thing that might keep you alive a little while longer. Where's the alchemist?'

Tsen shrugged. 'Still on the eyrie, I suppose.' Wiped from existence on account of falling into the storm-dark along with everything else probably wasn't what Chrias wanted to hear. Best not to mention that part. Unless Chrias had seen enough to work it out for himself. There was always that ...

Chrias eased himself to his feet. He moved slowly, stiff and awkward like an old man or one in a great deal of pain. The anger building around him was a slow and massive thing. 'Then what did you bring me, T'Varr?'

'Four dragon eggs.'

'And?'

Tsen held out his hands. 'And me, Chrias. You have me. For what good that does either of us. But I will help you in anything that will expose Shonda for what he is.' He closed his eyes, wondering why he'd even bothered to say that. Maybe he could offer Chrias something even more appealing? Like a few handfuls of desert sand to add to his already impressive collection? Or perhaps a simple punch in the teeth ...

'You?' Shrin Chrias Kwen stooped to pick up a lamp and held it out in front of him. Tsen turned away so as not to be dazzled by the flame. 'Look what she did to me, Tsen. Look what your rider-slave did!'

At last they were close enough for Tsen finally to see the kwen's face. His skin was scabbed and hard and flaking, split raw in places with dribbles of dried blood where wounds had wept. Kalaiya gasped, but Tsen had seen faces like this before, had seen them every day. The alchemist's Scales with their Hatchling Disease. Chrias had the Statue Plague. Well yes, he'd known that from the day the rider-slave had come back from Dhar Thosis, but not how bad it was, not how quickly it would take him without the alchemist to slow its course. He saw, and he knew that Chrias would kill him now, no matter what he said. Someone had to die, after all.

'Stick a part of you in a place where it wasn't wanted, did you, Chrias?' he asked, just to make sure they couldn't possibly come to any agreement. It wasn't as if either of them deserved any better.

47
A Hanging

In the great list of all the crimes that would one day condemn her Zafir wondered where this would rank. Abduction of the most powerful of the Taiytakei sea lords. Branding him with the mark of his own slaves. Having a dragon dangle him upside down in the air by one leg. Shonda started off, as all men did, by telling her how great and powerful he was and how terrible her suffering would be for what she was doing, then moved on to how worse still it would become if she didn't stop. She laughed in his face.

'What could you possibly do?' she screamed at him over the wind that whipped the eyrie. 'What else could you possibly do?'

The threats carried on long enough to draw a crowd in the dragon yard. After everything that had gone on, none of the Taiytakei were in bed. Which was good. It was a humiliation that demanded an audience.

The threats shifted to bribes. 'I will give you anything you wish for! This eyrie will be mine. You will fly for me and I will make you the richest sword-slave ever to live, richer than a sea lord!'

Zafir lifted the brand high over her head and had Diamond Eye turn his fire on it until it glowed. The dragon let Shonda down and Zafir gut-punched him and threw him onto his face. She straddled him before he could get up and ripped the feathered robe off his flabby back. 'I will never fly for you,' she hissed. 'No one will ever fly for you. You have nothing you could possibly give me.' She stabbed the brand into his skin and listened to him scream. No one tried to stop her. The Elemental Men watched and did nothing.

After a while, his sobs and whimpers grew annoying. Bellepheros hadn't given her much, but no dragon-rider flew without a salve for burns. She dabbed it over the brand mark. Not that it made it go away but for an hour or so the pain would ease. Then she had Diamond Eye dangle him again. 'You want me to be *your* slave, is that it? All this because you want me to be *your* slave and not Quai'Shu's slave? I'd taken you for a clever man, Sea Lord. Do you see Quai'Shu here? No. Because a dragon held him as mine holds you now and his mind broke in two. Then again, that dragon was awake. But I faced that dragon too, fat old man, and I did *not* break. Why should I be *your* slave? Why should you not be mine? Except what use would you be?'

Shonda screamed into the night, 'I will give you whatever you desire.'

'But you have nothing that I want!' She spat at him.

'Your freedom, slave. I will give you your freedom. Set me loose and I will take you on my ships and your monster too and sail you back to your own land!.'

Maybe she hesitated for a moment, because if there was anything she wanted more than a simple end to it all, fiery and unforgettable, it was that. Home. But of course he couldn't deliver. The Elemental Men were letting her do this to him because they knew he was done. He had no power any more, and even if he had, he wouldn't ever have given her what she wanted. He couldn't. No one could. It had never existed.

She took a deep breath and sighed. When she looked away, she saw the alchemist hurrying across the dragon yard. She held up the brand and waved it in Shonda's face. 'Why, fat old man? You had your kwen Mai'Choiro tell me to burn that city. What was it for? All the money in the world still not enough for you?' She held up a hand. 'No, don't answer. Don't fill the air with lies because I've sat higher than you ever will and I already know what it was for.

'Fear. Fear that you'll lose it. Fear that someone, somewhere, is better than you, or richer than you, or cleverer than you. Fear that they'll take it away again, that you'll slip behind and the men who used to quiver and tremble at your passing will laugh instead. Fat old man with all your power and your wealth, and what did you ever do with it? My dragon? That's what this was for? Then be happy, for you are closer to him now than Baros Tsen T'Varr or Quai'Shu ever got!'

She listened to him babble and squirm and wail and storm a little longer, paying scant attention to what he said. They were the same, he and she, or they had been once, clawing their way over the backs of those above them as fast as they could and always afraid of those clawing in their wake, and then she'd reached the top and had had no idea how else to be. She told Diamond Eye to let Shonda down. He crawled away and she let him be, empty of any idea of what to do with him any more.

The Elemental Men took him. Diamond Eye watched him go. The dragon wanted to eat him. It was, Zafir thought, an admirably simple desire. *My mother didn't give a fig for me or my sister beyond what we'd be worth to her in some dragon-prince's bed. Perhaps that's why I've never been fond of princes and their like.* Except it was more likely her father who'd drilled that into her, her father, who wanted to be very sure that his pretty princesses knew what to do once they'd been sold. Oh yes, very kind and loving when they did the right thing. Not so much when they didn't. *Liked to keep us locked in a dark room when we were naughty girls.* Still made her heart knot thinking of that, but not like it used to. She stroked Diamond Eye's nose. *But we've been there together now, you and I.*

The Adamantine Man drifted into her thoughts again. Tuuran. He came to her most days, ever since she'd seen him in Dhar Thosis. Always the same memory. The Pinnacles. That moment of selfless kindness, coming to her aid when her own father had had her pinned against a wall; and she'd taken that moment and killed with it, taken Tuuran's knife and stabbed her father, and someone had had to take the blame and be hanged for the death of a prince of the Silver City. Let it be him, let it be *his* fault, *his* knife. Make it go away and pretend it never happened. And she'd been afraid, but she was a dragon-rider destined to be a queen, and a dragon-rider knew better than to let fear grow and fester. So she'd taken what she'd done and faced it down and picked through the reasons and the causes, pored over everything that had been done to her, every day caged in the dark and the far worse thing that passed for love that came after. She'd looked at it all and given herself the choice of swallowing it whole or breaking into pieces, for what use was a dragon-rider who was afraid? None at all.

Her little sister, Kiam, just coming into bloom. She would have been next. *I spared her*, she told Diamond Eye. *But she had no idea. She just hated me for what I'd done. And in time I hated her back for not seeing the truth. For never seeing what he was.*

She'd taken what she wanted. Anyone who got in her way, she crushed them exactly as her mother had done. She'd had the Adamantine Man sent to Furymouth to be sold as a slave. Done it behind her mother's back and paid dearly for it, but at least it was better than letting him hang. She wished now that she could see him one more time before she died to tell him she was sorry. Not to ask for forgiveness, because that was too much. Just to say sorry.

After the killers took Shonda away, Zafir went to her shelter where no one would see her and curled up inside it. She slept a little while, a fitful doze full of dreams of her treacherous lover Jehal, of being her own mother. She woke up sobbing beside Diamond Eye and somehow couldn't stop, and so that was how Bellepheros found her, huddled up tight in a corner in her nightclothes, shaking.

'Holiness?'

When she looked at him, she wanted to rip the concern off his face with her bare hands, strangle him for seeing her this way, but she couldn't make herself move. She looked up at him with tear streaks down her cheeks. And he bowed but didn't go away, didn't turn, didn't stand outside. He just stared right back at her as though he'd never known that a dragon-rider could cry.

'It's done, Holiness,' he said. 'It's all finished.'

She had no idea what he was talking about, and then the only thing it could be hit her like a soft ripping-out of her stomach. 'You've poisoned Diamond Eye,' she said, knowing she would be next.

Bellepheros looked confused for a second and then shook his head. 'No, Holiness. Sea Lord Shonda has confessed his part in what you did. I gave him truth-smoke. Everyone was there to hear.' He hung his head. 'I took it myself and now they know everything there is to know about what I am. I will not be with you much longer. The Elemental Men say we must all wait for their Arbiter to return and hear it all again, but it's done. They will kill us all now. I am sorry.'

'Not as sorry as I am, alchemist. Go! No, wait!' It took a huge effort to force herself to stand. She was still shaking. 'Do one more thing for me. Do you have Frogsback? Blue Midnight?'

The alchemist shook his head. His mouth opened as if to speak. No words came out but she saw in his eyes that he understood.

'They took everything, Holiness. Everything I have.'

'Something else then. I will not be their toy. Let me go with my Diamond Eye. Together side by side. You must find something! Painless and quick if you can.' *And say yes, alchemist. Do it quickly before I decide to go the other way, with fire and fury and death to all around me.*

Bellepheros closed his eyes. 'Holiness, I—'

'One last service for your speaker, Grand Master. I hunted the hatchling down for you, and you owe me for that. Diamond Eye bit off his head brought back his body. You took an oath, alchemist.' *For once not for me, alchemist. For once I ask for others.*

'I took an oath to Speaker Hyram.'

'You took that oath to whoever sat in the Adamantine Throne.' But already the moment was slipping away. *Poison? Really?* She took his hands and gripped them tight. She might have begged if she could have brought herself to, but no, a dragon-queen couldn't ever beg. 'Neither of us knows who sits on the throne in the City of Dragons now, but for a time it was me and I am here.' She held out her trembling hand with the speaker's ring still on her finger. 'Bring me what I ask for and be released from your duties to me.' She took a deep breath. Forced the word out. 'Please.'

The alchemist was shaking as well. 'As you wish, Holiness. I will try.' She let go of him and he bowed, and then he ruined it. 'I will do this if I may ask a favour in return.'

No! No, no, no! She could have cried. 'Do not ask favours of me, alchemist, not for this. Little good comes to those who do. Haven't you seen that?' *Just give it to me and go before it's too late. I can't beg for it, I simply cannot.*

'Four eggs were stolen in the night.' He had no idea how hard it was for her to ask for death, for a way out that was easy for everyone. None; and now she was back to having to keep herself from strangling him. *Fire and ash, alchemist. Smoke and blood. So be it.* 'The Scales say I ordered them loaded into a gondola but I did not. Go, Holiness, with Diamond Eye, and bring back those eggs. I cannot allow them to hatch unwatched. Do this, Holiness, and I will find you a poison no matter what I must do.'

Zafir snorted. 'Do the Elemental Men approve, alchemist?' She could have screamed in his face, *Why should I even care?*

'They are searching too. But Diamond Eye will find the eggs far more easily. You know this.'

'And is that what you have told them?' She wasn't listening any more. It could all have come quietly to an end, peacefully and painlessly and possibly even with a touch of grace, but the moment had passed. It wasn't much to ask, was it, to be allowed to slip silently away? But no. They wanted something from her. Always, always they wanted something more. No peace. No rest. No mercy for pretty Zafir.

'I have.'

A dragon-queen to the end. 'Then let them hatch. Let dragons burn this world to ash. I spurn your poisons.' She turned her back on him. She heard him go and sank back into her corner and held herself. One more betrayal. Nothing left.

Inside her head the Adamantine Man was shaking his head and wagging his finger at her. An Adamantine Man went with his axe in his hand, screaming bloody defiance to the very last gasp of air in his lungs. An Adamantine Man *fought*, damn it, and a dragon-queen should do no less. She sat for a long time, thinking of Tuuran, thinking of that night in the Pinnacles and of all the things she'd done and what they had cost her. And of him again in Dhar Thosis, bowing at her feet. Did he even remember? And then last of all when she'd chased the hatchling into the abyss of the Queverra. The fleeting sense of him.

She was still wondering about that as she put on the glass-and-gold armour of a Taiytakei dragon-rider and climbed onto Diamond Eye's back. She scratched the dragon's scales, not that he ever noticed.

'Eggs,' she said. 'And him. Find both.'

48

Hatchling Disease

Tsen let the Kwen's soldiers bind him. It occurred to him that he ought to put up at least some sort of fight, but what would he do except make an even bigger fool of himself? At least a man could go with a little dignity. More than Chrias would have when the disease finally took him.

An insidious plague, the alchemist had said. *Takes a long time for the first symptoms to show. By the time you know it's out, it's spread through half a city.* And it had been a horrific thing to watch the Scales fall slowly to pieces. When the disease had begun to spread through the men of the eyrie Tsen had ordered everyone who carried it to be eaten by the dragon. It was the most brutal thing he'd ever done by far. Ever, and yes, kwens and t'varrs across Takei'Tarr did things like that all the time, but not *him*. Not Baros Tsen.

There were signs of it, when he looked, among some of the other men here. And he knew by now that the alchemist had the disease himself and kept it dormant with potions. So did the rider-slave. Shrin Chrias Kwen didn't have any potions and so it was killing him, and soldiers weren't so good at keeping themselves to themselves. Unless the kwen had told them, probably none of them even knew what they carried. Not yet.

He thought all these things as they tied him up and then he thought about the rider-slave. Zafir had done this. The dragon-queen had sent her plague out into the world. His world. He wondered whether she'd planned it that way all along or whether it had been merely personal vengeance on Chrias. Both perhaps? And it occurred to him then that for all these months when he'd thought he was matching his wits and cunning against Shonda of Vespinarr, he'd actually been fencing with Zafir, the slave who was once a dragon-queen, and that she'd thoroughly and comprehensively beaten him. She'd burned Dhar Thosis. She'd set this plague among his people. She'd brought down his house and everything in which he believed, and that was barely even the start.

Maybe she's dead. Small consolation. In a way he was happy for Chrias to kill him now. Dhar Thosis was bad enough. The rest? The rest he didn't want to see.

Chrias's soldiers dragged Tsen outside and threw him down. They were almost done with filling in the mass grave. Tsen supposed the dead were Sivan's men who'd hadn't fancied changing sides. He didn't feel sorry for them. Didn't feel sorry for Chrias either, nor any of the men he'd brought with him. Didn't even feel that sorry for himself. There hadn't been much chance of any other outcome. Kalaiya. It was all for her.

Chrias emerged from the tent. 'You must have wondered why I let you know I was still alive,' Tsen said. 'Why I let you see where I would be. Did you not think it was a trap?'

'Of course it's a trap.' Chrias glanced up at the sky and spat. 'But without your alchemist I'll die. So why not? Maybe your dragon egg will get me something.'

Tsen laughed. 'It makes no difference. I dropped the eyrie into the storm-dark, Chrias. I let the glasships go and watched it fall.'

'I was watching through your eyes, Tsen. I know what you did.'

'Even if he got out, the alchemist can't do anything except stop it from getting worse. The Elemental Men have him now. You should have gone somewhere quiet and died having some fun.' *And so should I.* And, dear forbidden gods, he found it bothering him again, now of all times, why the rider-slave hadn't given him the disease when she'd had the chance, why she'd changed her mind and knocked the glass out of his hand. It made him peevish. *Is that the best you can do for your last thoughts?*

'At least I get to watch you go first, Tsen.'

'Was I so bad to you?'

Chrias laughed. 'We both wanted to be the new lord of Xican, Tsen. No harm in that. No grudges, no regrets, but no remorse, and you still die.'

'You were right. Liang was right.' Tsen looked the kwen over. 'The dragon-rider did this to you. But couldn't you see how much she hated you?' He might have told his tongue to be careful but all things considered there didn't seem much point. Not that his tongue ever listened to him anyway.

'I saw. You should have put her down like the rabid dog she was right at the start.'

'Yes.' The people of Dhar Thosis, Tsen thought, would probably agree. 'But I didn't. Because of you. She played me well, Shrin Chrias Kwen. She made me into a fool.'

'She played us both, T'Varr.' And Tsen couldn't find much to argue with there.

Chrias walked stiffly back into his tent and returned dragging Kalaiya. 'You know the next thing I'm going to do, Tsen? I'm going to have you beg. I'm going to have you beg for your woman.' He patted himself between the legs. 'It hurts but it all still works, and there are plenty here who have the sickness already yet barely notice. Shall I pass her around between them in front of you while you watch? You can think of me dying slowly of this cursed plague and you can think of her dying of it too.' He bared his teeth. 'Everyone knows about you, Tsen. About time she had a proper man, isn't it? Beg me not to do it. Beg, T'Varr!'

Tsen twisted on the ground and spat at him but Chrias dodged the spittle. He came suddenly close and ripped Tsen's tunic open, looked between Tsen's legs and laughed.

'Some people said you were secretly a eunuch but now we all know better. So it just doesn't work, eh? But you've still got a hole in that fat arse of yours. Beg well enough and I'll spare your woman and pass *you* around instead. Maybe being buggered by a dozen soldiers will finally light some fire in you, T'Varr.'

'Your many bastards must be so very proud of you, Chrias!'

'I hope so.' Chrias pushed Kalaiya away. 'What makes me hate you, Tsen, what really makes it beyond the pale between us, is that you actually think I'd do that. You loathe me for being a kwen. You think I'm an animal and yet you barely know me at all. What wrong has she ever done me? None. What sort of monster do you think I am? I'll hang you, quick and simple, and then I'll let her go, Tsen. You can have that much as you die.' He turned and walked away. 'String him up.'

Out across the desert, somewhere under the storm-dark, Tsen heard the shriek of a dragon.

Diamond Eye launched himself off the edge of the eyrie, spread his wings and glided out over the pre-dawn glow of the storm-dark. Zafir felt him looking, searching. Eggs were difficult. Eggs weren't living things, not yet, just waiting vessels of flesh and bone until somewhere a dragon died and its soul came looking for a new home. The glasship then. Bellepheros had said that's how they'd been taken. Glasships had a taste to them. She'd found even before Dhar Thosis that Diamond Eye could feel their presence even when he couldn't see them. Something about the enchantments that made them fly, though other pieces of gold-glass seemed dead.

They flew to the edge of the storm-dark, dropped beneath it and immediately found the glasship floating over the desert with its gondola open, resting on the sand. No one came out to gawk and Diamond Eye already knew there was no one here alive. Zafir landed and slid off his back to see anyway. There were a handful of bodies outside the gondola and two more inside. Zafir ignored them. She ran her fingertips over the walls. They came away grimy with a greasy black ash.

The eggs weren't here. She stayed a while, circling the gondola on foot, looking at the tracks. There were a lot – and it would have been easier to see them from the back of a dragon but she was afraid that the wind of Diamond Eye's wings would disturb the sand and wipe them away. As she looked she felt a sharpness from the dragon. Diamond Eye surged towards her as a killer appeared.

'You came back with Sea Lord Shonda and without the elemental Man who escorted you. You will return to the eyrie now and I will come with you. You will await the Arbiter. You will do this or I will end you here.'

Zafir stamped her foot, shook her head and snorted. 'Your kinsman died under Shonda's lightning. You have his body. See it for yourself.' But perhaps in the confusion of the stolen eggs, of the eyrie plunging to its doom, of Shonda's confession, perhaps they didn't know. Perhaps the killer's broken corpse was still lying in Shonda's savaged gondola, unnoticed. Pity. She should have had Diamond Eye dangle him as well in front of that crowd – a sea lord and an Elemental Man. She smiled. 'My dragon will find your missing eggs for you.'

'No. You will not fly again. My knife awaits you.'

Zafir climbed onto Diamond Eye's back, buckled on her harness and then held up her arms in surrender. 'So be it.'

She smiled again as he sat behind her and strapped on his harness nice and tight.

The Elemental Men appeared around Shrin Chrias Kwen's camp simultaneously. There were only three but that didn't matter. One rose from the sand not far from the gallows close to the camp's heart. Another flickered in at its edge, behind the kwen but in Tsen's line of sight. He didn't see the third until later.

'Do not run!' ordered the first.

'Killers!' roared Chrias. 'Circles!'

Tsen watched, fascinated. Surely the only sensible thing to do was to throw yourself face down into the sand and lie very still, but Chrias's soldiers scurried together into tight circles of fighting men, blades drawn. The kwen had four soldiers close around him.

'The Way!' he shouted, whatever that was, and the clusters of soldiers all started moving at once, racing for the pavilion at the heart of the camp.

The Elemental Men vanished. One appeared out of the sand in front of Chrias and stabbed up. A soldier screamed and sank in a spray of blood. By then the Elemental Man had already flickered over the top of them. His bladeless knife flashed down. He vanished as a second man fell with blood pouring out of his mouth, appeared behind a third and ran him through from behind. Chrias and his last bodyguard ran, not that running would save them.

Kalaiya was suddenly on her feet. 'Stay down!' Tsen screamed at her, but she ignored him. She picked up a sword from one of the dead soldiers and ran to his side.

The killer appeared again in front of Chrias and the fourth soldier, knife outstretched. The soldier ran straight into the bladeless knife. It passed through his armour without a pause and sliced his heart in two. The kwen's hand flicked sideways, quick as a striking snake. The Elemental Man vanished and appeared crouched at his side. His bladeless knife flashed at Chrias's ankle and the kwen was suddenly missing a foot. Chrias screamed and went down. The Elemental Man rose slowly, stumbled, then sank to his knees and toppled into the sand.

Kalaiya sawed through the ropes around Tsen's wrists and feet. She gripped his arm, shaking like a leaf in a gale, eyes wide, quivering with fear. Her fingers were as rigid as an iron band. 'What do we do? What do we do?'

Tsen wished he knew. Lie down and stay very still and wait for it all to be over, that was what they *ought* to do. Trouble with that was what happened later, when the killers realised who he was and hanged him. First Sivan, then Chrias, now the killers. He had, he decided, enjoyed better days.

'We run,' he whispered, wondering if those were the most foolish words he'd ever say.

Diamond Eye powered into the sky, past the edge of the storm-dark and on. Higher and higher. The Elemental Man behind her was tense. The dragon felt his unease and so Zafir felt it too. She angled towards the eyrie to ease his mind, still climbing until they were a little above it, and then she dived, gently at first to build a little speed.

The great cliff, she murmured. *Do you remember it? Do you remember what we used to do?* The plunge, a mile straight down without a pause. There was a way to lie to keep the wind from slipping between rider and dragon and tearing them apart. Riders went there to learn. The ones who didn't get it right, sometimes they learned, sometimes they died, but everyone went one way or the other sooner or later because when it came to a fight gone wrong then down and fast was the only way to live.

Diamond Eye tucked in his wings, twitched his tail and dived, a sudden plunge straight past the eyrie and on at the waiting storm-dark, ever faster until she felt the wind tearing at every part of her. She leaned forward as far as she could, turning her head and pressing her visor against Diamond Eye's scales. If the killer behind tried to stab her now, the hurricane would rip his arm out of its socket. Through the dragon she felt the Elemental Man's fear. It drove her on, faster and faster until she didn't dare even move a finger.

Break him. She couldn't speak. *Until the wind rips him apart.*

The killer tried to turn into air but he couldn't, not so close to a dragon. He moved at last, reaching in despair for the harness she'd tied so tightly, and that little twitch was enough. The wind caught him, ripped him up and flipped him back and snapped his neck and his spine both at once. Diamond Eye felt him go. The dragon spread his wings, arced and spiralled and slowed their fall and settled into a long gentle glide across the surface of the storm-dark. Zafir felt his glee. Maybe he felt hers too. She unstrapped herself and the dead Elemental Man, slowly and carefully lest she lose her balance, then pushed him until his body fell, tumbling into the dark clouds of the maelstrom. She watched him go and then rose to stand on Diamond Eye's back and spread her arms, braced against the rush of air, feeling it push against her. She took off her helm and closed her eyes and let the wind tug her hair and scour her face. She howled. In her mind she stepped into the void and fell beside the killer down into the clouds and whatever end waited there. Fell and fell into a place where even her ancestors would never find her. She tried to see a reason to do it, or a reason not to, or anything that would make a difference one way or the other. All she saw was the Adamantine Man, wagging his finger.

He was a slave now. Ten years, give or take, for the gift he'd given her.

When she opened her eyes, she eased herself down and strapped herself into the harness once more.

49

The Easy Way

Deep beneath the maelstrom the darkness was close to absolute. The Godspike was far behind, very gently aglow, a faint haze in the distance. On the horizon ahead, out over the desert where the storm-dark ended, Tuuran could see stars. Crazy Mad urged his humpbacked horse into a gallop and Tuuran followed as best he could. Apparently it didn't bother Crazy that he couldn't see his hand in front of his face. Apparently it didn't bother his linxia either.

'Come on, big man!' Crazy looked back over his shoulder, his eyes shining with silver moonlight. Fine – so maybe Crazy *could* see his hand in front of his face.

'It's not so easy for us mortals, you know!'

At the far edge of the storm-dark, Flame knew how many hours later, Crazy stopped. Tuuran let out a good long sigh, slumped sideways in his saddle and let himself fall to the sand. There were stars again here, at least in the part of the sky that wasn't blotted out by the storm-dark's purple gloom, and he could see where he was going again. On the whole he liked that better than careering through the pitch-black on the heels of a madman.

'It's up there,' Crazy said. Tuuran had no idea how anyone could know, but Crazy's eyes were still bright burning silver, and this was the Crazy Mad who now and then turned people into ash, and Tuuran thought he sometimes did that for no particular reason other than that they were there, and so he was happy to take Crazy's word for it. But then, as he watched, a star winked out and winked back again, high above, and then another, and he knew that Crazy was right and he'd seen a dragon.

Crazy turned his linxia around and went pelting off almost back the way they'd come.

'Where the bloody Xibaiya …?' Tuuran scrambled back onto

his mount and shouted, but now they were going full tilt again, and Crazy Mad couldn't hear him, and apparently it didn't bother him that they'd been out here all bloody night with not a moment to rest. On the bright side, Tuuran's legs had stopped complaining about all the climbing, if only so his back could gripe about the riding instead.

Miles and miles and miles more passed under the storm-dark until Crazy suddenly stopped and pointed: up in the sky beneath the cloud a bright star was coming down. A glasship. Crazy's eyes faded to a glimmer and he set off after it, which seemed pointless to Tuuran, a glasship being what it was, and so he felt a bit stupid when the glasship mocked him by coming right on down to the ground and stopped with its gondola an inch above the sand.

Crazy pulled up a good way short, watching, and now Tuuran could hear the distant rumble of other riders not far away and then shouts coming closer. He couldn't see much except the glow of the glasship until a haze of figures arrived around it, lit up by the glare of its spinning heart. Must have been pushing a hundred men and half a dozen wagons with them.

After a bit the riders and their wagons went away, splitting off in four separate directions like they were in a real hurry or there was a devil after them, but none of that seemed to bother Crazy. He eased closer to the glasship once the riders were gone, walking his linxia through the jumble of tracks until they reached the gondola. He dismounted and went inside and Tuuran followed. Crazy hardly seemed to notice the dead men lying in the sand outside, nor the live one in the gondola, sitting propped against the wall, gasping with a spear stuck through him. 'We can use this, right?' he asked. 'We can use this to get up there.'

Tuuran shrugged. 'Never saw how they worked.'

Crazy poked the man by the wall. 'You. You dying or living or what? How do you make this thing work?'

The man got slowly up off the floor. He kept twitching and writhing as though he had some sort of madness inside him. Tuuran moved to one side. The man had a big slash in the back of his robe as well as the spear in his gut. He was soaked with blood. Odd thing – the robe looked a lot like an alchemist's robe but the man inside was clearly Taiytakei.

Crazy Mad prodded him. 'Stop jiggling and answer!'

The madman spasmed and doubled over. He picked up a sword and rammed it into Crazy Mad's belly as he came up. Or at least he tried to. He might have done a good job of it too if Crazy hadn't been who he was, wriggly as an eel, but Crazy saw it coming, dodged sideways and caught the madman's arm. His eyes flared brilliant silver. The sword turned to black ash and the madman gasped and gaped, pretty much like Tuuran did inside each time he saw it happen. The madman stumbled back, tripped and scrabbled back to the wall of the gondola. Tuuran winced, imagining how much it must hurt, all that banging about with a spear stuck through the middle of you. Amazing the man wasn't already dead.

When he couldn't scrabble any further, the man with the spear through him closed his eyes. He started mumbling something to himself over and over. Tuuran didn't much like the sound of the mumbles but Crazy didn't seem to mind. The words meant something. Tuuran backed away, but Crazy went and crouched beside the madman and lifted his face.

'You know me then? Who am I?' asked Crazy.

'Black Moon,' whispered the madman. He was weeping tears of blood. Tuuran edged to the gondola's ramp and checked outside, making sure he had a good clear open space in case he suddenly had to run like buggery. Crazy put his other hand to the madman's brow. The silver in his eyes, bright as lamps, lit up the gondola, but the madman didn't look away.

'You'd best tell me everything, earth-touched.' Crazy's voice was gentle and hard all at once. Kind and yet irresistible. The madman whimpered. For a long time he didn't say anything and the two of them stayed as they were, Crazy with one hand on the madman's brow and the other lifting his chin, the madman looking into Crazy's eyes like he was having his soul sucked right out of him. Then, very slowly, Crazy let go. 'Loyalty is a touching thing,' he said softly. Tuuran took another step back. 'Clever thought, using a dragon's soul. Clever of you to know what they really are. But it won't work without the dead goddess. It took both of us, and she's not there any more. Where did she go, earth-touched?'

No answer. Crazy shook his head. And then he chuckled, a nasty little sound that set the hairs on the back of Tuuran's neck scrambling down his spine looking for a way out. The light faded from Crazy's eyes. He stood up and sounded like his old self again. Berren the Crowntaker, or Skyrie, or the Bloody Judge, or whatever he chose to call himself that particular day. 'You have a debt, skin-shifter,' he said. 'Pay it and then be gone.'

The madman looked as though he hadn't the first idea what Crazy was talking about, and then something flashed in his eyes and he nodded. Crazy went outside and hauled in a pair of corpses. The madman crawled over and put his hands on them. Their skin started to move and writhe as though filled with maggots. Tuuran's eyes bulged. He gagged and took another step back but he couldn't stop himself from staring. The faces of the dead men were changing; worse, they were changing into faces he knew – the eyrie's t'varr and his slave woman. Months had passed since he'd last seen them but he still remembered.

'Good,' said Crazy and caught the madman's arm. 'Now be done.'

There wasn't any ceremony to it. Nothing more than that simple sentence and then the madman dissolved into black ash before Tuuran's eyes. Tuuran let out a howl and ran. Then stopped. Took long deep breaths. *Adamantine Man. Not afraid of anything. No fear at all. Made to kill dragons. But Flame, holy Flame …!*

Crazy caught his arm. Tuuran whirled and reached for his axe, not that it was going to do him a blind bit of good, but the silver light was gone now. Crazy was just Crazy again, whatever that meant. He looked at Tuuran. 'What's up, big man?'

'What's up? What's *up*? Shit, Crazy, you just turned a man into dust. Or ash. Or some other crap I don't understand. Like you did in Dhar Thosis. Like you did to those slavers. Like you did to who the Flame knows else!'

Crazy shrugged as though it was barely worth a mention. 'Well, now I know we can't get up there with this. But I also know another way. Things to be done, big man. Things to be done.'

He turned away, mounted up and rode hard off into the desert, and Tuuran watched him go and swore a lot and clenched his fists, and then, when he really couldn't think of anything else to do, rode after him; and after a bit, the sun came up and they reached a camp in the desert where all hell was breaking loose.

*

Soldiers ran screaming in all directions. A few had the sense to throw themselves down. Those were the ones who lived. Briefly. Tsen wasn't sure how many Elemental Men were here now, but at least two. They appeared, killed and vanished again, flickering in and out, there and gone as fast as a bolt of lightning. They ripped two fighting circles to shreds so fast that the last soldier died while the first was still falling to the sand. Those who saw didn't wait for it to happen to them too. Tsen wondered what made them think they could get away from the killers, but since he was running too then maybe it was best not to ask because maybe that made him every bit as stupid as they were. Missing foot or not, even Chrias was doing his best, limping and falling and crawling and hopping. He was heading for the same place as Tsen and Kalaiya – the pavilion with the cave where the dragon egg had gone.

A killer appeared behind and above the kwen and landed on his back, knocking him down. Tsen threw himself to the ground. Chrias roared. The Elemental Man wrenched the kwen's helm off his head and brought the pommel of his bladeless knife down hard. He vanished again. Chrias twitched, lifted his head, dropped it, lifted it again, clawed his way another couple of paces across the sand and then fell still. Kalaiya pulled Tsen up again and they kept running. He wasn't sure why the pavilion and the cave. Maybe it was a place to hide but inside, Tsen was already laughing at himself. *Hide? From a killer? Next stupid thought?*

Zafir wheeled Diamond Eye over the storm-dark. She'd killed an Elemental Man where no one would know but it was only one. She didn't know how many there were. Dozens. For all she knew there were thousands. No matter. From now on, as the chances came, she would take them one by one.

She turned back over the maelstrom. Diamond Eye whipped the fringes of its darkness with the wind from his wings. She aimed him for the nearest place where there were men and dived over the lip of the storm, thinking she might burn them, all of them, whoever they were, and lay out her challenge to the killers that remained: *Take me if you can.*

Khalishtor. The Crown of the Sea Lords in Khalishtor, their

great palace of government with its shimmering glass jewel floating high overhead and filled with navigators – she'd seen it and
dreamed of smashing it down, of Diamond Eye rending it to splinters with tooth and claw and tail, shattering the thirteen towers of
the Crown and smashing the glass bridges they called the Paths of
Words. Khalishtor ...

There was already a fight sprawling across the ground. There
were killers. How long before they came looking for her? How
long before someone had enough of her and made the circlet on
her head constrict and crush her skull.

But doll-woman's not here ...

Perhaps Khalishtor was too far. Vespinarr then. Closer. Burn the
richest city in all the worlds to cinders. She pulled away, skimmed
over the heads of the men fighting in the sand and veered west
but Diamond Eye circled back. Just the once but he did it on his
own, as though searching for something. Zafir let herself sink into
him and found a whiff of a taste that he wanted, that he wanted
enough to forget her for a moment, and when she let herself drift
deep inside him, she understood the scent was the one he'd found
in Dhar Thosis. The short man who'd been with Tuuran. The one
who called himself Crowntaker.

She shivered. The Adamantine Man was here?

Tuuran frowned. He had his axe at the ready for the soldiers scattering out of the camp but he was beginning to see he wouldn't
need it. The Taiytakei were scared as rabbits and didn't give a shit
about him and Crazy, or anyone at all except themselves and getting away as fast as they possibly could. Seemed odd to be riding
into the middle of them, but that was Crazy for you. It took until
they were a little closer to see *why* the soldiers were running and
screaming. Other men – Tuuran couldn't count how many because
they moved so quickly – were moving between them, appearing
out of the air to cut someone down and then vanishing again. Well,
he'd seen a man like that before. The Watcher had been one, and
the Watcher had carried him when he'd been dying from an assassin's knife in Zinzarra. All in all the Watcher hadn't seemed so
bad, but Tuuran had seen what he could do too. You didn't piss off
an Elemental Man, not unless you were mad or really dim.

He eyed Crazy and slowed, waiting to see what he was going to do, because this he had to see – Crazy with his eyes turning people into ash and a gang of killers who could appear and vanish at will. Interesting one to watch, that, but preferably from a good safe distance. But Crazy simply rode up to the edge of the melee and threw his swords into the sand, climbed off the back of his linxia and calmly lay down with his hands spread wide. He looked back at Tuuran. 'Come on, big man. This is how we get up there!'

A Taiytakei soldier in armour howled past Tuuran, face twisted and stricken with fear. An Elemental Man appeared in front of him, sliced his head clean off without moving anything except his arm and then stepped aside to let the body fall. He lingered long enough to catch Tuuran's eye and then disappeared. Tuuran got the message, dropped his axe, lay down and kept half an eye on Crazy in case he suddenly got up and kicked off again, but he didn't.

Off in the centre of the camp he could have sworn he caught a glimpse of the fat old Taiytakei t'varr Tsen from the eyrie, and then a dragon flew overhead and he couldn't see shit for all the sand in the air.

The dragon flashed overhead and Tsen couldn't help but look at it, so massive and so close with its wings and its neck and its tail out-stretched. Vast. Overwhelmingly huge. And he was still paralysed when the wind that came behind picked up the pavilion, tossed it into the air and threw it away, picked Kalaiya and even Tsen himself off their feet and threw them bouncing and rolling across the sand. He heard Kalaiya yelp as she landed on him, but before he could blink, the air filled with sand.

Tsen stumbled to his feet. He could hardly see a thing but he knew the pavilion had been right in front of him, and behind it, in a cleft between two rocks, was the cave. Or maybe it wasn't a cave; maybe the rocks were the old walls of some long-ruined tower and it was an entrance, but it didn't matter, it really didn't – a way out was a way out. He dragged Kalaiya, coughing and spluttering and never mind the Elemental Men – now was the time to run when none of them could find their own feet, none of them could see, these few seconds before the air cleared – and sprinted faster than he ever thought he could. The cleft loomed out of the haze. They ran inside and a gloom fell over them. The passage sloped slightly down. When his eyes adjusted to the dark, he saw a soft glow ahead from the rim of a shaft, lit from the bottom.

'Tsen!' Kalaiya was looking back. It took him a moment to re-alise what she was showing him: recessed into the stone either side of the entrance were two huge bronze doors. They were clearly ancient but at the same time pristine and shiny. He tugged at one to see what would happen and of course it wouldn't move, exactly as he'd known it wouldn't, except that when Kalaiya tugged too, it suddenly did, and once they got it going it swung easily as though the hinges had been oiled that very morning, and then it occurred to him that maybe they had, because maybe this had always been the skin-shifter's way out, because glassships didn't travel fast, and he was hardly going to get very far drifting out over the desert in full view of every Elemental Man who happened to pass by.

The other eggs. He'd said he only needed one really but more would be useful. They were decoys. Distractions ...

The second door closed as easily as the first. It had a huge bronze bar across the back. Together, he and Kalaiya swung it in place. The strike of it rang like a bell as it slid home and locked the doors fast. For a moment he stood and looked into the blackness, won-dering how he'd managed to get away and which of the gods he wasn't supposed to believe in was favouring him right now. Had to be one of them, though knowing the luck he'd had of late it was only so he could find the dragon egg in time for it hatch and eat him.

The shaft with the light at the bottom was bigger than he'd realised, big enough for the sled with the egg to descend through it – that or the sled had vanished into thin air – and was lined with the same white stone as the passages inside his eyrie. Someone had built crude wooden steps held up by rickety scaffolding spiralling around the inner circumference.

Kalaiya took his hand. 'Tsen ...'

'I know,' he whispered, and squeezed. 'I know. If Sivan was coming this way then perhaps he has someone waiting to meet him.' He glanced at the doors. 'But I can't go back, not out there.' He stopped to take a long look at her. 'You can, though. They're not looking for you.' But back to what if Sivan's plan had worked and the eyrie was gone? 'Perhaps you'd be safe?' Couldn't see how, though.

Kalaiya shook her head. Tsen took a deep breath and they started down.

There were fifteen of the Taiytakei left by the end, and they were all as terrified as small children. Tuuran reckoned he'd counted nearly a hundred dead too stupid or full of their own luck to throw themselves on the mercy of the Elemental Men. He wondered how many had got away and decided it was probably none. The survivors were rounded up and kept out in the desert sun for half the morning, sweating fit to drop, until a glasship picked them up and carried them away. It was the same glasship he and Crazy had found in the night, left under the storm-dark, with greasy black ash all over the walls. Tuuran kept away from that. He'd looked about for the fat old eyrie master but hadn't seen him, so Tsen had got out some other way. That or he'd been caught in the fight, but Tuuran reckoned Tsen to be a smart one, too smart not to know when to give up.

Another thing that struck him was the man in the fancy armour who was missing a foot and probably wasn't going to last all that long. The other Taiytakei were making a big fuss of him and seemed very keen to make sure that however long he lasted, they could at least get him up to the eyrie. It wasn't odd that he only had one foot – more luck than anything that, under the circumstances – and it wasn't odd that the Elemental Men treated him so well, not with all that flashy armour and those silks and the length of his braids. No, what was odd was that his skin was all hard and flaking. Take off that armour and he'd be a Scales. One with not long to go at that. He was bleeding a lot too. Tuuran kept well away. No one seemed to be bothered where all that tainted blood was ending up.

Crazy nudged him. 'Told you we'd do it the easy way,' he said and grinned. Time was, Tuuran had liked that grin because it meant trouble and mischief round the corner, and he'd had a soft spot for Crazy Mad's brand of trouble and mischief once, back when Crazy Mad's brand of trouble and mischief had meant bashing heads. Time was, but not any more. Now it meant turning people into ash.

'And then what? What's waiting for you when we get there?' But Crazy only shrugged. Didn't help that the bugger kept touching that golden knife of his. He held it out in the open but somehow the Elemental Men just didn't seem to see it.

The shaft went so far down into the desert that Tsen didn't much like the idea of climbing back up again. It was wide enough for a dragon, if one had wanted to squeeze down it, although that would have been a quick and thorough end to the steps and their uncertain scaffolding. Halfway down, when he could see the bottom more clearly, he called out, but no one answered. A thousand steps, maybe? Deeper than the shaft the skin-shifter had found out in the desert near the ruins of Uban, but he wasn't surprised when he got to the bottom and there were two more bronze doors like the ones he and Kalaiya had already closed behind them. They were open. Tsen stepped through into a tunnel – wide, reaching off in both directions, straight as an arrow and going on for as far as he could see, lined with white stone walls alight with their own soft starlight glow. Exactly like the one he'd seen with Sivan. Tsen discovered that he wasn't much surprised. If he'd had any doubts that Sivan had meant to come this way himself, the tunnel silenced them.

The sled with the dragon egg was in front of him. When he climbed onto it, he saw a black rod. He wasn't really expecting it to work but he tried it anyway. The sled shivered and lifted a few inches off the ground. He held out his hand to Kalaiya and tried to estimate how many times the steps had circled the shaft and which way the tunnel ran. East to west, he thought, and if he'd got it right then one way went off towards Uban and the other way headed east toward Dhar Thosis and the Queverra. Madness, it was all madness, everything he'd seen and been through these last few days. What did he want with a dragon egg? Nothing. What if it hatched? Well then it would eat them, wouldn't it? And there wouldn't be a thing he could do. Then why in Xibaiya take it?

But the egg was too heavy for him to move. And whichever way the tunnel went, they were hundreds of miles from the edge of the desert and they had no food and no water. They weren't going to just leave the sled and walk, not if they wanted to get anywhere alive. Tsen chuckled to himself and shook his head, took Kalaiya's hand and sat on the front, feet dangling over the edge. 'I have no idea where we are or what this is or where it leads, my love. For all I know this tunnel leads to nowhere and this egg will hatch and we will die.'

Kalaiya's eyes were bright with determination and wonder. 'I thought I was going to die so many times, Tsen. So many times in these last weeks. I've grown accustomed to it and it doesn't frighten me any more. I was a slave. A nothing to be played with for sport. No more, Baros Tsen. You are no longer t'varr to the sea lord of Xican and I am no longer a slave.'

Tsen took her hand and squeezed it tight. 'So be it. A desert man and his desert wife. That's probably the best we can hope for.'

'Isn't that enough?'

Tsen thought about that and then tapped the sled into motion. 'I'm not so sure about the desert. I'll miss my apple wine and I'll miss my baths. But it will do to start. You must tell me: what happened to my eyrie after the shifter took me?'

With a dragon egg behind them they drifted away. It would be a long journey with nothing much to see, but that was all right. They both had plenty to say.

Diamond Eye rose above the desert. The orange dawn light had long given way to the gold of early morning, the burnished copper of the sands turning electrum. A dozen men on linxia trotted across the dunes below, heading for the north. They had days of hard riding before they reached anything but desert. Zafir knew that because she and Diamond Eye had flown that way. They'd flown everywhere.

The riders scattered as she came, abandoning their sled with its egg. Zafir let them go. Diamond Eye swooped down and took the egg in his talons. He could be gentle if he wanted to be.

The Elemental Men hadn't come after her again. Were they losing their edge? Too much to do and too few of them? Stretched too thin? She knew perfectly what that looked like. She should keep going then. Fly on to the sea. Fly so they never found her and then set Diamond Eye free, but there wasn't really a way out for her and there never had been. Run away? Hide? Diamond Eye would wake up and she'd die. Abandon him and vanish among the Taiytakei, just another slave? The Statue Plague would get her and she'd die. And all if the gold-glass circlet she could never take off didn't crush her skull.

She rode the wind back to the eyrie, placed the egg back in the dragon yard for the Scales and went out for the next. As she did, she passed a glasship. She dived and circled its gondola, making sure that anyone inside had a good long look. A dragon and a dragon-queen. Rare things indeed and soon to be rarer still. The blinds on all the windows but one were closed. From inside Zafir saw a dark face looking back at her. The face was too far and too fleeting to recognise but the gondola was unfamiliar. Not the doll-woman. Today wasn't the day she'd be hanged.

She found the second egg out in the open desert to the east on another sled with another dozen riders. When the riders scattered, this time she let Diamond Eye chase them. He swooped and took a rider and his mount in his claws, bit them in two and ate them on the wing then arced to chase another, flipped him into the air and took his linxia between his teeth. A mist of blood flew back and spattered Zafir's visor. The linxia's rider fell to the sand, lost and forgotten, bones shattered, left for the vultures and the flies. The dragon took another and another that way, leaving the riders each time and eating their beasts. It played with them, lighting the sands with fire, leaving cherry-glowing glass, forcing riders to turn away and then turn again, boxing one in and making the box smaller and smaller until there was nowhere left to go and the rider simply stopped and waited for the end.

For no better reason than she felt like it, Zafir made Diamond Eye let that one go. The dragon snarled at her but sometimes a dragon had to remember who was in charge. She had him take the egg and fly home, turned and hunted down the third to the south, brought it quickly back and then returned and caught the scattered riders as they regrouped and burned them. She chased the stragglers. Diamond Eye tossed them into the air, caught the riders in his claws and their mounts between his teeth and crushed them.

The gondola had reached the eyrie by now and landed, and Zafir looked at all the dreams she'd had of tearing the Arbiter out of the sky, of setting the desert ablaze from end to end and found they'd lost their lustre. They seemed flat now, devoid of point and purpose. It didn't matter what she did. Lots of people would die or they wouldn't but in the end nothing would change.

I want to live. Not that she was afraid to die but she *did* want to live. That was why she kept looking over the edge and then backing away. Why she was still here.

I want to go home. Except if there was one thing the Taiytakei had shown her, it was that she'd never really had one.

Diamond Eye offered nothing. He didn't understand. How could he?

She went back to where Diamond Eye had sniffed out the trace of the Crowntaker, to where little camps lay scattered outside the shadow of the storm, the places where the tribes of the desert came to trade in goods and slaves, to hold their truces and their weddings and now and then betray. A horde of white-painted men was swarming across the sands, laying waste to everything. Diamond Eye raked across their minds, searching, but the Adamantine Man wasn't there. He was somewhere above them. The Crowntaker too. They'd come to her.

Zafir looked at the white-painted men, killing the Taiytakei. 'I could burn them all, every last one of them,' she offered, but no one answered, and so she went back to the eyrie and to her shelter and stripped away her armour and basked in the sun, waiting for her death or her salvation, whichever would find her first.

50

A Distant Sound of Thunder

The glasship rose from the abyss. Liang watched the scarred cliffs drift past her gaze until they gave way to the more jagged slopes of mountainsides and then to snowy peaks, and suddenly the sunbright glory of the Konsidar stretched out before her. When they were high above the mountain tops, the glasship turned to the east. Lin Feyn looked out of the window beside her, silent and pensive. They floated steadily towards the desert until the mountains fell away and in the far distance Liang saw the bright flat expanse of the arid badlands that led to the cliffs of the Tzwayg. They crossed that too, then the endless hours of the Empty Sands, until they reached the eyrie and the storm-dark. Killers came to them now and then with news. Shonda, Tsen, the eyrie falling, Zafir, the eggs, all of it. As they reached the eyrie at last, Red Lin Feyn dressed herself in her finery and guided the glasship down. She brought it to rest and then sat at her table, fingers steepled in front of her.

'I will no longer be the Arbiter after this, Chay-Liang,' she said. 'Do not trust the killers when I am gone. Do not trust any of them.' They went outside and moved between the glasships holding the eyrie aloft. Liang set each one loose and guided it back to its proper position. Lin Feyn touched the gold-glass blocks and secured the chains back where they belonged, sealing them with enchantments that not even Liang would ever break. One by one until all were back as they'd been before Tsen had set them free.

'You should think about where you wish to be, apprentice,' Lin Feyn said when they were finished. 'After this is done.'

The trial of Sea Lord Shonda of Vespinarr and Mai'Choiro Kwen, of Sea Lord Quai'Shu of Xican and Shrin Chrias and – in his absence – his t'varr was a quiet thing. Liang sat beside Red Lin Feyn. Six Elemental Men sat three to each side. A few dozen other Taiytakei quietly listened. Some men of Vespinarr, a few of

Xican, some of other cities. Most wrote a great many notes and two sword-slave scribes meticulously recorded every word spoken. Red Lin Feyn summoned them all and made them sit and then she summoned all those whose words were relevant, and nothing Liang heard came as any great surprise. When Belli came, Liang wished she could reach out to him or go to him but Lin Feyn wouldn't let her. He described the truth-smoke he made, something Liang had never known, and the Taiytakei hissed through their teeth at him and muttered to one another. There was no mention of the dead speaking – the Arbiter spared them all that at least, and so perhaps the Elemental Men would never know. Zafir stood before them all and told, as best Liang knew it, the truth, unvarnished and without shame. She was a slave. She'd done as she was commanded, nothing more, nothing less, and if what she'd done was wrong then perhaps the sea lords of the Taiytakei should look among themselves before they cast their stones. She showed no sorrow, no regret, no fear. Such things, she said, had no place in a dragon-rider's heart.

Bellepheros brought his truth-smoke and all the Taiytakei spoke again. Quietly and in private, the judgement of the Arbiter was given. The dragons to be poisoned and the eggs destroyed. One in ten of Shrin Chrias Kwen's men to be hanged and the dragon-rider too. Baros Tsen T'Varr, Shrin Chrias Kwen, Mai'Choiro Kwen, Sea Lords Shonda and Quai'Shu to be sent in chains to Khalishtor to have her verdict read out in the Crown of the Sea Lords before all the assembled lords of the thirteen cities. The fleet of Vespinarr to be stripped of a hundred ships to be given to the new sea lord of Dhar Thosis. All debts of Xican and Dhar Thosis to Vespinarr to be annulled. Stewardship of Xican and ownership of all properties of Sea Lord Quai'Shu to be assigned to Senxian's heirs. The House of Quai'Shu to be dissolved and struck from the Council of the Sea.

And so it went on in ever deeper detail, petty clauses and conditions that Liang barely understood. She listened to every word, heart in mouth, waiting until it was done, but nothing was said of shifters or the Queverra or the Konsidar or of any sorcery, nor of the alchemist Bellepheros until at the very end of it all when Red Lin Feyn spared her a pitying glance. 'Ownership of the alchemist slave Bellepheros and of the slaves known as the Scales to be transferred to the Dralamut.'

Red Lin Feyn lifted the headdress off her hair and rose. She left the headdress on her chair and walked slowly away, the Arbiter no more. The Elemental Men filed solemnly after her, walking for once instead of shifting into air. When they were gone, the other Taiytakei left. Liang hurried in Lin Feyn's wake.

'Lady!' She ran out into the dragon yard, following her. 'Lady!'

'I will leave by dusk, Liang. I have given judgement and I am no longer the Arbiter of the Dralamut. That burden may now pass to another. I mean to travel to the Queverra. Do you wish to join me, apprentice? You may if you so desire it.' She walked into her gondola and, when Liang followed, raised the ramp and shut the blinds and started to undress. 'It's done, Liang. My work is finished. I have listened and sought the truth and my judgement is passed. I have served my purpose. Did I do well?'

'Promise me!' Liang fell to her knees. 'Promise me you'll let him live until we return.'

'Who?' Then Lin Feyn shook her head and a half-smile flickered across her lips. 'Your alchemist? He's the property of the Dralamut now. And so are you and so he's yours. The killers won't touch him. You'll come back with me, both of you. After that …' She took Liang's hands in her own and lifted her to her feet. 'I'm not sure, Chay-Liang, that I can make promises now. The killers are no longer on my leash.'

'Then take him home, lady. Take him home! There's no reason to keep him here. You're a navigator.'

'As you will be, Liang.' She let go of Liang's hands and took the storm-dark globe and pushed it into them. 'Practise, Liang. You're close. Tell me, if I *did* send him home, would you stay in the dragon-lands with him?'

'I …' Liang looked up and down and to either side as if she might find an answer somewhere inside the gondola. She closed her eyes. 'I don't know, lady. He wishes to live among his own people and I wish to live among mine.'

'No gold-glass in the dragon-lands, Liang. What would you do?'

'Think what we could learn! Truth-smoke!'

Red Lin Feyn arched her brow. 'Bringing the dead back to speak, Liang?' She shook her head. 'Will you come with me?

There is a great deal for you to learn and it's pushing three days to the Queverra.'

'How long will you be, lady?' She already knew the answer. Too long.

'As long as needed to find the skin-shifter who did this, Liang.' Lin Feyn looked long and hard into Liang's eyes. 'But no.' She smiled. 'You love him, do you?'

'I ...' It was a question she tried not to think about. 'I hold him in very high regard, lady, and I have a great affection for him. Love? What is that? Would I die for him, do you mean?' She shrugged. 'Perhaps. For the beliefs he holds? Yes, because many are already my own. He is kind and generous and asks for little. He has great burdens and carries them lightly and will sacrifice himself for them if he has to, of that I have no doubt.'

Lin Feyn leaned forward and kissed Liang on the cheek. 'Then he sounds very much like an enchantress I have grown to like.'

'I know. Lady, I cannot ... The next days will be hard for him. He will lose everything. He will say we are right to do what we will do, but ... It will be hard, I think. He will need a friend. He will need someone to be his resolve.'

Lin Feyn nodded solemnly. 'He's not the only one, Chay-Liang.' Then she smiled. 'Go in peace, apprentice. I look forward to getting to know this alchemist when I return. Both of you.' She patted the globe in Liang's hands. 'And practise, apprentice. Practise!'

They embraced. Liang walked slowly away. As the ramp closed and the glasship lifted Red Lin Feyn away from the dragon yard, Liang smiled and waved and wished her well.

Better, she thought, to be here.

Zafir sat leaning against Diamond Eye's leg. No one told her how it had ended but when she watched the Arbiter fly away in her glasship, she knew it was over. She'd stood before them all, proud as a dragon-queen should be. She'd told them how she'd burned and smashed their city to the ground. She was a slave and had been told she must, and so she'd done as her master had instructed her without shame or regret, and all of that was true, but there was a bigger truth that lurked among her words, hard and ungilded. The willingness. The pride to have caused so much hurt to those who'd taken her from her home. It *was* the truth, and as she'd spoken it, she'd watched the faces around her and saw it bite. Too much? They only had themselves to blame. It was done now. She didn't know exactly who would hang and who wouldn't, only that a good few of their own deserved it a great deal and she'd cheer for every single one of them, even as she dangled from a gibbet of her own.

But for there to be any dangling, they had to take her, and Diamond Eye would know if anyone came close to hurt her, and so Diamond Eye would be the first. After that, the hatchlings and then the eggs, and somewhere in the middle of all that, her. And it would be the alchemist who was sworn to serve her, who'd taken an oath, *he* would do it. He'd kill her dragon and he'd do it because he wanted to, and so the next time he came out into the dragon yard, out into the open, he would die. No more potions, no more poison. The doll-woman would use the circlet and crush her, and Diamond Eye would awake. It made her laugh.

'When he comes, I want you to eat him.' She pictured Bellepheros walking to the wall to feed Diamond Eye his daily potion and the dragon snatching the alchemist in his jaws. But no, the alchemist was too clever for that. He'd be ready. 'No. Don't eat him. Throw him off the wall. Drop him into the storm-dark and then fly away as far and fast as you can. Fly to the sea. Fly to the water. Sink beneath it and wait until you awake.' She stroked the dragon's scales. Diamond Eye didn't understand.

The eyrie was full of bustle today. The doll-woman was gone. Other gondolas sat in the dragon yard, slaves hurrying to and fro, milling Taiytakei from a dozen different cities, all whipped up by a wind filled with shouted gossip of the Arbiter's judgement. On the far side of the yard, as far away from the hatchery as could be, a gang of slaves was building a wooden platform. Zafir watched them work and knew exactly what it was. A scaffold and gallows, just as Mai'Choiro had once ordered. Maybe, when they were nearly done, she'd climb onto Diamond Eye's back and smash it down. There didn't seem much point in waiting any longer.

The dragon was watching something too, out in the hustle and bustle. A sense stirred inside both of them at once, of something old and yet familiar. 'Is he here, old friend? The other one who fascinates you so?' She touched the dragon again and knew that he was. The man from Dhar Thosis. The Crowntaker, but the dragon knew him by a different name that made no sense. It couldn't quite remember but knew there was one there to be had, ancient and as powerful as the mountains and the sea ...

Days and days and the Adamantine Man hadn't come to her. She hadn't even seen him. But he too was here. Diamond Eye knew him.

She spotted Bellepheros coming into the dragon yard. He walked among the hatchlings, supervising the feeding, tipping potion from the bucket he carried over the slaughtered carcasses of the animals they ate. She could see the little dragons chafe at the food placed before them as though they were cattle. Where was the hunt? Where was the lunge of tooth and claw, the burn of fire? They were too dulled by the alchemist to understand what was wrong but they felt it nevertheless. They snapped at one another and shrieked and tugged their chains. They were angry today. Restless.

Glasships lifted off and gondolas drifted away. Zafir watched the alchemist work. She was dressed in her armour of glass and gold and dragon-scale, all of it repaired or replaced. The parts the enchantress Chay-Liang hadn't finished had been done by others – Shonda's enchanters, perhaps. No matter. She had Chay-Liang's helm and gauntlets waiting for when the time came. She wore the overlapping diamond-shaped scales of gold-glass, the same design she'd worn over Dhar Thosis. The greaves and the vambraces were cruder, artless pieces, but they'd keep the lightning at bay and that was all that mattered.

The slaves finished their scaffold and set to work on the gallows. They were only erecting one gibbet. One noose just for her. Zafir slipped back off the wall to her little shelter and drew out the bladeless knife she'd taken from the Elemental Man she'd dropped into the storm-dark. It felt heavy in her hand. If you looked hard and close, the blade shimmered sometimes when it caught the light, sparkled when the sun touched it just so. It wasn't bladeless at all, merely made of something so thin that it was all but invisible, yet so sharp and so hard that it would cut through glass and steel as though they were air.

She'd do it herself. In front of everyone, she'd kill her own alchemist.

The wind whipped across the wall, battering at her. It wouldn't make any difference. The Elemental Men would snuff her out quickly enough, but a dragon-queen shouldn't ever go meekly. She settled beside Diamond Eye again, using his bulk for shelter. The Taiytakei roundly cursed the ever-whipping gale by the Godspike, but to Zafir the wind was a friend. She liked it up here. The desert sun was hot and fierce, the air cold and fast, the contrast a delicious pleasure. Strong and pure and full of the energy of life.

The slaves finished their gallows and started on some wooden cages. Five of them. Bellepheros was still with the hatchlings, talking to the Scales, taking his time, dragging his heels perhaps, watching the last of the visiting gondolas fly away. The cages were quickly made, and as soon as they were, armoured soldiers dragged four chained men out into the sunlight. The cages were thrown open, the men hurled inside. Two of them almost had to be carried. Zafir tried to see who they were but they were too far away. She thought she knew, and Diamond Eye certainly did. Sea Lord Shonda. Sea Lord Quai'Shu. Mai'Choiro Kwen. He knew their thoughts and tasted their fear. He didn't know the fourth. *And the last cage is for me.*

She looked around the eyrie and put her mind to the battle to come, made herself note the lightning throwers that hadn't been destroyed, tried to make herself look up to the glasships that still flew overhead, to show Diamond Eye where each danger lay. Tried, but she knew the answers already. Instead she found herself looking at the knife again. Maybe it was better not to fight at all. The Taiytakei deserved what Diamond Eye would bring them but what point was there if she wasn't there to see it? In the end what difference did it make? In the end they'd always win. Flames and death all around, but her heart wasn't really in it. Even if she couldn't quite admit it, she knew that must be true because she was still standing on this wall and thinking and not sitting on Diamond Eye's back, screaming rage and fire.

Waiting for the Adamantine Man. That was it. Because he was here, and he would find her before she died.

She ran her finger along the flat of the blade, finding the tip. Tried hard to see it. Flexed her hand, felt its weight, looking for the flash of light where it caught the sun. It would be easy to drive it

through her own heart. She had a strong heart, she thought. Made
so by the dragons around her. It had needed to be strong to survive.
She'd been stabbed through it enough times, but none of them had
ever quite finished her. She could do it better. Do a proper job of
it. For some reason that made her laugh even if her eyes brimmed
and a tear trickled down her cheek. Betrayal everywhere, but she
survived.

No mercy for pretty Zafir.

She turned the knife carefully back, tipping its lethal point
away. The alchemist was leaving the hatchery, heading for the
tunnels behind. He'd come soon now. He'd put out his potions for
Diamond Eye to drink and she'd tell the dragon to wait. He'd come
to the wall and she'd take him to the rim and they'd talk, and then
she'd tell him she was sorry and kill him quietly and put on the last
of her armour, her golden helm and her gold-glass gauntlets, and
climb onto Diamond Eye's back and ... and they'd fly away? Just
that?

Her eyes ranged over the dragon yard, looking for Tuuran,
waiting for him to come to her, hoping he would before the alchemist made it all too late, and yet when he came up the steps
and crossed the wall towards her, big and with the sun across his
face and his hair all lank and straggly and his chin covered in a
month of beard, she didn't recognise him. Filled by an odd sense of
familiarity she watched this stranger come, until he stopped twelve
paces away, exactly as close as an Adamantine Man was allowed to
approach the speaker of the nine realms, and dropped to his knees
and pressed his head to the stone of the wall top. And then she
knew.

'Holiness. You told me to find my way back to you, Holiness.
Here I am. I have passed your test.'

And her heart was full of fire again.

Bellepheros had stayed in his laboratory after the trial, making
poison for the dragons. It wouldn't take long, surely. And then
Li had walked in. She'd sat with him, and she wouldn't say what
the Arbiter's judgement had been but nor did she need to. They'd
come and tell him to kill the dragon. Her Holiness would die. He
and Li would live. He could read it all in the set of her face and

there wasn't anything to be done about it, and so he asked Li to leave him be and quietly made a second poison to give to Zafir if she asked for it again. He couldn't save her and wasn't sure that he should, but he could give her that much. A quiet death of her own. Private and without spectacle.

The Elemental Man came early the next morning. He knocked on the iron door through which he couldn't pass, and when Bellepheros opened it, he walked politely inside instead of vanishing and appearing somewhere else. 'The judgement of the Arbiter has been given, alchemist.' They'd quietly stopped calling him slave since the truth-smoke.

Bellepheros gestured to the tables against the far wall, what he'd been able to repair of his laboratory. 'I told Sea Lord Quai'Shu, when he first brought me to his palace, that he would regret what he asked me to do. It ends then, does it?'

The killer bowed. 'They are all to be destroyed. You can do this?'

'I've been making this poison ever since I came here. I'm glad there's one among you whose wisdom exceeds his greed at last. There's still a missing egg. I trust you haven't forgotten.'

'It will be found.'

'And if it hatches?'

'It *will* be found.'

Well, that was surely true enough. They'd suffer for it but an egg was only an egg. No matter how big the dragon got before they stopped it, a single dragon couldn't mate with itself and hatch more, and so, one way or the other, the plague would end.

When he was ready, he made his rounds, delayed by all the busy fuss in the dragon yard as the Taiytakei who'd come to witness the trial bustled away, their gondolas and glasships cluttering the sky. He dawdled, talking to the Scales about things that didn't matter, but there was no ignoring it for ever. He had the poisons ready.

He was about to go when he saw the strangest thing. A man stood in the entrance to the tunnels behind the hatchery, short for a slave, his once-pale skin tanned brown by years in the open sun but not night-black like the Taiytakei. The man carried a naked knife, a strange-looking thing with a golden handle and a blade more like a cleaver in which patterns swirled like smoke in moonlight.

He wasn't Taiytakei but he wasn't dressed as a slave either, and his eyes ... There was light coming from them. For a moment they stared at each other. Then the man beckoned. Bellepheros wasn't sure why but it seemed important. He frowned and walked over.

'Who are you?' he asked.

The man looked up and Bellepheros gasped. His eyes were bright burning silver. 'Hello, brother,' he said, and drove the knife into Bellepheros's chest.

Three little cuts, Bellepheros heard a distant voice say. *You. Obey. Me.*

After Bellepheros went off to poison the dragon and put an end to it all at last, Chay-Liang surveyed her workshop. She'd asked to be with him and he'd refused, and it rankled because she knew he was quietly punishing her for being so pleased with herself. She picked up a few pieces of unshaped glass and moved them from one bench to another. She put away a few lengths of gold wire. She started to tidy up a pile of books and then spotted a glass beaker still half full of cold qaffeh, left forgotten on the floor beside one of her benches long enough to be growing mould. She looked around the workshop to make sure she was alone and then looked at the beaker, but no, she couldn't bring herself to drink it, not when it looked like that ...

The rider-slave was finally going to hang. It pleased her immensely and she wasn't hiding it very well and so Belli was punishing her.

Still, she wished he'd let her be with him for this.

Far beneath the earth and deeper still, across the divides between the world above and Xibaiya below, the dragon Silence circled the stuttering spirit of the Watcher, the Elemental Man once killed by the dragon Diamond Eye.

Earth-child. Silence spoke softly. The killer's spirit was fading, part consumed into the fabric of Xibaiya from which it had been made. Hiding in forlorn wait for the dead goddess.

Dragon. Its memories were broken and scarred and as thin as cloud in places, but they were there, jumbled in their jagged pieces. The dragon called Silence, as it reached for them, was gentle.

Tell me, the dragon whispered. *Tell me what it was you left un-done.* It showed the spirit a face: the Adamantine Man it had found in the desert. *What was he looking for? What did you want of him? Why?*

Flashes. Through the spirit's eye, the dragon saw three figures in silver and white. The moon sorcerers of the Diamond Isles, echoes of ghosts of half-gods who'd stayed behind when they should have known better. Faded ashes of themselves, yet they had once hurled Silence to Xibaiya with a single sorrowful thought.

They gave me a task. Words spoken. Or thoughts. *The grey dead come with the golden knife. They call the Black Moon to rise again.*

The Black Moon, chasing the sun across the sky, a little closer with every dawn until the Splintering had come and ripped the world apart and the Black Moon had shattered and its pieces had fallen across the earth ...

Silence wormed deeper. Other flashes. Memories. Little ones with white skin, with tattoos on their necks and faces and running down their sides. Strange words, old writing, sigils never seen except in places as old as time. The Azahl Pillar. The skin of a killer. The Adamantine Man had seen them in the living world where the men who mastered dragons lived, but not one of them knew those signs for what they were.

The grey dead have called the Black Moon to rise again. Do not let the splinters become whole, dragon. The spirit of the Watcher showed the future it saw. A terrible thing. Death and war and oblivion. The Black Moon reborn and rising from the southern sky to blot out the sun and smother the world in another age of ice and darkness. The dragon watched and wondered. It was a future that fed its hunger.

Why should I care? The glimpsed echo of the Black Moon that night in the desert, inside the little one whose eyes burned silver. Others existed in those thoughts. It had seen a different face that the little one claimed was his own and yet was not.

It will devour everything.

Silence turned from the stuttering spirit. The prison of the Nothing was broken. The splinters of the Black Moon were loose on the world.

You were once a half-god too.

The dragon Silence pondered the Watcher's words and cast its senses around for a new skin it might wear in the land of the living. It found one egg alone, separate from the rest, and tossed its soul through the veil of Xibaiya, leaping eagerly into the call of waiting flesh.

Red Lin Feyn sat in her gondola where the killers couldn't reach her, meditating and sleeping, thinking about the Queverra and what she might find there. She gave the killers most of the next day to clear the eyrie and do what needed to be done, and then she closed her eyes for a moment and with a thought set loose the enchantment to crush the dragon-rider's skull.

The Dragon-queen and the Unmade God

51

Blood and Dragons

'Holiness. Here I am. I have passed your test.' Zafir gazed at Tuuran. Out in the dragon yard, the alchemist was coming. The Adamantine Man's friend was beside him, guiding him, the one Diamond Eye hungered for, the one who called himself Crown-taker though he really didn't look like much. She'd ask him, maybe, whose crown he once took and who he'd stepped on to reach it and how he'd ended up as a slave. Maybe they could have a bitter laugh about that together.

The Adamantine Man stayed on his knees, head pressed to the stone. Zafir crouched in front of him and cupped his face between her hands and lifted him. Pulled him to his feet until he towered over her, yet she'd never felt so fierce. Her fingers dug into his skin.

'You are no longer a slave.'

He hung his head and wouldn't look at her until she forced him. The alchemist was dawdling ever closer, weary and slow, his old knees giving him grief again. Zafir's other hand dropped to her side and gripped the bladeless knife.

'You are not a slave.' She wasn't sure whether she was talking to herself or to the Adamantine Man.

'Holiness ...' Behind Tuuran the Crowntaker bounded past the alchemist and up the steps to the wall behind the Adamantine Man. Diamond Eye lowered his massive head to rub the stone, showing his submission.

'I waited for you. I should have come to find you.'

'Holiness ...'

The Crowntaker paused for a moment behind Tuuran. He looked at them both, Zafir then Tuuran then back again. He barely seemed to notice the dragon. Zafir had never seen anyone so unafraid. At the same time she felt a strange play of emotions from Diamond Eye, things she wasn't used to. Submission. Acceptance.

Resignation. Acquiescence. As though the dragon knew something was coming and was powerless. Helpless. Something was very wrong.

He was a threat. To her dragon.

The Crowntaker eased past them. Zafir let Tuuran go. A certainty surged through her, a certainty she'd been missing for far too long.

'I shouldn't have waited,' she said, and lashed out with the bladeless knife. The strike was good and the edge went through the Crowntaker's throat as though there was nothing there at all. Zafir stepped back, waiting for him to fall.

A tiny cloud of black dust swirled around his neck.

Her hand closed on empty air. She opened her fingers and looked at them. The bladeless knife was gone. All that was left was a fine film of sweat-streaked black ash across her palm like the greasy soot she'd found in the gondola under the storm-dark. The Crowntaker wasn't dead, wasn't bleeding, his head wasn't falling off his shoulders. He wasn't even looking at her, but his eyes burned pure bright silver ...

Silver! Zafir let out a little gasp and staggered back a step. Her legs almost failed her, empty of any strength. 'Isul Aieha!' The Silver King, and now she *was* going to die or something far far worse.

The Silver King had a knife in his hand now, a small cleaving thing with a golden handle. Patterns shimmered in its steel blade. He raised it and then stopped and looked at her. The fire in his eyes faded. He was a man again, ordinary and small, but Zafir knew she'd not forget what she'd seen, not ever. 'What did you call me?'

Diamond Eye. The dragon knew. That was why he behaved as he did.

The Silver King cocked his head. 'What did you call me?' he asked again.

Zafir pulled herself together as best she could. She was shaking. She couldn't remember the last time she'd been afraid, not truly and helplessly afraid like this. 'Isul Aieha,' she whispered. She forced herself to look at him. He had little wrinkles at the corners of his eyes, the first signs of age creeping up on him. His skin was weathered by the sun. He was darker than she was but not by much, not black like the Taiytakei. He had old scars on his hands and his skin there was hard and calloused. He held himself a little awkwardly, favouring one leg. His eyes, now they'd stopped being silver, were grey like the sea under a storm.

'You ride the dragon.' It wasn't a question. The knife turned towards her and she knew she should do something, kick out or try to get away, but she couldn't make herself move. Scared like a child, made helpless by a quiet voice full of pity and contempt at how pathetic she'd become. A dragon-queen, about to die, squealing inside like a little girl? Whimpering like a newborn? *You're better than that. We taught you better! We made you strong!* Her mother, contemptuous as ever. But the thrust didn't come. The little man froze. The bulk of the Adamantine Man loomed behind him and the big man had a sword too and now it was at the little man's neck. 'You don't touch her, Crazy. Not her.'

Zafir couldn't pull her eyes away. He didn't look like much – scrawny and tough in the way of any slave who spent their days hard at work and didn't get enough to eat. Yet he looked at her with eyes that had conquered worlds and didn't flinch at the Adamantine Man's sword against his skin. 'Why's that?' he asked, still looking at Zafir.

'Because I say. Does there have to be more reason?' For another few moments none of them moved. Then the Adamantine Man took a deep breath and slowly let it out and lifted his sword away. 'Because I'm asking, Crazy. That better?'

'She tried to cut off my head, big man. You have to concede that's … well …' He looked at Zafir, right though her, it seemed. She tasted the sweat dripping down her face, rolling into the corners of her mouth, mixing with the tears that had come before. Salty. It was hot in the lee of the dragon with the sun above, but it wasn't *that* hot. The armour. Must be. *That* was why she was sweating …

The Silver King. For a moment she'd seen the Silver King, the half-god who'd tamed the dragons, standing right in front of her. It was hard to look away, to stop searching for another glimpse of those burning silver eyes. She wondered if she was wrong. Some trick perhaps, but Diamond Eye knew better.

The Silver King didn't move, though he still had his knife pointed at her, still had Tuuran standing behind him. He was shorter than her. Not by much but it helped. Somehow that made him less dangerous. She reached out a hand to steady herself and touched Diamond Eye's scales. They were warm and rough under her fingers the way they always were. Reassuring. 'Isul Aieha,' she said again, because she knew she must be right. 'I am ... I mistook you for someone else.'

Abruptly the little man tucked the knife back into his belt. He took two quick steps closer to stand right in front of her and then reached out a hand to touch her face. The silver fire flared in his eyes again and his fingers against her skin were burning hot. She flinched. Pieces of her curled up into sobbing balls and others ran screaming in fear but she made herself stand firm, forced herself to face him eye to eye because that was what a dragon-queen learned to do, and if she could do it with a dragon then she could do it with a man, any man, however hard it was. She took his hand in her own and squeezed. She meant to pull it away but she didn't. She could feel him searching inside her for something.

'The Earthspear.' The word crawled between his teeth. She had other names for it but she had no doubt what he meant. The Adamantine Spear. The Speaker's Spear. He lowered his hand and the silver fire in his eyes burned ever brighter. 'You serve the Earthspear.'

Serve? The word cut through her fear and tapped the anger, the deep lake of it that was the bedrock of who she was. *Servant. Slave.* 'I am the dragon-queen Zafir,' she hissed at him. 'Speaker of the nine realms. Queen of the Adamantine Palace, carrier of the Silver King's spear ...' Her mouth stayed open but the words stopped. *The Silver King's spear.* For a moment again, all her anger wasn't enough to drown out the fear.

'Where is it?'

She had no idea. In the dragon-lands somewhere. Probably in the Adamantine Palace in the little cellar under the Speaker's Tower or the room far below the Glass Cathedral where Aruch had taken her the day she'd become speaker. Someone else must hold it now. Some other speaker, and with that thought, even as the silver fire in the little man's eyes held her transfixed, the tears began to well again. 'I will take it back,' she whispered, as if whispering might somehow make it true.

'You don't need to,' said the Silver King. 'It's yours. You gave it your blood. You're tied to it. It won't drink from another while you live.' He nodded sharply and took a step back. 'Side by side it shall be then. You may carry it once more and be my vassal and share in my dominion.' The silver flared brighter still then stuttered and vanished and the Crowntaker stood in front of her with his own eyes again, a bewildered frown on his face. He blinked a few times and then turned away, clutched at his hair and bared his teeth and let out a furious snarl. 'Leave me alone!'

Zafir took a step closer. She reached out a hand and touched his shoulder. There was a man in there too, struggling and afraid. 'Who are you?'

The Crowntaker jerked away. 'Not who you think.' He spun and looked up at the Adamantine Man. 'Not who *you* think. Either of you. I'm not your Silver King or your issle ayer, but whatever it is I carry, it remembers that name and not kindly!' He whipped back to Zafir. 'I'm done with this. I want myself back.' He bared his teeth and shouted, 'I want my face back!'

At the foot of the wall the alchemist was preparing a trough of bloody water for Diamond Eye to drink. Every morning the same – blood and water riddled with alchemy – and every morning Diamond Eye waited eagerly for it, but not today. Today he only had eyes for the Crowntaker. Zafir forced herself to look away from him. Past him at Tuuran. 'The alchemist. He's about to kill my dragon. Give me your blade. I must stop him.'

The Adamantine Man nodded and looked pleased with himself, then remembered he was supposed to bow. 'No need, Holiness. He won't be any trouble.' His eyes kept shifting to the Crowntaker.

'How so?'

'I think Crazy here is about to show you, Holiness.'

The Crowntaker lurched and threw back his head. He screamed as his eyes blazed silver again and he took his knife and stabbed it into Diamond Eye's neck.

52

Silver King

Diamond Eye felt the knife strike but Zafir had no sense of pain from the dragon. She lunged for the Crowntaker's arm but Tuuran caught her hand. 'No, Holiness.' Anger overwhelmed fear. She slapped him.

'You dare touch me, Adamantine Man?'

He fell to his knees and bowed his head. He said something she didn't hear. Thoughts and feelings washed over her, spilling from the dragon. They felt sharper. Sharper and sharper until they cut like knives and became memories. She didn't see them but she felt the shape of their presence as though a cloud had pulled back from covering the sun, or maybe as if they'd been flying high with nothing but a sea of white beneath them, and the dragon had plunged and punched through and out the other side, and now there was the land and the sea with all its contours and wrinkles and familiar places. Unfamiliar ones too.

The dragon was remembering. Understanding stabbed through her. She lunged again and seized the Crowntaker's arm to pull him away, too fast this time for Tuuran to stop her, but the moment she touched the Crowntaker she froze and couldn't move. Whatever he was doing to Diamond Eye, it sucked her in. She saw the ghostly shape of a second dragon, and within that dragon a web of silver strands as intricate and complex as the whole of history, woven together in impossible detail. She cried out and tried to pull away but instead moved helplessly deeper within the web to places where gossamer curtains hung. Everywhere she went, she cut those curtains down.

The Crowntaker was making Diamond Eye remember.

You want your alchemist gone? There will be no need for alchemists after I'm done.

Stop! She tried to draw her thoughts away but nothing worked. She was powerless.

Stop? Why? I will have them as I made them. All of them.
Who are you? Stop! Let me go!

As each curtain fell away, she glimpsed the memories that lay beneath. A thousand years, dozens upon dozens of lifetimes. Hundreds of years of servitude, dimly remembered. The great betrayal of the Isul Aieha, the silver half-god who carried the Earthspear – *her* spear, when she saw a flash of it. Before that, hunting and searching and eating. Glimpses of something lost and forgotten, growing stronger as the memories went back ever further. Searching for a purpose. Searching for their maker and for the enemies they were created to destroy. A world broken. Knowledge of that. A desire to change it but they couldn't. Anger. A place called Darkstone. Flying but never reaching it as the land shuddered and shifted and was rent apart, as an impossible wall of black cloud and lightning spread up to the sky with no end, too high for even a dragon to pass and the touch of which meant death for ever.

She reeled. She was seeing the Splintering.

And then before – the battles, the war, the towers of white stone and the rivers of steel-clad soldiers, lakes of fire, the earth torn open, the sky split apart. And back further – the very first awakening in a quiet place. A familiar presence. Its first sensations. The Crowntaker welcoming Diamond Eye into the world at his very first hatching, except the Crowntaker had borne a different name:

The Black Moon.

There. That part is done.

Rage seethed through the dragon, washing through Zafir. Rage and hunger and fury, an incandescence as it understood what had been done to it for lifetime after lifetime.

One more thing. Three little cuts that even the sun-child within me knows. You. Obey . . . The knife paused and then seemed to change its mind. *Her. My gift to you, spear carrier. Take me to it. Carry it at my side and we shall cross the world and I will be whole again and everything will be as it was before and this time there will be no mistake. We will heal this world and cast the old gods aside for ever. We will shape it to our vision.*

Who are you? Whole again? She didn't understand anything except that he'd woken Diamond Eye and made the dragon remember who and what it was and how terrified she was of that; and then she was back on the walls of the eyrie, wind howling and tearing at her, staggering away while the Crowntaker's eyes burned silver bright. He was whispering words in the dragon's ear, words she couldn't hear, but she understood them anyway because Diamond Eye understood, and everything the dragon knew so did she with crystal clarity. She clutched her head and gasped at the size of what was inside her.

'Go, dragon. Burn those here who would do us harm. Spare those who would serve.'

In her mind's eye she saw the who. The Elemental Men. The Taiytakei soldiers. Diamond Eye was awake. She felt the ferocity of his thoughts, the sifting of his returned memories, the outrage as he jumped from the wall and slammed into the dragon yard. The whole eyrie shook with his landing. He stamped on the trough of blood and water and potion, spattering Bellepheros with his own concoctions. Zafir heard Bellepheros cry out. She ran to the edge, expecting to see Diamond Eye crush him into bloody ooze, but the dragon passed him by, tail swishing back and forth with suppressed murder, and stalked across the yard straight at the Scales. The hatchlings, clustered around their food, tearing at the meat like vultures, stopped and backed away, huddled together, uncertain like cubs before a furious mother. The Scales looked up too, as dull and stupid as their dragons. Slaves hurrying across the yard on their errands paused to stare and then turned to run. Soldiers stopped their pacing and their gossip and touched their hands to the wands at their hips. It seemed that even the wind held its breath. For a moment there was stillness ...

Diamond Eye reared up and spat a torrent of fire. He swept it over the hatchlings, the Scales, the feeding troughs, the chains, the potion buckets, everything, on and on. Maybe the Scales screamed, but if they did then Zafir didn't hear over the roar of fire and the wind. The men around the scaffold and the cages bolted for the safety of the tunnels. The soldiers on the wall faltered. Some ran. Some turned on the dragon. Some turned on their comrades as though they'd been waiting for this all along. Zafir saw a flash and heard the first futile clap of lightning as the crystal order of the eyrie shattered into howling burning chaos.

Chay-Liang looked at the beaker with the mould growing inside. Still didn't know what to do with it. She collected the books scattered about on chairs and benches and even the floor and arranged them on her shelves.

The rest of the mess was all still there, resolutely not tidying itself. She started on her tools: tongs and blowers and pincers, the tiny hammers and the wickedly sharp little knives with enchanted glass blades that she used for the fine work of cutting gold. Once they were all back in their rack on the wall she swapped a few about and looked at them again and sighed. The thing she really ought to be getting on and dealing with was the wire. Seven different metals and alloys and probably the same number of different thicknesses of each, and there were bits of it scattered absolutely everywhere. The pig of it was putting each piece away in the right drawer.

A tremor shook the eyrie.

An Elemental Man appeared on the battlements. His bladeless knife pointed straight at Zafir. 'Make it stop or you die here and now.'

Could she? Diamond Eye's fury ran though her whether she wanted it or not, crushing every fear. Stop him? Even if she could, why would she? He had woken; and it dawned on her then that this was exactly what she'd wanted, only instead of sending Diamond Eye away to waken weeks after she was dead, now she could see it with her own eyes. Not for long, but she would see the terror unleashed.

She spat back at the killer, 'Instead of tomorrow when you decide to hang me?' And then she laughed and shook her head, carried off with a gleeful madness. 'Diamond Eye! This one wants to kill me. Will you let him?' Maybe Diamond Eye would hear and obey and move with a speed that even an Elemental Man couldn't match. Maybe not. It didn't matter any more.

The Elemental Man vanished. She felt the air pop behind her and the slight touch of something at the base of her spine before she could even start to respond. Then nothing and she was miraculously still alive. She turned. The Elemental Man stood frozen, his face a mask of rigid pain. The Crowntaker was behind him, eyes ablaze, one finger against the side of the killer's head. Zafir looked down. On the tip of the bladeless knife was a touch of blood. *Her* blood. Straight through the gold-glass of her armour as though it was air.

'Would you like him, spear carrier?' asked the Crowntaker. Zafir staggered back a step, trying to feel how deep the killer had cut her. She felt no pain, only a head full of dragon-rage. She shook herself, shook her head. 'No.' And the Crowntaker shrugged, and the killer jerked and burst into a cloud of black dust and smoke. The Crowntaker turned away and jumped over the wall after the dragon and its fire, into the terror and the lightning and the screaming men and women with no thought in their head but to run away.

'Holiness!' Tuuran took her hand and pulled her towards the steps. His eyes were wide. He ran, dragging her with him. 'You have to hide, Holiness. *We* have to hide!'

At the bottom of the steps she shook him off. *Hide?* 'Dragon!' she cried. 'Come to me, dragon!'

Diamond Eye turned. The burning stopped. There was nothing left of the hatchery but black shapes and the cluster of hatchlings pressed together, their wings raised to shield themselves. The Scales were stumps, not even things you could see had once been men. Screaming slaves in the dragon yard vanished into the tunnels, fighting with each other to get away, t'varrs and kwens and other Taiytakei with them, swallowed by mindless panic. The soldiers on the walls, the few with the courage or stupidity to hold their ground, were running for the lightning cannons. Diamond Eye took two huge steps and towered over Zafir, eyes ablaze and furious. Tuuran was still trying to pull her away. She slapped him. 'Are you mine, dragon?'

Resentment poured from him, a river in full flood that fed a fury of her own. His thoughts were as clear as polished sapphire. The alchemists of the Adamantine Palace had shown her a woken dragon on the day they'd made her speaker. She'd felt that dragon's thoughts like angry knives but never as clear as these.

I am.

'Then we do this as one. You will not hurt this one.' She jerked a thumb at Tuuran. Then, as an afterthought, at Bellepheros. 'Or him.'

And what then, little one? Such anger, piled on itself over and over for a dozen lifetimes. The dragon's tail slashed the air back and forth and then slammed straight at her, so fast and sudden that she hardly saw it. The spear-sharp tip lashed through an Elemental Man as he materialised beside her. His head and torso exploded in a shower of gore and splintered bone. The rest of him scattered in bloody pieces across the yard around her. Zafir launched herself at the legbreaker hanging from Diamond Eye's neck. The soldiers on the walls were turning the lightning cannon.

'Those,' she said. 'You remember those?' She climbed onto Diamond Eye's back. No helm. No gauntlets. No time for that.

I remember.

'Preserve them but kill those who man them!' She turned back to the Crowntaker and Tuuran and cried out to them, 'Side by side? Then this moment is mine! We will need men, Tuuran! Find those who will side with us against whatever this world will throw against us! Look to the slaves!' A madness filled her, the dragon's fury. This was always how it would end, in flames and ruin, and whether she lived another day or another hour or merely a minute, it no longer mattered a whit.

Diamond Eye picked up the mangled remains of the Elemental Man and launched it through the air. He surged forward, one mighty flap of his wings powering across the eyrie. The Crowntaker was among the hatchlings now, moving from one to the next, stabbing each with his knife, making them remember and setting them free.

'Who is he?' Zafir shouted. 'What is he? You know, don't you?'

Names come and names go and he has had many. He is not whole.

'But who is he?'

The Black Moon. Diamond Eye smashed into the eyrie wall beside one of the lightning cannon as its glass disc glowed bright. Cracks spread through the pure white stone. He reached inside the cannon's cradle. Two Taiytakei scrambled away, falling onto the wall. A spray of fire and they screamed and crisped. Pieces of glass-and-gold armour glowed cherry-red. Molten gold smeared and ran and the men inside flared and burned. Gusts of scorched air brushed Zafir's skin, mixing with the cold of the roaring wind. Diamond Eye was burning hot under her and everything was fire.

Chay-Liang paused a moment in her workshop, then went back to putting pieces of wire in a heap on a bench. Some pieces jumped out at her – that, for example, was obviously a length of half-finger gold and could be put away at once, and the copper was obvious enough too, except that when she started looking at it, the end was skewed by where pincers had cut it . . .

Two armoured soldiers burst through her door and crashed into the workshop, knocking over a stack of unfinished gold-glass. They looked terrified. One of them was a kwen.

'Enchantress, you are needed! The hatchlings are loose. The dragon has turned on us!' The soldiers ran back out and vanished into the tunnels. Liang stood open-mouthed. Surely, *surely* the killers had been ready for this?

Taiytakei soldiers ran out of the tunnels from the barracks. Diamond Eye's head whipped round. Fire scoured the top of the wall and then down the sides and into the yard, scattering them, sending them scurrying back. A thunderous crack of cannon lightning arced and struck Diamond Eye in the leg. Zafir felt its sting, felt him buckle as the leg turned limp. The dragon launched himself off the wall and poured fire around him. Waves of heat blew across her face. Smaller lightning bolts cracked into his side but the soldiers' wands were insect bites, nothing more. He landed again and ran along the wall, hosing fire down its length. Taiytakei howled and ran. They jumped into the dragon yard or tumbled down the shallow outer slope to the craggy edges of the rim to hide in the rubble and mounds of rubbish, and Zafir could only laugh because a dragon could pluck out your very thoughts, and only the alchemist had a remedy for *that*.

An Elemental Man appeared close to her, his face a rictus of strain. Diamond Eye bit him in two. Another appeared a dozen yards away. The dragon was already moving but this killer carried a wand and fired it at once. Zafir jerked as the lightning hit her and sparked across her gold-glass scales. Her eyes fluttered and then the feeling passed. The Elemental Man vanished. Diamond Eye crashed into the eyrie wall beside another lightning cannon but the soldiers manning it had already fled. Zafir saw Tuuran run up the far wall and jump into another to wrestle with the Taiytakei inside. The Crowntaker had moved away from the hatchlings. Another handful of soldiers ran out into the dragon yard, these with gold-glass shields as big as a man. The Crowntaker gestured and the hatchlings scattered, racing at them. Lightning thundered and flashed. Hatchlings fell and leaped up again, throwing themselves among the soldiers, shredding them with tooth and claw, shrieking with glee. Diamond Eye jumped off the wall. A moment later, something exploded where he'd been, and then his tail cracked like a whip overhead and a rag-doll flail of broken limbs arced away over the eyrie edge and on down to the maelstrom below.

On the walls, in the dragon yard, amid the mayhem, the Taiytakei were fighting among themselves. Why?

The Black Moon has turned them to his cause. Diamond Eye whipped around and spat a stream of fire into the air, incinerating an Elemental Man as he appeared overhead. *I hear their thoughts.* The dragon's own were tinged with a vicious glee. *I know where they will be.* In the middle of the dragon yard three killers appeared around the Crowntaker at once, one behind, one crouched in front, one upside down over his head, all three with their blades stretched to greet him. The next instant all three were gone, puffs of black smoke and dust torn to shreds by the howling wind. Diamond Eye wheeled in the air. He soared low over the walls, cleansing them, pouring flames. *I hear their thoughts.* A hatchling skittered down the entrance to the hatchery tunnels and disappeared into the bowels of the eyrie. *I hear them die.* Other hatchlings climbed the walls and dived over the sides. Their cries mingled with the desperate howls of men. The last Taiytakei too stupid or slow to have fled into the tunnels were cornered and torn limb from limb. The Crowntaker stood in the very centre of the yard now, watching it all, silver fire pouring from his eyes like burning moonlight.

'He bound you to me.'

Yes.

'And if I release you, what will you do, dragon?'

You cannot undo what he has done.

Liang snatched the box of fire globes she'd stolen from Tsen's rockets. There was the bomb she'd made before she'd left for the

Konsidar. She put that on a sled with a crate of unshaped glass. She could hear the soldiers outside, shouting at slaves to get out of the way, to stay in their rooms, to hide and barricade their doors. Liang hadn't the first idea how to kill, hurt, stop or even merely annoy the adult dragon, but wasn't that why there were lightning cannon on the walls? And the Elemental Men – surely, *surely*, it had crossed the mind of at least *someone* that Zafir was neither stupid nor likely to go meekly to the scaffold?

She ran out into the tunnels. A burst of screams echoed around the twist of the passageway. The walls lit up with a flare of orange light and a crack of lightning shook the air and then another. Another scream ...

A torrent of flames poured around the curve of the passage. It rushed at Liang with nowhere to go except on and through and past. She cringed, willed the gold-glass in her hand into a bubble and cowered inside it. Another crack of lightning rattled her ears and then an armoured soldier raced around the curve of the passage towards her, arms flailing, eyes bulging in terror. 'Dragon!' She caught his arm as he passed and tugged him off balance. He tripped over her sled and sprawled. She was already shaping the glass in her other hand into a wider shield.

'Hold your ground and give me your wand!'

She barely had time. The hatchling hurtled around the twist of the passage in pursuit, claws scratching and scraping and scrabbling on the stone. Liang fired lightning at its face and slammed it into the tunnel wall, a tangle of wings and claws. The soldier was back on his feet. Liang shifted her shield to engulf them both, grabbed his lightning wand and stuck it through the glass beside her own. The hatchling untangled itself and hissed. Liang let fly with both wands and the air rang with thunderbolts, echoes loud enough to rattle bones. She picked up the bomb and threw it. The thunder of the explosion slammed into her. Pieces of semi-molten wire flew like shot. One side of the shield shattered and Liang found herself on the floor. Something hot stung her face and a deep burning pain started in her calf. She scrambled to her feet. She couldn't see through one eye but the other was working well enough. The hatchling was crumpled. Half its face was shredded to the bone and one of its eyes was missing. It crawled and clawed its way a few feet towards her and then shuddered and stopped. Liang's leg buckled under her. A piece of glass like the blade of a knife was sticking out of her calf.

She wiped the blood off her face and wrestled the dazed soldier to his feet. 'Go! I'll make as many as I can. Send someone back to get them. And for the love of Charin, kill the dragon's rider. Find an Elemental Man and send him after the Arbiter and tell her that Chay-Liang said to please make her pretty little head explode.' As the soldier started off, Liang shouted after him, 'And make sure you destroy the eggs too!' Because it was quite enough to have to deal with a dragon once, even a little one, without having to deal with it all over again a few hours later.

Diamond Eye tipped his wings and circled the eyrie rim, rooting out the soldiers who'd sought shelter in the piles of rubbish. He flew slowly as though stalking them and then landed, and each time the eyrie shook under his weight. Whenever a Taiytakei broke cover, the dragon simply watched to see what his prey would do. The first fled in such panic that he ran right off the edge of the eyrie and plunged howling into the annihilation of the storm-dark. Others Diamond Eye lashed with his tail, batting them far into the air. Some he caught with tooth and claw and ripped apart, or held them down and burned them until their glass and gold melted into a smear on the stone.

A sled rose into the air across the eyrie and sped away. Then another and another and then more. The hatchlings shrieked and dived in furious pursuit. Diamond Eye leaped from the rim, curled and arced under the eyrie's black stone belly, weaving among the flickers and rivers of purple lightning. He came at the fleeing Taiytakei from beneath, overhauling the sleds one by one, plucking away their riders and throwing them into the sky, shattering glass with a swing of his tail or simply sending men tumbling through the air with the wash of his wings. His joy howled through Zafir's head, but this wasn't Dhar Thosis where it had engulfed her and become her own. She felt a coldness now that Diamond Eye was free. An awe and perhaps even a fear. A dread of what would follow. The dragon didn't need her any more.

'Stop!'

He turned, sullen and resentful, and landed in the dragon yard, simmering while the hatchlings cavorted in the air, tearing down the last of the fleeing sleds. Zafir slid from his back. She walked away through the carnage of fire and lightning and death. Tuuran and the Crowntaker lived. Oh, and when she peered, the alchemist was cringing in a corner, pressed up against the wall, and the poor bastards in their cages by the gallows seemed unhurt. Everything else was dead, lightning-charred, fire-scorched, ripped to shreds or all of that and more. Men torn limb from limb, scattered in pieces and then roasted.

The hatchlings wanted more. They crashed across the eyrie, talons scrabbling on the stone, tumbling in their eagerness, and raced for the tunnels with their heads full of blood and slaughter. They'd kill everyone, man, woman, slave, soldier, kwen, t'varr … A delicious coldness filled Zafir. They deserved it. All of them. Every Taiytakei, every slave, every man, every woman.

Dragon thoughts. She pushed them away. *Make them stop, dragon! We do not need this massacre.* She reached the passage which led to where the Scales had lived. There were hatchlings down there, two at least. She'd seen them go inside. She ran across the dragon yard to the tunnels where the slaves were quartered. *Tell them to stop.* She raced inside to the room that had been hers before she'd taken to living on the wall at Diamond Eye's side. She'd had a door at least, which was more than most slaves ever had, and by some miracle no one had kicked it in. She tried it but it wouldn't move. She hammered her fist against the iron. 'Myst! Onyx?' *Make. Them. Stop.*

No answer. She barged her shoulder against it and felt it give a little, as though held shut by someone then a voice came back: 'Mistress?'

'Let me in.' They were alive. The slaves who'd been hers since the Taiytakei had taken her from her home. The rush of relief took her by surprise – how strongly it shook her. She heard the scrape of wood on stone and the door opened. Myst and Onyx looked at her, wide-eyed at her scorched blood-streaked armour.

Alive. That was what mattered. Zafir squeezed past. And what she really wanted now was to strip off her armour and throw it aside and have them wash her clean, scrub her skin with cold water and soft oils, dress her in silks and lie beside her as she closed her eyes. Somewhere safe. That was all she'd ever really wanted. She whispered, though no one was listening, 'Make them stop.'

Distant screams echoed through the tunnels. Furious hatchling shrieks as Diamond Eye called them back. Zafir pulled her hand-maidens close.

'Stay here,' she whispered. 'And I will keep you safe.'

Liang lurched back to her workshop. She looked at her leg. Bloody and messy but she'd just have to make do. So Bellepheros had tried to poison the dragons and it hadn't worked, was that it? Or maybe it had and this was the result? Easy enough to have the rider-slave take the dragon out into the deep desert to do the killing, wasn't it? Why did they have to do it here? Oh yes, for the *show* of it. She ought to go up and see for herself but she could barely walk.

She rushed the first bomb. Bigger than the last but not as hard to carry. Bigger was probably better, wasn't it? Neatly ended her wire problems too – hardly mattered whether it was quarter-finger electrum or third-finger white gold when it was fizzing through the air like a ball from a cannon. She set to work on the next. She'd made seven and had run out of spare wire when she realised the eyrie had fallen quiet and that the soldier hadn't come back.

Her leg was killing her.

53

Old Wounds

The light of the white stone walls was bright and cold. It carried a touch of silver to it now and didn't seem to Zafir quite as she remembered it. More moonlight than sunlight, though the sky outside was still brilliant dazzling day. She wasn't sure how long she stood there holding Myst and Onyx. Not long. Couldn't have been. She turned back and opened the door again and there was Tuuran standing right outside. She walked past and then stopped and turned and looked him in the eye. He bowed and carefully looked away. Stupid old traditions had no place here but he was an Adamantine Man, drilled without mercy as to what was expected of him.

Eventually all wounds healed. They had to, didn't they?

'I'm sorry,' she said. It was a little thing that changed nothing and yet it was huge. She couldn't remember the last time she'd said that, not to anyone. *Sorry* had died in the Pinnacles.

Tuuran's bow grew deeper. Perhaps he didn't know what else to do.

'Look at me,' Zafir commanded. 'I said I'm sorry.'

Tuuran looked at her. 'A speaker does not apologise to an Adamantine Man,' he said gruffly. 'Not for anything, your Holiness. We serve. From birth to death, nothing more, nothing less. We are your most loyal servants.'

'But I was no speaker when I took your knife from your belt. I was merely a young princess who apparently inspired the wrong thoughts. I know you held your silence. I know my mother knew you were innocent. *I* knew you were innocent. I should have had you freed. Instead I had you sent away as a slave.'

Tuuran looked away. 'Had you not, I would have been hanged for my crime.'

'There was no crime.'

'But there was, Holiness. He was a prince. I spoke out of turn. It was my knife and I didn't stop you. That was enough.' He dropped to the floor and pressed his head to the stone. 'I have not forgotten, Holiness,' he said as he rose. 'I have never felt a shred of regret for what I did. I was content for my life to be forfeit and I have not forgotten that it was saved.'

Zafir couldn't breath. An unfamiliar lump choked her throat. This wasn't how it was supposed to be. *She* should be the one abasing herself. *He* was supposed to be angry with her, furious for his years of slavery. A little forgiveness. That was all she wanted. Gratitude? She couldn't begin to understand gratitude. How? 'Forgive me, Tuuran.'

'There is no forgiveness to be had, Holiness. None is required.'

Zafir clenched her fists. 'Forgive me anyway!' She screwed her eyes shut. Stupid! *That* way didn't mean anything. 'No. Never mind. I did not speak. Look after my slaves, Tuuran. They deserve a better mistress.' She fled from him outside into the brilliance of the afternoon sun, where the wind caught her and pulled her a step sideways. The wind invigorated her. It blew away the smell of burned men and charred skin. She felt the sun on her face.

A handful of slaves was at work around the charred remains of the scaffold, taking it down. The cages still stood beside them. By some miracle the men inside remained alive. Maybe they hoped for release. Maybe they were right to hope. She didn't know. Diamond Eye perched on the wall above them with the hatchlings beside him. She counted. Three were missing and she idly wondered where they were, whether they were still combing the tunnels or dead or had simply flown away. The eyrie felt oddly still. Paused, as if holding its breath for something.

Diamond Eye slowly turned to look at her. *Your thoughts will always be with me, little one.*

'Get out of my head!'

A handful of soldiers emerged from one of the tunnels with a pack of slaves in their wake. They began dragging the bodies in the dragon yard into neat lines and stripping them. The slaves worked while the soldiers looked on sombrely. Why weren't they terrified? They worked quietly, muted by their own survival perhaps, but not sullen or resentful or afraid. They didn't seem like prisoners.

She didn't understand what the Crowntaker had done. She didn't understand how or why or who he was or why she was alive. In a way it didn't matter. He was the Silver King, a half-god who did as he pleased.

She walked to the cages and looked up to the dragons. The hatchlings watched her with barely suppressed fury. She could see the intelligence in their eyes, the hunger. Awake and yet somehow bound to the Crowntaker, this Silver King. They whispered in the corners of her thoughts, free and full of eager joy tinged with the ever-present rage and the urge to burn.

She stopped before Diamond Eye, a dragon she'd known since the day he hatched. He'd been her favourite until Onyx had grown bigger and stronger but he was a stranger now. Vioros, her mother's alchemist, had once said that woken dragons felt none of the things you might expect of them, that they understood neither forgiveness nor revenge, neither spite nor mercy. They were simply dragons and did as they pleased.

Diamond Eye towered over her like a winged mountain.

'I release you,' she said, and forced herself to meet his eye. He'd eat her now. Or burn her, or flick her with his tail and fling her high out into the sky to fall into the storm-dark.

It is not your binding to unmake.

'Then I ask nothing of you. I will give you no commands. You are free from me.'

Diamond Eye looked at her for a long moment of silence.

Why?

Because now I understand what it is to be a slave.

You have always been a slave.

Tears blurred her eyes.

Do you think this frees you?

'No.' The doll-woman's circlet felt heavy across her brow but they both knew that wasn't want Diamond Eye meant. She'd feel that circlet there for ever, long after it was gone, if it ever was. She was slave to who she was.

'Why? Why do I matter to him at all?' Not to the Crowntaker but the thing he carried with him. The Silver King, the Black Moon.

Diamond Eye didn't answer but Zafir caught a fleeting idea of something sharp. The Adamantine Spear. The dragon should have hated her, as Tuuran should, but instead she was offered gratitude from one and indifference from the other; and if she had a purpose or a value left to her then neither had anything to do with who she was or how she thought or what she felt, only an ancient spear that sat far away in another world. The Adamantine Spear of the Silver King, claimed by her blood.

She turned her back on the dragons. The soldiers were helping the slaves with the bodies, all of them working together. The dead were now mostly in rows, stripped and with what survived of their belongings in tidy piles beside them. No one looked at her except the four men in their cages beside her: Mad Quai'Shu, who sat almost naked in his own filth; Mai'Choiro Kwen, who cowered in a corner as far away from her as he could get; Shonda of Vespinarr, formerly the mightiest man in the world, now held in a cage by the Elemental Men for everyone to see before he was hanged. She looked at Shonda. Stripped of all his power and his peacock robes and his rainbow silks and gold and silver threads, he was fat man in a shabby tunic, old and weak and crumpled; and yet as he met her eye, he straightened and puffed himself up, and there was still something about him. An aura of command, of a man accustomed to having the world at his fingertips.

'Rider-slave. I remember you.'

'Every time you look at the brand on your arm?' Zafir bared her teeth.

'The one on my back hurts more. You were a queen once. The queen of all queens in your own world.'

Zafir shook her head. 'And look at us now, Shonda of Vespinarr, look at us now.' She tapped the gold-glass around her head.

'I think you have the better of it.'

'For now. For how much longer I couldn't say.'

'Where did you get your sorcerer, dragon-queen?'

Zafir tried not to laugh at that. She waved a hand as if he was nothing. 'One of my Adamantine Guardsmen brought him. To be truthful, I haven't had time to ask.'

Shonda roared with bitter laugher. 'I curse your dragons, dragon-queen. Quai'Shu was a friend and they broke him. Vey Rin was my brother and they broke him as well.' He gave her a little bow. The irony made Zafir chuckle and shake her head.

The lord of Vespinarr shuffled closer and sat cross-legged as close to her as he could get. 'I did not get where I was, rider-slave, by kindness. Shall we bargain? A way across the storm-dark? No navigator will take you, not if they know who you are, but I can slip you aboard a ship so no one will ever know. It will be *your* ship, your crew ...'

A bark of laughter came from the next cage. The unknown fourth man. 'Save your words, Shonda of Vespinarr. You and I were better off when the Elemental Men merely meant to hang us.' And Zafir smiled because she recognised him now. Shrin Chrias Kwen, whose men had raped her and then put Dhar Thosis to the sword while she'd burned it from above. He was changed. He'd lost a foot and the Statue Plague was working its way through the rest of him. His face was swollen, his hair ragged, but his voice gave him away, and eyes, now that she looked, yes, his eyes too. She turned her back on the cages and rested her hands on her hips. Underneath, she and Chrias were alike. He hadn't had all his power simply given to him at every turn, he'd fought and bled and killed for it and worse. There were dark locked rooms in his past, she was quite sure of that, and they'd made him into a monster just as they'd made her into one too.

The slaves and the soldiers had almost finished stripping the bodies. The Crowntaker was with them now, taking pieces of Taiytakei armour and offering them about, though the slaves seemed reluctant to take them. Zafir looked deep inside to see if she could find any shred of pity for Shrin Chrias Kwen and what she'd done to him, but all she saw was Brightstar's blood pooling across the floor of her little cabin on Quai'Shu's ship the day they'd arrived in Xican, and then, much later, when he'd come to her with his men and told them to rape her, one after another. She turned her head to him. 'Should I just let you go, Chrias Kwen? I've nothing left for you. I'll not touch you, nor torture you, nor even notice your end. But I think you might stay in that cage a while so I can come out and see you and remember what you are. When you can give me a reason why my slave had to die, one that makes you more of a man and not less of one, I might ask my alchemist to ease your suffering.'

She turned away. Chrias spat at her back. 'You have the plague as well! You gave it to me, so you must. Guard your alchemist then, lest I reach from beyond the grave one day and take him from you and laugh as you follow me to hell! Everything I am, you will become!'

Zafir left the cages. She would be with her slaves again, she thought, and set them free as well; but before she could cross the dragon yard, the Crowntaker cut her off. His eyes no longer burned silver and he was simply a man. Wiry and skinny and shorter than she was but with a face that looked as though it had walked through Xibaiya and back again, chasing ghosts for fun. She stopped and let him stand in front of her. 'And you, Crowntaker? What do *you* want of me?' She looked at the golden knife on his belt, closed her eyes and shook her head. 'Shall I be your willing slave? You wouldn't be the first to try it.'

The Crowntaker flipped the knife out of its sheath and offered it to her, hilt first. 'A warlock stabbed me with this knife and made me his slave a while. A dozen years later I killed him with it. That day he cut me, he told me my future. "Dragons for one of you. Queens for both. An empress." Those were his words. Are you an empress?'

'I am a dragon-queen.'

'I saw myself confronted by a man with own face but many years older. I had a javelin in my hand. I raised it to throw and the man spoke. Half a lifetime later I met myself on the road. I had a javelin in my hand. I raised it to throw and the man with my face spoke the words I'd heard more than twenty years before. You and I are meant for something, Dragon-Queen Zafir.'

Zafir cocked her head. 'Men have wooed me in a lot of ways over the years but that one's new. You're the Silver King. You make the world as you want it. You've taken my dragons. If you don't mean to use your sorcery on me then I'll be away to my own realm, if I can. I would like to go home. I would like to find one. To have one. And it is not here.' She stepped around him and walked away.

'I don't know who I am, dragon-queen.'

'Then I'm the last person in the world you should ask for help,' she called over her shoulder. 'If you ever find the answer, tell me how you did it.'

Slaves and soldiers alike were gathered around the dead, men trying on armour, cracks of lightning as the wands from the fallen were tested. A steady trickle of men walked up to the walls and over them, each carrying a body. She didn't see what they did with them. Tipped them into the abyss below? But that was a waste when there there were hungry dragons to feed. She climbed up to an empty stretch of wall out in the teeth of the wind and looked across the storm-dark to the Godspike. She sat in her armour, filthy and sticky, flaking crumbs of cooked and crusted gore whenever she moved, and stared out over the roiling clouds and the far-off desert. Twinkles in the sky marked glasships floating not so many miles away. Dozens of them. The Taiytakei.

'They'll come back, you know,' she sighed to the wind. Or maybe she was talking to her dragons. 'They will. Will our Silver King come out to fight them again when they do?'

He is the Black Moon, whispered the dragons in her mind, and Zafir laughed because here was a thing that no alchemist could know, no Adamantine Man, but *she* did because she'd seen it deep within the Pinnacles, in the murals on the walls in the places forbidden to any but the queen of the Silver City. Pictures of the Silver King carrying the Adamantine Spear to war against a man of two faces, and one of them was the moon.

'Tell him to take me home and I will show them to him.' The murals had a sadness to them. A regret, as if of something gone terribly wrong.

The wind shifted. Zafir shivered. Out of the wind the heat was wilting, but in it … Even under her armour she had goosebumps. She sat a while and watched the sun slowly climb across the sky. Off in the distance the tiny stars of the glasships were moving. Zafir got up, turned and looked down to the dragon yard, at the slaves and the soldiers working dutifully as though nothing had changed and the morning of slaughter had never happened.

'Where's the witch?' she asked, but the dragons had no answer. She'd find out for herself then. She went looking for Tuuran.

54

Stowaway

Tuuran bowed as his speaker came to him. When she held out her hand, he touched his lips to the ring on her middle finger, the Speaker's Ring of the Adamantine Palace. As he did, she touched the back of his head. It felt odd. Off, and his hair was greasy and stiff with dirt and sand. 'In this realm there are no others,' she told him. 'I have you alone. You are the first of what will become a new ten thousand. I name you Night Watchman.'

She released him and he fell to his knees and pressed his head to the ground in front of her feet. 'I cannot, Holiness. I cannot take this honour. I am not worthy.'

'Worthy or not, this is what you have become. There is a price.'

'Holiness?'

'I know the creed of your kind. You are the swords. You sate yourselves in flesh and move on. You will not sate yourselves in the flesh of any slave from this eyrie. There are women here who were bred and taught for no purpose but to moan beneath fat uncaring men. They are not whores to be had as the fancy takes you. There are no slaves any more, and I will make a cage for any who act otherwise. You will see to this.'

Tuuran slowly got back to his feet. Erect, he towered over her, a full foot taller. A strange play of emotion flickered though him. Hope and passion and … was that adoration? No, not that. Pride. An Adamantine Man's pride in his speaker and in himself.

'Take what joy you can, Night Watchman.' Zafir's words sounded bleak and cold. 'It won't last long. Joy never does. Now find the witch Chay-Liang. The night-skins will come back for us soon enough.' She walked off and Tuuran watched her go, wondering how to become what she'd asked. Crazy Mad did it by stabbing people with his warlock's knife and disintegrating anything that annoyed him. This had its merits, he supposed, chief being that it scared the living shit out of everyone who saw it. Her Holiness got things done by burning people with her dragon if they didn't do what she said, the old-fashioned dragon-rider way of doing things, tried and tested. His old oar-master had been very fond of his whip. All struck him as the same thing: obey or be hurt. Which was fine until some pissed-off slave whacked you on the head in the middle of the night and tipped you into the sea.

Well, he didn't have a dragon and he couldn't disintegrate people who looked at him wrong, and he didn't fancy an unexpected night-time plunge off the edge of the eyrie, so none of those. He watched the slaves and the soldiers. They did what they were told because Crazy had quietly gone round and stabbed them with his crazy knife before he'd freed the dragon and not left them with a choice, but that was just making slaves in a different way and her Holiness had said not to do it.

He collared a couple of Crazy's tame soldiers and told them to find the enchantress Chay-Liang. 'Tell her what's happened. Tell her she won't be hurt as long as she behaves. Tell her Tuuran said so.' He didn't have much doubt she'd remember him.

He watched the men go and sighed. Letting the hatchlings rampage was all very well and they'd done a fine job of shredding the last Taiytakei soldiers who'd wanted to fight, but it seemed more like luck than anything that they hadn't slaughtered absolutely everybody; and now that her Holiness was done burning everything that moved and Crazy was done disintegrating everything that didn't, the eyrie needed slaves to make it work, to cook and fetch and carry and shovel shit and build things and wash things and herd things and all sorts, and generally those slaves needed to be alive.

Generally. Of course, Crazy had once managed to find a place where that wasn't so, and there were whispers of others too, but best not to think about that.

Since everything in the dragon yard seemed to be getting on well enough, Tuuran climbed to the wall and looked out over the distant desert and the maelstrom of the storm-dark. The wind in his face made him think of being at sea. He missed that. He'd had enough of the desert, thanks. Never enough to drink and when there was water it was tepid and stale, and sand in everything except when it was ants or scorpions. No, he'd definitely had enough of the desert.

He glanced at the two of them, Crazy and then the dragon-queen: a starving shackled wretch he'd saved from the bilges and a princess he'd found pinned against a wall by a drunkard. Gave him a strange feeling. Odd, like they were his children, and that was just daft, wasn't it?

There was a sliver of etched glass in his boot. The Watcher had given it to him, a pass to passage among the Taiytakei to take him anywhere he asked. He pulled it out and was about to throw it away, as far and hard as he could, then stopped. Zafir wanted to go home. But as far as Tuuran knew, Crazy couldn't cross the storm-dark. He tucked it away again and set his mind to getting the eyrie in order. *You never know, eh?*

The dull thuds of the lightning cannon had stopped. A handful of slaves ran past Liang's workshop, and then the eyrie fell into uncertain silence. After a while, when no one came, she limped to the door and looked up and down the passage.

Empty. She thought about heading up to the eyrie to find out what was going on and then imagined another hatchling lurking and went back for a second lightning wand instead. And maybe a sled. And maybe she could take several gold-glass spheres and make a shield around the sled, and then she wouldn't have to walk any more. And rockets. She could put the bombs on the ends of rockets. They wouldn't go very far but it would be better than throwing them. And she could sit inside the shield and stick wands out the front and rockets on the side and make a sort of sled for fighting dragons.

When she was done making her armoured sled, it crossed her mind that two lightning wands were all very well, but ten would be better; and it took a while, making all that, and she was still working when she heard new voices outside and another pair of soldiers came to her door. Not the soldiers she'd seen before, but at least they didn't look like they were running for their lives this time. Even if they were both Vespinese. She'd given up hating the Vespinese – it was just too much effort.

'Enchantress!'

'Did the Elemental Men kill it? What's happened to the dragon? Is it dead?'

The soldiers looked confused as if they didn't understand what she meant. 'Lady, you have to come to the dragon yard now. Night Watchman Tuuran gives his assurance you'll be safe.' The soldier sounded calm, almost asleep, as though he'd been chewing Xizic since dawn. No sign of the terror and the panic she'd seen in the others.

'Tuuran?' Liang shook her head, puzzled. 'Where are the Elemental Men?'

'Gone, lady.' The soldier offered a hand. 'Some were killed, others fled.' Calm as anything, as though it hardly mattered. Liang had to lean on a bench. This was too much. Her voice broke to a whisper.

'The dragon?'

'The dragon serves the Black Moon. As do we all.' They came towards her, arms reaching to take hold of her. As soon as they touched her, she reached her mind into the gold-glass armour they wore and froze it solid. She wrenched herself free. One of them toppled over. The other simply stood, stiff as a stone, an expression of bewilderment on his face. Liang shook her head.

'Now there's a lesson for you,' she muttered, wincing at the pain in her leg. 'I *could* make that armour of yours squeeze until your ribs burst, but why not tell me without all that messiness, eh? What in the name of Xibaiya and the unholy Rava are you talking about?'

They told her that a silver sorcerer of the moon had come, one of the half-gods to whom the smiths of Scythia quietly prayed when they thought that no one was looking. Belli's half-god, who might once, if you believed in the rumoured words of the forbidden Rava, have ruled everything and everywhere. It couldn't be true but that was what the soldiers believed. The worst was how it didn't seem to bother them.

When they were done, Liang dragged the two of them in their frozen armour into the far corner of her workshop and hobbled away to hide.

Tuuran headed into the tunnels with a few of the soldiers Crazy had stabbed with his knife. He found slaves barricaded in their dormitories to keep the dragons out and told them he'd keep them safe; and they came out because some of them remembered him and what a pain in the arse he'd been. The night-skins he found now and then generally threw lightning at him, but there were a few who remembered him from back when he'd been the alchemist's bodyguard, who did at least say hello before they tried to kill him. He herded the survivors up to the dragon yard and Crazy Mad quietly stabbed Taiytakei and slave alike and handed them back over to Tuuran, heart, mind and soul; and it was like his old galley – Crazy and her Holiness the galley masters, and him with a band of frightened slaves left to make sure that stuff got done.

'That's your dragon-queen, is it, big man?' asked Crazy. Tuuran nodded. 'This eyrie. It's hers now. Make it work.'

Out over the storm the glasships were coming. Her Holiness was shouting something, pitting her lungs against the wind. Tuuran listened for a bit, thinking she didn't sound much like a speaker of the nine realms and that old Vishmir the Magnificent or Narammed the Great would have given a much finer battle speech. He climbed the walls and looked around the rim at the cannon. *Right then.*

Liang limped across the ice-cold morgue of what had once been Baros Tsen T'Varr's bathhouse into the spiralling passages where the slaves lived. The tunnels were quiet and empty, the rooms deserted. She stepped around scorched bodies and pieces of men, some so mangled as to be unidentifiable. A few rooms here and there had been gutted by fire but most were simply empty. She went to where the kitchen slaves slept, found a stained white tunic and rubbed some of their cheap perfume over her skin to make herself, as best she could, seem just another slave. She returned the way she'd come and started looking for Belli. He wasn't in his laboratory so she tried his study and found him sitting on the end of his bed, his head in his hands, rocking gently back and forth. For a moment he didn't recognise her. Then his eyes sharpened and he jumped to his feet. 'Li! You're hurt!'

'I killed a dragon,' she said and then giggled a little shrilly at how ridiculous that sounded. And yet it was true. 'It was only one of the little ones,' she added sheepishly.

Belli might not even have heard for all she could tell. Just like the last time. He was on his hands and knees already, looking at her leg. She'd wrapped a piece of cloth around it to try and stop herself spattering blood all over the floor of her workshop, and it was saturated. A trickle of red dribbled along her calf and dripped from her ankle. Belli shook his head and tutted. 'You never look after yourself, Li.' He tried to untie the knotted cloth and merely ended up with her blood all over his fingers. He went to get a knife.

'Why didn't you kill it?' she asked.

'Kill what?'

'The dragon. Was it because of her?'

'Zafir?' He shook his head as he cut the bandage. 'I would have argued for her life with my own, but the dragon? The Elemental Men told me it must be done and they were right. It was the slave who said I should not.' He looked up at her and there were tears in his eyes. 'The Silver King, Li. The Silver King! How could I not obey? He returns. Or so I thought ...' He looked down again and shook his head. 'And then Zafir tried to kill him, and, Flame help me, I think she was right! Somehow she had a knife from an Elemental Man. She tried to kill the Silver King. The Silver King, Li! With a killer's blade but it turned to ash in her hand.' He was trembling. 'Only this is not the Silver King I thought to serve.' He shook his head and shuddered. 'He set them free, Li. He woke the dragons with a snap of his fingers and set them free.'

Belli was trembling. He cut himself with the knife and smeared his own blood over the wound in Liang's leg and Liang squealed at the sting of it. After that he bandaged her up again and then dabbed and fussed at the cut on her face until she sat him down, held his head in her lap and made him tell her exactly what had happened, over and over until she understood.

'I don't know what to do,' he whispered when he was done.

'We must each pick a side,' she answered softly.

'I will pick whatever side has you, Li.'

'I will fight them, Belli.'

'I cannot defy this Silver King to his face, Li, not for anything.' He shook his head. 'I cannot. He is ...'

She kissed him on the temple. 'Then keep me safe and I will fight them for both of us.'

For a long time they sat together and she stroked his thinning hair and rocked him back and forth until he began to doze, and it was only when she heard brisk footsteps coming towards the door that she let him go and quickly hid under the bed.

The Taiytakei Crazy stabbed with his warlock's knife did what Tuuran told them because Crazy had said they had to, but Crazy hadn't told them they had to pretend to like it. The slaves were a bit of this and a bit of that. Some put on armour of glass-and-gold with an eager glee, others slunk away. Tuuran let those ones go and sent them back down into the eyrie to carry on pulling out bodies and setting the place to rights. The ones who had the will to fight he set to work learning how to use the black-powder cannon. The eyrie shook every time they fired, and even over the wind the noise made him jump. From the corners of his eyes he watched the dragons. The hatchlings circled the eyrie. The big one stayed sat on the wall, still as a sentinel.

The bodies in the yard were almost gone, the dead sorted and stripped, the corpses thrown over the side. He hadn't had much of a chance to look at them and he wasn't sure he wanted to. He'd had a lover when he'd been here before. Yena. Didn't much like the thought of finding her again, charred and hacked into bits. They'd parted badly, but still … Maybe she wasn't even here. Maybe she was dead. Maybe she was cowering in a room deep under the dragon yard, terrified of what he'd do when he found her, terrified because she'd been too afraid to run away with him.

Which reminded him … He called up a pair of soldiers from the yard. 'The white witch. Where is she?' Yena had been a slave to the enchantress, and it struck him now that he hadn't seen her even though he'd sent men to find her. Hadn't seen Grand Master Bellepheros for a while either.

The soldier shrugged.

'Best you and I go and have a look then.'

Bellepheros woke as Li shifted under him and scrambled under the bed out of sight. The footsteps stopped outside his door. He straightened himself but no one burst in. Instead there was a polite firm knock. His knees creaked as he stood up. Every part of him carried a weight today, a heaviness. Failure. His purpose, above all other things, had always been to keep the dragons dull and stupid.

To fulfil the legacy of the Silver King. And now the Silver King himself had come in the guise of a man and undone everything he'd ever stood for. All of it gone at a stroke.

He opened the door. Tuuran grinned and opened his arms as though offering an embrace to an old friend, as though nothing had changed and he'd left only yesterday and the whole ugly business with the slave woman had never happened. But it had, and most of a year had passed and everything was different. Bellepheros stepped back out of reach.

'What do you want?'

'Grand Master Alchemist!' Tuuran was still grinning as he stepped in.

'Don't pretend we're friends, Tuuran. Not any more. You brought him here. I saw you with him. The monster.'

Tuuran's face turned solemn. 'The Isul Aieha, Grand Master Alchemist.'

'No.' Bellepheros shook his head. Couldn't be. Couldn't accept that. 'You've brought a monster that will end us all.'

'I've brought freedom, Grand Master. Freedom for you. For me. For *us*!'

'I don't *want* freedom, you stupid man! I want us to be safe! All of us! Safe from the fire that comes from the sky! Safe from tooth and claw and tail! Don't you see what you've done?' But he didn't. The look on Tuuran's face showed that. No shame, no guilt, no fear, just hurt and anger.

'Grand Master Alchemist, the eyrie and its people have been handed over to her Holiness Zafir, speaker of the nine realms and—'

'No, no, *no*!' Bellepheros turned away and raked his hands across his scalp. If he'd had more hair then he might have pulled it out. 'Great Flame! And now what? Has she declared war against the entire Taiytakei race yet? How many must burn before it ends?'

Tuuran's face hardened. 'I do not know, Master Alchemist, but what she has done so far is to command me as her Night Watchman to prepare this place for the defence that must come.'

'You? Night Watchman now?' Bellepheros laughed at the twist of it. 'Well as you must very well know, grand master alchemists and Night Watchmen have a long tradition of antipathy, and I see it set to continue. Go. Leave. I do not want you here. I serve my order and the realms, not you or your speaker.'

Tuuran shook his head. 'You serve the memory of the Isul Aieha. And he is returned.'

'It's not him!' Bellepheros screwed up his face and clutched his head again. But he *couldn't* refuse. Not if the demon came at him in person.

The scowl on Tuuran's face was so dark now that Bellepheros thought the big man might pick him up and carry him away but at last Tuuran bowed his head.

'I came here to ask you as a friend,' he said. 'As a man who was taken against his will by these Taiytakei as I was, for your help to keep our new freedom. The Isul Aieha will take us home, where we belong. I know this. I knew this man before you and I ever met. I ask, as a friend, that you help us to survive. Where is the white witch, Master Alchemist?'

Bellepheros shook his head. 'You have woken dragons. I stand opposed. Go, Night Watchman. You'll have no help from me.'

Tuuran's face tightened. He sighed and nodded. 'I'll do what I can to keep you safe. I've not forgotten how we sailed from the dragon-lands together, slaves both, nor how you spoke to me of the land we left behind and taught me our stories and legends.'

Bellepheros turned his back. He didn't move or speak until Tuuran was gone. After the door closed, he waited a while longer, then quietly crept to it and opened it. No one was listening outside.

'Patience, Belli,' whispered Li from where she hid. 'The killers will come. And when they do, I beg you to hide.'

Under the sound of the roaring wind and cannons firing, Zafir hauled Sea Lord Lord Shonda from his cage and the Crowntaker stabbed him in the back with his shimmering knife. When there wasn't any blood, Zafir frowned. The Crowntaker's eyes had silver in them again.

'This Taiytakei will be mine,' he said. 'He will do everything we ask. He can help us, no?'

Zafir looked at the other Taiytakei in their cages. Mai'Choiro and Shrin Chrias. 'A kwen would—'

They come. Diamond Eye, in her head, a warning the others

didn't have, and she was already sprinting before she wondered why the dragon had bothered to tell her. He was in the air, throwing himself from the wall towards her, wings stretched out. She understood at once. *Killers.* The only safe place was beside him.

The first Elemental Man appeared behind the Crowntaker. Shonda let out a startled cry. The killer vanished and Shonda's head rolled off his shoulders in a fountain of blood. Diamond Eye smashed into the dragon yard and slid across the stone. Zafir threw herself forward and rolled. In the dragon's thoughts she saw the killer rushing like the wind towards her. The dragon read his mind and showed her, and she saw where the killer would be and how his knife would cut her head from her shoulders and the exact moment he would be flesh and bone again. She ducked and jinked, timing perfect. Diamond Eye roared inside her. The killer vanished and appeared ahead of her, and again she saw it unfold a moment before. She twisted away from the blade but it cut through her shoulder, through her armour and sliced open her skin. She struck back at the air where the killer had been standing an instant too late. When he came at her a third time, Zafir threw her knife the moment before he became solid. His outstretched edge sliced a thin shallow cut in her side as she dived away. The Elemental Man looked down at himself, at the hilt of Zafir's blade sticking from his chest. He mouthed a word as he fell.

How?

Diamond Eye flattened his head to the stone as she reached him, inviting her onto his back.

Why? she asked.

55

The Secrets of the Queverra

Tsen was beginning to think the tunnel under the desert went on for ever. The sled moved slower than a glasship but it was faster than walking. His inner t'varr, who calculated things like this in his sleep, estimated two days to reach the Queverra, five if he'd got it wrong and they were heading for the Konsidar. He couldn't be sure. It wasn't a terribly comforting thought because it dawned on him in a slow and roundabout way that if he'd chosen wrong then he'd sentenced them to die of thirst, whereas if he'd set off in the right direction then they *might* survive. He sighed and agreed with himself that next time he'd give it some more thought before he charged off down a mysterious tunnel into gods-knew-where. Yes – when next there were killers hunting him, maybe he could ask them all nicely to wait a moment while he got his bearings and made sure he had plenty of food and water. Maybe a permission note from the Arbiter. A writ or a warrant or something. *And perhaps some dancing boys and a few singers to relieve the boredom too, eh? A full circus – why not?*

'What did you say?'

Talking to himself aloud again? He squeezed Kalaiya's hand. 'A while longer, my love. It will take us to a place we can rest.' Nothing like a little groundless optimism to pass the time. Maybe, he supposed, if he said it enough, he could delude himself that he had an ounce of a clue where he was going. Damned Desert of Thieves was a maze of cliffs and mesas and canyons and chasms and dead ends and old dried-up river beds that went nowhere. He wondered how quickly a sled might fly there using this tunnel. At least as fast as a galloping horse, which was about as fast as the enchanters ever made them. Cheaper and safer than flying sleds over the dunes. They could travel in chains linked together, one at the front towing twenty behind it and only one man to guide them.

He sighed. T'varr-ish thoughts and he wasn't a t'varr any more. Wasn't much of anything, but he knew he'd be stuck with thoughts like that for ever. He *was* a t'varr, like it or not.

The tunnel widened. Pairs of great bronze doors the height of three men passed on either side, each carved into a relief of a giant four-armed guardian wielding scimitars in each hand. Tsen stopped the sled and spent a while looking for a way to open them, but they had no handles, no locks, no keyholes, nothing.

'Where do they go?' Kalaiya asked, and he had to admit that he didn't know. He couldn't think of anywhere useful they might pass on the way to the Queverra – not that might have water. Yes, he could think of all sorts of names for all sorts of places and point to them on a map but he'd never actually visited them because there was nothing actually there. Nothing useful to a t'varr, anyway. Just aesthetically interesting rocks and carved cliffs and giant statues and the occasional long-abandoned ruin.

Thirst slowly drained them. The sled drifted steadily on, Tsen and Kalaiya draped across it. After the second day, Tsen could barely keep his head up. He stopped at another set of bronze doors like the first and couldn't find a way to open those either. At the third and fourth he didn't bother. By then he was drifting in and out of sleep. Maybe there were more, maybe not. The tunnel crept into his dreams. Sometimes he woke with a start and a shout with no idea whether he'd been asleep a moment or an hour. He lost all sense of time and distance.

'Tsen! Tsen!' Kalaiya shook him. He sat up, rubbing his eyes, trying to work out if this was a dream or whether it was real. Two bronze doors barred the tunnel. They hung open and were decorated like the doors he'd seen with Sivan, carved with snakes. Beyond them it was dark. Tsen slowed the sled and let it drift to a stop. His heart was suddenly beating a lot faster. He forgot he was tired and thirsty and nearly dead. The desert men had all sorts of stories about the Queverra: gateways to Xibaiya, half-living half-dead things, man-monsters, terrible sorcerers, a clan of white-faced scorpion-priests who worshipped the forbidden old gods, and that was just the start of it. If even a few of the stories were true then the depths of the Queverra were as busy as Khalishtor on a Mageday market. Nonsense, of course, all of them.

'Tsen!' Kalaiya clung to his arm. She was younger than he was, faster and probably stronger and definitely more likely to get away, but he appreciated the gesture anyway. He stroked her hair. It soothed him. Maybe it soothed her too.

The sled drifted on. It carried them through the open bronze doors and into a darkness like the inside of a cave, and Tsen could smell stone. *Damp* stone, which meant there was water; and as the sled emerged into the bottom of the Queverra and Tsen saw the faint glimmer of daylight above and heard the rustle of a river, he rolled off the sled and fell to the sand and crawled on his hands and knees until he found it.

Water.

Freedom.

When they were both sated, Tsen started looking for a way out and something to eat, and that was where everything started to go wrong again.

Red Lin Feyn stepped out of her gondola at the edge of the desert abyss. The first surprise was the slaughter. The camps of the slavers had been torn down and abandoned. The corpses littering the sand and the stone had been dead for a good few days and the vultures had had their fill. Most of the bodies were picked to the bone. No one had come back to burn them.

The second surprise was finding two of the killers beside her. She felt them an instant before they appeared, a moment long enough to wonder whether they were here to murder her. They bowed though, and their knives stayed sheathed.

'The dragon and its rider,' she asked. 'Is it done?' She didn't want them here.

They didn't know. They'd followed her from the eyrie all the way, whispering breezes around the sanctuary of her gondola. She tried ordering them to leave but they wouldn't. She'd passed her judgement, they reminded her. She was no longer the Arbiter of the Dralamut, merely an exalted navigator, and so they would do as they pleased; and what pleased them now was to know why she'd come to the Queverra and not returned home.

'Well you might as well make yourself useful,' she told them, 'and find out what happened here.' She walked among the bones and tatters, picking at the ruins of the camp, trying to piece the story together. When the desert men fought among themselves, they tried not to kill each other because there was no money to be made from a corpse while a healthy living man could be sold. This was something else. Hundreds of men had come through and all at once. There were no tracks except the ones that led away. Some of the corpses wore rags torn by the vultures. A few had pieces of armour. There weren't any weapons. A lot of the dead had either been stripped or been naked to begin with. She found a corpse under a collapsed tent. When she gingerly pulled back the canvas, what was left of the dead man's skin was painted white.

She began to see.

Lin Feyn moulded a globe of gold-glass into a sled. She stepped on it, sat cross-legged and guided herself up and out over the Queverra's abyss. 'I believe I will find the last of the missing eggs here,' she told the two killers. 'And the skin-shifter who took them. That is why I am here. I do not require your help.'

The killers didn't answer. After a short time she felt them go. Doubtless they'd be waiting for her at the bottom. As she sank into the depths and a twilight gloom closed around her, she looked for firelight from further below and saw nothing. She let herself fall, gently and steadily, calm and composed. The twilight turned to near-dark, split by a bar of brilliant sky miles above. Near-dark turned to night-black, gashed by faraway dazzling sunlight. As she approached the chasm's bottom, Lin Feyn slowed to let her eyes accustom themselves to the deep darkness. The ledges and terraces were abandoned and lifeless. She reached with her ears and heard only the rustle of water over sand. She knew what had happened now.

She reached the bottom. As she stepped off her sled the killers reappeared. She bowed to them and they bowed back. They kept their forms as flesh here out of courtesy, for the Queverra was a place where neither the Taiytakei of the surface nor the shifters of the Konsidar exerted dominion yet both claimed it as their own. In truth, the depths of the Queverra were a forsaken place, but Lin Feyn considered the shifters had the better claim.

'The painted men have gone,' they said. 'There is no one here.'

'I had deduced as much.' Lin Feyn kept her face perfectly blank. 'Do you know why?'

'No.'

'Then I will tell you why. Someone has walked out of Xibaiya. Or some*thing*.'

'The skin-shifter.'

Red Lin Feyn said nothing. She took off her slippers and stood in the cold water of the river, letting her toes sink into the sand. The water was only a few inches deep and the sand was as black as night. She looked slowly up and down the length of the Queverra, careful not to linger on the dazzling line of the sky. Dim shapes of stone arches loomed overhead. There were shadows that might be caves flanked with white stone pillars scattered here and there along the length of the abyss, peppering the walls. Some were beside the river, but others were up along the cliffs, or even faced onto the stone spans above. They glowed with a soft light, unsettling. She'd been here before. The light was something new. The nearest pillars marked an entrance, a tunnel into the stone. She walked to them and touched one.

'Lady!' The warning was sharp in the killer's voice. Lin Feyn drew her hand away slowly. The marks on the pillar were like the Azahl Pillar of Vespinarr.

'This is one of their gateways.' Another world lay beyond. Xibaiya, the realm of the dead. The navigator in her almost couldn't resist.

'It was, lady, but they are dead now. The Queverra is abandoned.'

Red Lin Feyn touched the stone again. Dead? Perhaps once, but not any more.

But this wasn't why she'd come, and she could ask the skin-shifter when she found him. Reluctantly, she turned away. The killers bowed in unison and led her back to the rustle of water and downstream through the darkness of the Queverra's depths, lit up by specks of cold white moonlight scattered like stars across the chasm walls. They stopped at a waterside shrine of white marble built into the rock wall. Flat sandy banks ran along both sides of the river. More pieces of shining moonlight dotted the walls, as if the black stone was a dark skin, chipped and flaked to reveal the gleaming beginnings of some skeletal colossus beneath.

The killers brought water from the river. Red Lin Feyn ate food of her own, flakes of raw fish marinated for three years in salt and oil, and then padded barefoot across the sand to the shallows. The river here was never more than inches deep across a bed of smooth rounded stones. She washed. Above her, the brilliant light of the sky was fading. Night fell sharply in the depths of the abyss, the last feeble echoes of daylight strangled high above so all that remained was the moonlight of the pillars and the flecks on the walls above her. She allowed herself to sleep, lying on her glass sled, then broke her fast on a plate of shredded mushrooms and a bowl of warm milk.

The killers were waiting outside the shrine. 'Why did you come here, lady?'

Red Lin Feyn gathered herself. 'I have no reasons to share with you beyond those I have already given.' They walked beside the river together, following its flow in the near-dark of the abyss until a gleam of light marked the entrance to the old ways, the passages deep under the earth left by the half-gods before the Splintering carried them away. The killers stood patiently. They made no move to cross the threshold. 'Why did you?' she asked them.

'Lady?'

'Why did *you* come here?' She turned away from the entrance with an odd sense that she was too late, that something had already been and gone. She started back, heading in among the caves set into the cliffs, creating bright little globes of enchanted light-filled glass and sending them on their way ahead of her, looking for something. Anything.

'We come as your guardians, lady.'

'But I am the Arbiter of the Dralamut no longer. My judgement has been delivered.'

Far off in the depths of one cave she thought she saw a flicker. She shaped a glass globe into a farscope and peered through it. A sled. She could see the shape of a dragon's egg. Two figures sat slumped beside it. They didn't move.

'It is well,' said one of the killers, 'that you came alone.'

Lin Feyn nodded. 'I thought as much.' The figures on the sled were Tsen's slave Kalaiya and Baros Tsen T'Varr himself, who would hang with Lord Shonda and Shrin Chrias Kwen and the dragon-rider as soon as she got him back to the eyrie. Or at least those were the shapes they wore. She wondered which one was the skin-shifter. Whichever it was, she felt sorry for the other. She supposed the shifter was the woman, that Tsen was really Tsen. They looked either asleep or dead.

She let the farscope settle back into raw glass that felt warm in her fingers and carried on walking. 'I will tell you why you came,' she said. 'But first answer me this: do you know why a skin-shifter stole a dragon egg?'

A silence followed, broken only by the rustle of water in the river. In the darkness Red Lin Feyn could barely see the killers but she felt them. She felt them look left and right and then up into the gloom of the open space above, the miles of still air between the river and the open sky – at how far away they were from everyone and everything.

'I think you do.' Red Lin Feyn felt it too, how isolated they were. Who, apart from Chay-Liang, even knew any of them was here?

'The Righteous Ones would hatch a dragon in Xibaiya, lady.'

'Yes, but why?'

Silence. She walked on into the cave. If the two bodies were awake, they must know they weren't alone.

'You helped Quai'Shu bring dragons to our realm, killers.'

'An error, lady. It will end here.'

'No.' Lin Feyn drew back her hands and threw the globes of glass she'd kept hidden up her sleeves. The killers shifted at once but one of them wasn't quick enough. The globe struck him and transformed in the flick of an eye into a hollow glass sphere, trapping him inside it as he swirled into air. The other was faster. He was behind her in a blink. Lin Feyn stayed absolutely still.

'I am saddened, lady.'

He struck. The bladeless knife touched her skin and, with a glint of twilight on glass, shattered. The shards of the Arbiter which hung over Lin Feyn's shoulders and neck flashed into a whirlwind of knives and sliced him to pieces before he could think. It was done in an instant, and then the shards returned, dripping bright bloody streaks across the white of her dress. Lin Feyn stepped away and looked. She was glad of the twilight. It hid the worst of what she'd done. She touched the glass with the second killer trapped inside and shrank it back to a sphere the size of a fist, crushing him into nothing, and put it in her pocket.

'I am saddened too,' she whispered to the emptiness. She reached into her sleeves for two more spheres of glass.

56

Fire and Lightning

The Elemental Men moved so fast. They flashed into existence and flashed out again with such speed that Tuuran couldn't begin to count them. A dozen? Two? A hundred? With every move they cut a man down and there wasn't a thing anyone could do. One moment you were alone, the next the air beside you turned into a blade and ran you through, and those blades cut through armour as if through butter. Tuuran saw Zafir somehow kill one as she raced for her dragon, and then all was chaos and terror and blood. Through it, Crazy Mad's eyes burned silver. He stood calmly, watching and doing nothing. The Elemental Men left him alone.

Tuuran bolted after Zafir. Futile to think he could protect her from something like this but she was his speaker and it was his duty to try and to die. As he reached her, she was screaming orders. Her dragon stood poised in the middle of the yard, wings folded, tail flicking back and forth, eyes staring ahead but almost closed as if it wasn't even paying that much attention. Then suddenly its tail lashed out as an Elemental Man appeared behind a running slave in gold-glass armour. The dragon smashed them both.

Another Elemental Man appeared a few feet from a hatchling on the walls. The hatchling lunged, its jaws already closing around flesh as the killer emerged from the air, biting the killer in two but not before a bladeless knife drove into its skull. They fell together, both dead. Two more killers blinked in and out along the walls. Men ran, slaves and Taiytakei soldiers alike, terrified as the killers sliced them to pieces. A hatchling swooped and they scattered from that too, every bit as terrified of the dragons. The hatchling burned the face off one Elemental Man as he appeared and lashed a second with its tail, breaking him almost in half, and then a third lunged in and severed the hatchling's head. The men who'd taken arms were slaughtered in moments. Tuuran watched how quickly they died, sick inside.

'Make them come to us!' screamed Zafir, and Tuuran didn't know whether she was screaming at him or at the dragon. The hatchlings paused. Tuuran felt the savagery in their eyes as they raked the eyrie, but one by one they settled around Diamond Eye. Zafir was shaking him. 'Make your men come to us!' she screamed.

Men? He didn't have any men, not any more. There might have been pushing a hundred just a moment ago, but every single one of them was dead, or fled for the spiralling tunnels as if that would somehow save them. Everyone except him and Crazy, eyes savage silver-bright, and her Holiness and half a dozen sword-slaves who'd understood they were safer under the belly of the dragon and had somehow found the courage to stand there.

Zafir had a hand on the great dragon's scales. 'They've gone down into the tunnels,' she said. 'They mean to kill everyone.' She bowed her head. 'Slaves and soldiers, women and men. Everyone.' Abruptly she looked up again. 'And I will not stand for it.' She let the dragon go and headed for the tunnels herself, and Tuuran couldn't imagine what she thought she was doing; but then the hatchlings followed her, all five of them and the dragon too, and then so did he, because what other choice did he have?

Bellepheros held his head in his hands. There was nothing he could do. Nothing. Even Li, when she crept back out of where she'd hidden and held him, even she couldn't change that. 'It's not your fault,' she whispered. 'Not your fault.' And no, perhaps it wasn't, but that didn't change anything and didn't make it any better. There was no one else. It was his duty, his alone to keep the dragons dulled, and he'd failed.

'I should have killed them long ago,' he whispered. 'I felt it in my bones but I didn't do it.' His voice had a quiver to it. 'I kept them alive because Zafir was my speaker. Because I took an oath. Because if I poisoned her dragons then I was killing her too. I'm sorry, Li.' He clasped her hand. 'I should have listened to you. I should have listened to my bones.' There were tears if he wanted them. He might have simply closed his eyes and wept at his own stupid pride and stubbornness but he couldn't, not even now. While he lived, he had to fight them. Who else?

'The end isn't the end until all are gone,' Li whispered in his ear, an absurd platitude. He brushed her away but she pulled him back again and shook him. 'Belli, you know these creatures more than any other. We will find a way. My people are not helpless. And you're not alone, Belli, you're not alone.'

'She burned a whole city, Li, she and that monster.' The burden, always heavy, was crushing. The duty to everyone, and he'd failed. Yet as Li turned his face and forced him to look at her, he saw all that old determination he'd slowly come to love, all that belief, and it gave him strength. She hugged him tight.

'You are not alone!'

And he realised that no, he wasn't, as a breath of wind brushed his face, as the air popped and a man appeared crouched in front of him where no man had been a moment before and then stepped back again. Blood dripped from the killer's invisible blade. As the killer vanished, Bellepheros looked down at himself. The front of his robe was drenched in crimson. He coughed and spat a gobbet of blood. He looked faintly surprised for a moment and then his eyes rolled back and he slumped sideways.

The killers had gone into the tunnels, scourging and cleansing. Killing. Zafir knew because Diamond Eye was inside their thoughts.

Myst. Onyx. She strode away, throwing her will at Diamond Eye. *If you are afraid to face them then I will face them alone.*

Afraid, little one? Diamond Eye was laughing at her, but the dragons followed, that was what mattered. She felt them talking to each other. As she reached the entrance, the Crowntaker was there, eyes burning bright. It was hard not to bow, hard not to fall to her knees in front of the Silver King, but she didn't. She leaned into the furious strength of the dragons around her and met him eye to eye. Diamond Eye lowered his head. The Crowntaker reached out and stroked the dragon's nose. He looked at the Adamantine Man.

'They come again, my friend, and this time they bring their lightning.' He spoke as though observing that there might be a little rain later, as of some trivial nuisance, of the mildest inconvenience.

Across the swirl of the storm-dark, the swarm of glasships drifted closer. Zafir knew perfectly well what they could do. She took a deep breath and felt a snarl build up inside her, and then suddenly she was on him, pushing the Crowntaker against the wall, pressed up against him and right close in his face, breathing fast and hard, heart pounding while the silver light of his eyes reached inside her. She rode him the way she rode the terror of a dragon. 'Isul Aieha. Silver King. Whatever you are. Make them stop. Make them stop!'

Silver light bored into every part of her, burrowing under her skin, her flesh, her bones, her soul. *Who are you, child of the sun, to demand anything of me?* The voice in her head was alien. It was like the voices of the moon sorcerers back on Quai'Shu's ship when they'd first taken her.

One has found the alchemist. She sensed the dragon's amusement. *He thinks he has killed him, but the alchemist ...* Then a moment of shock. *They are touched! He carries a sliver of a half-god within him!* Wonder. Awe. Great Flame, fear?

The Isul Aieha.

Diamond Eye shut her out. The Crowntaker pushed her aside.

'Belli!' Liang had an instant, that was all, before the Elemental Man killed her too. 'No! Stop!' She held up her hands.

The killer appeared across the room. 'I know you,' he said. 'You were the enchantress here. You served the traitor to the peace Baros Tsen T'Varr. Yet you were also the chosen aide to Arbiter Feyn. Why?'

'Because Tsen was no traitor! I testified before the Arbiter's court! Were you not there, killer? Did you not hear?' She looked at Bellepheros. He was slumped away from her, eyes closed now. He looked peaceful, as though he was sleeping. Tears ran over Liang's face now. 'I would help you stop this madness. He would have stopped it too, if he could.' She closed her eyes and shook with a heaving sob.

'He is a sorcerer, lady. You know the law.'

'The Arbiter assigned him to the Dralamut!'

'But now she is elsewhere and no longer holds her rank.' The killer bowed. 'I am sorry, lady, for your grief. It was a necessary thing.'

Liang spat at him. 'Necessary?' And maybe yes, in the eyes of the killers, Belli *was* a sorcerer, and maybe their law said so too, but he was also the kindest, most thoughtful, most compassionate, most considerate … 'Wait!' Under her hand, as the killer vanished into air, she felt the alchemist twitch.

The Elemental Man appeared again. 'What, lady?'

'I would help you if I can.'

'Do you have the power to destroy the dragon?'

Liang shook her head. 'When they're small and new from the egg, yes. The adult …'

Belli twitched again. This time the Elemental Man saw it. He flickered into smoke and vanished.

'No!' screamed Liang. 'If you kill him I will turn against you all!'

The killer appeared by the door. 'Threats, lady enchantress?'

'Threats, killer.'

Bellepheros groaned and slowly sat up. 'A sorcerer who takes his power through his own blood is very hard to kill, assassin. You're not the first to try it. I thought your sort might know better.' He looked down at himself and then struggled unsteadily to his feet. Liang jumped to help him but he waved her away. 'No, no. The last time was worse.' He hobbled to his workbench and rummaged around in the shelves and drawers, pulling the stoppers off bottles and sniffing them. Then he pulled a box from under his bed and found the potion he wanted. He offered it to the Elemental Man. 'I never made very much of this. Never saw the need.' He glanced at Li. 'The one her Holiness used when that hatchling came for her.' He met the killer's gaze and growled. 'They know your thoughts, killer. That's how they know what their riders want. When they're dull and stupid it's a haze of emotion and desire. But these are awake. Their minds are sharp. They can see you, killer. They are in your mind whether you're flesh or air or anything else. They know where you are and they know what you mean to do before you even do it. But this …' He held out the bottle. 'You will become a haze to them. They might not even know you're there at all. A thimble will be enough to last a day or so. There should be enough for six of you. Do what needs to be done.' When the Elemental Man didn't move, Belli brandished the bottle at him. 'Well? Do you want it or not?'

'Elemental Men drink water from the stream and eat food from the earth. We do not touch that which other men have prepared. That is not our way.'

Bellepheros shrugged and shuffled back to his desk. He poured a measure of the potion into two ornate qaffeh glasses, handed one to Liang and drank the other himself. 'If I was offering you poison, I dare say I might have a way to survive it, but Li wouldn't. Also there's this.' He glanced at the Elemental Man and there was a hiss and the killer jumped and yelped in pain. 'You have my blood on you. I could have made it burn far more fiercely than that.' He offered the bottle again. 'What matters to you more, killer? Your precious rules and traditions or your purpose? It's a question much on my own mind. There's enough for four of you now.'

The three of them stared at each other until the Elemental Man blinked across the room. He snatched the bottle from Bellepheros's hand and vanished. Liang waited a moment in case he appeared somewhere else but he didn't. After a few minutes, when she was sure he wasn't coming back, she turned to Belli and held him tightly and then kissed him. When she let go, he looked at her full of surprise.

'I've been wanting to do that for a while,' she said. 'Do you mind?'

'Well I … I mean it's … Um.' His shoulders slumped. 'Water, Li. Please. I need to …'

Liang shut him up with a finger on his lips. 'Yes yes, you've been stabbed. Again. Yes or no, old man, and then I'll get you your water.'

'Well. Um. No.'

Liang poured him a cup of water and then another. After he'd drained them both she was about to kiss him again but Belli's eyes were fluttering. He was falling asleep. Healing himself. Liang swore.

'What is it, Li?'

'I made some bombs. I was going to give them to …' She looked at Belli and stroked his face. 'How long before this potion—'

With a flash the soft-bright walls of the eyrie lit up and burned as harsh and fierce as the sun. Liang froze, wondering what it could mean. She heard a distant scream.

Zafir saw it all. She rode with Diamond Eye's thoughts as he flitted between the Elemental Man, Bellepheros and Chay-Liang. As her master alchemist betrayed her, she felt no bitterness any more. He was following his heart and his duty. She saw how little he thought of her, his disappointment and his sadness. She saw how the enchantress despised her and found it meant nothing, but she saw too how the enchantress cared for her alchemist and how deeply they felt for one another. The love cut her in two. Envy. *No mercy for pretty Zafir.* Oh, she'd been wanted enough, more than enough. Constantly and far too much, but never for who she was, only for *what.* For being her mother's daughter. For being a princess or a queen or a speaker. For being pretty. For her legs, her breasts, her face, her hair, her eyes, for the power she held, for the spear she carried, for the pleasure she promised but never for *her*. Not once for her soul. She looked away, then found she couldn't.

With their thoughts cloaked and invisible, they will kill you. Diamond Eye was talking to the hatchlings.

'No.' The Crowntaker took his gold-hafted knife. He thrust it into the white stone of the eyrie and the dragon yard burned suddenly as bright as the sun, and now the Crowntaker was with Diamond Eye too and they were coursing through the eyrie's veins, riding the white stone. One by one Diamond Eye sought the thoughts of the Elemental Men. He took the Crowntaker to them, and as he found each one, white-hot silver moonlight burned from the walls. One by one the killers faltered as the light seared them and stole their power and forced them into flesh. One by one the Crowntaker reached out of the light to touch them, and they twisted and cried out and burned into a soft settling of black greasy ash. One by one, Diamond Eye found them and the Crowntaker, the Black Moon, destroyed them.

There. They are gone.

Zafir quivered with rage and shock. For a moment the Crowntaker rounded on her, eyes blazing. His fingers closed around her throat, crushing her. Then he let her go and turned her face to look at the glasships drifting in across the sky.

'You have a little time, spear carrier, but those are yours and this storm has barely started.'

Diamond Eye shifted beside her. *I will take them in the air as I did before. You will not ride me for this.*

'Yes, I will.' Zafir walked into the tunnel.

Then you will die.

'So be it.' Better to die on the back of a dragon than helpless and alone.

57

The Storm-Dark

Zafir pushed open the door to her little room, beckoned to Myst and Onyx and wondered why they'd come to mean so much to her. The answer was complicated and she found herself shying away whenever she came close to it. Maybe it didn't matter, but she wasn't who she used to be. Her old lover Jehal would have laughed and then maybe frowned and been a little scared to see her like this. Her mother would have had nothing but contempt for her, but neither of them mattered any more. That felt strange too. And then she thought of Brightstar and wondered if this new Zafir was such a stranger after all. She held Myst and Onyx close. 'What can I promise you? Not much. Hide until it's done. I will do what I can.' It most likely wouldn't be enough but that didn't seem to matter either.

Onyx dropped to her knees and kissed Zafir's feet. 'We are yours, Holiness.' Holiness? That was new. They must have picked it up from Tuuran.

'We have a little time.' Zafir stripped off her armour and stepped back and held out her arms. 'Tend to my wounds and then dress me again for war. Please.'

They unlaced her tunic and lifted off her shift and Zafir looked at herself naked. The cuts from the Elemental Man were the worst, long and razor-sharp. They weren't deep, but every time she flexed her shoulder or twisted, she tore them open again. Onyx cleaned them with the last of their water. Myst went out and came back with curved needles and thin silk thread. She gestured to Zafir to be still and set to work sewing the wounds closed. Zafir looked over the rest of her skin while Myst worked. The bruises from riding Diamond Eye over Dhar Thosis were gone, but she had new bruises instead from other things, from the wild ride to seize Lord Shonda's gondola and from the hunt for the missing eggs when the wind had killed the Elemental Man behind her. She had two little scars on her ribs from when Diamond Eye had saved her from Mai'Choiro's noose and, older still, a trace of white skin on her side from when she'd almost hanged herself on the Taiytakei ship all those months ago. Her ankle twinged now and then, never quite right from her duel with Queen Lystra, Jehal's wife. She laughed.

'Holiness?'

She shook her head. Lystra. How she'd hated Jehal's little starling bride. Now? Easier to imagine them sipping sweet tea together, sharing smirks over Jehal's shortcomings, than going at each other with sword and axe.

'I was thinking of home,' she murmured, though she knew she'd never had a home as Myst or Onyx or even Tuuran would understand it. Never a safe place of comfort and kindness – wasn't that what a home was meant to be? But such things made for weakness and a dragon-rider could never be weak. The nature of dragons made it so. Strength born of cruelty.

Onyx tore strips off Zafir's filthy silk shift to make bandages and handed her a new one. It was stained with a streak of dried blood. In the Adamantine Palace she'd have hanged a servant who offered her something so dirty to wear but not any more. It was her own blood after all, and the best cloth they had. After the shift came the wraps of dragon-scale she'd worn over Dhar Thosis, scratched and marked. They stank of her sweat and didn't fit very well – the alchemist's enchantress was no tailor. She had Myst rip the rest of the torn shift into strips and pad her hips and under her arms where the chafing was worst. After the dragon-scale, she did the rest of the armour herself because it was a point of pride for a dragon-rider to dress alone when they went to war. Perhaps once there might have been a reason for it – perhaps a traitorous servant who had sabotaged a rider and made her armour fail. If so then the story had long been lost. A dragon-rider stood on her own two feet, that was all. They needed no one, not ever, not for anything.

She was almost done when Tuuran knocked. She let him in. When he saw her not quite fully dressed, the look on his face made her laugh. He dropped to his knees at once and pressed his face to the floor. 'Holiness, they come.'

Zafir put a hand on Tuuran's head. 'Get up, Night Watchman.

If there's anyone left, find them. When the glasships come you must hurt them if you can. The black-powder cannon are for that.'

Tuuran rose and bowed. 'There are few of us left, Holiness, but I will try.' He jogged away into the depths of the eyrie. Zafir wrapped the last gold-glass plates around her arms and slipped her hands into her golden gauntlets. She put on her old helm from Dhar Thosis. The dragon carvings had smeared a little in the heat of Diamond Eye's fire and no one had repaired them but the visor at least was new. She drew it down over her face and marvelled as she always did at how it almost wasn't there. The joy of being able to ride a dragon through wind and fire and to see, for the first time to really *see*, made everything else almost worth it. A mirror would have been nice. She took a bladeless knife from the passageway where an Elemental Man had been turned to a smear of ash, buckling its sheath around her waist. A rider rarely carried anything more than a pair of simple knives for cutting themselves free of a damaged harness, but she thought she might make an exception. It was, if nothing else, a trophy of all that she'd done.

Somewhere outside she felt Diamond Eye surge with glee and leap into the air, and then the first cracks of lightning began.

'Hide,' she said. 'Not here. Somewhere with an iron door. Hide and bar the door, and come out for no one until I come back.'

They were almost in tears. Myst fell at Zafir's feet and clutched her ankle. Onyx only stared. 'Live, mistress,' she said. 'Live.'

Zafir pulled gently away and bowed to them. 'And you. Both of you. I could not have asked for better slaves but you are slaves no more. You are free.' A lopsided smile curled her lip. 'Though it may not last for long. But remember, nonetheless.' She turned her back and walked away to where the battle had already begun.

Liang slipped out of Bellepheros's study and crept back to her workshop. She woke a sled and loaded the bombs she'd made. There was an easier way than simply throwing them, there had to be. She pulled the sled through the chill of the bathhouse morgue, through the empty passages where the Scales had lived and up to the dragon yard. She lurked in the shadows, waiting for the monstrous dragon in the middle of it all to be gone.

*

Waves of gleeful joy pulsed in Zafir's head. Chaos. Sleds sped through the air, racing over the edge of the eyrie. Hatchlings wheeled and snapped at them, peppered with lightning. It hurt them and they were all almost lost to their rage. Diamond Eye seized a soldier and crushed him, lashed his tail and smashed two sleds at once into pieces and their riders too. His head whipped round and fire washed over the white stone.

Zafir stepped out of the tunnels. A bolt of lightning struck her at once, dazing her for a moment as sparks crackled over gold-glass. Armoured Taiytakei soldiers were landing in the dragon yard, running for the tunnels. Three charged straight at her, waving their ashgars to smash her to pieces, clumsy weapons but deadly even to a glass-armoured knight. Zafir dodged aside and rammed the bladeless knife into the ribs of one and drew it out. He took another two paces before he even noticed. The other two rounded on her. She ducked another blow and sliced at a leg, cutting it clean in two. The third soldier caught her a glancing blow that knocked her flying. A sled zipped overhead. The soldier on the back leaned and swung at her, almost taking her head off, and then he suddenly wasn't there any more as a hatchling shot out of nowhere and seized him, bit off his arm and threw him aside. The sled spiralled and smashed into the eyrie in a shower of glass. The first soldier she'd cut faltered, looked down at himself and then dropped to his knees, crimson flooding in sheets from his side and down his armour. The last of the three jumped in to finish her. She scrabbled aside as his ashgar slammed into the white stone and lashed at him with the bladeless knife. She barely felt any resistance as the knife's blade severed glass and gold and flesh and bone. He screamed. Another Taiytakei roared and came at her as she rolled to her feet. She didn't try to defend herself this time. Didn't need to. As he lifted his ashgar to smash her, Diamond Eye's tail swatted him, hurling him through the air, a rag-bag of broken bone.

Across the dragon yard, the Taiytakei around the Crowntaker were fighting among themselves. Zafir didn't understand how so many men could have arrived so quickly, but she saw the Crowntaker walk calmly through the chaos, eyes burning silver. Here and there he reached out and touched a Taiytakei and they burst into a cloud of black dust, hanging for a moment in the shape of a man before the wind whipped them away. Lightning struck him and flared like an aura around him; fierce silver light travelled back along frozen thunderbolts and soldiers burned in hostile moonlight fire. Others he simply touched with his gold-handled knife, pausing a moment as he made them his slaves.

Another lightning bolt hit her. It blurred her sight. She didn't run but walked, as the Crowntaker did, to the side of her dragon, expecting death at any second – lightning or the bolt from a crossbow or a hidden knife. She found it didn't trouble her. She felt … serene. Men in glass and gold swung their ashgars at one another and let off lightning at anyone and everyone. A gang of slaves with Tuuran at its head burst out of the tunnels, mad with fear and fury. They ran this way and that, some of them bolting again for shelter, others throwing themselves at the first Taiytakei they saw, dragging them down, pulling off their helms and battering their faces against the stone.

And then the Vespinese still in the air turned and sped away. The Crowntaker raised his hand and silver flashed from his fingers. The last fleeing sleds dissolved into ash, tipping their riders screaming into the abyss below, while those ahead tore off and vanished into the distance. There seemed no method to the Crowntaker's fighting. He killed or enslaved or showed mercy or did nothing, all on a whim. The last few stranded Taiytakei left in the dragon yard fell to his knife. Zafir climbed onto Diamond Eye's back. The glasships were closing. Fifty, maybe sixty of them. Too many. Soldiers turned by the Crowntaker's horrible knife bowed at his feet as he sent them to Tuuran. Tight clusters of slaves huddled together in the mouths of the tunnels, transfixed by this killer they couldn't understand, this half-god come among a people for whom the idea of any god at all was anathema.

'The cannon, Tuuran,' she cried. 'We do what we can.'

Diamond Eye crossed the dragon yard and climbed the wall. He spread his wings and leaped and, when clear of the rim, allowed himself to fall, diving towards the storm-dark and then soaring up again in lazy circles, higher and higher as the glasships came closer. The hatchlings were taking to the air, circling the eyrie. The cannon were turning, slowly coming to bear.

The earth-touched are not all gone. A few remain.

How do you know?

I feel their thoughts, bewildered and full of dread. They are few now but they will return. Diamond Eye banked sharply, tucked in his wings and fell out of the air as the first bolt of lightning flew at him. Over the roar of the wind Zafir barely heard the thunderclap but she felt it prickle her skin. Diamond Eye pirouetted and shot up, jinked as another bolt of lightning flayed the sky so close that the flash of it dazzled her. She clung to his back, and then he was in among the glasships at the edge of their formation.

He fell on one of the silver gondolas and sank his talons into it. Metal groaned and bent. The glasship swayed and sank under the dragon's weight, and then one by one the silver chains snapped. They whipped past her, one of them striking Diamond Eye's neck hard enough to tear his scales. Drops of dragon-blood spattered her visor. Diamond Eye fell like a stone as a cascade of lightning showered the air around him. He curled up into a ball in the air and his wings wrapped tightly around his back, covering her. She felt his pain as lightning struck him. Then he unfurled and hurled the mangled gondola fizzing through the sky. It smashed into the disc of a glasship. Fractured fragments of lightning arced madly as the glass cracked and then fell apart in a glitter of shards. Diamond Eye snapped out his wings, crushing her as he stopped his fall. He threw himself up into the midst of the glasships again, fast and close, twisting and turning like a shark in a shoal of jellyfish. His tail lashed and glass exploded. He crashed into the top of one ship and tore out its heart with his teeth, held it as a shield against a dozen flashes of lightning as the glasship fell, then tossed it arcing away to smash into the side of another and send both tumbling away into the abyss.

The first cannon fired from the eyrie, a distant boom and flash scattering a spray of iron. Nothing happened. More flashes and puffs of smoke and still nothing. Diamond Eye wheeled and Zafir clung to him. Lightning hit him and he screamed and fell, and she howled at him until he found his wings and surged up high and dived among them again, the rage surging through them both so nothing mattered except to bring every last ship to the ground and smash it into sand. And there had been a time when she would have guided and fought that fury, as every rider learned to do, but not today, not any more.

A rain of iron balls fell past her, dozens of them, each the size of her fist. Three clipped the rim of a glasship, cracking it so great chips fell away. Zafir saw it tip and slowly spin, falling in a leisurely spiral to its death in the maelstrom beneath the eyrie. Diamond Eye began to sing, the same murmuring joy of being unleashed for war that he'd sung over Dhar Thosis. He didn't seem to know that he was doing it, but the song curled around Zafir. It was the song of a fight to the bitter end. It writhed inside her, hot and welcome.

Tuuran didn't understand where the soldiers Crazy Mad sent to him had come from. One minute he was standing in the dragon yard swinging his axe to split a man in two, ready to bolt for shelter before someone fried him with lightning, the next moment the Taiytakei were all running away and he was chasing them, and then the one after that, the dragon yard was almost empty and the lightning and the fire had stopped, and there was Crazy, wandering about to the last few men who hadn't got away. He didn't make any pretence about what he was doing. He stabbed them in the chest with his golden knife and whispered in their ear and pointed at Tuuran. And when the soldiers came to him, their eyes were glazed and dull and each one said the same: 'I am your slave,' and then stood slack and patient like a golem.

'The cannon, Tuuran!' The great red-gold dragon climbed from the yard onto the eyrie wall and launched itself over the side, swooping out of sight and then climbing in long slow circles as the glasships came closer. Crazy was out in the middle of the yard now. He sat down as Tuuran watched him, tipped back his head and put his hands on the white stone almost as though he was praying. His eyes blazed. Tuuran looked away. His own world hadn't had much use for praying, but if you were already half a god then maybe that made all the difference. Maybe Crazy could make all these glasships simply vanish. He'd do what he'd do, whatever that might be, and after what Tuuran had seen these last few weeks, he reckoned that could be almost anything or nothing at all.

Cannon then. He shook his head and started yelling, dividing his men into four squads, one for each of the cannon that still worked – three groups of Crazy's Taiytakei with their dull eyes and a fourth he took himself with the last free fighting men on the eyrie. He sent them with orders simple enough even for an Adamantine Man. *Hold your position. Destroy as many glasships as you can. Keep firing until either you or they are dead. Nothing else matters*. He might have added something about running away at some point, only to where?

The hatchlings took to the air to circle. The dragon and the dragon-queen dived. The rims of the glasships glowed a brilliant white like the sun, and Tuuran heard their thunder rumble over the roar of the wind as the first bolts arced. The dragon twisted as though it knew what was coming, jinked, wheeled and dodged and shot suddenly up through the glasships. Tuuran squinted. Dazzling shards exploded in its wake. A first glasship began to fall, and the soldiers around Tuuran jumped and punched the air and howled and cheered. Then the dragon fell and a cascade of lightning flew after it. Another glasship shattered and broke apart and the soldiers let out another cheer. The dragon flared its wings and began to rise again, powering up with a strength Tuuran didn't remember from any dragon in the realms of his home.

He felt the air tingle. Lightning arced from the nearest glasship but it fizzed into nothing before it reached the eyrie rim. They were coming low, level with the eyrie where the cannon couldn't bear on them. Black-powder cannon were designed to fire from the ground at glasships attacking from the sky. No one had thought that on an eyrie already flying a mile over the ground that wasn't so clever. The alchemist had explained this to Tuuran long ago and they'd had a bit of a laugh at the Taiytakei for not being as smart as they liked to think; but the alchemist had also whispered a little secret in Tuuran's ear that he'd never have thought of himself but was so patently obvious. What goes up must come down. And glasships, unlike dragons, were big and slow.

They had the cannon turned toward the glasships, the barrels cranked for the furthest range they could manage. He'd seen it done with scorpions before and archers did it all the time, arcing up-and-over shots instead of shooting straight. No one had ever hit a dragon with a scorpion doing something so daft, but dragons were fast and agile and glasships weren't. And there were a lot of them and they were clustered together, concentrating their lightning to drive the dragon away.

He winced as the first cannon fired, as loud as any thunder, then squinted to see whether it made a difference. He hadn't the first idea, but the glasships were coming straight towards the eyrie, and all he had to do was keep making it rain iron balls somewhere between them and eventually he'd hit something. And he had a lot of iron balls and a crew of a dozen men for each cluster of cannon and a whole pile of conveniently abandoned sleds to carry all the powder and shot.

Sleds.

He didn't know where the warning came from but it made him suddenly look back behind him, away from the glasships.

Liang ran out into the hatchery, hugging the eyrie wall, eyes darting everywhere for the next thing that would try to kill her. Sleds shot overhead and lightning rained from the sky. The hatchling dragons screamed and burned and lashed their tails and tore apart any who came near the cannon. A killer appeared and slashed, severing a hatchling's wing as he burned in the dragon's fire. Out over the rim and beyond the wall, soldiers on sleds swarmed around the black-powder cannon. The air fizzed and flashed with thunder as the Taiytakei swung their ashgars and slaughtered each other. Dozens of men fell, and then a spark must have set off some powder and one of the cannon exploded. Liang reeled. Over the roar of the wind and the lightning, the detonation rang in her ears. Debris – irons balls, bits of cannon, shards of mangled gold-glass, limbs and broken bodies – fizzed across the eyrie and showered over the far side of the dragon yard and the rim beyond. The Taiytakei around the cannon were pulverised and the blast picked up and shook every sled within a hundred yards, flinging them through the air, shrugging off riders to crash to the yard or the walls or fall screaming to the all-devouring storm-dark a mile below. More soldiers on sleds swarmed around the other cannon. Hatchlings shrieked and tore them down.

Liang kept as far away as she could. She scurried to the closest set of steps, well away from any of the cannon clusters on the rim. The crippled hatchling turned its head to look at her, more curious than anything, as if trying to understand what she was doing. Liang climbed to the top of the wall. She slipped and slid down the outside and then she was on the rim. The cannon here were already ruined, destroyed in the Vespinese attack weeks ago when Tsen had vanished. It was almost quiet here except for the wind. There was one other thing out on this side though.

Liang looked up at the glasship floating overhead, one of the five now keeping the eyrie aloft.

A sled shot past Tuuran's head as he dived around the bulk of the cannon. Lightning cracked and sparked along the barrel. Another sled whizzed past. The soldier on it levelled his wand and then vanished, torn off and thrown away by a furious hatchling. It was all wrong, fighting *with* a dragon and not against it. Then again it was all wrong fighting men on flying glass sleds who threw lightning, especially when he didn't have any of their nice fancy armour. A solid brigandine had done him fine in Dhar Thosis, but now he was buggered.

He cringed behind his gold-glass shield. Lightning slammed into it, dazzling him. He picked up a stone, ready to throw it, but the sled had shot off over the dragon yard and now another raced overhead. The soldier on the back swung his ashgar and sent one of Tuuran's sword-slaves flying. The Taiytakei had wands, armour and their sleds. Tuuran's soldiers had sleds too, but the Vespinese Taiytakei were practised with them, and knew how to fly, and that made all the difference.

The lightning from the glasships was getting closer. They were coming in range. Another minute or so and they'd start hitting the eyrie rim. Another minute after that and they'd reach the cannon and then ... well, never mind then. Had to last that long first.

'Keep firing the cannon!' he screamed, not that anyone could hear him over the roar of the wind and the cacophony of screams and dragon shrieks and thunderclaps. Four bolts hit a hatchling all at once. It crashed out of the air and smashed into the rim, rolled and jumped up and shook itself and was back in the air at once, mad with fury, but for a moment the Taiytakei had him and his men at their mercy ...

A thunderous explosion shook the eyrie. He felt it through his feet a moment before he heard it and then a thumping wall of air hammered into him, staggering him, almost knocking him down.

Pieces of stone and flying metal fizzed overhead. Something hit his shield hard enough to crack it, almost knocking it out of his hand. He saw a plume of bright fire, smoke trails arcing away before they were torn apart by the buffeting wind. Men and sleds tumbled and fell all around him. A Taiytakei landed heavily in front of him and groaned, dazed. Tuuran brought his axe down before the man could get up. Two cannons were still firing but his own sword-slaves were too busy fighting for their lives to tip bags of powder and iron balls into the barrels. He saw one on a sled turn and flee and then another, and he couldn't say he blamed them for it, and then one of the hatchlings shot out from the eyrie and tore them both to pieces. 'Our side!' Tuuran screamed, not that the dragon could hear, but he was sure it knew exactly what it was doing. They had no mercy, no fear, no remorse, and certainly no kindness.

He cowered behind his shield as another barrage of lightning flew at him. He was right next to the powder store. Deliberate choice, but now the Taiytakei knew what they had to do and they were firing at him again and again, and all he could do was hide behind the shield and wait for a spark and ...

Shadow engulfed him. The red-gold dragon swooped and shot over the top of his cannon as it sped back towards the glasships. The wind of its wings tumbled sleds, tossed riders into the air and scattered them to the stone below, Taiytakei and his own sword-slaves alike. One sled smashed into the cannon. Tuuran looked about. Half his men were dead. The rest were running. He was on his own. He picked up the broken sled, thought for a bit about propping it over the powder store and then reckoned that was pointless given there wasn't anyone left to load the cannon anyway. He jumped on it and tried to make it fly but it just sat under his feet and did nothing except make him feel stupid. The hard way then.

On foot he bolted around the rim for the cannon that were still firing.

Liang moulded her bomb until it was wrapped around all of the silver chains that connected the eyrie to the glasship above. Every-one was missing the point. They were fighting over the eyrie but why did it matter? The dragons, Zafir, the sorcerer sitting quietly in the middle of it all while anarchy and chaos and the end of the world exploded around him … no one would ever truly own any of them. They had to go. No eyrie, no more dragons.

She fired her lightning wand at the bomb, reeled from the light and then staggered and fell as a wall of hot air slammed into her. As she lay dazed, she wished she hadn't fought Tsen so hard for so many glasships to keep them from falling into the storm-dark and cursed Lin Feyn for setting enchantments she couldn't break.

She picked herself up. The silver chains were severed. Four more to go. She'd stand a little further away for the next lot.

A second cannon exploded. The blast knocked Tuuran off his feet and more of the Taiytakei off their sleds but they still kept coming. There were several on the ground again now and Tuuran kept waiting for Crazy to do something instead of sitting there with his head back, staring with his silver eyes up at the sky, but he didn't. He just sat, and anyone who went near him simply vanished into black vapour and blew away in the wind.

The rim was still littered with junk and all manner of detritus. Liang spotted a slave hiding, curled up under the ruin of a crane that had once lifted supplies from the desert. The eyrie had never struck her as particularly large, but running around the rim with a bomb in her hands to the second mooring, it felt vast. She couldn't remember the last time she'd run so fast, or if she'd ever been as terrified as she was now.

She glanced at the approaching glasships. Their lightning was almost at the walls. She couldn't see the dragon rampaging in their midst but she didn't dare hope it was dead. Nothing ever seemed enough. Dragon and rider alike, somehow they survived everything.

She reached the second mooring, set off her bomb around the silver chains, stayed long enough to see that all of them were severed and then ran back the way she'd come, flooded with relief to be free of the cursed thing, only to have the great red-gold dragon shoot up from under the rim straight over the top of her, flattening her and almost making her heart stop. There were holes in its wings, charred and ragged. The dragon circled the eyrie once, caused havoc among the Taiytakei on their sleds, knocked half of them out of the sky with the wind of its passing, and then shrieked and arrowed away. On the far side of the rim another detonation shook the ground as a second cannon exploded. Liang picked herself up, shaking. Three more moorings and then it would all be over, and it was just a matter of finding a sled that still worked and getting Belli to stand on the back of it with her – never mind his terror of heights – and then not being eaten by a dragon or shot down by lightning as they fled, and maybe, just maybe, escaping all the way from the Godspike to the Dralamut.

It made her laugh sometimes, her own boundless optimism that somehow everything would end not too badly after all. Helped with the shaking though. She ran back around the rim and over the wall to the mouth of the tunnel where she kept her bombs and her sled; and it was only as she reached the entrance to the spiralling passages that she saw the crippled hatchling, waiting for her there.

Tuuran's cannon were silent. The lightning from the glasships had reached the wall now and they were climbing. He saw a hatchling struck again and again by Taiytakei wands until it crashed into the dragon yard, and then a dozen soldiers struck it with more lightning from the air, over and over, keeping it writhing and helpless while three men on the ground with ashgars clubbed at its head. Another hatchling shot through them, scattering the soldiers on the sleds and tearing two of the Taiytakei from the ground in its talons and hurling them away, but too late. The fallen hatchling didn't move.

Tuuran half ran and half fell down the steps to the dragon yard. What defence was left was clustered around the last cannon now, two hatchlings and a few dozen soldiers, but they were being swamped, the men cowering behind their shields under a deluge of lightning. The glasships were still falling, one by one, smashed by cannon fire or torn from the sky by the raging dragon, but nowhere near fast enough. Once the eyrie was in range of their cannon, everything would be over. He raced into the middle of the yard.

'Crazy!' Somehow the wind was blowing more strongly in his face. 'Crazy! Do something! Look!'

But Crazy Mad didn't look up, and as Tuuran tried to get closer, he found the air thicker and thicker until a few feet away from Crazy it was like trying to walk through a wall and he simply couldn't. 'Crazy! You've got to ...'

The eyrie shook as the cannon behind him blew apart.

Liang's eyes bulged. The hatchling came at her, and the air was full of men on sleds and lightning, and any moment now one of them was going to see her, just another slave in the open, and shoot her down. She reached for a piece of glass to mould and throw at the dragon, but as she did, the hatchling suddenly turned and Liang saw the flicker of a man appear beside it and then vanish again. The hatchling jumped back and spat a gout of flame. The moment was enough. Liang threw the glass into the tunnel entrance, shaping it as it flew to seal the tunnel shut and the hatchling inside it. It wouldn't hold for long but maybe long enough. She turned and ran back for the wall, up the steps and over the other side, looking for a place to hide.

The air popped beside her. A killer. She whimpered and looked down at herself but there was no cut, no bladeless knife drawing away already dripping red with her blood. He looked at her. The knife was in his hand, ready. 'For whom do you fight, enchantress?'

She was shaking so much that she could hardly speak and she couldn't stop looking at the knife. Any moment now and he'd use it and then she'd die, but worse Belli would die too. She had more glass and she could make a shield, but it wouldn't matter because she didn't have time and he could appear anywhere he liked and the bladeless knife would cut through metal and glass as though it was air, and then she'd never finish severing the moorings to sink them all into the storm-dark, and even if he didn't kill her here and now, she'd sealed the hatchling into the tunnel and the bombs she'd made were in there too and she'd never get to ...

She stopped. Froze for a moment, consumed by her own quivering and the pounding of her heart. The knife ...

'I would sink this eyrie into the storm-dark,' she quavered, still staring at the knife. 'I was trying to do that. I was cutting the chains. But *you* could do that. You could cut them all. In a blink. Any one of you could.'

His face was a blank mask. She had no idea whether he understood. She went from terror to wanting to shake him.

'Cut the chains that tether the eyrie to the glasships! Finish what Tsen tried to do! It will all sink into the storm-dark and be gone for ever.'

He didn't move. She closed her eyes and waited for the cut to end her life, but it didn't come. When she opened them again, he'd vanished.

Diamond Eye was gone, lost to hunger and rage. Zafir felt his sense of death, his own coming end, but greater still his hunger to be a storm as he fell upon the glasships yet again, a frenzy of tooth and claw and lashing tail. Twice he tumbled towards the storm-dark below, helpless and dazed and dazzled with pain, mind ragged and jumbled and askew, and twice Zafir had screamed him back. She'd torn through the cacophony and the madness and rammed the order of her will into him. *Fly! Fly! Spread your wings and fly!* The second time they'd fallen they'd almost touched the maelstrom, but she'd done it. She'd saved them both and the dragon knew it. *See. We have a use.*

Diamond Eye didn't answer. He powered up in renewed fury towards the glasships as another one splintered and cracked under a hail of iron from the eyrie cannon. There was nothing their enemies could do but hang helplessly in the sky and hurl their lightning. Diamond Eye flew higher then turned and fell upon them, crashing into the highest, slashing and biting at the discs at the heart of it until the glasship tipped and began to slide to its end. He fell upon another and tore out its heart and gripped it with his claws, dragging it towards the next, shielding himself with it from the lightning that flashed and thundered around them. The glasships crashed together and exploded into shards while the dragon stormed on, slashing with his shattering tail, swooping and soaring as their gold rims glowed with white-hot light and Zafir felt the air prickle and scratch in the hail of lightning. They were almost over the eyrie now, the glasships raining death over everything, the battle already lost, the end coming close. Zafir closed her eyes. Her heart sang. They were primal beings now, both of them, locked together in this, dying as a dragon and a dragon-queen should die. Lightning shattered the air above her, beside her, all around her. Noise deafening, light blinding, yet Diamond Eye jinked and dived and rose and rolled between the thunderbolts. The air smelled of fire and sorcery, that burning tang that rose sometimes from the depths of her old palace where the Silver King had made his miracles.

Lightning from the glasships was hitting the walls. Crazy didn't flinch. Tuuran shook his head and turned his back and ran for the tunnels because now there was nothing he could do except find a sled and go. The eyrie shuddered again. He had the strangest feeling as though it was tipping, like a ship rolling in the swell of the sea.

A thunderbolt struck Diamond Eye's wing near the shoulder, punching another hole through the skin. Sparks arced along his wing and rippled over his scales. He tipped sideways. The glowing golden rims of the glasships brightened to fire again. Another bolt hit him in the belly. He shrieked and tumbled into one of the glass discs, a savagery of tooth and claw and tail and fire, blindly smashing it down. Straps in Zafir's harness groaned and snapped as he wheeled and tried to recover. She felt his rage at these ships-that-flew, burning her on the inside as his flames scorched the air without. Another bolt hit him at the base of his tail. She felt the shudder. Sparks ran over his scales and then there was another thunderclap and she felt her skin prickle ...

A bolt hit his neck a yard in front of her. For a moment her mind went blank. The noise drowned everything. She almost flew from the saddle but the remains of the harness held. Her heart stopped and then began beating again. Every muscle turned rigid. Diamond Eye fell, blind, dazed with pain, one wing paralysed. He couldn't lift his head.

We tried, she told him. *We tried and we died well.* Then she urged him: *Fly! Fly! Flare your wings and fly, damn you!* But Diamond Eye was too far gone to hear or care for her tiny voice. He almost managed to right himself at the last, flaring one wing to break the fall, but he couldn't flare the other and rolled. The dragon yard was suddenly above her, spinning wildly. He slammed into the stone on his side. The crash smashed her hard against his scales and yet her harness still held, and though bones and muscles screamed and tore, somehow she was alive. Luck, this time. Diamond Eye had forgotten she was even there.

He moved sluggishly, unsteadily. Trying to right himself. Lightning flared again, striking the last cluster of cannon. She heard them die, exploding in showers of fireworks and flying twisted metal. The dragon yard was littered with shattered glass and dismembered dead. She tried to make her arms move, to make her hands uncurl from the fists they'd become.

Lightning struck from above. Diamond Eye spasmed. Zafir gasped as the shock of it ran through her. Her fingers were too numb to undo the harness but there was still the bladeless knife. She forced her shaking hand to pull it free and cut, slashing at the ropes, cutting the dragon's scales and the flesh beneath in her frenzy to be free. Another bolt struck and then another. Diamond Eye writhed and curled and the sky went dark as one wing covered them both and she fell, sliding and tumbling over his burning scales to land on the stone, pressed up beside him, too broken to even move. Her eyes closed as thunder burst around her.

Liang made it to another tunnel. She felt the shift of the eyrie through her feet as she reached it, the lurch as it started to fall. Tsen had shown them all how long it would take, that the eyrie would fall slowly like a stricken glasship, not plunge like a stone, so she knew she had time. She paused and looked up before she entered the tunnel, watching the glasships overhead, dozens of them raining lightning in a storm around the dragon as it finally fell, and then picking out the glasships that had once belonged to Baros Tsen T'Varr, drifting up now, their dangling chains slack beneath. She stayed until she'd counted them and knew for certain that the Elemental Man had finished what she'd started.

The shock as the dragon hit the stone of the yard almost knocked her off her feet. She turned and ran as fast as she could and never mind how her legs burned and her feet hurt. She was in tunnels that had been the barracks once, an unfamiliar place, but that didn't matter. They all spiralled in the same downward fractal pattern to the chamber at the eyrie's core where Baros Tsen had built his bathhouse amid the ring of white stone arches. She met no one. Everyone was dead or had fled to the darkest corner they could find. She stumbled and fell as she ran, legs pumping too fast for the rest of her to keep up until she sprawled across the white stone floor. She got up again, dimly aware of the pain, raced on, deeper and deeper, dodging and hurdling the ripped bodies that still lay scattered about until she reached the open doorway to the bathhouse. Cold air billowed out, chilled by the enchantments she'd made for the bath house to become a morgue.

She stopped. The arches. She'd seen them on the very first day she'd come to the eyrie, when Tsen showed her around. *What do you make of these, enchantress?* And she'd made nothing of them at all because they were simply a ring of white stone arches around a white stone slab. An altar to old forbidden gods perhaps, that was all she could say, and Tsen had laughed and declared it as fine a place as any to build his bath and drink his apple wine. After that, she'd not spared them a second thought.

The archways shimmered silver now. Shining liquid moonlight. She went up to one and almost touched it to see if it would ripple, then shook herself and shivered in the unnatural cold and ran on. She was here for Belli, to get them away before the eyrie plunged into the storm-dark, because when it did, everything here would be gone as though it had never existed. She ran past Tsen's old rooms, past her workshop to Belli's study, praying to the forbidden gods that he was still there, that he hadn't moved, that she would find him; and there, waiting for her, was the crippled hatchling.

Liang skittered to a stop. The hatchling almost didn't see her, but then it turned and shrieked and its talons scrabbled at the stone, clawing for purchase. Liang dived back into her workshop, looking for a globe of glass to throw, grabbing the first that came to hand. She stumbled, turned as she fell and threw the glass back at the doorway as hard as she could, willing it into a cage. The dragon pushed inside but it was slow and hampered by the narrow entrance. The glass missed its head and hit its flank and burst in a thunderclap of imploding air. The dragon lurched and seemed to shrink in on itself. It fell dead at once, a gaping hole in its side where a festering dark black mass now floated in the air, lit from within by tiny flickers of purple.

Horror gripped Liang as she realised what she'd done. The glass she'd thrown had been Red Lin Feyn's captured piece of the storm-dark and now a tiny cloud of it hovered free in the doorway, the dead hatchling underneath blocking the rest of the way out.

She had to find a sled. She had to get to Belli. She had to ... but there was no way she could move the hatchling on her own ...

Lin Feyn had never said what would happen if the globe broke. Something bad, surely. Maybe not so bad if they were all doomed anyway, but now she couldn't get out and so Belli would die and so would she, and she wasn't ready for that, not after everything they'd been through. She reached her mind into the storm-dark as she would into her enchanted glass. There was a twist, Lin Feyn had told her. A reaching in and then doing something different. Not a bit different but completely alien.

Glass was all about control. Delicate, intricate, precise thoughts.

Maybe she could pile up some furniture and climb over. Maybe there was enough space ... But the eyrie was falling and it would all take too long.

She reached out and touched the storm-dark. She screamed all her pain and desperation and anguish, knowing that she'd never make it move, that it had her trapped.

Before her eyes the storm-dark obediently curled into a ball and floated in her palm.

Kill me, whispered the dragon through the lightning and the screaming pain. Zafir opened her eyes and shuddered awake. Everything ached, but worse than that was the dull numbness inside. When she tried to move, her arms flailed. Her legs twitched. She tried again and cried out at a stabbing pain that ripped through her insides. The doll-woman's circlet felt tight around her skull. Squeezing her.

I can't. I'm dying.

Kill me, little one. We are falling into the abyss.

Then the storm-dark will kill us both. You'll come back.

The storm-dark will unmake me. It will be the end.

She saw the dragon's thoughts and understood. A final end and the dragon was, at last, afraid. With gasping effort she forced her eyes to open and looked for the bladeless knife. It was right beside her. Her fingers clawed at the circlet. Somewhere, the doll-woman was trying to kill her. She'd always supposed it would be sudden and quick. Not like this.

Her hand closed around the hilt of the knife.

Drive it deep, little one.

Diamond Eye shuddered as lightning hit him again. She'd have to leave the wing that lay over her, shielding her. She'd have to haul herself out. Have to drive the knife through his skull. She started to crawl. Standing up was too much. She pulled herself with her arms and pushed with the one leg that still worked, inching along his body. She wondered briefly why she was doing this, what difference it made, then threw the thought away. Diamond Eye was hers and she was his. She pushed her way out from under his wing, hauled herself up with her hands, tugging on his scales until she was standing on one leg. The other would barely take any weight. She whimpered at the pain around her head. The pressure was crushing her skin.

I'm cold, she told him. She was bleeding inside. Had to be. She could feel blood inside her armour too, drying, tacky, sticking her silk shift to her skin.

I will keep you warm.

Yes. As he burned from the inside after she'd killed him. She hopped a little further and looked up.

The glasships were high overhead, far higher than they'd been before, receding into specks. The eyrie was falling. The lightning had stopped. Maybe they were out of range. She glanced at the walls but everything around her was lifeless ruin.

She dragged herself to Diamond Eye's head. She'd have to climb on top of him to drive the knife through his skull. She wasn't sure she could. She threw off her helmet and wiped her eyes, brushing away the pain, reached for the ruins of his harness to pull herself onto his shoulder, took hold of a rope and then howled in frustration when her arms didn't have the strength and she fell back. Another wave of pain washed over her. She could feel herself failing. *I can't.* And she couldn't. Just couldn't.

You were worthy to ride me, little one.

She wept. Nothing anyone had ever said had meant so much. And at the same time the pain in her head was like drowning.

'Hush.' She felt a shadow move over her. The Crowntaker stood there, eyes burning silver.

'Why didn't you ...?' She let out a long breath. What was the point? 'You could have been my Vishmir.' She lifted the blade-less knife to him. 'Finish us. Both of us.' Above them the glasships were little more than specks now, glints catching the sun. The Crowntaker, the Silver King, the Black Moon, whatever he was, crouched beside her. The circlet tightened a little more. She cried out and arched and then cried out again at the fresh wall of pain.

'I'll not be your Vishmir; I'll be your Isul Aieha.' And she might have laughed if they weren't all about to die. A darkness seemed to swell up around the eyrie. The storm-dark.

He reached out and touched her brow and the gold-glass circlet dissolved into ash. 'Be free.'

The storm-dark swallowed them.

Liang found Belli where she'd left him, sitting in his study, rock-ing in despair. She pulled him up by the arm and dragged him onto her sled and into the tunnels. They were glowing brilliant silver now. 'Come on, come on! The eyrie's falling. It's all going to the storm-dark now.' Driving the sled faster, holding him tight. 'Dragons, hatchlings, eggs – everything, all of it.' Up the spiral to the surface. 'Everything it touches.' Past the rooms where Tsen's t'varrs and kwens once lived. Maybe they were still there, for all she knew. 'We have to get off before it's too late.' Past the rooms where some of his favoured slaves once slept. 'We have to fly—'

She reached the end of the last twist and emerged into the dragon yard. The madman with silver eyes stood in the centre, arms stretched wide, head pitched up, light blazing out of him. The red-gold dragon Diamond Eye lay curled up on its side behind him, still. Two hatchlings flanked him, watching like sentinels. A hand-ful of men and women stood nearby – a few Taiytakei soldiers, a dozen slaves from across the different worlds, maybe a few more – the last survivors. They seemed entranced. Enraptured.

Belli stepped off the sled and walked to join them but Liang barely noticed the people. She barely even noticed the wind.

The sky above and beyond the eyrie walls was black churning

cloud and flashes of purple lightning. They were too late. *She* was too late. She knew what happened next.

The wind stopped.

The darkness turned absolute.

Silence.

58

The Silence That Comes After

A light flared and flickered somewhere about Baros Tsen, bright enough to stir him. When he opened his eyes, a figure stood at the edge of the darkness. 'Baros Tsen T'Varr!' A voice echoed through the tunnel. There was something not quite human about it.

'Kalaiya!' Tsen sat up. He nudged Kalaiya awake.

The figure held out its hands. Two specks of light flashed across the space between them. Tsen tried to duck. Kalaiya opened her eyes and screamed. Something as large and solid as a fist hit him in the chest and he felt it run up his skin like a giant centipede, irresistibly quick as it wrapped itself around his neck. He clawed at it but it was as hard as metal. He struggled, panicked for a moment, then, as nothing else happened, calmed himself. He looked at Kalaiya. She too had a collar around her throat. It was made of gold-glass.

'Do you know who I am, Baros Tsen?' rang out the voice.

Tsen clawed at the glass collar around his throat and then gave up. All this way and then days starving in a cave in the dark, unable to find the way out, and now this. He closed his eyes and squeezed Kalaiya's hand and wept, because really, after everything he'd done and all he'd been through, he'd well and truly had enough. The Arbiter of the Dralamut stood, a shadow amid the dancing lights of her enchanted globes. There didn't seem to be anyone with her but wherever the Arbiter went, killers were always on hand. Stupidest thing of all was that he'd never wanted to run away in the first place.

'I'm sorry, my love.'

The Arbiter reached out a hand. The sled began to move, drifting closer until it stopped in front of her. There was a dead man on the sand behind her. He looked as though he'd been ripped to pieces by a thousand knives. It took another moment for Tsen to realise that the shredded blood-soaked clothes were the robe of an Elemental Man.

The Arbiter of the Dralamut cocked her head. She didn't wear the headdress or the flaming feather robe, only the plain white tunic of an enchantress. For all he knew this was another skin-shifter. She *was* draped in the Arbiter's shards of glass, though. And they were stained red and dripping with fresh blood.

'Another Baros Tsen?' she asked. 'Or is it truly you?'

Tsen dropped to his knees and bowed. 'Lady Arbiter. Judge me as I know you must but my slave is innocent.'

'I am Red Lin Feyn, daughter in blood of Feyn Charin and the Crimson Sunburst, enchantress, navigator. Arbiter of the Dralamut until two days ago but I no longer claim that right. I have discharged that duty.' Her eyes narrowed. 'Who are you?'

'I am Baros Tsen T'Varr,' said Tsen.

'Really?' The collar round his neck contracted. He choked and clawed at it. Beside him Kalaiya screamed but Tsen found he couldn't make a sound. Couldn't breathe no matter how his lungs pumped and his ribs and belly heaved. He flailed, staggered to his feet, lurched a few steps forward, but the Arbiter simply backed away with such grace that she seemed almost to be floating. The darkness closed on him. He fell forward. As he closed his eyes he saw Kalaiya too clawing at her throat.

He came round perhaps a minute later. The Arbiter was sitting between them, perched on the edge of a gold-glass disc. 'Baros Tsen T'Varr.' She smiled and then laughed. 'Welcome to the Queverra. You are free to go.'

'What?' The collar had gone from around his neck.

'The Arbiter has passed judgement. I found you guilty in your absence of complicity in the razing of Dhar Thosis. They found your body in a gondola close to the Godspike. They'll take it back to Khalishtor to be hanged by the feet so I doubt anyone is looking for you. Although given that that was already the second time your body was found, I'd be careful. Nevertheless, you may go. I suppose the second body was the shifter, was it?'

Tsen shrugged. Last he'd seen Sivan, the shifter had looked like himself and had had a spear stuck through him. Seemed best not to mention that though.

'Free, lady?'

'In the end I believe you. I believe you tried to stop it. Because of your enchantress's faith. Because of your rider-slave's honesty. You were stupid, Tsen, but not evil.'

'Yes.' Wisdom suggested shutting up and taking Kalaiya's hand and walking away as fast as he possibly could, and yet the devil inside wouldn't let go. And he had a hundred questions about how she'd found him and why she'd thought he was a shifter and how much she knew about what lay beneath it all, but one thing more than anything else ... 'You called yourself daughter of Feyn Charin and the Crimson Sunburst, lady.'

Red Lin Feyn paused and then chuckled and nodded. She let out a long deep breath. 'A change is coming. A catastrophe, perhaps. You see it in the swelling of the storm-dark and in the cracked needle beside the Godspike. You see it in the rise of the sorcerers of Aria and the Necropolis of the Ice Witch and in the dead that do not rest, in Merizikat and also even here. In other things. In the storm-dark itself. The skin-shifters know.' She looked across the darkness at the shredded man on the sand, paused again and smiled. 'In your history, when the Crimson Sunburst appeared at the foot of Mount Solence with her army of golems, what became of her, Baros Tsen?'

'The Elemental Men fought her and she was defeated.'

'So she was.' Red Lin Feyn turned away. 'Disappear, Baros Tsen T'Varr. You'll find it's not so hard.'

'Why do you want the egg?' Tsen blinked. The question wasn't his. It had popped into his mind from somewhere else. He looked about himself. Nothing.

Red Lin Feyn shook her head.

'But the answer is in your thoughts, little one. The grey dead have called the Black Moon to rise ...' Tsen gasped. A hand flew to his mouth because the words didn't belong, made no sense, weren't his at all. 'I ...' Then he jumped as a sharp cracking noise broke the quiet. It came from the sled, and it took Tsen far too long to understand what it was and so he simply gawped as the dragon egg cracked and burst apart in a flurry of wings and claws and two furious eyes gleamed.

I am Silence.

Epilogue

The dragon Snow circled high over the mouth of the Fury, enraptured by the ripples in the water. On a clear fine day like this there was still a dark stain across the earth where the city of Furymouth had been. The ruins were overgrown with weeds and grass and briars now, but underneath them the stones remained black with soot and the air carried a tang of ash. There were little ones down there. She could feel their thoughts, pick them out and read them if she wanted to. They lived in cellars and damp old tunnels and came out to hunt for food when they thought it was safe.

Nowhere was safe.

A speck in the sky far out to sea caught her eye. Another dragon. She reached out her thoughts to greet it. Perhaps they would hunt together, digging these little ones out of their holes ...

She stopped her circling and almost fell out of the sky in surprise. The dragon had a rider.

Fly! it said. *Just Fly!*

Snow saw what was in the dragon's mind, what was coming out of the storm-dark, and fled.

Acknowledgements

With thanks to Simon Spanton, devourer of unnecessary prologues, who asked for dragons and got more than he bargained for. To Marcus Gipps and Robert Dinsdale for their editorial work. To Hugh Davis for copy-editing all my dragons and to the proofreaders whose names I've rarely known. To Stephen Youll for his gorgeous covers. To Sea Lord Jon Weir, even though he's gone to other things.

With thanks to all the people who read *A Memory of Flames* and talked about it and weren't afraid to be honest. *Dragon Queen* and *The Splintered Gods* are different books from the ones they might have been because of you.

It's still very true that none of this would have happened without the trust and faith of the same special few as always. Thank you again. Thank you to lovers of dragons everywhere. Thank you to all the alchemists and enchantresses out there. Thank *you*, for reading this.

To any who want to explore the world of the dragons for its own sake, you can do so at the online gazetteer at www.stephendeas. com. There are other goodies there from time to time too.

If you liked this book and want there to be more, please say so. Loudly and to lots of people.